# A STREET WHERE YOU LIVE

### A PSYCHOLOGICAL SUSPENSE COLLECTION: UNDERNEATH, MINE, BULLIED

### ANDREA M. LONG

This book is a work of fiction. Names, characters, places and incidents are either the product of the author's imagination or are used fictitiously, and any resemblance to actual persons, living or dead, events or locales is entirely coincidental.

No part of this book may be reproduced or transmitted in any form or by any means, electronic or mechanical, including photocopying, recording or by any information storage and retrieval system without the written permission of the author, except for the use of brief quotations in a book review.

Copyright (c) 2022 by Andrea M. Long

All rights reserved.

Cover photo from Deposit Photos. Cover design by The Pretty Little Design Company.

## AUTHOR'S NOTE

This book is written in British English and is set in the U.K. My psychological suspense reads contain flawed characters and situations that are all the more disturbing for the fact they could happen in real life, on **a street where you live**.

# UNDERNEATH

# PROLOGUE

Driven by adrenaline, my hands won't stop shaking as I turn off the alarm I'd set for three-thirty am and consider what I'm about to do; part two of my plan. I suck on my top lip, trying to get some saliva into my dry mouth. Pushing back the duvet, I reveal the black DKNY top and J. Crew trousers, chosen so I look hot if arrested. I imagined Monique's voice should I face the police dressed in 'Value' jeans and so assembled an 'attractive assassin' combo. My armpits feel damp, and my heart races to the point that I can feel its thud within my neck. I'm reminded of old movies when the monster moves slowly before attack. I breathe deep, this is self-defence, remember? My hands shake so much, I can barely tie the converse I slip on my feet, and for a moment I surrender. I lay down on the floor in child's pose, trying to regulate my breathing. It does no good. I must go now. I pull my wavy blonde hair back in a bun, grab my bag, slide on my D&G sunglasses and exit the house.

Behind the wheel of my faithful Nissan Micra, I drive to the bitch's estate and park around the corner, leaving the car obscured by a row of garages. Then I glance around checking for potential witnesses. Though I see no-one, I can hear the inebriated screams and laughs of people on their way back from nightclubs. I walk casually to her house; my posture straight so should anyone see me they wouldn't question my being there. As I arrive at the front garden I appraise how immaculate it looks, planted with symmetrical bedding, all oranges and purples. Box hedging as neat as a newly cut fringe ensures my cover from the rest of the estate. She must either love gardening herself or pay a fortune for someone to keep it so pristine. As someone who has grown vegetables from seed and tended to them like an expectant mother, I hesitate before I put on the rubber gloves. Can I really do this? Are things really this bad? As I consider past events, I feel my jaw clench and my teeth grind. She deserves everything she gets. I reach down, my fingers gripping the neck of the plants and I lift and smash them onto the path where the soil parts from the roots and spills out like spewed guts. I'm horrified to feel a grin that I cannot stop form on my lips. I carry on, full of energy, until the bedding plants are no more and the piled-up soil resembles a grave of the newly buried. I move onto her dustbin, retrieving food waste which I push through the letterbox, imagining the smell on her return: putrid and decaying.

Next, I open my bag, extract weed killer, and pour it over the meticulous green lawn. I try and dribble it to spell out the word 'bitch'. Give it a few days and yellowing dead patches will hopefully reveal my handiwork. I re-check that no-one watches me and move around the back of the house. A screwdriver from the front pocket of the bag is used to disable the security light in order to prevent its on and off SOS. Pre-dawn light allows me to write 'whore' in carefully disguised font across her white PVC back door. For my finale, I empty fake vomit out of a plastic container, covering her patio furniture, silently thanking the person who posted the recipe on Pinterest.

Back in the driving seat, I punch a fist in the air before I burst into tears. I turn down the visor and peer at my reflection, seeing the reasonably happily married woman turned revenge seeking missile.

Ground down and exposed to my rawest state. Right now if you looked closely, I feel you'd see every part of me, each individual cell. Be able to look within the membrane to the protoplasm. See what's underneath ...

# CHAPTER ONE

We all do it. Look at other people and envy their lives. The ones at work, the ones hanging around the school gates, the Facebook friends. We see their smiles, their perfect teeth, their immaculate clothes. We hear or read their stories of how they just returned from Florida, how their new fiancé proposed on a beach in an idyllic spot. Our teeth clench and we wonder, what made *them* so special. Why is it not us?

I seem like one of these people. The ones who have it all.

How do you tell people who think you have the perfect life that actually you're bored shitless?

I've spent so much time lying on my bed I'm surprised I don't have bedsores on my backside, as I stare at walls in a state of catatonia. Let's be honest, being a mother can bore you rigid, no matter how much you love your child. Where's the fun in telling your son fourteen times to get out of bed? Trying to get Joe ready for school while he ignores my every instruction, means my throat will be hoarse by around half eight. He's like his father in that respect. Niall has avoidance as his most-perfected trait.

I spend my days doing chores, while running my little vintage empire and my line in refurbished Barbie dolls via eBay. I do coffee with my bestie when she's not working. People are always telling me how lucky I am that I have such freedom, but sometimes I get so bored I put my pyjamas on and go back to sleep. It makes the clock tick faster.

If Niall's home for dinner, he expects a home cooked meal on the table as I 'don't work'. My eBaying is seen as a hobby. I've learnt to ensure I'm mid-chore when he gets home, or he'll comment that it must be nice to have time to sit or read. That's another reason I sometimes take myself to bed. Might as well do what I'm accused of anyway.

Attempts at adult conversation with Niall are for the most part rejected. I can count one minute tops before he's huffing and puffing that he's missing the news, that he's been at work all day and wants a few minutes peace to catch up. With Joe in the other room watching the Simpsons or playing on his DS, I retreat to Facebook, but there's limited solace found in what people I've never met have eaten that evening.

Once I hear Niall snoring on the sofa I'm back in bed, reading until my eyes close. I'm embarrassed to admit it, but I skip past any rude bits. They make me depressed and unhappy. How bad is that? I think I've got a more than alright figure for a thirty-one-year-old mother of one, but Niall doesn't appear to have any interest in seeing it at the moment. I wonder if he's addicted to computer porn or, being as he's ten years older than I am, just too knackered after work.

Niall feels life is mapped out – wife and kid, steady job, house and cars – I'm totally lost.

But tonight is going to be different. It's time to bring sexy back.


I run my hands down the black satin chemise I've bought. The stretchy, glossy material pushes my breasts up like Moll Flanders and does a good job of holding in my post-childbirth stomach. On goes a pair of hold ups with a lacy trim and some black stilettos with a pink sole, 'Car to Bar' shoes that I've never actually worn because I can hardly balance in them. I bought them because they were pretty and on sale. Looking at them makes me happy and I'll take joy where I can find it these days.

Checking myself out in the full-length mirror at the top of the stairs, I'm surprised to see I look quite fit. Enthused, and just a little turned on, I return to our room. I lie back on the bed and wait for Niall to come in to set his alarm clock. This is his evening ritual, post settling Joe down, and prior to switching the TV back on.

The door opens, and Niall enters the room. His blonde, wavy hair is all floppy, as if he's just run his hands through it. He still has a hint of a tan from our holidays. His newly appearing lines add to his handsomeness in a craggy, but sexy kind of way. He barely glimpses at me as he tiptoes past and reaches for his clock. I flex one of my shag-me shoes in his direction.

He nods towards the shoes. 'I'm nagged to death if I sit on the bed in my work clothes, but it's alright for you to have your shoes on then?'

I grit my teeth, kick off the shoes and sit up straighter. My breasts spill out over the top of the outfit, and I curl my legs up under myself. I let a lock of my own blonde hair fall across my face. In my mind I am a total sex kitten. Niall sets his alarm and after placing it on the bedside table turns towards me. I attempt what I hope is an alluring look, raising my eyebrows and giving him a hint of a smile.

'Love...' He looks at me like he's found me wandering the streets confused. 'You don't have to get dressed up for me. It's just going to come off anyway.' He sits on the bed at the side of me, then points and smirks. 'How much of my overtime have you spent on that thing? It's like a taped-up bin bag. I could've made you one just like it for about seventeen pence and still had enough left to line the bins.'

My mouth drops open as he undoes his trousers, and not because I'm about to suck him off.

'Fuck you.' I throw myself under the duvet. The tears in my eyes sting against the non-waterproof mascara I've left on. He mutters that he can't do anything right, re-zips, and walks back around the bed. The door clicks and his footsteps tread down the stairs. Within a minute, the low hum of the television travels through the floor.

I cry, wondering if I'm just not attractive anymore. I replay the scene over and over in my head, trying to work out how it went from the hot, mind blowing sex I'd been imagining, to this. Rage takes over again, making me tremble. I sit up, breathing rapidly, and wondering whether to go downstairs and ram my heel through the television set; at least then they would have proved a useful purchase. My eyes dart around the room, searching; my jaw firm with tension. I grab hold of Niall's pillow and pretend it's his face. I punch it until I'm out of breath.

Spotting his alarm clock, an idea forms. Pressing buttons, I change it to go off at seven pm. He'll oversleep and think he set it wrong. It's a small thing, but it makes me smile. My head throbs with tension, and as I lay my head on my pillow, I imagine it will take me ages to get to sleep. However, my brain must wish to block out the evening's trauma and I am out within minutes.

The next morning, I slip out of bed, wake Joe and head downstairs. Part of me feels guilty about the alarm clock and I pause on the stairs. Sucking at my lip, I consider going back up and waking Niall, but I just can't bring myself to do it. Instead, I decide to make Joe his favourite pancakes with strawberry sauce for breakfast. I creep back up to Joe's room to tell him. Whereas it usually takes forever for him to get out of bed, I get a 'Yay' and a thump as his feet hit the floor. He's out of bed, and in two minutes he's dressed and racing down the stairs for pancakes I won't be able to cook up fast enough for him. At nine, Joe is all skinniness and angles. His face has elongated over the last couple of months, looking more adult, and his shoulders have broadened. In contrast, his legs and feet resemble golf clubs, but his brain activity seems to be decreasing as his body grows. Yesterday I discovered him trying to saw Lego in half with my best knife when he'd supposedly gone in the kitchen for a biscuit. My heart melts when I see him enter the dining room. His short blonde hair is mussed up from sleeping and he's only half-awake. He looks at me with one eye scrunched up, as he does when he's trying to get used to the light.

'Can I have three pancakes today please, Mum?'

I laugh, telling him to try to eat one first and see how he goes, and head to the kitchen to start cooking. He does indeed manage to eat three, thanks to a soft mother who makes them small enough so he can manage it. He's so pleased with himself that he gets ready for school easily this morning, which is a godsend.

Just before we put on our coats to head out of the door, I pop upstairs to the bedroom and feign alarm, whilst inside rejoicing with an inner monologue of 'Take that you bastard'.

'Niall,' I say. 'Niall?'

There's a grunt from under the covers, of which I can't make out a word.

'Niall, its eight thirty. Shouldn't you be up?'

Niall shoots up so fast that in trying to pick up the clock, his muscular hairy arm sends it flying across the floor. 'Shit,' he says. 'Why didn't you wake me?'

I note the fact that he immediately blames me for his predicament, even if this time he is correct.

'I saw you set your alarm last night, so I never gave it a thought until now.'

'Damn,' says Niall, the clock now in his hand. He rubs his eye with the other hand. 'I set it for pm instead.'

I hitch the strap of my bag further up my shoulder. 'Well, I have to go, or Joe will be late for school,' I say. 'I hope you don't get into much trouble with work.'

He waves his arm at me. 'Nah,' he states. 'I'll just phone and tell them I had to go to the doctors.' With that, he lays his head back down on the pillow.

I feel my chest tighten and try to swallow the acid rising up from my gut. Does nothing ever rattle this man? I'm beginning to think I have a Stepford husband.

'Well, see you later,' I say. My smile fixed and teeth gritted, I close the door, head back downstairs, grab my bag and keys and take Joe to school.

Joe dropped off, I get back into my lovely metallic blue Nissan Micra and pull the lever until the seat is further back and I have more leg room. I lean back into the comfy padded upholstery and reach into my bag for my mobile phone. I pull out my iPhone and fire off a quick text to my friend Monique.

**Fed up. U free for cofi n chat?**

Within seconds I have a reply.

**God, yes. Get here asap.**

Texting that I'm on my way, I pull my seat forward and set off; calling at the supermarket bakery en-route for two pain au chocolats.

My friend's apartment is part of a large Victorian building that from a distance looks like a stately home. An elegant stone staircase leads to the front entrance. The grounds have large swathes of green grass and established shrubbery and trees. A consultant at the local hospital, where Monique works part-time as a research assistant, told her he thought she owned it all after giving her a lift home. Monique would make you think that though. She is immaculate. Tall with short brown hair in a pixie crop, she is the colour of the finest milk chocolate and has a row of freckles across her cheeks that add to her exoticness. She has exacting standards and will not leave the house without full make up and painted nails. Her clothing looks like it cost hundreds of pounds, and yet I know that the majority of it comes from the charity shops located in her local area. She lives in Ecclesall, a district full of yummy mummies who want the latest of everything and dispose of their attire the moment the next season is on the runway.

I first met Monique at yoga class five years ago, when I was desperately trying to shake off my frumpy mummy self-image. We hit it off and she took me under her wing, seeing me as both a friend and a little project. Now I feel I can hold my own with clothes and make-up, though I have to confess to making more of an effort on the days I'm seeing her.

She opens her door and I'm greeted with a wide smile that makes her look even more gorgeous.

'Hi, Lo.'

She never gets bored of this.

I roll my eyes. 'You letting me in or what? I have breakfast.' I hold up the bag and crinkle it before her eyes.

She scrunches her nose up. 'Ugh. An Asda carrier bag? Where on earth is that swish shopper bag I got you with Paris on it?'

'That's not as much fun as seeing your face when you have to touch a carrier bag.' I giggle, and hand it to her as I step through to the foyer.

She mock shivers and leads the way to her apartment, all the while holding the bag like it's a used nappy.

Monique's apartment is on the ground floor. She takes the bag through to the kitchen while I go straight through the hallway, removing my sandals to carry in my hand. I move past the sitting room and through the patio doors to outside. I claim one of the two wrought iron chairs and slip my footwear back on.

Within a few minutes, Monique comes outside bearing a cream vintage tray covered in tiny pink roses—a gift from me. Upon it are two steaming cups of coffee in pink tipped cream tea cups, nestled on pink tipped cream saucers with space for the Amaretti biscuit which lies beside it. Our pain au chocolats sit on matching side plates. No mismatching crockery for Monique.

She raises an eyebrow. 'What's up with you then, misery guts?'

I fill her in on my night of seduction. Monique is no fan of Niall and the way he fails to ever give me compliments. She shakes her head as I get to the part where I told him to get out. She stays silent for a moment and I wait to hear her verdict, and then she looks at me and falls about laughing. I can't help it. Her laughter's infectious and I start giggling too. Huge fat tears roll down my face as I think how funny it was, and then I think about how utterly humiliating it was and die a little more inside.

'Lo, he's Niall. He doesn't do seduction. He never notices your normal clothes, never mind your night attire,' she says. 'You've spent the last God knows how many years just getting into bed and getting on with it, and then you go and dress like a porn star. It probably blew a gasket in his brain. If he didn't want you, he wouldn't have tried to get into bed. It's obvious he sees the attire as an unnecessary barrier. You do remember who your husband is, right? Mr Unromantic. Mr Moody. You expected him to turn all Christian Grey on your ass? Seriously?'

'Okay, okay, I admit in hindsight I was a tad deluded. I just thought he'd think whoa and—'

'Take them off? As I keep saying, Niall just thinks you're wasting VBT.'

'VBT?'

'Valuable bonking time. Now stop talking and eat your pastry. I need to tell you about my Friday night hottie, and I don't mean a wheat bag.'

I partake of my delicious, pain au chocolat, chasing the sauce escaping from the corner of my mouth with my tongue. Monique tells me about the twenty-six-year-old medical student she got off with on Friday night. She hasn't had a serious relationship since Toby left her ten years ago after her refusal to have children. I didn't know her then. She was thirty-two; Toby was thirty-eight. He felt it was time. He left, and within six months had a pregnant girlfriend. Monique moved to Sheffield to start over. She's ten and a bit years older than me, although you wouldn't know it to look at her. She says she's inherited her mother's skin: there's barely a line on her face and sometimes

I feel very jealous. My crow's feet and frown lines have deepened over the last few years. I think having children must be an ageing factor. All that stress is enough to give anyone a few extra lines. Monique is blunt about why she doesn't want children and I love her for it.

'They make a mess and I can't deal with it. Plus, they want constant attention and I want all my attention.'

That said, she still makes the effort to see Joe a few times a year, and she really makes a big effort when she does. I selfishly and secretly like the fact that she's my child-free friend. She's the one I can talk to about books, fashion, and the latest on Netflix. I don't have to chat about school, SATs, and the things about having a child that bore me rigid to be honest. I don't do well with routine and having to get up at the same time to go to the same place twice a day nearly sends me demented.

'So how's Joe?' she says, like she's reading my mind.

'Oh. Well he totally loves school and must be the only child not looking forward to the summer break. He says he wishes school was carrying on. I think he's scared he's going to be stuck with me. I'm becoming less cool the older he gets.'

'Yeah, right. Joe totally adores you and you know it. You are Cool Mum personified. When are the holidays anyway? And more importantly, are you going to be able to ditch him for some girl time?'

'There's seven weeks left of the term, and yes, I've lined up some holiday clubs, so we can skive off. You'll have to let me know when you're free, so I can put it in my diary.' Monique looks satisfied at this and I know it was the correct response, though Joe hates holiday clubs and I feel torn between them both. 'Joe was extra excited today because a new boy was starting in class. I told him to be nice to him.'

'Strange time to start school?'

'I know. I can only think that his mum's doing it to get him introduced to the kids before the break. I hope he's a good kid, because that class has its fair share of troublemakers as it is.'

Monique starts looking around the room, my signal that she's getting bored.

'Anyway, enough about men and children,' I say. 'Show me the new clothes you've bought this week, you know you're dying to.' She claps her hands on her knees, smiles and goes off to get them whilst I move inside to the sofa and make myself comfortable. This is what I love, fashion. I smile to myself as I wait to see her latest collection.

She doesn't disappoint. A black knee length Wallis jacket sits amongst the items she piles at the side of me. I feel my mouth get wet as I look at it. She grins. 'See you don't need sex when you have fashion porn. Try it on. I picked it for you.'

I pull it around myself. The waist nips in and the bottom of the jacket flares out ever so slightly. I shimmy so it swings. Monique looks at me like a mother at her child's first school uniform fitting. I hug her. 'Thank you, it's beautiful.'

'You're very welcome. Now, how about another coffee and Real Housewives of NYC?'

'Mon, my life is complete,' I giggle, sitting back on the sofa and keeping my new jacket on so I can keep touching it.

Back at home I catch up with the 'Chore of the Day' (my latest project to alleviate boredom, courtesy of Pinterest). Today's exciting chore is vacuuming the house. Then I check my eBay account. I've not got much for sale at the moment, and I hope the weekend's nice for trawling car boots in search of bedraggled Barbie dolls and pretty vintage pieces. My business started off as a hobby when Joe was younger. A lot of my friends had daughters at a similar time and I was secretly jealous that they got to play with dolls. I don't think I've ever totally grown up. I'd got into eBaying while Niall had been nurse training. We were broke, so I'd sold anything I thought might make some money to help pay the bills. I noticed that Barbie clothes sold well and started looking around for them at summer fairs and car boots. Then I took to buying dolls that looked like they had seen better days; washing them, brushing their hair, mending their clothes and then selling them online in the run up to Christmas. I made a few hundred pounds and earned a good reputation for selling them, so I started my little eBay shop, *Lauren's pre-loved.* My obsession with all things vintage followed: pretty tea-cups, jewellery, the odd piece of clothing. It had grown into a little part-time job that fitted in perfectly around Joe and helped keep me sane.

I make a mental note to list the nine or so items in the box at the side of the desk later on, and then head off to school to collect Joe.

I meet Tanya, one of the other school mums, at the bottom of the school drive. Tall and slender, with her red hair tied in a ponytail with a huge scarf, she's easily identifiable from some distance away. I get on well with most of the school mums and we have the odd coffee, but I keep a distance as I have Monique and that's enough for me.

The walk up the drive only takes a few minutes. It leads past the main school building into a playground complete with two small benches, a wooden climbing frame and a large grassed area. In the corner of the playground are two Portakabins, one of which is Joe's classroom. We all gather nearby and await the release of our little angels. For once it's not raining.

'Did you know there's a new boy in school? Our Billy told me.' Tanya says.

'Yep, Joe said. I think he started today.'

'I've heard his mum's a footballer's wife,' she adds.

'What?' I laugh. 'A WAG, in Handsworth? You've got to be kidding; surely, she wouldn't come to live here? Not being funny, because I love living here myself, but it's hardly chock full of McMansions is it?'

Tanya shrugs. 'Just saying what I heard. We'll find out in a minute anyway, because she's over there.'

We head over to the tiny woman standing sideways to us. It has to be her as she is a stereotypical WAG. Her hair is almost yellow blonde, spiraled tendrils reaching the bottom of her back. She flicks it with her fingers, dazzling us with pink glitter painted fingernails, then turns to us showing an over-tanned face. It's either sunbed or real tan, because her skin resembles the part of my leather sofa where Niall's bottom has worn the seat out. Her mouth opens to reveal white teeth that might be okay in London, but in Sheffield, and against the tanned skin, look ridiculous, like snow on a beach.

She turns towards me. Her eyes open wide. 'Lauren,' she shouts, rushing over and throwing her arms around me. My forehead creases and I tense as I'm locked in her embrace, because I don't know who the hell she is. She releases me, and I step back to look at her. Her eyes look familiar and I'm just trying to place her when she adds, 'You muppet, it's me. Liz Parker, from Brook.'

I stare at her, and then try and plant a smile on my face as I realise an old echo from my life is back – one I didn't wish to hear again.

## CHAPTER TWO

'Gosh, Liz, er, I haven't seen you for years,' I state, my hand held to my chest.

'Yeah, well Danny went to play for Leeds United, so we were there for a while.'

There's a silence while I process the fact she's in front of me. The Liz I knew was a spotty, mousy-haired loner. I made the mistake of standing up for her when a rumour spread around school that she'd been caught masturbating in the toilets with her lunch box banana. She thanked me by reporting the culprits to the teachers and misguidedly told them I was being picked on too. I can only think she said it in some pathetic attempt to be my friend, but I was furious and joined in the rumour-mongering instead. I remember how she looked at me as she walked out of the headteacher's office while I sat outside awaiting my fate. I was threatened with suspension and had my Prefect badge taken away. Liz's parents took her out of school shortly after that and I didn't see her again. I'd heard a rumour later that her parents had discovered she was pregnant to Danny Southwell, one of the school hard cases who played football any time he could, and just like that, the WAG thing clicked. 'So, you and Danny stuck together? Wow.'

'You hadn't heard how successful Danny was?'

I shook my head. 'Sorry, I don't follow sport.'

She stares at me like she doesn't quite believe me and sighs. 'So you didn't hear about me being made to marry Danny because I was pregnant? You must have been the only person in South Yorkshire who didn't.'

I grit my teeth and shake my head again.

'I lost the baby, but we stayed together and had Tyler. Danny did well at Leeds, but we're divorced now. I've moved back to Sheffield to be nearer my mum. She isn't getting any younger and she dotes on Tyler.'

Good God, an over-sharer. I've only been standing here five minutes and I have her whole life history.

'Fancy you being here anyway. So you've children too?'

'Just the one, Joe. Well, I hope you get settled soon.' I look towards the classroom door as the kids start coming out of class. Thank goodness I can get out of here. 'I'm sure Joe will keep an eye on Tyler.'

'Oh, that's so kind,' she says as a child comes sloping towards her with a face so sneering it looks like the kid's had a stroke.

'Well, see you later, Liz,' I state.

'Oh,' she makes a small tinkly laugh. 'It's Bettina now. Bettina Southwell. I gave myself a fresh start when we moved to Leeds.

I dread to think what my face looks like in response to this. Niall says I am incapable of masking my emotions.

'Hey,' she adds, 'before you go, let's swap numbers. I'm out of touch with people around here. We must do coffee sometime.'

I hesitate as I've no wish to get involved with a girl I barely knew at school. 'I've not got my phone on me at the mo, but I'll bring it some other time.'

'Sure,' she says and smiles. 'Catch you tomorrow.'

When we get to the car, I ask Joe what his new schoolfriend is like.

'He's ace, Mum, dead cool. He's got over five-hundred Pokemon cards and loads of spares he says I can have.' Pokemon is Joe's new obsession, so Tyler will be a God now in his eyes.

'He seemed moody when he came out of school,' I mention. 'Was he like that in class?'

'Nope, he said his mum gets on his nerves. She's always making him do things he doesn't want to do, like moving.'

'Well, he'll be missing his friends from Leeds.'

'Suppose so,' Joe sucks on his bottom lip. 'But he's got me now.'

I walk into the house and for once I don't chastise my child as he leaves his coat and bag on the stairs and his shoes strewn in the hallway. Instead, I put the kettle on, make myself a coffee and reach into one of the high up kitchen cupboards. I take out a bottle of whisky, my tipple of choice on the few occasions I drink. I throw a good measure in, before finally plonking myself in a dining room chair.

'Can I play with my Lego?' Joe asks, seeing a chance to take advantage over the mother who usually gets him to practice his reading first.

'Whatever you want.' Joe looks at me strangely but runs off to his room before the alien leaves and his real mother returns.

I sink back in the chair, coffee in my hands, and close my eyes. I can feel a tension headache starting. I've loved being part of that school since Joe started, but now I feel a sense of dread. I was never friends with this woman, so how do I put her off without seeming mean? I can only hope she befriends some of the other mothers. Or maybe, I chastise myself, after all these years she's turned out okay and I should give her a chance. I take a large swig of my coffee. The whisky warms my mouth as much as the hot drink, and I decide I'm ditching tonight's planned tea and will walk to the chippy. Then I'll have a top up.

Niall comes home from work and I realise that Monique's chat and the latest school events have overtaken my frustration with him.

As I ask him my usual 'Have you had an okay day?' I can see the relief in his face, and then he looks at me with a furrowed brow. 'Have you been drinking?'

This behaviour is completely out of character for me on a school day. My anxieties about needing to be able to drive in case of an emergency with Joe mean I only usually drink on special occasions, or if I have a cold to help me sleep. I fill him in on the events of the afternoon, but I'm not sure how much of it he's taken in as he turns the news on at the same time, and then sits in the chair I vacated to let him in the house. 'Niall, what'll I do?'

'You're worrying over nothing, Lauren. Just smile at the woman, say hello, and leave it at that,' he advises in his *men provide solutions not empathy* voice. 'That Danny Southwell's a proper headcase though. He was always getting red-carded, so we best keep a close eye on Joe's new friend.' Then he turns back to the news.

I pick up my bag ready to head to the chippy. I can see that my problem is already solved in Niall's eyes, and that's the only advice I'll get.

Later in the evening I go to the secret Facebook Group I set up with Monique and leave her a message about the new kid and his mother. Of course, she knows nothing about my history with the now-named Bettina. I leave Facebook open whilst adding my eBay listings, and flip back when I see someone has posted. Sure enough, it's Monique.

***Jeez, if you're gonna change your name, change it to something nice, but normal. Who the fuck would actually want to be called that?***

**She looks like Donatella Versace.** I add with venom. Secret Facebook just makes me bitchier; I can't resist it when there's no-one else reading.

***Lol. So what's the WAG thing all about?***

**It's in her head; Danny played for Leeds. I googled him. He did okay, but he's hardly Beckham.**

*PMSL.*
**Dreading tomorrow.**
*Ask her to come for coffee with us next Monday. I need to meet her. It'll be a right laugh.*
**Noooooooo.**
*Yesssssss... pretty please?*
**Oh, Mon, I dunno. I doubt she'll do our coffee shop anyway. It's not in Harvey Nicks.**
*She might turn up with a Chihuahua in her handbag. I bet she wears a Juicy Couture tracky with Uggs. And hair curlers in her hair.*
**ROFLMAO. No I think she likes leopard print, like you.**
*Piss off.*
**Nite, Cougar.**
*Nite. INVITE her.*


Niall comes to bed about ten which is ridiculously early for him. I keep my face firmly on my book, but he undresses and snuggles up beside me, placing a hand on my breast. I'm feeling quite squiffy from all the whisky I've consumed. I do feel quite in the mood but choose to ignore him. 'I'm sorry about last night,' he says. 'I didn't mean to upset you. I just wanted you to know you don't have to dress up for me.'

'S'okay.' I turn the page of my book.

'Anyway, to make amends...'

He jumps out of bed to reveal a pair of crocodile pants, a joke I bought him once as a Christmas gift that have laid abandoned in a drawer. He runs around the bed with them on and I watch them snap, snap, snap. I collapse with giggles.

He lands next to me. 'So, d'ya think I'm sexy?'

'Quit while you're ahead, mate,' I state and turn towards him, pushing him back on the bed.

The next morning, I drop Joe off at the bottom of the school driveway. I know it's pathetic and in doing so I had to pull up on the very zigzags I berate the other parents for parking on, but I just can't face seeing Bettina this morning. I decide that the scheduled housework can stuff for the day as well. The weather is beautiful, and I drive up to Ecclesall Road, which is chock full of second-hand shops, gorgeous chocolatiers, and coffee shops. I browse for vintage items and wander from shop to shop, just enjoying the day. I pick up some pieces of jewellery: a gorgeous bronze coloured sequined clutch bag and a handmade crocheted cream shrug. I have my latest book in my bag; a chick lit about someone travelling to Paris. At lunchtime I walk the few minutes to the local park, sit myself under a tree and eat a prawn baguette. The sun warms my skin and my head floats to the Champs Elysees. When it's time to drive back to school, I lean back against the tree, ignoring the bark digging in my back and sigh. I really don't want to go there. I take my phone out of my bag and ring Tanya instead.

'I'm stuck in traffic and going to be late. Will you take Joe to yours and I'll pick him up from there?'

'Yes, of course, don't worry. Take your time. We'll see you whenever.'

I try to get back into my book, but my mind is distracted by thoughts of the past. I can't avoid Bettina forever, but after all these years I still feel like I want to shout at her for what she did to me. I still remember my mother's reaction. She was furious when she discovered I'd lost my prefect status and accused me of taking after my father, calling me a bully. I take a breath and tell myself I'm being completely irrational, that it was all such a long time ago. I resolve to see her tomorrow, ask her for coffee, and stop being so ridiculous. I might even ask Tyler for tea if Joe continues to get on well with him. I pick up my baguette wrapper and my spoils of the day and head back to the car to drive to Tanya's.

Later, I feel so much better for having a me-day. I help Joe with his spellings and let all my Lego figures lose to his in battle. Then I spend the evening with Niall, even though he's watching a run of TV shows about pimping up cars. Before I get in bed, I have another little peek at my treasures from the shops. I cradle a delicate necklace in my hand and admire the white teacup pendant. Pink roses adorn the cup and saucer, and gold leaf swirls around the rim and edges. I decide to keep it for myself, to remind me of how lucky I am that I can spend my days this way.

The following morning, Bettina spots me at the bottom of the drive. I decide to make an effort and wait for her to drop Tyler off as she's still taking him up to the classroom door.

'Has Tyler enjoyed his first few days?'

'He loves it. I'm so surprised. I thought he'd really miss his friends in Leeds. Joe is helping a lot. He's introduced him to the other lads.'

'It must be hard being the new kid.'

'Yeah,' Bettina says, breaking eye contact with me for a moment.

I remember she had to start again after she left our school. 'Are you doing anything now, or do you want to grab a coffee?' I say quickly, to get her mind back from wherever it is before I chicken out and abandon her.

'I'd love one,' she replies. 'Where shall we go?'

'I'll think of somewhere. Leave your car here, and we'll pick it up later.'

'Oh. I don't drive.'

'Okay, well I can drop you back at yours after. I'm parked this way.' I point up the hill. We head up the road to the car and once inside, I set off trying to think of a decent coffee shop. She asks me about my mum and dad and other things from the past. I move the conversation on to current times and ask where she's living. It's a house a few streets away from school in a popular catchment area, so she must have done okay by Danny in the divorce.

Handsworth only has the local supermarket cafe, so I drive further afield, to a garden centre cafe in Wentworth that I enjoy visiting. Bettina and I dodge branches from shrubs and take care not to knock into garden ornaments on our way into the cafe. I take us to the waitress service section where we order two coffees and two teacakes. Just as I wonder what on earth I'm going to talk to her about, she speaks.

'Have you seen the sign for help with the summer fair at school?'

I pull a face. 'Yeah, but I don't usually get involved to be honest.'

'Oh.' Her posture sags. 'I thought it might be a good way for me to get to know some of the teachers, but I didn't want to go on my own. I wondered if you'd come to the meeting with me? You don't have to sign up for anything. Just come for moral support.'

I chew my lip as I try to think of a way to get out of it, and then remember I'm meant to be making an effort. 'Go on then, when is it?'

'Tonight at six.'

Inwardly cursing, I decide we can have a quick pizza tea, and that the curry I took out of the freezer will keep for tomorrow. I don't want to arrive at the meeting smelling of garlic. I don't realise I'm daydreaming, mentally planning the evening meals, until Bettina touches my arm.

'Is that okay? It's not too short notice, is it?'

I shake my head. 'It's fine. I'll text Niall and let him know to get straight home after work. I'll meet you outside the school at five to.'

'Thank you so much. I'm so pleased I've found someone I know. You and Joe are being so kind to us.' She reaches across the table and gives my hand a squeeze.

'Honestly, don't worry about it.' I feign a cough, so I can take my hand away, and take a sip of my coffee.

'But you really are being so helpful.'

'Well, I believe in treating everyone as I'd like to be treated myself.' God, I can hear my mother's platitudes coming out of my mouth.

'Oh, I agree with that,' she replies, looking towards the window for a moment. She turns back. 'Any ideas as to what we'll get roped into at the fair?'

'Hey, no *we*. I'm the moral support, remember? But I'll put your hand up if there's any custard pie throwing.'

'Don't you dare,' Bettina flicks a stray currant at me. We start laughing, and I relax a little. Maybe she's not so bad after all.

The meeting starts at six pm sharp. In the school hall, there's Mrs Sullivan, the headteacher; and an assortment of other teachers, assistants, and parents. Amongst them is Mr Kingsley, who'll be Joe's form teacher next year. He started halfway through the year to cover maternity leave, so I've only seen him once or twice. He's a bit of a nerdy looking thing, with his gelled back tufty brown hair, and glasses. The green pullover and grey slacks don't help either. I guess he's over six feet tall because he looks similar in height to Niall. I find myself thinking that he must be around his mid-thirties because he doesn't have the beginning of Niall's middle-aged spread. It'll be a nice change for Joe to have a male teacher though, another male mentor. Mr Kingsley pulls up a chair next to mine and gives a small nod in greeting. Bettina looks at me.

'Who's the geek?' she whispers.

'Sssshhh, you'll miss the pie casting.'

She sticks her tongue out at me and laughs. 'I'm so putting you up for something now.'

Mrs Sullivan explains how she's hoping that this year we'll raise even more funds for the school as the library is in need of a makeover. I adore books and reading and decide to volunteer to run the book stall. I whisper the idea to Bettina and she gives me a thumbs up. Mrs Sullivan says she has a number of roles to fill and will then discuss any further issues. She's a formidable looking woman, I guess in her late fifties, with bobbed light brown hair. She frowns a lot which has left two vivid crease marks over her brow. We're given the date of the fair – just under three weeks away, on Saturday the twenty-second of June. I quickly check my diary, but we have nothing down for that day, so I know I'm clear to volunteer.

'Right, I'll go through the roles we have to fill. Please raise your hand if you're interested. Okay, firstly there's the cake stall…'

Mrs Sullivan goes through a few of the more usual stalls including tombola and 'guess the amount of marbles in the jar'. Bettina's yet to volunteer, and I'm waiting for the book stall to be called out.

'Now we need a very willing volunteer for the sponge stocks…'

Quick as a flash Bettina lifts my hand up. 'Lauren'll do that. She said she wanted to do something crazy.'

'Brilliant, Mrs Lawler, that's so kind. It's usually difficult to get a volunteer for that one, so thank you.'

I look at Bettina, a half-smile on my face, wondering what she's playing at.

'And now the book stall,' says Mrs Sullivan.

Bettina lifts her hand while biting her lip. 'Err, actually could Lauren help me with that instead of doing the sponge stocks?'

'I hardly think a small book stall requires two people,' Mrs Sullivan berates in her scary headteacher voice.

Bettina visibly shrinks and then turns to me mouthing, 'I'm so sorry.'

'Don't worry about it,' I say. 'You can always swap with me.'

'I would, but I'm scared of water,' she replies, her eyes filling with tears.

'I'll help Mrs Lawler with the sponge stocks,' says the male voice to my right. Mr Kingsley has finally spoken up. 'The kids would much rather pelt a teacher, and Mrs Lawler can collect the money and pass me towels to help me dry off.'

'A good point,' says Mrs Sullivan. 'Well, that's the roles all decided then. I suggest you take some time to consider what you need for your stalls, and we'll reconvene at the same time next week. If there's nothing else, I'll see you then.' Her tone suggests that the 'discussion' part of the meeting isn't something she's required for, and we're all dismissed.

I turn to find Mr Kingsley hovering beside me. 'Can you spare me ten minutes to go through what we need to do?'

'Sure,' I say turning around to Bettina. 'I'll catch you tomorrow, missus, and you'd better watch out on fair day for stray flying sponges.'

'I really am sorry. I'll do you proud with the book stall,' she says in a quiet voice.

'You'd better,' I say to her retreating back.

'Right, well, school's closing. Any chance you can nip around the corner to the Queen's Head?' Mr Kingsley shifts from foot to foot.

'Why not?' I reply. I feel riled with Bettina and consider I need a drink after being roped in to being hit with wet sponges all day. At this rate I'll be in The Priory by the end of the term.

The Queen's Head is about a five-minute walk from school. It's an old-fashioned pub that's been there for years and is badly in need of redecoration. The burgundy leather seating is worn, but comfy, and I deposit myself on it. Mr Kingsley takes the seat opposite me on a purple and gold chair in major need of some TLC.

'What would you like to drink?'

I go to get my purse from my bag.

'Oh, no, this is on me.'

'Oh, okay, thanks. A whisky with ice then please, Mr Kingsley.'

He bursts out laughing, which suits him. His teeth would be flawless except for one at the front that twists just slightly.

'Seb, please,' he says, 'or I just won't answer you.'

'Okay, Seb please,' I josh back. 'I still want a whisky.'

He smiles and heads to the bar.

Drink placed in front of me, I watch as Seb looks around and removes his glasses. 'Phew, that's better.'

'Do you wear contacts?' I ask, taking a drink.

'I'll let you into a secret, Mrs Lawler,' he leans over the table towards me and whispers near my ear. 'I don't need glasses, they're just for show.'

The mouthful of whisky I've taken splatters ungainly from my mouth. 'It's Lauren. Sorry, I don't understand.'

'Well, Lauren sorry I don't understand,' he deadpans back at me. 'See, I'm just dressing for the job.'

'What?' My forehead creases. I lean back and cross my legs. Seb gets up from his seat.

'Give me a couple of minutes,' he says.

The brown-haired man who returns to the bar from the gents' bathroom bears little resemblance to the man I sat next to at the school fair meeting. His hair is tousled in very sexy waves. At a guess I'd say it's been wet and dried in the bathroom. Without the glasses, I see that he has the most beautiful dark brown eyes. He's removed the pullover and undone the collar of his shirt. I suddenly get the thought that Niall would not be happy to find me sitting here with this version of Mr Kingsley.

I rise from my seat and take a last swig of my drink. 'I need to go.'

'But I've not explained yet,' he says.

I hesitate, casting my eye at the wall clock to check the time. 'Okay, five more minutes then,' I reply as I am a little intrigued. I sit back down.

'I've not been a very reliable employee in the past, so I decided to try a new tack.' He shrugs. 'I dressed up in my best impression of a stereotypical teacher, gelled my unruly hair down, put on a pair of fake reading glasses, and went for an interview. I gave it everything I had. The head said she'd keep me on if I knuckled down and earned the respect of the other teachers. I've had to dress like it ever since. It works though. The other teachers love me; but it's killing me dressing like Clark Kent.'

'It serves you right for being fake.' I take out my ponytail and re-fix it.

'Hey, we're all fakes in some way,' he replies, his brown eyes on mine. 'People can be completely different with others. Look at you, acting like you were interested in being part of the fair tonight.'

I shuffle in my seat.

His mouth turns up at the corner and his eyes sparkle with mischief. 'I'd like to know what's underneath the surface of you, Lauren Lawler.'

I look down my nose at him. 'What you see is what you get. Anyway, now that I have your life story, what do we need to do about the fair?'

He stretches his hands behind his head. 'Well, we turn up on the day. Get the stocks, sponges and the bucket out of the store room and we're ready. Can you bring some towels?'

My voice turns sharp. 'You could have said that in the school hall.'

'But then I wouldn't have had the pleasure of your lovely company.'

'I'm married, Mr Kingsley.' I place emphasis on his name.

He puts his hands up in front of me. 'Have I stated any improper attentions towards you? No. It's very presumptuous of you, Mrs Lawler, to imply I was angling for a shag or something.'

I feel the heat rise in my cheeks, although I'm not someone who usually blushes.

He carries on, 'I just thought the pub would be nicer. I fancied a pint and don't like drinking alone.'

'Well, I need to head home now,' I state, and get up to leave.

'Of course, if you do fancy a ....'

'Goodnight, Mr Kingsley.' I almost run towards the door. I turn back just before I leave to make sure he's not following me and catch his eye. He winks. I'm too shell-shocked to respond and head home where the whisky bottle comes out of the cupboard for the second time that week.

## CHAPTER THREE

Niall is red in the face with mirth. 'Hey, Joe, did you hear? We can pay to hit your mother in the face with wet sponges. Don't need any practice, do you, love? We could always go out in the garden and hit you with the bath and kitchen ones?'

'Ha, bloody ha. I'm not being pelted. I'm the money collector.'

'It's a good job with your 36Ds. The husbands would all be skint, the wives would swap the sponges for rotten fruit, and the kids would be scarred for life.'

'Aren't you jealous about me towelling down Seb Kingsley?'

'What am I supposed to be jealous of? Joe says he's lame. You're hardly planning on putting his arms in the stocks to have your wicked way with him, are you?'

I huff and waltz into the kitchen to do the packing up. Niall follows me in.

'Don't suppose you can borrow those stocks?' He grins.

'Only thing on you I want to lock up is your mouth,' I fire back.

'Kinky,' he replies, smacks me on the rear and returns to his favourite chair.

. . .

That evening I sit on the sofa near Niall as he watches some sports programme. He doesn't utter a word. I'm wondering if he's no longer interested in my conversation, or if we've just run out of things to talk about. I know if I was to start talking now he'd get annoyed because I'd be interrupting his listening. I decide I'm going to talk anyway.

'Why do we always sit here in silence?'

'We don't sit in silence, love, because you can bet the minute I'm trying to listen to a crucial point, you yack on about something and interrupt me, like right now.'

'My conversation should be more important than anything on the television.'

'I've been at work all day -'

'Yeah, yeah, yeah, that's all I ever hear,' my voice rises as my temper does. 'Don't interrupt the news. Don't interrupt Gordon Fucking Ramsey. Don't interrupt me being a boring fart.'

'You're being ridiculous.' Niall mutes the television and turns to me. 'I'm sorry, what is it that's so important?'

Reasonable, never ruffled Niall. He drives me mad. I want him to argue back, to fight and show me some passion.

'It doesn't matter now, it'll seem stupid,' I say. 'I'm going to bed.'


I don't pick my book up straightaway but lie back against the pillow, pull up the duvet, and wonder how long it will actually be before we have sex again. It's become about once a month, so after the other day that's June done with. It doesn't help that Joe's always getting out of bed and is settling down later and later, so by the time he finally falls asleep, it's my own bed time. I'm exhausted by then and just want to sleep, not go and see if Niall's up for it. I worry about us not doing it enough, but if I ever raise the issue Niall just dismisses it and says he's happy and we don't need to be at it like rabbits. It makes me feel insecure though. I know I'm not bad looking for my age, and my figure is still trim and firm, but I worry I'm getting to the point where the wolf-whistles stop, and no-one will find me attractive. I think about the evening in the pub. I was totally shocked. Who'd have thought that nerdy Mr Kingsley had all that going on under his clothes? As much as I felt irritated with how he spoke to me, I keep replaying the conversation in my head and I like the fact he flirted with me. I need to be flirted with. Maybe Niall would be a bit more interested in me if it were possible to dress up as a 1956 Ford Zephyr. I wonder how Seb would have reacted to my boudoir outfit? I realise I'm smiling and berate myself for thinking like this. I love my husband.

Monday comes around fast, and I meet Bettina at the school gates, so we can travel in my car together to meet Monique. Bettina is quiet at first, twirling a piece of her hair around and staring out of the front window. After a few minutes of awkward silence she asks, 'You're not mad at me about the sponge stocks, are you?'

'How long have you been worrying about that?' I reply. 'And no, I'm over it. I'm not going in the stocks and it should be a laugh watching the kids pelt Seb.'

'Seb,' she says, considering the name. 'I wouldn't have thought him a Seb, more a Gordon or a Steve.'

'How stereotypical of you,' I mock. 'Whatever have the Gordons and Steves of the world done to you?'

'You know what I mean. He's dead straight looking. Sebastian's quite a cool name.'

'Yeah, well he's not quite as straight-laced as you might think,' I state, raising an eyebrow at her.

Her eyes fire up. 'Tell me more.'

I turn to her and wink. 'You'll have to wait til we get to the coffee shop. I want to fill Monique in, so I'll tell you both together.'

'Ooh, I hope she's on time.'

We pull up just down the road from the coffee shop that is mine and Monique's favourite haunt on Ecclesall Road. Tucked in between all the charity and other shops is a modern red brick building with almost floor to ceiling glass windows. Today is sunny, but not all that warm, so I walk past the outside tables and head inside towards my favourite corner. I'm happy to see it's free, and sink down into the warm, comfy, tan leather sofa that I wish I could transport home. It makes me feel snug and protected. I quite often remove my shoes and sit sideways with my feet up on it when I'm chatting to Monique. Bettina has seated herself at the side of me where Monique usually sits.

'God, they need new sofa's, I don't think I'll get back up from here.'

'It's lovely and comfy though.'

'You and your love of old things. Shall we wait for Monique before we get drinks?'

Monique charges through the door at that point. Dressed in a pale-yellow dress with an A-line skirt and cream wedge sandals on her feet, she is once again immaculately turned out.

I watch Bettina's eyes widen and she sits up straight, rising partway to shake Monique's hand. 'Hi, I'm Bettina, lovely to meet you.'

'Likewise. I've been looking forward to meeting someone who knew Lo at fifteen, you can give me some new material for taking the piss out of her.'

Bettina looks at me, her brow furrowing.

'I'm joking,' says Monique, mock thumping Bettina's arm lightly. 'Right, what are we having to drink?'

One thing about Monique is that she never shuts up talking, so within minutes of being seated, Bettina has relaxed and is joining in with the conversation, which has so far consisted of a critique of my outfit: a long black skirt with black sandals and a stringy-strapped lilac t-shirt that I thought looked okay.

'Good God, woman, it's summer. What're you doing in a long black skirt? As soon as you're home get it packed away. In fact, throw it out, those legs of yours should be seen. That top does nothing for your skin tone either. Where's the jade-green one you bought last time we were round here? And *why* are your toenails not painted?'

'I didn't have time,' I plead.

'Did you go on Facebook this morning?'

'Erm ...'

'Thought so, and if you were on there any longer than ten minutes you most certainly had time.'

I turn to Bettina. 'See what I have to put up with?'

'You two are hilarious,' she grins. 'It's like watching some kind of reality TV show. In fact, I think you should make a demo.'

'Hey, we could be the new Ant and Dec. We could call it The Lomon Show. If you say it in a Jamaican accent it sounds like Lemon,' I say.

'Right, you're in trouble,' states Monique turning to Bettina. 'You've started her on the lame joke telling. You don't know what you've done.'

'We could call it Bit r Lomon.'

'Shut up, *please*,' pleads Monique.

'Or learn sumo-wresting and call it Lomon squash.'

'Stop,' they yell out in unison.

I pretend to look hurt and take a sip of my coffee and then smirk at them both. 'Bettina, say beer can.'

'Beer can.'

'See you can talk Jamaican too. Say I want a beer can sandwich.'

Monique lifts her shoulders and drops them with a sigh. 'I give up.'

There's a break in conversation for a short time. 'I wonder if I could do with a makeover?' says Bettina quietly.

Monique re-energises. 'Well to be honest, if you're intent on sticking around Sheffield you could do with going down a hair shade or two and dropping the tan about three shades.' Monique's like my own personal Gok Wan and is always direct with her answers. I envy her confidence.

'I was wondering if I was a bit full-on, I've already sent the sunbed back. Thanks for being so honest,' Bettina replies. 'I'll get booked in. Do you know a good salon?'

'Bella's on the top of Handsworth is excellent,' I say. Monique nods in agreement.

'They are good, they've won awards. I'd definitely book in there.'

'Cool, I'll do that this week,' she says. 'Anyone fancy another coffee? Then you,' she points at me, 'need to fill us in on the gossip about Seb.' She gets up to order the drinks.

Monique appraises me. 'Who's Seb?'

'Aha, I've saved that gossip especially for today.' I bat my eyelashes at Monique.

'Get those coffees dead fast or else,' she shouts across at Bettina.

'Right, spill,' says Monique once Bettina returns with fresh drinks.

'Just before I do, where was it you got those great yoga pants from again?'

'Yeah right, get on with it, woman.'

I recount the pub events to them both and they listen without interruption, which for Monique is new territory, although she does sit twiddling her friendship bracelet round and round her arm.

'Oh my God, I just can't believe that of Mr Kingsley,' says Bettina. 'He looks so... boring.'

'Yes, well, I did find it boring.'

'Would you shag him if you were single?'

'Mon!'

'Well, would you? Does he live up to his hype?'

'Well there's definitely no faulting the TV', I state, 'but the picture's a bit dubious.'

'Oh jeez. Can't you just talk normally?'

'Stop picking on me,' I pout. 'You're causing interference.'

Bettina rolls her eyes and laughs. 'Reality show,' she repeats.

'So, what're you going to do about Sexy Seb's seduction?' Monique pronounces each 's' like an Adult Chat-Line operator.

'You'll have to tell Mrs Sullivan. It's inappropriate to attempt to seduce a pupil's mother,' adds Bettina.

'Nah. It was amusing, and he's not going to get anywhere, so let him do his worst,' I say. 'I'm quite looking forward to his next attempt actually.'

'What did Niall say?' says Monique.

'Nothing really. He doesn't feel threatened by a,' – I make air quotes – '"lame teacher". Not that I told him what he said to me. I'd just have been wasting my time. I'm thinking of entering Hell's Kitchen or being arrested by the police for speeding to get him to pay me some attention.'

'If you wanted a romantic, you picked the wrong bloke,' says Monique.

'What's your husband like?' asks Bettina.

'He's a dickhead.' Monique is as delicate as ever.

'That's my husband you're talking about, Mon.'

'Okay. He's a nice guy who acts like a dickhead. He doesn't appreciate what he's got in Lauren. She's beautiful, a fab mother, and she runs a small business as well as keeping the household running. He continually ignores her. I think a compliment would kill him.'

'Oh don't listen to Monique,' I protest. 'I do all my whinging to her, so he comes across worse than he actually is.'

'You let him get away with ignoring you and I can tell it makes you feel crap. It upsets me seeing you down and unconfident. That's why I think he's a dick.'

'Okay,' I sigh. We've had this conversation before and it's not worth getting into an argument about it. She doesn't really know him. They've only met a handful of times, so I let it go, and enjoy another taste of my decaf.

'Anyway, what about you, Bettina?' asks Monique. 'I gather yours was a dick too if you divorced him?'

'Nosey much?' I berate. 'Did toy boy not give it up then? Is this why there's a sudden obsession with the male anatomy today?'

We look at Bettina. She's gone quiet. 'Hell, sorry,' says Monique.

'I didn't mean to pry. I can be brash sometimes, take no notice. Sit back, drink your coffee and watch the show.'

'No, it's okay', says Bettina. 'I don't mind talking about it. I've nothing to hide.' She twiddles a lock of her hair again, a sign I now realise indicates her nervousness. 'It's quite simple really. He kept cheating, and I put up with it because of Tyler. He hit me... a couple of times... I didn't want Tyler at risk living there, so I left. He offered to pay me to leave Tyler behind.' She looks us in the eye in turn. 'As if I'd sell my son, and when that didn't work he started setting me up, saying I was a psycho. He doused himself in scalding hot coffee and told the police I attacked him. I was at the police station for hours.'

'Were you charged?' I ask.

'They let me off with a caution at that point.'

'So then what?' asks Monique.

'Oh that's the best bit,' she answers, with a sniff. 'When I went back home to fetch Tyler, I told him he couldn't do a damn thing about it, so he got a kitchen knife and stabbed himself through the hand. It wasn't a serious wound, I mean, he wouldn't have wanted to do anything that would threaten his glorious career.'

My mouth is wide open. 'Oh my God!'

Bettina's eyes are teary, but she carries on. 'He got his friend who lived next door to come around and say he'd been a witness to it all. The police dropped the case as a domestic in the end; I mean, they knew he wasn't a saint from what they heard about him from the press, but he still managed to get me committed to a mental health unit.'

Her voice cracks on the last word. I lean over and squeeze her hand.

She smiles weakly at me. 'It was only for a couple of days, thank goodness.' She closes her eyes and takes a breath. 'I went to court to retain custody of Tyler. It was a hard fight, no thanks to him, but I got it, although he has to spend every other weekend with his dad. I moved back near my mother as she'd told the courts she'd be close by.'

I'm at a loss for words. What must it be like to be married to such an awful man? Poor Tyler too, what sort of effect has this had on him? I reflect on what I have. It might be boring at times, but at least I'm not in an abusive relationship.

'This girl needs a good time,' says Monique. 'Let's hit a few charity shops, then Etta's wine bar.'

'No wonder you love it around here,' Bettina is in awe. 'Designer gear for like five pounds an item?'

'Yep, and all because it's not in season.' I'm in my element having got myself a little Karen Millen khaki cardigan for three ninety-nine, which Monique pointed out to me, and another two bags full of vintage style stuff, including a tea service, more jewellery, and a few crocheted style handbags.

We are positioned in a window seat at Etta's. Our spoils rest on the window behind us as we sit on high bar stools with a glass of rosé wine each. I don't usually drink and drive, but it seems apt to have one given what Bettina revealed this morning. We've ordered an Etta special for lunch: an open baguette with roast beef, rocket, horse-radish sauce, and caramelised onions, served with a side salad and beer battered chunky chips. My mouth is salivating just thinking about it.

'What exactly do you do on eBay?' asks Bettina.

'I have a little shop,' I explain. 'The overheads have gone up a lot recently, so I have to make sure I sell quite a few things a month to cover my costs and make a profit, but I do okay. I sell vintage looking items, as you've seen.' I point to the bags.

'She also plays with dolls,' smirks Monique. 'Buys them from car boots all bedraggled and unloved from little girls who've moved onto Monster High.' She coughs, and I elbow her in the side. 'Ahem, I mean she *refreshes* them, washes them, brushes out their hair and gets them looking absolutely gorgeous again. She's like Extreme Makeover for Mattel. But it works, she's got a good eBay rep and you do okay, don't you?'

'Well, I'm not about to give Richard Branson a run for his money, but it's a bit extra that comes in handy for treats and holidays. I doubt we'd have got to Tenerife in May without my additions to the bank account.'

'That sounds really cool,' says Bettina. 'I loved Barbie when I was little.'

'They're really popular,' I smile. 'Before you know it I'll be on the run up to Christmas and it'll really take off, like the Princess of Monaco on her wedding day.'

Monique groans.

'So how much do you sell each month?'

'About fifty items a month I guess, until the end of September. Then I can sell two-hundred a month in the run up to Christmas as it gets so busy. I've only got about twenty things listed at the moment, but I've got another couple of bags full to list now, so that's my evening sorted. I hate listing though, it takes forever.'

Monique tilts to the side. 'Nope, it doesn't, look just took me a sec.'

'You're so funnneeeee,' I state, 'and you tell me off for my jokes?' I shake my head.

Our food arrives at this point and we're silent whilst we consume the deliciousness that is the Etta special.

We're ready to leave and Monique asks me if I fancy going to the pictures on Friday evening to see the latest Romcom.

'I can't. Niall has a work leaving do,' I state in a sad voice.

'If it's alright with you, I'd love to go,' says Bettina, looking at me for permission. I turn to Monique who shrugs. 'It's okay with me.'

'That's great then,' I say. 'I can avoid the latest Romcom where it leads me to believe there are men in this world who *do* treat women like the most desirable objects on earth, only to go home and see the reality.'

'Excuse me. Aren't you the one with a solid fella *and* another sexy bloke who wants to get in your pants?' says Monique. 'Quit your moaning.'

'I haven't had a night out for ages. I'm really looking forward to it,' adds Bettina, whose face then falls. 'Oh no, I can't. I've no-one to look after Tyler that night.'

'I'm stuck in. Why doesn't he come around to mine for the night? You can pick him up after the cinema, as long as you're not going to be mega late.'

'I was thinking a seven-ish showing,' says Monique. 'Then, if the Romcom gets me in the mood I can booty call Dr Love.'

'Ewww,' I say, trying to keep a laugh down, while making it look like I may vomit.

'Thanks so much,' says Bettina.

'No problem. I'll take him from school and give him some tea, so you have plenty of time to get ready.'

'You're such a pal. I'm so glad you're back in my life.'

I smile at her and touch her arm. We say our goodbyes to Monique and head home.

Later that evening I'm back on Facebook to see what Monique made of our new friend.

***She seems okay. Obviously got over the school victim thing to become another victim, which is a shame. You'll have to introduce her to some school gate mums though. As nice as she seems, I don't want her with us all the time. Three's a crowd and all that.***

**Well maybe you should have made an excuse for Friday instead of taking her to the cinema.**

***Awww, you jel, hun? I felt sorry for her, so just this once I've made an exception. Plus, I really want to see the film and admit it, you didn't want to go.***

**I didn't want to go.**

*When you seeing Sexy Seb next?*

It's the meeting tomorrow night, but I'll be quite safe because the other parents and helpers will be there.

*I'm going to call you Lo-is, as only you know his real identity.*

**And Bettina.**

*Yes, but only you have been charmed by Super Seb. Wonder if he has a muscly, manly chest under that nerdy teacher outfit?*

**I am not going there with this conversation.**

*Love ya, Lo-is. I want any gossip tomorrow night. Hot off the press for the Daily Planet.*

**Ha ha. Goodnight.**

*Is that kryptonite in your pocket or are you just pleased to see me?*

**GOODBYE.**

## CHAPTER FOUR

It's Wednesday night. Six pm rolls around and I find myself once again entering the school hall for the summer fair update. I've dressed down in jeans and a t-shirt, my hair is loose, and I'm make-up free apart from foundation and blush. I spot Seb sitting in a chair with the Clark Kent look alive and well and see tonight's nerd look is helped along by a maroon tank top. He gives me a nod and a small smile and looks away. I sit at the side of Bettina who has saved me a chair. Her hair has been cut to shoulder length and is now honey blonde. She looks so different. As I sit, I notice her nails are French polished, rather than the pink I've become accustomed to. She's dressed in jeans and a t-shirt, though I recognise her jeans are DVB.

'You look amazing.' She really does look fresher.

'Thanks. I'm pleased with it.'

'Did you go to Bella's?'

'Yes, who'd have thought you had such a treasure on your doorstep?'

'Yep, well ssh, we need to keep her local.'

Bettina appraises my hair. 'I've just realised it looks very similar to yours. We could be twins.'

I touch my hair. 'Er, yes, well it's similar, but mine's lighter, and wavy. I like that honey colour she's used though, it suits your skin tone.'

'I'm going lighter once I've let the tan fade.'

I feel uncomfortable and at a loss at what to add. I've never understood people who copy others. I look around, inadvertently catching Seb's eye. He gives me a wink.

Mrs Sullivan arrives dressed in a brown woollen suit that would bake anyone else half to death, and have them fainting, but she is as composed as always. Her hair remains in its immovable position as she turns to us like she's about to give a presidential address. 'Okay, so can everyone give me a progress update?'

Volunteers fill her in about where they've got to over the past week. Bettina has placed notices on the boards in the main building and in the classroom windows, asking for unwanted books and says that quite a few have been donated already. Of course the stocks are easy to set up and need no further discussion.

'This week's task is to create some posters,' states Mrs Sullivan. 'So if everyone can start by doing a poster for their own stall, and ensure it shows the price of the activity. While you're doing that, I'll be having a think about any additional posters we might need, such as arrows for the toilets, refreshment signs et cetera.'

'Right, I'll catch up with you later,' I tell Bettina as I get up to make my way over to Seb. The paper for the posters is being placed on the tables. I'm pleased I wore my dodgier clothes as I know from previous experience with Joe that the paint is notoriously difficult to wash out, even though the school professes it's washable.

'Ooohh, Sexy Seb,' she giggles.

'Don't you start,' I playfully hit her on the shoulder. 'Just remember, this is your entire fault for landing me in the water. You didn't realise it was hot water, did you?'

A groan indicates Bettina's response to my humour. 'Monique is right, *lame*.'

I laugh and go over to Seb's table.

He looks me up and down. I squirm under his gaze.

'Well if it isn't the lovely Lauren Lawler. Oh, the alliteration. I could make a beautiful poem out of your name.'

'Leave it out.' I sit down at the table with my side to him, so I don't have to look directly at him. 'Pass me the pencil to sketch out the poster before we paint it. The quicker we get this done, the quicker I get home to my family.'

'So we're not going to the pub then?'

I purse my lips. 'We are so *not* going to the pub.'

Seb watches me outline the sign for the fair. I sketch out the words *get revenge on a teacher, sponge stocks: one pound for five sponges.*

'Twenty pence a throw? Dear God, I'll be drenched,' Seb says. 'Then you'll have to go in the stocks. Lauren Lawler all wet. I like the sound of that.'

I glare at him. 'One more pathetic, lewd comment and I'm out of here. I don't know if this ladies' man charm works with other mothers or women, but to be honest, it's as attractive to me as you in that get up.'

'Ouch, that hurts.' He makes a stabbing through his chest motion with his hands.

I push the poster towards him. 'I've sketched it, you can paint it. It's done.' I get up to walk away.

He puts his hand on my arm. 'I'm sorry. I can't seem to help myself. In my defence, it does usually work very well on the fairer sex.'

'How many times do I have to point out I'm married?'

'Yes, but are you happily married, Lauren?'

I wince at his words.

'You see if there's one thing I've picked up on since I've been *charming* the ladies as you so nicely call it; it's which ones are happy, and my guess, is that although you don't want to like me, you can't help it. You're getting attention from me and I'm guessing you're not getting it at home.'

I clap three times, slowly. 'Bravo. That deserves a standing ovation. What a crock of shit.'

He rubs his jaw. His usual patter not having worked, his shoulders slump. He fixes me with his chocolate eyed gaze. It hits me again just how attractive he is. It's a shame his mouth doesn't match up to his features.

'Well, gosh, I don't think I've ever been turned down before, married or not,' he says. 'I'm sorry, Lauren. Can we just get on with the painting and forget about the total ass I've made of myself?'

'That would be nice,' I state.

We spend the rest of the painting time chatting about Joe, Seb's job at the school, and my eBay work. It's companionable and pleasant, and I see a different side to Seb. He is so much nicer when the act's turned off. Mrs Sullivan announces that we have five more minutes left.

Seb pauses from painting and looks up at me. 'So you have a happy marriage then? I'm pleased for you.'

'Some of the time he's a complete arse.' I state, placing my bag on my shoulder ready to leave. 'And the last time I got a compliment was about 1995. But he doesn't play games. No-one likes a player.'

He nods, his forehead wrinkling, as I walk away.

The following night I find myself at home alone. Bettina insisted on having Joe round at hers for tea, to take her turn before I had the kids Friday, and somehow Tyler and Joe have managed to negotiate a sleepover. Niall's shift had been changed to afternoons, so I text Monique to see if she wants to meet up for tea, but she's busy, which I translate as shagging Dr Love.

I sit on my sofa, a coffee-coloured corner placement like the one in the café. I look around the house. We live in a three-bedroomed semi. The walls were painted a neutral beige at Niall's insistence, so I've jazzed it up with abstract red canvasses and assorted cushions in different textures. I had to fight Niall's obstinacy to get a rug in the living room, a lovely thick brown one with stripes graduating into shades of red. He thinks they make rooms look too fussy. I like it because it makes the room cosier. I can lie across the rug, rise onto my wrists and read or watch TV. Once upon a time Niall and I would have christened such a rug within days of it being put on the floor, but I've had it over seven months now and its only other use has been as a racetrack for Joe's cars. I realise I'm back getting maudlin and decide if no-one's available to go out with me, I'll just go on my own. There's a pizza place in Meadowhall I go to frequently with Joe, and I reckon I can sit at a dark table at the back. I grab my book to read in lieu of a partner and head off.

Minutes after entering the shopping centre, window shopping on my way to the pizza restaurant, I pass a shop that sells intimate items. Usually I pay this shop no attention and walk past. Today, I stop. I haven't had a vibrator for years. I think about how times change. I threw out anything dubious looking when Joe was around four and started going through all the drawers asking what everything was. I suck on my bottom lip. Maybe if I'm not getting much at home from Niall, it wouldn't hurt to have a solo companion. I smile, thinking next time I'm home alone I might not feel the need to rush off shopping.

I go in, and I'm immediately approached by an assistant. 'I'm just looking thanks.'

She moves away and leaves me to browse. The vibrators are situated at the back of the store, obscured by a corner so you can't be seen by outside shoppers. There are rows upon rows of them in assorted shapes and colours. I don't know where to start. I look at the assistant and she must be used to reading faces like mine because she heads straight back over.

'Bit overwhelming isn't it?'

I nod. 'I've had one before but...'

'Not a first timer then, that's useful to know.' She looks through the racks and hands me a few to look at, describing what they do. I decide on a simple pocket rocket after finding that some of them quite frankly scare me. I feel empowered when I've bought one and leave the shop proudly clutching my carrier bag. My stomach growls, so I walk quickly towards the restaurant.

'Lauren?'

I turn around slowly to find myself facing Seb Kingsley. Of all the people to bump into right now. For God's sake. He looks at my carrier bag. My face reddens to a deeper shade than ketchup.

'Normally, I would say something lewd and witty, but seeing as it's you, my mouth is closed.' He makes a zipping motion with his fingers across his lips.

'Well, of all the people I could have met at this exact moment, of course it would have to be you,' I huff.

'Could've been Mrs Sullivan...'

The thought of Mrs Sullivan near a sexy store reduces me to laughter and the awkwardness evaporates.

'Right, well I must get going before I faint with hunger.'

He raises an eyebrow. 'You haven't eaten yet?'

'Niall and Joe are out. Now don't think I'm being rude, but I need to get going.'

'Well, that'll definitely get you going,' he nods towards the bag. 'Sorry, sorry, couldn't resist it. I saw an opening and had to take it. Oh my God, I actually didn't mean to say that one,' he says with a hand across his mouth, doing his best to hold down a smirk.

'There's obviously an underlying sexual repression or something with you,' I state. 'Go home, have a wank, and get it over with.'

'Mrs *Lawler*. I am shocked that you said that to me, a teacher at your son's school.'

I close my eyes for a few seconds and wish myself somewhere else. 'You're right, that was inappropriate. I'm sorry.'

'I promise not to tell Mrs Sullivan, but only if you eat with me.'

'What? Don't be ridiculous, you're not going to tell Mrs Sullivan.'

'I'll just follow you then and sit opposite you anyway.'

I sigh. 'Oh my God, you are so annoying. Whatever. Come on then, before I come to my senses and change my mind.'

I no longer need a corner table for one as I don't want it to look like an illicit encounter, so I ask for a seat in the middle of the restaurant, near several noisy children, and infants in high chairs. The smell of garlic and tomato permeates the air. It makes my stomach rumble and my mouth water. I so need to eat. 'Are you going to behave normally?'

He holds up three fingers. 'Scout's promise. I'll even talk about the summer fair.'

The waitress comes to take our order. I ask for a plain margarita pizza and a coke. Seb orders the same.

'So, I gather there's no significant other in your life, with your persistent need to annoy me?'

'Nope.' He sits back in his seat, legs wide open. 'I can't be doing with serious relationships. It gets to six months and then the pressure starts.'

I raise an eyebrow at him.

'I'm being serious. One kept inviting me to her friends' weddings and always managed to catch the bouquet. Another tried to make my mother her best friend. It does my head in; I'm just not that kind of guy. It's why I started having affairs with married women. I like non-committal sex, but sometimes even they get carried away.'

'Have you listened to yourself?'

'I'm just being honest.' He opens his hands apart in gesture.

The waitress brings our drinks and I have a long sip of mine.

'Are you enjoying being at Woodley?' I think a change of subject is a good move.

His face opens up into a large smile. 'I love it. The kids are mainly awesome.'

'It's nice to enjoy a job as well as just earn money from it,' I say.

'Absolutely. Total bonus. I love looking at a kid and seeing how there's all this information about the world they don't know yet, and I can teach them some of it. Some of those kids might make decisions in the future based on what I've taught them. It's just amazing. Sometimes I can't get up fast enough in a morning.'

I smirk, and he realises what he's said. 'Oh, so now you're starting with the innuendo? Steady on, Mrs Lawler, you might just have some fun.'

I pick up my drink quickly and lose my grip on the glass. As it starts to drop, his hand hits mine as he reaches over to catch it. We place the glass back down while somehow still having our hands touching. I move my own away. I can't look at him as my traitorous mind thinks I actually wouldn't mind touching him again. He hesitates and then leans over the table. I look up at him and I don't know what to say.

'You careless sod,' he chucks me under the chin and the mood is broken, which is just as well as our pizzas arrive.

Seb insists on paying the bill and walking me to my car. The shopping centre closes at eight pm, with the exception of the restaurant area, so there aren't many cars left around.

He breaks the silence. 'That poster you drew is really good. You have a talent for art.'

'Thanks, I love doing anything like that.'

At this point I realise I'm swinging the carrier bag containing my vibrator around.

Seb nods towards it. 'Is that vintage patterned as well then?'

I roll my eyes at him. 'Thanks for walking me to the car,' I say, and open the driver's side door.

'My pleasure,' he says, looking at the bag again. I feel my breathing get heavier.

'Well, night.'

'Good night, Lauren.' He turns and walks across the car park, his hands in his pockets. I try not to notice that this causes the material of his trousers to pull tight, displaying a mighty fine bottom.

I get home feeling wired. Niall has not yet returned home from work. I go upstairs, remove the packaging from my new toy, clean it and put batteries in. It has noise reduction and whirrs quietly. I feel stupid as

I lie back against the pillows and shut my eyes. Thoughts of Seb come into my mind and I drop a hand to my breast and imagine he's touching me with those soft fingers. I stop; feeling guilty. I'm thinking of a man who's not my husband. It's not even a movie star, which I'd give myself a pass for, but my son's next teacher. I turn the vibrator off, jump out of bed, and throw it at the back of the wardrobe. I'm tired and feeling foolish. I'm too tired to check Facebooking tonight. I didn't manage to get on Facebook last night either, so I know Monique will be waiting for an update on things. Oh well, I'll catch up with her tomorrow. After getting ready for bed, I go to turn my phone onto silent and see I have a message from her asking to know what happened at the fair meeting. There's another text message from a number I don't recognise. I open it and read:

**Remember your phone can vibrate too, so I might have to keep texting. Keep it in your pants ;)**

Seb? How did he get my number? Shaken, I get into bed for what turns out to be a most restless night's sleep.

## CHAPTER FIVE

I spend Friday wasting time on the computer and watching daytime television, which is the one thing I have never succumbed to before at home. At three-fifteen I arrive at school and take Joe and Tyler home. They had an amazing time the previous evening and can't wait for round two. I'm just dropping the schoolbags into the house when my mobile rings.

'Lauren?' The voice is so loud I wince. 'Oh my God, Lauren. Tyler's missing. The teacher didn't see who took him. I've called the police. I think Danny's got him.' Bettina is sobbing hysterically down the phone and I have to shout to be heard.

'Bettina, I have them. It's Friday, remember? You're going to the cinema with Monique.' There's a pause.

'Oh my God', she bursts into tears down the phone. 'I totally forgot. Oh my God. I've rung the police. I reported him. I—'

'Take a breath, ring them back, and then ring me and let me know you're okay.'

'I... I'll, yes, I'll do that now.'

She puts the phone down and I get the children a drink and a snack. When she phones again she is much calmer.

'I'll come through and see him, if that's okay. It's really,' her breath catches, 'got to me. I thought he had him.'

'Well of course you can. I was sure Mrs Baxter had seen me, you know.'

'As long as he's safe, I don't care.'

'But doesn't Danny see him every other weekend anyway? Why would he take him?' I know I should be apologising. How would I feel if it was Joe? But how can she have forgotten? Surely Tyler and Joe would have been talking about it this morning?

'He threatened to do it before. He told me he might just take him and go abroad. It's not like he couldn't afford it.'

'I'm sorry, Bettina. I didn't know. Okay, get yourself around here, and I'll get the kettle on.' I end the call and sit on the bottom step for a few moments.

When she arrives at the house, she's shaking and teary. I keep her in the hallway for a minute, apologise again, and get her to compose herself. Tyler will only worry if he sees her upset.

'I don't think I can go out now. I'll stay here with the kids. You go.'

'Not a chance. Everything here is okay; it was just a mix up, that's all.

'I just want to be with Tyler.'

'He's fine, and he's with Joe. Look, I think you need this night out. Go have a break from things. Plus, there is no way on this earth I am seeing that damn film, and Monique will kill you if you don't go. So, cup of tea coming up, and you can have something to eat here if you like. It's casserole, so there's plenty, and you'll be able to meet Niall as he'll be home from work soon.' I shut up as I realise I'm rambling on and she's only half listening.

She rubs her eyes with the back of her hand and draws in a deep breath. 'Thank you. I just... I panicked. I keep thinking Danny's going to pull some kind of stunt to get Tyler.'

'Right, come through to the living room.' I say, 'but mind where you're walking, because there is Lego everywhere and it flipping hurts when you step on it.' I wait for her acknowledgement. Mothers have a universal hatred of Lego on the floor, but there's nothing. She rushes straight for Tyler, who endures a hug from his mum, which is obviously so not cool in front of his mate. I see him look over her head and roll his eyes at Joe. I head into the kitchen to warm through the casserole and decide to give the kids their meal first as they're complaining they're *starving*. Bettina and I can wait for Niall to arrive home from work.

Kids seated and eating, I'm about to sit down when the phone rings. I curse under my breath but pick up anyway. 'Hello?'

'Hello, Mrs Lawler, are you okay to have a quick word?' It's Mrs Sullivan.

'Yes, of course.'

'It's about the incident at school tonight. We are obviously going to have to look into it because it could have potentially been very serious.'

My brow furrows. 'I understand, and I'm so sorry. I was sure Mrs Baxter had seen me.'

Bettina comes and hovers nearby.

'You may have actually done us a favour. At least this time it was a mum from school and everything was alright. I just need you to tell me exactly what happened.'

'Of course. Well it's very simple really, Joe came out of class with Tyler and I took them both home. I'd made arrangements with his mother for Tyler to stay for tea.'

'Hmm, well obviously security has got a little lax. We'll be reviewing our procedures in light of this incident and we will be making sure Mrs Baxter or her assistant are standing at the doorway at home time to ensure each child is collected by a person they know, which is what should happen anyway.'

'I should have made a point of telling Mrs Baxter I had them.'

'Not at all. The teacher should have been paying more attention.

The situation won't arise again, but I do need you to pop in tomorrow to fill in an incident report.'

'Of course. Is there anything else?'

'Not at the moment, Mrs Lawler. I'll see you tomorrow.'

I put the phone down and exhale sharply.

'I gather that was the school?' Bettina says.

'Yes, they've got to do some kind of report about the incident.'

'Oh, well good. They can't be letting kids go off with just anybody.'

'Bettina,' I say. 'It was a mix up, and anyway it sounds like it's Mrs Baxter who's in trouble.'

'Why?'

'For not paying attention to who's collecting the kids. Anyway,' I say as a thought occurs to me. 'Why weren't you at the school gates if you'd forgotten I was getting Tyler?'

'I was running late. I'd had to get the bus from town and it took forever. By the time I'd got there, hardly any parents were around.'

I'm starting to wish I'd just gone to the cinema myself. There was probably less drama in the movie. I turn as I hear keys jangling in the door. 'Niall's here,' I smile. Bettina sits up straight and flicks her hair, putting a smile on her own face.

'Oh, hi,' Niall looks questioningly at Bettina as he walks into the room and then he sees Tyler. 'I'm guessing you're Bettina. Aren't you supposed to be at the cinema?'

'Hi, I am,' she stands up and holds out her hand for Niall to shake, which he does. 'Not for about another hour though.'

I stand also. 'I'll serve the meal. Do you want to go and sit at the dining table?'

As they do, I hear Joe saying, 'This is my mate Tyler.'

'Well how do you do, Tyler?' replies Niall. 'Are you two responsible for all this Lego mess?'

'I'll get them to clear it,' says Bettina quickly, and heads towards a seat.

'He's only teasing,' I say. 'We can't get Joe to pick anything up without nagging at him for hours.'

'Apart from swear words at school,' Niall quips. 'Those he picks up just fine.'

Bettina giggles, a silly high girlish giggle that I've never heard her make before.

We send the kids off to play. Niall sits next to me as usual, and Bettina takes a seat opposite. I feel like I do when I'm waiting in the doctors, wanting it to all be over quickly.

'So, you're a nurse?' Bettina asks in her new girly tone.

'A charge nurse, yes. Dead important, I am,' Niall winks, then turns and smiles at me. 'I have to work hard so Lauren can go out and buy pretty bags and jewellery.'

'Ha ha,' I say, a bit miffed by his insensitivity about my business.

Bettina lifts up her hand daintily. 'I'm sorry for mentioning work things, but my wrist has been hurting and …'

'I need to stop you there,' I say. 'Niall works at a psychiatric unit for the elderly. He only did a few weeks placement in general nursing, so he's hopeless unless you've gone bonkers.'

Bettina flinches and I realise what I've said. Oh God, she was a psychiatric patient. Foot in mouth again. *Well done, Lauren.* She can tell I'm about to say something but gives me a warning with her eyes, and a slight shake of her head. She doesn't want Niall to know. I've told him anyway, but maybe he wasn't listening at the time, he usually doesn't. Right now, he certainly seems to have no idea what's going on as he reaches to turn on the TV.

'Excuse me, ladies. I don't mean to be rude switching on the TV during our meal, but I'm going out soon and haven't managed to catch up with the news yet.'

I raise an eyebrow. He puts it on every bloody night and never says it's rude then. Hypocrite.

'Where are you off to, Niall?' asks Bettina.

'A leaving do at The Chantry,' I state, speaking louder so it reaches Niall's ears. 'Which he needs to be at in about thirty minutes.'

He turns to me. 'I can answer for myself you know. Actually, I have to pass the cinema to get there,' he says looking at Bettina. 'Do you want a lift?'

'That'd be awesome,' she says.

*Awesome?*

When they've gone I catch up on eBay. The kids are great, and with an ample supply of junk food, they keep themselves occupied with the toys in Joe's bedroom. The evening passes quickly. Bettina picks Tyler up at nine-thirty and takes him home in a taxi, saying she had a nice time. Niall arrives home not much later at ten. He's not one for staying at a do. I begin to tell him about the drama of the afternoon that led to our extra dinner guest, but he stops me. 'Bettina told me in the car. Messed up there, didn't you? Nearly gave the poor woman a heart attack.'

'She's the one who forgot,' my voice gets higher.

Niall walks into the kitchen and sticks the kettle on. He grabs a mug out of the shiny red kitchen cabinet and plonks a tea bag in it.

'For someone who didn't want much to do with her, you are certainly very involved.'

'You were the one who told me I was being stupid, so I decided to make an effort. She seems okay, though a bit paranoid about her ex-husband.'

'She seemed fine to me. Her husband sounds like a complete knob.'

'Yes,' I sigh. 'Tyler and Joe are getting on like a house on fire anyway.'

'Owww, speaking of houses...' Niall picks up a Lego window that he's stood on with a bare foot.

'What do you tell Joe all the time?' I mock. 'Should've had your slippers on.'

'Go and fetch 'em for me, I'm knackered,' he states, fishing the tea bag out of his cup, and throwing it into the bin. I watch as tea drips down the side of the bin and grit my teeth.

I huff but fetch his slippers. When I come back from the hallway, he's sat in the living room, cuppa in hand, and the television on.

I stand in the doorway. He's transfixed by the pixelation.

'Night then.'

'Night, love.'

Another sigh escapes me as I leave the room.

I get my pj's on, check Joe is settled, and get into bed. I check my Inbox through my phone. There's a private message from Monique.

**Ring me, ASAP!**

I pick up the house phone and call her. 'Is everything okay? Did you have a good time?'

'The film was great, and you missed out on my fabulous company which is a sin in my book,' she says. 'Anyway, I need to talk to you about Loser Liz.'

'Mon,' I say, shocked. 'That's a bit blunt, even for you.'

'Yeah, well after tonight I've a new name for her—Besotted Bettina'.

I laugh. 'Yeah, she was a bit taken with Niall.'

'Not with Niall, with you.'

'What?'

'I know we couldn't talk while the movie was on, but every other bit of conversation was about you. When you met Niall. How long you'd been married. Were you happy? Had you ever cheated? Did Niall resent the fact you didn't work? How long had I known you? It went on and on. I asked her what the twenty questions was about, and she said she was trying to fill in the years she hadn't known you. She was worried about seeming nosey and didn't want to ask you directly. It was so weird, Lo. She was going on about the grief you'd caused her today, and how she was sure you hadn't meant it, but that it had really upset her. She was asking if you'd ever done anything to upset me.'

'I'm sure it's nothing more than getting all the gossip on me from my best mate, and she was really shaken up this afternoon. With what she told us about her husband, it doesn't surprise me. Honestly, don't sweat it.'

'Well, I don't like her. She's odd. Sorry for putting on you like this, but please don't bring her for coffee or anything again.'

'You feel that strongly about it?'

'There's something very off about her, Lo. You need to watch her.'

'Okay, okay.' My voice rises slightly. 'I get the message.'

There's a pause. 'I'm only going on about it because I love ya, babes.'

'I know, hun, love ya too, BFF,' I say. 'Sleep tight.'

'I certainly shall. I shall be thinking about Ryan Reynolds in that film.'

'You saddo.' I laugh and put the phone down.

I lie back in bed and think about what she's said. What else would Bettina talk about? She had nothing much in common with Monique apart from myself. Monique has such a strong personality I don't think she realises sometimes how difficult it is for others to converse with her. She doesn't really have any other friends than me. I also think that maybe I pushed Bettina into going out tonight. I should have just driven her and Tyler home. After what happened with Danny she must feel so insecure about everything, and she's only been around me for a couple of weeks, which isn't really long enough to trust anybody. I still have to see Bettina because our kids are friends and in the same class. I'll just have to make excuses if she asks to meet up with me and Monique again.

Saturday morning rolls around. I get up and head to the kitchen while Niall takes Joe to his swimming lesson. I'm pleased we have no pre-arranged plans for the weekend and that when they get back we can just chill and have some family time. It's a lovely day, and I decide that instead of taking Joe car booting, I'll make a picnic. There's a large park within a twenty-minute drive of the house we can go to. I prepare the food, sit at the table and boot up Niall's laptop to check my eBay account. Out of the forty items I've listed, nineteen of them have sold overnight. I look, staggered by what I'm seeing. Three different bidders have bought several items each, and they've all paid by PayPal, so the money is in my account already. I leave positive feedback, praising them for being prompt payers, and then make my way upstairs to prepare their purchases for sending. The local Post Office is open on a Saturday morning, so I'll be able to get them sent quickly. I like to be punctual in posting, in order to maintain my one hundred per cent feedback rating. Hopefully I might get some regular customers. If that happens, I can up my game and regularly look for items, rather than just visiting the odd charity shop or car boot. I feel really energised and positive.

The guys get back from swimming and Joe is in a strop. 'He must be tired after his late night with Tyler,' says Niall.

'I've packed a picnic for us,' I say. 'Do you want to get the bikes out, and we'll go to Rother Valley?'

'Are you joking, love? We've just come back from swimming. He's in a right mood, and I just want to have a sit down. I've been working all week.'

My shoulders slump. 'I thought it'd be nice for us to have some family time.'

'What's this then? Are we not a family now?'

'You know what I mean; going out, having fun.'

'Well, let's compromise. We'll have the picnic in the garden, and I'll kick a football around with Joe for a bit. He'll like that.'

'You can do that,' I say, thinking about the dwindling stock on my eBay account. 'I'm going to have lunch and go to the car boot this afternoon.'

'Oh, Joe'll enjoy that.'

'I'm not taking Joe, he's tired, remember? I'm going on my own.'

'Here we go.'

I walk into the kitchen before I throttle him.

I eat lunch and gather my boot stuff together. I take three fold-up cotton bags that fit inside each other, and a small handbag with lots of loose change. As I go to get in the car I see a shadow cross the concrete. I turn quickly with my keys turned out, ready to stab out in self-defence.

'Hey, steady on. Gosh, you haven't changed one bit, Lauren,' says Danny Southwell.

# CHAPTER SIX

I back up against the car. I see the same lad I knew from school, only now he has lines on his face, grey flecks in his hair, and stubble. He's small for a man, only about an inch taller than my five feet seven, but as he stands wide-legged, with his hands in his pockets, his demeanour makes me wary.

'What are you doing here? Do I need to shout for my husband?'

He grins. 'You look like I'm about to kill ya, Lauren, mate. Calm down, I'm here about Bet.' His eyes focus on my face. 'Gosh, you really haven't changed much since school. It's weird us being older, innit? I still feel about fifteen.'

My jaw is clenched, and my shoulders are fixed. I feel like I cannot move. Is Danny here to hurt me or for a school reunion? 'How did you know where I live?'

He clasps his hands tightly. 'After the police accused me of kidnapping my son, I rang Bet's mother. She said you've been a good friend to her. A little digging on the internet got me your address, so I thought I'd come and see what the score was.'

'Have you any idea how psycho that sounds?'

'Lauren, I'm not without resources now, and seriously, an eight-year-old could find out where you live on the internet these days. Anyway,' he nods towards the house, 'nice looking place you've got. How ya been doin' all these years?'

I feel myself start to loosen as memory takes over and I'm back just talking to Danny from school. He has a small scar on his lip which I know is from where he fell off his skateboard in year seven, and he has the tiniest hint of acne scars. I'd always had a soft spot for him at school—he was a loveable rogue. Not that our paths had crossed often, but he'd been in a couple of my classes.

I straighten up and move nearer to speak to him. 'I'm alright, Danny. Yesterday was a misunderstanding. She'd forgotten I was picking the kids up. What did the police say?'

'They rang and said they were on their way round to check out the house and I had to stay there until they arrived. Not long after that call, they phoned back to say he'd been found. How the dozy cow managed to lose him at school I don't know.'

'Like I said, it was a misunderstanding.'

'Bet's mother said, but I've got a right to know what's going on. He's my son too.'

'Yeah. I don't mean to be funny, but I don't think Bettina would like you being around here. I know you have visitation rights over Tyler, but that's just at the weekend isn't it? She was so frightened yesterday—'

'That's what I want to talk to ya about. I wanna know what she's been saying about me; given it's probably a load of crap. I can tell with how her mother talks to me that she doesn't exactly get the truth.' Danny runs his hands through his hair; his face looks pained.

'Look, I'm trying to be a friend to her, so I don't want to know the ins and outs of your marriage. I'd rather not be involved.'

'Well, you see, that's the problem,' says Danny. 'Like it or not you are involved.'

My forehead creases. 'I don't see how.'

He tilts his head. 'Why did she say she came back to Sheffield?'

'To be near her mum of course. It makes sense that that's where she'd go if you'd split up.'

'Well she's lying. She came to Sheffield for you.' He points his finger at me.

'What on earth are you talking about?' I'm starting to get exasperated and check my watch. If he doesn't go soon it won't be worth me going to the car boot, and I really need more stock now I've sold so much stuff.

'Has Bettina told you she was having some problems? Had to see a psychiatrist?'

I look at him and remain silent. I'm divulging nothing. I look back at my house. Niall and Joe haven't noticed that I'm still here. I wonder how long I'd lay dead for before they discovered me? Probably not until the evening meal didn't turn up. Maybe not even then if they gorged on chocolate and bits from the fridge. Perhaps it might get to Monday morning when they had no clean shirts for school and work.

'Lauren, listen to me. Just hear me out and then I'll be getting off.'

I look back at him, my fingers tapping against my arm. 'I'm listening.'

'When Bettina left our school, she was mad at you. She thought you'd dissed her, left her to the clutches of Jodie and the gang. Her mother pulled her out of school after they'd waited for her one night and threatened to do things to her with a broom they'd had in their hands. I saw them and broke it up, but it was the final straw for her mother. Bet was grateful to me and showed me in more ways than one; that's how she ended up pregnant,' he looks at me, smiling, but he doesn't find it reflected back.

I fold my arms around myself. 'And?'

'One time when we were talking about our school days, she was having a right go about you. I stuck up for you, saying that I'd always thought you were alright and that it wasn't you who'd bullied her anyway. She went mad, accusing me of fancying you and saying I was only with her because I was forced to be. She developed a bit of an obsession about you, saying you'd let her down and that all this was your fault, that you were ruining her marriage.'

'What?'

'I know. I told her she was being ridiculous. We tried for another baby and got our Tyler. She calmed down for a bit after that.' He sighs. 'Then a couple of years ago I had an affair; first of a few to be honest. Alicia had blonde wavy hair, and Bet went ballistic. Said I had it bad for you and was shagging your lookalike. She threw a hot drink over me; I had to go to hospital. I thought it was just temper until the crazy bitch stabbed me in the hand.' He wipes a drip of sweat from his forehead with his t-shirt sleeve. 'I got the police involved and she had to go to counselling for a while. She came through it though, said she was fine. Then the next minute she's left and come back to Sheffield and taken Tyler away from me.'

I move to sit on the front step trying to take in what he's saying to me. How am I supposed to know who to believe? Did she stab him? Is he twisting things to get me on his side with Tyler? Maybe that's what was happening now. I'm at a loss for what to do and what to say. I put my head in my hands feeling like it's about to explode. Then I think about what Monique said to me about Bettina's constant questioning and I feel my mouth go dry.

I lift my head back up. 'What is it exactly you want me to do? Do you want Tyler? Is that why you're here?'

'I love my kid, and course I want him back, but that isn't why I'm here. When she walked out she told me I'd pay for what I'd done to her, and believe me I have – I am. She's doing everything in her power to make sure my contact with Tyler is as brief as possible. If she had her way I wouldn't see him at all. But that wasn't all she said, and I thought you needed to know, now you're hanging round with her.'

There's a pause.

'Go on then, what else did she say?'

'She said she was going to destroy you, slowly, one part of your life at a time, until you knew how she felt.'

## CHAPTER SEVEN

When he's left, I get in the car and sit there for a few minutes, thoughts whirring through my head. There's no way I'm going to the car boot now—I've lost my enthusiasm—so instead I drive to my favourite coffee shop and let out a silent prayer that my favourite sofa will be free, even on a busy Saturday afternoon. By a miracle it is. I toy with ordering a hit of espresso before deciding I'm shaky enough already, so I stick with a large decaf black coffee. I sink down into the sofa's cosy depths, close my eyes, and think of everything I've been told over the last few days. Is it really possible that Bettina is out to get me? She doesn't seem crazy, yet how do I know what crazy looks like? Why would she be obsessed with me over one incident that happened when we were younger? But how can I not consider it when my best friend and Danny have both warned me? My breathing is ragged and unsteady and I feel the first tingling of a panic attack, something I haven't had for years. My heart races and I begin to feel sick. I have an overwhelming urge to rush home. I remember my training and push through it, breathing steadily, and remembering that it's the fast breathing that causes the dizziness, while the stomach churning is caused by adrenaline. It takes a few moments, but I feel my heartbeat calm down and relax enough to take a sip of my coffee. I need to decide how to handle this information, but I just can't take it all in. Danny seemed okay, but then I've only seen him for ten minutes out of the last God knows how many years. If Bettina's telling the truth then he's trying to destroy her, and what better way to do it than to turn her only friend against her? On the other hand, Mon only has my best interests at heart, so she has no reason to lie. I make a decision to keep my distance from Bettina for a while. It'll be difficult with the kids and the fair, but I think it's the best course of action for now. I think of when I'll next need to see her. If I ask Tanya to get Joe from school again on Monday, then I can turn up as late as possible on Tuesday. I can sit with Seb at the fair meeting, and she can't really take offence at that seeing as it's her fault we're doing the sponge stocks together. I figure I just need a couple of days to assess the situation and get my head around things. In fact, that's an idea. I'll have a day off from everyone. On Monday I'll have another day to myself at home. I need some time alone, to work through my foggy brain. I take my phone out of my bag and text Mon.

**Soz can't meet u Monday, something came up.**

A few minutes later I get a text back asking if everything is okay.

**Yes, just busy, sold lots eBay. Catch up FB soon.**

When she replies to say that's okay, I feel relieved. I reckon we'd have spent Monday talking about nothing but Bettina, and to be honest, right about now I feel like I've had a belly full of it. All I want at this moment is Niall and Joe. It's the weekend and I want to be with my family, whether they go out with me or we just share the same time zone. I leave my half-drunk cup of coffee on the table and head straight home.

When I get back, it's no surprise that Niall and Joe don't realise I've returned empty-handed. I was going to tell Niall about Danny's visit, but decide that I can't be bothered going through it now. When I work out what's going on I'll tell him. Right now, I want to forget about it. I walk through the house and out of the patio doors, removing my shoes and walking barefoot along the grass towards Joe, who is happily bouncing around on his ten-foot trampoline. 'Hi, Mum,' he waves. 'Are you coming on?'

'Sure am, hun,' I smile and climb through the netting that keeps him safe.

'Mum, you aren't allowed on without socks.'

'I'll be okay this once.' I realise how hypocritical I'm being to go on barefoot when I'm forever telling Joe to make sure he has socks on, but I don't care. I want to break the rules and I don't want to miss being with my son for one more second today. We bounce around the trampoline. I pretend to try and get off and Joe drags me back by the arms and pulls me around the floor of it, then he bounces over me, as if he might fall on me like a mini wrestler. As we look at each other, with our hair raised with static electricity, we start giggling and my heart is full to bursting with the love I have for him. I feel someone watching and look up to see Niall in the dining room. He smiles and waves, while taking a sip of a cup of tea. I wave back and return to Joe, diving on him in a wrestling move and listening to him giggle uncontrollably.

'Did you bring me anything back, Mum?'

Damn. 'No, love, there was nothing decent. It was nearly all traders there this week.'

'Oh well, I'm glad you're back.'

'Me too.'


Monday turns out to be the perfect day for lounging around. I return soaking wet from dropping Joe off at school. Typical British summertime has returned. It's pouring with rain and six degrees outside. I shrug my coat and shoes off at the door, and to make sure I'm toasty I switch on the central heating. Wearily, I pad upstairs in my slippers, walking on the only carpet in the house, the stair carpet, and enter the bedroom. I let my clothes drop to the floor and dig out my Christmas pjs from the bag on the top of the wardrobe. They're made of fleece and really snuggly. I realise this is all completely over the top, but I don't care. I quickly dry the ends of my hair and fringe with the hairdryer and get into bed. What the hell. I climb under the duvet, designed to feel like duck-down, and check out the clock. Tanya has offered to give Joe his tea so I have until six pm all to myself. It's not even nine. Glorious. I snuggle down inside the bed and go back to sleep. When I wake, it's lunchtime.

I eat chocolate for lunch with a coffee. When I'm stressed my diet is the first thing that goes out of the window. I'm usually so meticulously organised with what we are eating for breakfast, lunch, and evening dinner, and have it balanced so we eat a good diet, but this past week I'd been slipping: chip shop, pizza. I'd felt guilt after each convenience meal but not guilty enough to cook properly for us. I'd thrown food away this weekend and felt guilty about that too. I hated waste. As I lie here, I wonder what to do next. Having rested I need an activity. I look at my wardrobes and an idea forms.

I spend a few hours rearranging my wardrobe into ready to go outfits. I'm especially pleased with a blue gingham shirt and white jeans that I put the teacup necklace with and decide I must wear that very soon. Feeling better, I spend the next two hours making a chicken pie for tea and an apple crumble for dessert. The cooking completely relaxes me. While I bake, I seem to go into another world, just one of sensations; feeling the ingredients as I rub them together, taking in the smells that permeate the room as it cooks. I'm rolling the pastry when I hear a knock at the door. Groaning at the interruption, I wipe my hands down my apron, walk to the front door and look through the spy-hole. It's Bettina and Tyler. What the hell are they doing here when it's obvious I wasn't around to fetch Joe? I hear Bettina through the door. 'She doesn't seem to be in. I hope everything's okay. Stay there and I'll have a look around the back.'

God, if she goes to the back window she'll see my half-rolled pastry. I have no choice but to answer the door.

'Hi sorry, I was caught short.' I shake my hair.

'Just wondered if you were okay? Only I haven't heard from you for a few days.'

'I'm fine, just been having some family time, and I've had a bit of a dodgy stomach today.'

'Oh, Tanya said she was getting Joe as you had a backlog of work to get through?'

'Well, yes, that was the plan before my stomach started.'

'Well, I came to tell you that they've moved the summer fair meeting to tomorrow night. Same time though.'

'Oh right, thanks for letting me know. Hopefully I'll be okay by then.'

She looks at me as if she expects to be invited in. I feign a cramp and whimper. 'You must excuse me, it's happening again. I'll catch up with you tomorrow.' I close the door on them and rush upstairs where I peek out from behind the curtain of Joe's room and watch them walk away. Bettina looks back at the house before she strolls off. I'm not entirely sure she hasn't seen me. I realise then that I'm still wearing the apron, smeared in flour.

Twenty minutes after I've got Joe back home, Niall comes through the door. 'Something smells nice.'

'Chicken pie, and apple crumble.' I say

'My favourites. Come on, what do you want?'

'Your body,' I state giggling. For some reason Niall doesn't laugh back. Instead, he turns to Joe and asks him how his school day has been.

'Fine,' says Joe, his stock answer for a school day. Niall and I roll our eyes at each other and I head to the kitchen to finalise the dinner, while he heads upstairs to get changed.

We have a relaxed evening, and for once Joe is really tired and fast asleep by eight. I climb onto Niall's chair and move onto his lap to snuggle up.

'That's not very comfy, Lauren.'

'I just want a snuggle.'

'Your bony elbows and butt are digging into me, it hurts.'

'For God's sake, why do I bother?' I shout and walk out of the room, back to the retreat of my bedroom.

I power up my laptop, switch to my Facebook tab and see that Monique is online. I start typing.

**Hello, did you miss me today?**

*Course I bloody did. You aren't allowed to ditch me again. EVER.*

**I won't. Missed you too, although spending the morning sleeping was fun.**

*You ditched me to sleep? You said you were working. You prefer sleeping to my delightful company? I AM INSULTED.*

**Hey, shouty caps, I've said I won't do it again. You'll be proud of me tho, because I spent the afternoon making up outfits.**

*Well obvs I'll need to see if they're acceptable first, seeing as I'm convinced ur colour blind.*

**Cheeky. What's been going on with you then?**

*\*sulks\* Well you'd know that if you hadn't bailed on me.*

**Forgive me?**

*Maybe, if you buy the coffees next Monday...*

**Done.**

*Did some overtime at the weekend, wasn't much else to do. Yoga class was cancelled due to illness. Oh, and I had 'lunch' in the disabled toilet with Dr Love as there are no other staff around on a weekend ;)*

**Filth. Please stop, I do not wish to be tainted by association.**

*What? Don't you have 'lunch' with Niall?*

**Not even getting a snack at the mo :(**

*What's up with him now?*

**God knows, he just doesn't seem up for it.**

*Oh well, at least you have sexy Seb to look forward to on Wednesday.*

**Don't you start. Anyway, it's been changed to tomorrow O.O.**

*So that's why you've been working out outfits…*

**No it is NOT. I found out after. Confess though, little bit excited re potential flirt.**

*You seen Bettina?*

I wonder whether to mention the few minutes at the door earlier but decide against it.

**No. I've avoided her after what you said. I'll see her tomorrow at the fair meeting, but I'm going to sit with Seb and keep my distance.**

*Any excuse.*

**Well, he can be my bodyguard lol.**

*How's the business empire?*

**Brilliant, I sold loads this week.**

*Oh yes, you said when you were blowing me out, but ended up sleeping. Well done, Branson. Did you get a lot at Saturday's boot? It was a lovely day wasn't it?*

**A few bits, but not as much as I would have liked.**

God, now I'm lying to Mon as well.

**I'm off to read for a bit now, finish my day off with an early night.**

*Ditching me again? Watch it, I'll have my revenge.*

**Scared.com.**

I feel so much better the morning after. The sun is out again, though there's a cool wind. I grab my gym kit and sling it in the back of the car and do an hour's swimming and a yoga class. Today I have bags of energy, probably from doing bugger all yesterday. I grab a fresh juice at the gym and spend ages in the shower and the changing rooms, making sure I don't resemble the sweaty mess that emerged from class. As silly as it sounds, I seem to have even more energy after this. I head home and spend some time on eBay. I've received a few more orders, so I get the parcels organised and ready for the post office. I can drop them off before going to school. As I'm heading out of the door later, I realise I've not checked my phone. I eventually find it right at the bottom of my bag, which may be why I've not heard the twenty-seven missed calls I have on it. Twenty-seven? I check, and every single one of them is from Bettina. There are also four texts. I open them up.

*__Where are you?__*
*__Are you not speaking to me?__*
*__Have I done something wrong?__*
*__Why are you not answering?__*

I ring her straight back.

'Bettina, is everything okay?'

'Where the fuck have you been?'

I hold the phone away from my ear. 'I beg your pardon?'

'Oh gosh, I'm sorry, Lo.'

Lo? She called me Lo? That's Monique's name for me; not even Niall calls me that. My voice is low, measured. 'I don't appreciate being sworn at.'

'I'm sorry. I've just been really worried that you were avoiding me for some reason. My mum told me Danny's been snooping around. Has he said anything to you?'

'Nope, I haven't seen him. Why would I?' I lie.

'My mum said he was asking about you. She thought he might try to get in touch. I just wanted you to know.'

'Well thanks. If he turns up, I'll get Niall to sort him out.'

'You wouldn't want to do that. He's not right, Lauren.'

'Well, I haven't seen him, and if I do I'll tell him to get lost.' She pauses, and I wonder if she's thinking of when I wouldn't let her in earlier. 'There's nothing going on, Bettina. I've been ill, you saw that for yourself. I told you I'd see you at school later and there's the fair meeting after that. I do have a life away from you, you know?'

Her voice breaks up on the phone and I feel heaviness, like dark clouds are working their way over my head. I can tell she's choking back tears. 'I'm sorry. I know I overreact, but he frightens me. And I know we're not really friends, but I've enjoyed spending time with you. I just wanted to make sure he wasn't poisoning that.'

I relent then as the guilt washes over me. 'We are friends, Bettina, but I can't be available to you all the time. Listen,' I hesitate. 'Are you still in touch with your doctor?'

'No, I'm on a waiting list here,' she sniffs.

'Well, I think you need someone to talk to about Danny,' I say. 'Someone impartial who can guide you on how to deal with it. That's not me, Bettina. I can't take that on.'

'I understand,' she says, her voice going quiet. 'Thank you for saying we're friends. It means a lot. I'll try not to bother you so much. Probably see you later.'

She hangs up and I feel like the worst person on earth.

## CHAPTER EIGHT

I have absolutely no enthusiasm for the summer fair meeting whatsoever, and only turn up because Joe is excited that his mum is part of the team; that and he wants to pelt me with a wet sponge. I see Bettina sitting in the corner. As I move closer, I see her eyes are rimmed with red and are slightly bloodshot. She sees me looking.

'Hayfever.'

'Look, I'm sorry about our conversation earlier, but I've been feeling crap and fed up myself.'

This seems to animate her somewhat. 'Why? What's the matter?'

I decide I'll put it on a bit about Niall. Maybe if I let her know my world isn't perfect she won't feel so bad, or if she is out to ruin me, it'll put her off. 'Me and Niall aren't getting along so well at the moment.'

'Really? I didn't pick that up from him in the car. Maybe he's just tired from work?' She hesitates a moment. 'You don't think he's having an affair, do you?'

'No.' I am shocked by this statement. 'Nothing like that. He likes to watch TV all evening and Joe's getting to sleep later and later these days, so it's just hard.'

'Or not as the case may be,' she sniggers.

I smile. The lack of sex in my life seems to have cheered her up a bit, at least. Great, glad it's of use to someone.

'You can join my boat. Danny's put me off men for a long time. So right now, the only one getting any is Monique with Dr Love.'

'That she is, lucky bitch,' I state.

'How is Monique by the way?'

'I've not seen her for about a week.'

'Oh? That's not like you.'

'I was poorly yesterday, remember? So couldn't make it to see her.'

'Such a shame. I know you love your coffees.'

Mrs Sullivan comes in at that point wearing a black suit and red shoes. 'Get her,' says Bettina.

'Right, last minute checks, ladies and gentlemen,' she says. 'If you can set up your stalls as much as is practical. We'll do it here in the hall though rather than outside. Should the weather turn against us we'll have to bring it indoors anyway.'

I glance around the room looking for Seb, but he's not here.

I spend the next half hour dragging out the stocks, setting them up and practising opening and closing them. I get a sponge and pretend to throw it. Our posters are finished and there is nothing left to do. We're ready for the fair. I put everything away and check to see if Bettina needs any help, but she doesn't. Her books just need boxing up for display, and she's done a great job of sorting them into genres and alphabetical order for easy selection. The rest of the meeting passes quickly. We say our goodbyes and head home.

As I walk to the car, I feel let down and disappointed. I look down at my outfit, black skinny fit jeans, a red bat-sleeved cotton top, and black ballet slippers. I'd tied my hair in a side ponytail. I look casual, yet cool, but it's been a waste of time. The person I'd hoped to look attractive for; the one person I could count on to boost my confidence—even if he was a bit of a man slut—wasn't there. I open the car door to go home.

'Did you miss me?'

'Arrrrrrrrrrgh.' My heart beats frantically. 'Oh my fucking God, you idiot,' I screech, and smack my fists into Seb's chest.

He lifts his hands. 'Sorry, sorry, I didn't mean to scare you.'

'Scare me? You've taken ten years off my life expectancy at least. What did you think would happen if you snuck up on me?'

'I didn't think I was sneaking up on you. I thought you'd seen me and were ignoring me.'

'I looked up the road before I crossed to see if there were cars coming. I wasn't paying attention to bloody pedestrians.'

'Well you should. One of them could be an attacker and you wouldn't be able to give a description.'

I thought back to Danny surprising me in much the same way on Saturday and decided I wasn't getting in my car again without an attack alarm firmly in my hand.

'Where were you tonight then?'

His cool brown eyes bore into mine. 'I'll tell you if you come to the pub.'

I hesitate, the keys swinging in my hand. I think of the alternative, going home and talking to myself. 'Oh, go on then.'

We walk to the Queen's Head where I insist on buying the drinks as he bought them last time. I don't want to feel I owe him anything. At the bar I try to stand so my backside sticks out a little and I add a little wiggle to my walk as I return with the drinks. We sit in the same seats as before, and I think how much calmer he is now compared to the idiot I had spoken to in here just two weeks ago.

'So, what happened to you tonight then?'

'Truth? I couldn't be arsed. I'd had enough of school today; the kids were total twats. I practically ran out at home time. I told Mrs S. I'd got a migraine.'

'I had to lug all the sponge stocks around to set them up because you didn't show.'

'You keep making out you're an independent woman, Mrs Lawler, I'm sure you were fine.'

'That's not the point.'

'You missed me,' Seb beams at me.

I feel my cheeks flush. 'Don't be stupid.'

'You did, you missed me,' he jumps up and does a twirly dance. 'She missed me, she missed me.' It reminds me of when Tom Cruise went bonkers on Oprah. The other pub residents either try their best to not look or give him a dirty look to indicate it's not suitable behaviour for this establishment.

'Seb, sit down,' I hiss.

He does and grabs his pint. 'How long have you been with your husband?'

I feel a whoosh, like a popped balloon, as I realise that is where I should be, at home with my husband, not here with Seb acting like some teenager with a crush. I decide I will tell him just how much I love my husband and go home.

'We've been together twelve years,' I say. 'We met when I was nineteen and he was twenty-nine, in a bar in Sheffield City Centre. I thought I was grown up and he still acted like a kid, so the age difference didn't matter. I found out I was pregnant with Joe at twenty-two and Niall said he was about to propose anyway, so we eloped to the registry office.

'Weren't your parents mad?'

'I have nothing to do with my parents, and that's a subject that's not open for discussion. Ever.'

'Okay, sorry. So, you and Niall have been married for ten years?'

'It'll be eleven in August, not long after my thirty-second birthday. How old are you anyway?'

'How old do you think I am?'

'Twelve.'

'Ha ha. I was thirty-five last November. Now stop changing the subject.' His voice lowers huskily, 'Are you happy, Lauren? I can't work it out. You say so, but then you're here with me.'

I fix my gaze firmly on Seb. 'Yes. I love my husband. If you're waiting to hear that I don't, you're going to be disappointed.'

'I'm disappointed.'

My mouth curves at the edges. 'You are so good for my ego, Seb Kingsley.'

'I could be good for a lot more.'

'Don't.' I put my finger across his lips. They are soft to the touch and he looks at me. The feeling is too intimate. He opens his mouth and my finger falls onto his tongue. He closes his lips and sucks lightly, circling my finger with his tongue. I feel a pulse between my legs and butterflies in my stomach. I withdraw my hand.

'You're going to go now, aren't you?' he says.

'No,' I reply. 'I'm not.' I take my finger and run it around the rim of my glass. I don't know which of us is more surprised by my answer.

We chat for another thirty minutes or so, and then I say that I really will have to leave. Outside the pub, Seb offers to walk me to my car, his own being parked nearer to the school.

I look up at him. 'No, I can walk back by myself.'

'You don't have to be scared of me, Lauren.'

We end up walking beside each other as we pass houses, some with curtains open. Some of the kids from school live around here, and I feel like I'm on display. I waffle on about complete nonsense the whole way to the car, trying to diffuse the tension between us.

He runs his hand through his hair. 'Well, night, Lauren. Thanks for coming for the drink.'

I sigh. 'I just don't know what to do with you. I like you, you could be a good friend. But nothing else, Seb. Nothing can happen between—'

I'm not finished before his lips touch mine. I thought feeling sparks of electricity was a cliché before now, but as I feel them zip through my body I change my opinion. Seb runs his hands up the back of my top, causing me to shiver. He takes this as I'm feeling cold and wraps his arms further around me. I should be protesting, I should be backing off, but his warm mouth feels so good against mine, and I've missed this kind of tender touch. I need it. Seb backs me up against the car door. His tongue fights to get between my lips and I allow it. A small moan escapes me, and I kiss him back, my tongue entwining with his. He breaks the kiss, backs away from me and smiles.

'Friends then,' he says. 'I'll see you around, Mrs Lawler,' and just like that, he leaves me hanging.

## CHAPTER NINE

I sit in the car, unable to drive as adrenaline takes over and I begin to shake. I can't believe what I've done, but I can't lie, at the moment I don't regret it. I feel alive. I relive the kiss in my head over and over and feel the wetness pool between my legs. I wanted to carry on kissing him, it was divine; like sucking on the most succulent strawberry. I pull down the windshield and look at myself in the mirror, expecting to see a bedraggled harlot, but I look exactly the same, with only a few wisps of hair out of place. I re-tie my ponytail, start the engine and begin to drive home. As I turn at the end of the road, I see a parked Mazda 5 at the corner on the opposite side. It's him. He flashes me twice with his indicators and I roar off, leaving him behind.

When I get home, I pop my head around the door. 'I'm back,' I state breezily.

'You're late; you missed Joe going to bed. Thought you'd be back by seven thirty-ish, it's nine.'

'Sorry, some of us went to the pub after. I should've called.'

'Nah, don't worry. We had a good time together, played scrabble. He's getting quite good at it now.'

'Well I've got some stuff to sort out on the computer so I'm going straight up.'

'You've had a busy day with the school and the little empire,' he laughs. 'It must be exhausting.'

I bristle at his stab at humour and go upstairs to bed where I continue to replay the kiss in my head until I fall asleep.

It's a few moments after waking before the memories of the night before hit me. I berate myself for what I did. What an idiot I am. I turn over and see Niall laid next to me, his head on the pillow with his mouth open, dead to the world. Strange snorting noises come out of his nose. His elbow is pointing out from the pillow, an annoying sleeping habit of his that drives me mad. If I turn around in sleep, I'm often woken by being elbowed in the face. I lie there for several minutes, looking at my husband and wondering why I've felt the need to kiss another man. It can't be justified by the fact that I have an overwhelming need to be adored, to feel that someone cares. Niall provides for our family, showing he cares every day. I am being selfish wanting more. I lay back and stare at the ceiling, wondering what I'm going to do about my actions, but I'm interrupted by the buzzing of the alarm clock. I switch it off and get out of bed, back to the morning routine.

Back from school, I text Monique.

**Emergency.**

She texts back.

*I have some time owing. I can get out for twelve-thirty.* We arrange to meet at Etta's. I spend the next three hours watching the clock go round.

'So what's the great emergency, then? Better not be because you've forgotten my rules and bought eight identical V-neck t-shirts in different colours.'

I stick out my tongue. 'You're so funny. Thank God, you could meet me.'

'I was bored out of my brains. I'd have met you if you were just hungry.'

'Well, I wish I was just hungry.' I took a deep breath. 'I snogged Seb.'

Monique starts laughing. 'Is that all? This is you, "Mrs needs attention", who hasn't been getting any, and a cute guy comes along and wants in your pants. I'm not the slightest bit surprised.'

My face falls. 'I've not done anything like this before.'

'That's because Niall generally comes around and there isn't a stud muffin waiting in the wings. Did you nearly have sex?'

'God, no.'

'Well then, what's the problem? It was just a snog.'

'The problem is that I feel guilty about it, but don't regret it. It was amazing,' I snap.

'And this is Joe's teacher next year? Shame Joe's an angel really. You won't get kept back after school.'

'Can you not take anything seriously?'

'I'm trying to balance you; you take things too seriously. Look, are you going to snog him again?'

'Certainly not.'

'Well then, no harm done, and you've had a bit of fun. Can we eat now?'

Sometimes Monique can be really supportive and other times, like today, she just doesn't understand. I wonder what her relationship with Toby was like. She doesn't talk about him much, but I'm guessing it made her build walls because she's kept every relationship since really light. Our cheese and onion toasties arrive. I'm ravenous and dive straight in. Monique smells hers and pulls a face. 'This smells weird,' she says. 'I'm not eating that.'

I pull her plate towards me and sniff it. 'Mon, there's nothing wrong with it,' I say. 'It smells fine.'

She takes a bite and pulls a face. ''I'll get some crisps.'

'You are beyond weird,' I state. 'Were you perhaps drinking with Dr Love last night? Mon?'

'Sorry, I was miles away. No. He was working yesterday afternoon and the same tonight. I might not see him until Monday. Absence makes the heart grow fonder and all that. Actually, I'm starting to feel a bit shit, I think after here I'll go to bed.'

'You okay?'

'Yeah, fine, its working at that damn hospital with all those bloody bugs.'

I finish my sandwich and we leave, Monique gives me a peck on the cheek and a hug. As we part she whispers, 'One more snog wouldn't hurt.'

---

I get home and clean the house from top to bottom, pushing my body through scrubbing at marks on walls and floors, and ignoring the fact that if I wasn't feeling so guilty I wouldn't be doing this. I wonder if I'll see Seb when I fetch Joe from school. I don't usually but will he make it happen? I bet I'm another notch now, just one he had to work a bit harder for, and now he's cracked it.

I crash onto the sofa throwing off my cardigan as I'm so damn hot from rushing around. I grab a hair tie from the coffee table and fasten my hair into a bun at the back of my head. My chest is pumping up and down through the exertion. I grab the laptop and log on to catch up on mail. I have a Facebook friend request from a Mr Uri Kent. Where I would usually reject it, a suspicion makes me send a message back.

**Your name is offensive. Do I know you?**

Later, I log back on to find a reply from Mr Kent.

*I think you know me quite well, especially my tongue.*

Jesus, it's him. I accept his friend request and set up a private group between us.

**For goodness' sake, post your messages here where no-one can see them.**

*A secret group? So I can say what I want and no-one but us knows? I like it.*

A few minutes passes.

*Are you anticipating my messages? Waiting for one to appear? Heart beating quicker?*

I squirm on the sofa, guilty.

*I loved the feel of my tongue in your hot mouth. Entering your warm parts and feeling you writhe against me. You had goose bumps on your arms.*

There's another pause then,

**Did you feel me get hard as I pushed you against the metal? You revved my engine.**

He logs off, leaving me hanging.

Monique calls me later, unusual after we've seen each other so recently. 'Are you feeling alright now?' I ask.

'Yeah fine, not sure what that was all about,' she says. 'Anyway, what are you doing Friday night and Saturday day?'

I stretch my unoccupied arm. 'Nothing much, I've kept them clear because the school fair's on Sunday and I know I'll be busy.'

'I've found a cheap London break, only sixty pounds each, including travel. Wondered if you fancied an overnighter?'

I smile. 'Oh my, yes, that would be fabulous. Let me check with Niall.'

I go downstairs and ask Niall, who has no problems with it. 'Abandoning me again to spend my money, eh?'

My jaw sets. 'I'll not go if you don't want.'

'Don't be daft, I'm joking. Get yourself off.'

I rush back upstairs. 'I can go. What time are we leaving?'

'Train station at eleven. I've taken annual leave for Friday, so we can have all of Friday afternoon and come back on the two-thirty train Saturday. You'll be back in time for tea.'

'I can't wait,' I say, suddenly excited by a couple of days away from Sexy Seb and the maybe Bonkers Bettina.

'I know, we haven't been away for ages,' she says. 'Get ready for ...'

'Chaos,' we shout in unison.

With all our previous minibreaks we've endured some drama or another. Monique blames me every time. She says that for all my organisational skills, when it comes to mini-breaks, I lose the plot. She says I attract chaos like Uri Geller bends spoons, it's a phenomenon. The last time we went away, I realised at the station that the tickets had been booked on a card that had expired. After a trip to Customer Services, who said I had to ring the ticket issuer, we got the tickets with three minutes to spare. Then there was the time we went to a country retreat and I attempted to turn the car around, not realising it was on a one-way system. It was winter, and I got the car stuck partway in a drainage ditch, causing the traffic to come to a halt until the site tractor could pull us out. We term these moments my 'chaos'. I am determined this time there will be no such thing. Monique has booked the trip this time after all, so I'm cleared for that.

Thursday morning though, I begin to throw up. Damn Monique, she obviously had a bug yesterday and passed it on. I throw up three times before collapsing back into bed. Niall drops Joe off at school and says he'll try to finish early so he can pick him up. After lunch, I ring Monique. 'I'm sick. I don't think I can go.'

'There's no way I'm going without you. Get plenty of water down yourself, I need this night away.'

'But I feel terrible.'

'So did I yesterday, but I still came out for lunch with you. When were you last sick?'

'A couple of hours ago.'

'Right, so it's probably out of your system now. Get some sleep, there's nearly twenty-four hours until the train. We're going, and that's that.'

'Jeez, you're so bossy and mean.'

'Sleep.'

The next morning I feel wiped out, but drag my stuff together and drop Joe at school. I buy a can of Red Bull from the corner shop, and then book a taxi to the train station as I'm not in the mood to catch a bus. I make myself a slice of toast and jam, the first food I've had since yesterday's breakfast. I catch sight of myself in the kitchen mirror. Under my eyes are dark circles. My skin looks sallow and my wrinkles all seem really prominent. I look five years older than usual. I grab my make-up bag and launch for the Touche Eclat. I need the big boys if I'm not going for the 'extra in Thriller video' look.

I arrive at the train station at eleven sharp. Of course Monique looks like she's stepped off the cover of InStyle. She's dressed in a V-neck knitted purple tunic, with a tan belt at the waist, and some slightly flared indigo jeans. This is set off by a pair of tan ankle boots that make her look taller than ever. She has a matching purple Samsonite spinner and a little shoulder purse in tan, no doubt carrying just the bare essentials. This girl knows how to travel. I, in contrast, have my 'free with a catalogue' navy wheeled holdall, my Levi's, one of the V-neck tees she is always taking the piss out of me for in red, my black M&S Footglove flats (they're comfy) and a large fluffy black cardi, even though it's quite warm today. I feel a bit pants still and want a material hug.

Monique looks at me from top to bottom for a few minutes. 'Well, it could be worse under the circumstances,' she drawls. 'Let's go.'

When we are on the train she fetches me a coffee and gets a water for herself. She passes me a Berocca. 'The coffee ain't decaf,' she says.

At twelve, she fetches me a bacon butty and I'm ready for it. I scoff it greedily. 'You not having one?'

'I ate a good breakfast.'

I sit back satisfied, and feeling a lot better, though if someone passed me a pillow right now, I'd marry them. Monique opens her shoulder bag and brings out a small carrier bag from Accessorize.

'You owe me eleven pounds for the repair kit'. She takes out a comb and sidles in the seat alongside me. 'Right, let's sort that bloody mop out.'

She plaits my hair and twists it up onto the back of my head, fixing it in place with grips. She sprays it with an industrial strength mini hairspray and curls up a few tendrils around the front of my face.

I point to the carrier bag. 'Is that a small carrier bag, or the Tardis?'

'I just know how to shop, and you do realise I've carried a plastic bag for you? The sacrifices I make.'

'It's like that bag Hermione had in Harry Potter, where she could reach in it over and over and get out whatever they needed. What else you got in there?'

She pulls out some black beads and fastens them around my neck, then hands me a pair of black drop earrings. 'Get them in.'

'Yes, Boss.'

She looks over me appraisingly. I feel like I'm about to be introduced to my future husband as part of an arranged marriage. 'Much better,' she says, and heads back to her own seat.

I take out a copy of Good Housekeeping magazine from my Betty Barclay.

'What the fuck is that?' Monique grabs it and throws it down the train. It narrowly misses an elderly gentleman's head and lands on an empty seat. She moves down to the luggage rack and opens the front compartment of her case, taking out issues of Grazia and Vogue.

She rolls her eyes at me. 'Read one of those. At least you can appear to have some style.'

'God, are you going to be like this for the entire journey?' I snap. 'I know I'm not looking my best, but I've been sick and you're being a right bitch about it. What's got into you?'

'A fucking baby, that's what's got into me,' her nostrils flare. 'And being sick's not an excuse because I've been puking for the last three days now and I look divine.'

## CHAPTER TEN

'Fuck.'

'Yes, well that's how it usually gets in there.'

'You know what I mean.'

Monique sighs and fiddles with the bag the jewellery came out of. 'This is why I wanted to come away, so you can help me decide whether I'm keeping it or not.'

My voice softens. 'You think you might?'

She shrugs. 'I've no idea what I'm going to do.'

I touch her hand. 'Why didn't you tell me before?'

She withdraws her hand and crosses her arms. 'Because I only confirmed it a week ago, and to be quite honest with you, lately it's been Bettina this, Niall that, and Seb the other.'

I lower my gaze. 'I'm sorry. I have been a bit me, me, me.'

'Yeah, well it's typical that the one time I needed you was the day you decided to cancel.'

I ignore the mean streak she's displaying as she's in shock and hormonal. She's just hitting out and I'm the nearest target. I remember pregnancy mood swings well enough, even if it was over nine years ago.

'What did Dr Love say?'

'I've not told him yet, and I don't know if I'm going to. If I do decide to keep it, I do not want a significant other interfering.'

'You'll need support, Mon.'

'I've never needed anyone, and if I want some support I've got you.'

We don't speak as the train pulls into St Pancras. *Chaos*, I think.

We get off the train, but I notice a few magazines left on seats and run back on to get them. I pick up my Good Housekeeping, which is now minus its cover, having been ripped off while flying over the seats. Monique just rolls her eyes at me again as I get off at the other end of the carriage armed with five magazines. 'I'm recycling,' I pout.

We arrive at the hotel to see if we can check in early, bearing in mind its only fifty minutes off the check-in time. The hotel is a converted house in Bayswater. It looks nice from the outside. Several storeys high, it's a white painted building with a wrought iron railed basement. We walk inside. The reception area is light and airy, although I notice the couch for visitors has a large rip across its red leather.

'Your room is available now, Madam,' says the receptionist, a young blonde lad who gains an icy look from Monique who believes she should be addressed as Miss. He hands Monique a room key and points. 'If you follow the corridor to the first turning on your left and then take the stairs down.' We do as instructed and walk towards the basement.

We enter the room. It smells of damp.

'What the fuck is this?' Says Monique.

I just gasp. I swear to God that I have never seen anything like it in my life. It's a small room, containing a double bed with plain white sheets and an itchy looking beige blanket folded across the bottom. I pick up the blanket. It's covered in hair.

'Aaarrrgh'. I drop it as if it's scalding hot and wipe my hand down my leg.

The window is made of etched obscure glass that resembles the squared graph paper we had at school for drawing angles, but there is no mistaking what's behind it as we recognise the whirr of a generator. We look at each other.

'Monique, open the bathroom door.'

She approaches it as if we are hiding from terrorists. She carefully opens the bathroom door and I see a green bathroom suite. She checks out the loo and nearly barfs. A look of complete fury crosses her face and she storms out of the room, swiping a box off the side table on her way out. I follow her back to the reception.

'That room is completely unacceptable,' she screeches at the receptionist. He takes a step backwards. 'I am pregnant, and I do not wish to share my bed with umpteen other people's pubic hairs, and as for this …' She slams down the cardboard box and the tea and coffee sachets fly across the counter. 'I am fully into the concept of re..cy..cling.' I see her spittle hit the guys shoulder as she enunciates every word. 'However, I think for the purpose of holding my tea, coffee and sugar sachets, you could at least have the decency to *find a plate or a bowl,* and not make it out of a piece of cardboard that won't even hold together.' She waltzes off and sits on the couch, avoiding the huge rip. 'We shall wait here,' she announces, 'until you find us another room.'

The receptionist goes rushing into the back room, his chin trembling. A few minutes later he comes out with another key. 'This is our best room,' he states, pointing at the opposite corner of the reception room. 'Please, enjoy.'

The new room is quite spacious and has two single beds, no hairy blankets in sight and a huge window overlooking a park that looks green and serene. It appears really nice. We are unpacking about fifteen minutes later when I suddenly realise there's a small problem.

'Mon?'

'Mmmm, hmmmm?'

'Where's the bathroom?'

We look around the room: bed, dressing table, window, wardrobe, no bathroom. 'We must have to share the one along the corridor,' I state, heading for the door at the same time Monique opens the right sided wardrobe door to hang up some clothes.

'The bathroom's here, behind the wardrobe door.'

It's true. One side of the wardrobe is exactly that. The other side covers a small recess which houses a tiny sink and a shower. To say it's small, it is actually quite clean.

I begin to giggle. 'I'm not moving again.' I walk around to the desk and pick up a bowl containing the tea and coffee. 'Look,' I state. 'It's otherwise perfect.'

She narrows her eyes at me. "All I could think about was that bloody cardboard holder.'

'Our room is *not* acceptable. We do *not* have a bone china tea holder.' I guffaw as I collapse on one of the single beds. 'I'm done in. I'm having a kip.'

'Yes, me too,' Monique abandons packing and flings herself on the other bed. By half past three we're both fast asleep.


'Lauren. Come on, it's gone seven. We're not sleeping in any longer.'

'Nnoooo, go away,' I put the covers back over my head. The next minute they are entirely on the floor.

'Up.'

'God, were you an Army major in a past life?'

'I'm starving,' she says. 'I need to eat something so I can throw up later.'

After splashing my face with cold water and reapplying some lipstick, I put on my black Monsoon mini-dress and get ready to hit London. Bayswater is a lovely area, brimming with little cafes and restaurants. We pick a chain we know well and head there for some pasta. We both eat like it's the Last Supper. The sleep and food reinvigorate us and we head for a small shopping complex where I buy a pair of black silky pyjamas with a matching dressing gown. It's sexy, but doesn't look like I'm trying too hard. I also buy some new pants, a few pieces of jewellery, and a lovely ornate headband.

Monique eyes my stash. 'Good gracious, we've only been out ten minutes.'

'I was born to shop,' I reply. I smile; I'm starting to enjoy myself.

'Who are the new pants for?' Monique asks and winks.

'All of this is for me *personally*. I figure if I start feeling better about myself, I'll stop trying to lean on other people. Like you for instance.' I throw my arms around her and give her a hug. 'I still feel bad for not being there when you needed me, but I'm here now. Tomorrow we'll have a good chat and a think. Tonight should be about fun; so how about we go back and watch Big Brother?'

'Sounds like a plan, and don't laugh, but I'm really sleepy again.'

The next morning we head down to breakfast where I'm informed by Monique that due to the hotel's religious beliefs there will be no bacon, but an alternative made of turkey. I walk downstairs to be served a green coloured egg yolk, some unidentifiable turkey/bacon substitute and an equally green looking Monique. 'Let's eat out,' I state.

We return to the shopping mall, to the diner we'd spied yesterday that served breakfast. I peruse the menu and ask the guy behind the counter for two decaf coffees and two croissants.

'Just toast,' he says.

I peruse the menu again which details approximately fourteen different breakfast options you can have. 'Toast?'

'Toast.' He repeats.

I point to the picture. 'Not a croissant?'

'Toast.'

I look at Monique. She shrugs. I turn back to the man.

'Okay, toast.'

'You sit. I go there.' He points outside. 'Fifteen minutes, yes? I get croissant.' He gestures to the central seating area and walks off.

'I spied a Patisserie Valerie on the way past,' I whisper to Monique. We give the guy time to leave and then escape.

We are ensconced in one of my favourite cafes, and all Monique keeps repeating is toast and chuckling.

'Oh God, I just thought, we could have gone with the alternative of... bread,' I say. We cackle together causing the other breakfasting patrons to look at us, some frowning, some with eyebrows raised and half smiles on their faces.

'Enjoy your breakfast,' says the waitress as she puts down two huge mugs of coffee, a cake stand containing a dozen mini fruit scones, little pots of jam, and two small pots of cream.'

'Still think I'd have preferred toast,' I say and we laugh.

After breakfast I take Monique to Harrods toy department and let her walk around while dozens of overexcited children run amok around her feet. She looks scared to death. 'If you can survive this toy store hell, you can survive your own baby,' I state. 'The mothers here don't know what to do when the nannies and au pairs aren't around, so they bring them here and fling money at them in the vain hope they'll behave.'

'Can we go to the pet department?'

'Yep, can I just look at these Barbies first?'

After Harrods, I take her to the National History Museum. We wander around all the stuffed animals and end up at the giant dinosaur skeleton. 'Look at all this history you could pass onto another person,' I say.

'Google can do that. I don't need to.'

'I give up. Let's get lunch.'

We hole up in Costa for one of their delicious toasties. I have a glass of fresh orange juice whilst Mon orders milk. 'Heartburn.'

'Okay,' I say when we're settled. 'Time for baby chat. Why, when you were with Toby, did you adamantly not want a kid?'

She fidgets with her glass. 'I just never did. I still don't think I do now. I love being by myself.' She pauses, rubbing condensation from the glass. 'Toby knew to give me my distance; we led quite independent lives. He had lots of sporty friends and I did my yoga. I had lots of quiet time to myself. He started wanting more, I couldn't provide it, so he moved on.'

'So why the hesitation now?'

'Because it's here inside me, a real thing. I could dismiss a thought, but I'm not finding it so easy to dismiss a real baby. I'm scared shitless, Lo, but I know at my age that if I don't have it, that it really is my very last chance.'

'I think you should have it,' I say.

'Why?'

'You have lots of love inside you. I know because I get some of it. I really think you could do it, Mon.'

She gives me a half smile. 'If I do, will you be there for me?'

'You need to ask?'

'Even if Bettina and Sexy Seb want your attention?'

'I'll ditch them. I'm all yours,' I joke. 'Although I do still need to see my husband and child.'

'Well obvs, but at least Niall is a good egg. He'll let you come when I need you, like this weekend.'

'Mon,' I say my eyes widening. 'Those pregnancy hormones must really be getting to you. You've just given Niall a compliment.'

'Fuck,' she says, 'So I have. This parasite's making me soft.'

We arrive back in Sheffield at a quarter to five. Monique heads off for the bus and I go to the entrance of the short stay car park. Joe comes dashing out of the car and runs towards me like we've been separated for years. 'Mum, Dad's bought me five packets of series seven Lego figures.'

'Someone's been spoilt,' I say.

After a huge hug he looks at me from under his fringe. 'Have you got me anything?'

I laugh, 'What about four packets of series eight Lego figures?' I say getting them out of my pocket. 'London's a bit ahead of us.'

'Wow, thanks, Mum,' he runs back off towards his dad. 'Mum got me series eight."

'Sorry,' I mouth at Niall as I get to the car.

'Bloody fickle children,' he pretends to flick Joe's ear and then drives us home.

---

I've been home a while and then it hits me. Tomorrow is the school fair. I call Bettina,

'Hi, just a quick call to say see you tomorrow.'

'Hey stranger. I tried you at home, but Niall said you were away? You feeling better? Niall said you were ill again.'

Oh crikey, I'd told her I had a bad stomach the week before, obviously karma had given me the sick bug. 'Yep, had another bug. Must be run down. I've been away with Monique. She made me go, even though I wasn't fully better, the bully. Anyway, I feel okay now.'

'Oh good. Listen, I've been given some extra books by a few neighbours. Could you pick me up in the morning and help me get them to school?'

'Course I can. I'll see you in the morning then.'

'See you then.'

---

Niall is gobsmacked by my news about Monique. 'If she rings, don't mention it. I said I wouldn't tell anyone.'

'No secrets between us, love. She must know that. Do you think she'll keep it?'

'I've no idea, but I said I'll be there whatever.'

'Course, not a problem. You know if I'm around I'll take care of Joe if she needs you.'

'Thanks, love,' I say, and reach up to give him a kiss. It's familiar and I breathe in the remnants of his aftershave.

'Do you want to come upstairs?' I say.

'Would you be offended if I said no? Only I've been playing football with Joe and to be honest, I've pulled my groin.'

I reach out and stroke his cheek. 'I could kiss it better?'

'No, honestly, it really hurts,' he says moving my hand away. 'Do you want to sit on the sofa with me and watch CSI?'

'No, you're alright, I'm tired from the trip. I'll go on up. I need an early night so I'm ready for tomorrow.'

'Oh yes, how could I forget. Me and Joe have a quid each ready to smack you upside the head with a sponge.'

'I feel you are getting rather too enthusiastic about this.'


I power up the laptop to check all my messages. I am inundated with emails and Facebook notifications after ignoring them for thirty-six hours. I ignore them all and click into the secret group for Seb and I. I've named it 'eBay queries'. I figured if I left it on by accident that would be too boring for Niall to click into. I read the list of messages.

**Where are you luscious Lauren?**

**I feel all alone :(.**

**I'm tapping my fingers on the keyboard, still waiting.**

**Bored now, gonna have to think of something to do.**

**Oh, my hands have found something to play with …**

**Hmmm right now I'm thinking about your hot tongue snaking around the inside of my mouth again. Now I'm imagining it somewhere else …**

There were no more updates. I caught up with the rest of the emails and wondered what in the hell tomorrow would bring.

## CHAPTER ELEVEN

We couldn't have asked for better weather for the fair. It's a bright day with sunshine, accompanied by a cooling breeze, so everyone who attends can join in without feeling like they're going to melt. We arrive an hour before the start to make sure everything is in place. I spend the morning filling up balloons and tying up banners. Seb is there, dressed in black and grey stripy pyjamas. He smiles at me as I arrive and carries on with what he's doing. I'd dressed myself as planned, with my swimming costume underneath my clothes. I'd just gone for black jogging bottoms and a black baggy tee. Not ideal clothing if it turned hotter later, but at least if it got wet I'd still look respectable.

I think back to when I used to take Joe to fun sessions at the local swimming baths. Many children were almost left to drown by their dads as my costume barely fit my 36Ds. I had to go to M&S and buy a more respectable swimsuit, more akin to what a sixty-year-old would wear. My current costume has a decent bra bit to it, and the black makes my waist look a lot slimmer than it really is. It suits my figure, making it look a bit fifties pin up, but that doesn't matter today because I'm neither swimming nor bathing, so no one will be seeing it.

Bettina is busy setting books out on her stall. Her blonde hair is loose, and she must have used some tongs as it's lightly waved. She's wearing a floaty summer hat in pale pink, and a vintage style tea dress with soft pink roses and bluebells on it; a dress I'd have killed for. With pale pink peep toe sandals and nails, and a large blue shopper style bag which matches the bluebells on the dress, she looks exquisite. I feel dowdy and lifeless by comparison. I'd had to tie up my own hair in a bun and had left my make-up off as I figured water didn't mix very well with blow dried hair and a face full of slap. I walk over to her.

'I really do adore that dress.'

'I know, you said when you picked me up, but thanks,' she twiddles with a piece of hair.

I watch as she pulls an embroidered tablecloth out of her bag. It's patchwork, with loads of different vintage style squares of pretty florals. It's divine, and I touch it. 'Where did you get this from, it's delightful?'

'I've had it years,' she says. 'You're not the only one who does vintage you know?'

I take a step back. 'Well, of course. It's just that I would have liked to get some for my shop if they'd still been around. I'm sure they'd have sold amazingly fast.'

'I think I'm just about there with the stall.' She looks away.

I gather I'm dismissed, so I head over to the kids' canteen where the school cooks have kindly volunteered to cook us a breakfast before they start serving teas and coffees to the patrons of the fair. I turn back to Bettina, but she doesn't look up. She's smoothing out the tablecloth. I watch her rip off a tag hanging down from it. I recognise it as a Dunbar's tag, a store not too far away in Derbyshire—a store that opened last year.

Breakfast is so tasty and appreciated. Fried egg, fried bread, bacon, beans, and fried mushrooms, with a slice of toast and butter, and all washed down with a coffee. Why does it taste so much nicer when it's cooked for you?

At ten-thirty Mrs Sullivan asks us to stand by our stations because some parents always turn up early in the hopes of getting the best bargains from the toy stalls. She is resplendent in a navy suit with a gold scarf; her hair immaculate as always. She wishes us luck. I head over to the sponge stocks where Seb has pulled up two child-sized chairs to one side. I can barely sit on mine but it's better than standing all morning.

'You've been quiet,' he says.

'I went to London with my friend. It was a nice break, I enjoyed it.'

'You didn't reply to my updates.' He says quietly.

I raised a brow. 'You seemed to be doing okay by *yourself*.'

'Would've been better if you were there.'

'Oh I know,' I wink at him, warming up to the idea of tormenting Seb for entertainment.

A young girl comes up with her father. 'Morning, Mr Kingsley,' she says quietly.

'Hi, Deborah. Let me guess, you want to hit me with a wet sponge?'

'Yes please,' she giggles.

The sight of Mr Kingsley in his pyjamas is a target for all the young lads in the school, who can't wait to turn their nerdy teacher into a soaking wet victim. However, without his glasses, and with his hair becoming wet and unruly, there's a sudden surge of mothers drawn to the stocks. I watch as he peels off his pyjama top and replaces it with a dry one. He gives us all a quick reveal of his ripped body. The tattoo of a dragon stretches across his skin. Its body and tail snake around a muscled left arm, while its head comes to a stop just above his left nipple, sitting atop a defined pec. I swear some mothers actually swoon. I get so hot I imagine the dragon could have scorched me with its breath, and toy with the idea of switching the hosepipe we've been using to fill the bucket onto myself to cool down.

'Hey, Mum.' Joe is here, and I sweep his gangly body up into my arms. I am so pleased to see him.

'Put me down, it's embarrassing.'

Oops. Mother mistake made already. Hugging child in front of others at school. 'How about a free go of the sponge stocks then? You can salvage your integrity.'

'Don't know what that word means, but can I have the sponges?' he asks.

While I'm getting them ready, I ask Joe where his dad is. 'Oh, he's gone to get a couple of coffees; says you'll be ready for one by now.'

My husband is so right. I am desperate for a drink, and I could do with a wee too. Listening to this water sloshing around is not helping.

I head over to Seb and ask him to put me in the stocks. 'Oooh kinky,' he whispers.

'Shut it, Joe's over there. He doesn't need to know his future teacher's a total lech.'

He mimes stabbing his heart. 'I am wounded.'

I hate it in the stocks, I feel so vulnerable. Yes, I know it's only a pretend thing, and I could break out of it if I wanted to, but I feel trapped and claustrophobic. I'm not a good swimmer and can hardly bear water on my face. I swim breaststroke with my head so far out of the water, I always have a bad neck when I've done. However, this is for Joe, so I try to calm myself. 'Okay. I'm ready.'

The first four sponges miss completely, although some spray still splashes me, but the fifth hits me squarely in the face. I can't stand it. I shake my head and desperately want to wipe my eyes, but my arms are in the stocks. Niall has come up and I ask him to wipe my face with a towel. He knows how much I hate water but tells me that would be cheating and then pays Seb a pound for another five sponges. I'm frustratingly unable to see what Seb makes of Niall as I'm stuck in these things. Niall walks in front and guides Joe's hands to show him how to throw more accurately. 'I'll do the first one,' he tells Joe, then raises his arm in an overhand throw as if he's playing cricket and I'm the wicket. Whoomph, straight in my face.

'Yeeeeeaaaaaaaahhhhhhh,' he does a sad dad dance and slaps Joe's hand in a high five. I find it remarkable that Joe is so caught up with the perfect shot that he lets his dad off with one of the most embarrassing jigs ever. Joe takes the next four shots and two of them are right on target, straight in my face.

'Hey, what's all this? Pick on your mum time?' Bettina strolls over to us.

'Shouldn't you be on the book stall?' I splutter, as drips fall down my nose from my fringe.

'One of the other mum's is doing it for ten minutes. I'm having a quick walk around and a coffee. I need the loo too. I just couldn't resist seeing the always well put together Mrs Lawler looking like a drowned rat.'

'You want to see her at home,' chips in Niall. 'She walks about in leggings and a t-shirt all the time you know.'

'Niall,' I shout.

Bettina giggles. 'Tell me more of her secrets while she's locked up in the stocks.'

'I'll tell you what,' says Niall, handing Seb another quid. 'For every sponge you get in her face, I'll tell you something embarrassing about her.'

'Niall, no,' I squeal. 'Seb, let me out of the stocks.' I wriggle, but it hurts my neck and wrists.

'They've paid their pound fair and square,' he says, then I feel him at my back, touching the stocks where my arms are, as if checking them. He whispers. 'Your husband's a dickhead.'

Of course, Bettina gets four of the five sponges right in my face. She does a girlish twirl, like a ballerina on the top of a music box and asks Niall and Joe if they want to join her for a quick coffee so they can tell her four of my secrets.

'I know some too,' says Joe. 'If you buy me a penguin biscuit, I'll tell.'

Seb releases me from the stocks. My hair and the top of my t-shirt are soaking, but will be fine with a towel down and ten minutes of sunshine. As I reach for a towel, I fail to see Tyler run up out of nowhere. He picks up the hosepipe and turns it on Seb. 'I dare, I dare'. Bettina goes to knock it out of his hands, which turns the hosepipe towards me and before I know it I am absolutely drenched from head to foot, but worse than that, the water is freezing, so I scream.

'Tyler Southwell,' shouts Mrs Sullivan. 'What on earth is going on?'

'They dared me, Miss.' Tyler points to a group of giggling schoolchildren.

'Do you do everything you're dared to do? I think your mother needs to take you home.'

Bettina looks horrified.

'No need,' I say shivering. 'Boys will be boys. If all their parents stick a couple of quid in the tub, we can let him off.'

'That's very understanding of you,' says Mrs Southwell. She then turns to Bettina. 'I realise you are on a stall, but you also need to be responsible for your son.'

Bettina looks at the floor. 'Of course, Mrs Sullivan. He can stay on the stall with me for the rest of the fair.' She digs in her bag and brings out a five-pound note. 'That's Tyler's contribution. It can come out of his pocket money.'

'Muuum, that's not fair,' Tyler harrumphs. She drags him over to her stall and her furious face leaves no doubt about the fact that Tyler will be lucky to be given any more pocket money this month.

At least she didn't get any inside info on my life, I think.

Mrs Sullivan decides that the sponge stocks have been a success, but in the circumstances it's time for them to finish. We can dry off, get changed and have a wander around the rest of the fair ourselves. I spied some delicious looking chocolate cupcakes on the cake stall earlier and hope there's still one there with my name on it. Niall tells me he'll find me in a bit and heads off with Joe. I grab my plastic Tesco bag, containing my change of clothes, hairbrush, towels, hairdryer, and spare plastic bags for the wet clothes (Monique would throw a fit but hey she isn't here) and head into Seb's classroom, which has been set up as our changing area. He follows me in.

'Erm, excuse me. I need some privacy to get changed,' I tell him.

He leans against the wall. 'I don't think you do. I think you'll need some assistance getting out of those wet clothes, *and* I can help you dry off,' he replies.

'Seb, my husband and son are outside.'

His tongue wets his lip. 'That makes it even more fun, don't you think?'

I'm trying to pull my t-shirt over my head, but it's so wet it rolls up and gets stuck. I sigh in frustration. He comes over and helps me take it off. Struggling with a wet shirt isn't exactly like the clothes ripping off scenes you get on TV, but my nipples visibly harden under my swimsuit. I flush. 'It's the cold.'

'No it's not, Lauren.'

I realise at this point that I can take my belongings with me, go and find Niall, and we can go home. There he'll no doubt re-enact the sponge stocks in the garden with my kitchen sponges and state that while I'm wet I might as well let them have another turn. I inhale deeply. 'Lock the door.'

'I already have.'

He comes towards me and grabs my wrist, leading me towards the storage room at the back of the classroom. As his classroom is at the rear of the school we are unlikely to be seen anyway, but it's good that he's thinking of things like that because my own sense seems to have disappeared. He pulls me into the cupboard where he strips his pyjama shirt off and throws it to the floor. I put my hand against his chest and feel the cold, damp skin underneath my fingers. I stroke around the head of the dragon, tracing my fingertips around the outline. I've never seen a tattoo up close, the black ink is like a trail of temptation, of darkness. Seb's breathing intensifies. I move my hand to his cheek and touch his face. I can feel the beginnings of stubble. I pause and look at him. His eyes darken as his pupils dilate. I can still leave, I remind myself, but instead, I lean into him, raising myself up on tiptoes and lick the side of his neck. He tastes of water and salt.

'You started it this time,' he says, his voice gruff.

'And at any time, I may well end it,' I say, trailing tiny kisses down his chin. He catches my mouth with a groan and his tongue is strong and insistent between my teeth. He helps me remove my leggings and they join his shirt on the floor. I stand in just my swimsuit. Seb's eyes appraise me as he takes in the curve of my breasts, with their slight swell over the top of the swimsuit. He places his body oh-so-closely next to mine, and then his mouth is on mine again. My breathing is getting raspier and I can feel his heart beating against my chest. He drops the strap of my swimsuit and runs his hand over my breast, caressing an erect nipple. I arch my breast into his hand, savouring the touch. His other hand moves down my back, grabbing my ass and pulling me towards him.

'Put your hand here,' he moans, showing me the opening of his PJ bottoms, which had been fastened previously, but now gives me a tantalising glimpse of what lays beneath.

I trail my hand over his stomach, touching the fine hair there, and move my hand lower.

My phone rings. Loud and shrill, playing the *Star Wars* theme tune, it reminds me that my son and husband are just outside. I leap for the phone while Seb tries to grab hold of me and keep me close to him.

I shake him off. 'Hello?'

'We're done here and ready to go. We walked up this morning, so thought if you were nearly ready we could get a lift back with you?' says Niall.

'Yes, of course. Give me a minute. I'm just changing into some dry clothes.'

'Don't get too dry, I've promised Joe we'll make our own sponge stocks at home.'

'Yes, I thought you might.'

'I'm allowed to be a little predictable at my age, aren't I?' he laughs.

'Of course. Well, I'll see you in a few.' I end the call.

I daren't look at Seb's face. He comes over to me and lifts my chin. 'It doesn't matter to me, Lauren. I just like spending time with you, though you're driving me mad,' he indicates the bulge in his trousers. He sighs, 'Go on.'

I grab my things and leave to find my husband. As I get to the door he whispers,

'I'll contact you tonight, on Facebook.'

'Please don't,' I say. My eyes beg him not to, before I close the door behind me.

I ruminate all afternoon. I can't believe what I did. I feel guilty, yet it was exhilarating to be that naughty and abandoned. Why can't it still be like this with Niall? After re-enacting the sponge stocks in the garden, I go upstairs to shower. Niall comes in to use the loo.

I peer around the shower curtain. 'What's Joe doing?'

'Building a Lego train we got at the fair.'

'Well, why don't you come and get in here?' I flash him a breast.

He looks at me. 'I'll get wet.'

'That's the idea, idiot. Come on. Let's have a quickie while Joe's busy.'

'Don't be ridiculous, Lauren. What if he comes upstairs?'

'He won't. Once he's in Lego world he's in a world of his own.'

'It's not very responsible though, having sex while our child is downstairs. Maybe later, eh?' He walks over and reaches round to slap my wet bottom. 'Damn, I've got my bloody sleeve wet now.'

Then he walks out. I'm left frustrated. I close my eyes and feel the force of the shower on my shoulders, waiting for it to work on my muscles and release the tension. It doesn't work, so I pad out of the shower, trailing wet footsteps and droplets everywhere, and reach into the back of the wardrobe. Returning to the shower, I switch on the bullet vibrator and place it between my legs. I lean against the tiled wall of the shower, remembering and repeating Seb's touch of my breasts, imagining he's here and we didn't stop. I run the bullet over my clitoris again and again imagining it's his fingers until I come in a delicious wave. The tension leaves my body instantly. I sit down in the bath and let the shower wash over me.

The temptation that night proves too great and I log on to Facebook and click on our group. The green button indicates Seb is online. I type.

**I'm here.**
*I'm pleased.*
**I shouldn't be though.**
*Why are you then?*
**I don't know.**
**I want to finish what we started.**

I feel between my legs get slick again, and the pull from earlier returns.

**I can't do that.**
*Look, if it's virtual, it doesn't count right?*
**I suppose not.**
*Imagine what we were doing before your phone rang.*

It doesn't take much to imagine it. I've thought of little else all day. I'm brimming with lust again.

*My hand is on my cock and I'm pretending it's yours. Tell me what you were going to do.*

I can't do this.

*Your hand's here, I can feel it. Oh, God, tell me what you want.*

My mouth is dry. I need to decide whether to turn off the computer or stay. I close my eyes for a second and breathe. All it does is make me focus on the heat in my core. I begin to type.

**I trail my hand down your stomach and dip below the waistline of your bottoms. I grasp you within my hand. You feel cool to the touch, but I move my hand around and your cock soon warms up and gets hard.** I feel stupid typing it at first.

*Feels so good. Now I have moved my hand from your breast. I'm sliding it down your stomach, below your navel, and my fingers are slipping under the edge of your panties.*

My embarrassment wears off quickly. I feel my pants getting damper while my breathing gets faster. I move my hand exactly as he says.

*Now imagine I'm touching you there, stroking you, first quickly and then slowly until you are begging for release.*

I can barely type. **God, yes, and I'm pumping your cock with my fist. You want to fuck me, but I won't let you. You have to come in my hand.**

*Christ, Lauren.*

**I need to come.**

*Me too. Now think of this afternoon and how we could have ended it. See you soon.*

I lean against the bed and imagine that indeed my hand is his hand, that this is a continuation of earlier, and that he's stroking my breasts while bringing me to a climax. I rub myself faster and faster until I feel the pressure building and I come in a fierce explosion all over my fingers.

I quickly switch off the page and lay back against the bed feeling sated.

When Niall comes to bed he disturbs me. I cuddle into his back which he welcomes, holding on to the arm I've wrapped around him.

Now feeling guilty, I move my hand down his stomach, but he grabs it and tells me he's tired. I move away, sitting up in bed with tears in my eyes. 'What's going on, Niall? You're constantly turning me down.'

He huffs like I'm being a nuisance. 'I've just got a few things on my mind at the moment.'

'Well tell me about them for goodness' sake, because I can't go on like this.'

He sits up. 'I was thinking about seeing the doctor about a vasectomy.'

'Oh. Okay.'

'I really don't want any more kids, Lauren. I love Joe to bits, but I feel too old to start again.'

'That's fine with me, Niall.'

'Really? You're still only young. I thought you might end up wanting another.'

'Really,' I say. 'We've discussed this before. Joe's nine. I'd have changed my mind before now don't you think?'

He sniffs. 'One of the guys at work's wife has just got pregnant. Claims it's an accident, but he's not so sure. They're both in their early forties. He reckons she's had a last-minute panic attack about getting older. I've been worrying about accidents and ending up in the smelly nappy zone again. I'm just too old. I feel settled, Lauren. I like how we are.'

'I said it's fine. Arrange the vasectomy. I have enough with Joe. He's perfect.'

'Oh thank God.' He exhales deeply. 'That's such a weight off my mind. Now Monique's pregnant, I thought you might get the idea of pushing prams together.'

'Do you know, I just can't imagine Monique with a baby.'

'Me neither.' He pats my arm and turns over. In seconds he is asleep. I stay awake most of the night.

# CHAPTER TWELVE

The post-school run finds me in a quandary. I'm supposed to be meeting Monique as usual, but Niall has woken in a happy mood and wants us to spend the morning together as he's on a late shift. I don't want to ruin Niall's good mood when he seems genuinely upbeat for the first time all month, and maybe if we spend more time together I'll stop my stupid behaviour with Seb. As I'm not due to meet Monique until ten-thirty this morning anyway, I delay telling Niall I'm going out, put the kettle on, and begin to fix us breakfast. I hope he'll understand that I still need to see her though.

Brrrriiiiiiiing. The doorbell cuts into my thoughts.

'I'll get it,' says Niall. 'Morning, Bettina,' I hear. 'I'll get her for you.'

I throw the croissant packet down on the side. What does she want?

I wander into the hallway. 'I wasn't expecting you, was I?'

Bettina stands at the door in jeans and a blue cotton blouse with flower trim. Her hair is in a ponytail. I expect her to burst into a country and western song any minute.

'Lauren, it's rude to keep visitors on the doorstep,' she replies and walks past me into the house.

'Did you put the kettle on?' says Niall, from the living room.

'Yes, love.'

'Oh fab. Coffee: milk, one sugar, please.' Bettina moves through into the dining room and sits on one of my comfy brown tub chairs.

'Two things,' she says, brimming with cheer. 'I saw Mrs Sullivan this morning. The fair raised three hundred and seventy-three pounds. She said that about forty-six of that was from your sponge stocks. The book stall raised seventy-eight.'

'That's fantastic,' I say, hoping my enthusiasm has reached my eyes. Inside I don't give a stuff, and just wish she'd go away. It's now a quarter past nine and my quality time with Niall is being eroded by her presence. My arms are folded, and I tap a finger against my left arm.

'I know and loads of mums at the school have said morning to me today. I feel like I'm actually starting to get settled in now. I've arranged to have coffee tomorrow with one of them, so don't worry, I'll be out your hair soon.'

'Don't be silly, I like hanging out. It's just I have a lot on.'

'Like Monique? Which is understandable, because she's your best friend after all.'

'Even Monique has to take a back seat sometimes. Family comes first.'

'Don't you usually meet her on a Monday?'

'I'm not sure if we're meeting today, I need to ring her.' I take a sip of my coffee and then it comes to me. If she knew I was meeting Monique, what is she doing at the house? 'So, you said two things?'

'Oh yes, I wanted to apologise for Tyler again. I think he was just trying to look cool in front of the other kids. It's hard being the new boy.'

'There was no harm done. It was only water. If the weather had been any hotter I'd have quite enjoyed it.'

'I'll be honest,' she whispers, looking over her shoulder to check

Niall is out of earshot. 'It looked pretty hot from where I was. Mr Kingsley still pursuing you?'

I look away. 'Nah, he flirts, but I've put him straight on that score,' I lie. 'Look,' I say finishing my coffee. 'I've got stacks to do today, but how about we meet up on Wednesday? There's a lovely little market at Chesterfield if you fancy it?'

'That'd be great,' she says, rising from her chair and picking up her bag.

The telephone rings. 'Excuse me a moment.' I lift up the cordless.

'Lo? It's me. Are you coming over?'

'I was just about to ring you, I've got a bit held up at home and so I thought I'd just pop over for an hour this afternoon before I fetch Joe home, is that okay?'

'I need you now, Lo,' she sniffs.

'Well, it's just a bit tricky right now.'

'I've lost the baby.'

I gasp. 'Oh my God. When? Are you at the hospital?'

'I'm at home, but I need you. Please?'

There is just the sound of sobbing at the other end of the line.

'I'm on my way, Mon.'

I sit on the sofa. I feel the blood drain away from my face. Poor Monique, the decision was made for her in the end.

Bettina shouts. 'Niall, come quickly, something's wrong.'

Niall comes rushing in. 'What's the matter? Is it Joe?'

'Monique's had some bad news,' I eye Niall, trying to transmit what I can't say out loud to his eyes.

He nods and says, 'Well, you'd better get over there.'

I start to gather my things together. Bettina asks if there is anything she can do, and I shake my head.

'Well I'll just finish my coffee, Niall, if that's okay with you?' she says, sitting back down on the chair. 'Only I'm food shopping next, so it might be a while before I get another.'

'I'll make a fresh pot, shall I?' says my husband, in such a sarcastic tone that I can't believe she doesn't hear it.

'Fab,' she smiles. 'I'll keep you company for a bit while Lo's out. You don't mind if I borrow the company of your husband for a bit do you, Lauren?'

'Erm, not at all. If it's okay with Niall, it's fine with me.' He looks at me and I see his nostrils flare.

'You're so lucky to have such a trusting relationship. I couldn't have left Danny with my friends.'

I stop and look at her. 'I'm very grateful for what I have.' I think of Monique as I say it. I am so damn lucky to have Niall and Joe. I feel tears welling up behind my eyes. 'Well I have to go. I'll see you later.'

'Give Monique my love. I hope she's okay.'

I give Niall a peck on the cheek. 'I'll see you tonight.'

'See you later, Lauren.' He tucks a piece of hair behind my ear.

Bettina clears her throat. 'Hey, audience here you two. Anyway Niall, while Lo's out you can tell me her secrets. I believe I'm owed some from yesterday.'

I get in the car, closing the door a little stronger than necessary. I take deep breaths. What is wrong with that woman? Is it me or does she have no social boundaries? I decide my frustrations may be more about Mon. Bettina's not to know what's going on.

I set off. It takes me fifteen minutes to drive to Monique's as the traffic lights decide to turn green for me today.

Rushing to the main door, I ring the buzzer. Today she doesn't come to meet me; she just buzzes me in.

Her door is slightly ajar and after removing my shoes at the entrance, I walk into the living room to find her curled up on the sofa weeping quietly. The curtains across the patio door are drawn, casting the room in dim shadow. I pull them open to let in some light and sit next to her on the sofa, putting my arm around her. She turns and collapses against my chest, her sobbing gaining momentum. I feel uncomfortable, which makes me feel guilty. Monique's always been there to listen to my problems, but we've never been at this stage of raw emotions needing physical comfort. I'm not a hugging type of person, except with Joe. I'm at a loss to know what to do, so I just let her weep.

After a few minutes she lifts her head then moves to sit away from me. She smiles weakly. 'I don't know why I'm so upset, when I was considering getting rid of it anyway.'

'Yes, but you'd not decided, and it's a loss, Mon. Don't try to minimise it, you need to grieve.' I walk into the bathroom and grab some toilet paper for her nose and pass it to her. 'Do you feel up to telling me what happened?'

She sniffs, wiping the tissue under her nose and her voice quivers. 'I got a lot of pain yesterday afternoon and then I started bleeding. I passed this huge clot.' Her eyes go huge. 'It was so frightening. I went to the hospital and they did an ultrasound, but the baby was gone. They said there was nothing they could do and just to go home.' She starts crying again. 'I felt so alone.'

'Why on earth didn't you ring me?'

'You had the fundraiser and I know how hard you'd worked on it and how Niall and Joe were looking forward to getting you with the wet sponges. I didn't want to spoil that. It was the longest day of my life. I'm so pleased you're here today.'

'I'm here until school time and I'll come back tomorrow. I presume you're staying off work?'

She nods her head.

'Right, I'm going to run you a bath.'

'I can't have one, in case of infection.'

'Oh right, okay then.' I drum my fingers against my arm. 'Do you have a hot water bottle?'

'Bottom right cupboard in the kitchen.'

I walk into the kitchen. There are a few dirty dishes in the sink. I can tackle those later. I put the kettle on with enough water to make us both a drink and fill the hot water bottle. I have to smile as I lift it up. It has a fluffy leopard print cover, truly Monique. That makes me think of how she didn't argue when I passed her the toilet paper, she didn't demand a tissue. I sigh. While I'm waiting for the water to heat up, I walk into Monique's bedroom. The curtains are already closed. I check the bedding. There's no bleeding on the covers, but I change them anyway. I light the Yankee Candle she has on her bedside cabinet and fluff up her pillows. Back in the kitchen I sort out the hot water bottle and drinks and carry them through to her room.

As I walk back into the living room, Mon's eyes are drooping like she's struggling to stay awake. 'Right, let's get you in your room,' I say, and help her to her feet. I settle her down in her bed and we sit quietly while she drinks her coffee.

'I just want to sleep; I want it all to go away.'

'I know, honey.'

She puts her head down on the pillow. I pull her duvet up, close the door and leave her to sleep. I go and tidy the few pots and put the old bedding into the washing machine. For a while I sit on the sofa and look out onto the patio, feeling helpless and wondering what I'll do when she wakes. It sounds selfish, but I can't wait to see Joe, to hug him and be grateful that he was born so perfect. Once again, I reflect on how lucky I am.

I leave it until the last possible moment before I leave to collect Joe from school, but Monique remains asleep. I don't want to wake her because I'm a firm believer that sleep aids recovery. I write her a note to say I'll be back in the morning, but to call me if she needs anything, and then quietly close the door behind myself.

I meet Bettina in the school yard. 'How's Monique?'

'Not good. I can't go into details, but she's really upset about something. I need to spend some time with her. Is there any chance you could have Joe after school tomorrow? I could get Niall to pick him up and I could stay over at Mon's.'

'Joe can sleep over, it's cool. Tyler would love it. I'll take them to school Wednesday morning and you won't have to worry about being back. Spend a couple of days with her.

'We were having coffee on Wednesday.'

'So? Don't worry about that, your friend needs you.'

'I feel like I'm letting you down though.'

'Well don't. You can't look after everybody you know, and sometimes we are more than capable of looking after ourselves.'

'Sorry,' I shrug. 'Thank you. I'll meet you here in the morning and bring you his stuff.'

'No probs. You want to have a bath or something tonight and take care of yourself for a change, instead of everyone else.'

'I might just do that,' I say, knowing full well that I plan on spoiling Joe to death with attention tonight.

Joe is in his element that evening. I've built a den in the living room, something I haven't done since he was little. I set it up in front of the television and give him his tea in there. I slide in alongside him and stick his current favourite film, 'Iron Man 2,' on. I watch his face more than I watch the film. I see his eyes light up at various points, listen to his occasional chuckle, and witness his amazement when Iron Man does something demonstrating his amazing strength. Later, I bring in a few small bowls with different chocolates in them. He hugs me. 'You're the best mum ever.' I break out in a huge smile and wonder why I don't do this stuff more often. I'm always on the computer these days. I realise that as much as I've been blaming Niall for just sitting around, that I'm to blame myself. I've turned boring and disappeared into a virtual world. No computer tonight I decide. Iron Man finishes. I tell Joe he needs to change into his pyjamas and head upstairs. 'Awww, is it bedtime?' he pouts.

'Nope, time for Monopoly,' I say. The world's longest game that I usually refuse to play, protesting I don't have time, but in truth find so boring.

'Awwwwweeesssooome,' Joe yells. He jumps up to give me a huge hug before bounding upstairs.

Niall comes home just before ten to find Joe tucked up in bed reading, and drinking a hot chocolate topped with squirty cream and marshmallows. 'Someone's projecting,' he half smiles. 'He'll be up all night with that sugar rush.'

'Button it with the psychobabble. We've had loads of fun.'

'I've seen the evidence of that fun all over the kitchen and living room.'

'Yeah, well once we settle Joe down, I'm going to tidy up and then get a few things together. Bettina's going to have Joe overnight tomorrow, so I can stay with Mon.'

Niall frowns. 'Let's talk about that downstairs.'

Joe looks at him. 'I can go can't I, Dad? I can't wait. Tyler's got loads of Ninjago.'

'Yes, you can go,' he says. 'Poor Dad left all alone,' he mock cries. 'You best give me some hugs tonight, enough for tomorrow too.'

'What? Am I two?' says Joe and we all collapse into giggles, then Joe jumps on Niall and gives him a cuddle.

Downstairs, I quickly tidy up. Niall comes into the kitchen and follows his usual routine of getting home and sticking the kettle on while mooching around the cupboards and fridge for snacks. He's in luck tonight as the remainder of four packets of chocolates remain. I see him eyeing them greedily. 'They're all yours,' I state.

'I should think so. I do of course provide the money for such snacks.'

'Watch it,' I elbow him. 'Right, what was with the face up there?'

He points towards the dining room chairs and I go to sit down.

'Look, I don't want you to take this the wrong way, but doesn't Monique have some family of her own to look after her?'

'Niall, she's lost the baby.'

'I know. Now hear me out. Are you absolutely sure she's actually lost it and not just got rid of it? She's never been maternal.'

I draw a breath and close my eyes for a few seconds. These two have never seen eye to eye and for a moment it really gets to me.

'If you could have seen the state of her, you wouldn't ask me that.'

'Well, that's just it, Lauren. I don't see her, do I? She likes to have you for herself.'

I shake my head with disbelief. 'Are you jealous of the time I'm spending with my friend?'

'No. I just think that sometimes when you're in full Florence Nightingale mode, you forget your loyalties are to your own family.'

My voice rises, 'How can you say that?'

'Easily. You've known Bettina for two minutes, and let's face it, you can barely stand her half the time, but now she's having our son overnight, and might I point out that *none* of this was discussed with me beforehand. I might be easygoing, Lauren, but I am certainly no pushover. You need to rein it in with Monique. She needs to stand on her own two feet, which is just how she likes it, and you need to be home with Joe. He's your responsibility, not her.'

I'm shocked. I don't remember Niall ever having spoken to me this way. I want to rage against him, yet deep down I know he's right. How can I abandon my friend though, when she's always been there for me?

'I do hear what you're saying, but she really is in a bad way.'

'Where's her family?'

'They all live in Suffolk and she's not close to any of them.'

'Does that not tell you something?'

'Yes, it tells me that at this moment in time she needs me.'

Niall sighs. 'You're still going then?'

I look at him. 'I'm going tomorrow after school and staying until Wednesday. It's all arranged now, but I swear I'm listening to you, and when I'm back my attention will be where it belongs, with you and Joe. I promise.'

'I hope so,' says Niall, who gets up, moves to the living room and switches the TV on.

I stand in the kitchen, thoughts swirling around my head. I feel like I'm outside myself looking in. I've been so busy with my friends, eBay and Facebook, that some of what's happening between Niall and myself really is my own fault. I assume he sits in front of the TV all night because he's tired from work. But is it possible I've spent so much time the past year on the internet I could be partly responsible for this? He's right about Bettina too. I don't know her that well, and if I listen to Monique and Danny, she's bad news anyway. Tonight with Joe showed me the fun I'm missing out on and before long he'll be too cool to spend time with me and I'll regret the missed opportunities. I whizz up a quick pancake batter ready for the morning and stick it in the fridge. Then I take out a stew from the freezer and stick a post-it on the front saying 'enjoy, love Mum xxx'. I pop that in the fridge as well. Now I don't want to go. I feel so mixed-up and unsettled.

That night I know it's going to be impossible to fall straight to sleep and despite all my new resolutions I switch on the computer. There's a message from Seb.

***I've thought about you all day today. I couldn't get you out of my mind.***

I think of the previous night. I feel dirty and I'm appalled at myself.

I message back. **I'm sorry, some things have happened at home that make me realise just how much I love my husband, and these silly adolescent games I'm playing with you have got to stop. You totally rock, you know that, and if I was single it'd be different, but I'm not and I need to grow up. I'll leave this message on until the morning and then I'm deleting the whole group from Facebook and yourself from my account. Please don't try to stop me. You need a woman who can be all yours, Seb. I am using you to replace the void I felt I had with Niall, but recent events have shown me I need**

**to spend time with my husband and son. I hope you understand.**

I sign off and close the computer. I head back downstairs to Niall. He's sitting in his favourite chair.

'I've been thinking about what you said and you're right. We need to spend more time together as a family, and I need to make more of an effort to be around.' I place my hand on the waistband of his trousers. 'Because you are so clever you've won a reward.' He shuffles to let me pull down his trousers and pants and hutches forward to the edge of the chair.

'Is it my birthday?'

'Ssshhh,' I tell him as I take him in my mouth. For once he doesn't complain about missing a programme.

## CHAPTER THIRTEEN

I'm back at Monique's by half past nine the next morning, having first made sure to delete the secret group and Seb, aka Mr Uri Kent, as a friend from Facebook. He'd very simply put :( underneath my statement. I felt a little disappointed that he had no more to say than that, but let the thought go. Today is about Mon. She buzzes me in and I am surprised to see her up and dressed. She's wearing black Sweaty Betty yoga pants, a Carrot Banana Peach fitted yoga tee, and some slipper boots with little pompoms at the back of them. She is fresh-faced and her short dark hair lies flat. She looks about fourteen.

'How are you doing?'

'Um, okay, I suppose. Thanks for yesterday. I felt a lot better after that cry and sleep. I'll make us a drink.'

'I brought our pastries.' I dangle the Asda carrier bag at her, but she doesn't bite.

'Great,' she moves into the kitchen. It's a small galley kitchen, so I leave her to it as when two people are in it you can't move around very comfortably.

I pull the coffee table up to the sofa as it's not warm enough to sit outside this morning; there's been some slight drizzle and it's quite cloudy and windy. I holler, 'Have you got a large plate and some bowls?'

She brings some crockery through. 'Here, you go. I'm not sure I'm all that hungry though.'

'You need to eat. Do you want me to sort out drinks?'

'No, it's okay.' She returns to the kitchen.

I empty out the rest of the carrier bag: a selection of magazines including a fashion weekly, a couple of gossip magazines, and a monthly that was on offer. I place the pain au chocolats on the plate and empty the mini croissants and little brioche into the smaller bowls, then bring out a small pot of jam. I also have three girly DVDs.

Monique returns with the coffee and sees the stash. 'You spoil me,' she says, and I shrug.

We spend the morning quietly, as you can when you've been friends for a while, watching one of the movies and steadily working our way through the food. I pause it partway to make fresh coffee.

I bring it through. 'God, I love coffee, it sorts me out. I feel all warm and happy when I've had one.'

'Perhaps you can get me a barrel-full then?'

'Oh, Mon. I wish I knew what I could do to help.'

'You're already doing it. Just being here. I'll be okay. Just need time.'

I nod. 'Well, it's stopped drizzling out so let's go and get some fresh air. You need some time out of this flat.'

She agrees and goes to get her trainers. I relax a bit as she seems to be coping a little better today.

The local park is just five minutes' walk from Monique's apartment. It's a lovely park with a cafe, a playground for the kids, and a large duck pond. If you walk further through there are a few pieces of outdoor exercise equipment for adults. There's a lovely leafy walk alongside a stream that after an hour or so leads you up to a fishing lake and another cafe where they sell the most amazing butties. This fresh weather is perfect for such a walk. 'If you can manage a walk up the Dam Cafe, I'll buy us a chip butty and some coke.'

'How on earth do you manage to remain so slim, Lauren? Pastries, and then chips and coke?'

'Well it's not every day is it? I just feel like spoiling you right now.'

'Oh enough about me now,' Monique straightens and lengthens her stride. 'I'm fed up of being pathetic. Tell me what's happening with sexy Seb?'

I tell her some of it, leaving out the Facebook group stuff, and just mention that he'd kissed me in the classroom.

'Oh my God, Lauren. Did you kiss him back?'

'I did at first, but I stopped myself.' I rub my nose, it feels itchy. 'I told him it was a mistake. I love Niall, so that's that.'

'Yes, but that's twice you've kissed him now. I'm having a hard time being convinced you're not going to go for round three, so how's he going to be feeling? What if he won't give up?'

'I'm sure he will. He'll get nothing further from me and I won't see him so much now that the fair's over.'

'Until September. You'll see him every day then.'

I sigh. 'I'll have to cross that bridge when it comes. It's ten weeks away; hopefully it will all have settled down by then.'

'So how are you and Niall?'

'Loads better. We've talked about stuff. Hey, guess what? He wants the snip. Apparently, he's been avoiding nookie because he was paranoid I was going to get pregnant.' The words are out before I think about what I'm saying. I gasp and cover my mouth. 'Oh my God, I'm so sorry. It just came out.'

'Lo, you can't avoid the subject; there are lots of babies about. Look.' She points to a pair of yummy mummies strolling with their buggies.

'Yes, but I should be thinking about what I'm saying.'

'It's fine, carry on. What was the hapless idiot thinking this time?'

'He's decided he's too old for any more kids and thought at the last hurdle I might panic and want another, which I don't. So now he's okay and going to get the snip.'

'So the old love life's back on track?'

'We're getting there slowly.'

'I thought you were on the coil?'

'I am, but he's paranoid because of a workmate's missus.'

'I'll not have helped.'

'Don't be daft. He was being like this long before your situation. Thinking about it, maybe in some ways you even helped. Maybe that made him bring the conversation up? Anyway, who knows? At least the end is in sight and I can get back to some shenanigans.'

'I'm surprised though. You'd think he'd want a brother or sister for Joe after having such an angel the first time.'

'He grew up with three brothers. Never a moment to himself. He can't cope with the noise kids make. Even if Joe has a friend round I can see the tension get to him after a while.'

'Seems like Joe might suffer for that.'

'I've never particularly got on with my sister. I just make sure Joe goes to lots of social events, sports groups, and has friends over. I think it's enough. He seems to like his own company, just like his dad.'

'Which is great because then you have more time for me,' she smiles and jogs up to the cafe.

On the way back, the drizzle starts again, getting heavier until the rain is pouring down. Monique's short hair looks fine wet, but I can feel mine hanging in strings with water running off it, reminding me somewhat of the sponge stocks. Monique takes one look at me and giggles, 'Now you'll wish you listened to me about waterproof mascara, you look like a clown.'

'Thanks, friend. I'm going to shake myself out all over your Yankee Candles when I get back to yours so they won't light.'

'Evil witch.'

'Troll.'

. . .

It's heaven to get back to Monique's. Her apartment is furnished throughout with a navy blue, thick pile carpet. I can feel my feet sink into it as I walk. I nip in the shower, then Monique does the same. We sit back on the sofa in our pyjamas with towel turbans on our heads. Spa time I shout, and out of my travel case I bring out face packs and a French manicure kit.

'Yay,' says Monique. 'It's like being on a minibreak. I'm going to call my flat the Coffee Rocks hotel.'

'Well I think I need to sample some as Hotel Inspector to check if you are deserving of such status.'

I'm given coffee and an accompanying caramelised biscuit. 'I give the Coffee Rocks Hotel the full five stars,' I declare. 'In fact, I shall award six as the bathroom is not in the wardrobe.'

The evening and the following day pass quickly. We have had a pleasant time, although there were some occasional tears and silences on Mon's part. Monique hugs me as I leave.

'Thank you. I can't tell you how much I needed that.'

'You're welcome. I was glad to spend the time with you.'

'Do you think Niall would let you come up for the weekend?'

I step back. 'I doubt it, Mon. He'll expect me to be with him and Joe. I've already spent two days away this week.'

'Course, I'm being stupid, sorry.'

'Don't be daft, it's understandable. You just don't want to be on your own. I'll try to sneak over at some point for an hour, okay? But I need to spend time with my family, especially now me and Niall seem to be getting on a lot better.'

'Well, anytime you can get over will be great,' she says.

As I pass the main school doors on our way home, Seb crosses my path. 'Could I have a quick word, Mrs Lawler? It's about the fundraising?'

I step to one side, out of the way of the streaming crowd of other parents, carers and children, and tell Joe he can go on the play equipment. As he's usually banned from this before and after school, he thinks it's amazing and runs off.

'I get what you said on Facebook, Lauren, but can't I just see you occasionally? I know you felt something too.'

I look at the floor. 'There's absolutely no point. So, please, just leave me alone? Nothing happened thank goodness, so let me be.'

'That's not entirely true though, is it?'

My shoulders slump and I feel a bit teary. The last couple of days have left me feeling raw and emotional. 'Seb, I'm asking you to leave it, please?'

'But I know you feel something for me.'

I touch his arm. 'The truth is I think of you so much and I shouldn't.' I feel the heat of him through my touch and move my hand away. 'I love Niall. I've never cheated, and I don't intend to. It hurts because I'm so tempted to see you. That's why I closed the internet page, because I knew I'd not be able to keep away.' I rub the middle of my forehead with my fingers; I can feel a headache brewing. 'I have to though, Seb. For my marriage, which I value, and for Joe.' With that we both look at him playing happily on the frame.

He sighs. 'I'll try to leave you alone,' he says. 'But only because I care for you so much.'

'Oh please don't say that.'

'Is everything okay here, Mr Kingsley? You look a bit upset, Mrs Lawler.' Mrs Sullivan has appeared.

I step back. 'Yes, it's fine. I was just chatting about Joe being a bit behind with his maths and I got all emotional; silly really.'

Seb adds. 'I was saying that next year I'll make sure he gets some extra help if it's needed.'

'Well, don't forget my office door is always open, Mrs Lawler. I understand Mr Kingsley is Joe's next teacher and you worked together at the fair, but the first route for concerns is to Joe's current teacher, and then me.'

'You're right. I apologise for monopolising your time.' I state to Seb. 'Joe,' I shout. 'Time to go home now.'

Of course, as I'm walking down the drive wanting to hurry home, Bettina calls out for me 'How's Monique?'

'We had a really good time thanks. She's feeling a lot better. Thank you for helping out with Joe. I hope you don't feel I'm putting on you? Niall thinks I'm taking advantage.'

'Oh I think we're okay now that he knows me a little better,' she replies. 'You'd forgotten to pack Joe some clean pants, so I popped over to yours last night. I thought Niall was bound to have not eaten so I called to the fish shop on the way. We all ate together before I brought the boys back. I think he was a bit narked that Joe still wanted to come back with me though.'

'You had tea together?'

'It was a right laugh. You have some lovely crockery. It seemed a shame to put chips on it, but I can't eat them out of the wrapper.'

'Niall always does.'

'Well he didn't yesterday. Oh, and your bedroom is so pretty. I'm thinking about doing mine a similar colour.'

I grit my teeth. 'You were in my bedroom?'

'Oh God, don't look so panicked. I wasn't seducing your husband. I just asked for a guided tour.'

I give her a beaming smile. 'Well, I must get back. Thanks again for having Joe.'

'Any time you need me to mind him, it's no problem. It was a pleasure yesterday; he's a lovely boy.'

I ask Joe about everything on the way back. 'We were only there ten minutes, Mum, eating our chips. Then dad said he really needed to get on with some jobs he'd started while we were all out of the house and we went back to Bettina's.'

'Okay, darling,' I say. Once again, I'm reading too much into things. So what if she took the kids to our house for tea? She was just getting Joe stuff I'd obviously forgotten to pack in my rush to get to Monique's. *Failing as a mother again*, I hear in my head. Also, I've a bit of a nerve worrying about Niall when I consider what I've been up to with Seb.

All thoughts of Bettina are forgotten as I enter the house. Monique's okay, business is good, and I'm looking forward to seeing my husband when he gets in from work. Therefore I'm surprised to find Niall already at home and in the living room.

'What're you doing home this early?'

'I took some time owing. I had something I needed to do.' His face is frozen into a tight mask. He turns to Joe. 'I've charged up your DS. It's on your bed if you want to play for a bit before your homework.'

'Cool,' Joe goes running upstairs. It sounds like a stampede, not the small feet of a nine- year-old boy.

'What's wrong?' I ask.

'This came in the post today.' He hands me a piece of paper.

I unfold it. It's typewritten in capital letters and says YOUR WIFE HAS A SECRET. TRY 19, 5 AND 2.

My brow creases. 'What? ... I don't understand.'

'Letters of the alphabet. Didn't take much working out,' says Niall. 'It spells Seb. What secret do you have with Seb then?' He spits the word Seb out like a venomous snake.

My heart is pounding. 'Niall, there is absolutely nothing going on between me and Seb Kingsley.'

'You've had plenty of opportunity with those fair meetings.'

I thrust the paper at his chest. 'I have opportunities to cheat all the time while you're at work and Joe's at school.' I feel air pumping out of my nostrils. 'That however, does not make me a cheat.'

'Well, you'll not mind if I check your laptop,' he says. 'You're always on that bloody thing. I'm going to see what you spend your time doing.'

'I'm running my business.' I feel myself tremble. 'If you do this, you're showing that you don't trust me, Niall. That's a heavy weight to put on our relationship. Do you really want to do that?'

He hesitates. 'If it's not true then why would someone do this?'

He waves the paper around. 'Why would they go to the trouble of posting a note?'

'I have no idea,' I say, but then it comes to me.

'Oh my God, it'll be her, Bettina.'

'What?'

'She's trying to ruin things for me. She told me she turned up for tea last night and you were all cosy together. She turned up at the house the other day when she thought I was out. It's just like Danny said, she's trying to ruin me.'

'Danny? *Danny Southwell?* Her ex? When have you seen Bettina's husband?'

'Last Saturday. He turned up here as I was about to set off to the car boot. He came to warn me about her. Told me that she's nuts and was out to get me. Oh my god, it's true.'

'That psycho turned up at the house? Where was I?'

'In the house with Joe.'

'So you're telling me that Danny Southwell was outside our house, and you didn't shout for me or come and tell me, and you didn't bother telling me afterwards that he'd been?' He shakes his head. 'Did you even go to the car boot that afternoon, Lauren? I thought it was funny you returned without anything.'

So he had noticed.

'You talk about trust,' he looks at me with a sneer, 'where was it that day?'

I'm silent. I don't know what to say that at this point that won't make things worse. How can the day have come to this when I was so positive about everything? I can't stand seeing Niall look at me this way.

He folds his arms across his chest. 'I want to see your computer, Lauren,' he says, 'so go and get it.'

## CHAPTER FOURTEEN

I open the computer with my password and hand it to him. I walk away, open the back door and sit on the doorstep. I often come out here to think. I breathe in the cool, fresh air and listen to the sounds of traffic passing the busy parkway near the house. It was going to be such a nice evening.

Niall will find nothing of course, thanks to my fortuitous deleting. I had ensured all comments to Monique were deleted too, so all that remained was our usual chat about life in general with inane comments about shoes. If he came across some crass comment in there about himself, well it served him right for reading my private stuff.

For some reason, even though I know full well I kissed Seb, I am damn angry that Niall was so quick to think I would cheat on him. He didn't trust me at all. My teeth are clenched, and I feel the need to hit out at something. Over in the corner of the garden, behind the shed, is an old tin bath that we haven't got around to taking to the tip. I stand up and walk over to the garage, unlock it, then heave the door open over my head and walk to Niall's shelves where I grab a large hammer. I stride to the back of the garden and take great heaving swipes at the bath. It reverberates loudly, how I imagine standing next to a church bell would sound. The bath begins to dint, and I feel my anger pouring out like an overflowing red-hot bath. Bang. Bang. Bang.

Niall comes running out of the house and I notice his first thought is to look up at the neighbours' windows to see if any of them are watching. All reason leaves me, and I throw the hammer, watching as it sails through the shed window. The plastic cracks, and it leaves a gaping wound.

'For God's sake, what are you doing?' He yells as he runs up to me and grabs my arms.

'What does it look like?' Tears stream down my cheeks. I begin to smack my fists into his chest. 'You think I'd have an affair? You're a total bastard. I hate you.'

Niall wraps his arms around me so that mine are trapped and drags me into the house while I kick him in the shins the best I am able. 'Stop it, Lauren. Calm down.'

'Calm down?' my voice gets even higher.

'Think of Joe,' says Niall. 'He's just asked what's wrong with you. I've told him you're sad and angry about something that's happened with Monique.'

I am shaking. I take some deep breaths for he is right, I will be frightening Joe.

We are silent for minutes, each not knowing how to get past this.

'How could a note do this to us? You didn't believe me... after all these years?'

'Well, it wasn't just that,' Niall puts his hands in his pockets and shrugs his shoulders. 'When Bettina came over with the kids the other night, she kind of warned me about him. Said she felt he was really into you and was flirting while you were arranging the fair.'

'*So what*? He flirted with me, big deal. At least he paid me some attention, which is more than you've been doing lately.'

'I suppose I deserve that.' He adds quietly. 'Did you flirt back?'

'I had a bit of banter, yes, but nothing major. Just like how you are with nearly every female you ever meet. I'm not going to apologise for it. I'll tell you right now that it was nice knowing that someone found me sexy. It made me feel good about myself. Like I said, this is all down to Bettina. Well good for her, she's managed to drive a wedge between us, score one for her.'

'She was just looking out for you.'

'You're going to stick up for her, even though I told you about Danny coming to warn me?'

'He's supposed to be a bloody psycho; I wouldn't rate anything he said.'

'Yeah? Well Monique warned me weeks ago that she thought Bettina was shifty. That night she went to the cinema with her, apparently she never stopped asking questions about me.'

'She was like that in the car on the way there with me too. She just seemed nervous and we didn't have anything else in common but you. It was probably the same with Monique. You can't assume from a small piece of conversation that she's out to get you. She's had plenty of opportunity to kick your arse if she wanted to.'

'She's going for a less obvious way instead.'

'It doesn't appear that way to me. Lauren, you're being paranoid.'

'I had a fucking poison pen letter sent about me today, I think I'm entitled to be a little bit paranoid.'

'Look,' Niall runs his hands through his hair, 'I overreacted big time, Lauren. I'm sorry. It was just the thought of that nerd having his hands on you.' His own hands ball into fists as he speaks.

'Sorry doesn't really get us anywhere right now though, does it?' I reply. 'Like you said, I've broken your trust.'

'I'll get over the thing with Southwell.'

'Yes, but you didn't trust me in the first place.' I walk over and pick up my laptop and put it on the side to take upstairs. 'That's going to be a lot more difficult to fix than the shed window.'

I go into the kitchen to start the evening meal.

. . .

I speak when I need to. Inside I feel wrecked, like I've just heard news of someone's death. I put on smiles when Joe is talking. Niall is over exuberant. He thinks I'll immediately put it behind me, like I usually do after an argument, and move on. Life is short, but I don't feel that way this time. When Joe goes to bed, I run myself a bath and immerse myself, topping it up with warm water every so often. I stare at the white tiles on the bathroom wall as if I am drugged with anaesthetic, too numb to do anything but lie beneath the water. I let my skin wrinkle up until it's too uncomfortable to stay in it any longer. I wrap myself in my towelling robe, looking at it as I do so. Its purple colour has faded, there are pulled threads hanging down from it all over. It has seen better days. It needs renewing. I feel an affinity with my robe. I place my feet in my slippers and pad into the bedroom where I dry my hair without being bothered to comb it through, knowing full well it will frizz and resemble tangled wool. I leave the hairdryer plugged in and on the floor, pull on my pyjamas, and get in bed, pulling the duvet up to the top of my neck, seeking immediate sleep that will take me away from my problems. Luckily my body complies.

I wake in the night as Niall gets into bed. I wait to see if he gets on my back to cuddle me, but he turns the other way and I let myself drift back to sleep.


On Thursday, I ring Monique and ask how she is. She seems a lot brighter, but obviously picks up the tension in my voice.

'Is everything alright, Lo?'

'Yeah, just a bit fed up today. Nothing to bother you with, you've enough on your plate.'

'Lauren Lawler, what is going on?'

'I don't want to put on you, Mon, it's not fair.'

'I'm a big girl and can decide what's fair. Tell me what's going on; I'm getting worried now.'

I fill her in on the note and Niall's accusations.

'Jeez, Lo,' she says. 'It's got to be her, hasn't it? What a bitch.'

'Well, apparently, I'm overreacting.'

'It's a bit suss that she just happened to mention Seb, and the next day, poof, here's a letter stating you're up to no good.'

'Did you really just say poof?'

'It's an official magic term.'

'Joe would call you lame, don't you know it's "booya" now,' I scoff.

'Is that a hint of a smile I can hear in your voice? See you need your Monique,' she says.

'I do,' I agree.

'Well get your ass over here then. I'm bored. Let's talk this thing through.'

I mull it over, but I don't feel like going anywhere. 'Thanks, Mon, but I just feel like moping.'

'You can mope just as well here as there.'

'No. Thanks for the offer, but I'm just going to living room about at home until school pick-up.'

'Suit yourself. You know where I am if you change your mind.'

'Thanks, Mon, and sorry for putting on you.'

'Will you leave it with the sodding guilt trip. Go forth and eat chocolate.'

'You've read my mind,' I state.


I take myself off up to my bedroom armed with a mug full of decaf and a share bag of Minstrels that I have no intention of sharing. I stick on my latest Private Practice box set to see what Addison and Co are up to and lose myself in the drama of Oceanside Wellness for an hour or two. The phone disturbs me mid-afternoon. I look at the screen thinking that if it shows an unknown number, or anyone I don't want to speak to, I'll ignore it. 'Niall mobile' flashes on the screen. I hold the phone in my hand, hovering over the answer button. I decide to let it go to the machine.

'Lauren, if you're there, please pick up. It's an emergency.'

I press the green button, all annoyance temporarily forgotten. 'What is it? What's happened?'

'I'm in the hospital car park. Someone's just run into the back of the car. Then they've come round and played hell with me and said I reversed into them. I don't know what the hell's going on. They've someone with them who's saying they're a witness and that it was me. I was reversing, but I stopped when I saw them coming towards me. It was them. There's no-one else around to witness it and they're phoning the police.'

'Calm down Niall, surely there's CCTV?'

'Oh, course, I didn't think of that. I'll mention it to the police when they get here.'

'What are the people like, do they look rough? It's only a car. If they look like they might stab you, don't make a fuss.'

'It's a bloody doctor. I've seen his badge. Dr Matthias Bailey.'

'Are you all right? You're not injured?'

'I feel shaky, my legs are wobbly, but I didn't do anything, Lauren, I swear.'

'Is there much damage to the car?'

'It needs the boot sorting, it's crushed. It went with a right bang.'

'Just wait for the police, Niall, they'll sort it out.'

'Okay. Obviously, I don't know how long I'll be. I'll see you as soon as I can get away.'

The line goes dead. I sit back on the bed. I'm not surprised at this doctor saying it's Niall's fault. No-one in this world seems to tell the truth anymore or stands up and admits when they've made a mistake. I hope the CCTV's working so justice can prevail. I feel my anger return. I wish I could turn up to the car park with a baseball bat and knock seven bells out of the git who's blaming Niall. I bet he's a cocky doctor who thinks the sun shines out of his arse. I notice it's time to get Joe from school and think that now, if Niall's car needs repair, he'll take mine, and I'm the one who will end up inconvenienced. Annoyed, I stomp to the car.

I say hello to Tanya in the schoolyard and let her witter on about pointless rubbish while I wait for Joe. She's looking at me weirdly and I realise she's waiting for me to answer a question.

'Oh, err, what did you say?'

'I said, you don't seem with it, Lauren. Is everything alright?'

'I'm sorry. Niall's just had an accident in the car, my minds wandering. I didn't mean to seem rude.'

'Gosh, don't worry about it. Is he okay?'

A hand clutches my arm and makes me turn, as if defending an attack.

'Good God, Bettina. You made me jump.'

'Sorry, did I just hear Niall's been in an accident?'

'Yes, someone's just reversed into him in the hospital car park.'

'Is he okay?'

'Just shaken up, thanks.' I fidget from side to side and turn to the school Portakabin windows. 'Is this bell ever going to ring? I just want to get home, so we can get things sorted out.'

'Do you need me to do anything, Lauren?' says Bettina.

The tight wiring of the coil inside my body bursts free. 'I think you've done quite enough lately, thank you.'

Bettina backs off, shocked, and her face sets like stone. 'What the hell are you talking about? I've not banged into the car.'

'I'm on about your little chat with Niall about Seb. He accused me of having an affair with him yesterday.'

'I only said he was flirting with you. I felt he should know. Niall adores you and don't think I haven't seen you flirting right back. You want to stop having a go at me and look at your own behaviour.'

Tanya walks over to the other mothers, raising an eyebrow at them. It seems Bettina and I are now sparring in a ring with all the spectators looking to see who will win the next round.

'How dare you judge me? You keep coming around to my house and having cosy little coffees with my husband. Go and get your own. Oh, I'm sorry, you can't can you? He won't have you because you're a bloody psycho.'

I feel the slap hard against my cheek; it jars my head and stings. I clutch my face.

'You've no idea what I've had to put up with.'

'Unfortunately I do, Bettina, because you keep bringing it to my door. I had the pleasure of your lovely husband's company after you *forgot* I was collecting your son.'

She's silent for a moment, her mouth open with the sharp breath she's taken. Then her eyes narrow. 'I made a mistake. Have you any idea what it was like for me, thinking he'd taken my child?'

'But he takes him every other weekend you thick cow. Anyway, thanks to you, Niall and I are hardly speaking. Did you post the note through the door and then decide to say it to his face instead, or was the note a back up to make him believe you?'

'What note?'

'Oh come off it. The cryptic note that you stuck through the letterbox saying to watch out for Seb.'

'I don't know what you're talking about, or what you're accusing me of, and if anyone around here's a psycho then you want to take a good look at yourself, Lauren, because from where I'm standing, the only loony is shouting at me right now.'

Brrrrrrrrring. The school bell goes.

I jab a finger towards her face. 'I've not finished with you. Stay away from me and my family.'

'With pleasure.'

I feel shaky and hot and guide Joe back to the car. As the mobile classes are away from the main classrooms, I am only gawped at by the parents from Joe's class and the one next door.

Tanya comes running up. 'Are you alright? What was that all about?'

She's only interested in getting gossip to share with the rest of the parents, so I point at Joe and mouth. 'I'll tell you later.'

Once behind the wheel of the car, I burst into heavy, noisy sobs.

'Mum, what's the matter?' I turn to see Joe's face all scrunched up in concern and looking like he might cry himself. 'I saw you and Tyler's mum arguing. I can still play with Tyler, can't I?'

'Course you can, love,' I stroke my thumb down his cheek. 'Mum's just being silly, take no notice. Dad's had a little bang in the car.' Joe tears up. 'Oh he's fine, honey, but it upset me a bit, and then Bettina said something to upset me too, and I lost my temper. I was silly. I'm a grown up and should act better. I'm sorry, Joe, you shouldn't have had to see that.'

He wipes away my tears. 'We all make mistakes, Mum.' I hear my own words reflected in his own. 'Remember what you tell me and just walk away, okay?'

'I will, I promise.' I smooth his hair behind his ears, this wise boy who is right now looking after his mum when it should be the other way around.

'You'll need to say sorry to Tyler's mum tomorrow.'

'I don't think it's as simple as that, son,' I shrug.

'Why not?'

'It's grown up stuff.'

'Aaarrrgh, I hate it when you say that. Are you okay to drive now because I'm starving? Can we stop for a sausage roll?'

Niall gets in at six. His face is grim. He has shadows under his eyes and his skin looks sallow.

'What did the police say?'

'They took both our statements, breathalysed us.'

'They thought you'd been drinking?'

'It's standard procedure. They said they'd contact security to see about the CCTV and get back to me.'

'What about the witness?'

'Still adamant it was my fault.'

'Are you sure you weren't just tired and didn't realise?'

'Lauren, don't go there okay? I didn't reverse into that car.'

'Okay, don't bite my head off. I'm just thinking you probably didn't get a lot of sleep.'

'I was stationary.'

'Don't argue with Mum again,' chips in Joe. 'I hate it when you argue, and you did it for ages yesterday. Anyway, Mum'll be losing her voice if she shouts anymore. She's already fallen out with Tyler's mum today.'

'What?' Niall looks at me.

'We had words in the school playground.'

'They were arguing really loud, Dad. I couldn't tell what they were saying, but I thought they were going to have a fight.'

'What were you arguing about?'

'The note.'

'Oh, Lauren, you don't know she had anything to do with that note.'

'Well I had a go at her for saying things to you about Seb.'

'But I'm glad she did, Lauren, because you weren't going to.'

'Are you talking about Mr Kingsley?' says Joe.

We both look at him. 'Erm. Yes. Yesterday we were arguing that we thought he should have worn his clothes to the school fair, not his pyjamas,' Niall says.

As a spur of the moment excuse it's the worst I've ever heard, but Joe takes it seriously.

'He did look stupid, but he was probably trying to save his clothes for best.'

'Gosh, we never thought of it like that. I guess you're right,' I say.

'You grown-ups are so lame sometimes. All that arguing, and I could have told you that yesterday.'

'We're very silly,' I agree. 'Let's get some tea and then how about a game of Tumbling Monkeys?'

'I'll go set it up.' Joe scampers off into the living room.

Niall follows me into the kitchen.

'So you had a catfight in front of the entire school?'

I throw the bag of pasta onto the worktop. 'Not the entire school, just the Portakabins. I'm considering calling the police because she slapped me.' I touch my cheek. 'I shouldn't let her get away with violence. Hey, that's a thought,' I say, warming up to the idea. 'They might phone her shrink and get her back into some kind of therapy. That's what she needs for posting poison pen letters.'

'Have you heard yourself, Lauren?' Niall takes me by the shoulders. 'You sound obsessed. You have absolutely no proof that she sent that note. It could be anyone from that school. Maybe one of them's got a thing for the nerd and took umbrage that he has an eye for you?'

'It just fits in with what Danny said. She's come back to Sheffield for some twisted revenge against me.'

'Or maybe she left a bad marriage and just wanted to be near her mother.'

'Why are you sticking up for her all the time?' I slam the pan on the top of the cooker and watch water spill onto the gas flame, which goes out. 'Sodding hell.' I move the pan to another ring and light it. 'Do you fancy her or something, Niall?'

'Oh don't be so pathetic.' Niall's face is twisted in fury and he slams his hand against the wall. 'Look, I don't want to argue any further because it's affecting Joe. Let's just eat our meal, play the game and sleep on everything. I've had a hell of a day.' He walks out of the kitchen.

'Yeah, you're not the only one,' I state quietly to his retreating back.


I'm dreading school the following morning and tell Joe that I'll drop him off at the end of the school driveway. I just can't face seeing anyone. I've not had a shower and my hair looks like I've sprayed cooking oil down my centre parting. I look in the windscreen mirror and think that I must get my roots done soon.

On returning to the house, I walk round slamming cupboard doors. I pull everything out of one of the bottom kitchen cupboards and listen to all the tins slam out over the floor. I look at the dates on everything and opening the back door, throw anything out of date outside with a satisfying surge of adrenaline. I tidy the rest back up and potter into the living room. My mobile rings; its Monique.

'How're you doing today, babe?'

I sigh. 'I don't know.'

'Are you going to come over?'

'Nah, I just feel like being at home.'

'Yeah, well open your front door. I thought you'd say that, so I'm here.'

I go to the front door and sure enough Monique is standing there, looking resplendent in a blue and green silky blouse, and jeans. I feel wet on my cheek and gulp to hold it in, but she puts her arms around me in a hug and the dam bursts again.

'If they complain about a water shortage this year, they should come find us two. I think we've provided enough over this last week or so to see England through the summer.'

I retract myself from her hug and walk into the kitchen and lift the kettle. 'Coffee makes everything better.'

'And bacon sandwiches.' Monique holds up a material bag with a peacock design on it complete with feathers and sequins. From inside it she brings out the familiar green logoed supermarket carrier bag. 'Bacon and breadcakes. I thought the hard stuff was needed.'

I smile. I feel like a rainbow is peeking out from behind a thundery cloud. 'I'm a mess.'

'Well you can rectify that by sticking yourself in the shower, Stinko, and I'll fix the butties.'

I turn the shower up extra hot and welcome the feel of the almost burn as the water touches my skin. I spend time lathering myself up in a vanilla scented shower gel and give my hair a really good wash. I dress myself in some clean clothes: a red Topshop sweater and some three-quarter length black skinnies, and head back downstairs to the tempting smell of freshly cooked bacon. Monique has put it on the dining table and is seated, and already partway through her butty. 'Sorry, it smelled too good to wait for you.'

'That's okay; I couldn't get out of the shower once I got in.'

'You feel a bit better for it?'

'Yeah, I feel clean. I need to stop wallowing and do something.' I take a bite out of my butty. 'Mmmmmm.' I realise I feel ravenous and wolf it down. 'Is there any more bacon left?'

'Yeah, and another two breadcakes.'

'You want another?'

'Nope,' she points to her washboard stomach. 'This takes dedication and hard work.'

I point to my own stomach which has an extra podge around it that's been there since Joe. 'This affords me the occasional slip up.' I go and fix myself another butty.

'So what do you think we should do today?' Monique shouts into the kitchen.

I wander back out. 'Well first I need to check my eBay account, because I didn't do it yesterday with everything that went off. Then if I have any parcels to do, I want to get that out of the way, so this morning might be a little boring.'

'You can have an hour doing that while I catch up with the Housewives of New York, and then we're going out.' Monique passes me the TV remote. 'Put the TV on, would you? I'm just going to visit the bathroom.'

I clear the dishes into the sink. I'll wash them later and clean down the dining room table. As Monique returns, I head upstairs to get my laptop. I power it up at the kitchen table and log in. The first thing I see is my feedback rating. My lovely one hundred percent rating is no more and in the red column I have twenty-six negative feedback ratings. What? There must be some mistake. I feel like I've been caught cheating at an exam when I'm innocent. I click on the feedback to see what's going on.

**Horrendous product. Arrived broken. Do not use seller.**

**Covered in cat hair. Buyer beware.**

**Product cheap and nasty, not as described.**

The list goes on. Most of the feedback is from the two business sellers that ordered loads of items, but there are some from other recent buyers too. I am horrified. I feel cold and sick, and the room goes hazy, as if I might faint.

Monique looks over from Housewives. 'Christ, Lo, what's up? You look like you've seen a ghost.'

'My business... it's...' I can't form words and just point to the machine.

She hurries round to look at the screen. 'Oh my God, how has that happened? It must be a mistake, just contact eBay. They've obviously put someone else's feedback on your page.'

'It's not, Mon, look.' I open one of the orders on screen. 'Those are mainly the items I sold in the big orders that I thought might drum up more business for me in future. It's all ruined, what am I going to do?'

'Surely you can complain to eBay about them?'

'It's my word against theirs. eBay won't do anything and anyway, others have posted negative feedback too.'

Monique looks more closely at the feedback. 'Your feedback rating is still high. Why don't you just offer an apology and offer to refund them or something?'

'I could do, but they spent close to two hundred pounds. That's just such a lot of money.'

'But that and a nice quote from you saying sorry they didn't like your stuff should bring your page round, clear up the negative stuff. You'll soon make it back.'

I slump back into my seat and look up into Monique's face. 'Why is this happening? I can't take much more.'

I put my head in my hands and bring my palms down to rub over my face and eyes. 'God, it's got to be Bettina? She's set me up. I bet all these accounts are hers.'

Monique looks at me carefully. 'I have to admit, this does looks like a set up.'

'I'm not giving a penny back.' I clench my teeth. 'I'm going to get that bitch.'

'Oooh. Are you going to kick her ass? Can I watch?'

'I can't be that obvious after yesterday.'

'Why, what happened yesterday?'

I fill her in on the details of the spat. Her eyes widen as my tale goes on.

'Lo Lawler, get you. You're a wildcat. I wouldn't want to be on the wrong side of you.'

'Yeah, well, she's going to regret it,' I say. 'I'm just not sure how yet.'

I turn back to the computer and start adding the same feedback to each comment.

**I am sorry you have found this product unsatisfactory. I send items as I would expect to receive them, and yours was sent in excellent, 'as new' condition. On this occasion I can assure you your item was sent in immaculate condition.** I sign off and put the computer to sleep with a satisfactory click.

'Right, any idea what we should do next? I'm ready for getting out of here. I feel like I could hit the gym or something,' I say.

'You're hitting Bella's. I called them while watching Housewives and made you an appointment for eleven-thirty. Those roots are appalling, and I'm not being seen in public with you until they're sorted.'

I smile and check out my reflection in the living room mirror. 'Excellent. First line of defence, look absolutely amazing. When I see her this afternoon at school, she'll wonder why I'm so happy. I don't know what revenge I'm going for yet, but she'll not be ready for it.'

'Now that sounds more like the Lauren I know. I'll see if I can think of anything you can do. I'm getting my nails done while you're having your hair sorted. Hey, we should get claws.'

'I'm not dragging you into this, Mon. You've been brill, but you've had enough of your own problems. By the way, I'm paying for your nails.' I put my hands up before she can interrupt. 'No. I insist, you've been fab.'

'Okay. Gosh there's more action here than in today's episode of Real Housewives.'

'Come on, let's get to the hairdressers.' I stand and run my hands through my hair. 'I need to get armoured up.'

# CHAPTER FIFTEEN

I feel better after my haircut. My new soft highlights make me look golden skinned and healthy. I'm naturally blonde, but my hair goes darker as the years pass, so now I require a blonde 'top-up' every six months. I say goodbye and thank Monique for turning up and dragging me out of the doldrums, with a promise to ring her tomorrow.

I have twenty minutes before I need to pick up Joe. I slam the car in gear and head to Bettina's house.

It's a detached house, on one of Handsworth's better estates (we couldn't afford one). Determined, I march up the driveway, and ignoring the doorbell, pound on the door. I can see her moving behind the glass panel. She opens the door and looks at me warily.

'What do you want, Lauren?'

'I came to ask you to just stop it. You've probably ruined my business now, so there you go. You've created more trouble for me than I ever did for you at school, so please can you just leave us alone? I don't know how you managed the different eBay addresses, whether you had me send the stuff to relatives or what, but enough's enough. Can you retract your feedback, so I can at least get on with my life, and I'll let you get on with yours?'

Bettina fold her arms across her chest. 'What on earth are you rambling on about? Do you want the number of my psychiatrist, Lauren, because you seriously have some kind of mental issue.'

I hold up my hands. 'If that's how you want to play it so be it. I'm just letting you know that it stops now, because I'm not putting up with any more of your nonsense.'

'I'd like you to leave now. I need to get Tyler from school. We're away this weekend.'

'Not a problem. I'm going.'

'You need to sort out your issues and stop dumping everything at my door. You're not the only one with problems, but all anyone ever hears about is me, me, me; poor old Lauren with her terrible life.'

I glare at her. 'How dare you? You were the one who moved back to Sheffield. You didn't have to be near me.'

'You don't own Handsworth, Lauren. My family is here, which is more than can be said about yours. They ditched you long ago, didn't they?'

I stagger back. I feel like she's slapped me. I try not to think about my parents, the dad who walked out on us, and my mother. She couldn't be bothered with me or get rid of me fast enough once I was old enough to cope on my own. It's one of those things schoolchildren know about each other, but I thought I'd left my school years behind a long time ago.

I walk away. It's started to pour with rain and my lovely new hairstyle is gone. My new armour failed the practice round. I head for the car.

Her voice comes from behind me. 'Lauren, come back. I'm sorry. I shouldn't have said that.'

I look back at her. 'But you did. I believe Danny, you're obviously no friend of mine. You are definitely one psychotic bitch. Go rot in hell.'

'You're making a mistake,' she shouts after me.

I ignore her, I need to get to school.

Despite what she has just said, she hasn't finished. 'By the way, just so you know, Seb asked me out. I was going to say no because I didn't think you'd like it, but sod it, he's not yours.' Her mouth twists up at one side and while I'm looking at her with my mouth wide open, she walks back to her house and slams the door.

At home Joe rushes off to play and I sit on the sofa. I can't even be bothered to put the kettle on. All the mess of the past few days runs through my mind: the note, the car, the argument at school, my eBay business, and now she's targeted Seb. I don't know how true it is or whether she's just said it out of maliciousness, but I need to find out. I have his mobile number but can't risk phoning him. I pace the living room. Did she ask him, or him her? If he has done it, he's done it to make me jealous, I'm sure. He doesn't realise he's playing with a petrol fuelled bonfire. Oh, why do I care? I accidentally knock a pile of Joe's magazines on the floor.

'For God's sake, Joe, can you tidy these up?' I shout. I walk over to the stereo, put in my Rhianna CD and turn it up loud.

Joe walks past. 'Oh, Mum, I hate that CD.'

'Well stay in your room and you won't have to listen to it. Take the magazines up as you go.' Now I'm snapping at Joe. I need to sort myself out.

Niall comes in about ten minutes later, barging through the doors at warp speed. 'Can you turn that down, love?'

He misses my glare. I stab the off button.

'Cheers. Okay, listen, they didn't have the cameras on in the car park, so there's no evidence to prove I'm telling the truth, so that's it, it's all on me.' He flops into the chair. 'At least we've got a courtesy car for a week or so while mine's being repaired.'

'Well that's something I suppose.' I want to tell him about Bettina, but then I remember what she just said, that it's 'me, me, me' all the time, and I keep quiet. I can't help thinking that it's yet another thing gone wrong. Another round to Bettina. I feel myself tense.

Niall smacks his hand on his thigh and stands up. 'Anyway, are you ready?'

'Ready for what?'

'We're going to see my parents this weekend, remember?'

Oh heck, I'd forgotten with everything that had been happening. I don't feel ready to see his folks right now. They are lovely people, but they get in my space, and right now, I need people at arm's length. I need to get my head around what happened this afternoon, regroup and think of my next move.

'You've forgotten, haven't you?'

I nod. 'Don't worry though, it won't take long to pack.' I pause, 'Actually Niall, would it be okay if I drive down tomorrow, only I'd promised to sort out some stuff with Bettina tonight?'

'You're talking again? Good. I'd rather you came tonight though, Lauren.'

'I know, but I don't want to ruin things when the situation is so delicate.'

'Well, can you be at Mum's for lunch tomorrow?'

'Absolutely. I'll aim for late morning, okay?'

'Okay, love. Can you get our stuff together then?'

'Of course. Is she doing your evening meal?'

'Yes, so no worries about that.' He heads to the bottom of the stairs. 'Joe, come on, we're going to Grandma and Grandad's.'

Joe comes rushing down the stairs. 'Yay, I love going there. How long are we staying?'

'Until Sunday. It'll be a nice break for everyone. I think I speak for me and your mum when I say we could do with a nice break and a change of scenery.'

*A change of scenery.* Suddenly I have an idea for Project Revenge.

'I'll pack your things,' I say, and leave the room with a smirk on my face.

. . .

They're safely on their way when I set to work in the kitchen. I have a new Pinterest idea to try for my project. When that's done, I dig my mobile out of my bag. I call Seb's number to get part one of my plan sorted.

'Well, you're one person I wasn't expecting a call from on a Friday night.'

'I need to talk to you. Can you come over?'

'Hey, I'm not going anywhere near your husband.'

'Niall and Joe have gone to his mother's. It's just me. I need to talk to you about something.'

'Is this something called Bettina?'

'Just get over here and bring wine. Have you got my address?'

'I looked it up on the school computer a while ago.'

I sigh. 'I might've known.'

'See you in a few. What sort of wine?'

'As long as it's alcoholic, I don't care.'

My mobile rings a minute after.

'Yes?' I say.

'Hey girl, how'd it go at school earlier?'

'Oh, not great but I have a plan.'

'Oh yeah? Tell me more.'

'I'm going to have to ring you back, Mon. I'm on with it all now and I'm in a rush.'

'Sure, okay. Catch you later then.' She sounds sullen, but I just don't have time to worry about Monique right now.

Thirty minutes later he's at my door. He smells strongly of aftershave and looks as hot as a chilli pepper, dressed in a Guns n Roses tee and jeans. I can see a tiny bit of dark ink just below his collarbone and my mouth gets wet. He comes in and sits himself on the sofa without asking.

'Guests usually remove their shoes in the hall.'

He throws them off and gives me a slow smirk. 'Anything else I should remove?'

'Look before you go there ...'

'I know, I know, you're not interested. Is that supposed to stop me from getting hard every time I see you?'

My eyes stray to his groin. I bite my lip.

'Just tell me why I'm here.'

'Give me a minute to get the drinks sorted.' I dash from the room.

Handing him a glass, I tell him about my past with Bettina and how I think she may be behind the note and the eBay saga. Seb listens without interruption; I notice his frown lines creasing as he ponders what I'm saying.

'So she took great delight in telling me you'd asked her out. That's not true, is it?'

He looks at the floor, avoiding eye contact.

'Oh my God, it is.'

'Not one of my better moves then? Shit, if she's a psycho I can't afford to have anything to do with her.'

'Why did you do it anyway? Was it to get at me?'

'She seemed nice, a bit vulnerable. You know that's my type,' he half laughs. 'I admit it did cross my mind that it might wind you up, but I'd heard rumours from the schoolyard about us two and thought I'd head it off by making a play for Bettina.'

'This can't be doing your career any good.'

'Doesn't matter. I handed my notice in. I'm going abroad to teach for a while.' He looks at me, all wide eyes and honest desperation. I feel as if I'm seeing the true Seb, and not the ladykiller.

'I can't be around you and not have you, Lauren. It'd be impossible for me to be Joe's teacher and have to see you every day. Meeting Niall at parents' evenings, thinking all the while you're sat there about your amazing tits and the fact I want to fuck you over the desk.'

I sigh. 'What a mess I've caused. I'm sorry. You know if I wasn't with Niall—'

'Yeah, you said. But you are, and I feel a fresh start is just what I need. I'll cancel my date now anyway, if it helps.'

I take a sip of wine. 'That's what I wanted to ask you. It really will help, thank you.'

'I guess that's it then?'

I feel empty that he's going. It seems like we really had some chemistry and in another time and place we might have had something. 'Do you reckon we were together in a past life?'

'You say some weird shit, you know.'

I laugh. 'So is Seb the ladykiller going abroad to devastate hearts all over the world, or are you actually going to be true to yourself and let some lucky lady see the nice guy you really are?'

'That will depend if I can meet another woman like you'. He winks. 'I suppose it may happen eventually, but until then, I shall be happy to be there for any unhappy lady that crosses my path.'

'You need to pick a happy lady, so she can make you happy.'

'Maybe. Anyway, as this is probably our last time alone together, let's have a toast to what might have been.'

'To what might have been,' we chink glasses.

Seb stands up, puts down his empty glass and starts to put on his shoes. I go and put the glasses in the kitchen sink ready to wash. I walk towards the window to draw the curtains, Seb walks up behind me.

'Can I have a goodbye kiss?'

It's my last chance, so, why not? He tips his head down and his lips touch mine. I can taste the wine. It starts as a sweet chaste kiss but though I want nothing more from Seb, I can't resist this final chance to touch him. I snake my arms around his neck and pull him towards me. Once again, I've lost my control around him. The kiss lasts for minutes until finally we break apart, panting. 'Goodbye, Seb.'

I turn to close the curtains, but really I'm turning away so he doesn't see that my eyes have filled with tears. I grip the curtains a little too tight as I pull them together.

'Bye, Lauren. I hope you're wrong about Bettina, but be careful, won't you?'

'I will.'

I walk him to the door, and then as I turn to go back into the house, I see that my car has been keyed the whole way down the side. I go out to examine it and see there's a note behind the windscreen.

### Advantage me

Oh, it's like that is it? I've only had one glass of wine, but it fuels my temper and I mutter 'Game on bitch.'

Driven by adrenaline, my hands won't stop shaking as I turn off the alarm I'd set for three-thirty am and consider what I'm about to do; part two of my plan. I suck on my top lip, trying to get some saliva into my dry mouth. Pushing back the duvet, I reveal the black DKNY top and J. Crew trousers, chosen so I look hot if arrested. I imagined Monique's voice should I face the police dressed in 'Value' jeans and so assembled an 'attractive assassin' combo. My armpits feel damp, and my heart races to the point that I can feel its thud within my neck. I'm reminded of old movies when the monster moves slowly before attack. I breathe deep, this is self-defence, remember? My hands shake so much, I can barely tie the converse I slip on my feet, and for a moment I surrender. I lay down on the floor in child's pose, trying to regulate my breathing. It does no good. I must go now. I pull my wavy blonde hair back in a bun, grab my bag, slide on my D&G sunglasses and exit the house.

Behind the wheel of my faithful Nissan Micra, I drive to the bitch's estate and park around the corner, leaving the car obscured by a row of garages. Then I glance around checking for potential witnesses. Though I see no-one, I can hear the inebriated screams and laughs of people on their way back from nightclubs. I walk casually to her house; my posture straight so should anyone see me they wouldn't question my being there. As I arrive at the front garden I appraise how immaculate it looks, planted with symmetrical bedding, all oranges and purples. Box hedging as neat as a newly cut fringe ensures my cover from the rest of the estate. She must either love gardening herself or pay a fortune for someone to keep it so pristine. As someone who has grown vegetables from seed and tended to them like an expectant mother, I hesitate before I put on the rubber gloves. Can I really do this? Are things really this bad? As I consider past events, I feel my jaw clench and my teeth grind. She deserves everything she gets. I reach down, my fingers gripping the neck of the plants and I lift and smash them onto the path where the soil parts from the roots and spills out like spewed guts. I'm horrified to feel a grin that I cannot stop form on my lips. I carry on, full of energy, until the bedding plants are no more and the piled-up soil resembles a grave of the newly buried. I move onto her dustbin, retrieving food waste which I push through the letterbox, imagining the smell on her return: putrid and decaying.

Next, I open my bag, extract weed killer, and pour it over the meticulous green lawn. I try and dribble it to spell out the word 'bitch'. Give it a few days and yellowing dead patches will hopefully reveal my handiwork. I re-check that no-one watches me and move around the back of the house. A screwdriver from the front pocket of the bag is used to disable the security light in order to prevent its on and off SOS. Pre-dawn light allows me to write 'whore' in carefully disguised font across her white PVC back door. For my finale, I empty fake vomit out of a plastic container, covering her patio furniture, silently thanking the person who posted the recipe on Pinterest.

Back in the driving seat, I punch a fist in the air before I burst into tears. I turn down the visor and peer at my reflection, seeing the reasonably happily married woman turned revenge seeking missile. Ground down and exposed to my rawest state. Right now if you looked closely, I feel you'd see every part of me, each individual cell. Be able to look within the membrane to the protoplasm. See what's underneath ...

. . .

Back home I put my clothes in the washing machine and set them on a wash and dry programme. I put the weed killer and gloves back in the shed, then wash out the fake vomit carton. Then I wash Seb's glass and put it back in the cupboard. I go to the computer where I bookmarked the page from Pinterest (I didn't pin it), delete it and clear my history. I'm too wired to sleep, so I drink the rest of the bottle of wine and go upstairs to bed to read. At the top of the stairs, I pause outside Joe's room. It's weird seeing his door open and his window with no blind down. I miss him already. Then the regret comes over me; what I've risked, how it could affect Joe. I begin to shake and feel sick. I just reach the toilet in time to bring up the wine I've consumed. Sitting on the floor feeling clammy and cold, I imagine myself rotting in a police cell for causing criminal damage. I punch the toilet seat in disgust at myself. She's brought me to this level, so now I'm no better than her. My arm reaches to the back of the bathroom door, where I grab a hand towel, fold it, and place it on the bathroom floor. That's where I wake a few hours later with my neck and back hurting like hell, and with a head that feels like someone has jumped up and down on it.

I groan and move to my bed. The alarm clock says seven fifty-two. I've got to set off to Niall's mothers in just over two hours. I open my bedside cabinet where I keep Calpol sachets for Joe. I swallow two of them like Joe's allowed. I'm too scared of liver damage to risk another, and there's no way I'm going downstairs. Setting the alarm for ten, I pull the quilt firmly over my head. But instead of sleeping, I ruminate over my actions, eventually deciding that she definitely deserved it. I vow not to bother with her anymore personally, and to ring the police should anything else happen. I have a family to protect, especially Joe.

. . .

I finally drag myself out of bed at ten twenty-four and hit the shower in order to attempt to make myself feel more human. I take a couple of Ibuprofen on an empty stomach because I can't face food, get a breakfast bar out of the cupboard and a bottle of water out of the fridge for the car journey, and get on my way.

The drive to Brockton takes just short of two hours usually, but today I pull into a parking bay halfway and eat my breakfast.

On my way, I periodically feel nauseous, but finally arrive at Niall's parents' village just before one. They live in a small village surrounded by farmers' fields and everywhere you turn there's a cow or a horse. I love this village. There's something about it that is so relaxing. Just down the road from Niall's parents' home is a small art studio that sells pottery. I like wandering down there, past all the pretty cottages with their gloriously tended gardens, admiring the beautiful flowerbeds and shrubbery.

I pull into Glen & Rebecca's gravelled driveway and slide my car in alongside Niall's courtesy car and Glen's BMW. They have a three-bedroom bungalow with a bay window. There are overflowing red and yellow hanging baskets at either side of the door, with bees hungrily swarming around them. Flashbacks of decimated flower beds hits my brain and I shake my head as if I can dislodge them. I leave my case in the car, walk to their front entrance, and ring the bell. I hear crockery clatter, and then Joe pulls open the door, with Niall coming up behind him.

'Muuum, you're here. Hurry up, you're missing lunch.'

'Well don't let yours get cold. Run back along and eat up.'

'You're late,' Niall says, 'but I suppose you'll have an excuse.'

I look up at him and I see him frown as he looks at my face. Maybe he's noticed the blackness underneath my eyes and the white pallor of my face.

'Are you okay?'

I shrug. 'Not really.'

'I gather it didn't go well with Bettina.'

'I have a lot to catch you up on,' I confirm.

Niall looks over my shoulder. 'What the *fuck* has happened to the car?' He goes running out to assess the damage down the side of the paintwork.

I stand alongside him and watch as he runs his hand along the groove. 'That's what we need to discuss. I think it was Bettina.'

'Lauren...'

'There's more to tell you before the car stuff, so don't give me any lectures about having no proof. Let me get inside and get some lunch and we'll talk this afternoon. Perhaps we could go for a walk around the village?'

Niall turns to me. 'This is getting serious, Lauren. I think we need to contact the police.'

'We've the rest of the weekend to figure out what to do.' I look back at the bungalow. 'I can't tell you how pleased I am to be here.' I realise this is true. I've found Niall's mother quite stifling at times, but today her home is a refuge. The scent of summer hangs in the air, a slight breeze blows the scent of the flowers my way. I breathe it in. I'm now ravenous and head inside to get some lunch.

'I'm so sorry I'm late.' I greet Glen with a smile, but Rebecca gets up and gives me both a hug and a peck on the cheek.

'We missed you last night. Are you feeling okay, darling, you look awfully pale?'

'I've had a headache all morning. I've taken some tablets and I'm feeling a lot better. I'll be fine after this lunch I think.' I indicate the glorious spread of quiche, various salads including Waldorf and potato, jacket potatoes, nachos, salsa, and a large bowl of chicken and bacon pasta, plus some garlic bread. I sit beside my family and tuck in.

Afterwards we walk through to the garden. The Lawlers' have a stable door that leads out to the patio through the kitchen. I love this door. For some reason, even though we didn't have one, it reminds me of childhood. I like the idea that you can open it halfway and lean on it to chat to people. Niall's parents have a fat black cat called Tristan who must be around eighteen now. He is laid out on the patio looking like a comma, toasting his belly in the sunshine. Tristan is so pampered that when I bring him a tin of cat food he thinks that's a delicacy and laps it up, finding his usual salmon to be completely beneath him now. Later he'll come brushing around my legs and wonder why the tin lady hasn't brought his treat.

The patio consists of square grey flagstones that extend from the outside of the kitchen door, all the way to the end of the living room where there are patio doors. We go to sit out on their furniture: a green rectangular glass table with six canvas chairs. Joe spots a new football lying on the tennis court sized garden and he's off. Glen comes out of the house carrying a glass jug containing what I guess to be Pimms judging by the fruit in the bottom. In his early sixties, his dad is similarly built to Niall; a tall, handsome man with wavy hair that has faded from blonde to grey. He has the same crinkly eyes when he laughs, and I can tell by looking at him what Niall will look like in twenty years' time. I'm wondering if I can face a Pimms, when he pours and hands me one anyway.

'Kill or cure, Lauren. I reckon my Pimms Punch will put you straight.'

'Or on your back,' announces Rebecca, coming out of the house with a tray of strawberry jellies, which I know will contain rose wine as they're her 'house special'. Niall's mum is around the same height as me, five foot six, with short brown hair (topped up by the local hairdresser). She favours smart but casual, and today is wearing some beige cotton trousers and a three-quarter sleeve silk top. Her reading-come-sunglasses are perched on top of her head.

We all take a seat around the table. I face out towards Joe, so I can enjoy watching him run around the space, kicking his ball with abandon.

'Grandad, come and play.'

'That's my sit down finished already,' Glen says with obvious pleasure. He heads off to join Joe.

'Actually, I think I'll join them, looks like fun.' Niall is away too, and then there's just me and his mum sitting at the table.

I lift my spoon and taste a bit of the strawberry jelly. It is refreshing and delicious, and I tell his mum this.

'Oh it takes no doing, Lauren. It's one of those recipes that looks good and tastes nice, but only takes about five minutes of prep. I just can't be bothered with cooking these days.'

'Yes, well, make sure to pass me your mushroom soup recipe if you've stopped making it, because I can't live without that.'

Rebecca takes a sip of her Pimms, considering me over the top of the rim.

'So what's going on, Lauren? Niall and Joe arrive without you and he says you're having trouble with some old schoolfriend. Then you turn up today looking like, if you don't mind me saying so, hell.'

'It's complicated,' I reply. 'I wouldn't know where to start.'

'Well,' she leans over and puts her hand across mine. 'I won't pry but I want you to know that I'm here for you, Lauren, if you need me. You've become the daughter I never had. I know you had a difficult childhood, and I just wanted to tell you that if you need a mature opinion or a chat, I'm always on the end of a phone.'

My eyes fill with tears. I've known Rebecca a long time now and she has always been motherly towards me, insisting on hugs and cheek kisses. I have always held her at a distance, being scared of letting a 'mother' figure into my life, for fear of being abandoned by another one. Now I look into her soft grey eyes and wonder why I've never let her in before. I need this person in my life right now. I put my other hand over hers, making a gesture of intimacy towards her that I never have before. Her hand initially jumps as I touch it, but then she smiles at me. 'I'm scared,' I tell her, like it's bedtime and the monsters are hiding in my wardrobe.

I tell her all about Bettina, my history with her from school, how she's been hanging around Niall, the eBay business, the scraped car, the note, her telling Niall that Seb was flirting with me, Danny's warning.

'Oh, Lauren. I really think you should phone the police.'

'That's what I want to talk to Niall about. He doesn't know about my business and the story behind the keyed car yet. I've been thinking the same myself. I thought I'd maybe look into if I can get an injunction or something. I'm just a bit nervous that I don't have any proof.'

'She's obviously been playing a very clever game. Well I know it's not going to help now, but when school breaks up you are more than welcome to come here for a week or two to have a break from everything.'

'I think we'd like that very much,' I say. I breathe in the fresh air. 'I love it here, it's so peaceful.'

'Not when the farmers plough the fields it's not and getting stuck behind tractors on your way to the shops isn't a barrel of laughs.'

I raise my eyebrows at her.

She smiles. 'Okay, I admit it is lovely around here. We are very lucky. I do wish I could see my grandson more though. There's a hospital here, you know?'

I laugh. 'Very tactfully put. Look, I can't think of anything right now with what's going on, but I promise to consider it in the future, okay?' I mean what I say.

She tops up my glass. 'Cheers to that.'

We spend another hour or so companionably chatting about this and that. She fills me in on village life, her local yoga class that I'd love, and the village festival they are putting on in the next week or so. It brings to mind the summer fair and for a moment, clouds threaten to challenge the sunshine for my soul.

'I've bought Joe a new Lego set for after our evening meal,' says Rebecca. 'It should keep him busy for an hour or so, and then I'll help him run a bath. He loves our rolltop. There's a really pleasant walk around the village, and the Dog and Duck has a decent real ale selection. I think you and Niall would enjoy it tonight.'

'Thank you.' She's giving me the opportunity to catch Niall up with recent events on our own and I am extremely grateful to her for it. I feel my eyes threaten to spill over with tears again, so I pick up the jelly glasses and carry them into the kitchen. I look out of the kitchen window, at Rebecca relaxed in her chair, looking out over the men and at them laughing and joking around. They're tormenting Joe with piggy-in-the-middle and I wish I could stay here forever, wrapped warm and cosy like in an electric blanket. The other life, the hard life, seems far away and surreal, and I wish I could toss it away like garbage and start anew here. I go to get my overnight case from the car and begin to spend time unpacking, feeling for the first time in a long time, as if I can relax.

## CHAPTER SIXTEEN

After a dinner of thick vegetable soup with an array of different breads; followed by pork, stuffing and apple sauce sandwiches, Niall and I head out for a walk. It's still humid outside, the perfect temperature for a stroll, and we meander around the village lanes, where quite often the pavement completely disappears and you have to keep a close watch for cars and cyclists. On the way to the pub we chat about how lovely the area is, and how spoilt Joe gets at his Grandma and Grandad's house. Inane stuff, as we are both aware we need a major chat and beer is required. The Dog and Duck is a small village pub, very spit and sawdust, with brass plates on the walls, and a landlord and landlady that have been there for years. Although we don't come here very often, Gary the landlord—a robust, balding red-cheeked man, who looks like he samples quite a few of his own wares—gives Niall's hand a firm shake as we approach the bar.

'Well you're definitely not the milkman's. I swear you're morphing into your dad, Niall; and you, Lauren, are looking as gorgeous as ever.' He lifts my hand and kisses it.

Thinking of the pasty and sallow face I arrived with, and doubting much has changed, I smile at the charmer. After how I felt this morning, I can't believe I'm going to have yet more alcohol, but as I walked into the bar and smelled the real ale my mouth watered, so I ask for a half of Theakston's Old Peculiar, a drink I used to have long ago when Niall and I were first dating. We get ourselves a seat in a little nook that has a good window overlooking a little stream and flowered area. I take a sip of my drink. It's thick and treacly and I smack my lips after.

'Okay, well update time,' I tell him. I take a deep breath. 'Firstly, I know you won't be impressed with me, so I apologise right now for what I'm about to say, but things have been really difficult, and I didn't want to get into it all yesterday with the car and going to your mothers.'

'Get on with it because I'm sure what I'm imagining is far worse than what you've done.'

'Right. Well, yesterday morning I went on my eBay account and it had been ruined with negative feedback from four different buyers, including two so-called business leads I'd had, so it would appear I've been set up.'

'Lauren, are you sure you haven't done something to upset someone, because this is getting disturbing?'

'Well, yes actually, I have. Bettina. But it was a long time ago. Anyway, let me finish.'

He nods.

'So, I contacted eBay, but I'm not sure what will happen with that. If they make me refund them, I'll lose two hundred pounds.'

Niall huffs. 'That'll go nicely with the four hundred excess on the car.'

'Yesterday afternoon, I went over to her house to ask her to stop it and leave us alone. She denied it all, as expected, and then when I said we should just avoid each other, she told me she had a date with Seb. You know, the same Seb she told you was mad about me? Well he's so obsessed with me he's asked Bettina out.'

'Are you joking?'

'Nope.'

He takes a gulp of beer. 'This is getting weirder. I'm starting to feel I'm on some wind-up TV programme.'

'Right, well, here goes the rest of it. Last night I didn't go to see Bettina to sort things out. She said she was going away with Tyler, but with what happened after I'm not so sure I believe her. I phoned Seb, because I had his number from the fair, and I told him about what she'd been saying. He was stunned and said he didn't think he wanted to date her now. I said that was up to him and I hung up. I had a really bad headache, so I went to bed early, and when I woke up the car had been keyed. I reckon she'd heard from Seb and did it.'

'I'm not very happy that you lied to stay at home and phoned that man.'

'I think we have more to worry about at the moment, Niall. What are we going to do?'

'I don't know.' I can see his tongue poking around the side of his cheek. 'Maybe we need to ring the police?'

'I wondered about an injunction?'

'I don't feel we've proof enough for that. I'll tell you what. As a start, I'll get a security camera fitted on the house. They're quite cheap now on the internet. If there's any more damage to the house, we'll have surveillance footage.'

'That's a great idea.'

'Well hopefully that'll deter vandalism, and if she turns up at the house, we'll have evidence for the courts to get an injunction, so I definitely think that's the place to start. You'll have to find some way of avoiding her in the schoolyard. There's only three weeks of term left so just get Joe to meet you at the bottom of the drive or something, so you don't have to stand near her.'

I smile to myself at Niall's male solution planning in evidence.

'With eBay, I'd contact them and let them know what's happened, and that you seem to have been targeted maliciously. Hopefully with your meticulous feedback record they'll wipe the slate clean.'

'I hope so, I love my little business.'

'Now, without sounding like a jealous prick, no more talking to that Seb.'

I nod. 'Message received and understood. I shouldn't need to now anyway, and by the way, he's leaving so he's not going to be around.'

'Leaving? Good. Well, I think that's all we can do for now, isn't it? I'll ring a garage on Monday and ask how much it is to get the keying removed from the car. I really don't want to put another claim in on the insurance or we'll lose our no claims bonus, although it's so deep I suspect the whole side of the car will need a respray.'

'That's another expense then.'

'Yes, fate has decided we shouldn't have any money just now.'

'Fate or some spiteful cow.'

'Well she didn't blame me for reversing into her car, so we'll have to let her off that one.'

'Just that one.'

I let Niall have another pint and I have a still mineral water to help me hydrate. We consider sitting outside, but the midges are hanging around the water and the moths around the lights, so we stay in the nook. We go back to normal conversation and it feels so nice here, to be away from everything and have this time alone with my husband. We need more of this sort of time, 'date nights', I've read it called in magazines. If we lived nearer to Niall's parents, we'd have regular sitters.

'I've been thinking that I quite like it around here, Niall. Would you consider moving out here with Joe?'

'Now where's that idea come from?' he says. 'You know I moved to the city to escape the quiet country upbringing I had. It can be a bit remote living in the sticks.'

'I think it's lovely, and it's away from the city fumes. It'd be so much better for Joe. Perhaps we could be nearer to Stafford town centre anyway? It doesn't have to be here, just near enough to see your parents more often.'

'I didn't have you pegged as a lover of my parents, Lauren, you normally try and avoid visiting them.'

'I know,' I giggle. 'I've realised today that I've resented your mum trying to be a mother to me. I felt like she couldn't bridge the gap of hurt I feel when parents get mentioned. What if I got close to her and something happened and she hated me? I couldn't go through that again.'

'My mother's not like that, Lauren. She's really maternal.'

'I guess she'd have to be with four of you.'

'I don't know, we were quite a handful. One thing I do know is that Mum took to you as soon as she saw you, the swan who thought she was an ugly duckling.'

'Yes, well today she made me feel like the swan, and I feel like I've made a breakthrough, that maybe I can feel loved by others, if I can trust them first.'

Niall squeezes my hand. 'You've no idea how happy that makes me feel to hear that. You can't let what your parents did to you torture you forever. You must be a good egg if I've stuck with you, being the golden child that I am.'

It's Niall's way of saying he loves me, and I take comfort from the feel of his hand over mine. 'Shall we walk home now and snog on street corners and in doorways like teenagers?'

'Lead the way,' he says, downing the last of his pint.

We arrive home. Glen lets us in and we walk through to the living room; a spacious room painted beige with a traditional style brown leather suite and a brass fire with cream marble surround. I can't work out what's different and then it hits me. I look at Rebecca. 'Oh, I didn't bring flowers.' Usually these would have pride of place in the centre of the mantle shelf within five minutes of my arrival.

'Don't you be worrying about that, Lauren; you've enough fetching and carrying after these two. I know they turned up without you last night, but I bet I know who packed.'

I grin as Niall pouts. 'I'd been working hard all day, Mum.'

'Of course, my darling boy, you provide for your family and that's an amazing thing.' She winks at me behind his back.

After a long game of Trivial Pursuit, we head off to bed. I am by now absolutely shattered, and I'm aware that Niall is still in the en-suite as I feel myself drift off to sleep.

Morning starts with an array of breakfast cereals, sliced fresh bread, croissants and jam, and we are told in no uncertain terms by Rebecca that we are staying for Sunday lunch, and that she's bought an extra-large chicken and a gammon joint. I'm pleased to hear this as I'm in no rush to head back. After breakfast, Niall, Joe and I go to our room to shower. Niall takes Joe in to supervise his, and I put my phone on to check for messages, having switched it off the night before. After a minute or so it starts beeping; I have seventeen message notifications. I open them in turn. They are all from an unknown number.

*__Enjoy what time you have left with your husband.__*
*__You are a selfish bitch.__*
*__It won't be long now.__*
*__Tick tock.__*

They go on, all warning in tone. I feel an icy chill travel up my spine and I shiver. I head to the bathroom. 'Niall, do you have a moment?'

He comes out of the bathroom drying his hands on a towel. 'What's up love? I'm just making sure Joe actually washes himself.'

I show him my phone.

'Right, that's it; as soon as we're home I'm ringing the police. They can come round tonight. If they can trace that phone, we can find out who's behind it. In the meantime, turn it off.'

'I'll text Monique first because I forgot to tell her we were going away.' I type a quick text that we're at Niall's mums and that I hope she's free for a coffee tomorrow as usual. I soon get a reply.

*__Of course. Thought I'd got to report you as a missing person. Hope you're having good time. Usual place nine-thirty?__*

I type back yes and that I'm switching off my phone and will fill her in tomorrow. Then I turn it off and throw it to the bottom of my handbag as if it's made of dirt. I lie on the bed and await my shower, looking forward to the cleansing water and the feel of the heat warming my skin.

We set off back home around four with hugs from Rebecca and leftover food parcels for supper. Joe has a carrier bag full of toys he didn't arrive with. Rebecca reminds us that we are more than welcome to stay for a week or two in the school holidays. It's been a glorious weekend. I drive down the country lanes with the windows open to catch the last of the country fresh air before the motorway clogs my lungs with fumes. Niall and Joe are in the courtesy car, which races me for a short while before disappearing off ahead.

I arrive at the house and I'm met with a stony-faced Niall. 'I've phoned the police. Go upstairs and look, but don't touch anything.'

'Mum, your bedroom's a right mess,' adds Joe.

I run up the stairs, enter my bedroom and see a scene of total carnage. What looks like my whole wardrobe is laying cut on the floor. Not cut to shreds but cut enough to make it unwearable. My jewellery box lies empty on the floor and all my trinkets, both valuable and vintage costume jewellery, are gone. The jewelled hooks I have on the side of the wardrobe to hang large necklaces on are also stripped bare. I lift up the duvet cover. Luckily my shoes and bags are still hidden under the bed; saved by the king size duvet, they remain thankfully untouched. I think of my teacup pendant that I'd just bought and not had much time to wear yet, and of the sentimental pieces of jewellery I've had from Niall, including a diamond pendant he bought me when I had Joe. My wardrobe doors are open and there are only about ten items of clothing left hanging. Perhaps they got bored or ran out of time. I glance at my gold band, the only remaining piece of jewellery I have, and I'm thankful I never take it off.

I close the door on the scene, sit on the top step and cry. Angry tears pour down my cheeks, mixed with the total sorrow of things I can't replace. Niall joins me, sitting a few steps further down with Joe behind him.

'Dad says someone's broken in and been really mean to your stuff.'

'How did they get in?' I ask.

'They jimmied the kitchen window open, but they haven't touched anything else, only your stuff. I'm sorry, but your laptop's downstairs. It's been smashed.'

'Surely this proves there's a vendetta against me? It's got to be her.'

'Who, Mum?'

Niall frowns at me, clearly indicating I should shut up. 'Oh, nobody you know. Don't worry, Joe. Someone's been a bit nasty with mum about her eBay business.'

Joe looks at me. 'I don't want to sleep on my own tonight.'

Niall folds his arms protectively around our son. 'No one can harm you when we're with you. We'd kill them before we let anyone get you.'

'Can I sleep with you tonight though?'

I look at Niall, who nods, and I turn to Joe and stroke his cheek. 'We'll wait until we're allowed to clear up and then we'll put you in with us, just for tonight, okay?'

Joe's deer-trapped-in-headlights look disappears. 'Thanks, Mum.'

It comes to me then. 'Niall, did the burglar alarm go off?'

'It was flashing when I got here. You know how it is though; no one takes any notice anymore.'

'How come the autodialler didn't contact us? Oh damn …' I think of my mobile phone lying switched off in my bag. 'It will have, but my phones not on.' I turn on my phone and wait for it to load. There's a message. It's from the unknown number.

***Do you like your surprise? Everything you value is disappearing one by one: dignity, job. What next, husband?***

'Oh my God,' I squeal, but I'm drowned out by the sound of the doorbell. The police are here.

Niall takes Joe into the dining room, so I can talk to the police about everything that's been happening. They ask for my telephone and look at the keying on the car and the mess in the bedroom, plus the broken laptop. They take notes of everything, and then PC Sheldon, a young slim guy with straight dark hair and a mole above his lip, indicates that I should take a seat in the living room. His colleague PC James goes to sit with Joe, allowing Niall to join us, and I hear him reassuring Joe that he's safe.

'Okay, Mrs Lawler, so you believe that a Mrs Bettina Southwell has been committing these acts against you?'

'That's right. I'm hoping the phone tracing will prove that as I know I don't have any evidence.'

The policeman stares at me while stroking his chin. 'The thing is, Mrs Lawler, we were called out earlier this afternoon to another property in Handsworth that was the scene of suspected criminal damage. It belonged to Mrs Southwell, and when asked who could have done it, she cited both her ex-husband... and you.'

'More like she did it herself before or after she came here to make herself look innocent.'

Niall leaps to my defence. 'We've been away all weekend, so how does she reckon Lauren did that?'

'Yes, well Mrs Southwell also says that she has been away all weekend. We need to do some more investigating. I will be back to visit Mrs Southwell regarding this break in, but I have to say, from where I'm standing this looks very much like a dispute between you two ladies.' He checks out his notepad. 'You had a witnessed argument in the schoolyard, and on Friday afternoon, visited Mrs Southwell at her property and threatened her.'

I open my mouth to protest. 'I did no such thing. I went to ask her to leave us alone.'

'You can see the difficult position we are in, Mrs Lawler?'

'I can see that psychotic idiots are allowed to get away with anything. What's she got to do before you do anything to her? Murder me? What about her latest text where she's threatening my husband?'

Niall looks shocked. 'What text?'

'It came at the same time as the police arrived.' I ask the policeman to hand me the phone back and show Niall.

'Does this mean split us up, or is it a death threat? I don't think we should stay here tonight, Lauren. We'll get a cheap hotel.'

'There's no need to overreact, Mr Lawler. I'll get someone to sit outside on surveillance tonight. Tomorrow, you should fit the security camera your wife was telling me you were thinking about purchasing. Hopefully we'll have more news for you by then.'

'I'll feel better if someone can stay outside for the night,' I say.

'I'll stay until ten, and then a colleague will be taking over my shift until six.'

'I'll be up by then to get things ready for school, so that's great. Thank you.'

PC Sheldon stands up and opens the door to his colleague, indicating that it's time to leave.

'Right, we'll leave you to it. We've got everything we need, so feel free to tidy things up now, though you might want to take your own photos and keep items for the insurance company.'

'Yes, we will do. I'm going to have to take tomorrow off work now to deal with the car insurance, house insurance, and key damage to the other car. This is just unbelievable,' says Niall.

'I'm sorry I can't do more. Please don't visit Mrs Southwell while we investigate.'

'But what about collecting my son from school?'

'I'll get the community bobby to stand with you. They often attend your school anyway. Goodnight to you both, and you, Joe.'

'Niall brings our double mattress down into the living room and I throw a duvet on the sofa for Joe. Niall makes Joe a hot chocolate while I go upstairs and clear up my stuff the best I can. I strip off the beds and change the bedding as the room feels defiled, and I open the windows for a while, as if I can let the bad out into the night. I sweep and mop the floor and dry it. I'm out of breath with the flurry of evening activity. Dragging the black sacks of ruined clothing, I dump them on the bed in the spare room. I'm desperate to talk to Niall and can see the frustration in his face; we can't speak freely in front of Joe.

At ten we're all back in the living room, waiting for Joe to fall asleep. After chatting excitedly for a few minutes, with the novelty of us all being in one room, we tell him he needs to settle. We wait. Our eyes grow accustomed to the dark and we see him begin to twitch. We know he's dropped off enough to not be disturbed by our low murmurs.

'I hope the police find something from the phone.'

'What if they don't, Lauren? They're affecting Joe with all this now. He was scared to death tonight. What if I go and see Bettina's mother?'

'No. If we need to contact someone I'll find a way to get in touch with Danny. He can ring her doctor and get her admitted. He's the money to sort it.'

'Well we've got to do something. I can't just sit and take all this.'

I run my hand down his clenched jaw, stroking his face and trying to free it of tension. 'We'll sort it, somehow, we're strong.'

I turn around and curl up into his body. He spoons protectively around me and if I open my eyes I can see Joe. 'We'll be alright. We're a team.'

. . .

I was nervous about taking Joe to school with Tyler being there, but I saw Bettina's mother dropping him off. She smiled as she passed us in the car, so was maybe unaware of what was going on between us. I was pleased to drive away from the school and stuck an old Sugababes CD in the player and turned it up loud, singing along to 'Hole in the Head' as loud as I could. When it finished I'd enjoyed singing along so much I pressed repeat. I had a few strange looks from drivers and passengers in other cars, but just smiled and carried on singing. Maybe I was verging on hysteria by then? Who knows?

. . .

I pull into Endcliffe Park's car park near the coffee shop and find Monique already there. She gestures to the waitress and then gives me a hug, 'I've already ordered, so it shouldn't be long now.'

'Thanks, I'm so ready for it.'

'So how was your weekend away?'

'Loved it. Just what I needed. Time away from the psycho; except when I got back the house had been broken into, my clothes were shredded and all my jewellery's gone. We had to phone the police.'

Monique's mouth drops open. 'What? Lo, oh my, that is sick, what did the police say?'

'Looking at evidence, going to talk to her, will let us know. Anyway, if it's okay with you can we talk about other things? I'm so fed up of thinking about it all.'

'No problem. Let's get this coffee quick, and then do you need to look for some new clothes?'

'I was going to suggest we did that. I don't have a lot left to wear.'

We wander around the shops and I find a couple of pairs of trousers and some t-shirts. They aren't my Levi's though, and I hope the insurance doesn't take long to sort out. I know my attachment to clothes is a little pathetic, but it's something to depend on. I feel naked without my nice things.

'How are things with Dr Love?' I ask.

'Oh, we're pretty much done there, I think.' Monique carries on looking through the racks and holds up a silk khaki top. 'That'll suit you; try it on.'

'Never worn that colour in my life. Won't that cling round my bust? How come this one's on his way out?'

'Try it on, and then moan if it doesn't look nice, which you know it will, because I am a stylista extraordinaire. He's started to bore me, and after the whole miscarriage thing, I've not been that interested in nookie, so his attention has waned somewhat. Anyway, I'm more than happy right now with my own company, and that of my fairy godfriend, Lo Lawler.'

'Why thank you,' I wave an imaginary wand. 'You shall be

rewarded with further coffee and a sprinkled donut from the new cake shop and cafe across the street.'

'Lo! Cheating on your favourite coffee shop?' Monique pretends to swoon, placing her hand across her brow.

I pout. 'I'm just testing it out to see if the competition's any good.'

'Is that what you were doing with Seb?'

'Ha ha, you're funny you, aren't ya?'

She rifles through some belts. 'What's happening with the eBay stuff?'

'I've not heard anything yet. I have to use Niall's laptop now. I've lost so much stuff.'

'Are there any summer fetes coming up you could do?'

'I don't have any more booked. Anyway, I've lost my mojo with it at the moment. Until things are settled I'm forgetting about the business.'

Monique sighs. 'She's messed you up good and proper, hasn't she?'

'She's done exactly what she set out to do. Hopefully the police are on the case and she'll stop now.'

'I hope so, Lo, because if she does the same to your shoes and bags, I'm going to have a breakdown looking at the state of your clothes.'

'It's not my fault she only left me with my George specials. Anyway, at least they're comfy.'

'Please, stop, I'm only jesting. If only you were my size, I could lend you some of my things. I feel so helpless.'

'You help just by being around, Mon,' I say. 'Now come on. Donuts and sprinkles.' I wave my imaginary wand again.


The community policewoman, PC Smith, is a young enthusiastic brunette with her hair tied back in a ponytail. She meets me at the bottom of the drive. She is on a bicycle, 'Easier for getting around.'

She accompanies me to the Portakabin. All the other parents and carers try to look as if they aren't staring, even though they couldn't be more obvious if they tried. Once again, it's Bettina's mother who is there to pick up Tyler, so I needn't have worried. 'We'll be fine now,' I tell PC Smith and she cycles away.

Joe comes out of school. 'Mum, Mrs Sullivan wants to see you.'

I bet Joe's mentioned something about the break in. We walk around to the school entrance and I press the buzzer. I walk in and report to the receptionist. She asks me to take a seat in the waiting room. There's a box of baby toys in the corner that Joe starts playing with, despite the fact that they are years too young for him.

Mrs Sullivan appears from her office, dressed today in a black power suit with a white and black spotty blouse that reminds me of spilled ink. 'Joe, are you okay to wait there? Mrs Tweedy will keep an eye on you.' She beckons me into her office, a small room fitted with a glass partition that overlooks the school office and path to the dining room and classrooms. It's fitted with a blind for privacy. She closes it and the door.

'Mrs Lawler, please take a seat.'

I sit myself down on the blue fabric-covered chair facing her as she takes a seat behind her desk. I feel like a pupil in trouble with the headmistress.

'I have a couple of issues to talk to you about. The first I'm afraid, is that a complaint has been made about you.'

I sink into the seat. 'What sort of complaint?'

'I've received an anonymous letter that states you have been having an affair with Mr Kingsley, and that some of it took place within the school building. As it's anonymous, I am not going to go down any official route, but I need to know if it's true?'

I sit up straight. 'I would never cheat on my husband. And the only time I've spent with Mr Kingsley has been at the fair.'

'That's what he said, so your stories corroborate. What I'd like to know is why you think someone would send such a letter.'

I feel I have no choice but to fill her in with all the things that have been happening.

'That must have put you and your husband under a terrible strain, but also brings me to the other thing I wished to talk to you about. I understand you and Mrs Southwell put on quite an exhibition last week.'

My face goes red. 'I must apologise for that.'

'Just...no repeats of it, please. I trust that your problems are now being handled by the police. I must ask you to act courteous and adult in the school grounds. You set an example to the children here; we cannot have parents fighting in the yard. If there are any further problems between you then you must come to me, and I'll see what I can do. As there's less than three weeks of school left, I'm hoping we can manage until then?'

'I'm sure it'll be fine,' I say, 'thank you.'

I'm about to walk out of the door when I turn to her. 'Seb Kingsley seems like a really nice guy. He deserves a good reference.'

She smiles a slow smile. 'Thank you for that, it's nice to hear, although I'm well aware of Mr Kingsley's strengths and weaknesses.'

'Sorry, I didn't mean to tell you how to do your job.'

'Oh, it's not that,' she says. 'Seb is my son.'

## CHAPTER SEVENTEEN

'Seb is what?' I walk back into the room and stand with my back to the door.

'My son has spent much of his adult life wandering around the world, not quite knowing what to do with himself. He trained to be a teacher and it's suited him, being able to move around, but with a vocation. I asked him to come here because he'd had a bad time of things lately and needed to get back on his feet. We agreed not to tell people that he was my son. I felt it would cause embarrassment for him, so please don't say anything.'

'I won't mention it.'

She sighs in obvious relief. 'I know he's not a bad lad, but he does try and get by more on his charm than his intellect. I was hoping he'd leave that side of his personality aside working with me, but alas, it seems not.'

'I think you'd be surprised. I got to know him a bit at the fair and I'd like to think I saw some of the real Seb, kind-hearted and quite vulnerable. Yes, he could do with losing the ladies' man patter, but I reckon in a couple more years he'll settle down. I do believe he wants that, eventually.'

'Well, time will tell I suppose. Anyway, I won't keep you any longer, Lauren, you have your own lovely family to get back to.'

'Yes I do,' I smile. 'There's a lot of stress going on for us at the moment but at least we're in it together.' I walk over and shake her hand. 'Thanks, Mrs Sullivan, and I promise to keep things away from the schoolyard.'

'Appreciated.'


I collect Joe from the waiting room, thank Mrs Tweedy and we head home. Pleased to be back through the door, I kick my shoes off in the hallway and sag down onto the stairs as Joe goes running through to greet his dad. I hear a female voice and wonder if it's the policewoman, so I put my slippers on and head into the room.

I am greeted with the sight of Bettina on the sofa, looking pale, red-eyed, and dishevelled, with a tissue in her hand. I look at her and she flinches.

I turn to my husband. 'What is she doing here, Niall?'

'I think you'd better sit down, Lauren. Bettina's had quite a lot to tell me. Joe, Tyler's in the dining room on the Xbox.'

'Wow, cool. Can he stay for tea?'

'Probably not, son. Just go and play for now.'

'Aww, please?'

'Joe...'

'Ohhkaay,' he goes off to find his friend.

We're left all together. I want to grab Bettina off the sofa and throw her out of the house, but the silence is pregnant with some untold tale, so I place myself on the floor with my head resting near to the bay window and wait for her to say whatever it is she needs to say. 'Right, what's going on?'

Niall is the first to speak. 'Bettina has a cast iron alibi for not breaking into the house over the weekend. She was with Tyler in Leeds.'

I look at Bettina. She is struggling to catch her breath between quiet sobs. 'So you have absolute proof you didn't trash my room?'

Niall answers for her. 'Yes, she has proof. She had to deal with some issues with Danny. She's come to tell us today, as it's about to break in the press. Danny is in police custody, on suspicion of manslaughter.'

I hug my knees with my arms, so I'm tightly curled up, grateful that I'm already sitting on the floor. *Danny? Manslaughter?* I know he had a reputation for being a hard case, but manslaughter? I feel my stomach flutter. If Bettina was away this weekend then who damaged my car? Who broke into our house? I start laughing; I have no idea why.

'Oh my god, what is happening?' I rock slightly backwards and forwards. There's silence for a moment, then I bite my lip and turn my head towards Niall. 'How do we know she didn't pay someone else to do it? She's not without money.'

'Lauren, please?' Her voice cracks as she turns to me. 'I've come here because I'm desperate. I can't take any more. Just hear me out and then I'll be gone.'

'Just give her a chance, Lauren, love, okay?'

I nod.

Niall disappears into the kitchen and returns with three glasses and some sherry. 'Medicinal.'

I turn to Bettina. 'Let's hear it then.'

She takes a deep breath. 'Niall's told me about all the trouble you've been having. I honestly had no idea. I'm not the one behind it, but if you want to believe that I am, please yourself, because the police know it's the truth. Anyway, I wanted to come and clear things up for Tyler's sake.' She takes a drink of her sherry. 'I told you Danny had a nasty side, and he's got an extremely volatile temper. For God's sake, he stabbed himself in the hand. Tyler was brought up in that household. He heard our arguments and he's spent the past couple of years thinking he has to look after me. I don't want that. I'm the mother,' she trembles. 'It's my job to protect him. That's why I didn't want Danny having any custody of Tyler, and why I was so scared when I thought he'd taken him from school. I've been trying to get his access stopped.'

'So, what happened?'

'He was arrested Friday lunchtime for punching someone in his local bar. The man hit his head and died on route to hospital. I'm torn between feeling sorry for that man's family, and being grateful it wasn't me or Tyler,' she wipes her eyes with the tissue, then sits up straight.

'When you came to the door on Friday afternoon, I was just getting everything ready to head to Leeds. The police wanted me to come and talk to them, and I thought I might be able to get the rest of our stuff from the house: clothes and Tyler's toys. Danny didn't let me have anything when I left. I thought he may have thrown our stuff out; but no, it was there to taunt me. Or maybe it was there in case I was stupid enough to go back.'

I rub my forehead. I can feel a headache coming on. 'I'm sorry. I believed Danny. What he said seemed plausible at the time.'

'Niall said Danny told you that I came here for you. I moved to be near my mum, so me and Tyler had some stability, some security. I'm not lying, Lauren. I do have issues from school. What happened there affected my life. You were a potential positive in my moving here. I'd mentioned you to my doctor and she'd said if I could come back and make amends it would help deal with some of my childhood issues.' She snorts. 'Well that went well. I'll be able to keep her employed for years after this.'

'Bettina, I wasn't to blame for you leaving school. You got me into trouble.'

'I don't have the energy to go there now, Lauren. To be honest I'm starting to believe with what's happening now, that a schoolgirl spat wasn't much in the scheme of things.'

I look at the floor and pick at some flaking nail polish on my toe.

There's more silence for a while as she worries at her tissue and I find my feet more and more interesting.

Niall breaks it. 'What've you got to do now then, Bettina? What did the police say?'

'I'm free to do what I please. He's my ex-husband. I've no ties to him anymore beyond the large one,' she looks towards the dining room door. 'I'm going to give up my rental. I've got a while left on the lease but I'm going to look for something larger to share with Mum. I'd feel better with someone else in the house. My mother can't wait.' She turns to me. 'You need to know I'm not moving Tyler from school; he's settling in nicely. If you don't like me here, then move yourself. Anyway,' she bristles, 'why were you so damn sure it was me causing all this grief? I told you it wasn't.'

'It started the same time you moved here. Monique told me you were asking lots of questions about me, and then Danny turned up and said you were crazy and out to get me. Things kept happening and it all just seemed to point at you.'

'Well as for the eBay stuff, you should know that I don't even have an account. I've never been on eBay in my life. I wouldn't have a clue how to order anything, never mind do it under several aliases.'

I start to cough. Despite the sherry, my throat is really dry.

'Do you want a coffee?' Niall asks. I nod. 'Bettina?'

'Yes, alright.'

'I'll check on the kids and fix them a quick sandwich, if that's okay with you, Bettina?'

She nods. 'Thank you.'

Niall leaves and I feel the draft from the door sweep over me. From down here I can see dust gathered under Bettina's chair. My carefully ordered life has broken like a smashed meringue over the last few weeks.

'Seb called me on Saturday,' she says.

I try a naive look, but it obviously fails.

'Please. Save it. I know full well that you've been in touch with him. I could tell by the way he suddenly ran a mile. Why I thought he was genuinely interested in me, I don't know, bearing in mind he practically tripped over his own tongue every time you walked past him.'

Something else dawns on me. 'So you didn't report us to the school, saying we were having an affair?'

'Of course not. Look, Lauren, I'd normally hate to sound this rude, but right now I really don't give a fuck. You can do what the hell you want with your life: screw Seb, stay with Niall, switch to battery powered. I couldn't give a toss. Your life is of no interest to me beyond Tyler's friendship with Joe. Other than things that connect the kids, I don't want to speak to you, or be involved with you in any way. I just need to keep Tyler's life in order. I don't need any more of your grief, your temper tantrums, or for that matter your selfishness. I'm sorry someone seems to be targeting you at the moment, Lauren, I really am. It must be very scary, not least for where Joe is concerned. I know, because I've been there with Tyler and I'm not trying to top you here, but have you no idea how good you've had it? Moaning about Niall. He's one of the best blokes I've ever met, no one's perfect. You don't have to work, you can just swan around the shops all day going for coffees with your best mate. Then you have an extremely well-behaved son, a gorgeous home with two cars, and yet you feel the need to practically dry hump the schoolteacher? Grow up, and don't get a life, enjoy the one you have.'

She stands up, as Niall heads back through the doorway. 'Sorry, Niall, forget the coffee. I'll be off in a minute,' he looks between us, at Bettina's now angry face and my downcast one. If I slide any further down the wall, I'll become some of that trapped dust.

'There's just one last thing I wanted to bring up before I go, and it's the last time I intend to speak of it,' she says. 'The damage that was done to my own house over the weekend... I know it wasn't Danny because he was in the cells, so that really only leaves me with one suspect,' she glares at me. 'What you did makes me sick to my stomach. I hadn't realised you hated me that much, Lauren. I realise some of why you felt you needed to do it, but I thought you were better than that.'

'Lauren?' Niall looks at me and then at Bettina. 'What exactly was the damage at your house, Bettina?' I listen as she tells him and I watch his face drop. I feel like I'm watching a car with a puncture, where the tyre was filled with love and trust and then it deflates and bleeds until there's nothing much left. How is he going to trust me now?

'Is this true, Lauren?' He turns back to me, searching my face for the one glimmer that'll reassure him it's not me; that it's entirely stupid to suppose I could ever do that. I can't meet his eyes. I look away.

'I've lost my bond money and have to pay to fix the damage to the lawn.'

'I'll make sure you're reimbursed, Bettina, as soon as I can,' says Niall. 'Though God knows where the money's going to come from with everything else we've lost or had to pay for lately.'

She goes to get Tyler from the dining room. 'Thanks for his sandwich,' she says and heads out of the door with him.

Niall turns to me.

'I'm not sure I know who you are right now,' he says. 'I think it's best you go to our room.'

Just like that I'm dismissed like a child sent to bed for bad behaviour, though my own has been far worse.

As I walk into our bedroom, I realise I can't sleep here. I can't face Niall again when he comes to bed. This room has always been my refuge, but I feel I'll blight it with darkness if I lay my head here. I grab my pyjamas and head off into the spare room. My spare room has always been my workspace, with a bed under the window and the rest of the room taken over by an enormous corner desk where I keep my laptop, printer, and boxes of craft supplies from previous creative endeavours. I have shelves covered in craft, and cookbooks, a pile of notebooks which I collect just because they are pretty, and two square Perspex boxes on the desk, which are usually full of the vintage trinkets for sale on eBay. They're now as empty as I feel. I pull down the blind to plunge the room into darkness and switch on the small light. I look at my pyjamas. They are far too cheery looking: blue and red tartan bottoms and a grey top with the appliqué 'I've been good all year'. What a joke. I go back into my room, take out a pair of black pyjamas and slip those on. It feels right.

## CHAPTER EIGHTEEN

Trying to sleep is a waste of time. I stare around the room in the dark trying to make out shapes as my eyes become more accustomed to the lack of light. Thoughts whirl around my mind. Bettina maintains her innocence and it seems to point that way, but is it coincidence that she delivered another blow by telling Niall about the damage to her property? If it's not her, then who the hell have I offended? Or is it Niall who has an enemy? Maybe some patient of his has a grudge; he did get crashed into in the car park? I warm to the idea that it has something to do with Niall. But then how would they know so much about me? Has someone been spying on us? I think back to Bettina. If she is innocent, then all along she's just been an anxious mother trying to get settled near her mum and start over. If so, look what I have done, screaming at her in the schoolyard and destroying her property.

I put the light back on, wincing at the brightness, and look around for something to do. I grab my nail polish tub from my shelf. I get out the black and paint my nails to match my mood and pyjamas. If I could make myself disappear I would. My thoughts won't leave me alone. I feel like I'm going crazy. I want to take a holiday from my own head.

In the morning, Niall remains in bed. He should have been on an early shift, so I assume he's taking a further day off. I get Joe ready for school, just having to call into the bedroom once to grab some clothes. I choose black again, easily identifiable by its darkness in my still colour co-ordinated wardrobe, though there's not a lot to choose from anyway. I sweep my unwashed hair back into a ponytail. A glance in the bathroom mirror shows the truth of the last few days in my face, every agony is mapped out in frown lines and misery.

I walk Joe right up to the school gates on this dark and drizzly morning. I'm scared in case someone is following us. I need to make sure he is safely delivered inside. I tell him I just wanted the fresh air by way of an excuse, and he takes this on board in the innocent way children do. It worries me. I feel reassured by the new password system which ensures no stranger can take my child out of school. When Joe's inside, I walk back down the driveway, folding my coat around myself, pulling my hood up, and keeping my head down. I'm behind three of the other mothers and hear them talking.

'Thought there must have been something going on when they had that fight outside.'

'Fighting over a teacher they reckon. I've never taken to her, seems like she thinks she's better than everyone, swanning about in that vintage shit. Her poor husband... and little Joe, he's so sweet.'

'Well just shows you don't know what's happening behind closed doors. Who'd have thought it of Lauren. I thought she was a good one....'

I recognise Tanya's voice coming out from under an umbrella. I turn left and shortcut through the nursery school. We're not supposed to go this way unless we have nursery kids, but I need to escape the narrow minds and prying eyes.

The window is open when I get home, telling me Niall is up and about. Honestly, it's like living in a fridge when he's around. It's quite cold, yet he has all the windows and the back door open. I usually hate it because once I'm cold it takes hours for me to warm up. Today it will make no difference; I'm numb on the inside anyway. I walk into the room and see Niall fixing his breakfast.

'Joe went off fine.'

'Why wouldn't he?' Niall says, his expression pinched.

'I'm just telling you. How long are you going to be like this? Can't I try to explain?'

'When I'm ready, Lauren. I've enough on my mind sorting out all the insurance and other finances, so don't pressure me right now.'

At no time during this conversation does he ever look up at me.

He points back into the living room. 'Your phone's on the side. The police just dropped it off, said there's nothing further they can do. No evidence of anything. The phone used was a pre-paid; they obviously knew what they were doing.' He goes back to buttering toast, and I go into the room and pick up my phone.

I can't face putting it on. I'll sort out a new one today with a new number. I get Niall's laptop and look at my emails. I see one from eBay customer services and click on it.

**_Thank you for your email regarding the negative feedback on your account. While we investigate the matter we have set up a temporary limit on your account of three items per week. This will be in place for the next three months while we monitor your account for suspicious activity. Please be aware that this limit is provided for your safety and security online._**

Three items a week for three months? My business is over. Not that I think I'd have the confidence to sell much again after this. I've lost almost everything. The person texting was right. My dignity is shredded, my personal life is a shambles, my business is over, and the cars need insurance work. The only things I have left are Joe and Monique, and hopefully in time Niall will come around. The doorbell rings and I rise to answer it.

'Delivery for Mrs Lauren Lawler.'

I look at the black chrysanthemum wreath being delivered to my door by the local florist.

'There must be some mistake.'

'Are you Lauren Lawler?'

'Yes, but...'

'Then it's for you.' He taps his pen on his clipboard. 'Are you going to sign for it, or shall I take it back?'

I sign for it and take it back in the house to look at the card. I remove it slowly from the envelope, nervous that it's going to contain poison or something. There's just a plain card and on it is written 'deepest sympathies on the loss of your best friend'. My heart lurches and I feel I need to rush to Monique to warn her, but I remember she's at work. I rush to Niall and show him instead.

'Leave it on the window ledge, I'll show it to the police later. Maybe they can trace who made the order.' He heads through the house towards the hallway. 'I'm going for a drive, Lauren. I need to clear my head.'

He leaves me standing there.

I hear him removing just delivered post from the letterbox and opening an envelope. I go through to see if there's anything for me. Niall has gone deathly white, as if he's in great pain. I'm worried for his health.

'Niall, are you okay? Does your chest hurt?'

He thrusts a photograph at me. It shows me and Seb on Friday evening. Though our kiss was captured through the living room window, it's perfectly clear what we were doing. I open my mouth to explain, but before I can utter a word, Niall beats me to it.

'I will collect Joe from school tonight. Right now, I don't want to see your face or hear any more of your lies. Get the fuck out of this house,' he spits. 'Be gone before I get back or I swear to God I will throw you out myself.' He slams the door and is gone.

I collapse to the floor, all my strength is gone. I am no longer real, just a speck where there once was life.

. . .

I don't know how long I lay there for—catatonic—before I feel like I'm looking down on myself and seeing the pathetic wreck that is laid there. I'm transported back to my childhood, when my father could make me feel this way by the sound of his shouting voice, or the crack of his hand; or by my mother's endless words about my patheticness. I sit up in shock. I will *not* go there again. I am Lauren *Lawler* now. I have left my previous persona behind.

I get up and pace around the living room. What shall I do? I realise I want my friend. I want to tell Monique everything; she'll know what to do. I know she'll let me stay over. That will give Niall time to calm down. I go upstairs and pack a bag of things I need, and then drag out an empty suitcase from the garage. Monique won't be back until around half-five. I decide not to ring, but to surprise her instead. We can have a fun girly evening and right now I decide I'll go around the charity shops again to try to replace more of my wardrobe. I can also get a new phone. It's a positive thing to do and the thought of it propels me into action. I drag myself into the shower and put on some clean clothes. Before I head out of the door, I write Niall a note telling him where I'll be and that I'll text him my new number. I check that my address book with everyone's telephone numbers is in my bag, and catch sight of my black nails, now the only reminder of my previous mood.

After getting a new phone, I go around the charity shops. It's a perfect shopping day and there seems to be lots of lovely items in my size. I get some Per Una jeans, a Diesel shirt, and several pairs of casual trousers. I buy so much I have to go back to the car mid-trip to drop it off, so I can start again. I open the suitcase and place the new items inside, then zip it up.

Before round two, I decide to hit my favourite cafe for a cup of life juice, AKA coffee. My favourite sofa is available, and I feel buoyed that the shopping has gone so well. I feel it a sign that my brown couch is free to comfort me. I look at my new phone. It needs charging before I can put the numbers in, so I'll have to do that at Monique's. Relaxing, I sit back and look around. There's a new piece of art on the wall, a kind of tribal mask, carved out of wood. It has a sign under it 'protector of the innocent' and a price tag of a hundred and twenty pounds. It's by a local artist. Is it a total coincidence that not only do I love it, but that it appears meant for me? We can't really afford it, but I reason the insurance will come through at some point, my jewellery was worth a decent amount of money. I flag down the waitress and buy it. I head back to the car a second time and place it in the boot.

I spend the rest of the afternoon in the shops buying more items, getting a thrill out of each purchase. I add shoes and bags to the pile. I don't need them but each one gives me happiness. At five, I decide to head to the local pizza restaurant to pick up a takeaway for me and Monique. While I'm waiting, I watch a family of four eating their meals. They are all so happy, and this is communicated without words. A wipe of one son's mouth, a mother pouring some of her coke into her other son's glass. She and her husband looking at the kids and smiling at each other. Their happiness shines out of them like the winter sun, and just like that, it hurts my eyes. I look down at my bags and realise that apart from the things I need, the rest of it won't make me happy. Once again, I'm attempting to comfort myself with materialistic things that will only provide happiness for brief moments. It can't compare to the love I have for my family. I feel I've made the right decision to stay at Monique's tonight, and then tomorrow I'll go home and stand in Niall's way and protest until he listens. I will fight for my family, they are my life. I take the pizza and go and get the car, putting the purchases in the boot and the pizza on the seat at the side of me.

I pull up to Monique's and press the buzzer. She comes through on the intercom. 'Yeah?'

'It's me. I need a place to stay tonight. I brought pizza.'

There's a moment of silence and she buzzes me through. I walk to her door and I'm surprised to see a guy there. He's tall and good looking; with dark, mussed hair and a flush to his cheeks.

'Oh my God, I'm so sorry, I never thought you might have company.' I cover my mouth with my hands. Once again, I've assumed everyone is there to look after me. 'Sorry, I'll leave and call you later.'

'Matty's just going. Don't worry about it.'

I hold up the box. 'Sure you don't want to share pizza?'

'No, I'm okay,' he says, and winks at Monique. 'I've had my fill.'

She rolls her eyes at him and I feel my own face flush. I'm guessing this is Dr Love and look at his ID card hanging from his waistband. He sees me and quickly whips it off. 'Gosh, I'll be losing that if I'm not careful. She didn't give me chance to organise myself, that insatiable friend of yours.' He bounds off saying he'll catch us later and I step into the apartment.

'Well, you were right. He is damn hot,' I say, and place the pizza box on the side in the kitchen. I decide I'll not share my woes with Mon and will enjoy a girly night instead. For once, I'm not going to be selfish. I've already maybe spoilt her planned evening.

'He is all that, which is why even though I'd ditched him, he's found his way back into my bed.' She grins. 'Anyway, to what do I owe this honour?'

'You've been a great friend and I want to spoil you. I've bought a couple of DVDs this afternoon,' I get them out of my bag. 'Pick one and we'll have a cinema night.'

She looks at me like she wants to ask me something, but chews on her lip and walks into the kitchen instead to get plates. No eating straight from the box for Monique.

We have a great evening and I feel able to distance myself from what is happening at home. In my mind I'm on a mini-break, with no focus other than Monique, fashion, and fun.

After the film ends, Monique stands up. 'I'll go and fix up the spare room quickly. I wasn't expecting you.'

'Sorry, I really should have called.'

'Well, I would appreciate a call in future, but I forgive you this time. It's been a great night.'

I watch some trash on the TV. I hear Monique banging around putting stuff away and dragging out the sofa bed. She returns. 'It's ready when you are; but leave your clothes and stuff you don't need out here as all the drawers are full. You'll be fine if you stick to the area around the bed, but I don't want you tripping up.'

'No problems, I'll be careful.'

We settle down to watch Big Brother as I haven't seen it for a few days. At eleven, I decide to turn in. I don't want to keep Monique up as she's back at work in the morning. I want to get back to see Niall as soon as I can.

I go into her spare room. It's covered in clothes; they are draped all over the surfaces. She's much worse than I am at buying clothes, shoes, and bags. I remember I need to charge my new phone, creep back into the living room, and get it. I can hear Monique brushing her teeth. I return to my room and look for a suitable socket. As I place the phone on the dressing table I see one of her jewellery holders, one of those that are shaped like a lady's body and a teacup necklace catches my eye. It's just like mine. I feel another pang at its loss. I sit back on the bed thinking about the coincidence. We share the same tastes and have often bought the same thing. I wonder if Monique would let me buy it off her.

I settle under the duvet and think about how embarrassed I felt when I first turned up. A few minutes earlier and I would have interrupted her and Matty 'at it'. I really must learn to think of others more. Another resolution going forward. I know it's early days and he's a lot younger than Mon, but there was a great spark between them, and I hope he'll be able to break through her barriers. Finally, Dr Love has a name, Dr Matty Bailey. I frown. The name sounds familiar, but I can't place where from. Then it comes to me. My eyes open wide and I shoot up in bed. The bloke who crashed into Niall's car—he was called Dr Matthias Bailey. A wave of unease comes over me as I think of this next coincidence. I sit in the dark with my heart beating fast for a long time, until I'm sure that Monique must be asleep. I tiptoe to the bathroom and on my return listen at her door. I can hear the sounds of her snoring; something we've laughed at in the past, but now I'm glad of the clear sign of sleep. Back in my room, I switch the small lamp on and systematically go through all her drawers and cupboards. I find nothing. I'm about to dismiss my suspicions as stupid when I remember something she said to me when I told her about the break in, that she hoped they didn't come after my shoes and bags. I never mentioned they had been left, so how would she know? A feeling of nausea begins to accompany my rapid heartbeat. I resolve to carry on looking. After about ten minutes, I'm about to give up when I spy a vintage style vanity case at the back of the wardrobe. I bought it for her the first Christmas after we met. I open it up and inside find more of my missing jewellery and some photos. One of the photos is the one of Seb leaving my house. My hand shakes as I look through the pile of photos I am clutching. There are a couple of Bettina from what must be a few years ago as she looks younger. As I get to the bottom I find a well-thumbed photo of Monique gazing lovingly up at a man. The man is Danny Southwell.

## CHAPTER NINETEEN

I carefully replace the items in the case, remembering the order of them, and get back into bed. Part of me wants to take the case and run, but instead I lie there, thinking there has to be some other explanation. Monique is my best friend. She's shown no sign of knowing Bettina, yet there are old pictures of her. The picture with Danny shows Monique was either a fan, or worse, a lover. It makes no sense. Why do things to me? What have I done to Monique other than be a good friend? Is this part of Bettina's plan? Are they in on it together?

I stare at the ceiling, my heart thumping. What should I do next?

I need to get out of here.

Or do I confront her?

There must be some logical explanation.

I decide I'll stay here tonight. It's not like I have anywhere else to go. Tomorrow at breakfast, I'll tell her the news about Danny if it hasn't broken already and watch her reaction. Maybe she'll give some clue in her behaviour that'll point me in the right direction?

Or maybe I just should get out now, while I have the chance?

But then I'll get no answers. No, I'll stay.

My thoughts circle like a car on a roundabout.

. . .

At six I get up as I've barely slept anyway. I fix some coffee and toast for myself and Monique. Around half an hour later she enters the kitchen and stretches, reminding me of a slinky cat. She smiles at me and I smile back, hoping my face gives nothing away, while feeling like tormented prey.

'Did you sleep okay?' she asks.

'Yes, thank you. That spare bed is surprisingly comfy. Other than a quick wee I was out like a light.'

'That's good. I really enjoyed you coming over.'

'Er, yeah, it was great. I'm going to have breakfast and then head back home though. I fancy doing some baking.' Another lie, in truth I have nowhere to go, and I'm not sure what to do.

'Are you baking your cupcakes? I can't remember the last time I had one. You should have made some yesterday before you came over.'

'Never thought. I'll bring you some soon, promise.'

'Right, well I'll head to the shower. Do you need one?'

'No, I'll just freshen up and get showered at mine. I'll see you in a bit.'

I stick on a bit of TV while I eat my breakfast and then get dressed. When Monique leaves the shower, I head in and have a quick wash, brush my teeth, and stick my hair back in a ponytail. Looking in the mirror, I think if the circles under my eyes get any darker, I'll look like I've been run over by dirty tyres. I gather all my things together ready to leave and then head back into the living room to say goodbye to Monique and mention Danny to her. I see she's reading the newspaper. Her face is deathly white and her head is in her hands. I reverse my steps back into the bathroom quietly and make more noise on my way out. When I re-enter, her face is perky. She looks up at me like a gossip columnist who's been in the toilet next to a drug smoking supermodel, scoring an exclusive. 'You'll never guess what? Bettina's husband's been arrested,' she says.

'Yeah, she told me yesterday.'

'You spoke to Bettina yesterday? Why would you see her? Why didn't you tell me last night?' she shouts with uncharacteristic force.

'I didn't think you'd be interested. It's not like you know Danny.'

If I hadn't known to look for it, I would have missed the split-second hesitation before her reply.

'Course not, but it's major gossip. Sorry, I got a little overexcited, because we kind of know him through Bettina.'

'No worries. Anyway, I need to get off so thanks for every—'

'No, no, no. You can't leave me without info. How come you saw her? Tell me what she said. It says he pushed someone. Does she think he'll get off? Seems unfair if it was an accident.'

'She was there when I got home yesterday, saying she wanted us to know, and that whatever has gone on between us, she still wanted the boys to be able to play as Tyler needs some stability, especially with what's happening with his dad. She didn't have much to say, other than he's being charged with manslaughter because he punched the guy and he banged his head.'

'Is she going to see him?'

She's not interested. She's his ex-wife now, so it doesn't really concern her.'

She shrugs. 'She's got Danny's son.'

'Her priority is to keep Tyler away from it all, and from the press.'

Monique plays with her top lip. 'So do you think he'll get out?'

'I've no idea, but he's not known for his mild manners, is he?'

'If you believe Bettina? But look what she's been doing to you. You only have what his poisonous ex-wife says. I'm sure he's an alright bloke really. Maybe she set him up too?'

'She can rot in hell for all I care. She came and told Niall yesterday about Danny. I asked her to leave as soon as I arrived home. I doubt I'll have anything to do with her again, and I'll phone the police if she starts anything.'

'That's good. Hopefully you'll get back on your feet if she's out from under your hair.'

'Well I live in hope. Anyway, you're going to be late for work if you keep on yakking. Who'd have thought, Monique Henry, gossip queen?'

She folds up her fist like a microphone and talks in a reporter style voice. 'Keep in touch and let me know if there are any new developments.'

'I will.'

She tilts her head to one side looking at me and sucking on her bottom lip. Shit, is she onto me somehow? 'She was alone with Niall when you came home, you said? You need to watch her.'

I nod relieved, grab my overnight bag and head out of the door. I walk calmly down the path towards the stairs, thankful that the driveway isn't visible from Monique's apartment and then I run, my feet crunching in the gravel, across the car park. I throw my things in the car, jump in the driver's seat and reverse out of my space. I need to tell Niall what I've discovered and fast.

I race through the door when I get home, seeing the car outside and noting that Niall has not gone to work for a third day. I find him in the garden digging the hole required for the garden pond he wants. He looks at me and wipes the sweat from his brow and walks towards me.

'Lauren.'

I can barely get out my words due to being out of breath. 'It's Monique... Niall, I was in her room last night and...'

He throws down the spade and clutches his temples. 'Good God. You nearly drove Bettina to a nervous breakdown, and now you're starting on Monique?'

'But I—'

'No. I'm not listening to this right now. Look, is there somewhere you can stay another night or two? I'll tell Joe you're on a mini-break. He's used to you abandoning him to babysitters while you float off anyway.'

Tears fill my eyes. 'My son is everything to me, don't you dare.

Sulk away today, Niall, I'll be back tomorrow. Hopefully by then you'll have grown up.'

'I need some time to think.'

'You can have today.' I stride away from him, picking up my overnight bag from the doorway. I run upstairs and add some clean undies and then go back out of the door. I now have another day to find something to do. I need to make a plan of what to do next. However, glancing at my watch, I see that it's only just turned half nine. I decide to drive down to the local cinema which is about ten minutes away. There are always some early showings, so I decide to kill a couple of hours in there.

After the film, I look around the entertainment complex and decide to lunch in the local pizza place. Honestly, I have never eaten so much rubbish in my life as I have the last few weeks. I order a coke, and while I wait for my pizza, I take my cupcake design notebook and pink biro out of my bag and turn it onto a fresh page. I need to think and make a plan, and when I make plans I make lists. I consider who can help me to get through to Niall and come up with either the most logical or most stupid plan ever. Seb. Seb could help me to make Niall see sense. He'll be gone in less than two weeks. Anyway, what do I have to lose? I write on the list:

1. *Ring Seb.*

I also need to see Bettina. I need her to wrack her brains to see if she remembers Monique from anywhere.

2. *Try to find a way to get Bettina to meet me.*

That's a start.

3. *Maybe speak to Dr Love?*

I'm unsure of this as a plan. If Monique has set Niall up, then this could tip her off that I'm onto her. Now I'm annoyed that I didn't bring the photos and jewellery with me, but I didn't want her to get suspicious. I just don't understand why she would do this to me. My pizza arrives, and I pick at it, struggling to find an appetite. Then I start thinking again and regret not taking any evidence. Maybe then Niall would believe me.

There's only one thing for it.

3. ~~Maybe speak with Dr Love?~~ *Go back to Monique's.*

I stare at my piece of paper while eating a little more pizza. I doodle in the corner, drawing a sun and turning it into a happy face. Then before I know it, I've drawn lightning striking it and rain pouring. I get out my phone and send Seb a text.

**I'm sorry to bother you yet again, but I need to ask you a favour. Can we meet at our usual pub?**

Luckily for me it's the school lunchtime and I get a text back quickly.

*I can be there by four. PS You never bother me, Lauren.*

A minute passes. I get another,

**Actually, that's not true. You make me extremely hot and bothered.**

I smile and wonder if he will ever actually change. I wipe my mouth with a napkin and ask for the bill.

It's just gone one and I have until four to do something. I go back to the cinema to pick something else. This morning I chose a comedy in a feeble attempt to cheer myself up. This afternoon I'm plumping for an ass kicking spectacular. On my way out, sitting in the car, I send Monique a text.

**Trying to sort stuff out at home. Be in touch soon xxx.**

I need to keep things as normal as possible. I drive to the pub with my mind so full of current happenings, that when I arrive I'm not entirely sure how I got there. I don't remember even being conscious of the traffic lights.

Seb is already at the pub. He looks as gorgeous as ever. Dressed in his nerd gear, I want to take off his glasses and rough up his hair. Still furious with Niall, I order a glass of wine. However, I'm mindful of the fact I can't drink much more as I need to drive to a local hotel for the evening.

'So, as much as it's nice to see you, Lauren, what's this all about?'

I take a large mouthful of wine. 'Niall was sent a picture of us kissing at my house. Now he's convinced we had an affair. I want you to come and tell him it's not true.'

He splutters. 'I don't bloody think so. Not sure I fancy a cosy meet up with your hubby.'

I bite my lip and try to stop my tears. 'Please... I'm desperate. He's kicked me out and won't let me see Joe.'

His brown eyes seem to darken to black. 'He's a total fucking dick then. Can't he see what he has?' He taps his foot on the floor. 'I'll think about it okay?'

I wipe my eyes. 'Thank you.'

'Is that all you want me for? I have marking to do.'

I grab hold of his fingers across the table. 'Please, don't go.'

'Christ, Lauren, what do you want from me? I feel like a bloody yo-yo.'

'I'm on my own.' I neck my glass of red. 'Please stay and have a meal with me. I hate being alone.'

He sighs. 'I need to get away from this... from you.'

'Yes,' I spit. 'That's what everyone seems to want, to get away from me. At most points in my life I appear to have been some diabolical person that everyone needs to be rid of.'

I go to the bar to order another glass of red wine. Sod it. I'll have a bottle. I'll order a taxi to the hotel and leave the car here. I smirk. I might just leave it with the door open and the engine running so Niall gets a call from the police and goes frantic—it would serve him right. I sit back down and drink another large mouthful. The blackcurrant and cinnamon flavours warm my mouth.

'Don't you think you should slow down? You'll be flat on your back before long,' Seb warns.

I look defiantly at him. 'Isn't that where you want me anyway?'

I hear his breath hitch. 'I'm going to order some food and get you some, so you don't fall over.' He rises from his seat and goes to the bar.

While he's gone I finish off my current glass of wine and pour myself another. I can already feel it going to my head. I feel this slight sensation of being in a greenhouse, as if I can see everyone but there's a distance between me and them. I like it. I'll stop after a third glass as I know I'll be prone to vomiting if I drink any more, lightweight that I am. But one more glass with some food, I should be able to manage and if not, who cares? Seb can call me a cab.

When he returns I follow on from my train of thought.

'I'm going to stop at the Novotel. If I'm a bit squiffy, dial me a cab.'

He picks up the remainder of the wine and moves it out of reach. 'That's you done for the night. Don't do anything you'll regret tomorrow, Lauren.'

I smile up at him and give him the benefit of a full toothed grin. 'I'm a bit pissed, and I'll tell you something,' I lean over the table and mock whisper, 'I've done nothing but be a good person and look where it's got me. My life is ruined. Well stuff it. I'm not behaving right now. I'm getting drunk and having some fun.'

I wander over to the game machine and feel in my pocket for the change I got from the bar when I bought the bottle of wine. I stick a few quid in, pressing random buttons as I've never gambled apart from a few goes on the Grand National over the years. There are a series of flashes and noise and then coins come tumbling out into the tray. I've won twenty quid.

'Whoo hoo,' eyes turn towards me and I get a few "well done's" and grins. Seb comes over and takes my arm. 'Our food's here.'

I heartily tuck into my scampi and chips. I smear it in tartare sauce, using up three sachets.

'I had no idea you were such a pig with your food.'

I stick out my tongue and then get a chip and suck all the tartare sauce off. 'Mmmmmmm'.

Seb shuffles in his seat, adjusting himself. 'Jesus, Lauren, what're you trying to do to me?'

I look down at the chip in my mouth and begin to giggle hysterically. I can't stop. I take another chip, dip it in the sauce and lick up and down its length. A woman at the next table gives me a dirty look. I give her a wink back.

'Eat your food. It's time to go before you're kicked out. It's only tea-time for Christ's sake.'

'Why is everyone so boring?' I roll my eyes. 'Do you know, today I made plans and lists? Well to hell with them.' I take out my little notebook and upend it in Seb's pint of beer. He looks skyward. 'I'm going with the flow, by the seat of my pants, throwing caution to the wind.'

'I think you've swallowed a book of clichés along with that wine, missus. Come on, let's get you home before you fall over.'

'I have no home.' I stand stock still as an idea comes to me. 'Take me to your home.'

Seb raises his eyebrows. 'You want to come home with me?'

'Yes.' I puff out my chest sexily. 'I want to see your bachelor pad.'

'Jesus, how drunk are you?'

'I'm just merry—merry and bright; bright like the wine was sunshine, and its brought light into my life.'

'I'm going to take you to my flat, but just to make you some coffee and help you sober up. Then I'll drop you off at your hotel.'

'Oh, yes, take me to your home,' I say. 'Now.' I start giggling.

Seb holds my arm to help me out of the pub. I see him roll his eyes at the landlord as he wishes him a good evening.

'Rude.' I mutter.

Seb's place is nothing like I would have guessed. It's a ground floor apartment which we enter through a hallway, like Monique's. It's a lot shabbier though with cracked paintwork and graffiti. Yet when he opens his apartment door, I'm pleasantly surprised. The door opens straight onto a decently sized living room with a dark brown carpet and neutral walls. He has a large screen television and a green canvas couch. I look at him questioningly.

'Came with the flat. Beggars can't be choosers.'

He goes to switch the kettle on, telling me I'm to have a couple of cups of coffee. I made him take my overnight case out of my car and bring it in here, so I wander off to take it into his bedroom. His room is decorated in purples, again no doubt the work of whoever owns the flat. It puts me in mind of an Arabian night's scene, and I giggle thinking of Seb as Shahryar surrounded by nubile young virgins. I don't consider what I'm doing. I put my case in the corner of the room and lay on the bed. I'm not thinking of Niall or anyone else this time, not even Joe, I'm doing what I want; to hell with everyone.

That's the last I remember until the early hours when Seb accidentally wakes me up as he comes into the room. I see his alarm clock reads two sixteen.

I am thankfully hangover free. I turn to face Seb, who is picking up pillows. I am laid on the top of the bed.

'Sorry,' he says. 'I was trying not to disturb you.'

'That's okay,' my mouth is dry. 'I guess I missed out on the coffee then?'

'Yes, and you'd have loved it, a rich Ethiopian blend. It serves you right for falling asleep.'

I sit up.

'Where are you going?'

'Bathroom. I need some water. Then I'll head to the couch. It's your bed.'

'No, you can have the bed. I'm okay with the couch. I think you need a good night's sleep.'

I head to the bathroom, which has a smart white suite. Although basic, it looks really effective with a black and white checked shower curtain and a black venetian blind. I splash water on my face and have a few sips from the tap. Then I use the loo. I sit for a few minutes, thinking about where I am and that a man who is not my husband is only a few feet away. I strip myself down to my bra and pants, wrap a towel around myself and walk back into the bedroom. Light peeks through the curtains, casting a glow on the room so I can see my way around. I hesitate as to whether to get my pyjamas out of my case, and stand in the room, completely unsure of which way to turn.

'Everything okay?'

One look at his open caring gaze and mussed up hair and the temptation is too much. I'm done resisting. The towel drops to the floor and I climb onto the bed beside him.

I run my hand up his t-shirt and stroke his chest. He has a slight covering of dark hair across his chest and down his navel. He shivers and grabs my hand.

'Are you sure about this, Lauren?'

'Sssshhh.' I place my index finger across his mouth. 'You'll be gone in a few days. I need this to remember you by.'

He bites my finger and turns and backs me into the bed, crushing his chest across mine. His mouth smashes into mine and I thrust my tongue between his teeth. He tastes of his Ethiopian blend. I can't get enough. We kiss on and on, trying to drink each other in. I want as much of him as I can get, knowing this is a one-time only deal. He moves his mouth onto my neck and I twist with delight as he kisses and licks it. It makes me squirm where I'm laid as the ticklishness of it fights with desire. I raise myself up, so he can remove my bra. He pauses and looks me in the eyes and says. 'Oh God, Lauren. I can't believe you're here.'

I silence him with another deep kiss and stroke my hands down his back. Next, I help him remove his shirt and move to sit astride him. I trace the dragon tattoo with the tip of my tongue. He flips me back over and moves himself further down the bed. I can feel his desire pressing against my leg. He takes turns to suck, lick and tease my nipples. I can feel my excitement between my legs, I am so turned on. Pulling him back up the bed to kiss me again, I slip my hand under the waistband of his pants and stroke him there.

He jerks away from me. 'No.'

I try to put my hand back.

'I said no.'

I look up at him. 'You want this.'

'Yes, but I don't think you do, Lauren.'

He moves himself away from me and runs his hand through his hair. 'Shit, that was so nearly a huge mistake.'

My voice trembles. 'But... why?'

'Because you're hitting out, Lauren. Tell me, how will you feel if Niall apologises and we've slept together?'

I look at the floor.

'If your marriage is over, Lauren, and you want us to be together, that's different. But I won't do it this way, do you understand?'

I begin to cry. 'I don't know what I'm doing any more, Seb. I just keep making everything worse.'

'Well I can't decide for you,' he says. 'Next time I won't stop, Lauren. I'll fuck your brains out. I'm not a good guy, don't you get it?' He turns over, his back to me.

I breathe until my tears subside and finally, I fall back to sleep.

When I wake, I move out of Seb's warm arms. My eyes feel swollen and gritty. I pick up my wash bag and go to the bathroom. My reflection in the mirror shows I look tired and drawn. My eyes are bloodshot. I stare at myself, wondering what on earth is happening to me. What am I doing? I feel I need to wash last night away. Thank goodness Seb stopped me. I feel the tears welling again. I'm such a fool.

As the water washes over me, I rub my wash mitt down myself and scrub away at my skin, relishing the pain. I need to feel something. I massage shampoo into my hair, kneading my skull. I'm pulling Lauren Lawler back together. I'm letting my enemy win and that's not going to happen if I can do anything to prevent it. I dress, dry my hair, and head back into the living room as Seb's kitchen is very small and has no table. Seb pulls up a coffee table, one of those sets of three that fit neatly under each other, and he puts down some coffee and a plate of toast. My stomach growls at the coffee aroma. 'Wow, that smells good,' I say. 'And strong.'

'I think it should be named after me,' he says.

I smile, pleased that he's being normal.

'I'll leave you a key if you like. You're more than welcome to stay here.'

'Thank you. I need to regroup, and to think.'

'Well, I'll be gone a week on Saturday. You need to decide if you want to fight for your marriage and get your life back together, or,' he pauses, 'you can come with me.'

I fall silent because while I know I want my marriage to work, there's a small part of me that wants to be with Seb; a tiny chink of obsidian fighting to be seen amongst diamond. I know Seb has been a little deviation from the route of my life, a wrong turning on the journey, that to me, has begun and will end with Niall.

'Well, things are slightly more complicated than that,' I say and fill him in about Monique.


'She must be mentally ill if she's been doing things like that.'

'I feel like the Monique I've known for the past five years was a mirage, and now I'm left with this new person who I don't know at all. What I do know though, is that I need to get Bettina to speak to me, and then I need to see Niall.'

'It sounds like you have some things to occupy you today. As I said, stay here as long as you need to.'

'Will you come with me to see Niall later?'

'That's a bit of an ask, Lauren. Look, I'll think about it while I'm at work. Go see Bettina and take it from there. Maybe it's time to step out from all the protection you place around yourself and take some chances.' He kisses me swiftly on the cheek and leaves for work.

I get out my mobile phone and call Niall.

'I'll be picking Joe up from school and coming home.'

'I've got school covered, Lauren. I've taken the rest of the week off.'

'You don't seem to be listening. I will be picking my son up at three fifteen. I don't know why on earth I've let you boss me around this week. Sure, I've not told the whole truth, but I've done nothing to deserve being shut out of my own home. So tonight, I *will* be home and you'll listen to what I have to say if you have any ounce of compassion in your bones. If not, then you can pack your own bags, Niall, because I'm staying with my son.'

There's silence at the other end of the phone. I feel sick while I wait to hear what his reply will be.

'I'll see you later.'

My outtake of breath makes me go dizzy.


I drive to Bettina's and pray that she's in. As I walk up her driveway, I see evidence of the damage I've caused to the garden, as yet not repaired. There are yellow dry patches on the garden where the weed killer is taking effect and turned over earth where I pulled out the plants. It looks like a mole's had an acid trip on the lawn. I knock on the door and step back.

Within a minute she opens the door. 'Get away from my house or I'll phone the police.'

'Bettina. I know we aren't friends, but I desperately need to talk to you.'

'I'm not a sounding board for the woes of Lauren Lawler, you have Monique for that.'

'That's why I'm here,' I pause. 'I think Monique's the one who's been doing all this.'

She stares at me, her eyes narrowing. 'Why on earth would she do that?'

'Because of Danny. She may have been his lover.'

She sighs, the cheated-on wife discovering yet another infidelity of her husband.

She steps away from the door. 'You'd better come in.'

## CHAPTER TWENTY

Stepping through the hallway, I realise that this is the first time I've actually been inside Bettina's rented house. We go into the living room. There are packing boxes piled in the corner and the room is noticeably bare. It's decorated in the old nineties style of burnt orange wallpaper with a floral border around the middle. It has laminate flooring, an orange sofa, and a beanbag. There's an array of toys around the beanbag and a folded back copy of Hello! lies on the sofa.

'I've just made a pot of coffee. I suppose asking if you want one's a silly question?'

'A bit.' My mouth attempts a smile.

'Take a seat. I'll be back in a sec.'

She brings in two mugs of coffee and a plate of chocolate biscuits on a tray, setting it on the floor in front of us.

'Sorry. I've packed the table.'

'Oh, yeah, course.'

'I haven't seen you at school the last few days? Niall said you were on a mini-break?'

'Niall threw me out after a photo arrived of Seb leaving our house.'

'Oh.'

'It's not what you think. He came around because I needed some advice; but presented with that picture on the back of everything else... Niall found me guilty as charged.'

'I'm sure he's just angry and bewildered. I've been there. You don't know what to believe.'

'Yes, well aren't we all? Anyway, I'm going back home tonight to talk to him and try to get him to see reason, then the ball's in his court. I'm tired of it. If he wants to pack his bags, he can go.'

'You don't mean that, Lauren. You love Niall.'

'Yeah? Well maybe that's not enough. Right now, I'm just focused on Joe. I want to be near my son, and if that means it's just him and me, so be it.'

'He'd miss his father like crazy. Tyler does, and look what a moron he is. Forget your bitterness, Lauren. Niall's not your mother and father. He's hurt. This has affected him too and he must be scared of what could happen to Joe, just like you are.'

I wince as she mentions my parents, but perhaps she's right. I'm building up a wall ready to protect myself again.

'I'll see how it goes later. Right now, I need to talk to you about Monique.'

I explain about finding the photos in the vanity case, about several of them being of a younger Bettina, and then tell her about the one of Monique and Danny.

'Well if she had an affair with him, I never knew about it. All the ones I knew about were stereotypical blondes with big boobs.'

'I don't understand why she would attack me though. I've no real connection to Danny.'

She lifts her shoulders. 'Who knows how a weirdo's mind works? All the time you've known her, has she ever displayed any strange behaviour, stalked anyone or anything?'

'No, she's just been my best mate. We've been there for each other for everything over the last five years. As soon as I met her at yoga I felt like we'd known each other forever.' My voice cracks. 'I can't believe she could be behind all this. I mean, she's just been through a miscarriage…'

There's an uncomfortable silence for a minute or so.

'How sure are you that she actually had a miscarriage?'

I think back. I never saw evidence of any blood or a mess, all I had was Monique's tears and her word. 'Making something like that up would be totally sick.'

'You reckon?'

I frown. 'But why? If it wasn't genuine, what did she achieve by faking it?'

'I have no idea. We need to try to get more of a clue.'

'I'm thinking about going back and gathering some evidence, see if I can find out any more, but I don't know. I feel like I need to talk to Niall first. He's always so good at thinking of what to do.' This makes me feel sad. I've always depended on Niall, maybe too much. Will he be there now when I really need him, or should I do things myself?

'We need to get this sorted as soon as possible. You talk to Niall tonight, and I'll call you in the morning. When you've gone, I'll ring the prison and try to set up a visit for tomorrow morning. Danny's allowed three visits a week at the moment, so hopefully I'll be able to get to see him. I'll ask him how he knows Monique.'

'That'd be great.' I realise I've not drunk any of my coffee and leave it untouched. 'Maybe I need to speak to Monique's Dr Love as well, find out if he was asked to crash into Niall's car? It seems too coincidental now.'

'I wouldn't at the moment. He might tip Monique off.'

'You're right. Okay, I'll speak to you in the morning. I'm sorry I had to come and bug you yet again.'

'It seems we're in this together, Lauren, for whatever reason.'

'Yeah, well let's see if we can find out what that is.'

I get a hero's welcome from Joe at school. 'Mum, you're back. Please don't go away for as long again.'

'I won't, I promise.' My words are the truth. I won't be leaving Joe again for a long while. I need to know he's safe, and I need him to know he can rely on me to look after him. Once again, I feel rage at Niall for taking precious time with my son away from me.

Seeing Niall makes me feel like I'm facing the executioner. He ruffles Joe's hair as he goes to hug him. The usual "have you had a nice day, Joe" is answered with "fine," and then Joe's off to his room, regardless of the fact he hasn't seen me for days. It makes me feel warm inside, that the thought of me being here is enough.

'Let's hear it then, your latest version of the truth.'

I don't bite back. I take a seat diagonally across from Niall at the dining table. He sits back in the chair with his arms folded. He looks impenetrable and I need to get through to him. So I begin.

'The other night at Monique's, I found some of my stolen jewellery in a case in her wardrobe.' Niall opens his mouth to speak and I hold up my hand. 'Let me finish. There were some photos of Bettina from a few years ago in there too, and the photo of me and Seb that was delivered through the post to you. And... an old picture of Monique looking very loved up with Danny Southwell. My assumption then, is that for whatever reason, but connected to Danny and Bettina, Monique is behind everything that's happened. Also,' I take a deep breath, 'Monique's boyfriend is the doctor who crashed into your car.'

'I'll kill her.' Niall is out of the chair with his face in a grimace and his fists clenched. 'Get the phone. I'm calling the police.'

'That's the thing though, Niall. I don't have the photos or the jewellery. I didn't want to tip her off, so I left them there.'

'Well if we ring the police now we can show them where it all is.'

'But then I may never know why she targeted us. What if she's moved everything? I want to go back to the apartment to see if I can find anything else.'

'You must be bloody joking. You can't go there now. Who knows what she'll do?'

'If she was going to harm me, Niall, she's had plenty of opportunity to do that already. I don't know what her game is, but I do know it's not to hurt me.'

He folds his arms across his chest. 'Well, I don't know how you expect me to just sit here while you enter the monster's lair.'

'I'll be fine. I need to do this. I promise, any sign of something iffy and I'll be out of there. I thought I'd go tomorrow morning. I'll tell her we've fallen out, so she won't be suspicious of my turning up at her house. I'll find some way of getting the stuff and get out. Hopefully I won't be long.'

I uncross my legs as I'm getting pins and needles in one foot and shake it out. 'There is something I need you to do though. Is there anyone at the hospital who could look up whether or not Monique attended A&E, or the antenatal ward? Bettina reckons she might have faked the miscarriage.'

He peers at me, his forehead creasing. 'Faked a miscarriage? I just can't take this all in, Lauren.' He sighs. 'It breaks all the rules of confidentiality, but I'll ring our secretary. Write me her date of birth and the first line of her address.' He passes me a post-it note and a pen. I quickly scribble them down and he goes off into the living room. He returns a couple of minutes later.

'Monique hasn't been anywhere near a hospital since she's been in Sheffield. She's not even on the system.'

'Are you sure they inputted her details correctly?'

'She did what's called a soundex; it looks for anyone remotely relating to the details. There was nothing.'

And with that, one of the branches of my heart snaps. My best friend is not who she seems.

For the rest of the evening we imitate normal family life, with the usual sit-down meal and bath time, then I go to my own room while Niall sits in the living room. My own bed feels wonderful. I dive under the sheets, pulling the covers up around me and spend a long time wondering what the next day will bring.

. . .

I ring Monique the following morning and she's delighted that I'm coming over. I never usually see her on a Friday as it's her 'working from home day', but obviously being given a chance to catch up on developments means she'll do her work later. 'Bring some of your baking,' she says. 'I'm in the mood for something delicious.'

Damn. I forgot I was supposed to have been baking. I pick up a Tupperware box. I'll call into a bakery on my way over and hope I can wing it.

On arrival, I'm ushered into the living room where she is dressed in a long burgundy silk chemise with black lace trim and matching gown. She looks like she needs one of those long cigarettes they had in the nineteen twenties. I don't know if I should be afraid of her or act differently, but she just appears to be my same old mate. I just can't get over the fact that she could be anything else. She sits on the sofa and gestures for me to take a seat on the other one, then passes me a drink. 'I'm being decadent today, I've made Mimosas.'

'Oh, any reason why?' I ask

'A few things I've had in the pipeline seem to be coming to fruition. I feel we should celebrate. Also, it will help cheer you up. What's Niall done this time, anyway?'

*I must act normal.* 'He's had a big go at me about everything. I assume it's the stress, but I'm not putting up with it anymore.'

'Good girl. Right, what did you bake?'

I get out the cupcakes I've bought; all pink icing and coated in sprinkles. They smell amazing, either recently cooked or warmed through by the bakery. Thankfully made in the shop and not of uniform size, I can get away with having not baked them myself.

'Have you heard anything else about the break in? Are they going to replace your clothes?'

'They will do, but these things take time, don't they?'

She takes a bite of cupcake. 'Umm, these are gorgeous. You should think of selling them in a shop.'

*Does she know?* I need to act fast and get her out of here. I feel sick.

'Is everything all right, Lauren?'

'No.' I hold my guts as if I'm in severe pain. 'Owww, it really hurts.'

'What is it? Shall I get you a hot water bottle?'

'It won't go without medicine. I've had it before. Can you fetch me some if I give you the money? Your local chemist isn't far, is it?' I push the half-eaten cupcake and the bubbling Mimosa out of the way. 'I knew I shouldn't have had them. Serves me right for trying to have fun when my life's a pile of steaming dung.'

'Honestly, Lo, there's always a drama when you're around. Have you thought of applying for your equity card?'

I manage a brave smile. 'I feel a bit sick.'

'Go to the bathroom,' she orders pointing. 'I'll get straight dressed and go to the chemist. It shouldn't take me long in the car. By the way, if you puke, you're cleaning it up. I might be your best mate, but even I don't love you that much.'

I wander to the bathroom clutching my stomach as she goes to get ready.

The minute she leaves the flat I run straight into the spare room. The vanity case is still at the back of the wardrobe. I grab it, and with hands shaking so much I can barely open it, I record with the tiny Flip camcorder I have in my pocket and then remove the photos and jewellery and put them down my bra. I have about ten minutes or so before she's back if there's no queue, so I keep an eye on my watch as I move around the room. As I pass her dressing table I bang into the corner bruising my leg and making myself go lightheaded with the pain. As I do so, I hear something falling down the back of it. Mindful to not move anything visible, lest she get suspicious while I'm there, I pull out the dresser to see what fell. Behind is a cheap looking handset. I'd put money on it being the one used to message me. I run and place it at the bottom of my handbag, remove the photos and jewellery from my bra and stuff them inside as well. Once I'm back in the room, I shove the dresser into its original position. I look around the room again, but in full on panic mode with the adrenaline kicking my ass I realise that I really am about to be sick. I run back to the bathroom and get there just in time; a half-eaten cupcake mixed with Mimosa shoots into the toilet bowl. The look and smell of it is enough that I begin to heave again and that's how Monique finds me, sweating and bent over the toilet seat.

'Oh gosh, you really are ill, aren't you, Lo?'

I nod my head. I feel clammy and sweaty. I feel really rough now. 'I think it's best if I head home and go to bed.'

'Nonsense. You can have a rest here. The spare room—'

She looks towards the spare room and frowns. 'I'm sure I closed that door.'

'I've been in here since you left,' I lie. 'How can you know how you left a door, anyway? I don't know how I leave the house in a morning; never mind what chaos I leave behind.'

'It's just who I am,' says Monique. 'I always close every door. It's just one of my little rituals.'

My mouth feels dry. How have I never noticed this before?

'Anyway,' she says, 'either I forgot for once, or it's blown open. I don't know why I'm thinking of that while my best friend is ill. She rinses out a face cloth, folds it over and gives it me to hold to my head. You stay there. I'll get the spare room ready for you to have a sleep. I'll take the laptop into the living room and work from there.' She gets up and strides purposefully towards the spare room. I realise that my game is probably up, so I do the only thing I can think of under the circumstances, I grab my bag and run, closing the door silently behind me.

I dash to the car. My legs feel so wobbly they threaten to give way on me, but I manage to get in and start it straight up. Once again, I find myself blasting down the communal driveway. I really must get a job at a racetrack for my next career, I'd be damn good at it. I drive until I am well away from her apartment and park myself in a local supermarket car park, and then I sit and shake.

My phone rings and I nearly die with fright. It's Bettina.

'Hello.'

'Have you been running? You sound out of breath.'

'I've just legged it from Monique's.'

'Crikey, how did that go then?'

'I got everything, but I think she was onto me. I left the spare room door open and apparently she always closes them.'

'What do you think she'll do now?'

'Goodness knows. We need our evidence together for tonight, so we can go to the police before she does anything stupid. Anyway, I panicked. She might have genuinely been going in the spare room to get it ready for me staying, and now I've run off and given her a reason to be suspicious.'

'You'd better ring her with some kind of excuse, just in case.'

'Good idea.'

'Well, I was calling to let you know that I'm just about to go in and see Danny, so wish me luck.'

'Good luck.'

'I'll give you another call when I get out.'

'Actually... do you want to come over to ours when you've done? Niall will be there and then we can all decide where we go from here.'

'Okay, I'll see you this afternoon sometime. I'll ring when I'm on my way.'

I dial Monique's number. 'Hello,' she sounds agitated.

'Monique, it's me.'

'I know. It says on my phone, dumbass. Where the hell are you? One minute you're puking in my loo, the next you've disappeared.'

'I wanted my own bed.'

'Well, you could have said. I had no idea where you were. I looked around the apartment and the grounds thinking you might have collapsed somewhere.'

'I'm sorry, Mon, I didn't want to worry you. I just panicked and wanted to get back home.'

'Is that where you are now?'

'Yes,' I lie. 'In bed. Not that Niall is taking any notice of me being ill. He's a pig.'

'Well, I've told you that from the beginning. You should've stayed with me.'

'I know.'

'So are you staying at home all day now?'

'Yes.'

'Well, look after yourself, and Lauren—'

'Yes?'

'About the spare room.'

I think my heart actually pauses. 'Hmm?'

'It was me. I left the window open. Sorry for seeming paranoid.'

'I never gave it another thought.'

'Ring me when you're feeling better.'

'I will. Thanks for everything, Mon.'

When I put the phone down, I'm deeply worried. Because the window in Monique's spare room was definitely closed.

I drive back home carefully, on alert to anything untoward, and jumping if another car moves anywhere near me. I feel parched. The first thing I do when I get home is to run upstairs, swill water around my mouth and then brush my teeth. So I'm more than a little shocked when I eventually walk into the living room and find Niall on the sofa with a pack of frozen vegetables on his fist. Seb clutches another bag against what I guess is the beginnings of a black eye.

'Do you want to sit down, Lauren?' Niall asks.

# CHAPTER TWENTY-ONE

I'm not sure my poor heart can take much more of this stress today. I swear it'll be grey rinses from now on, not blonde highlights.

'How come you're not at work?' I ask Seb.

'Yes, Lauren, I'm fine, thank you,' he states with snarled sarcasm.

'I can see you're not fine. I can also make out that you've connected with my husband's fists, being that I am not entirely stupid.'

'The headteacher gave me the afternoon off.'

'Your mother let you finish early?'

'Mother?' Niall sniggers. 'Mrs Sullivan's your mother?' He bursts into laughter.

Seb clenches his fists.

I take note of the fact there are two cans of beer on the coffee table.

'So did you start drinking before or after the fight?'

'He punched me the minute he opened the door,' says Seb, looking at me like a wounded puppy. 'Didn't even give me a chance to speak.'

'Yeah, well, mate. Last time I saw you was on a photo kissing my wife, so what'd you expect?'

'I've explained that now. I have no interest in your wife whatsoever.'

I feel a bit insulted but realise it's best to keep my mouth shut. 'So you finally believe me?' I state.

'Yes, well, with all this Monique business, I was already thinking you'd probably been set up, but I was still wondering what he was doing at the house. He's explained it all now, and it's sorted.' He turns to Seb. 'Do you fancy another beer, mate?'

'No thanks, I need to be able to drive home.'

'Good point. I'll just shift these tins or she'll be moaning.'

While he pops into the kitchen I look at Seb and he winks at me with his good eye.

Niall comes back with a cloth and wipes the table down. However, not to make me completely think he's been abducted by aliens, he leaves the cloth on the table and sits back down. 'So, er, you got a lady then, Seb?'

'There was someone, but they didn't feel the same way about me, so I'm planning on going Down Under for a while.'

I have to cough to cover a snort and then I replay back what he's said, and I feel sad. I've used this guy and deserted him, so beach life should suit him well.

'We've talked about going to Australia in the past,' says Niall. 'I can go with work over there through being a nurse. I guess that's the same with you; are they crying out for teachers?'

'Yes. Are you considering it then, in light of what's happened?' Seb asks Niall.

They both look towards me and I feel uncomfortable under their gazes, and unsure as to who I should look at.

I turn towards Seb. 'No, though I am asking Niall to consider a move. I'd like to go to Staffordshire to be nearer his parents. I think it would be nice for Joe.'

'Sounds sensible to me,' says Seb, looking at Niall. 'I do think a fresh start away from this madness is what you need.'

'Well, we still need to talk about it, but it's definitely a possibility.' Niall looks at me and gives me a look and a half smile that—for the first time in a long time—gives me hope again for us.

'Right, well I'd better be off then,' says Seb. 'I'll leave you to it. Good luck with the police later. I'll be around until a week on Saturday if they need me for statements or anything.'

'Thanks, I'll show you out,' I say.

He stands up and shakes Niall's unbruised hand. 'See you, mate. Take care of this lady; she's a good one.'

'I know, that's why I married her.' I hear the Neanderthal coming out of Niall, so head Seb towards the door quickly.

As he stands in the doorway, he turns towards me and I get the full melting-chocolate-brown eyes. 'Here,' he says, and hands me a piece of paper, taking time to stroke my hand as he leaves it in my grasp. My hand tingles.

'What is it?' I whisper.

'My address in Australia. I'll be there for a couple of months. If it doesn't work out with Niall, you know where to find me. I'm not saying goodbye, Lauren.' With that he walks away and I know that although there's a chance I'll bump into him at school, it's possible that this will be the last time I'll ever see him. I close the door on him and on that part of my life. I tear the paper into tiny pieces which I place in my pocket to throw away later.

I walk back into the living room and into Niall's embrace. He covers me with his arms like my warm duvet. I hope this episode in our lives has passed and we can go on to the next. Anyone who thinks a marriage is always love and flowers is fooling themselves. Marriage is hard work. Sometimes you travel on different paths as you grow, but if you're lucky enough, those paths reunite and the journey is good again. I hope that Niall and I will get through this. After all these years, it's not our first bump in the road, although it's proving to be the largest to date. I sink into his hug and feel relief overwhelm me.

'So what do we do now?' asks Niall.

'We wait.'

Bettina arrives just after two. The day has turned pleasant, so we sit in the garden on my bench. Niall brings out a fold up chair, so he can sit with us. We sit expectantly. There are no pleasantries exchanged; we just want to try to get to the bottom of the situation.

'Well it took me to say Tyler may be in danger, but once he got that, it all came out. I think I'm going to need some more therapy after this.'

'Won't we all,' says Niall.

'Danny says he met Monique when I was pregnant with Tyler.' She sits stony-faced. 'So he was probably never faithful to me at all.'

'I'm sorry, Bettina.'

She shrugs. 'I got over Danny Southwell a long time ago. Anyway, they had, by all accounts, a torrid affair, for about a year. She wanted to get serious and asked him to leave me, and of course he said no. He told her she wasn't his only lover and he didn't need another wife because he already had one.

'What a charming man. Why on earth did you stay with him so long?' asks Niall.

'You do what you can for your kids. I thought Tyler needed his dad.'

Niall nods.

'She threatened to tell me everything apparently. Danny told her to go ahead because I knew anyway, and that there was no way he'd leave—he had his son to think about. She gave him a load of hassle, saying that kids always got in the way of things and she was sick of it.'

'Hang on a minute,' I say. 'This is like, nine or ten years ago?'

'So?'

'That's around the time her husband left her because he wanted kids. Looks like it became a pattern for her; rejected for children again.'

'Apparently, she sent him poison pen letters. She turned up at bars he was in. He had to threaten her with the police. She said he'd come around eventually, and she could wait.' He just put it down to her being another possessive bimbo. He's met quite a few over the years.'

'So has he any idea why she came to Sheffield? That was five years before you arrived. She couldn't possibly have known you'd move here.'

'No. That he has no idea about. He fails to see the connection with you, other than he believes he probably discussed my "obsession" with you.'

'I don't understand,' says Niall.

'It was one of his "my wife doesn't understand me" lines. I had issues with Lauren over school. He'd tell his girlfriends I was obsessed with a former schoolfriend, make out I made his life hell. Sound familiar?'

'That's what he told me,' I say.

'Yes, well that's the only connection to you that was made, so we have to assume that she befriended you to get to me.'

'That makes no sense. We weren't in touch.'

'Well, I don't have any other ideas.'

'At least we know what set her off now.' I'm still in total shock that my mate has turned into a crazy lady. 'I think it's time to ring the police.'

The police take the phone, the photos, and brief statements from us. They say they'll need to talk to us again later, but for now they just intend to pick her up for questioning. They call to say she's not at the apartment, but they'll keep checking in until she appears. Bettina and I go to collect the kids from school, aware that now it's just a waiting game.

The kids are full of it as they come out. 'I've had a great day, Mum,' Joe squeals. 'We had a class treat and watched a video.'

'Remind me to retrain as a teacher,' I tell Joe. 'Because that sounds like fun.'

We walk down the drive together and say goodbye at the bottom. Bettina and Tyler walk off in the opposite direction. As the weather's nice we walked to school to pick up the kids, so I look forward to a nice stroll home with my son. What I'm not expecting is for my path to cross with that of Dr Love.

'What the hell?'

'I need to speak to you.'

I turn to Joe. 'Mum, won't be a minute, hun. Just wait here while I talk to Matt.'

'Who are you?' Joe asks him bluntly.

'It's Auntie Mon's boyfriend, Joe, don't be rude.'

Joe stands at my side looking up the street and fidgeting. It's impossible for him to keep still. I smile and then turn back to Matt.

I speak in hushed tones. 'We've called the police, so they'll be looking for you in connection with the crash into our car.'

His face turns grim. 'It's my word against your husband's. I've got a witness, and anyway, I'm a doctor.'

'Yes, but you're linked with Monique, whose turned fifteen shades of crazy, so maybe your statement won't hold as much clout as you think.'

Joe tugs my arm. 'Mum, Mum.'

'Just a minute, Joe.' People are bustling around us in their quest to get home from school as quickly as possible. This is not the best place to hold a conversation, but I need to find out as much as I can from this man.

'Why did she ask you to crash into his car?'

'I'm not going into that with *you*.'

'So why are you here? Why bother coming all this way? You must have had some reason?'

He smirks and jumps in the car that has pulled alongside us. It tears off down the street.

I turn around to tell Joe that we need to get home, but he's not there. He's gone from my side while I was distracted by Dr Love. My world spins as I realise the words out of Joe's mouth weren't 'Mum, Mum,' they were 'Mon, Mon.'

My legs give way and a scream leaves my body at a noise level I didn't know I could reach.

Someone calls the police. It's all a blur. My voice screams for Joe, and then as much as I try to fight it, knowing I need to keep on top of things for Joe, it all goes dark.

I come to in Mrs Sullivan's office. I'm laid on the floor with my head on a jacket and my heels perched on the edge of a child's chair. I'm told Niall is on his way. A policewoman is sitting in the corner and I realise there is someone to the right of me, a paramedic. 'Okay, Mrs Lawler, stay where you are a moment."

I ignore him and sit up. I go dizzy and feel faint again. What sort of mother am I? My child needs me, and I can't help for fainting.

'I'll make her a cup of sweet tea,' says Mrs Sullivan, 'and get her a biscuit.'

My son is missing, and they think I have time to drink tea and eat biscuits? Yet I know that if I don't take this time, I'll be of no use to anyone. A trickle of water slides down my face. Niall, who has now arrived and been briefed, looks at me with concern.

'The police are looking for them, but can you remember the number plate or make of the car?'

'No,' I sob. 'It wasn't Monique's car.' I curl up in a foetal position. 'I only know it was dark blue. What the hell use am I? I don't even know the make of it.'

'Stop it, Lauren.'

'I let her take my child.'

'Before you fainted, you told the people with you that Dr Bailey deliberately distracted you. Is that true?' The policewoman moves over toward me.

'Yes.' My eyes open wide. 'She hates children, what does she want with Joe? What if she harms him? Oh God, I can't bear it.'

She places a hand on my shoulder. 'They won't be far. We've all the local airports and other travel stations covered.'

A fresh wave of horror washes over me. I never thought she might take him away somewhere. 'Joe, Joe, Joe.' I sit up and rock back and forth. 'My baby, my baby.' I stand up and a burst of adrenaline shoots through me. 'I'll fucking kill her.'

The policewoman guides me back to a seat. 'You need to calm down, Mrs Lawler.' She hands me my tea. I take a sip and wince as it burns my tongue. It's sweet and disgusting. The policewoman urges me to take another sip. 'It's what you need right now. We need you to calm down, so we can ask you some questions. Now don't worry about the make of the car. There were other witnesses around who recognised it as a VW Golf, so that's one further detail we have to go on. It's not Dr Bailey's car, so we're currently looking into car rental places to see if we can get a positive ID that way.'

Of course, I'm the key witness and so far I've been no use to anybody, least of all Joe. I take a few deep breaths and sip the tea slowly. I ask for a biscuit and force it down. After a few minutes and two biscuits I feel calmer. 'Okay, ask away.'

I recall the conversation with Dr Bailey and how he'd obviously been there to distract me while Monique got Joe in the car. I told them how I'd just thought Joe was being his usual annoying 'Mum, Mum, Mum' self, and I have to bite my tongue, deliberately hurting myself until I taste blood, in order to stop from falling apart again. 'He was saying Mon, Niall,' I say, looking up at him and seeing my pain reflected in his face. 'I wasn't listening properly. I'm a hopeless mother.'

Niall comes over and gets down on his knees so he's looking me in the eyes. His eyes flash with anger. 'You are not a hopeless mother. Our son has wanted for nothing. But now is not about your ability as a mother, Lauren. It's not about you, and it's not about your past. It's about now and Joe, and I need you to get yourself out of this funk and into a place where you can help get our son back. Do you understand what I'm saying, Lauren?'

I feel like I've been slapped in the face, but in a good way, if that's possible. As if I was sleepwalking, about to go off a cliff edge and the slap was to wake me up and bring me back from danger.

'You're right. I've got my mobile on me. We need to go looking for Joe ourselves.'

The policewoman shakes her head. 'Leave it to us, we've everything covered. Why don't you take her home, Mr Lawler?'

'I'm not sitting around while that cow has my son somewhere.' I snap. 'You have my number if there are developments.' I get up from my chair, feeling stronger now that I have a purpose. 'Niall, let's go, we need to find our son.'

He walks with me towards the door.

'I'll call you later, Lauren, and see how you're getting on,' says Mrs Sullivan. 'You know we're here for you if you need anything.'

'Thank you,' I tell her, and leave the school.

We sit in Niall's car thinking about what we should do next. 'What if she goes for Tyler next?' He says.

'We'd better let her know.'


Bettina turns hysterical when we tell her and then catapults into me, holding me in her arms. 'Oh God, Lauren, I'll help anyway I can. I feel responsible for getting you involved in all this.'

I stiffen.

'There's no reason behind this; she's a nutter,' says Niall. 'Anyway, you may need to think about getting some protection from the police until she's caught.

'I'm going to drop Tyler off with my mum,' she says. With the police there, they'll be safe. I feel partly responsible for her behaviour. So, no arguing, but what's the plan?

'We're going to look anywhere we can think of as to where she might have taken him.' I say.

'Well, I'm coming with you, so let's go.'

## CHAPTER TWENTY-TWO

I wait at Bettina's while Niall takes her to her mother's to drop Tyler off. I pace around the house wondering why I didn't go with them rather than hanging around here, but it had been agreed they would return to the house, so we could think of the best way to approach things. I just want to be out there looking for my kid. I'm surprised the police haven't called with any updates, and then I remember. Of course, my mobile. I try to call Monique's home number, but it just goes to the machine. I leave a message.

'Mon, it's me. I don't know why you've taken Joe. Please don't hurt him and please ring me. I thought we were friends.' I don't know what else to say and feel my voice breaking on the words, so I hang up. I open the keypad and text the same message to her mobile. I sit on my knees next to the window ledge and pray that she'll make contact and bring me back my son.

Niall and Bettina return within twenty-five minutes. He looks at me hopefully and I watch his face drop as I have nothing to offer him.

'I've called and texted,' I state. 'Nothing yet.'

'We need to come up with a list of places she might have taken him,' says Niall. 'She's obviously not stupid enough to go back home.'

We sit and think and come up with the following:
*Coffee shop*
*Gym*
*Supermarket*
*Toy shops.*
'It's a start,' says Niall. 'Let's go.'

We spend a few hours trailing around all the places we can think of, but find nothing. It's early evening and though still light, it's beginning to fade. It strikes me that I might have to spend the whole evening without my son. From there I start to think what if I never get him back, never see him again?

'I think for now we need to go back home,' says Niall. 'We'll leave it to the police and try again tomorrow morning.'

'We can't give up, Niall. We have to keep looking.'

'We need rest and some food. Remember what you're always saying to Joe? A car can't run without petrol? Well you need to take your own advice. We'll go home, get some food and rest, and then we'll take it from there, okay? If we think of anywhere else to look tonight, I promise, I'll be the first one out of the door.'

My shoulders slump and I sit back in the front seat of the car. My eyes scan the road all the way back to Bettina's mother's house.

'Ring me if there's anything, and if you go back out. I want to be there. I have my own issues with that bitch.'

'We'll keep you informed,' says Niall, 'but any issues you have, you need to keep a hold of. Joe's our concern right now. Not the reasons she wanted to hurt us.'

Bettina looks contrite. 'You're right, of course. I'm sorry, I'm just tired. I can't imagine what you're going through. When I think about it I just get so damn angry.'

'Get some rest,' says Niall, 'We'll ring you later.'

'Right now, I just want to hug my son,' she says. 'Oh my god, I'm sorry, that was really insensitive.'

'No it's not, it's what any mum would do,' I say. 'Go and hug him, Bettina, and don't let him go.'

With Bettina dropped off, we drive back to our own house in silence, both too busy searching the streets. We wander around inside. The house seems so empty, and quiet. My insides twist. I can feel the impression of Joe in the house, echoes of him running around making noises as his Lego figures begin battles with each other, or his voice shouting 'Muuuuuum, I need you.' I walk upstairs and into his bedroom. It's a complete mess. There are figures all over the floor. His pyjamas are thrown in a heap where he took them off, and the books and magazines he's read are strewn across the bookshelves rather than being placed back in a tidy order. I think of all the times I've nagged him to tidy his bedroom and now I just want to see him in this room, being Joe; a messy, nine-year-old kid. I don't need to close his bedroom curtains, yet I do. I see his bedtime pal, a soft blue rabbit that he still takes to bed; a reminder to me that he's still my little boy, no matter how fast he seems to be growing up. I curl up on his bed with the rabbit and hold it close, breathing in the smell of Joe on it, and wondering where my son will be spending the night, praying he is safe and warm. I tell Joe goodnight and hope wherever he is he can hear me. I fall asleep on his bed, stress making me blank everything out.

For a few blissful moments when I wake, I have peace, and then it all floods back. How can I have fallen asleep while my son is missing? I don't know what the time is, but it's becoming lighter. I run to our bedroom where Niall is asleep, sitting up in bed, my mobile at the side of his own. I pick it up but there are no messages or missed calls. It does inform me however that it has just passed five am. I ring Monique's number again.

'Mum?'

'Joe? Oh my god, Joe. Are you okay?'

Niall shoots up in bed. 'You've got him?'

I wave a finger to warn him to be quiet.

'Hi, Mum. You have to be quiet because Auntie Mon is sleeping. She was awake nearly all night. You've nearly woke her up. It's really early you know?'

'Joe, where are you? Do you know?'

'Have you forgotten silly? Auntie Mon said she'd told you where we were going. She said it was a surprise.'

'Is Matt with you?'

'No. Auntie Mon took him home. It's been awesome, Mum. She's bought me new clothes and toys and everything.'

'Joe, listen to me. I've forgotten where she said she was taking you. Can you tell me?'

'We're in Manchester. We've been to the Science and Industry Museum, and today she's taking me to Legoland Discovery. She's promised me loads of Legos.'

'Joe, something's happened and I need you back home. Nothing to worry about, but the police need to see Monique.'

'Has her mum died?'

'No, but it's something like that. I don't want you to worry her, so I'm going to come and get you both, and I don't want you to tell her anything okay? Not even that you've talked to me. Can you do that?'

'Course I can. I'm not two.'

'Do you know where you are?'

'We're in a hotel called Doubletree. It's easy to remember because you just have to think of two trees. It's near the train station because we didn't have to walk far. I need to go now, Mum, Auntie Mon's waking up.'

'Okay, sweetie. Try to stay at the hotel as long as you can.'

'Okay, Mum.'

He hangs up and I shout all the details at Niall. He calls the police and I ring Bettina, while throwing things in my handbag.

The police tell us to wait to hear from them. We have no intention of waiting in Sheffield, so they agree that we can travel to Manchester, and we arrange to sit in a cafe upstairs in Piccadilly Train Station.

. . .

I've never known such extremes of time. The journey was fraught and passed in the blink of an eye, we were so busy trying to rush there. Now waiting at this station, I feel like I'm in a scene from The Matrix, like time is passing so slowly I can see people moving in extreme slow motion. A policeman comes upstairs and approaches us; he's an older guy, grey and balding. He's overweight and I wonder how he can possibly run after anyone who might have my son. They surely should all be built like Superman. But of course he isn't a superhero, he's just an ordinary person. I simultaneously feel sorry for the fat copper at the same time as I want to grab every fit young person in the train station and get them to help us.

He sits down alongside us and introduces himself as PC Trevor Irwin. The three of us are sitting with untouched drinks, bought only because we felt we needed to justify taking up the seats.

We all wait for him to speak. It's the longest moment of my life to date.

He places his hands on his knees. 'I'm sorry, but they'd checked out before we got there.'

It's too much. I hunch over and clutch my head in my hands. 'They can't be far. How could you let them get away? Niall, oh God, Niall.'

He places his arm around me. 'Sssshhh, it's okay.'

'What if we never find him?'

I place my hands over my eyes. He's gone again. This morning he seemed within reach, and now he could be anywhere.

'We've got people stationed at Lego Discovery,' says PC Irwin.

'She'll not go there now,' I say. 'Joe either told her I'd called, or she figured it out. Either way, she'll be on her way somewhere else by now.'

'Well at least you can feel reassured that she's keeping him safe.'

'Reassured?' I shout and others in the cafe turn and look at us. 'She could be doing anything to him.'

He turns and places a hand on my arm. I want to smack it off.

'Does she have a good relationship with your son? You said he seemed happy when he called? Maybe she's genuinely taken him on a break.'

'Niall, get this man away from me, or I swear to God...'

'With all respect, PC Irwin, our son has been abducted by someone with a Personality Disorder. Hence the great police intervention.'

'Okay, Mr Lawler, fair enough. I just hoped it could be a mistake. We're doing all we can.'

'She could hurt him,' I say. 'When she's caught she's going to end up in prison, so what does she have to lose?'

'There's a big difference between kidnapping and murder, Mrs Lawler, and to be honest, if she's really lost it upstairs,' PC Irwin points to his forehead as if I don't understand what he means, 'it's a psychiatric ward that'll end up with her.'

'You mean she can kidnap my son and not even go to jail?'

'If she's mad, they usually end up in a secure ward like Rampton, near Nottingham. That'd be my bet with someone like her.'

'Do they let them out?'

'Depends on what they've done, and if they're able to function in society again.'

'So potentially she could walk free?'

'Yeah, if they feel she's recovered.'

'That's ridiculous.'

'Yeah, well that's the system. Between you and me I can't say I agree with it. I'll be glad when I retire in a few years. All I do is arrest folks and watch half of them walk free. The others aren't inside for two minutes before they're back out robbing innocent folks, but anyway, you don't need to hear my moaning. We'll keep in touch, but for now, you need to decide whether to stay in Manchester or head back home.'

I look at Niall.

'We'll head back home,' he says. 'I doubt she's still in Manchester.'

It's then that PC Irwin's radio crackles into action.

'Excuse me a moment.'

He walks over to the edge of the coffee section. I wait a moment and then jump up and follow him. If there's news, I want to listen. From this point you can look out over the crowds of people arriving in Manchester or rushing to catch trains out of here. They resemble little busy worker ants—everyone doing a job they think is important when really in the scheme of things, it's a small part of everything. I consider all these people with their own stories. I wonder if anyone else's is as hellish as ours is right now? Are Joe and Monique maybe down there somewhere?

PC Irwin turns to me. 'Well there's nothing with regards to Miss Henry and little Joe, but they've arrested a Dr Matt Bailey. Apparently, he had the brass neck to turn up for work today.'

'That's it then.' Niall stands up and looks from the copper, to myself and Bettina. 'He's our best lead, so let's head back to Sheffield.'

We actually start to feel a little hungry, so we stop off at a McDonald's drive thru for a small meal. I order a happy meal and put the toy that comes with it safely away in the glove box to give to Joe when he's finally home. I have to believe he will be back soon. While we're parked, I decide to send another text to Monique, not that she's answered the several I've sent so far.

**We can get past this, whatever the problem is. Don't make it worse, send Joe home. Put him on a train, he'll be fine. I'll wait at the station for him. Just please let him come home.**

'The police told you not to contact her, they have strict procedures,' Niall huffs and looks at me, 'but then again, when have you ever done as you're told? You're wasting your time, you know?'

I turn my head away from him in disgust and look out of the window.

Bettina rings home to check that Tyler is okay. 'He's not missing me at all; being spoilt rotten by his grandmother. Apparently, she's let him have chocolate for lunch. *Chocolate*.'

It brings a rare smile to my face. In the school holidays, Joe and I quite often eat a chocolate breakfast from the secret stash I keep hidden upstairs away from the two male chocoholics in my home. It means we can laze around in bed until lunchtime, watching TV. Then when Niall gets home from work, we tease him by saying we had a pyjama morning and he pretends to be disgusted that we had chocolate for breakfast. Good times, and I have to believe, to have faith, that those times will be back. I vow to let Joe have a chocolate breakfast once he's back with us.

'Sounds yummy to me.' I say.

'What is?'

'A chocolate lunch.'

'Lauren, I said that over five minutes ago.'

'Oh, sorry.'

'Why don't you rest your head and try to catch a bit of sleep?' says Niall. 'We've got about another thirty minutes before we're home. You look all in.'

I do as he says and shut my eyes. The food in my belly and the lull of the car take over and give me half an hour of peace from the current hell of existence.


We drop Bettina off at her mother's once again. It begins to feel like Groundhog Day. Niall promises to let her know as soon as we hear anything. We've been home less than half an hour when there's a knock at the door. Why does no one ever ring the doorbell? It's PC Sheldon, the local bobby who we first met when the burglary had happened.

'Hello, Mr and Mrs Lawler. I've just come to update you on our interview with Dr Bailey. Can I come in?'

We show him through to the living room. We are so calm and well mannered, when I know that all Niall and I really want to do is yell at him to tell us what's going on. Niall goes through the motions of asking if he wants a drink and he says yes. I am in turmoil inside, and this guy wants us to wait while we get him a drink? This is another Matrix scene that extends on for what seems like twenty minutes but can only really be about three.

PC Sheldon wriggles his bottom on the sofa to get in a comfy position and thanks Niall for the tea placed in his hands.

'You'd be amazed how many people don't offer you a drink. I'm parched. I've not had a chance to call anywhere for one, been really busy today.'

'No problem,' says Niall. 'What do you have to tell us?'

'Right,' says PC Sheldon sitting forwards. 'We've had Matt Bailey in custody since nine-thirty this morning when, as I believe you've been told, he turned up to work. He was accompanied to the station where he requested legal representation and was then interviewed.'

'Does he know what she wants with Joe, and did he say why he'd been helping Monique?' Niall asks.

'It appears he's been rather duped by Miss Henry. She told him that you, Mrs Lawler, had stolen Mr Lawler,' he nods towards Niall, 'away from her, and that you'd taken away their adopted son Joe.'

'What?'

'Indeed. He says he had no reason to disbelieve her. She showed him photos of herself with Joe—'

'Photos *we've* taken of her with our son?' I say.

'Well, anyway, he was convinced. In relation to the crash into your husband's car, she got him to ask a colleague to be a witness against Mr Lawler, so that you,' he again nods at Niall, 'would be blamed.' She told him she was trying to discredit Mr Lawler as a father figure in order to get her son back. Matt Bailey, for all his brains as a doctor, obviously must have left his decisions to another part of his anatomy.'

Niall looks at him, unamused, and the policeman flushes slightly and coughs.

'Anyway, she then told him that Mrs Lawler had been violent

with Joe, and he agreed to help get him back after school, thinking that she was going to take him home and call social services. She dropped him off home saying she'd be in touch when she had things sorted and that was the last he'd heard. He's rather shocked at the reality of the situation.'

'I'd like five minutes with that man alone,' says Niall. 'Can you arrange it?'

'I'm afraid not, although I do understand how you must be feeling.'

Niall looks at him with such menace and fire, I imagine PC Sheldon's eyebrows singeing off.

'I haven't had personal experience of kidnap, but I do have to handle delivering and hearing bad news day in and day out; some of the things that happen to people,' he pauses, 'well, let's just say that I've felt similar to how you must feel now.'

I look at PC Sheldon. His youth belies the fact that during his career he's no doubt been the bearer of bad news, over and over again.

'I know what you're trying to say,' I tell him, 'and of course you can't beat him up, Niall, however you feel. He's just another misguided fool who took in what she said—like me, in fact. Do you want five minutes in a room with me with what I've let happen to Joe?'

'Don't be ridiculous.' He stands up and smacks his fist into the door—the same fist that had punched Seb in the eye.

'Dear God,' I state. 'Give me strength.' I go and fetch a bag of frozen vegetables and a tea-towel from the kitchen. I hand them to him. Both he and PC Sheldon have sat in perfect silence while I've done this.

'I still don't understand why she's doing this to us. I haven't done anything to her. Do you think she's one of those people who have gone mad because they haven't got kids? She faked a miscarriage, you know?'

'I don't know,' PC Sheldon answers honestly. 'It's usually a baby that's taken in that sort of case.'"Well, if that's all,' I say, 'we'd like to be alone for a while.'

'Oh, of course. They're charging Dr Bailey with—'

I hold my hand up. 'I don't really care what happens to him. He's nothing to me. I just want my son back.'

He nods.

I let him out and return to the living room. My phone beeps. I run to it and look at the screen.

***17 Ruskley Park Road. Bring Bettina and no police. If I see a policeman I'm out of here with your son. You want him, I want Bettina. I'll swap you. Seven pm.***

'Niall,' I gasp. 'It's her.'

## CHAPTER TWENTY-THREE

We spend the next couple of hours debating whether or not to call the police. We agree we won't at this time, but make sure we have our mobiles close to hand. I put my panic alarm just inside the top of my pants. We agree to travel in separate cars. Niall still has his courtesy car that hopefully Monique won't have seen. He works out a route that means he'll be parked further down the street, while I will be there with Bettina. We call her and not surprisingly, faced with such a situation, she says she needs time to think about it and will call us back.

'No. I'm on my way to yours now,' I say. 'Do not phone the police and put my son's life at risk; but have a decision of whether or not you're coming when I get there.'

I pull up outside her mum's house at six-fifteen. There's no way I'm being late. I run up to the doorway and ring the bell. Bettina comes to the door; she's still in her slippers.

I fold my arms. 'So you're not coming then? Do you not care about my son?'

'I don't know what to do, Lauren. If she does something to me, she would potentially leave Tyler without a mother. He's already got a waste of space for a dad.'

I grip my head in my hands, messing up my hair. 'But if you don't go, she might harm Joe and I'd never see him again. Can you live with yourself if something happens to him? Well, can you?'

'No.' She sighs and grabs her coat and stuffs her feet in her shoes. 'I'm just going to tell them I'm going out.'

Five minutes pass. I can't keep my legs and arms still and keep looking at my watch.

She appears in the doorway with her bag.

'Come on, or we'll be late,' I yell.

'I've just been saying goodbye to my son and mother, Lauren. How do I know I'll even be back?'

'Because we aren't going to let anything happen to each other,' I look her directly in the eyes. 'We're in this together, whatever the reason, remember?'

We arrive at the given address and knock. Monique looks out of the door and quickly up and down the street, as if expecting armed policemen to be surrounding her house.

'We didn't ring the police, Monique. Where's Joe?'

She looks completely unruffled and unfazed. 'He's inside, all packed and ready to go. He's fine, Lauren. I wouldn't have hurt him.'

My eyes narrow. 'No, kidnapping won't have done him any harm at all.'

'He doesn't have a clue about that. He thinks it was a special trip with Auntie Mon, and if you've any sense you'll keep it that way.' She smiles. 'We've had a good time.'

I have to hold my own hands tightly as I want to punch her, but I want Joe more.

'Okay,' she says, 'so here's what we do. You come inside to collect Joe, and then you leave. 'She', she points at Bettina, 'stays. I need to speak to her.'

'I have another idea,' I say. 'I want to know why you've done this and why I was involved, so let Joe come out and walk down the road to Niall's car.'

Monique's eyes shoot down the street and she attempts to slam the door, but I'm too fast and hold it open. 'There are no police, it's just Niall. Let him take Joe home and let me and Bettina in.'

She considers this for a minute. 'Suit yourself. Just don't try anything funny.' She flashes us a kitchen knife from within her pocket and opens the door.

'Muuuuuuum,' Joe runs up to me with the biggest hug. I will never moan about hearing him repeat this familiar word over and over ever again. It's the most beautiful sound I've ever heard, next to his first cry as he entered the world and my life. 'I have had the best time. Auntie Mon has spoilt me to death.'

The word death makes me gasp; it could so easily have been that tragic.

'Well, your dad's waiting for you down the road,' I say, 'so get your stuff together because he can't wait to see you.'

'Oki-doki. Look at this Lego, Mum; it's Loki and Iron Man and—'

'Joe, I promise I'll spend as long as you want looking at your new toys later, but right now you need a cuddle with your dad and to have a bath.'

He runs off to get his stuff and we stand and wait for him in perfect silence. He's back within a couple of minutes with a heaving duffle bag and a carrier bag full of new things. He throws himself at Monique, arms outstretched. 'Thanks, Auntie Mon, that was brilliant. Can we do it again sometime?'

She reaches down to him and looks at me, her mouth forming a smirk while she strokes her hand down my son's hair. 'Well that'll be up to your mum now, won't it? But I'd absolutely love to.'

He comes and gets hold of my hand, something he doesn't do very often now he's nine, and definitely not in public. 'Right, I'm ready, Mum.'

'Okay, darling. Well, I'll be home really soon, but me and Bettina just need to stay with Monique a little while.'

'Oh, is that because of Auntie Mon's mummy? You were wrong. She said she's fine now, so you don't need to worry.'

'No, it's something else. Your dad's brought his car. I'll show you where he's parked.' I walk to the door. 'I won't be long and then I'm going to read you so many bedtime stories when I get back you'll be begging me to stop and let you sleep.'

'That won't ever happen, Mum. I can stay up until midnight. Are you having a bit of girly time? Dad says you talk about shoes non-stop. I thought it was boring, but I guess it's just like me liking Lego.'

'It is, and yes that's what we're going to do, just for a little while, because we've missed Monique.'

I open the door and I needn't have worried about him getting to Niall; he's outside the door. He grabs Joe in a hug. I give him a warning look and Niall bets him to a race to see who can reach the car first. I reach into my pocket and press the send button on the text I typed in earlier.

**Give me one hour after you get home and then call the police.**

It's timely because Monique picks up a glass bowl off her side and holds it out. 'Mobile phones in here please.' My heart thuds. If she looks at my phone, this will be a disaster.

We do as requested and thankfully she just places the bowl on a high up shelf.

'I don't like being left two against one, so for now, Bettina, I'd be very grateful if you'd go in here.' Monique opens a door to our right. It opens into a large closet. 'There's no window, so you won't be able to shout for help, but there's a light and a single bed in there to sit on.'

I nod at Bettina and she goes in.

Monique slides a hook and eye across the door closing.

'This way, Lo,' she says pointing to the living room, which is small and basically furnished. There's a feature wall painted light blue, and navy cord carpet with pink floral curtains. 'Oh, Lauren. You're dying to know what's happening, aren't you? This,' she sweeps her hand around the room, 'is one of my rentals. My dad left me some money when he died and I invested it in property. It's recently become vacant, though it's rented again from next month.' She smiles. 'Where did you think my money comes from? I only work three days a week.'

I had honestly never given it a thought.

'I wish you could see your face,' she laughs. 'You've been provided for, and for so long, that you've no idea what the cost of living is. Well I'll give you a little tip, Lo, when you leave here, try to stand on your own two feet, because the pathetic, hard done by, bored housewife thing is sooo last year.'

'So, you were never genuinely my friend?' I ask.

'Oh no, that's where you're wrong,' she says. 'Take a seat. Let's have our usual coffee, shall we? I always enjoy them.' She gets up to head into the kitchen and turns back, seeing me eyeing the door keeping Bettina in. 'Make any moves towards that door and I'll walk in there and stab her. Or maybe,' she gets the knife from her pocket and looks at it, 'I'll do you, and then there'll be no bedtime stories for Joe after all.'

I sink into the chair and wait for her to return.

She places the coffee in front of me. I have no intention of drinking it but take pretend sips. I don't trust her; it could have anything in it. She looks at me, smiling.

'If I was going to do something to you, I could think of better things than spiking your coffee; maybe cutting your car brakes, or something. That would have been interesting.'

I look at her in horror and she cackles with laughter.

'I'm joking, Lauren. Oh dear, I fear our friendship is forever ruined. Oh well.'

The woman is sick in the head. I don't know why I came for an explanation. We should have tried to overpower her while we had the chance.

'Why do you want to talk to Bettina?'

She runs her hands through her hair. 'I want Tyler.'

I shake my head. 'You are joking?'

She crosses her legs. 'That child is the one thing that's kept Danny and I apart all these years. I get Tyler. I get Danny.'

I roll my eyes. 'I can see you now, "Mum of the Year".'

Monique affords me a sickly-sweet smile. 'I don't need to be a fantastic mother. Danny can afford nannies. I just need the child to be ours.'

'You're insane.'

I'm not prepared as she punches me in the nose. I feel a burning sensation, followed by a trickle running from my nostril.

'Let's not forget where we are, and who is calling the shots here, Lauren. Now, I suggest you sit there and be quiet, or I'll kick you out and start on your friend.'

I nod. My nose is throbbing. Monique hands me a tissue from the coffee table.

'Clean yourself up. God, I'm always having to look out for your appearance.'

She looks at her hand as if I might have ruined her manicure with my nose. 'I've followed Leeds United since I was young, you know? My dad got me into it. After Toby left I didn't know what to do with myself, so I started going to games again. I met Danny in the local bar the team went to after matches. He was an amazing player, and so sexy. He told me what a bitch his wife was and that he was only staying with her because of their kid. He said she'd got pregnant to trap him, and that they'd been together since school. He tried to dump her, but he was stuck with her because of the kid. I told him I never wanted children and he thought that was fantastic. We fell in love.'

I want to laugh, to ask her if she's heard herself. She sounds like a fourteen-year-old with a crush, not a grown woman, but I keep my mouth shut and continue to listen.

'We saw each other for months. I asked him to leave her and move in with me. He'd still see the kid on the weekends, but he'd be child free the rest of the time. He told me I must be joking. He didn't want to be a part-time dad; the football took him away often enough. So I suggested he try to get custody of Tyler and I'd help him. He told me all about her fixation with you. He was going to exploit that and make her seem crazy. I thought then we'd be together.' She puts her drink down on the mat hard. 'But he told me he didn't need another wife, he could have his needs met by any number of bimbos hanging around the club, and he finished with me.' She smiles to herself. 'I decided I would play the long game. I knew the marriage wouldn't last, and in the meantime, I wanted to be friends with the girl who had never fallen for Bettina's charm. The one person who'd got into his wife's mind and messed with her head.'

'Me.' I state.

'It didn't take long to track you down. A bit of Googling and Facebook and I soon had your details. You really should tighten up your security settings, Lo.'

I did—after friending Seb.

'So that was that. I met you at yoga and surprisingly, I genuinely clicked with you. I really was your best friend.'

She looks at me for a few seconds. Does she expect me to thank her?

'But then of course Bettina came back and you made friends with her. The *one* person I expected to tell her to take a running jump, and you fucking befriended her. Then the stupid bitch asks to come to the cinema with me. *You* were *my* friend, not hers.' She wrings her hands. 'YOU RUINED EVERYTHING,' she roars.

I wrap my arms around myself. 'W-why the fake pregnancy and miscarriage?'

'To get you to spend some time *with me*; away from Niall and Joe, and Bettina, and from whatever the fuck was going on with Seb. I was losing you, Lauren. You hurt me.'

'Why did you take Joe? You know what he means to me. How could you do that?'

'I panicked. I knew you'd seen the photos and jewellery, so I got

Matt to help me to get Joe. God that man's gullible—great lay though. I figured if I had Joe you'd hold off the police, but you didn't, did you? So now I'm left in this situation. Anyway, I figured we could come to some arrangement, so here you are. You can say I was innocent, and we'll get Bettina to confess to the crimes.'

Monique's eyes glitter. 'If she wants to keep Tyler safe, she'll do it. I'll take Tyler to visit his dad in prison. Once he's released, which of course, he will be, we can live together somewhere.'

Her speech becomes rapid. 'He could get a transfer to Real Madrid, maybe even Barcelona.' She looks at me, a pitying smile on her face. 'Me and Danny have a connection. That's how I always knew Niall wasn't the one for you. You don't get each other like me and Danny do. He's the only man I've ever really loved, and once I have Tyler we can all be together.'

She gets up and reaches for my coffee cup. 'What a waste of good coffee,' she says. I snatch my alarm out from my waistband and blast it into her ear. She wobbles backward, dropping the coffee and I upend the coffee table, knocking her to the floor. I fly out of the room, past the spare room door and flip the latch. Bettina hurtles through the door, grabbing the bowl with our phones, and we race outside to my car. I'm fumbling with my key fob to get the car open and just manage it as Monique races out of the house shouting, 'I should never have let Joe go, you traitorous bitch.'

'Get in the car,' I yell at Bettina. She hesitates. 'Do it,' I shout.

I judge that I might not make it around to the driver's side, so I run to the back of the car and flip the boot open. Inside is the carved mask I bought in the coffee shop. As Monique rushes towards me, waving the kitchen knife, I swing the mask with all my strength. It hits her head and I watch her drop to the floor. Then aware that she might yet get up again, I run and dive into the driver's seat. 'Hold on,' I yell at Bettina. I check my mirrors. There is no one around. One more look behind me and I see Monique beginning to get up, clutching her head. I put the gear stick in reverse and start to accelerate. I take off the handbrake, let up the clutch and shoot backwards.

There's a large thump. We're lucky not to have hurt ourselves with the whiplash as the car jerks. I sit behind the wheel, my heartbeat thudding in my chest. I turn to Bettina. 'That was an accident.'

Her face has drained of colour and she looks like she's going to be sick, but she nods her head. 'Absolutely.'

She reaches for my hand. I squeeze hers tightly.

I hear sirens in the distance and in a few minutes police cars and an ambulance appear. Niall came through and called them. We get out of the car and they take us to the ambulance, where our shoulders are covered with blankets. A number of policemen gather around the back of the car. Monique is covered in a blanket as well, only hers stretches the whole way over her body.

# EPILOGUE

Things moved quickly after that. The police concluded that Monique's death was an accident, caused by us trying to get away from the house with her in pursuit holding a weapon. I sold the car soon after. I couldn't bear to see it again.

Joe and Tyler had the last two weeks off school due to the publicity surrounding the case. I sat with Joe and told him about Monique. I skirted around the main issues and just said that she had mental health problems and her death was a tragic accident. I've kept newspapers out of his way, but I know he'll find out the truth one day. Being nine years old, Joe accepted what I told him. He and Tyler seemed more bothered that they got eight weeks off school instead of six. They spent the last two weeks of term at each other's house, playing Lego. It must be good to be nine, able to deal with things so easily.

We put our house up for sale, and while we await a buyer, we are living with Niall's mum and dad. Niall got a transfer to a post in Stafford Hospital. His employers were really helpful with his transfer, possibly because his infamy was stopping a lot of people from getting on with their work. I am enjoying having the security of family around me. We are being spoilt rotten as Rebecca cooks most of the meals and insists that we have at least one 'date night' a week. This means that Niall and me are enjoying some alone time, though we desperately miss Joe, even if it's just for one evening. We can't help it. I think we'll always be a bit overprotective now.

I spend loads of time with Joe though. He started his new school a few weeks ago and has made a few friends already, though he says he misses Tyler. I make sure I'm there to take him and collect him every day. I realise it's not practical and hopefully sometime soon I'll be able to trust Glen or Rebecca to pick him up occasionally, but for now it has to be me. That's just the way it is and they understand.

Niall and I are getting there slowly. Like I've said, relationships take work and they're not always on an up, but the time we're getting together is helping us heal. We're seeing a marriage counsellor and Niall knows how close I came to cheating on him with Seb. We're both accepting some responsibility. I'm positive about our future.

Mrs Sullivan told me that Seb moved to Australia as planned and was settling in well. She wrote me a lovely reference to take with me to Stafford and I'm volunteering as a teaching assistant at the local school (the one Joe goes to, but I don't look after his class, that would be too embarrassing for him). I'm hoping that eventually it will lead to paid work, but for now I'm just enjoying the interaction with the children. I look out for the quiet ones who are singled out by others; I try to help raise their confidence. I realise that being in touch with Mrs Sullivan means that I have a link to Seb. I hope one day I'll hear that he's met someone and settled down. She'll be a lucky woman, and I'll always be slightly jealous.

I left the eBay account closed. I no longer find the need to search and scour for bargains and look closer to home for any comfort I need. I gave my jewellery away to charity as I felt it was tainted after being in Monique's hands.

Niall was cleared of being responsible for the car accident and Matt Bailey's insurers paid out. His job as a doctor is under review, but we know how hard it is to lose your license to practice in a medical establishment; maybe his forthcoming court case will be more productive.

The insurance paid out on the damage to my belongings. I've put most of it in the bank. Maybe we'll have a holiday, though being in Staffordshire so far, with the countryside, fresh air and animals feels like a permanent one anyway.

Once we left for Stafford, Bettina and I agreed to no longer stay in touch. It was felt that we knew far too much about each other's lives; it was an unhealthy relationship and would be difficult to maintain over a distance anyway. She can now have the fresh start she needs, now the fuss is dying down. We looked at each other in mutual understanding as we said goodbye for the last time; some things were never to be spoken about.

Danny is still on remand for manslaughter. He's expected to be sentenced and remain behind bars for a number of years.

I told Niall I deliberately reversed over Monique, for we have no secrets now. He was shocked but said if the circumstances were reversed and he was behind the wheel he's sure he would have done the same. Niall, Bettina, and I therefore hold this secret between us. I'm sorry but I can't even regret it.

Monique's family were notified of her death. We didn't attend the funeral, so I don't know which, if any, of her family turned out to say goodbye. I wonder what her own family history was, whether it had affected who she was as a person? I no longer feel defined by my own. I'm a strong individual now, as well as whole within my family unit.

I make my last visit to Sheffield. I walk through the churchyard, my boots kicking up gravel as I walk. I search for the mound of newly dug earth. Locating it, I place a wreath of black flowers on the grave. They're identical to the ones she sent to my house for my best friend. It's only right she received them.

'Goodbye, Monique. Rest in Peace.' I say. I know that I can rest in peace myself, now that Monique is underneath.

## THE END

Ready for another story that could take place on 'a street where you live'? Read on for SAVE HER.

# MINE

# PART 1

# MELISSA

# CHAPTER ONE

SAM

30 August 2014

People are abhorrent. Before, I was tolerant, friendly, with the human emotion of wishing to be liked, adored even. I thought I was. What a stupid, ignorant bitch. Now as people talk, I watch their mouths twist into different shapes as they deliver their subjective wisdom. If only they knew that while I pick up on small phrases I can acknowledge with a small smile or a nod of my head, my mind visualises wrapping my hands around their neck and squeezing until their eyes bulge, blood vessels bursting, and they beg for their life. Why not think of that the next time you speak to your friends. Is what you're saying so important that you'd fight to speak it if denied your breath?

I spend hours studying people. Like the fat woman who just stuffed half a pasty in her mouth with one great push of her hand. Don't judge me. I have no problem with anyone's appearance. I wasn't always this slim. What makes my face grimace is the inelegance of how she ate it. I want to force my fingers down her throat and make her throw up every morsel. I'd show her the regurgitated lumps where the food remained solid because she couldn't take the time to chew or taste her food. Then I'd make her eat it again, this time with style.

Then there are the clone-like faces of the technological revolution. Robotic on their bus seats. Tap, tap, tap, go their fingers. I'll sit near them, smirking. They're unaware of me considering how I could stab them, and they'd never see it coming. Their puckered mouths would form an 'O' as I smiled and rang the bell. I'd depart the bus, leaving them bleeding with no one the wiser as they're all too busy telling relatives they are on the bus, playing Candy Crush, or seeing what amazing statuses their fake friends have posted on social media. People they've never met get more acknowledgement than I do, although I travel with them every day.

But I distract myself. I have a story to tell. Because I wasn't always like this. Once, I was kind. Before *him*.

'S-Sam?'

I blink and come to. Remember where I am. I'd lost myself for a minute there.

I sigh. What sort of therapist stutters? Mine has sweat pouring down his face for fuck's sake.

The room is an ambient temperature. Light would enter the room from the small window if the blind wasn't closed. My fingers grip the edge of my chair as I attempt to control myself.

My therapist wipes the sweat off his forehead with a shaky hand. He disgusts me. He needs a good wash.

'So, Sam. Would you like to tell me why you are h-here?'

I smile. I should try to keep hold of my emotions, but I can't help myself. A laugh threatens to break. Instead, a smile hurts my cheek as it stretches my face.

'I think therapy will be so much fun. I can't wait to explore my fucked-up mind with you.'

A flash of terror crosses his face. A brief moment before his cold mask returns. But that one glimpse of fear makes my pussy wet.

His Adam's apple rises and falls. 'So, you made this appointment Sam. Where do you want to begin?'

I push my tongue into my cheek and consider my position while I stare at him. Then I sit up straight, and a smirk teases the edge of my lips a second time. 'I'll tell you how I met Edward. I think that's as good a place as any to start.'

The adrenaline pumps through my veins. It feels good. It's been a long time since I felt in charge. Like I was winning.

# CHAPTER TWO

SAM
July 2013

It's my first day of employment at Bailey's Accountants. The interview had been a breeze. Take a middle-aged man called Jacobs and present him with a slim, blue-eyed blonde. I'd run my fingers through my cropped hair. Thought about the questions asked while placing a finger against my perfect pout. I repeatedly flicked my tongue against perfect white teeth. Let's face it, he wasn't appraising me for the post, he imagined my mouth around his cock. I'd kept my skirt knee-length, but it still seemed inappropriate given the length of my legs. During the interview, I'd crossed and uncrossed my gym bunny calves so he could imagine them wrapped around him, squeezing out his orgasm. A perfectly orchestrated interview. I conducted myself impeccably, and so here I am – PA to Mr Edward Bonham. *Bon Homme*, good man. We'll see about that. I was surprised the man himself hadn't interviewed me but as I came to find out, assistants weren't that important to him.

I'm inducted to the job and given passwords to the computer systems. Introductions to other staff members are made. I've yet to work out who can assist me and who'll try to thwart me. Has he already fucked any of the staff here? Or does he keep his private life separate? That's what I'm here to discover.

First day. First mistake. I'm bawled out of his office for disturbing him before eight am. I'd thought I'd get brownie points for being early and efficient.

I storm into the staff room to get myself a drink of iced water. My hand shakes as I press and hold the ice button. Kerry, one of the other personal assistants, mistakes it for nerves rather than the murderous anger coursing through my veins.

'Did no one tell you about Mr Bonham's morning routine?' She bites on her bottom lip.

I smile widely at her. If she sees it doesn't reach my eyes, she doesn't let on. 'No, they didn't.'

'Gosh, sorry about that. Mr Bonham meditates for thirty minutes every morning. He's never to be disturbed. I think it's kind of like a ritual for him. Maybe he thinks it brings him luck? But for thirty minutes exactly, from eight to eight-thirty am he does it. Not one second outside of either time.'

I raise an eyebrow. 'So, I'm working for a weirdo?'

She shakes her head. 'No. You're working for one of the most focused men I've ever come across.'

I see the change in her pupils as she speaks of him. Girl crush o' clock.

I lean against the sink, blocking Kerry from filling the kettle in her hand. 'So, what's he really like? What do you think of him? Anything else I should be aware of?'

She stands and looks up at me through a thick fringe. 'There are some rumours about him. They're probably made up.'

I move away from the sink, giving her access to fill her kettle. 'Ooh, I love gossip. Tell me more.'

She bites her lip again as she turns the tap. Spray shoots out and wets her blouse. She sighs. 'I'm told he's just as focused in the bedroom as he is at work.'

'I thought he was married? He wears a ring.'

'He is. She's lovely. I think they're madly in love still. Have been since the day they met apparently, but there are rumours about his extra-curricular activities. I've never seen anything but devotion to his wife though.'

She gives another sigh, this time a dreamy one. 'Anyway, I'd better get back. Jack – Mr Simpson – he'll be wondering where his cup of tea is. I hope you enjoy your first day, Sam.'

I smile again before speaking. 'Thanks for the heads up. It's appreciated. It's hard being the new girl.'

She nods and leaves the room.

I pick up my drink of iced water, squeezing the plastic cup until it breaks apart in my hand. Water runs down my sleeve and drips onto the floor. I place ice in my mouth and hold it there until it burns my tongue. Pain. Now feeling focused, I throw the cup in the bin and return to the office.

Edward is six-foot-two. He has short dark hair, longer at the top and shaved at the sides. Every morning before work he trains in the gym. He has muscles on muscles. For a man who's going to turn fifty this year, he's in prime condition. Information gleaned because I've now been stalking him for a long time. I know many, many things about Mr Edward Bonham. But I need to break into his inner circle. Being a watcher is not an option anymore. It's time for action.

I stroll into his office, with my head held high.

'So, Sam, just so we can be clear -'

I put my hand up. Palm facing him, fingers outstretched. 'I've been briefed. My apologies. I wasn't aware. I won't set foot in the office until after eight-thirty am from now on.'

He nods. 'Thank you.'

'Just one thing though.' I fix him with a direct stare. 'I can take orders. I like order and I adore routine. But don't ever raise your voice to me again.'

He raises an eyebrow. 'But I'm the boss.'

I tilt my head, meeting his steely gaze. 'There are ways to be a boss and losing control and shouting at staff isn't one of them. I observed part of your meditation this morning. You seem like someone who prefers order and control in their life?'

The corner of his mouth twists.

'You can tell that by the fact I meditate in the morning?'

'No. I can tell by the fact it has to start at eight am and end at eight-thirty am precisely. I can walk through that door at eight-thirty-one every morning should it please you.'

He gasps and covers it quickly with a cough before he relaxes back in his seat. 'A morning coffee anytime from eight-thirty to nine am is fine, depending on the meetings or work I have scheduled. I need my PA to be adaptable to my timetable.'

'Noted. I'll make you a coffee right now.'

I head out of the room, but I don't go straight to the staff room. I hover at the periphery of the door and watch him.

He sits with his hand on his chin, absentmindedly stroking his jaw. Then he shakes his head and switches on his computer.

I'm aware my own plans may take time. But that's not a problem. There's never been a rush.

Back at my flat that evening, I prepared my usual salad. I also have a strict routine. Nothing but water passes my lips. From work, I'd visited the gym where my personal trainer put me through my paces for an hour. My evening ritual consisted of removing my blue contact lenses and then moisturising every part of my skin to keep it in pristine, soft, and supple condition. Next was to check my hair for root growth and apply dye if necessary. I did thirty minutes of yoga before bed and then prepared my work clothes for the next day, hanging them on the back of the bathroom door. Everything had to be perfectly so. All worked out and ordered. For every day was an act, a stage I'd prepared myself for. The performance had started.

## Present Day - 30 August 2014

'So why did you want to ruin this man?' His voice is calm again, controlled, no stutter.

I snigger. 'You're not a very experienced therapist, are you?'

He looks at the floor.

'Mr Therapist, we have to get to the crux of the matter slowly. You're supposed to guide me towards discovering the answers for myself. I'm not just going to come out and tell you why I've done the things I've done.' I leap up. 'Do you know what? I don't think this relationship is going to work out.'

'No,' he says firmly, through gritted teeth. 'As you say, I'm the therapist. Let me direct you, and we'll find the answers together.'

I sit back in my seat and smile. It would seem my therapist has found his balls. I'll delight in watching them retreat so far up he's in agony.

'Please continue, Sam. What happened next with Edward?'

I smirk. 'What indeed?'

# CHAPTER THREE

SAM

I knew it would be difficult to get to Ed. His discipline and regimented life meant that he didn't have room for anything outside of work and home. This is where meticulous planning and research came in. I had to know exactly what buttons to push to get him to consider something outside of his schedule, painstakingly plotted out in his electronic diary. Luckily, I have a friend, Bobby, who'll do anything for me.' My eyes drift towards the blind. 'He's a friend I made some time ago. We'll discuss him soon, but for now, all you need to know is that he's helped me a lot.'

Bobby made an appointment to see Ed. Under an assumed name of course. Ed was his usual highly professional self, taking his client out for dinner seeing as he looked like making a huge bonus from him. Then Bobby made a sexual harassment claim against Ed to Ed's boss, Jacobs.' I beam while I stare at my therapist. 'It was fantastic because meticulous, controlled Ed never fucks up and is so fucking loyal to his wife. His boss came to his office, and you could hear the raised voices all the way down the corridor. Aftershocks tore through the building's staff. Ed? Sexual harassment with another male? Surely there was some mistake. Wasn't he happily married? I owe Bobby so, so much. He gave me my way in. Ed tried to track him down but of course, he couldn't because the customer didn't exist. The damage was done anyway, because there's no smoke without fire, right? Staff chatted behind his back for weeks. He loathed it. I'd see him snap pencils while sitting at his desk, his jaw set and his mind deep in thought.'

I drift into past memories as I recount the story.

*After a few minutes, I went into the office unsure of what I would find.*

*'Mr Bonham? I heard the commotion. Is there anything I can—?'*

*'You can get the fuck out of my office, that's what you can do,' he snarled.*

*I slammed my hand on his desk. 'I warned you I wouldn't be spoken to like that. I've not fucked up here.'*

*His eyes widened. 'My, Ms Briers, you certainly take risks, confronting an angry man. What if I'd have lost my temper completely?'*

*I shook my head. 'I don't think you would. I think you know how to regain that control and harness it for use in other ways.'*

*He turned away, swivelling his chair towards the window. 'You know nothing about me.'*

*I spoke to the back of his head, my voice low in tone. 'I've seen how you are in your workspace, but you're right. I don't know anything about you. But I'm good at reading people. You like control. Today you lost it, for that brief moment when Mr Jacobs came in here. Now you'll claw it back. I bet you already have a scheme in your head on how to get your client to retract their complaint. I know you want Jacobs in here on his knees, apologising.'*

*Edward turned his chair around and narrowed his gaze. 'You're an intriguing assistant, Ms Briers. That's a lot you assume about me. Perhaps you have a crush and are building me up as a hero in your mind. It wouldn't be the first time it's happened. Women like a man in a position of power.'*

*I stood my ground. 'Don't belittle me or flatter yourself. Psychology interests me, yes. I did an A-level in the subject, and I watch programmes about it too. Watching your control is fascinating, but don't think for one minute I'd let you take me to bed. I'm not attracted to you so don't worry about any crushes here.'*

*His jaw tightened, then relaxed. 'Only my wife has been in my bed.'*

*'How lovely, and so rare these days. I hope she's as faithful as you are.'*

*He jumped back in his seat.*

*'What the hell-?'*

*My smirk returned. 'I'm just testing. I told you, I like studying people. Searching for their reactions.'*

*'You'd be as well not studying me.' A threat lay unspoken within his tone.*

*'Just make sure you treat me with the same respect you do all your other business associates, and we'll be fine. Now, I'll leave you to concentrate on what you're going to do to Jacobs.'*

*He opens a clenched fist and massages his fingers with his other hand. 'Why are you so interested in Jacobs?'*

*'Because something tells me it will be extraordinary. I get bored so easily, Mr Bonham. I've been unable to settle to any kind of career because I find most of my employment so mind-numbingly dull. Don't let me get bored here. I'm starting to enjoy myself.'*

*'Call me Ed,' he says.*

'For all his control, a simple bit of flattery at a weak moment and I had my way in.'

'What about guilt? Do you feel guilt over your actions?' my therapist asks.

'Everything I've done has been justified as far as I'm concerned. He didn't deserve to be happy, to have a happy marriage. I've taken from them what was taken from me. Why should they enjoy what I was denied?'

'How do you know they were happy? Most married couples have fucked-up lives behind closed doors.'

'Well, they thought they had it all. I witnessed enough of it.'

'Maybe you only saw what you wanted to see?'

I exhale deeply, my nostrils flaring.

'Perhaps we should move on. Maybe you could tell me something of your family? What were your parents like?'

At this, I laugh hysterically. Once I begin, I can't stop. Tears trail down my face and my jaw hurts from laughing so hard. 'Is that what you think therapy is? The psychotic have fucked-up childhoods that explain everything?'

He blanches. I watch another drop of sweat trickle down his cheek. I walk over to him, lean in, and lick it off his face.

He does his best to hold still. To give me no satisfaction from my action. Kudos. I'd have punched me.

I sit on the edge of the desk, peering down at him.

'I had an amazing childhood. My parents weren't rich by any stretch of the imagination, but they provided for me the best they could. I was loved. I had amazing toys. Fabulous holidays at the beach. I visited them twice a week until they died.'

'You lost your parents? You must have been very young. You can only be in your twenties now?'

'How and when I lost my parents is not something I'm willing to discuss. I'll get to it in due course.'

He sighs. 'I'm not sure what you want to get out of this therapy. Every time I ask you a question, you defer it, or you laugh at me. Is this all a joke?'

I narrow my eyes and lean toward him. 'It's far from a joke. I just thought it would be good for us to chat. In a controlled environment.'

'For how long? How long is this therapy session going to last? Can you answer me that question at least?'

He shakes his arm. The chain holding his right arm to the wall rattles. He's losing control. I don't know how much longer I can keep him here.

'It will take as long as it takes.'

He glares at me as his urine gushes down his leg and onto the floor. My punishment for his subordination.

I display no reaction. I leave the room, returning with a bucket, warm soapy water and a change of trousers. I don't speak to him again for the rest of the day.

## CHAPTER FOUR

MELISSA
February 1985

We move into our new home on the twentieth of February nineteen eighty-five. Number twenty-three Cyclamen Crescent. A beautiful name for a beautiful crescent of houses. As a self-employed electrician, Jarrod has built a reliable reputation, leaving many almost dependent on his services. This has meant I've stayed home to be a housewife. To cook, clean, care for him and to do the same for our children when they arrive.

Jarrod and I were childhood sweethearts. We met at nursery school, and our first wedding took place when we were six – in the year of decimalisation – with the class teacher as registrar and classmates as bridesmaids and guests. I doubt any of those people would believe we repeated the wedding and got married for real when we were the tender age of eighteen. Our wedding disco was filled with the sounds of Duran Duran, Spandau Ballet, and Culture Club.

After living with Jarrod's parents since we married, our new home is a diamond in a bed of coal. Jarrod has called in favours from his friends in the trade, and our house is stunning. I'm nervous about meeting the new neighbours, used to keeping out of the way and trying to be seen and not heard. It's strange when people come to our door to say hello and welcome us to the crescent. We're told it's always been a place where neighbours are close. They'll look out for us. Jarrod says that means they are nosy bastards, but I think it's sweet.

During the first week, I decide I'll bake and take my offerings around some of the neighbours. I'm not the best cook, but my baking's not so bad. I make several batches of jam tarts and place them in Tupperware boxes. I hope they'll give the boxes back - they were a wedding gift.

The first house I visit is Sandra's. I'm informed that Sandra and her husband Dave have lived here for the past seven years. She invites me in for a cup of tea. I enter, looking around to see if any of the other neighbours' curtains are twitching as they watch me go inside. It seems that kind of street.

'I'm so glad you called around, honey. You've picked a lovely place to come and live. Everyone here is just so friendly. Are you newlyweds?'

I smile and take a sip of my hot tea. 'We've been married two years officially, fourteen if you count our nursery school ceremony.' I take a worn Polaroid picture out of my bag and show her myself and Jarrod at our first ceremony. Then I take out a further photo showing us at the proper wedding.

'Oh, that's just adorable. You are both beyond cute.'

'Thank you.'

'Right, let's have a couple of those jam tarts of yours to go with this tea.' She hands me a side plate and then my own Tupperware box. 'So, where did you live before then?'

'Since the wedding, we lived with Jarrod's parents. We had two rooms upstairs, one as a bedroom and one as a sitting room.'

'Newlyweds? Sharing with the folks. That must have been difficult if you get what I mean.' She titters.

I blush.

'Oh, I'm sorry; I didn't mean to embarrass you. That's the problem with us all getting on so well around here. We're used to joking with each other.'

'I'm sure I'll get used to it.' I shrug. 'As you say, it's just different at the moment. I kind of feel like a nursery school child again. Playing houses.'

'Believe me, the novelty will wear off when you've done the washing for the umpteenth time, and then your husband gets home and gives you yet another set of dirty overalls, or in Dave's case, cricket attire. That's such a pain in the backside to clean.'

I can't imagine ever being bored of seeing Jarrod's face when he smiles at me or when I bring him his meal or fold away his washing. As for the sex, we didn't have it too often seeing as we were in his parents' house, but that should change now, once we get settled. With all the hours Jarrod works and the fact he gets home late sometimes, I'm not going to annoy him about it. I know he loves me. He tells me every day. In the next few years, we're going to start a family. Jarrod just wants to get a little more of a nest egg behind us as the new house has wiped out a lot of our savings.

'So, once you're settled in, a couple of times a week the guys have a card game. They take it in turns as to which house they play at. We ladies get together for an hour or two for a chat. Sometimes we'll have a clothes party. That's if you're interested? I don't want you to feel forced into anything.'

'Oh no, that'll be lovely.' I tell her. 'I'll get to know the other women on the street quicker. Jarrod often works late, but I'm sure he'll try to join in.'

'Well, just so you know you are welcome anytime. Mmmm, these jam tarts are delicious, Mel.'

Only my father and Jarrod call me Mel, so I bristle at this overfamiliarity. Then I chastise myself. She's being friendly. It's only a name.

I exhale. 'Oh, I'm pleased they're okay. I don't cook or bake very often. I was a little nervous they'd be too dry.'

'No, they're just right. If you want a few cooking lessons, I can teach you. I do a mean meat and potato pie. Will fill that husband up a treat. He'll be in your debt for days.'

I laugh. I like Sandra. She can only be about five years older than me. Maybe I'll get the nerve up to ask her the next time I see her. She's very maternal. I hear a wail.

'Oh hell, Joanne's awake. Those afternoon naps seem to fly.'

'I didn't realise you had a child.'

'Two of them. Becky's at school. She's five and Joanne is eighteen months. I bet it'll be your turn soon.'

'I hope so.' I confide in her.

'Would you like to meet Joanne? She might be a little grumpy at first, but once she's had a nappy change and a bottle, she should be good for a cuddle.'

'I'd love to.'

This becomes a regular event. The odd cooking lesson, a lot of chatter with Sandra, and cuddles with the baby. I feel instantly at home with Sandra.

Now and again I'm still around when Dave comes home from work. He's a banker and looks so rigid and formal in his suit that the first time I see him, I shrink back.

Then he clasps my hand in his and brings me in for a hug.

'So, this is the famous Mel I've heard so much about lately. My wife never shuts up about you.'

She elbows him and then goes off to make him a drink.

'Seriously, Mel,' he lowers his voice, 'Whatever you're doing, please keep doing it. I was worried she was getting a little lonely stuck in with the baby. You've brought a change to her since you started visiting.'

'That's great because I love coming around here. I was wondering if I might be overstaying my welcome.'

'Not at all. Not at all,' he tells me. 'Now, the next thing you need to do is to get Jarrod to one of our game nights. He's proving elusive.'

'He's just been really busy. I'll tell him. I'm sure he'll come along soon.'

'I hope so. I want to meet the man who is fortunate to have such a fantastic wife.'

I giggle, unsure how to handle the compliment.

'You're embarrassing her, Dave. It's true though. You are a very sweet person. Your Jarrod is lucky to have you. Now you better go and get his tea fixed, or he'll be calling us a bad influence.'

I see the time. Oh, my goodness, he could be home very soon. For once I pray that he is running late on a job, so I'm not caught out.

I rush home and reheat a spare pie I made yesterday. Sandra has been showing me batch cooking. Today it works perfectly. Her habits are rubbing off on me, as I spend more time cooking things that can be reheated to allow me to spend more time at Sandra's. Hey, isn't that what Tupperware is for?

# CHAPTER FIVE

MELISSA
June 1985.

Jarrod laughs as he eats his dinner. 'You never stop talking lately. It's great you're getting on with the neighbours. I don't have to worry about you while I'm at work.'

I wipe my mouth with a napkin. 'You worry about me? Why?'

'I did when we first moved here. We'd gone from being around family all the time to our own home. With me being at work so much, I thought you'd be bored rattling around here on your own.'

I bristle and put my hand on the table, smoothing out the napkin. 'But I love our home. I like taking care of it and you.'

He puts his hand on mine. 'I know you do. But being here on your own day after day would have driven you mad eventually. I thought you might start saying you wanted a job.'

'No. I know how you feel about that. I'm happy to be provided for.'

'I just want to look after the old lady.'

I smack his arm. 'Hey, you. Less of the old. I'm only twenty.'

He slices through pie crust with his knife. 'How are the neighbours anyway? Any gossip?'

'Gaynor and Trevor are expecting,' I inform him.

His eyes widen. 'The older couple from the corner house? I thought they had grown up kids?'

'They do, and apparently, it's been a huge shock. Eighteen and nineteen their sons are. She thought she was in the menopause.'

'I'd get an abortion.'

My jaw drops. 'Jarrod. That's a life you're talking about.'

'What about their life? They start to get time to themselves and then it's back to nappies. Ugh.'

'I was hoping we'd be joining them soon,' I mumble quietly.

Jarrod pushes his plate away and rubs his belly. 'Let's just concentrate on filling my tum for now. A couple more years, Mel. When I can afford every possible thing you'll want and need. We're still only young.'

'Okay.' I take the dirty plates into the kitchen.

Jarrod comes up behind me and nibbles my neck. 'In the meantime, we can enjoy practising.'

He pulls my skirt up to my thighs and lowers my pants.

I put my hands on his. 'Jarrod, the neighbours will see.'

'No they won't.' He leans over and pulls down the blind. 'If any of them were looking they'll have to decide for themselves whether I'm helping you with the dishes or your knickers.'

'Jarrod!'

'I want you there, Mel. Let me love you there. Please?'

I close my eyes. I've only ever been with Jarrod and him with me. I'd been nervous when I'd given him his first blowjob when I was fourteen. When we had anal sex last year at nineteen, I was surprised to find I enjoyed it.

'Okay.'

He wets his finger and moves it around the entrance of my anus as if this will be adequate lubrication. Luckily for him, I like the feeling of roughness and invasion. I'd never tell him. I'd be nervous that he'd think I was a freak. He slowly pushes into my tight hole. I feel like he's going to rip me apart. His fingers come around the front and he strums across my clit. He plays me like a musical instrument. After all these years, he knows exactly what movement gets me to relax, and pushes further in.

'Oh, Mel. Fucking hell. You're so tight.'

'Love me, Jarrod. Please.'

He pushes me against the sink cabinet. Water from the front of the unit wets the waistband of my top. My long brown hair shakes forward with every thrust. He inserts a finger up my vagina and fucks me with it while he owns my back entrance.

He withdraws his finger and strums my clit so hard I don't know how his wrist doesn't snap. The friction builds. I reach under my top and cup my bare breasts in my hands. They're too small to need the restraint of a bra. I pinch my nipples as I head towards my crescendo.

'Now, God. Now, Mel.'

He thrusts so hard my waist is slammed into the sink. I feel the warmth of his semen as he finishes. He withdraws straight away, grabbing some kitchen towel and wiping us both up.

'That is always worth coming home to. You know how to keep your man happy, Mel.'

I turn and smile as I reach up on my tiptoes to kiss his cheek. I didn't manage to come. I was so near, but as soon as he reached his orgasm, he left me behind. I feel like I want to go into the bathroom and fuck myself with my own fingers until I'm sore and replete. But I don't. I'd feel too embarrassed afterwards. Anyway, Jarrod is the only one I want to create my orgasms. He's all I've ever had and all I'll ever want.

'Tell me how it felt when I was inside you?'

He's always been so attentive to how he makes me feel. I describe in detail, embellishing my retelling with fictional details of my non-existent orgasm.

He's mine, and I'm his. It's how it's always been.

I follow him through into the lounge where he sits on the sofa, remote control in hand, flicking through TV channels.

'I was hoping to watch Brookside,' I tell him.

He switches it over to Channel Four. 'Be my guest, there's nothing on the other three channels.'

I lie on the sofa and put my feet across his knees. 'They're having a card game tonight. It's at Dave's. Why don't you pop over there and get to know some of the blokes?'

Jarrod scratches his chin. 'I don't know.'

'Hey, what's up? Why are you so reluctant?'

He turns to me. 'They're all a few years older than me. A lot of them are family men and have jobs that require suits and stuff. I'd hate to think they judged me. Found me immature or stupid.'

'Jarrod,' I chastise him. 'They'll love you like I do. Go and see. You could be missing out on a great time.'

He chews on his lip, then moves my legs. 'Okay, I'll go. If they make me feel stupid, you have to promise to pee in their lemonade next time you're over there.'

I giggle. 'I promise.'

Jarrod has a great night. He starts making sure he can get home in time to join in their card and poker nights twice a week. We settle in, and life goes on. One night Jarrod comes home drunk, stating that it's time to start making babies.

I waited until he'd sobered up to quiz him. My heart thudded in my chest, an excitement fizzing deep within me. Hope he could extinguish just as quickly now he hadn't had a drink.

I walked into our bathroom where Jarrod was having a soak in the bath. 'Jarrod?'

'Yes, darling? Have you come to wash my back?'

I picked up the sponge and squirted some shower gel on it, lathering his back and around the nape of his neck where his light blonde hair reached midway.

'Did you mean what you said about starting a family?' I kept my voice light.

He grinned. 'Yes. The guys had a word with me last night. Well, Dave really. He said you can't wait forever. He's right. That man makes a lot of sense you know? I've saved quite a bit up now. I can stop working such long hours. We can get pregnant.' He winked at me. 'Then I can go out playing cards and poker while you change dirty nappies.'

I squeezed the sponge over his head so soap got in his eyes. He grabbed me in a split second and pulled me into the bath with him. The water splashed over the sides, and I feared for the lino and floorboards.

Jarrod kissed the tip of my nose.

'Get into bed. We should get started now.'

His wish was my command. It always had been.

By the end of the year, I was expecting our first child.

# CHAPTER SIX

SAM

31 August 2014

I've opened the blind on the window so my therapist can see some daylight. Or rather can see me from his fixed viewpoint. I'm in my shorts and tee. They display my abs and glutes to perfection. As I dig the ground, he'll see my strength as my muscles cord with the push and pull of the spade. I'm digging a rectangle. For no reason other than to let him think I'm digging his grave. Psychology is the bomb. My house is an old miner's cottage. One house on its own, at the bottom of a country lane. There used to be others living here before the council bought them with the intent of developing the land. I planned to fight them, but they gave the idea up anyway, the land was deemed unsafe after a shaft collapsed on the old colliery. The other houses fell into ruin, but I looked after mine, even when I didn't live in it for a time.

I love it here. I'm a seven-minute walk away from the nearest house. I fixed a post-box at the end of the lane for any mail, so I'm left entirely alone. No one bothers to come all the way down here. Except children. Children and their enquiring minds. They come and play on Red Mountain. That's what they've named the red earth mounded into the hills surrounding my home; leftovers from Handforth's time as a mining community. I watch them sometimes as they climb up and then back down the hills, taking red dusted clothes back for their mothers to try to clean. They don't bother me. I have signs everywhere saying Beware of the Dogs. The children have assigned ghost stories to the row of abandoned-looking houses. I'm a wicked witch, and there's a curse on the rest of the row. The scrap cars piled up in the lot in the distance take their eye now and again, and they risk their lives to find a car they can make a den in. There's no fear when you're young and innocent.

I never look back at the room when I'm here, so I don't know if he watches me dig, or thinks of his potential demise. I couldn't face the disappointment if he chose to ignore my efforts. It's better I remain unaware.

I cease digging and go to shower. I have another session with my therapist after lunch.

'I worked for Ed for a year. A whole year where I proved I was the best assistant ever. He could trust me with anything. I waited patiently for him to show me that trust. Sure enough, a test arose. Ed invited his boss, Mr Jacobs, to dinner at a city centre restaurant with a casino. He asked me to accompany them. Called it a business dinner. The invitation came with the words, "I hope I don't regret this." I knew then that I was on trial. To see if I was made of the same stuff he was. I remember that evening so well. I wore a long black chiffon dress that gathered at the waist and split up to the knee. When I sat, the material shifted to reveal a shapely calf, and gave Jacobs a hint of my black lace panties. I don't know what Ed slipped him during the evening, but come the time to gamble, Jacobs was like a racehorse that had thrown its rider. He blew money while attempting to get me to blow him. I'd smile and say let's bet again, the next one's bound to be a winner. But once again, Ed proved himself my superior. I was completely unaware that Mr Jacobs had a prior gambling addiction. Ed had purposely taken him to that restaurant and not revealed the casino attached until they'd had a few drinks. At which point, Jacobs had tried to leave. Then I'd shown up. Apparently, his ex-wife was a short-haired blonde.' I laugh.

'Something amusing?'

'Yes. I thought I'd been playing a great game until then - getting Ed to trust me. I knew my employment was based on my appearance, but I wasn't aware that I bore more than a passing resemblance to Jacobs' ex-wife. No wonder he employed me. It had nothing to do with my talents. But Ed knew why and made it part of a long game to destroy him.'

'How did that make you feel?'

'Like I was out of my league. I went home that night and smashed up my apartment. I'd been totally played. I felt like he'd won again.'

'Again?'

'Jacobs put a rope around his neck the following morning. When he didn't turn into work, I went to his home to apologise during my lunch break. I wanted to see if I could salvage anything. Maybe find a way to exact my revenge on Ed for using me. Instead, I saw his dangling feet when I peered through the letterbox.' I'm quiet for a moment as if paying my respects over again. 'After a couple of months, Ed was promoted to Jacobs' job.'

'That must have been frustrating?' The chains rattle, 'For fuck's sake, take these off!'

I stand up and lick my bottom lip. 'Still such venom after all these days. You really are impressive. That's why I had to do what I did next.' I sigh. 'You're not much use as a therapist, Ed. You're not designed for considering other people, are you? I think you need some time out to consider your outburst.'

'No, not again, please. We can sort this out. What do you want, Sam? Is it money? I have money. I'll give you money.'

I upturn my chair and throw it at the wall at the side of his head. He flinches.

'I don't want your money. I want you to take some responsibility for your actions. Your actions and your decisions have consequences. You don't even care. How many decisions have you made during your lifetime that have impacted on other people, huh? Have you given a thought to Jacobs' kids? How it felt to have a father who killed himself?'

'Oh, my God, are you Jacobs' daughter?' A ghost of a smile hints at Ed's lips.

'Of course not. I showed him my snatch, you sick fuck. Stop trying to guess why I'm here and listen for once in your life.'

'I'll listen if you let me out of these cuffs.'

'You think you're unbreakable, Edward Bonham, and you still think you're in control. Open. Your. Eyes.'

I close the door on him and return to my digging. It's that or put the shovel into his skull, and that's not part of my plan.

# CHAPTER SEVEN

MELISSA
May 1986

I've been going around to Gaynor's a lot. Her son Andrew is now four months old.

'How did you decide on a name?' I ask her.

'Oh, we went through the baby name book and chose three each. We'd both picked Andrew. I'd picked it because of the royal wedding, but I didn't tell Trevor that, or it would have put him off. He doesn't believe in the royal family, thinks they're a waste for the taxpayer.'

I nod as if I know what she's talking about. I ignore politics and financial news. It's so deadly boring.

'So how are you feeling?' she asks me.

'Being pregnant is amazing.' I make a rubbing motion with the hand more or less permanently placed on my stomach. I'm showing now.

'You've been so lucky with no sickness.'

'I know. I've just been exhausted.'

'Make sure you rest. Get Jarrod to look after you.'

'Oh, he has.' I don't tell her how fussy he is, treating me like a delicate antique. He's so nervous about hurting the baby, and point blank refuses to make love while I'm pregnant. 'As soon as he gets home, he makes me put my feet up, and he won't let me lift anything.'

'Lucky bugger. Trevor just let me get on with it. Third child, all done twice before. You make the most of that special attention and get all the rest you can. Once that baby's here, you'll forget what sleep is.'

'I don't mind.' I reply. 'He or she will be worth it.'

I spend hours imagining who our child will resemble. Sometimes a boy who looks like his father, at other times a daughter with my dark-brown hair. I imagine she'll be beguiling and adorable, with huge chocolate brown eyes she'll peer through shyly while claiming her daddy's heart. I imagine us on shared shopping trips. We'll be able to have play-dates with Andrew, and Joanne before she starts nursery school. I visit the library and bring home several books on the subject of babies, careful to only choose light volumes, so I'm not carrying too much. I fill up on information, wanting to be as prepared as I can be. Jarrod laughs, saying you can't learn about babies from books. I have though. I know about feeding, winding, and how to bathe our baby. Literature is a joy and a wealth of information. My practical husband – who works with his hands – just doesn't see it; in my mind, I have several different scenarios of how and when to respond to our baby. I'll try them all until I get the best response. It's all in the research.

Over the last months, while I've been so tired, Jarrod has often met with one of the guys for a beer, or a card game. A new guy moved onto the estate at the beginning of the year. Edward. Jarrod says he's around the same age as us. He's an accountant. I sometimes watch him go to work from my bedroom window. He's a good-looking man. Tall. Walks very straight, as if there's a coat-hanger in his back. He and Jarrod hit it off. A fact that surprises me. They seem such opposites. A lot of the men's nights take place at Edward's home, as he doesn't have a wife to placate. Jarrod says Edward has told him he dates, but he wants to focus on his career.

## June 1987

I've become obsessed with watching Edward. He does everything with military precision. It's like he's a living robot. I think it's because I'm so bored. I'm getting quite large now, and I'm easily tired. I've become obsessed with people-watching, and Edward is by far the most interesting to spy on. Last weekend he had gardeners in. They fitted hedging. It is all uniform. The top of the hedge the same height all the way around. He waters his garden at ten pm every evening, even if the men are around playing a game of cards. They come out and drink their beer while he waters and they chat. At weekends, he heads off with his gym bag at nine am and doesn't return until twelve. Jarrod says he swims and then uses the weights. If he passes me in the street, he just nods his head. He's never actually spoken a word to me, and I want to know what his voice is like, the timbre of it.

It's Saturday, and he returned from the gym an hour ago. It's about time I properly spoke to him, given he's so close to Jarrod. Maybe I could invite him around for a meal one evening? After considering, I decide to ask him for some gardening advice. Wanting to look my best, I shower, dry my hair and use a scrunchie to tie it back into a ponytail. I've no need for makeup as my skin has a light glow from sitting in the garden in the sunshine, but I add a little Seventeen light pink lipstick, and I'm done. My sandals are next to the door, so I push my feet into them, noticing the tightness as the pregnancy has swollen them. Pulling the door closed behind me, I walk the three houses down to Edward's.

There's an open pathway to Edward's front door. Plain brown curtains hang at the windows. Net curtains ensure you can't see in. The door is painted an emerald green, which blends in with the garden. It's boring. I'd expect Edward to have a striking house, given his exactness. I press the doorbell and hear its buzz. Net curtains are pulled aside, then I hear the chain removed and the door opens.

I look up. My mouth drops. Up close, Edward is exotic looking. His skin is tanned from the sun and golden-brown. He looks almost apache Indian. His neck is thick, and I wonder what size collar his shirts are.

'Can I help you?'

His voice is deep like it comes from the earth itself. Commanding. I expect winds to swirl as he speaks. He has an unearthly presence like he's some kind of a god. I'm fascinated by his aura.

'Are you okay, Mrs Simmons?'

I jolt. 'Sorry. Pregnancy brain.' I pat my stomach as if he can't see the significant bump protruding from below my bust. 'I'm sorry to bother you, but I wondered if you could tell me if there's anything you're feeding your hedges? They are well, fantastic looking and ours, well...' I peer over my shoulder to my own house where our hedge is uneven and full of half-dead, brown twigs.

'You're taking a keen interest in gardening now?' He raises an eyebrow. 'I would have thought you had lots of preparations to do for the baby.'

His tone is flat and cold. Suddenly I don't want to be here. I feel foolish. He is looking at me as if he knows full well that I have no interest in gardening.

'I'm prepared for my baby, but I'm becoming restless and need something to do.' I reply, my voice running out of steam by the end of the sentence. Why did I come here? I should just go. I turn away.

'Other than sitting in the window watching people? Wait there. I've just bought a new packet of feed. I'll get it for you. I can buy another.' He closes the door, gently, but still in my face. I wait, though right now I want the ground to swallow me up. *This man is around the same age as you*, I tell myself. *Why are you so intimidated?* I straighten my shoulders as the door opens again.

'There you are. Instructions are on the packet. Follow them precisely. Will that be all?'

I note the name of the product. 'Thank you, but I'm perfectly capable of buying my own feed. I won't need to inconvenience you by taking yours.' I keep my hands firmly by my sides, not taking the offered item. 'Good day, Mr Bonham. I appreciate your time.'

A hint of a smile appears. 'Call me Edward,' he says.

'I doubt I'll need to call on you again at all, Mr Bonham.'

I walk away, trying to salvage what remains of my dignity. The man is awful. I don't want Jarrod around him.

## July 1987

From then on, when I pass Edward in the street he nods his head and says a curt, "Mrs Simmons". On one occasion, he passes as I am coming out of my house. He looks at the still messy hedges and raises an eyebrow before continuing down the street. My fascination with him turns into hatred, the hormones from my pregnancy no doubt fuelling what would ordinarily be an annoyance.

It's a Wednesday evening when Jarrod once again leaves me to play cards. I'm seven and a half months pregnant, feeling fabulous, and like I want to have sex with my husband.

'Oh, do you have to go around there tonight? I was hoping we could have a night in.' I smile in what I hope is a teasing fashion.

Jarrod pulls me towards him and kisses the top of my head. 'You know I'm not doing anything to risk that baby.' He strokes my stomach.

'You're always out with the guys.' I pout.

Jarrod laughs. He strokes his chin. 'You were the one who said I had no friends and needed to go out with them. Now you want me at home. Those hormones really do mess with a woman.'

A flash of anger crosses my face.

'Whoa, with that glare I'm out of here.' He dashes to the door and almost flings himself through it in his haste.

I throw myself down on the sofa, completely bored. There's nothing to do but watch a television programme until I fall asleep.

I come to wondering where I am. The side of my face is crushed into the arm of the sofa. Drool runs from the corner of my lip. I glance at the clock. It's after one am. I presume Jarrod went straight upstairs so as not to disturb me and after coming around for a minute or two I walk upstairs to the bedroom. He's not there. The bed covers are completely untouched. I run back downstairs. Jarrod is always back by midnight. My anger rises to the surface. Where the fuck is he? I stroll into the kitchen to get a glass of water. My mouth is dry from being asleep and it needs to be well lubricated for when he does get home and I give him a piece of my mind. I raise the blind and peer at Edward's house. There's no sign of anyone on the street. From the corner of my eye, I notice movement. Sandra is waving to me from her window and indicating I should come outside.

I walk out of the front door to meet her.

'They're late, aren't they? What are you still doing up? You should be resting that baby.'

'I fell asleep on the sofa. Shall we collect our husbands? It's that bloody Edward. He's leading them astray.'

Sandra laughs, 'They've probably passed out on his sofa.' She looks back at her house. 'I'll lock up. The kids will be okay for a few minutes, won't they?'

'We're only going three doors down. You can see your house from there. Don't let me go there alone. Jarrod will complain I'm embarrassing him, whereas if we both turn up, we can appear like overbearing wives together.'

'Okay. Let me lock the door.'

As we walk down Edward's path, there's jazz music coming from the house. Subdued lighting comes through the net curtain.

I knock on the door, but there's no answer.

I tut and turn towards Sandra.

'What shall we do now?' she asks.

'You can see a bit under the net curtain.'

Sandra looks at me with a raised eyebrow.

'I snooped a while back, so shoot me.' I laugh. 'It would seem I'm a nosy neighbour.' I wander to the front and bend to peer underneath. I feel the weight of my bump as I get into this uncomfortable position.

Jarrod lies on the floor. It takes me a while to process the fact that his lips are locked with another man's. That the other man, Edward, is fucking my husband up his backside. I can just make out small grunts accompanying the loud jazz music. Dave is passed out in a chair. I turn away and throw up in the garden.

Sandra rushes over. 'Mel, whatever is the matter?'

I point.

She looks through the curtains herself. Her scream rings out into the quiet of the street.

My thoughts rush at me. They'll know we're here now. I need to get away. If I run back to my own home, maybe I can pretend I've never seen this. Go back to my settled, normal life.

But Sandra is in front of me, battering on the window.

'Stop it.' I grab hold of her arms. 'We need to get out of here. Then decide what we will do.'

She nods. 'I'm going back to my babies.'

She runs towards her house. I attempt to run after her though with my pregnancy I'm not fast. A stitch starts in my side, and I pause in the middle of the street, rubbing my stomach. Edward's front door opens, and Dave dashes through it. Jarrod stands in the doorway watching Dave but avoiding my gaze.

It's this distraction that means I'm in the middle of the road when the taxi comes around the corner, hitting me sideways on. No one would expect a woman to be standing in the middle of the road of a quiet cul-de-sac at one-thirty am I'm sure.

The world goes black.

# CHAPTER EIGHT

MELISSA
January 1988

When a car collides with the side of a pedestrian, the impact to the lower body means that the lower half accelerates while the top stays relatively still. The body then wraps around the front of the vehicle, in my case, causing my head to hit the windshield, tearing my face in the process. The resultant fall to the ground causes my skull to fracture. The taxi will have a dent in the hood and a smashed windshield. This will be recorded by the insurance companies, along with the burnt tyre marks on the road from braking. It's the braking that caused my injuries, although not braking would have been far worse.

    I watch *St. Elsewhere* these days and consider this is what it must have been like on scene and in the hospital. Shining lights in my eyes to check pupil responses. Listening to my chest, hearing the diminished breathing caused by the diaphragmatic rupture. You kind of need the muscle that runs across the bottom of your ribcage to breathe. Blunt trauma creates a whole host of problems.

Losing a lot of blood sends a body into hypovolaemia. When this happens, it tries to save blood. My body considered my unborn baby to be non-essential to my survival and stopped the blood running to my uterus, diverting it elsewhere. If the car impact hadn't already caused the death of my daughter, then my own body would have killed her instead. It's a sobering thought and not one a mother wants to dwell on. My womb and my dead child are removed from my body. I do not get to cradle her because I am unconscious.

Torn knee ligaments, lacerations, abrasions.

I spend time in the intensive care unit as they wait to see if I'll live. I'm moved to the high dependency unit. Then to a general ward where I'm given physiotherapy. Finally, I'm allowed home.

Home.

After several months in hospital, I'm unsure of what to expect when I get there.

I know what not to expect.

My husband.

I lost him the night of my accident. He ceased to exist, just like our daughter. I was abandoned without a second thought, no explanation, nothing.

From that day, I distract myself from my thoughts every time he comes to my mind.

My parents open the door. The house belongs to me now. It's clean. My mother has obviously been through it with stealth. My house is stocked with groceries. A vase of flowers sits on the table. As soon as they leave, I throw them in the bin; they remind me of my days in hospital. I never want to see a flower in a vase again. Later, I gaze out of the window and stare across at Sandra and Dave's. I wonder how they went on. If they are still together. Then I look at Edward's.

Later, there's a knock on the door. A glimpse through the peephole reveals Dave. His hair is greyer; he looks ten years older than the last time I saw him.

I open the door, slowly. I'm unsure if I want to open it at all.

'Dave.'

'Can I come in?'

I pause before opening the door and indicating that he should enter.

Dave is a tall bloke, and he seems too large for my living room. I can't help but think about the last time I saw him. I mustn't let these thoughts in.

'How is Sandra?' I ask.

'That's why I'm here,' he says. His eyes close, tears on his lashes.

I don't want him to speak. I don't want to know what that tone of voice means. That given up, reluctant tone.

'She blamed herself for you being in the road. She'd look at the kids and say it wasn't fair that she had two daughters and you'd lost yours. She couldn't look at me either. She wouldn't believe I hadn't taken part. I didn't know, Mel, I swear.'

'How did she...?'

'She took an overdose.'

'When?'

'A month after the accident.'

I stand still though I don't know how. 'I'm sorry for your loss, but I'd like to be alone now.'

He nods and walks towards the door.

'Is he still here?' I ask.

'Yes.' Then he updates me.

Edward now lives with his girlfriend, Inez. While we all suffered, Edward moved on.

Damage to the brain after an accident can sometimes leave a person suffering from behavioural problems. It can be like they are two different people, Jekyll and Hyde if you will. I like to blame my accident, but I had issues with Mr Bonham from the get go. The man is inhuman. I vow that one day I will get that man to show some emotion. To apologise for the actions that resulted in my loss. But for now, I am too damaged, too broken and I hole up behind the walls of my home and try to survive each day.

Dave and I become close. We cling to each other, with the shared history of that evening. The first time Dave kisses me, I let him. He's a decent looking bloke, but I don't think I'm capable of love anymore, there's not much room beyond the hatred I keep deep within. I realise however that I can become a mother to Becky and Joanne. Babies I never gave birth to but can love as my own. Dave wants to move, but I insist we stay in his family home. I tell him the children need that stability. We get married. One thing I discover is sex is something that can be loving one minute and like animals attacking each other the next. I realise what a pathetic lover Jarrod was and that the right lover can make your body sing to the heavens. I crave Dave's contact, even if I struggle to sum up my feelings for him. With the girls, I try my best to show good and positive emotions. Our life together, bearing in mind our past, is a good one. But the hatred simmers beneath me like a pilot light, kept on, waiting to be turned up. I tell Dave the truth from the beginning of our relationship. That one day I will make them pay. He hates them as much as I do. He says he'd help me, but I'm not sure I'd let him.

After I moved into Dave's, I sold my own home and put the proceeds in a bank account, telling Dave my parents were struggling financially and I'd given them a loan. I learnt to type, and as the children got older, I began work as a medical secretary to a surgeon. Dave refused to take any money from me towards the household bills, telling me to spend it on myself or the kids. I bank my salary too. My parents pass away. I keep the home we moved to when I was fifteen, but I save the money from their investments. All saved. For what at that point in time I didn't know. But there, in case I should need it.

All the while Edward lives across the street with Inez. Inez with her long dark hair, gleaming white teeth and legs up to her armpits. They never even glance towards me or Dave. It's like they live in another world. They taunt me with their blandness. I wonder what they are like behind closed doors. The house remains the same from the outside. The same uniformity. Edward's routine never changes, despite now having his partner living with him. Turn your thoughts off, I tell myself. One day, but not now. A man like Edward considers everything. The fact that I do nothing will hopefully taunt him as he will expect my next move at any moment.

However, I let the years' pass. Because when I'm ready, I need to have nothing to lose.

# CHAPTER NINE

SAM
1 September 2014

I take Edward puzzles. Sudoku, crosswords, anagrams. Sometimes I sit and watch him while he does them. He can solve an anagram at a rapid pace. His intellect is sharp. That's what I want. I don't need him going into a confused state while he's here. I want him to know exactly what is happening. I want him to figure out this puzzle. Who I am and why he is here.

'I have a new treat for you today, Edward. A new puzzle. Let's see if you can figure this one out.'

I make sure his other hand remains restrained, and I am clear to do my work.

I bring out the shaver and shave the hair on his chest.

Edward blanks his face and pretends I'm not touching him. I sweep over his skin with a towel and rub him down with alcohol wipes. I love the smell, so strong like they mean business. I breathe it in. Then I get my pens. Slowly I outline the letter M all over his chest. As I do, I say it. 'M. M. M. M. M.' This gets his attention. 'What?' I ask. After a flash of annoyance crosses his features, no doubt directed at himself, he goes blank-faced again. I leave a decent space after the M as there are more letters to go there, four in total. 'I.I.I.I.I.' 'N.N.N.N.N.N.' 'E.E.E.E.E.' I laugh. 'E.E.E. That'll be the sound you might be making in a minute.' I outline the same letters on his back.

Nothing. The blank face remains.

While you are tattooing, good hand-eye coordination is required. However, the main talent is attention to detail. My purest trait. Attention to every single possible detail. I am completely focused on the tasks I need to execute.

My tattoo machine is one of the best you can buy. The best equipment for the best tattoos. Metal tubes. No disposables for me. Then I begin. I work solidly for two hours. This sounds like a lot, but when taking care, it means just a small amount of the body is now covered with permanent letters. I'll do this daily until my project is complete. I've almost done with Edward now, to be honest. I wrap his abdomen in cling film. I'll come back and wash my work with warm soapy water in a few hours and blot it. I need to make sure there's no chance of infection.

Adrenaline will be coursing through Edward's body now. I get up to leave him, and he gives me the filthiest look I've received so far. Apart from a tightening of his jaw, he remained impassive throughout my work. His strength is admirable, but it just makes me want to break him more.

'I have no idea what you are trying to achieve, but this smacks of desperation.'

I smile at him.

'Yet I know your body has always been a temple to you, where you can worship that god you follow. You know, yourself. Now when you look in the mirror, you'll always think of me.'

'You flatter yourself.'

'I'm pleased with my work. I am a fucking brilliant tattooist. I have you to thank for that, Edward. Had you not put me on the path I found myself on, I may never have learnt, and I was a natural. That's what my teacher said. It's really hard to get an apprenticeship, but I was that damn good.'

'Who are you?'

'Oh dear, Edward. Is it so hard to work out?'

'I don't understand your puzzles. Just tell me who you are and what you want.'

I smirk. 'What if I said that when I knew you my name was Melissa Simmons?'

Edward's eyes widen, and his jaw slackens. 'Don't be ridiculous.'

'Why is that ridiculous?'

'Melissa is decades older than you. Brunette. Different eye colour. I don't know who you are, but you are not Melissa Simmons.'

I sit back in my chair and cross my legs. This time my smile is genuine. A great big beam across my face. Then I talk. 'I'd better explain the puzzle that you aren't getting, Ed. Let's give you an anagram. Your clue: Sam lies. Have you worked it out yet? Melissa. Get it? Rearrange the letters of Sam lies. Yes, I fucking well do.'

Ed rattles his chain, trying to get away from the wall. Finally, I have the reaction I've been looking for.

'You're lying. You have to be. Who are you and what do you want?'

'All in good time, Edward. I'm bored now.'

I close the door on him and tidy my equipment away ready for tomorrow.

# CHAPTER TEN

MELISSA
June 2000

Dave always knew the day would come. At twenty, and sixteen years of age, our daughters were old enough to deal with my leaving. Becky had a child of her own now, and Dave doted on his grandson. I wanted to. I made it look as if I thought Jude was the cutest grandchild ever, but in truth, I was restless.

I had to win.

So, I left.

My travels took me to Suffolk, a place of childhood holidays. I recalled seeing the heavily tattooed punks from the shop on the sea front - my parents dragging me along when I wanted to peer in and see the permanent artwork being etched on people's bodies. My mother tutted at my interest and declared that they'd regret it when they were older. When they were sixty and had a past boyfriend/girlfriend's name on their arm. The tattoo shop was still there to my utter delight. Tattoo Heaven. I walked in and asked to be an apprentice. Bobby, the owner, took one look at my appearance - a thirty-five-year-old woman with medium length dark brown hair, perfectly manicured hands and Clarks shoes on my feet and he guffawed. He made me a coffee, and I never looked back. He had nothing to lose. I didn't need a wage, and I was a quick learner. I'd adored art at school and took to my new profession like a brick takes to cement. I built a firm foundation in a new career and developed a friendship that would last for years. Bobby told me he had no intention of settling down with one woman. There was too much pussy on offer, especially the babes who loved getting tats and hanging around the parlour. I moved in with him, rented a room in his house. It didn't bother me hearing him banging his whores. I stayed there for three years. Bobby knew everything, and he understood when it was time for me to move on.

'I'm here when you're ready for the next step. I'll help you all the way, you know that.'

'I know.'

'I love you like a sister. Going to miss seeing your face around here though.'

'Trade will be affected by the loss of one of your star tattooists.' I snorted.

'You're joking, but it's true. There's always a place for you here, Mel. Always.'

'I won't be the same when I return.'

Bobby shakes his head. 'You'll always be you, but like our customers, with a few modifications.'


From Suffolk, I travelled to New York. Now thirty-eight, I was more than ready to experience more of life. It was time for the scars of my past to heal. The ones on my body from the car accident had faded, but I made an appointment with a plastic surgeon. My years working as a medical secretary for a surgeon had prepared me for what lay ahead. After several consultations, the surgeon began the work of clearing my body of its scars. I lived as a New Yorker, soaking up the best places on earth, while I continued with surgery. I attended dramatic arts classes, learning how to speak in different tones and accents, and became a total gym bunny. I often ran around Central Park when I wasn't recovering from surgery. I had my hair cropped short and dyed blonde. I had a facelift, breast augmentation, a butt-lift. The fake tan took my pale skin away, and contacts turned my brown eyes blue. Living on salads and fruit, my skin became youthful and glossy. The process took years, during which, I kept in touch with Bobby and Dave, though I never sent photographs or anything in writing that could fall into the wrong hands. Dave kept me informed about Edward and Inez. Edward was becoming a big name at the accountancy firm he'd moved to after "the incident". They still appeared happy.

I got theatre work. It didn't pay much, but I got to be other people for months on end. It suited me. I never formed a relationship with another male. In fact, my feelings for Dave surprised me. It took leaving him for me to realise how important he was to me. I really did love him. However, I couldn't explore that while I was still so consumed by hatred. I tell Dave to move on, but not to tell me if he meets someone else. It would hurt too much. But my love for him is not strong enough to take me home. I hate, more than I love.

It's 2013 when I finally decide it's time to go home. To finish what I started so I can live the rest of my life.

I don't tell Dave I'm home. But Bobby is there when I need him. He stays in my apartment when required. He's a good friend, but the offer of money makes him a better one.

Now another person is dead because of Edward Bonham, and I've had enough. He needs to be held accountable for his actions.

There's no sign of Melissa Simmons, nee Jones. I'm Sam Briers now – Edward Bonham's right-hand lady. I've to move on from what happened to Mr Jacobs. Regroup, and figure my next steps.

It's ridiculously easy to purchase fake documents. Bobby saw to all of that for me. My CV and references are perfect for the personal assistant role. What I didn't expect was silence from Ed. Other than asking me to work, he barely addressed me at all. From my time working in the tattoo parlour to my time in theatre, I'd experienced nothing but noise. Bobby would always have music thrashing through speakers while customers chatted and equipment whirred. For the theatre, I'd learn my lines in peace, but practice and productions were always frantic.

I'd speak to Kerry in the staff room, but Ed didn't like idle office chatter. He'd give me plenty of work as if challenging me to not to be able to complete it. I did. Even if it meant staying late, that work was always done. We became a productive team despite the lack of friendly communication between us. I learnt all about his customers, and his business. Unfortunately, there were no skeletons. I'd quizzed Kerry, but any rumours about Ed seemed to be just that, rumours – no doubt made up by staff who couldn't get a real story on him.

As the year went on, I began to see no reason to keep working for him. I'd uncovered nothing in terms of exacting revenge. Then one day he went out to the bathroom, leaving his suit jacket on the back of his chair. As quickly as I could, I ransacked his pockets, looking for anything I could use. There was a thin, black address book. I flicked through it, my heart beating fast in my chest, my hands wavering. If he caught me, I was fucked. There was nothing of interest in the pages but in a pocket at the back was a photo of Ed in a Scout uniform. I noted the scout group then shoved his address book back in his pocket and dashed back to my desk.

When Ed walked back, he appraised me. 'Your face is very flushed, Miss Briers. What have you been doing while I was gone?'

'I'm, well, I'm handing in my notice, Ed.'

He stops moving. 'Sorry? Is there a problem?'

'No. I feel it's time for me to move on. Obviously, I'll work a month's notice, but this job isn't for me.'

'You're extremely efficient. You've been a real asset,' he says, a frown appearing on his brow. 'I hope I haven't done anything to offend you. I know I can seem cold at times.'

'No. It's the job. It's too quiet. I can't sit there every day with lots of work but no one to talk to. It's not me. You need an assistant like yourself.'

'Well, what sort of thing did you want to do?'

'Normal assistants would arrange meetings for you. Take messages from your wife. That sort of thing. You handle all your own phone calls, and well, I'm bored.'

'But you have plenty of work.'

'Paperwork yes, but nothing else. I'm going crazy. I live alone and basically work alone. I need more excitement in my day.'

Ed scratched his chin. 'So, if I give over more responsibility to you. Let you take the phone calls, arrange my diary, etc., you'll stay?'

'I'd give it a try.'

'Fine. Stay, and we'll try working your way. This isn't going to be easy for me. I abhor change, and I don't like to not be in control. You'd better not mess up.'

'I won't. Thank you.'


The first time I speak to his wife on the phone, a tingle shoots up my spine. At last, a way in.

'Hello. Is that Ed's Assistant?'

'It is.'

'Hi, I'm his wife, Inez.' It's said in a friendly voice but with an underlying tone of suspicion. I suppose I'd be suspicious if instead of getting through to my husband I suddenly got his assistant. I'm being viewed as a threat, and I love it.

'Good morning, Mrs Bonham,' I reply, making her sound her middle-age. 'Ed's out at a meeting. Can I take a message for you?'

'That's very kind, but I'll try his mobile.'

'Okay then. Well, it was very nice to speak to you, Mrs Bonham.'

'Please, call me Inez.'

'Okay, well I'm Sam. Sam Briers.'

'I know. Good day, Sam, I'm sure we'll speak again soon.'

The phone call ends.

Later in the month, there's a boring annual business meeting followed by a business dinner. Wives are invited, and the thought of seeing Inez while I'm in my new body makes me sweat. All staff members are expected to attend, but I didn't want to meet her under these circumstances. I needn't have worried. Ed informs me that he keeps his wife and personal life entirely separate from his business affairs.

I sit beside him at the meal. I wear a corporate black trouser suit with a grey silk blouse. Edward asks about everyone else's families while giving cursory replies about his own.

'Do you know I've only ever seen photos of his wife?' Jack Simpson bellows, slightly inebriated. 'Never met her. I don't think she exists. Either that or he's nipped to Thailand and bought one. Sure she ain't a ladyboy, Ed?'

Only I notice the clench of his jaw.

'I've met her,' I say. Ed looks at me, believing that I'm lying. 'And spoken to her many times on the phone. She seems lovely.'

'Oh, right,' Jack says subdued. I notice his wife has a tight pinch to her mouth and is obviously embarrassed about her husband's behaviour.

The rest of the meal passes quietly. At the end of the evening, corporate photographs are taken to be displayed on the office walls.

When Jack returns to work on Monday morning, he has a black eye and a split lip. He gives the story of having been mugged while leaving the party. His inebriation making him a target, while his wife waited in the car.

But I watch Ed stretch his hand out several times that day as if his knuckles are sore. Though there's no evidence of bruising, his skin tone masks any darkened areas.

It's become my aim to cause as much trouble between Ed and his wife as I can. I begin by sending a copy of the corporate photo through the post. In it, I'm standing at the side of Ed smiling at him. Inez can see that her husband's assistant is a slim blonde.

The calls to the office to check on her husband's whereabouts increase.

I make my tone friendly when she calls.

'Hi, Inez. No, he's not here. Gone to yet another meeting. I don't know what they find to talk about. Hardly ever see him these days.'

I hear the panic in her voice, a slight tremble to the tone. 'Can you get him to call me when he's back? He's not answering his mobile.'

'I will do.'

He's not answering his mobile because I knocked it onto silent earlier when it was on my desk. She can ring and ring, and he'll not know until he checks it.

Another time I put the answerphone on to say we're both at lunch. We are, separately, but Inez leaves a further message for her husband to ring her.

I know something's amiss when Ed's daily meditation runs over and I'm still waiting outside his office door at eight forty-five am.

Finally, he opens his door and asks me to come in.

His face is drawn. He doesn't look like he's slept well. He has a couple of creases in his jacket and a scratch on his left cheek.

He watches me appraise him, but says nothing.

'I'm sorry, Sam,' he tells me. 'But I'm going to have to ask you be transferred. It's my wife. She's very possessive, and well, she believes there's something going on between us.'

'But that's stupid. Do you want me to talk to her?'

He shakes his head. 'No. My wife has some issues. I don't wish to discuss them, but there's a reason she's like she is. I can write you a marvellous reference anytime, Sam, but from tomorrow you'll be working for one of the other accountants.'

'No. I quit, and I'm going off sick so as not to work any notice.'

'Why leave secure employment?'

'I've another job lined up. I was going to tell you.'

I can see he doesn't believe me. I can also see he doesn't care one way or another. His mind is on his wife.

Finally, I got through the mask and found his weakness.

Her.

# CHAPTER ELEVEN

## SAM/SELMA
June 2014

I can now focus completely on Inez Bonham.

I visit a top hairdresser's in London and have cherry red hair extensions. Filler gives me a plumper mouth. My eyebrows are darkened and my eyelashes tinted. I change my contacts to a pale grey and wear a lot of makeup and boho style clothing. I'm now Selma.

Bobby delights in the fact that I finally want a tattoo of my own. He tattoos a dreamcatcher on my upper left arm. I fully intend to catch Inez Bonham's dreams and turn them into nightmares.

Every single morning Inez walks her dog, a pathetic looking chihuahua, to a cafe where she stays for a drink. On this particular morning, Bobby rushes towards her, pinches the dog, and dashes off. Inez screams, her surrogate child stolen. I use my gym-honed body, dressed in a bright floral loose tee and tight pale blue jogging pants, and tear after the "thief". I snatch the dog back, and Bobby runs away as planned.

I jog back to her and return her dog. 'Here. You okay?'

Inez weeps. She's taller than me, and tall for a woman at six feet to my five foot five. She's always walked hunched over, afraid to own her height. Her long brown hair reminds me of my own when I was Melissa. Her passing resemblance to me makes me so angry I have to clench my hands behind my back, else I may attempt to rip her hair away and scratch at her face. I focus on my breathing. *Calm down, talk to her.*

My accent is now scouse. I adore playing these new roles. I was always supporting cast in the plays, now I'm centre stage.

'I... Oh, my God. He stole Bounty. She's my baby. Shit. Should I call the police?' she asks.

'There's no point. He was obviously an opportunist and is long gone. Waste of time. Listen, there's a nice cafe near here that takes dogs. Can I buy you a hot drink? I'd like to make sure you're okay before I leave you.'

She clutches my arm in a strong grip. 'Thank you so much for rescuing her. Yes, I think I will have a nice cup of tea with some sugar for the shock.'

'Let's head to Cafe Coco then. It's this way.' I indicate up the street.

'Oh, I know, I go there every day. That's where I was heading to. I don't think I've seen you there before?'

I smile. 'I only moved to this area last week. First thing I did was find a great place to have coffee. It's a priority you know? I can't survive without it.'

'I know what you mean. Coco's has become part of my daily routine. My husband works long hours, and I get a little bored.'

'Mine too.' I twist the wedding band on my left hand. 'He's a self-employed writer. We travel a lot as it depends on where he sets his next novel. For some reason, he chose Rotherleigh for his latest, so here we are.'

'Wow, that sounds so exciting,' she says.

We reach the doorway of the cafe, step inside, and take a seat. She sits Bounty in a basket on one of the chairs, and it stays there, its face vacant. I can't understand the fascination for these toy dogs. They look like they could break apart should you blow on them.

'So why the name Bounty?' I ask. Though the answer is pathetic and obvious.

'Because my little sweetie girl is brown with a white belly. She made me think of the chocolate bar.' She tickles the dog's belly. It still does nothing.

'Do you dress her up? I know a lot of small breed owners do that?'

'Oh, yes,' she tells me, her shock wearing off as she becomes enthused. 'She has little jumpers, pyjamas, the lot. Basically, she's like my baby substitute.' Her face falls.

'I can't have children,' I confide.

'You can't? I'm so sorry. Neither can I, and we've tried to adopt, but that hasn't happened either. So, Bounty is my baby.' She looks at me. 'I sound pathetic, don't I?'

'No, you don't. You've done more than I have. To be honest, I block out the fact I can't have children.' I smile and take a deep breath. 'I can't believe I'm telling you all this when we've only just met. I'm usually so private.'

'Me too,' Inez agrees. 'My husband is an extremely private man and likes me to be the same. He's always preferred it to be just me and him, and well, it can be difficult to make friends, you know?'

'I do. Well, all you needed was to get your dog almost kidnapped, and now you have one. If you want one that is? Maybe we could just meet here occasionally for a hot drink?'

'That would be lovely,' Inez says. 'Some female adult conversation. I'm here almost every morning. Same time, ten until around eleven. Any time you want to come along, feel free.'

'You might regret that invitation when I turn up every day because I'm bored.'

'No I won't,' Inez says. 'You're the first genuine person I've met in a long time. I could use a friend and, well, I'm sorry about your child situation, but it's nice to have someone who understands if you see what I mean.'

'I do. So, what will your husband say about you having a new friend?'

Inez chews on her lip. 'I'm not going to tell him. He'd want to meet you, and he can be rather aloof. He might scare you away. I'm going to keep you all for myself.'

'Fine by me. I'll not tell my husband either. We'll be secret best friends forever.'

Inez giggles. She looks so fucking ugly when she does so.

I take a sip of my latte. I can't stand milk, but Selma drinks it.

'Oh, my God, I haven't even asked your name, and I'm saying we need to be BFFs.' I put a hand over my mouth.

'I'm Inez,' she says.

'Selma.' I hold out my hand, and she shakes it. Her hand in mine makes me want to heave. 'Inez is a beautiful name. Very unusual for around here I would think.'

'Yes. My name was given to me with love. I adore it.' She smiles. I want to stick the end of my spoon in her eyeball. 'Selma is unusual too.'

'My mother always was a bit dramatic. She wanted to call me Thelma after the film *Thelma and Louise*, but my father ruled it out, so Selma it was,' I lie. I don't know how I make this shit up. I hope she doesn't check the film release date as I've no fucking idea if the timeline matches up with my story. I berate myself for being careless.

I finish up my drink. 'Well, I'd better go and get my housework done. That's the deal for me being a stay at home housewife. I keep the place clean. And believe me, when my other half's writing it's needed. He loads up on mugs and dirty plates. I don't see him for days. He's like a hermit. In fact, I end up smelling him before I see him.' I laugh.

'Mine works long hours. I get really bored on my own, but he leaves me a list of things to do while he's out.'

'Sounds very bossy.'

'He likes order and routine. Mess displeases him. He's a believer that a woman's place is in the home.'

I guffaw. 'Oh, my God. I couldn't live with someone like that. I'd rebel.'

Inez's face falls.

'Gosh, I'm sorry. That was insensitive of me.'

'No, it's okay. I like his order. It makes me feel safe.'

'Why would you not feel safe?' I put a look of mock concern on my face.

'Oh. Forget that. Daft turn of phrase. I can get a little agoraphobic. Hide away. That's why I have the dog and go out for coffee every morning. I'd be tempted to never go out otherwise.'

I stand up and lean over Inez and give her a hug. Then I tickle the zombie dog's ears.

'Well, I'll probably see you in the morning. If you're sure that's okay with you?'

She smiles. 'I'm already looking forward to it.'

I walk out of the cafe and walk back to my apartment. When I'm safely inside, I rush to the bathroom where I vomit up the drink I had. My body shakes with pent up emotion. I lie on my bed and let the thoughts of the morning swirl around my mind. When I feel calmer, I take out my journal and write down our entire conversation and my observations. I don't want to forget anything that I can use in the future.

Then I drink some water and eat an apple before firing up the computer to plan my next move.

# CHAPTER TWELVE

SELMA

August 2014

From here on in it's a breeze. We meet most days at the coffee shop. She's so desperate for a friend. To be liked. It's tragic.

From the copy I'd made of Ed's electronic diary before I left the accountants, I know he's due to attend a conference in London today and will be staying there for a further two days. When Inez brings it up at the coffee shop, I try hard not to smirk.

'My husband's away for a couple of days on business. Would you want to-' Her voice fades.

'Want to what? Go to the cinema maybe?'

'Erm, no, actually, I wondered if you'd like to come over to the house? I could make a meal. That's if you aren't busy with your husband.'

'No, I'd love to. He's in his writing cave for a change. I'm climbing the walls with nothing to do. He hasn't come to bed the last two days, he's slept in his chair.'

'Well, you could stay if you like? That way you could drink. We could have a girly sleepover. I never did that when I was younger.'

'No girly sleepovers? How come? They're a rite of passage. Midnight feasts and chick flicks.'

'I wasn't allowed.'

'Well then, I'm definitely staying over, and I'll bring films and nail polish.'

She smiles. 'I think for the first time ever I might actually be pleased my husband has to stay away.'

Inez lets me into the house. The outside is as uniform as it was all those years ago, but there are no longer net curtains, modern times have ditched that look. Instead, there are blinds, angled so as not to be able to see inside. The house is surprisingly masculine. All greys and sharp angled furniture. I thought Inez would have let herself free with decorating, but it seems her husband's control is in the decor too.

Bounty comes yapping at my feet. I want to swing my leg and kick her into the wall. She must sense it as she nips my ankle.

'Ow.'

'Bounty. Naughty girl, come here.'

I watch as Bounty is fed three pieces of steak. Well, talk about rewarding bad behaviour. *Don't worry, Bounty, I'll give you a treat later too.*

Inez cooks an amazing meal. To be frank, I'm astounded by her culinary skills.

'I watch a lot of cookery programmes,' she explains, 'and then I practice the recipes. I have nothing but time.'

'I quite like a good cookery programme too,' I tell her.

'We are so alike. I can't believe it,' says Inez. 'Do you like the film *Chocolate?*'

'Do I? Johnny Depp plus chocolate? What's not to like?' I laugh.

'I wasn't sure you'd have seen it, with you being so young.'

Fuck. I forget I'm only supposed to be in my twenties.

'Well it's a classic, isn't it?'

She leans back against the sofa and sighs. 'I don't know why you want to hang around with a middle-aged woman like me and not someone your own age.' Her face falls.

'Why? How old are you?' I ask as if I don't already know.

'I'm almost forty-nine.'

'Wow. You don't look it,' I lie. 'I thought you were early forties.'

'How old are you? If you don't mind me asking, that is?'

'Twenty-seven,' I tell her. 'Age is just a number, Inez. I don't make friends based on it. Most women my age are having babies, and well, you know what that subject does for me. I'd rather hang with you. You have life experience, history. We have lots to chat about. I bet you've done some amazing things in your life.'

I see a wobble to her lip. A nervous tremor to her hand. 'My life's been quite stale,' she lies.

It doesn't matter. I know all her secrets anyway, whether she confides in me or not.

'Could you tell me where the bathroom is?' I ask. 'I've drunk too much water.'

When I'm safely ensconced in the bathroom, I take out a prepaid mobile from my pocket and dial her house phone, praying there won't be any interference.

I change my voice to Sam's and make myself sound drunk.

'Hello?'

'Inez, sweetie, how's tricks?' I slur.

'S-Sam?'

'That's right. Remember me, darling? I miss our chats.'

'Erm, h-how's the new job?'

'What new job? Ohhh, that's right. Poor Inez. I didn't leave, honey. Ed just told you that so you'd stop being so paranoid.'

'What do you want?' Her tone goes cold.

'Oh, babe, well I'm drunk, and I just wanted to let you know that your husband's cock is a-maz-ing. I almost couldn't fit it in my mouth.'

'W-what?'

'No, I didn't think he'd have told you. That's why I'm calling. I think you deserve to know. There's no conference. We're holed up in a hotel in London just fucking. I've come out to get something to take back for us to eat, instead of each other. Such an appetite. Anyway, I thought you should know, Ed's planning on leaving you.'

There's an anguished squeal.

'He says he likes me best because I have a more responsive pussy.' I laugh and put the phone down.

I hide the phone and flush the toilet. Then I head back downstairs.

I find Inez in a heap on the floor, tears pouring down her face as she presses keys on her phone, no doubt trying to ring her errant husband.

I can hear the reply. *The number you have called is currently unavailable.*

And it is. Because Edward is otherwise engaged – against the wall of my old family home, with his phone locked in a drawer there. Turned off.


Ed always did insist on walking to the gym early every morning. That's the thing with routine. You know where someone is going to be at a certain time of day. So, I knew Ed would walk past the derelict industrial estate ten minutes away from my old home at six-fifteen am. That's where Bobby stuck a handkerchief full of chloroform in his face before we took him to my house. My parent's old home where no one lives close enough to bear witness to a large man being dragged inside. I paid Bobby a handsome sum of money. He may be a mate, but his silence needed to be bought. I sent him back to my apartment once Ed was secured to the wall.

I put a blonde wig on and my contacts in, so I looked like Sam again, albeit with puffier lips. At this stage I didn't really give a shit what Ed saw.

When he came around it was so cool to see him freak out about his new surroundings.

'Sorry. I forgot you like routine. I don't think you're going to the gym today, Edward, or your conference.'

I expected him to pull on his chains, but he didn't.

'What do you want, Sam?'

'Simple,' I told him. 'I want to destroy your life. Like you did mine.'


I spend the night consoling Inez. Telling her men are bastards and that she could do better. I lie and tell her I'm sure my own husband has had an affair. That I'm always feeling lonely. She soaks up every word and eventually falls asleep on my shoulder.

I ease her off and go and let Bounty out for a piss. I take out a piece of chicken from my bag that I prepared earlier. Fucking dog had kept barking near it, almost giving the game away.

'Here you go, Bounty. You'll love Auntie Selma's chicken. It's marinated,' I tell her.

She barely chews the meat. It's gone in seconds. Chicken a la antifreeze.

She returns to the warm house, as do I. I place myself back in the position we were in before. After an hour or so Bounty starts to wobble as if she's drunk. Then she shits herself; the smell is so offensive I want to throw up. A small part of me wants to rush the dog to the vets, but a larger part, the winning part, knows it has to be done.

'I'm sorry, Bounty,' I whisper. 'Sarah will take care of you in Heaven.'

Sarah. That's what I called my beautiful lost baby. I lost mine. Now Inez is about to lose hers.

I wake to another scream.

'Bounty. Oh, my God. Bounty.'

Inez is up and cradling her pet in her arms.

'She had a seizure. Something's wrong.'

'Where's the vets? I can run us there if you like?'

'Please.' She sobs. 'Can we get there fast?'

We arrive. Inez is a dishevelled mess with mascara smears down her face. The vet rushes Bounty into surgery, saying they'll call us.

They phone Inez at home hours later to tell her that Bounty died from kidney failure. That it looked like she'd been poisoned, likely by antifreeze. They tell her that it's so easy for it to happen. It's kept in people's garages. It drips from cars and the pets lick it.

'But she never goes out of my sight.' Inez looks at me, her face crumples as she cries again.

I put a look of terror on my face. 'Oh, God. I let her out last night while you slept. She was at the door, I thought she needed a wee. I wasn't going to tell you because you had enough on your mind, but she ran down the road, and it took me an hour to get her back. She must have done it then. I'm so sorry.' I begin to cry, easily done as I am truly sorry about what I had to do. I had a heart before they broke it. Sometimes it tries to beat again.

'Selma. No. It was an accident. You weren't to know.'

We sit, arms tight around each other and weep. Consoling each other, before I make my excuses to leave, to return to my 'husband,' when really, I'm returning to hers.

## CHAPTER THIRTEEN

SAM/SELMA/MELISSA
3 September 2014

My artwork is almost complete. Edward has been mute for the last couple of days, offering me no physical or emotional response to my news. Today that changes.

'We thought you'd finally moved on.'

It's the first words he's uttered that I believe are honest.

'Well, now you know.'

'To go to all that effort.' He appraises my body. 'There's no trace of Melissa Simmons.'

'Thank God,' I retort, 'Or my surgeon-'

He interrupts. 'I know you lost your husband and your baby, and I can't know what that must have felt like. The betrayal...'

He's trying to get to me. It won't work.

'That's right, you can't possibly know. That's why we're here, Ed, so you can gain some understanding.' I continue with my inking.

'Inez wanted to move. She couldn't stand you watching us. But I told her she'd done nothing wrong. We weren't going anywhere. If anything, I felt you and Dave should move, away from the bad memories of that place. Instead, you spent years taunting yourselves.'

'We spent years bringing up the children left without their mother because of your actions.'

'My actions? You stifled your husband. He couldn't be himself, having to fit in with your playing house games just like when you were at school together. He'd grown up.'

I swipe the alcohol rub from my desk and pour it over his fresh tattoos. I watch him try to hold back the pain but his face grimaces and he groans.

'You fucked my husband, and you fucked me over. If you hadn't instigated this. If you'd left us alone, there'd still be me, Jarrod, and at least one daughter. There'd still be Sandra, Dave, Becky, and Joanne.

'You're fooling yourself. There'd be no you and Jarrod,' he spits out his name. 'Because it was all a fucking lie.'

I grab my tattoo machine and swing it at Ed's head. A huge gash appears on his cheek as his head collides with the wall. He's knocked unconscious.

I check my machine, ensuring it still works and carry on with the final inking while he's quiet. Tomorrow I hope to let him go home - if he still has one.

4 September 2014

I walk into the room with a brilliant smile on my face.

'Ed. Darling. Today's the day. I'm letting you go.' I smile, noting the gash to his cheek. His face is no longer clean shaven. He has dark brown stubble. I bet he'd hate his reflection.

He awards me a cold, calculating look. 'Why? Did you finally realise you've gained nothing from keeping me here?'

'You silly billy. What do you mean? I've gained so many things.'

He looks at his chest. 'You tattooed me. I'll have to wear shirts for life. I'll live.'

'Hmmm. How will you explain them to your wife?'

'I'll tell her I was held hostage by Melissa Simmons. The same story I'll give to the police.'

'If you do that, then there's a bounty on your head, darling. You don't think I haven't covered myself, do you? Speaking of Bounty. It's a shame what happened to your wife's dog.'

He strains at his cuff. 'What have you done? You'd better not have been anywhere near Inez.'

'Oh, I've been near her alright. Very near.'

'You can do what the fuck you want with me, but not with her. Do you hear me? She'll have been frantic while I've been missing. She'll have called the police.'

'I think you'll find she doesn't want anything more to do with you, and she doesn't care where you are,' I taunt. 'What with you fucking Sam from work, which is where she thinks you are now.'

'How the fuck have you managed to see her? She'd recognise you.'

I shake my head and remove my wig to show him my cherry red hair. 'Nah. She's looking for a blonde she saw once in a photo. Not her best friend Selma.'

'Selma? You're fucking deranged.'

'I certainly am. Congratulations. You made me this way.'

'I don't know how you keep up with your multiple personalities.'

'It's all an act. I think I'm actually really fucking clever and that's what you didn't bargain for when you fucked over a meek little housewife.'

'Do it then, let me out. I won't go to the police. I'll sign something. Bring me a fucking legal document. I bet you have one.'

'Of course I do. Legal documents and your demise plotted should anything go wrong. Yours and Inez's. I'm not choosy over whichever one of you rots in hell.'

'All I want is my wife. All I ever wanted was my wife.' Ed's face shows actual pain as a tear runs down his cheek.

'Except to get your wife you had to steal my husband, didn't you?' I spit. 'So, I didn't just lose my baby. You fucked up my husband so badly he relinquished his whole self and became Inez Bonham. You screwed up my world.'

'He was never yours.'

'He was always mine,' I spit. 'Then he ceased to exist. Have you any idea what that was like? I almost died. I had to have counselling. I'd lost my baby and my husband. I find out when I'm conscious that my husband wears dresses; a long dark wig, that looks like my own fucking hair, and you've named him Inez. He didn't even choose his own fucking name. He looked a complete joke. You made *me* a joke. I had *nothing*,' I scream.

'I did what I had to do,' Ed says quietly. 'He was mine more than he ever was yours.'

'You. Stole. My. Life,' I spit out. 'Now you've lost her. Good luck with getting her back.'

'You stole mine first, you bitch,' Ed snaps. Then he looks shocked.

'What do you mean?'

He tightens his lips. His jaw tense. I can see he's not going to tell me anything.

'Oh, Ed. Just when I'm ready to let you go, you show me you have more to tell. I'm intrigued.' I drag my nails up his arm and hold his chin in my hand. 'You're not leaving today after all.'

I leave him in the room. My phone rings. Inez wants to go out to the pub. It's eleven-thirty am. She's having a bad day. I grab my things. I'm sure I'll be able to turn this to my advantage.

# PART 2

## INEZ

## CHAPTER FOURTEEN

Inez

I was born Jarrod Lee Simmons.

I remember finding it hard to make male friends at school. I didn't want to play football. I wanted to play with the girls and their dolls. I wouldn't let my mother cut my hair short, preferring it to my shoulder and wavy. Luckily mullet hairstyles were all the rage back then and my hair hadn't thinned like it did in my mid-twenties. Mel was my best friend from us being five years old. We met in the first year of infants and were inseparable. She had been fed fairy stories from birth and decided I was her Prince Charming. We even got married in class. She looked so pretty in her dress-up wedding dress. I kept playing with the net of it.

I kept my dirty secret to myself. In my teens, I couldn't understand why I'd want to wank to pictures of both men and women and yet hate my penis and wish it didn't exist. I'd steal clothes from Mel's house. She had so many she never even noticed. Every so often her mother would make her clear out her unworn clothes and put them out on the street in a bin bag for the charity collection. I'd come back later that night under cover of darkness and go through the bag, taking out the items I liked. When we were thirteen, Mel was actually taller than I was by a few inches, so the clothes lasted me a long time. When my own height shot up to six feet, while she stayed five foot five, I couldn't raid her clothes anymore. I'd pretend to buy makeup for my mother, saying it was her birthday. At night, I'd lock my door and put on makeup and a skirt or dress, and I'd sit in my room feeling normal.

The first time I realised that my sexuality was not defined by the sex of a person was when I went on a camping trip with the Scouts. I'd met a young guy from a different group a couple of times. I confessed to him about my feelings, and he understood. He kissed me, and we fooled around. I met up with him a few times afterwards, and we progressed to anal sex, but it couldn't last. I had to end it.

Mel and I became lovers when we were fifteen. I guess I'd resigned myself to the fact that my life would be spent with her. To be honest, I was fascinated by her soft breasts and her warm pussy lips. I tried to imagine I had them. I'd quiz her all the time on how it felt when I touched her. She thought I was an attentive lover, but actually, I was a jealous one. I didn't much care for sex. It was too confusing for me with my male genitalia and female mind. I'd get off and then feel guilty about it. Sometimes I'd imagine that scout boy was sucking me off. Other times I'd get Mel to sit on top of me, and I'd try and visualise that she was fucking me. That the penis was hers.

When Mel encouraged me to attend the street poker evening, she had no idea what a can of worms she'd opened. When Edward opened the door, my jaw dropped to the floor. He'd really not changed that much from the young scout who's dick I'd fondled. He confessed to having kept tabs on me, asking people we knew where I was and what I was doing. He told me he'd stood outside the church on my wedding day and wept. He said I'd been the only person to have ever given him love. I was confused at first. We'd been teenage boys experimenting, that's all, but then the other men on the estate had gone home and left Edward and me alone.

He'd held my face in his hand tenderly, leaned over and kissed me.

After having only ever kissed Mel other than Ed, he took my breath away. His mouth was firm on mine. Not the softness of Mel's but hard, commanding. Hunger opened within me that I'd never experienced before. Want. Need.

Edward had taken me to his bedroom, laid me down against his sheets and moved over me. We'd kissed hard for hours. His hands had roamed my body and mine his. He took my rock-hard cock into his mouth and sucked me off. I'd loved it, and I loved it even more when he lubed my anus and his cock, and he took me there. He faced me as he did it and it was like I'd made love, finally, like a woman. I knew then that I needed Edward. But I owed Mel. She'd been my constant all my life, and I couldn't imagine life without her. Edward needed to be my dirty little secret – for now.

I told Mel we could try for a baby. I'd put the idea off as I didn't want a child brought into a world where their father didn't know who the hell he was. But I felt I owed her. The guilt consumed me. I wanted my cock serviced by Edward, but I'd fuck Mel with it, pretending it was Ed's mouth. She was overjoyed when she found out she was pregnant. I couldn't imagine being a father, and I resigned myself to the fact that I'd handle it when it arose. Mel understood when I said I didn't want to make love to her for the health of our unborn child. Of course, it was a complete fiction. I had no more interest in shagging Mel. I was obsessed with Edward, with whom I was exploring the part of myself I'd not fully understood for years.

People expect transgender people to have a particular sexual orientation. Oh, he's now a woman. So he should like being fucked. It's so narrow-minded. Just like anyone else's sexuality, I find I'm attracted to a person, rather than what they have. I identify as a woman, and when I finally had my reassignment surgery, I physically became the person that I'd always identified with. Edward and I were able to make love as a man and woman, though Edward would still take me anally. For him, I was a person he'd fallen in love with, regardless of my sexual gender.

Edward was a complex man. How complex I didn't realise until we became a couple. After Mel's accident, my grief was crippling. I felt responsible for the death of an infant Mel had wanted from being small. She'd discovered my secret and had lost everything that night, and very nearly her own life.

She was in hospital for months. I waited for her family to visit and tell me what a disgusting individual I was. A pervert.

But Mel came back, and the only thing she wanted was the house. She didn't want me. She negotiated through solicitors, and we divorced. She'd ignore me in the street. I wanted to move, but Edward said we were going nowhere. This was our home, and once Ed made his mind up about something there was no reasoning with him. The truth was that our quiet crescent became a place of safety for me. The game nights and neighbourly drinks had ceased. Everyone kept to themselves, and I was left to become Inez. I'm not sure why Ed chose that name for me. He just said he liked it. I'd always thought I'd choose my own name and imagined being called Lynne, but Ed didn't like that. It was easier to please him. I was happy when Mel married Dave and became a mother to his children. I'd taken away the chance for her to become a biological mother and she excelled at looking after those two girls. I'd watch her from the window when she wasn't looking.

If she saw me and Edward in the street, she looked through us. It was hard having known her for all those years. Her knowing everything about me except for my sexual identity and in some ways, not really knowing me at all. But we'd shared the best parts of our lives together and her not being in mine was a strange loss, a bereavement almost. Edward wouldn't listen when I tried to talk to him about it. When I'd seen the counsellor prior to my surgery, I'd been able to explore it a little. So many opposing feelings in my mind, it was enough to drive me crazy. So, I stayed within my well-ordered life with Edward. Finally able to be the woman I'd always wanted to be, with my regimented but steady husband.

But then he'd got a new assistant. At first, nothing changed, but then she started taking his phone calls. Alarm bells sounded. Edward never relinquished control to anyone. The only times he gave himself over was inside my hand, mouth, pussy or arsehole at the time of release. Suddenly Sam was answering his phone and Edward was unavailable.

He became angry with my suspicion and paranoia, our once ordered household becoming a place of argument. But Edward had never shown interest in anyone but me. When the photo arrived in the post showing a slim, blonde woman I'd lost it and thrown crockery and glassware. She was so womanly. A woman who looked stunning and too good to be real. Bright blue eyes. Beautiful bone structure. A perfectly honed gym body. Glowing tanned skin. Impressive tits. She was the total opposite of me with my brown curly wig and six-foot frame. My hair looked pathetically thin and wispy when I'd tried to grow it, so I'd had to cope with the heat and itchiness of wigs to become the Inez of Ed's dreams. Hormones had given me A-cup breasts and thickened my waist, but exercise would have made me feel more masculine, so my body was soft, my thighs wobbly. Sam was in her twenties, myself approaching fifty. I imagined Edward was having a mid-life crisis, though he was only two years older than me. He was going to take Sam as his younger lover, and I would be alone. The freak show. All by myself.

He was angry. Told me I was being stupid. That there was no one else for him but me. He said she'd left and that he wouldn't be seeing her again. For my sake, he'd let her go.

I believed him. Until the phone call. Now my whole world has fallen apart, and I didn't know what to do next.

I thanked my lucky stars that God brought Selma into my life. I am no longer alone. I have a friend I can seek advice from. Thank goodness she's here.

# CHAPTER FIFTEEN

Selma
1 September 2014

After I left Edward last night, I spent the evening at my apartment. It was lovely to work through a yoga video. To stretch out all my muscles. Then I relaxed and watched a DVD. I sent a text to Inez, checking in and telling her I'd be around in the morning.

So here I am now. She's getting me a glass of water. There are photos of Bounty strewn across the sofa, but not one photo of her and Ed. That strikes me as strange.

She walks back in and hands me my drink.

I make my voice sound soothing. 'So, a stupid question I know, but how have you been?'

She sniffles. It's most unsightly and most definitely Jarrod. He never could be arsed to fetch a tissue.

'Ed won't answer my calls. I'd feel better if I could see him or speak to him but his phone goes to voicemail, and that bitch won't tell me where they are.'

'He can't stay away forever. He'll need his belongings at some point.'

Her face falls as if the thought of him leaving her has only just come to mind.

She turns to me, her mouth quivering. 'I don't know what to do.'

I lightly touch her shoulder. 'Well, do you want to fight for him or kick him out?'

She looks down and swallows. 'I honestly don't know.'

I stroke her arm. 'There's nothing to say you have to decide right now. Just get on with your normal day as best you can and make decisions when they need to be made.'

Inez chews on a fingernail then she stops herself and pulls at an imaginary thread on her top. 'Can I talk to you? Properly talk to you? There's something I want to check out.' Her voice comes out shaky.

'Of course,' I say, moving closer. What is she about to divulge?

'I-I'll understand if this drives you away and you never want to see me again, but well, I-I'm transgender.' She lets out a deep shaking breath. 'I was born male, although I've mainly identified with being female.'

*Fucking what? Mainly identified? Liar.*

I attempt to stay outwardly calm. *Breathe, Mel, breathe.*

'Really? It did cross my mind,' I tell her. 'You're so tall, and I can tell you wear a wig, but I didn't know for definite. It's not highly obvious like you see with some trans.'

Inez sits back, a frown on her face. 'But you seem so accepting of it. Doesn't it bother you? I thought you'd have left by now.'

I look at her as if she's stupid, which she is, but not for this reason. 'Absolutely not. I think my generation are a lot more accepting. I've slept with women as well as my husband,' I lie. 'It's about falling in love with a person not what gender they've been officially assigned.'

'Oh, my God, that's exactly how I feel. I really do believe fate sent you my way, Selma.'

*God, I want to suffocate her with a cushion.*

'So, you say you've always identified with being female? That must have been hard growing up.'

She sits back on the sofa. 'It was. I had no one to confide in. Things were different back then. I didn't believe anyone would understand. They'd have called me a freak.'

'Didn't you have a best friend? Oh, guys don't really do that, do they?'

Inez gazes into the distance before returning her eyes to mine. 'I had an amazing friend who later became my wife.'

'You were married to a woman?' I act shocked.

'For a short while.' She takes a sip of her tea. 'She was my best friend through school. Always had my back.'

'So, why didn't you tell her?'

I'm desperate to know the answer to this question. Why she made my early life a joke and a waste of time.

She slides her finger around the top of her cup as she speaks. 'She loved me, and I loved her. Mel spoke about getting married from the moment we met at age five, and she seemed my soul mate. She just got me, well the me I showed. I was born male, I expected to have to stay male. People didn't suspect my gender identity issues because I was always with Mel.'

'But didn't she guess? Sorry to get personal but what about sex?'

'That's one of the things people don't understand about being transgender if you don't mind me saying. I physically and mentally identify with being female, but I enjoyed sex with Mel when I had a penis. At least, I thought it was okay. It's just that, well, we'd been together and never known anything else. When I met Edward, it was all consuming. I fell head over heels. When I'd lived with him for a few years and had my reassignment surgery, my life became complete.'

I want to be sick. The confirmation that he no longer has his manhood. I know he'd alluded to it, but it shocks me that it's no longer there. The parts that made our baby: his cock and balls, and my womb, gone forever, just like our daughter.

'Wow, I can't imagine. So, how do you get to enjoy sex?' I put my hands over my mouth. 'Sorry, that's so rude of me. I'm so intrigued by the whole thing. You're amazing you know. So brave.'

Inez smiles. 'I've never felt brave. I've always felt a coward. I used Mel to hide my true self, and in some ways, I've hidden while I've been with Ed.'

'Well, maybe while Ed sorts out what he's doing, you should take some time to think about what you want?'

'Yeah.' She nods her head. 'Absolutely. I should. Anyway, would you like me to explain about the surgery? That's if you're interested. I hope you're not squeamish.'

'Would you? I'm intrigued. I may pull faces a little, but I'll try to behave.' I laugh.

'Okay, so I had hormone therapy, something which continues to this day. It helped me grow my breasts and made me more *womanly*, though like you say, at six feet tall, that's not something easily achieved. I had extensive counselling prior to my surgery. Ed supported me every step of the way.'

'That's good.'

'So, in the surgery, they slice the penis and remove the internal penile tissue.'

'Ew,' I say, grimacing, and this time my reactions aren't false.

'They removed my testicles, although they used the scrotal tissue to make my vaginal lips. They turned the penile skin inside out and stitched it back up. It's so clever, there's a piece of erectile tissue that they push through the slit, and that makes the clitoris. They constructed a urinary opening and used my abdominal muscles to make my vagina contract. I was in bed for a week and had to have a catheter. The pain was excruciating.' She looks at me and sighs. 'I'll not go into it any further because I can see it's a lot to take in.'

I grab her hand and squeeze it, then let go. 'Sorry, I have so many questions. You have the parts, but I guess you can't come, right?'

'No, I absolutely can. The stub of penile tissue they use as a clit is fully functioning. Ed and I made love after about eight weeks, and I was able to climax. That's when I realised that although I'd enjoyed sex with Mel…with Ed, and my being in the body I'd always identified with, well, it was mind-blowing.'

Part of me wants to smash his cunt up with a baseball bat, but another part of me is strangely inquisitive, especially when he's admitting how he felt when he was with me. I won't allow myself to think about all this right now. I'll block it until I get back to my apartment. I'm here to fact find. That's my aim.

'So how did Mel take the news of your surgery?'

Inez casts her face downward. 'She never knew. We divorced after she caught me with Ed. She never spoke to me again. Her parents said I was dead to her. I was never able to tell her how sorry I was.' She looks up. 'Is it okay if we change the subject now? I feel exhausted. I will talk about it more another time.'

'Of course. I'm sorry, things did get heavy there, didn't they?' I squeeze her arm. 'Thank you for confiding in me though. I'll have to do the same sometime. I have skeletons in my own closet.'

'Well that's what friends are for.' says Inez. 'Hey, do you fancy going to a cafe or restaurant for lunch? Not Coco's because they'll ask me where Bounty is. Anyway, it's time for a fresh start. It's time for Inez to treat her friend Selma to lunch. I'm not going to sit around waiting for Edward.'

'Good for you. Sounds great.'

'We could do a spot of shopping afterwards. I'd love it if you could come with me to find a new wig. Ed chose this one. I'd like to pick one for myself. One that's not so obvious.'

'You dress nicely. Do you choose your clothes yourself?'

'No, that's Edward too. He advised I dressed classy. The only clothes I had before were the ones I'd stolen from Mel. She was a shopaholic and didn't realise I'd taken things.'

I splutter out my water and quickly make it look like I'm giggling.

'Oh, my God, you nicked your wife's clothes?'

'Yes, and she was considerably shorter than me, so you can imagine what I looked like. Also, she was very girly in how she dressed. I looked rather drag queen until Ed took me in hand.'

I suffer through an afternoon with Inez. I encourage anything anti-Edward, and she uses her credit card to purchase new outfits and two new wigs. She says its revenge against the cheating bastard. Then she bursts into tears.

I spend time consoling her, giving her a hug, which is weird when she's so much taller than I am. Then I send her home and return to my apartment. Inez needs to atone for her actions, and I need a goddamn shower, I feel like my skin is crawling.

A phone call to Bobby and he arranges for a 'driver' in a suit to turn up at Inez's house on Ed's behalf. The driver tells Inez he's there to collect some of Ed's belongings and that Ed will be in touch soon about collecting the rest. When she asks for identification, he shows her the door key and alarm code. The key I'd taken an imprint of when I first went to her house, and the code she never hid when she opened the door with me behind her. Devastated at being told Ed doesn't plan to stay with her, she lets my driver in to collect some belongings. I make sure he takes all of Edwards clothes. As she stole mine, I'm taking his. An eye for an eye and all that.

When the driver brings them to me boxed, I put them in the back of my car. The next day I visit a charity shop and hand the whole lot over. The owner checks the labels, all designer. 'Are you sure? You could take these to the dress agency down the road and make a decent amount of money from them.'

'No.' I hold my hand up. 'That won't be necessary. We'd like you to make as much money as possible for your charity. It means a lot to us.'

'If you don't mind me asking, why so many clothes? You've not suffered a recent bereavement have you, sweetie?'

'No. My husband has lost weight, and these don't fit anymore.

Any excuse for him to go shopping. He's worse than any woman.' I laugh. It's true. Chained to a wall and only given minimum amounts of food, Ed has already begun to lose muscle tone. I love the fact that he can't get to his beloved gym every morning. The break in routine must be infuriating him.

'Well, bless you. Thank you so much for thinking of us,' she says. I nod and walk out.

As I walk away, I allow myself a last look at the shop's frontage – Angels – a charity set up to help the parents of bereaved children. Maybe the funds raised by the donation can prevent someone turning into me.

# CHAPTER SIXTEEN

Inez
4 September 2014

After spending the first couple of days inconsolable, my mood shifts to anger. It would seem I'm going through something akin to a bereavement. When Ed had his clothes collected it was a wake-up call that he really had moved on. Perhaps he needed to fuck another woman, get it out of his system and then come back? Maybe he needed a proper vagina now, a regular life? Who the fuck knew, seeing as he wouldn't speak to me. I had hours alone, to think things through. I realised that I'd spent my life playing a fiddle to someone else's music. Who was I? Who did I want to be? I was neither Jarrod, son of a fervent Christian father who would have turned in his grave if he had seen who I'd become, nor did I want to be Inez anymore - manufactured by Ed and a group of physicians. I wanted to be me.

I need to get out of this fucking house. Its greys make me gloomy, and the empty pet basket hurts my stomach. I need to let rip somehow. I pick up my phone and press my hotkey to Selma.

'Fancy a drink somewhere?'

'It's only eleven-thirty!' she mocks.

'It'll be after lunch by the time you're ready. I need to get drunk. Life's a bastard, and I need a rest from it.'

'Where and when?'

Fantastic. She's such a support. I don't know what I would do without her.

The first thing I do is order a beer. I stick to a half. Ed always poured wine and said beer was unladylike. He'd let me drink beer at his house when I was Jarrod, but once Inez existed, it was wine only, or a glass of champagne – which was like piss. I guzzle my beer down and order another. I can do what the fuck I like today.

Selma strolls into the pub as I'm finishing my second drink and grins. She looks amazing in a long maxi dress with a shrug style cardigan. I wish I had her sense of style.

'Goodness me. Can't even wait?' She nods at my glass. 'What're you drinking?' Then she heads to the bar. She returns with two more half pints of beer. 'I quite like a beer myself. Much better than a glass of wine.'

'Isn't it just?' I smile. 'Selma. I've made a decision. Even if Ed returns. I'm going to be me. Not Jarrod, not Inez. Just... me.'

She looks at me over the top of her half pint glass. 'And who are you?'

'I don't know yet.'

We fall about laughing.

'Well, for now, I think we should stick to the name Inez until you've had a chance to think about a new one. You don't want to keep changing it because you've thought of a better one.'

'I guess I can hold onto that name a little longer. I'm changing though Selma. It's like with Mel I was a caterpillar, camouflaged by leaves. Then with Ed, I've been in a chrysalis. Now I can finally be me. If he doesn't like it, he knows what he can do.'

'While I like your confidence, Inez, I do feel you're probably having a reaction to your present situation. You might feel different in a few days, or when Ed deigns to get in touch.'

My shoulders fall. 'Do you think so?'

She shrugs. 'Probably.' She puts a hand over mine on the table. 'That's not to say you won't do all those things, but you can't decide your future life in five seconds flat. You've been with Mel and then Ed. Are you going to manage on your own? Will you stay on the estate? Is it your house or Ed's?'

I sit back and sigh. 'It's Ed's house. I have nothing in savings. I gave our house over to Mel through guilt, and Ed wouldn't let me work.'

'Did you use to work?'

'I was an electrician. Not much call for a transgender sparky.' I wink.

'Well if you continue to have those negative thoughts you'll certainly never get anywhere. Anyway, if you're having a new start, you can have a new career. What would you like to do?'

I ponder for a minute. 'Actually, I love makeup. I'd like to work on a makeup counter and help people make the best of themselves.'

'Well, I'm sure you could get a job like that no problem. Why not start looking through the employment websites? Beats sitting at home pining for your pooch and waiting for Ed to call.'

I realise I've drunk another half pint. 'Want another?' I ask Selma.

'I've only had the top out of this one,' she says. 'Would you get me some water? I've got a bit of a headache.'

'Lightweight,' I tease.

'Lush,' She teases back.

The lunchtime rush has come in, and it takes a while for me to get back to Selma. When I return, she's just finishing her half. 'Took you long enough,' I say.

'It's nice to see you like this,' Selma replies. 'It's like a weight's been lifted off you. I'm surprised. After what's happened to you, I thought you'd be in a heap.'

I nod. 'I thought I would be too, but without Edward here, it's showing me what control he had over me. I can please myself now.'

'Oh yeah?' Selma winks.

'Oh, my God, no.' I blush. 'I haven't had any thoughts in that direction.'

'You'll have to excuse me. I need to pee,' she says. 'I don't know how you've not had to go yet.'

'I'm not a lightweight.' I laugh.

While I wait for Selma to return, one of the bar staff heads over to our table. It's not the one who served me but an older bloke. He looks mid-forties. 'Excuse me,' he says, his arms folded across his chest. 'I've had a complaint about you.'

My forehead creases. 'Sorry?' I look around. He can't mean me, I've not done anything.

'About who you are. What you are.' He spits. 'There's no place in here for your sort. I need you to leave.'

My eyes widen. 'But I haven't done anything wrong. All I've done is sit and enjoy a drink with my friend.'

He looks around. 'And where's your friend now?'

'In the bathroom.'

'Well, I'll ask her to meet you outside. Now let's not have any trouble. Pick up your bag and go, and don't come back – you're barred.'

'And you're a bigot!' I yell. Three halves of beer have gone to my head after drinking them in such a short period of time. My anger about Ed gets projected at this man, obviously the manager or landlord. I stand up, my six-foot frame swamping him by at least five inches.

A woman comes up with her boyfriend. She jumps up and pulls

my wig off revealing my own patchy medium length hair. It hurts like a bitch as it was gripped in place. 'Look, it's a ladyboy.' she laughs.

'Get out, queer,' yells her boyfriend.

I grab my belongings, whip my wig from the floor and dash out of the pub. I quickly pull my wig back onto my head and dive into an alleyway. I take deep breaths, taking out my mirror and fixing my wig back in place. That's what's more important. People have noticed me though and are staring.

I hear Selma shouting my name and peek out of the alleyway, beckoning her.

'What's going on? I came out of the loo, and the landlord said he'd thrown you out?'

I start to tear up. 'It was horrendous, Selma, I don't know how I ever imagined I could lead a normal life.' I explain what had happened in the pub.

'Hey,' she says. 'No talk like that. Days like this are going to happen. You have to learn to deal with them. Come on.' She grabs my arm. 'We'll go back to yours and grab a six-pack of beer on the way.'

## Selma

It seems so cruel to hit someone when they're down, doesn't it? A little like, for instance, when your wife's lost your baby and instead of visiting her in hospital you remain with your lover and forget she exists. When Inez went to the bar for our drinks, I rang the bar and told them there was a tall woman in the bar who was a trans prostitute picking up tricks for later. She was becoming well known for it, and they should watch out for her. I'd described her jacket. I didn't know if they'd take me seriously, but when I saw the man from the bar heading in our direction, I'd made out I needed the loo. Then in the toilet, I'd seen a young teenage woman, pissed or drugged out of her mind. She'd asked to borrow my lipstick. I told her she could have it if she did me a favour. It's a Kylie Jenner lipstick, and her eyes went wider than Kylie's lips. I told her there was a 'fucking tranny' in the bar. 'Go and have a look. Drinking beer, dressed in a floral blouse and tight grey skirt. Hilarious.' She giggled. Said it would give her and her boyfriend a right laugh. To be honest, Inez had looked elegant in her new wig, but the pisshead wouldn't worry about that.

By the time I came out of the bar, there's no sign of Inez. The drunk girl nudges my arm as I pass her. 'Saw that drag woman. She was getting thrown out. Fucking queer.' Her boyfriend pulls a face, 'Not fucking normal that.'

I don't acknowledge them further and walk out of the bar in search of Inez, where I intend to console her and act like the best friend she ever had. I laugh to myself. Oh, like I was before when I was Melissa. Only this time I'll be the one leaving and destroying everything in *her* path. I find her in an alleyway, wig dishevelled and with a small group of spectators. I barge past them and dash up to her. Ask her if she's okay. I tell her we'll go to her house. A drunk Inez is an out of control Inez. Time to encourage it and see what further destruction I can cause before I visit her husband and see if he's ready to give up his secrets yet.

### Inez

'Oh, my God, I'm completely smashed,' I tell Selma as if she can't tell when I'm swaying and having to hold onto the walls to walk around.

'Me too,' says Selma, who's let herself go and bought herself a bottle of vodka. She lies back on the sofa and sighs. 'You need some fun. What shall we do now?'

'I think we should have a spend of some of Ed's money, don't you?'

She sits up, 'Yes! Fantastic idea. Get his credit cards.'

'Right, let's max out his cards before he decides to cut me off.'

'What?' Selma looks at me and then closes her eyes as if the effort's too much.

'Selma.' I nudge her. 'Come on. Help me choose some new furniture. This manly shit's got to go.'

Selma opens one eye. 'You need to choose. Time for you to make decisions on your own.'

'But what shall I start with?'

She sighs and grabs the laptop, and types in the name of a top store that sells household furniture and delivers next day for a fee. 'Get on with it. Sofa. Chair. Cushions. Curtains. Rug. Bits of ornament shit. I'm going to sleep. When I wake up I expect you to have spent a shitload of Ed's money and then tomorrow morning, we'll need to throw all this furniture out. I know a charity actually, they'll come and fetch it.'

Selma falls asleep, and I sit back and relax, chilled out from the booze. I order heaps of stuff before I crawl onto the other end of the sofa and close my own eyes.

I wake to find the room in total darkness apart from a touch of light from the moon. I clutch my head and make my way over to the clock on the mantle. It's five am. Selma is still asleep on the other side of the sofa. She looks so peaceful. The moon casts its light across a cheekbone. She's so very beautiful. I reach over and gently touch her cheek to see if her skin is as smooth as it appears. It is. The pads of my fingers sweep across her brow. I don't know whether to leave her to sleep here or tell her she can use the spare room.

With my hand still on her face and while I'm lost in thought, I don't realise that Selma has opened her eyes. Her eyes widen.

'Sorry. I was just, well...' I flush red. 'I wanted to see if your skin was as smooth as it looked.'

Selma sits up a little and pushes her hair out of her face. Her grey eyes fix on mine. 'And was it?'

'Yes. Your skin is so soft and beautiful. I wish I could have skin like that.'

She brings her hand up to mine and runs her fingers down my face. 'Inez, you are beautiful. Can you not see that? Both inside and outside. I can see it. Let me show you.'

She leans forward and puts her lips on mine. I hesitate. Selma is my friend, and if I go here, I could lose her. Then I think of Ed and imagine him fucking that Sam bitch. Next, I stop thinking at all.

I move my lips against Selma's. Then press harder against her mouth. Her mouth opens, and her tongue seeks mine. I'm so used to being directed by Ed in what we do that I decide to take charge. To see what it's like to fuck someone how I want to. I stop and ask Selma to come to my bedroom.

I'm sure she's going to say no, leave, and I'll never see her again. Instead, she nods her head and follows me upstairs. She said she'd had both male and female lovers. Now she was about to fuck a mixture of both. I go with my gut feelings and my longings and don't question whether I'm playing a male or female role. I just have a need, an urge, to make love as myself. Not as a cuckolded husband and not as a controlled wife. I strip Selma of her clothes and find myself in awe of her body. She's toned, with definition to her arms. Her breasts are medium and pert, they could almost be false, but I guess it's the exercise that made them this way. She pulls my top over my head and unfastens my bra. I fold my arms across my chest.

'No. Don't hide yourself,' says Selma.

I remember my promise to own this and drop my arms. I lift Selma and place her on the bed, then lie at the side of her propped up on pillows.

'Let me look at you,' she says.

I lie back. Selma's gaze on my body is so intense I imagine I feel a burn. She strokes my cheek, a flash of longing on her face. Her fingertips trail down my neck, scratching there. I turn my neck and push up into her fingers, the feel of her nails on my skin is divine and causes goosebumps. Further down, she trails her fingers across my chest and then cups one of my breasts in her hand. She palms it, my nipple hardening under her touch. She moves to sit astride my legs so she can gain a better reach and takes my nipple into her mouth. Her hands still roam my body, gently scraping my skin with her nails. I'm on fire. I love being scratched. There's a connection between us as if she knows how to touch me. I'm lost. The alcohol and sensations have me in their thrall. She moves off me and reaches for the zip on my skirt.

I grab her hand. 'Not yet,' I say, and I flip her over.

I sit astride Selma's body as she did mine and trail my tongue down her neck, dipping into her ear. I feel her shiver beneath me. I move lower, trailing my tongue over her toned stomach. Parting her legs, I pause, staring at her pussy. Unlike mine, hers is damn perfect. Natural. I place a finger on her and rub the wetness there. Fascinated I suck on my finger tasting her juices. I never went down on Mel. Could never look at her pussy. I was too confused over how I felt about my sexuality and too damn jealous that she had one and I didn't. My head lowers to her pussy, and I lick there. She bucks against my mouth and tongue. I must be doing something right, despite my cunnilingus virginity. Ed has always adored my blowjobs though. Selma pants and comes against my face, then she grabs my head and drags me up her body.

'It's your turn. Tell me what you want me to do?'

I open my bedside drawer and remove a five-inch dildo and some lube.

Selma takes them off me and looks to me for direction.

'My pussy doesn't get wet like yours does. That's why I have the lube.'

'Do you come the same?'

I nod. 'You'll be surprised.'

The hormones I take make my orgasms strong and plentiful. Selma rubs plenty of lube over and into me and over the tip of the dildo. I lie back against the cushions, close my eyes and spread my legs. There's a pause. Selma is still, so I open my eyes to find her drinking me in. I guess it's not often you get to look at a made vagina.

'It's so realistic,' she says.

'Yes.'

'You really are female now?'

'You sound surprised?'

'It's one thing to be told it and another to see it with your own eyes.'

'Do you want to stop?'

'No,' she says. 'But I want you to close your eyes.'

I feel the dildo nudge against my entrance. Selma rubs it around my formed clit. She rubs her fingers around me too. She's clumsy, and at this point, I bite my lip as I really miss my husband. I wonder whether to stop the whole thing when she begins to push the dildo inside me and then there's no turning back. I love the feel of it inside. I feel home. Though it's Selma making the moves, in my mind, Ed is filling me with his dick, fucking me with his precise and controlled movements. He's ordering me that I'm not allowed to come until he says so. Anger burns through me as I imagine his cock in this Sam woman and in my mind I'm defiant. I won't be told when I can come, I'll do it now. I will fuck this other cock until my pussy hurts. My hips rise, and I grind against the dildo. I feel flesh against me and open my eyes to find Selma holding the dildo against her pussy like it's a dick and is fucking me like a dude.

'Close your eyes,' she whispers.

Her thrusts become more powerful. 'Come for me, Inez,' she shouts. 'Fuck me.'

'Oh, my God, Selma, Yes.'

I push myself on the dildo in a frenzy until I explode.

I sigh with the release and lie back against my pillow. Then I wonder what the fuck I've just done and regret hits me like a sledgehammer. Selma excuses herself to use the bathroom, and when she's gone, I weep like a baby.

## CHAPTER SEVENTEEN

Selma

I rush to the bathroom and switch on the shower, taking care to remove my watch and place it on the window ledge. I grab a folded, clean small towel from the shelf and scrub every part of my body until it feels raw. I sit on the floor of the shower cubicle gagging. I'd not considered that Inez might develop feelings for me, but when she'd reached over and put her lips on mine, I had to make the decision to go for it. His lips felt the same as they always had, warm against mine, taking me back to when we'd been Mel and Jarrod, and I thought we'd been happy.

To a time of lies.

I stared at his breasts and his surgically made vagina and could have wept for the fact that Jarrod was absolutely no more. Another reminder that the formative years of my life had been a complete waste of time. I'd lived with a liar in a sham of a relationship. My whole early life a deception. Of course, I knew one fact, one truth, that Jarrod had loved to be tickled and scratched. So, I used that information against him. My dramatic arts skills had come in useful when I'd faked an orgasm. In my mind my legs were wrapped around his head in a stranglehold, crushing his windpipe, laughing as he clutched for air.

Then I had to fuck him with a dildo. The only reason I was so enthused was because the watch on my wrist has a video recorder on it. I made sure to get a decent angle of the dildo thrusting in and out while she ground herself furiously on it.

'Come for me, Inez,' I had shouted. 'Fuck me.'

'Oh, my God, Selma, Yes.'

Feeling calmer, I turn off the shower and dry myself off with a clean bath towel. I feel cleansed of the dirty deeds of the last hour. Now I need to go back to face Inez, try and salvage the friendship because I'm not doing that again.

A smile breaks out on my face as I watch the video clip. I can't wait to visit Ed.


I walk back into the bedroom to find Inez with puffy eyes. She looks at me, a desolate look on her face.

'Can I say something?'

She nods.

'We were intrigued and pissed. Can we forget it happened? I much prefer you as a best mate.'

Inez rubs her eyes and sits up. 'Seriously? That would be okay with you? I'm so sorry. I was thinking about my husband the whole time.'

'I have to confess, it didn't do a lot for me. I prefer my husband too. Let's forget it. I guess it'll be weird for a bit, but I'm willing to try if you are.'

'Yes please.' Inez grabs my hand. 'You're my only friend, I don't want to lose you.'

'So, your furniture is coming this morning.' I remind her,

changing the subject. 'Shall we grab some breakfast and get ready for some interior design?'

'I think I'd better not drink so much ever again,' says Inez as she looks around at her newly furnished lounge. It's unrecognisable apart from the previously grey walls and light grey carpet. There's a comfy charcoal sofa and matching tub chair. Lime green curtains, with a matching rug and cushions. New ornaments. A woodland picture on the wall and a large, lime green, floor-standing vase.

'You certainly know how to shop.' I laugh.

The charity I help had been to collect the old furniture. I kept out of the way in case it was someone I'd met before, but it was two strapping blokes, who moved the furniture like it was made of cotton wool.

'I think we need pizza for lunch to celebrate,' announces Inez. 'It'll help the remnants of my hangover too. You fancy some?'

'I'd love some.'

Inez grabs her coat. 'I'll ring it in, but it's quicker to collect. Will you be okay here while I fetch it? I'll be about twenty minutes or so.'

'Absolutely.' I pick up the remote. 'I'll find some trashy TV programme we can watch while we eat.'

Of course, the minute she leaves I explore the house. I find Ed's office and look through his stuff. As I rifle through his drawer, I see a photo similar to the one in his address book. The picture is of Ed in his Scout uniform, but this time he's with another boy – Jarrod.

What the actual fuck?

I leave the room and return to the sofa downstairs. My mind flips out with this new information. They knew each other before? Edward moving to our street had not been the start of my life falling apart? Had he moved here deliberately? Had they been having a relationship all those years or was Edward a stalker? Maybe he'd met Jarrod at Scouts and then started an obsession?

With not being able to confess to having seen the photo, there's only one thing I can do.

I wait for Inez to return to ask how she and Ed met. I wonder if she'll tell me the truth.

Firstly, I make up some shit about my imaginary husband. How his book is coming along. How I miss him when he's in the writing cave because I love him so much. I say we met when I stumbled across an author event when I was on holiday, and he was a signing author.

Then I slip it into conversation. 'How about you? How did you meet Ed? How did you know he was the one?'

Inez sighs and looks at the floor, and for a moment I think she's going to tell me she can't speak about it. Then she looks up.

'I guess seeing as we got a bit too close physically, I may as well let you in mentally. It's not a pretty story, and I'm not proud. Promise me you'll not judge me? I don't want to lose your friendship.'

'I promise,' I tell her.

'Ed moved into this house. I lived down the street with Mel.' She walks over to the window. 'In that house, over there.'

I make a pretence of seeking out my old home.

'Mel encouraged me to attend one of the street's game nights. The guys would play poker and stuff. I hated the thought. I'd rather have been doing the baking she spent her time doing, but she insisted. When I went to Ed's house, and he opened the door, I was shocked. We'd met before, years ago when I was in a scout camp. I'd seen him on a couple of occasions at Scouts, and well, we'd experimented together. The first indication to me that I was not living the life I was meant for.'

'What an amazing coincidence. It was like fate,' I say, faking excitement.

'No.' Inez shakes her head. 'I didn't know, but he'd kept tabs on me. He admitted to having never forgotten me. He said he had to know whether I was genuinely happy with my wife or whether there was a chance for us.' She rubs the back of her neck. 'I started a relationship with Ed.'

## Inez

For a brief moment, I feel Selma is judging me, but the look disappears from her face. 'Did you not love your wife?' she asks.

'I did. It's hard to explain. We were best friends, and I don't remember ever not loving her. Like I said before, sex was okay but nothing amazing.'

Selma winces.

'I know. It's not kind of me to say that, but I was her only lover, and I know now I wasn't a good one. I was always trying to put her off. With Ed, something clicked. I fell *in love* with him.'

'So you left?'

'Not quite. One night we were drunk and got carried away. Anyway, Mel and another guy's wife saw us. Then she had an accident, and well, then there was no more me and Mel.'

Selma looks shocked. 'Oh, my God. What happened? Did she die?'

'Gosh, no. It was terrible though. She was in the road after she found us and a taxi hit her. In time, she remarried. I think in some ways it did her a favour. She seemed genuinely happy with her new husband.'

'How can you know that?' Selma snaps.

I sit back, my mouth open.

'Sorry,' says Selma. 'I'm being judgy. It's just you say she saw you and then ended up in hospital, and you think she was happier afterwards. Did you never talk to her? Explain?'

'No,' I said. 'I've always been a coward. Is that what you want to hear?'

'If it's the truth, yes. We're friends. Talk to me.'

'Fine.' My nostrils flare. 'I was a shit scared coward. She lost our baby, and I didn't want to have to see her. The truth is I hadn't wanted the child anyway. I was sad she'd lost it but happy that I wouldn't be tied to her now I was in love with Edward. Ed didn't want me to see her so I didn't visit and it was easier to avoid all the drama that would have come with it. By the time she came out of hospital all she wanted was the house. She'd grown indifferent to me. So, she got it.'

'Jesus, Inez, what a mess.'

'My whole life was a mess. From then on it was beautiful. Ed adored me. Until now. Until Sam.' I spit the name out. 'Do you know what?' I fold my arms across my chest. 'He's not ignoring me anymore. Tomorrow I'm going to his work, and I'm going to demand he talks to me.'

'Sounds like a plan,' Selma says and smiles.

### Selma

When I leave, I can't put my fury into words. I visit the pub I went to with Inez and hope to God the drunk idiots are still there. It's not really luck. Downbeats like them are never anywhere else. The woman spots me, nods to her bloke, and they saunter in my direction. They try to appear cool, but I can smell their desperation.

'Do you want to earn some money?' I ask them. 'I'll give you half now and half after. You never met me. If you ever grass on me in any way, there'll be an accident with petrol, a match, and your faces? Do you understand?'

I make a deal with them and leave.

Since I decided to keep Ed at my home a while longer, I thought it wise to make him more comfortable. I didn't want him getting sick. Bobby moved him to a bedroom where he could lie down last night, with a bedpan so he could swivel his hips to pee. Of course, for that to happen his bottom half had to be naked, but that couldn't be helped. We very kindly left a shopping channel on so he could spend his day learning about juicers and exercise machines. Tonight I've got him some extra special viewing pleasure.

'Evening, Edward. It's time for this to move along. I want my house back.'

He eyes me coolly. 'That television crap is worse torture than your tattooing.'

I give him a drink, pouring the liquid down his throat and then I feed him a sandwich. The look of loathing he gives me at having to eat at my whim makes a smirk curl the edges of my lips and my heart beat faster with euphoria.

When I'm satisfied he's had enough to eat I ask him my question again.

'What is it you're not telling me, Ed? I know you met Jarrod at scout camp. I know you corrupted him there.'

'He wanted to be corrupted.'

'Whether he did or not, my guess is you encouraged him.'

He smiles and answers my question by doing so.

'Why did I ruin your life? I don't remember you. Was it school? Did I accidentally cause you some kind of problem?'

'Let me go, Mel. This is tiresome, and you're getting nowhere.'

I sigh and sit on the edge of the bed, my shoulders sagging, as if in defeat. 'Were you and Inez always faithful to each other?' I ask him, letting my voice quieten. 'He wasn't faithful to me.'

'Yes. We adore each other. We were meant to be.'

'That's funny,' I say, my voice returning to its usual timbre. I hold up my mobile. 'Because earlier he didn't seem to think of you at all.' I play the video I transferred to my mobile phone.

He watches, his face sears in agony as his wife fucks the living hell out of a dildo that appears attached to my body, hearing her scream, 'Oh, my God, Selma, yes.'

'Guess she doesn't feel the same way,' I tell him.

'You win,' he spits, rattling the chain attached to the bedhead.

'You win, all right. I need to get out of here and get back to my wife. You sick fuck.'

I stand back and glare at him. 'Tell me the secret.' I demand.

'I'm your older brother,' he shouts and then he laughs at me, a self-satisfied smirk on his face. 'Your lovely mother was the school slag, and I was the result.'

'You're a liar,' I scream. 'Permanently creating chaos in other people's lives as if you're the great puppet master. Well, tonight it's time I end this once and for all.'

'Go find out. You're a clever girl. My father's name was Charles Devon.'

I switch the television off and leave Ed in the dark and silence while I dash home to confirm he's a fantasist.

# CHAPTER EIGHTEEN

Inez

The strangest thing happens this evening. I'm on my way to the chip shop, having decided I can't be bothered to cook and I see Dave on his driveway, washing his car. As I'm not with my usual protector, I find my feet crossing the street and stand before him. It's fair to say that he looks shocked to see me in front of him.

'Inez,' he nods, his tone cool.

'Dave.' I say. 'I-' I look around. What the fuck was I thinking? It's talking to Selma about the past that's dragged things up. Made me wonder about what happened with Mel.

'I know it's far too late, but I wanted to say I'm sorry. About everything.'

Dave throws his chamois leather into the bucket of warm soapy water.

'You're quite right, it's too fucking late. Where's your bodyguard, chicken shit?'

I take a step backwards.

Dave shakes his head. 'Oh, my God look at you. I raise my temper and you back off like a girl.'

'I am a woman,' I protest.

'No, you're not. You're a bloke. A bloke I drank beer with. A bloke who had surgery to be a woman. But you're not a woman so don't back off like you're scared of me when you're three inches taller than I am and could take me on any day. Woman or not, you aren't weak, Inez. You managed to turn your back on your family and friends easily enough. Or maybe you were weak and let Ed take complete charge of your life. I wouldn't know because you never spoke to me again. I thought we were friends.'

He turns back to his car, retrieves his chamois from the bucket and carries on cleaning the car's exterior though it's with a renewed vigour.

'Why did she leave?' I say quietly.

He turns around and looks at me like he's sure he's misheard.

'I beg your pardon?'

'Why did she leave? I thought you were happy together?'

'What we were is none of your business, but if you believe she could stay forever in a street housing her ex-husband and his psycho lover, then you're even more stupid than I gave you credit for.'

'Where did she go? To her parents?'

'Her parents are dead, not that it's any business of yours, so no, she didn't go there. You've no right to know what happened in her life and I'm not telling you.'

He picks up the bucket of hot water. He tilts it as if ready to throw it at me. 'Now get off my property.'

'He's left me you know?' I say. 'Fucked off with a secretary from work. Sam they call her. Sam with the perfect vagina.'

Dave puts the bucket down.

I fight back the tears, some of sadness but more of frustration that I'm breaking down in front of a man I've ignored for years. One who I never consoled when he lost his own wife. So I'm surprised when he asks me to come inside.

I settle on his sofa. As I glance around, I see no pictures of Mel, so I guess their separation was acrimonious. There are pictures of youngsters. Dave sees my interest.

'My grandchildren,' he says.

'Gosh. Time passes so quickly.' It's one of those statements you say without thinking, a platitude. I instantly regret it.

'Time hasn't passed quickly for me, Inez. It's mainly been fighting for survival. Keeping going for my children. Waiting for a day when everything resembles normality. When I'm curled up on the sofa with a loved one and all we have to worry about is what we're going to watch on the TV. Instead, I've found myself alone twice, and I blame you and Edward for both.'

'I couldn't help it,' I try to explain. 'We loved each other with an intensity that burned through common sense.'

'Well, it's obviously extinguished now, if he's taken up with this Sam. Is he not coming back then? Is he with her now?'

My voice thickens. 'I think so. He won't talk to me. Hasn't since he left. It's her calling all the time. I'm going to his work tomorrow to demand he speaks to me. I need to know what's happening. I can't stay in this limbo.'

He scratches his chin. 'I thought something was going on. I saw the charity van come and collect furniture and I've seen you've had a friend round a few times?'

'Selma. She's been my rock.' I tell him. Though I fucked up there as well.

I pour my heart out to this man as he sits in silence listening intently. When I tell him I slept with Selma, he grimaces. 'I know. I fucked up,' I tell him. 'But seriously, it's weird, we've slotted straight back into being friends. It's as if last night didn't happen.'

'So where's Selma now?'

'She's gone back home to her husband. He's a writer apparently.'

Dave shrugs.

I stand up. 'I'm sorry I blurted my problems out. I know it was inappropriate. Thank you for inviting me in and listening.'

As my eyes meet Dave's, I see his are cold and flat. He sneers. 'You always were a cry baby. Moaning that your wife wanted to start a family. I swear Ed must have been a cross dresser because you've always hidden behind his skirts. You never approached your ex-wife or me to see how we were. Then the minute your jailer fucks off, you're over here trying to say sorry. You attempt to satisfy your curiosity about what occurred during the years you've missed, and then you have the audacity to sit in the house of my dead first wife and whine that your husband's gone off with his secretary, that you've fucked your friend and now you're a whole ball of regret,' he spits. 'Your selfishness knows no bounds. Your ego is one of the largest I've come across. You're devoid of personality and empty of empathy. You should have died or been hit by a taxi. You. Not Sandra or Mel.'

I back off. 'I think it's best if I leave.'

Dave picks up a baseball bat from underneath the sofa. 'Take off that wig.'

I clutch at my hair. 'Dave, don't do anything stupid.'

He walks towards me and pulls it off my head. Not again. It brings back memories of the pub attack. Again it pulls, making my eyes water. As I see the menace in his face, I begin to tremble.

'You deserve to suffer for what you've done.'

He swings the bat at my body. The pain is indescribable. He inflicts ten blows in all, including three directly in between my legs. I begin to retch. He drags me by the arm to his integral garage. He pushes me in and looks at my shaking body. 'When it goes dark I'll take you back to your own house. Until then you can fucking stay on the floor like the piece of dirt you are.'

Then he locks the door.

I spend what must be a couple of hours on the cold garage floor with my legs curled up and my arms clutched around me, while I weep and wonder what the fuck is happening in my life.

Eventually, the garage door opens. As the light floods my eyes, I wince. Dave helps me up.

'If anyone asks. You're pissed, and I'm helping you home. Say a word, and you'll be in hospital next time.'

I turn to him. 'I won't say anything. I understand why you did it. I'd probably have done the same.' I gulp as a wave of pain hits. 'I know I'm pathetic, but I loved him so much.'

'Loved?' Dave queries.

I fall silent, and neither of us says another word. I open my front door, and once I close it behind me, I hear Dave's footsteps retreat.

I run a warm bath to try and soothe my aching bones. Livid bruises appear on my body. When my body hits the warm water, pain surges and again I'm brought to tears.

Once I'm out I lie on my bed, thoughts of food long forgotten. I reach for my phone to call Selma. To ask her to come over and help me.

There's no answer. Her phone goes to voicemail. I leave a message asking her to ring me, my voice desperate.

Then I sit back, realising that once again I'm a coward who's asking other people to protect her. It's true. Why do I believe that because I identify as a woman, I'm weak? That that's how I should act. Weak, defenceless and pathetic. Mel never acted that way. She always fought for what she wanted. Except for me, and that's no surprise after what I did to her. God if I could see her again, I'd fall to her feet and beg her forgiveness. I'm so sorry for the pain I caused her when all she ever did was love me. I am a selfish, introspected wimp.

Somehow I fall asleep. No doubt through the shock. When I wake, I get up gingerly and decide that this is the day I take no more shit.

I'm going to work to see Ed. He has some explaining to do.

. . .

'He's off sick? That's his excuse, is it? Where's Jack? Can I speak to Jack please?' The receptionist walks away from me. I catch her eye roll in the direction of her colleague. So what if I'm dramatic? I need answers.

Jack strolls through to the reception. 'Inez? My goodness, it's great to finally meet you. How is Ed?' Jack asks. 'Not like him to be off sick. Must be serious. Anyway, come through to my office. Would you like a drink?'

My gaze darts around the reception. 'Where's Sam? Is she in? I want to speak to her.'

'Sam?' Jack's forehead creases. 'Sam Briers?'

'I can't remember her surname. The woman Ed's been fucking. His secretary?'

Jack gasps. 'Ed's been fucking Sam? Well, I never guessed that.' He looks at me. 'Inez, I'm shocked. He only ever spoke of you. He adored you. So it carried on since she left?'

'Um.' I rub my eyebrow. 'What do you mean left? She's still here. She's been ringing me from the office.'

Jack shakes his head. 'She can't have been. Sam left a couple of weeks ago.'

'You're wrong. She called from here. Told me Ed wasn't at a conference. That he was staying with her.'

Jack sighs. 'Just a minute.' He speaks to the receptionist while I stand with my arms around myself. When he returns his tone changes to that of someone trying to communicate with an infant. 'Inez. Ed's been off sick, and our computer notes say you've been phoning in for him.' He tilts his head and stares at me. 'Are you feeling okay?'

'She's left, and he's not here. He's off sick?' I run my hands through my hair, then regret it as my scalp is painful. My painkillers are wearing off, and I can feel a sheen of sweat on my forehead. 'D-do you have a forwarding number for Sam? I need to speak to her.'

'I have her mobile number, but I can't give it to you. Confidentiality. How about you sit a moment in the waiting area and I'll go call her, see if she'll speak to you?'

I nod. 'Thank you.'

When he returns, his face is a mask of concern. 'I spoke to Sam, and she's not seen Ed since she stopped working here. She did, however, say that he had confided in her that he was planning on leaving you.' He places a hand on mine. 'I'm sorry, Inez.'

I pull my hand away. Ed's not with Sam? So where the fuck is he, and who's been calling me? I feel myself sweating even more. The pain is becoming intolerable. I feel sick. My thoughts run fast. Has anyone been calling me? Have I gone insane? Have I imagined it all?

I get up from my seat and head toward the door.

'Inez. I'm worried about you. Can I phone anyone to come and get you?'

I stop. Nodding vigorously. 'Yes. Yes please,' I say. 'Here.' I hand him my mobile phone. 'Can you call my friend Selma and see if she'll collect me? I'm not feeling so well.'

'Of course.'

Jack phones and speaks to my friend. He gives her directions.

'She asks if you feel well enough to wait for her downstairs, so she doesn't have to negotiate a parking space.'

'Yes, that's fine,' I tell him.

'I can wait with you if you like?'

I wave him off. 'No, I'm fine. Thank you for the drink. I'm sorry to bring my marriage woes to your door. If Edward calls, will you ask him where he's really staying as it's not with me. I'm going to head for some fresh air now.'

Jack nods. 'Take care of yourself, Inez. At least I realise why Ed's been off so long. Marriage problems are the worst.'

When I reach the foyer of the building, I lean against the stone pillar and breathe in fresh air. When Selma pulls up in her car, I open the door and more or less collapse inside.

'Please take me home,' I ask her. 'I need my bed and some painkillers.'

'What on earth's happened?'

I begin with the events of the previous evening up until the present time. She stays silent but attentive, both to myself and the road ahead. She takes my keys, lets me into the house and helps me upstairs. She runs me another warm bath, and then I climb below my sheets and sleep to block the world out.

# CHAPTER NINETEEN

Selma

Despite my searching on the internet for a Charles Devon I find no information. After a couple of hours, I give up, deciding it's a pile of rubbish Ed's made up to have me running around at his bidding. I had a fantastic upbringing, and my parents were very much in love. Staring at my body, I realise it's been a while since I hit the gym. I decide to go and work out and get rid of some of the tension. It works a treat, and I return to the apartment with a satisfying ache.

Answering two different mobile phones in my apartment amuses me no end. Jack had no idea he was talking to the same woman twice. Of course, I couldn't go to the office to fetch her as he could have recognised me. Inez was so confused. She was clutching her head in the car and wondering if she was going insane, then clutching her abdomen because Dave had pasted the shit out of her.

Dave.

My Dave.

I've kept away from him. Kept quiet while I've gone about my business. Inez spoke about Sam and Selma. Has he guessed I'm back? That I'm involved?

After Inez had her bath, I passed her two painkillers, except they weren't. They were sleeping tablets. I now have several hours at my disposal. Several hours to spend in Ed's office. I switch on his computer and wait for it to load. Luckily for me, his password for the home computer is the same as it was for work. Once it's loaded, I open his email account and type an email to Bailey's from Ed. Stating that due to personal issues he's handing in his resignation, effective immediately. I use his credit card details to order some cheap, nasty clothes, so he has something to wear later in the week. Then I write to Inez. As Ed's email account is web-based, she'll not be suspicious.

*Inez,*

*I realise I made a mistake. I genuinely believed I was in love with you and we did share some happy years together. But I've realised I needed a proper woman. There have been several over the years. I'm not proud of having cheated. I'm sorry. They meant nothing. It was just sex. However, Sam is different. I love her. So, I won't be coming back. I'll come over sometime tomorrow for the rest of my belongings. I've handed in my notice at work, and I'm going to start afresh somewhere with Sam.*

*I wish you every happiness and hope you can find the same sort of love I have. You'll realise then that what we had together wasn't it.*

That should do it.

At three am, my drunken couple turn up and daub the house with paint. I let them finish before I call the police on them. Stupid fuckers. They try and tell the policeman I paid them to do it. Unfortunately, I'm sober and educated, and they're drunk and stupid, so they're bundled into the back of a police car. A very groggy Inez lies confused on the bed while I deal with everything. I tell her it's okay. I'll get someone to remove the words tomorrow. Not to worry about it.

She nods and dozes. I tell her it's time for some more painkillers and this time I do give her painkillers. Very strong ones. Then a short time later I wake her up and do it again, and again. She's so groggy she's no idea how many she's taking. I give her sleeping pills and pain meds.

At nine am, I leave the pill bottles at her side and phone an ambulance, telling them my friend has had a very traumatic night and I've found her overdosed. They arrive, place her in the ambulance and head off at speed. I tell them I'll follow in my car.

Except I won't. Because Selma is not traceable and is no longer needed.

I stand outside the house and look up at the red daubed paint.

*Pervert.*

*Ladyboy.*

*Sicko.*

If she doesn't remember it from early this morning, it should make a nice welcome home present.

I turn towards my car and spot him standing at the edge of the path. He beckons me over.

I walk towards my husband.

He appraises me. Of course, I am nothing like my previous self. He has no idea it's me.

'How on earth can you look so different?' he asks.

My eyes widen. 'How can you know?' I ask him in my own voice.

'You walked towards me with your usual gait. Plus, I've been waiting. I knew you'd do something spectacular, but this? My God. When you stopped contact I knew it was time.'

'So what do you think of the new look?' I ask him and twirl. 'Although this is just one of my many disguises and I'm kind of done with it. I need to get my hair done. I fancy going back to dark.'

Dave smiles. 'It's what's within I fell in love with. Though the outside is hot. Fuck, I've missed you. So damn much.'

'What surprised me the most, Dave, is how much I missed you. I didn't think I was capable of-' I look away for a moment. 'Well, you know.' We stand and stare at each other. 'I'm almost finished. Just a couple more things I need to do and then I'm back. If I can I come back?' My voice trails off.

'The door's open, Mel. When you're ready, come home. Please be ready soon.'

I nod. I don't lean towards him, or touch him because if I do, we're going to end up in bed and I'll never want to leave. I turn and walk back towards my car. I have a busy day ahead.

After a few hours' sleep, my first call is the hairdressers, where I spend four hours having my hair turned to its original brown. Of course, I have streaks of grey now, but we all love the transformational power of a new hair colour, and I'm ready to be as near to the original Melissa as possible. My contacts are gone, and I'm back to speaking in my own voice.

I'm back.

# CHAPTER TWENTY

Inez

I wake up in a hospital bed. A scream tears from my throat and then the pain comes as I realise my throat is sore. A nurse runs in.

'It's okay, love.'

'Why am I here? What time is it?'

She puffs up my pillow, giving me a weak smile. 'Sit back and try to relax. The doctor won't be long. He's doing the ward round and will get here soon. He'll explain what happened. Now, here's some water, take a few sips for me. It'll ease that throat.'

I do what she says. I feel like hell on earth. What happened to me? As I move I wince and remember my bruising. Then I recall I went to the accountants where I felt confused, then back to mine with Selma. I had a bath, but my memories are vague after that. Did the police come around? I peer up at the nurse, 'I don't remember.'

She pats my arm. 'It's just after ten. They'll be round with the tea trolley soon. A nice warm, soothing tea will do you good. Try not to worry. You're in hospital being looked after, and you're fine. Now, I need to do your blood pressure, okay?'

The nurse checks me over, records details on a chart and tells me someone will be in shortly. I lie back on the bed. Out of seemingly nowhere, a feeling of terror rises and rushes over my body. It's a hot electrical shock type feeling. My skin sweats. I feel clammy, sick, and faint. My heart beats so hard I think I'm going to have a heart attack. I tremble. My breath comes in sharp, fast pants. I struggle in my sheets, trying to get out of bed - gasping for air.

The nurse rushes back in. 'You're hyperventilating. Inez. Breathe. Follow me. Steady. Deep breaths. You're in hospital. You're safe. Come on, breathe slowly. In and out.'

She brings me back to a calmer level of panic, but it's still there, simmering. Waiting to spill over. What the hell happened? Why am I here? I need Selma. Selma will tell me everything I need to know.

'Excuse me?' I ask the nurse once I'm able to speak.

'Yes, love?'

'I need to contact my friend. Is there a phone I can use?'

'If you give me the number I'll ring them for you, love. I don't think you're well enough yet. We can get you set up with the hospital phone system or get someone to bring your things from home. There wasn't any answer from your next of kin.'

'No. He's left me,' I say. My voice quiet.

'Oh.'

She gives me an understanding look as if she's privy to something I'm not. My teeth gnash together. I'm starting to get pissed off with not knowing what's going on.

'I'll be back in a moment.'

A few seconds after she's gone a doctor walks in. 'Good morning, Inez. I'm Dr Walton. Do you know why you're here?'

'No,' I spit out, frustrated. 'So, if you could tell me, that would help.'

'We received a call to say you'd taken an overdose.'

'A what?' I pull at my hair. 'That's ridiculous. I didn't take an overdose.'

The doctor sighs. 'I'm afraid you did. We had to perform a gastric lavage. You'd consumed sleeping pills and painkillers.'

I try and think back. 'My friend gave me a couple of painkillers, but that's all.'

'Your friend told us she'd left the painkillers on the side. She thought you were sleeping but then discovered you were unconscious. There were pills on the bed around you. That's when she phoned the ambulance.'

I sit back. Had I done it and didn't remember?

'What's a gastric lavage?'

'Sorry, medical term. It's a stomach pump. We cleared your body of the drugs. You're going to feel tender for a few days. Now, when we admitted you, we noticed you had bruising to your abdomen. How did that occur?'

'It's nothing. An accident.'

The doctor sighs. 'If you think of anything you need to tell us, Inez, please buzz. Now, because you took an overdose, the on-call psychiatrist will be visiting you this afternoon.'

I narrow my eyes. 'You think I'm mad?'

'We think you need some support. Something has obviously occurred to make you self-harm, and we need to look into that.'

I rub my eye. 'I'm tired. Can I go back to sleep?'

'Of course. Ring the buzzer if you need anything.'

Dr Walton leaves, and I close my eyes. I took tablets? Had my stomach pumped? I need Selma. She'll help me and explain what's going on.

None of this would have happened if Ed hadn't fucking pissed off. Where is he anyway? With this Sam, I guess. They must have been carrying on for months. I bet she's laughing about the fact she convinced me she was still working with him. He's probably taken her away on holiday. I bet he's not ashamed of her. Frustration boils over. I bet that's why he controlled me. Not because he loved me and wanted me to himself but because he was ashamed of me and embarrassed. Didn't want anyone to know I wasn't a real woman. God, I've been stupid.

The nurse from this morning walks back in.

'Have you spoken to Selma? Is she coming in? I need to see her. She'll be able to give me some answers about what on earth went off last night.' I waffle on.

The nurse swallows.

I still.

'I rang the number you gave me, Inez,' she says carefully. 'But it doesn't belong to anyone called Selma.'

I huff. 'Then you must have written it down wrong. Can I see the number you called, please? I call her on it all the time.'

'It's okay. She explained it all. She's on her way, Inez, and says she'll help you as much as she can. She's been really helpful and told us what stress you've been going through lately.'

'Who are you talking about?'

The nurse sighs.

'I'm going to go and get the doctor back, Inez, for when Mrs Tebbs comes in.'

Mrs Tebbs? I can't have heard right. That's Dave's surname. Mel's surname.

I swallow. 'Who?'

'Melissa Tebbs. Your ex-wife. She explained that you've been suffering with your mental health for a while now. She says she's sorry that she didn't get you help earlier.'

My heart thuds again. I feel the blood drain from my body. Melissa. My ex-wife. Coming here? Answering the phone of Selma. I really am insane. Or this nurse is.

'I don't understand. Why is Melissa answering Selma's phone? What's going on?'

'She explained. Sit back and relax, sweetheart. She says you've been calling her Selma for a while. That you've been hallucinating and imagining she's someone else. She wonders if it's a manifestation of who you wanted to be.' She nods at me. 'She told me about your op.'

The anger takes over. 'I'm not mad!' I scream. 'I've not seen Mel for years. I've been with Selma. She's been helping me since my marriage broke down. My husband. He's left me. Selma helped me. Where is she? Where's Selma.'

Staff rush in and I find myself held down until I agree I'm calm. They keep a nurse by my bed. Apparently, I'm now on one-to-ones because I'm not safe to be left alone.

Maybe I'm not.

# CHAPTER TWENTY-ONE

Melissa

It feels good to be me again. No pussyfooting about, ensuring I speak in the right accent and don't give myself away like I did with Dave. Now I can be me. Or rather, very soon I'll be able to live the rest of my life knowing that my sacrifices of the last few years were worth it, that they suffered what I did and now we're even. Just a couple more things to strike off the to-do list.

The first is to ask Bobby to drop Inez's phone off at the nurse station with a message that I'll be along later.

The second is to deal with Ed.

I unlock the door of my house and walk through, a smile on my face, knowing that the filthy infestation of Ed is on its way out. I open the kitchen drawer and take out the key for the handcuffs and then open the bedroom door. When I walk into the room, Ed is mumbling to himself. His head turns towards me. He looks like a deranged hobo.

'Did you find the truth? Am I finally getting out of here, sis?'

I give him a withering glare. 'You believe that if it helps you. You are getting out of here though, and this is how it's going to go. I'm going to uncuff you, and then you're going to get a shower. Bobby is arriving shortly, and he'll assist you with shaving. We need to get you looking as smart as possible. After that, I'll fix you a drink and a sandwich, get some sustenance in you, and then you can put on this suit. The last nice suit you own by the way as Inez got rid of all your clothes. Bobby will drop you home. You understand it wouldn't be right us being seen together, don't you? Wouldn't want people to talk.'

'And what if the minute you uncuff me, I break your nose instead?' he sneers.

'Well, then you'll not know how to locate your wife, will you? Or is that ex-wife, or even'— I chuckle –'Late wife.'

He strains on his chain. 'What have you done?'

'It's a little stupid to let you go, without having an insurance policy, isn't it? I've done what I set out to do, we're even-stevens. Now you can go.'

Ed stares at me. His eyes full of hatred. 'I'll do whatever it takes to get out of here.'

Ed is true to his word. He gives Bobby no problems and is dropped off at his door. Unknown to them I've followed in my car and parked down the street. I move nearer to their house, keeping behind foliage and out of sight. I watch as Ed sees the graffiti on the outside of the house. I watch as he picks up a parcel from behind his bin. A whole new set of cheap shit clothes. When he's safely indoors, and Bobby has driven away, I call his house phone.

'Yes,' he says tersely.

'Your wife is on Ward A2 at Southern. At least, she was when I left. They may have transferred her to the psychiatric unit by now. Anyway, I'm about to find out. I'll see you there.'

I cut him off.

# CHAPTER TWENTY-TWO

Inez

They ask me if I'm settled now. I nod. I'm confused still, but I feel a lot better. If Melissa comes, I'll ask her to explain. I don't think I've gone mad. There's an explanation here somewhere, I know there is. I'll bet the drugs they've given me here have made me imagine they've said Mel. It'll be Selma who visits, I'm sure.

Another nurse walks in with my phone. 'This has been dropped off for you.'

I brighten and smile. 'Thank you.' This is great. I can look through my photos and find the ones of me and Selma together. Then I can show them to the nurse. They'll know then I'm not mad. I skim through my photos but find none of us both. I swipe the phone faster. Not a single one. My photos consist of pictures of Ed, and Bounty – my poor beautiful dog.

I check my emails. There are no longer signs banning the use of mobile phones in the hospital, or if there is my nurse stays silent as I carry on searching through mine. I startle as I see that I have an email from Ed. I read it.

*Inez,*

*I realise I made a mistake. I genuinely believed I was in love with you and we did share some happy years together. But I realised I needed a proper woman. There have been several over the years. I'm not proud of having cheated. I'm sorry. They meant nothing. It was just sex. However, Sam is different. I love her. So, I won't be coming back. I'll come over sometime tomorrow for the rest of my belongings. I've handed in my notice at work, and I'm going to start afresh somewhere with Sam.*

*I wish you every happiness and hope you can find the same sort of love I have. You'll realise then that what we had together wasn't it.*

'I need to get home,' I scream. Jumping out of bed and trying to grab hold of my belongings. 'My husband's coming home to get his things.'

My nurse looks at the door. 'Inez, please get back in bed. You're getting upset again. They'll hold you down.'

I stop and turn to her. 'Read this email.' I hand her the phone. 'He's leaving me. This is the last chance I'll have to see him.'

The nurse looks genuinely remorseful as she gives me a sad smile and touches my arm. 'I'm sorry, Inez. You're neither physically or mentally ready to go home.'

To prove her point, I break down and cry right there in front of her. I've nothing left and can't see the point in carrying on, so they're right to keep me here.

I hear a nurse's voice. 'Look, I'll let you in, but if she becomes upset you'll have to leave. It's been a difficult day for her. Do you understand?'

I try to gaze past the nurse's shoulder to see who's behind her but I can't. The nurse is too tall. I breathe a sigh of relief when Selma's voice comes out. 'I understand, thank you.'

The nurse turns to me and says to press my buzzer if needed. I nod, and then she moves away.

My mouth drops open as behind her stands Selma, but not Selma. Her body is the same, but her eyes are a different colour, and her hair is long and dark. Her hair is like Mel's when she was married to Dave.

'I don't understand, Selma. I'm confused.'

'Hello, Jarrod.' The voice that comes out of her mouth is my ex-wife's. As clear as anything. My hand goes across my mouth. It can't be. I really am insane. It's not possible this is Mel. She's years younger and doesn't look like her. I'm mistaken with the voice. It's Selma. Selma with a new hairstyle.

Selma takes a seat at the side of my bed.

'We don't have long. If you create any fuss, our conversation will be over, and you'll be on your way to the psychiatric unit, so I suggest you shut up and listen,' she tells me. I listen with my eyes shut. It *is* Mel's voice.

I open my eyes and can't stop staring. How can this be Mel? Her skin is not the same. Her cheekbones are not the same. Her nose is different. Her lips are a completely different shape. She's toned and tanned, and Mel was soft, with plump edges and as pale as milk. Mel had no bust, this woman's are, I know, a decent handful. If this is Mel, I fucked Mel. There was no Selma. Never any Selma. It was Mel all along.

'You can't be Mel. I hear your voice, but you can't be.'

'You're not the only one to have reconstructive surgery. It's amazing what money can buy.'

I sit a moment, staring and shaking my head. 'But, why?'

'You killed my baby. I lost who I believed was the love of my life. I lost the ability to have any more babies. You took away my life. It was only fair you lost yours in return.'

'So you set Ed up with Sam?'

She guffaws with laughter. 'I am Sam.'

'What?' I sit up. 'You slept with my husband?'

'No, I most certainly didn't. But that's rich coming from you,' she snarls. 'I'll explain it to you like I did Ed. It's really quite clever when you think about it. It's a puzzle. Rearrange the letters of Melissa, and you get Sam lies. Oh, and how Sam has lied. She lied about having an affair with your husband. I did work with him though, that's the truth. It was so much fun working with Ed and him not knowing who I was.'

If I thought my mind was messed up before it's nothing to how it feels now. I'm reeling. I can't take my eyes away from my ex-wife. Trying to find any part of her I recognise, other than her now non-contact-lensed eyes and her voice. Even the shape of her eyes is different, though other than the colour it's difficult to associate it with the woman I knew.

'So, you weren't ever my friend?' I ask. 'You were playing a part?'

'Yup.' She sits back and smiles. 'Your mugging? Set up.'

I gasp.

'Well, thank you for at least being helpful when I lost Bounty,' I say. I watch as her face saddens. 'I'm still devastated.' I tell her.

'It's the one thing I regret.'

'W-what?' My breath catches in my throat.

She fiddles with the wedding ring I now notice on her left hand. Not the one I put there. 'I made a huge donation to a pet charity after that you know. For them to specifically look into how to develop antidotes to antifreeze poisoning.'

'Y-you killed Bounty?'

She looks at me with an intense stare. 'You killed my baby. I killed yours. Only you can buy another one. How is that fair?'

'So all of this has been for revenge?'

'That's right.'

My forehead creases. 'But all that effort. Surgery to make yourself different, murdering animals. Do you not feel it's slightly over the top? Could you not just have egged the house or something?'

'You still don't get it, do you?' she says. 'You're making jokes about a situation that has no humour.' Her voice is so low, it sends a chill down my spine.

'You tilted my world on its axis. You were my whole life. We were happily married and having a baby. In one night, I lost my husband, who became someone else, so I couldn't even mourn your loss properly. You were no longer Jarrod but still around. Living across the street, shoving your happiness down my throat, making me choke. I fought for my life. I lost my baby and any chance of having one. Then I found out I'd lost my friend. Do you even remember Sandra? She was so guilt ridden she killed herself. Next, I lost my home.' She puts a finger up as she sees me start to protest. 'Yes, I got it from you in payment for the divorce, but it was never my home again. I had to give away all the baby stuff, Jarrod. Do you know how that felt? Of course you don't. You didn't give a shit because you were so in love with Ed.'

I wince as she calls me my old name again, but I guess that's who she's talking to so I let it go. Right now, that's who's present in this hospital room. Jarrod and Mel. Having the conversation we should have had after the accident.

'I'm sorry.'

'No, you're not. You never wanted the baby. That's what you told Selma. Oh, by the way, that's another in-joke. Selma Is. Selma is Melissa. Another jumble of the letters. You'll see I've had to take my laughs where I can find them.'

I bite my lip as I think back to my conversation with Selma. I told her everything. Mel knows everything. Fuck.

'I think what hurt the most though, Jarrod, is that you couldn't have confided in me when we were younger. When you first started things with Ed. Instead, you dragged us through years of lies. Years I could have spent with another man, having another man's children, being happy. Now do you see why you have to pay? Yes, it's taken me years, and I don't care. You already took years of my life so what's a few more? You don't deserve happiness, Jarrod. Not one bit of it. Not with him anyway.'

'I love him.'

'Do you? That's not what I think. I've spent enough time with you the last week to get to know exactly what your relationship was like. He controls every one of your actions. You can't breathe without his permission. You swapped a life of imprisonment with me, for another one. You can be Inez, but you're still not yourself. You're Ed's toy, Inez. He even named you. So who are you?' Her voice rises on the you. 'You're no longer Jarrod. Are you, Inez? Or are you someone else? The person *you* hoped to be. You said you had an idea of a name of your own.' She laughs. 'I was going to say you don't have the balls to do it, to be yourself.' Another laugh, 'and you really don't, do you?'

I look at the bed, concentrate on the hospital emblem imprinted on the bedding.

'I wanted to be physically sick when I saw your vagina.'

I wince and hug my arms around myself, trying to become smaller.

'Not that they haven't done a good job. In some ways it's fascinating, to see how they can make a vagina that actually comes. Science and biology are incredible. But it was like another loss to me, you know. I had to acknowledge that the male part of you was completely gone.'

'I've never felt male, Melissa.'

'I know that now,' she says in a quieter tone. 'You explained it all to Selma.'

'So where's Ed then? Do you know?' I ask her.

'He's been in my old house.'

'The one at Handforth? Your parents old home?'

'Yes.'

'Why has he been staying there?'

'Not through choice. I kidnapped him. He's not the same man either now.' She glares at me. 'We'll see how you get on when he returns. By the way, he knows you fucked me.'

I breathe sharply. 'I'll tell him you lied.'

'I recorded it on a camera on my watch Jarrod. He's seen it.'

I place my head in my hands. 'Oh, my God. What else have you done?'

'Lots of things. An eye for an eye. As I said, I lost my baby, you lost yours.'

'I can't believe you murdered my dog.'

'Then I lost my husband. I can't force Edward not to want you, so instead, I'm sending him back with a reminder of what you stole from me. Let you look at it as you make love and remember. I'll always be there now, Jarrod. Always. In your bedroom with you. While Ed thinks about how you let me fuck you. How you cheated on him. When you look at Ed's body, you're always going to be reminded of me. If you survive it, good luck to you. But my hope is that it eats you alive until you can't stand to be together anymore. You see, I don't want your separation to be quick. I want it to take years. I want it to waste years. For you to realise that it's all been for nothing. Your whole sad fuck-up of a life. All for nothing. That you failed as Jarrod, that you failed as Inez. That you don't know who the fuck you actually are.'

'I never realised how much hurt I caused you, to make you like this.' I look at her in pity.

'Well, now you do,' she sneers. 'Oh, don't give me that look. The poor Mel look that you gave me when I asked you if we could have children and you made me wait. Now I can finally move on with my life. That's if Dave will still have me. I realised how much I loved him when I was away. I couldn't understand it as I'd only ever known the fake love between us. Dave and I - we have to start again, afresh. We're getting on in years now. We don't have any more time to waste. I'm almost done with you.'

'Almost?'

'Like I said. I lost my home. I could never settle in that house. I only wanted it so I could use the funds to pay for this.' She sweeps a hand over her body.

'What have you done to my house?'

'Let's save that for later because any minute now you're going to get a visitor. I can hear him asking where you are.' Mel laughs. 'It's such a shame that I'm going to tell the nurse you're extremely agitated and need a rest before you have any more visitors.'

'Mel. No.'

But she does. I watch her go out and have a word with the nurse outside the door. I hear Ed arguing as the nurse says he can't go in. That I need to rest. That visiting time starts again at six and to come back then. He gets angry, and she warns him that she'll ring security if he doesn't calm down. I hear him storm off, his footsteps heavy and then I hear Mel say, 'I wonder if that's where her bruises came from?'

She's so very fucking clever.

How I underestimated my stay at home housewife.

At six pm Ed bursts through my door. He dashes over to my bedside, his arms wide.

I veer back towards the bed head.

'You can't hug me?' he says.

'I'm not myself at the moment, Ed. I need a bit of space.' I look at him, seeing his drawn face, his weight loss. 'What did she do to you?'

'She tried to break my spirit, but she failed. Other than when she showed me the video.'

I cast my eyes down. 'I'm so sorry.'

'Don't be. If it had been another person, it'd be different. But it was Melissa. She's part of your past, and we'll put her back there again.'

'I want her to be left alone, Ed. She's suffered enough.'

'What?' Ed snarls. 'Are you kidding me?'

'No.' I snap, waving my hand around. 'All this that she did. She explained. It was a reaction to what we put her through. She's finished. It's over now. It's time for us to live our lives and let her live hers.'

He removes his jacket and begins to unbutton his shirt.

'Ed, what are you doing?'

'You need to see this.' He opens his shirt to reveal words. So many, many words. The same word. His abdomen and chest are covered with the words.

MINE.
MINE.
MINE.
MINE.

'It seems your ex-wife wants to remind us that we took from her,' Ed says. 'I'm sorry you'll have to look at these, but at least they'll cover with a shirt. I was scared the stupid bitch might tattoo my head.'

'She's not a stupid bitch,' I tell him.

'Oh, my God, you're seriously not sticking up for her?'

'No. But she's far from stupid. She's smarter than I gave her credit for and now we have to pay.'

'I'll find out the cost of laser removal and see if they can be removed or faded. I might be able to cover them with something else.'

'She told me.' I study his body. 'She said that every time we made love, she'd always be there.'

'What? Because she wrote MINE on my body? Do you know what? We can make this about us. I'm yours. You're mine. We'll work through it.'

I shake my head. 'No. You don't get it. It's part of her word games.'

He sighs. 'You're reading too much into this, Inez.'

'Mine.' I touch the M on his chest.

He clasps my finger. 'Yours,' he says.

'No.' I snatch my hand back. 'Watch.'

I touch the M. 'M is for Melissa.'

I trail my finger across the I and the N. 'IN for Inez.'

I point to the E. 'E for Edward.'

'All three of us.' I trail my hand across the letters and back away from Ed. 'Always there with us.'

'Inez. Don't be stupid. You're letting her get into your head.

That's what she wants. Now, what do we need to do to get you discharged?'

'Don't call me that.' Mel was right. I'm not being myself. I'm being who Ed wants. Right now, he wants little Inez to behave and come home like a good girl.

'Look. I've just got away from one nutcase, and I'd really like to go home. Although I note half the furniture has been changed, so it doesn't really feel like my home.'

I flinch at his words. 'Then go. Get away from this nutcase.'

'Inez.'

'I'm not Inez anymore. I always wanted to be called Lynne. That's my name from now on, get used to it.'

He sighs out loud. 'I'm starting to think you really do have psychiatric problems.'

'You're right. I have a lot of problems.' I shake my head in agreement. 'So I'm staying here to work through some of them. They have specialists here. They can help me come to terms with everything that happened and help me to become who I want to be.'

'And what about us?'

'When I finally get discharged, we'll see if you want to be with Lynne, and if I want to be with Edward, won't we?'

'She'll pay for this.' He spits out angrily as he makes his way towards the door.

'Leave her alone. We've caused her enough problems.'

'I'm afraid it's not that simple,' he yells as he storms from the room.

I should feel sadness that he's left after I've only just got him back but I don't. I feel relief. I feel a weight lifted. I smell a fresh start where I can try and make amends for everything that's happened, and I can focus on the rest of my life like Mel is doing.

If Ed will let her.

# CHAPTER TWENTY-THREE

Melissa

It was all set to happen the minute Ed left the house. Bobby had parked up nearby and returned as soon as he saw Ed leave the street in the taxi he'd ordered. Bobby has my key and the alarm code and leaves no sign of forced entry. He's dressed in builder's garb, and so raises no suspicion on our quiet little estate. Anyway, after the scandal that tore us apart, I know everyone would keep their mouths shut if they did see something. They live private lives now. So, Bobby leaves a pan on. It's his last job for me, and after this, he leaves to return to Suffolk. Stupid, stupid Ed. Despite his denial, it will appear he left the pan on and burned down his house. They'll determine due to the stress of a wife in hospital he got distracted and careless.

Dave watches and lets the house become overwhelmed with flames before he phones the fire brigade.

'Thanks, darling. That should do nicely,' I tell him. I walk over to him and place my arms around his neck.

My eyes stare into my husband's, and I try and show him how much I love him with that one look. 'I'm done. They lost what I lost. Now it's time to live my life, our life. Take me to bed, Dave. I need you.'

So while the house down the street is cooled down by the fire brigade, our house heats up.

Dave walks up the stairs, and I follow behind. We enter our bedroom, and I gasp. It's the same as when I left all those years ago, bedding and all.

'I hope you've washed this since I left.' I laugh.

'Yes. It's a little threadbare, but it's you. I wanted to keep everything us.'

I bite my lip. 'I'm sorry.' I sweep a hand down my body. 'I didn't do the same, did I?'

He takes a step towards me. 'You're still you.'

Slowly, he removes my top, pulling it over my arms and head and letting it drop to the floor. He pours over every detail of my body. He drops the straps of my bra off each shoulder and unclasps it at the back, letting it sweep past my breasts on its way to join my top. His hands explore my new breasts with utter devotion. It's like he's attempting to commit my new body to memory.

'I'm not going anywhere again,' I whisper.

'I can't believe you're here,' he says. The emotion is too much, and a tear trickles from one eye. 'Fuck, I missed you so damn much.'

Hunger flashes in his eyes and he undoes my trouser button, yanking down the zip. My pants follow. He sheds his own clothes with haste and backs me onto the bed, *our* bed, with a frenzy. His lips tease my body, replaced by his tongue. It's at this moment it becomes clear that no matter how different the outside of my body is, it responds to Dave exactly as it did before. Our bodies move harmoniously together, with the assured moves of lovers who know each other intimately. I moan as I accept his cock within me. I need him with a fervour I can't put into words. I indicate it with my body instead, raising my hips off the bed towards him.

'Open your eyes,' Dave says.

We keep our focus on each other as we build towards our climaxes. Our gaze on each other intensifies. Without restraint we thrash against each other, seeking the point where we reunite in ecstasy.

I feel Dave tighten as I build towards my climax.

I pulse around his cock as he releases his seed inside me.

He lowers his forehead to mine. Beads of sweat cross his brow.

'I love you. Please don't leave me again.'

'I told you, I'm going nowhere.'

He lies back against the pillow. 'I think we should move,' my husband says.

I stroke my fingers down his cheek. God, I've missed him.

'A new beginning. What do you think about moving to the States?'

'I'll go anywhere you want me to. As long as we're together, I don't care.'

I snuggle into his arms and sleep the soundest sleep I've had in a long, long time.

The sleep of a deluded person who believed Edward would let it all lie.

# PART 3
# EDWARD

# CHAPTER TWENTY-FOUR

Edward

I thought my parents loved me. Though my father worked long hours and was gone on many an evening, my mother did her best to bring me up, but she struggled. She overdosed on painkillers when I was twelve. By fifteen I had a stepmother. She ignored me completely until I was sixteen. Then, all of a sudden, as I grew, so did her interest.

When my father returned home after one of his trips away he finds me balls deep in his wife. She'd been quite the teacher, and I had an array of skills that would stand me in good stead in the future.

My father grabbed me by the shoulder and threw me into the door. I'd stood up, ready to escape. But I saw fear on my stepmother's face. Watched as my dad stalked over to her like a cat teasing prey, as he'd taken off his belt and thrashed her until the skin on her back ripped apart, blood trickling down onto the floor. Her screams were beautiful. That's what I remembered, but they couldn't replace the satisfaction I'd got from seeing that fear, knowing that my dad was in charge and would mete out punishment as he saw fit. I got harder from that than I did from thinking about fucking her.

From then on, I ignored her, which my stepmother did not take kindly to. Despite her punishment from my father she continued to pursue me. I'd find her half naked in my room. To her annoyance, I'd walk away. Until one day she said the words that changed everything.

'You're adopted, you know?'

I called her a lying, scheming cunt. Then I hit her as my father had. I took a belt from my drawer and lashed her with it. She was petrified, but she let me do it. Wanted me to fuck her afterwards. So in order to find out exactly what my background was, I fucked my stepmother while her back bled into the sheets.

My real mother was some young slut who'd fucked another pupil and come unstuck. She didn't want the child because the father was part African American and part Native American. She'd been intrigued enough to get impregnated by him but not enough to stay with him. Did I find all this out on my eighteenth birthday? Fuck, no. My stepmother was the social worker involved in my adoption. Now thirty-eight, she'd been fucking my 'father' since she was twenty-two years old.

So I did what any kid would do. I went to see my real mother. There was no forwarding address for my father. No way of contacting him, but my stepmother, Inez, gave me her address.

Inez.

Are you confused?

Not my wife.

My stepmother. The stepmother I couldn't control. The only person who ever played me. The person who made me the scapegoat, the victim. The name for my future wife was clear, as was her appearance. She was tall like my stepmother. I made sure her hair was dark like hers, and then I gave Jarrod her name. An Inez I could completely control, even to the point where she got herself a vagina.

That had been all me. Encouraging Jarrod to be what I wanted him to be - her.

My stepmother had broken me for all women. None of them ever had that fear. I wasn't a rapist, and when I brought out restraints, they always seemed to enjoy it. I began to despise them. There may be a spark of worry, but they knew their fuck was coming and went along with the ride. Never any fear. Until Jarrod.

When I walked down my mother's street and stood at her fence, I found a dark-haired girl and a fair-haired boy chatting away while the girl hosed the garden plants.

'Hey. Excuse me. Do you know where Hendon Street is?' I asked.

The girl looked at me coolly, as if annoyed that I'd disturbed them. The boy moved away from her and over to the fence. 'Sure, it's down the street, left and then left again.'

'Thanks.' I said and wandered away. I'd taken note of the scout group badge on the shirt he was wearing. I wasn't sure why. I just collected it. Another piece of information. I hung around the house a few times at different hours of the day until one day I got lucky. My real mother was in the house alone; the daughter and her husband, along with the girl's male friend, had got into a car filled with fishing equipment. They were going to be a while, and I had the opportunity while they were out to net my own catch.

I can remember it so clearly. I rang the doorbell, and it was pulled open quickly.

'What did you leave this-? Oh. Can I help you?'

Her request was a hope that her eyes were playing tricks on her. For my colouring, the same as my adopted father's, was also the same as her ex-lover's. She didn't want it to be true, but she knew.

'You have his eyes,' she said.

She invited me in. I kept myself cool, controlled. I would wait to hear what she said before I made decisions about her future and mine. I found out over a cup of tea and a slice of apple pie that she had wanted to keep me. Had fought to do so, but at fifteen, she had lost the battle against her parents and had given me up. She cried as she explained how she'd tried to get over it by marrying at seventeen and having another baby. But that it hadn't worked. For as much as she loved my half-sister Melissa, it had never replaced the hole left by the loss of myself.

My mother had wanted me. It was like she gave me approval. She hadn't abandoned me. She had fought for me. It was my grandparents who were to blame. She was estranged from them, she explained. Would never have anything to do with them again.

So I asked what would happen now we had found each other again. My mother faced me with a look of stoic regret.

'We go back to how it was, Edward. I have a daughter now and a husband. They don't know about you. If word got out, I'd be a disgrace. You need to return to your life, and I'll return to mine. Just remember, I wanted you.'

Wanted. Past tense.

She went into a drawer in the kitchen and extracted an envelope from deep at the back. I saw her scratch the top of her fingers as she pulled it out. She checked the envelope and passed it to me. 'There are a couple of photographs of me and your father, and there's some money. I saved it for you, for if you ever came here, though I didn't expect you for another two years at least.'

'My stepmother told me.'

'Oh?'

I didn't explain further.

'Could you wait a moment?' She stood on a kitchen chair and reached to the back of a high up cupboard, bringing down a faded blue elephant. 'For the short time I held you in the hospital you had this toy.' I saw her swallow and tears swam at the bottom of her eyelids. 'Your adoptive parents wouldn't take it. Said they wanted a totally fresh start.' She bit her lip. 'You say you have a stepmother? Your parents split up then?'

'My adoptive mother killed herself,' I said bluntly. 'I don't seem to have a good track record with mother figures. The first abandoned me when I was born, the second when I was twelve, and my stepmother likes to fuck me for her own amusement.'

My mother stepped back and clutched a hand to her chest. 'I'm sorry I can't do more, Edward. I have too much to lose.'

I nodded because I understood. It was a choice she needed to make, and I fully got her position. To keep the life she had intact, she couldn't open the door to the past. No. I didn't blame my mother at all.

I blamed Melissa. Because if she hadn't existed, my mother would have let me in. Instead, I was a dirty little secret. Sent secret parcels at birthdays and Christmas.


I forced myself to date girls from Melissa's class, without her ever seeing me with them. I found out everything I could about her. She was the perfect student. She was on all the school sports teams. She'd been Head Girl at school. She had the most amazing boyfriend, Jarrod, and they already knew they'd get married and live happily ever after. I'd go home and hit my stepmother, unleashing my anger. Then frustrated with my own weakness, I'd steal from my father's wallet. He always carried far too much money. He didn't know what the hell planet he was on half the time he was so busy with work and my stepmum. It wasn't a lot of money, but it was a start. Myself, I was strong in one subject only - mathematics. So I gave it everything I had. Though I spent my seventeenth year calculating a lot more than sums.

I joined a scout group and became an explorer. I genuinely loved it and wished I'd joined when I was younger. The rules appealed. I felt pride every time I earned a badge. They taught skills - camper, chef, leadership. They made me feel like an expert. We had to abide by the Scout Law, agreeing that we could be trusted, loyal, friendly and considerate, that we'd have courage and be respectful.

Within Explorers, I adhered to it all. Outside of it, I adhered to none. However much I enjoyed the place, I'd joined for one reason only – a reason that came up on our first joint camping trip with other groups in the neighbourhood. To get to Jarrod. My aim had been to befriend him and show him how much more pussy there was out there than boring old Melissa. Not that I expected he'd done much with her at fourteen. The only intimacy I'd ever witnessed was from Melissa - grabbing his hand, jumping up to kiss his cheek, and putting her arms around his neck and making him kiss her. Oh, he tried to get into it, I could tell, but he wasn't fully committed.

Though at that stage I hadn't known the *why*.

The first time I went to camp for the weekend, my scout group was one among a few from the locality, including Jarrod's group.

A treasure hunt set up for the Saturday daytime proved to be my way to get near to him. I found him sitting on the stump of a tree by himself. He wasn't distressed. If anything, he looked bored.

'Hey, do you live near Hendon Street?'

Jarrod looked up. I could see his face registering he knew me and trying to place where from. 'I don't. My girlfriend Melissa does.'

I pulled a thinking face. 'Ah, that's it,' I said. 'I asked for directions once, and you were very helpful. I remember you and your friend.'

'Thought you looked familiar,' he said, 'But I'd never have remembered that. You've got a good memory.'

'I have, and unfortunately, I remember how crap camp is.'

Jarrod tore off a piece of tall grass. 'Tell me about it.'

'Are you forced to come here too? My parents thought it would be good for me to meet people. They say I'm too "insular".'

He nodded. 'My dad is very religious. He's a scout leader. Insists I need to uphold his beliefs.'

'Is he here?'

'No. He hurt his back, so he stayed home, but *I've* still had to come.' Jarrod got up and kicked the tree stump. 'It fucking stinks here. They all bully me because I'd rather hang with the girls and the girls don't want to know me because of my dad. They say he's a pervert, you know?'

'Standard name calling for scout leaders or teachers that.'

'Yeah, well, it's not fair on me.' He looked at the floor.

'So I guess you're not doing the activity then?'

Jarrod looked at me as if I'd asked him if he was going to the moon. 'No chance. I'll just turn up at the meeting point. They expect me to be useless anyway.'

'I'm sure you're not. Look, how do you fancy going round together? See if we're better as a team. I hate the kids in my own group.'

Jarrod tilted his head. 'I thought you said you were insular?'

'I usually am. But I must recognise you as being cut from the same cloth I am. There's an old saying for you.' I laugh.

'My dad talks like that. He's an idiot.'

'Well, he's no doubt expecting to hear you failed at the activity, so let's go and do our best. Let word get back to him that you aren't what he believes you are. Then I can go back and say I've made a friend and shock my own parents.'

He nods and follows me. He never was a challenge.

On the second camp, we acknowledged each other as we arrived. I got to see Jarrod's father. I overheard him calling his son a pansy and saying that he would stop him hanging around with Melissa unless he manned up.

It disgusted me to see him treated that way. Yet in front of everyone else, his father portrayed himself as a friend to all and holier than thou.

We met up where we could during the weekend. I found Jarrod easy to talk to. I looked forward to meeting up with him. He was completely transparent with me. Admitting to his weaknesses. No lies. No falsehoods. I told him so.

His face fell, and he looked on the verge of tears. 'Oh Edward. I'm sorry, but that's not true. I'm a walking web of lies.'

My forehead creased. 'I don't understand. Have you not been telling me the truth?'

Jarrod turned to face me with a look of sheer terror. 'I daren't tell you the truth, Ed. You'd hate me, and I couldn't bear for that to happen. You and Mel are all I have.'

I bristled at the mention of her name.

'You can tell me anything, Jarrod, anything at all.'

He began to cry. I couldn't bear it and pulled him into my arms. I couldn't explain it, but it felt right. I felt his suffering as if it poured from him and through my own skin.

'Not even Mel knows this,' he said.

Then he told me how he wished he'd been born female. He was attracted to Mel, but also found himself drawn to some men. That he didn't feel he really knew who he was. I had to hide the shock on my face. What he'd given me was the perfect story for revealing to Melissa. To take away her relationship. But I stared at the mixed-up teenager who had disintegrated into a ball of nothingness, not believing he had any worth and I realised I could build him up, make him stronger, make him who I wanted him to be. So I stroked his hair and reassured him that he was not alone. I confessed that I was adopted – that my whole world was a lie. I didn't tell him I was Melissa's brother. I wasn't that stupid. That weekend he looked up to me like you would a pop star or film star that you've made into your hero. He hung onto my every word as if I was the Lord himself.

On the third camp, when we escaped to the woods to talk, I made a move that could have killed my plans, but it was my last scout camp, and I needed to make progress. We'd been chatting for ages. He'd been telling about how he'd been dressing in Mel's clothes. How he felt guilty after.

'Why do you feel guilty for being you?' I asked him. 'You need to embrace who you are. If it has to be in secret for now, so be it. I'll keep your secrets. I'll always be your confidante.'

'I know I rarely get to see you, but I don't know what I'd do without you,' Jarrod had said. 'Just knowing when I lie in bed at night, that someone out there knows how I really feel. It helps, you know? If it weren't for you, Ed, I think I might have done something stupid by now.'

I pulled him towards me and wrapped my arms around him. 'You must never talk like that, Jarrod. You hear me? Being different does not mean you should have to conform to other people's versions of acceptable. You can always be yourself with me.'

'But I hardly see you. I wish you lived a bit nearer and that Melissa didn't get so jealous of other friends. I haven't told her about you, do you know that? How bad is it that I can't even be honest with her about making a good friend? She'd get jealous, so it isn't worth the hassle.'

'Then we'll stay a secret, and one day maybe it will be different.'

It's then I took the chance. I turned Jarrod's face to my own, leaned in, and kissed him.

Jarrod pulled his head back sharply and stared at me, anger displayed in his eyes, and tension in his jaw. Then he threw himself towards me, his lips back on my own, with an ardour I'd never experienced with any woman. I realised later, the anger he'd displayed was not at me, but the period of being at war with himself.

I backed him up towards the tree. Dusk was coming, and there was no one around. We didn't have long before we'd have others looking for us though. I pulled down his tracksuit bottoms and returned to kissing him. I wet my finger, having read about such things in the top shelf magazines passed around the classroom, and I pushed it up his arsehole. Jarrod arched towards me, his dick erect. Lowering myself to the ground, I took his cock in my mouth and sucked him until he erupted into my throat. It didn't take long.

When he cried afterwards, I licked up every tear. I told him I was sorry for doing it.

'No. Ed. You don't understand. I loved it. I felt things with you

I've never felt with Mel. Almost everything I do with Mel is a lie. I'm so confused.'

I placed his hand around the girth of my own cock. 'Please.'

He pumped, tentative at first, and then his breath came harder until I came. I pulled out of his hand as I felt my balls tighten and sprayed cum against the tree.

'Meet me here again in the early hours of the morning. Please?' I begged.

He gave me his phone number and very occasionally, for the next year or so, we met up. We'd progressed to me fucking his anus while he pleasured me with his hand and mouth. He didn't want to take me the same way, and that was fine. We'd determined this was the way we fit best. I fell in love with him and begged him to move in with me when he turned eighteen.

'I can't,' he said with tears in his eyes. 'I'm going to marry Melissa.'

My heart shattered, and I placed barbed wire protection over it. Blocked him from my mind. Blocked out the words that said the world wasn't ready for us. We'd be beaten up. Spat at.

I told him I couldn't see him anymore, and with a final farewell fuck, he agreed that was how it had to be.

'I'll come for you,' I said. 'When the world has a better tolerance, I'll come for you. So don't do anything stupid.'

Yet it appears I only delayed what he would do anyway, years down the line. That bitch made him believe he'd lost me forever. Now he's in hospital, and it's her fault. Well, if she thinks we're done, she's a fool.

## CHAPTER TWENTY-FIVE

Edward

I'm exhausted. Adrenaline had pushed me to the hospital. Now I was fading fast. I needed to get to bed. Tomorrow, I would start afresh with my diet and strength building. Get back to the man I was before. I'd look into laser surgery for the tattoos too. Today, I admitted defeat. I needed my own bed.

'Christ, what's happening here, man?' the taxi driver mutters.

I look out of the front window and see people out of their doorways, standing on the pavement.

'Fire engine up ahead. Looks like a house fire,' he says.

I know before I get out of the taxi. I pay the driver and thank God I took some money out of the house and stuck it in my pocket. As I walk as near as the barricades will allow, I realise it's all I have left. The heat from the fire hits you from metres away.

A fireman approaches me. 'Keep back, mate. No one can go any closer. We've had to evacuate.'

'It's my house.'

I look towards Dave and Melissa's house as I wait. Their curtains are closed upstairs. Are they fucking while my house burns down? Are they celebrating that they won?

What is the loss of our home going to do for Inez's mental state?

With my details handed over to the fire brigade and a contact number taken, I make another call to a taxi firm and get taken to a hotel. Then I sleep until the phone interrupts me. It's the fire brigade with an update that the fire is out. Then I sleep again, my body wracked with exhaustion. I've paid for a week's stay at this budget hotel, added to my credit card. In the morning I'll phone work, make up some excuse as to where I've been and get back to my desk. I need to get earning again while we await the insurance on the house.

In the end, I decide to call into the office in person. I end up in a heated argument with Jack.

'No. I did not hand in my resignation. I assure you.'

'It came from your email address, Ed,' says Jack. 'I don't know what's going on with you and your wife, but you need time out. She was in here last week not making any sense either.'

'I didn't hand in my resignation. Someone else did.'

There's a pause. 'Someone broke into your house and used your computer to send a letter of resignation?' He shoves his hands in his pockets. 'You agree that sounds a bit weird, don't you? Unless... Was it Sam? Is it true you've had it away with her, you naughty boy? Whoa, bit Bunny Boiler her breaking into your home to do that. Or did you have her round while the missus was out shopping, you sly dog, Ed.'

I sigh. At least he's offered me a decent excuse. 'Yes, Sam probably did it. So can you destroy it? Can I come back to work?'

'Sure you can, mate.' He comes towards me and bumps shoulders. I want to push him into the wall. 'We'll have to get down

Spearmint Rhino now I know you're one of the boys. Unless you're still with that Sam, you lucky bastard. Those tight thighs, fuck, I'd have liked those around my head.'

I endure ten more minutes of this before we agree I'll return to work on the following Monday. That's my job back. It's time to phone the insurance company so I can see about getting the house rebuilt.

'I'm sorry, Mr Bonham. A chip pan fire is excluded from your policy. You cannot claim on this occasion.'

I try so very hard to hold my temper, but my voice rises anyway. 'I've told the fire brigade. I didn't leave a pan on. I hadn't had anything to eat. I don't even eat chips.'

'Look, you'll have to take it up with them. We have their report. It states major damage to the kitchen and dining area, and the rest of the property is badly affected by heavy soot and smoke deposits on all surfaces. There's nothing more we can do from our end. Good day, sir.'

I throw a water glass at the wall where it sprinkles in shards. Before, only my stepmother made me lose control. Now *she* had. My *sister*. Now I had a fucking glass to pay for on top of house repairs if the fuckers didn't cough up. I pick up the shards one by one. Might as well put them to some use seeing as I'll have to pay for the glass. I wrap the shards in tissue and place them in my pocket.

She still has fucking everything. A loving husband that she's with because of me. Why did she never see it like that? Her ex-husband was not the route to her happiness. It was a fucked-up way, but she ended up with a husband who loved her, and stepchildren. But she still wasn't happy. I see the surly face of a young Mel in my mind. The one who didn't want to give me directions. She has no room in her life for anything not carefully considered. I guess in that way we're quite similar. Maybe it's a trait from our mother? I wouldn't know because Mel kept me from knowing her.

I mutter to myself. Shaking my head as I think things through.

*Tomorrow I get my car back.*
*Time for some visits.*
*Inez. I'm coming to see you, Inez. I'll bring my belt.*
I chuckle.
*Then sister dear, I'm coming to see you.*
I shake the shards in my pocket. I have just the idea.

# CHAPTER TWENTY-SIX

Melissa

The For Sale sign swings in the breeze outside our house. I'll be glad when someone purchases it, and we can be on our way. Far from here and from them. I don't know what's happening with Jarrod, Edward, or the house, and I honestly don't care. It's as if a huge weight has lifted from me. Our daughters found their stepmother's makeover strange, but they quickly came around. My grandchildren are adorable. I've missed so much. Jude is now fourteen. He's taller than I am. Becky also has a ten-year-old son called Marc. Today little Millie is here. She's Joanne's daughter and is three years old. She delights with her singsong voice and theatrical ways. I realise that we'd miss them so much if we moved to the States. Why should we miss out on time with our grandchildren? Haven't I missed enough? We need to stay nearer.

I'm making an apple pie when Millie runs in clutching a wrapped gift box.

'Millie. Where's that come from?' I laugh, assuming grandad is spoiling her once again.

'Man passed it through window.'

I drop the pie dish and snatch it from her hand. 'What man?'

She stands startled. Her lip wobbling and tears threatening.

'He said give you box. He said friend, Grandma.'

I clutch her towards my apron. 'I'm sorry, Millie. You did nothing wrong. The naughty man shouldn't have come to our window. He's still a stranger, okay? I'll lock the windows now. Don't go near him again if he comes back, Millie.'

'Okay, Grandma. What's in the box?'

'I'll look later.' I stuff the box in my apron pocket. 'Can you help me finish this pie?'

Thank goodness three-year-olds are easily distracted.

When the pie's in the oven and Millie is on the sofa watching children's TV, I hover in the kitchen doorway and remove the box from my pocket. When I remove the lid, shards of broken glass are contained within. A gift tag says simply, 'Ed'. The message is clear. He gave my granddaughter broken glass. He's not finished. We're not safe.

I hate him. Why did he decide to ruin my life?

It's time to move. To escape. Also, it's time to seek answers.

We'll have no choice but to temporarily move to the house at Handforth. I don't know what I'll do with it going forward. Maybe I'll see if a developer wants to take a gamble on it? It's uninsurable, so I doubt it, but maybe they can make the surrounding area safe again? If not, I'll have to leave it behind. It reminds me too much of Edward now. This was my parents final home, but their happy place has been soiled by that man. He's like a slow spreading toxin. I need to know one way or another if we're related. For that, I'm going to need to see him again.

I'm going to get rid of this man once and for all.
But how?

# CHAPTER TWENTY-SEVEN

Edward

'Edward Bonham speaking.'

'You got your job back then?' Melissa's voice teases down the line. My hand tightens around the telephone.

'No thanks to you.'

'Thank you for the gift. If you ever pull a stunt like that with my granddaughter again, you'll be back at my house eating a cake with those very ingredients.'

'Is that why you're ringing, Melissa? To warn me off? Good to know I got to you.'

There's a sigh down the phone.

'No. I need to know something once and for all. Can you give me your current address? I need to get something delivered to you.'

'I'm not sure about that. You'll forgive me for being suspicious.'

'It's a DNA test kit. I've been in touch with a company. Results within 24 hours for sibling tests.'

'Oh, in that case I'll definitely tell you. Can we meet for the results? I want to see your face.'

'How's my ex-husband doing?'

I stay silent.

'Oh, my God, he won't see you, will he?'

'Inez is a she, Mel. Can you get your head around that? Jarrod lived a lie.'

'Yeah, well he/she lived one with you too. Who knows who's coming out of that hospital.'

I tell her my address and hang up.

Two days later we arrange to meet in a cafe. Melissa has the results envelope in her hand. I watch as she walks toward me, her face devoid of any emotion.

'Lovely to see you again, sis. Have you missed me?'

'Save it, Edward.' She sits down and re-opens the envelope. 'Our score indicated that we are indeed half siblings.'

I clutch onto Melissa's arm and act like it's the best news I've ever received. It isn't difficult because knowing what this will do to her, makes it some of the best news I've ever received.

Melissa gets up to leave.

'Where are you going, sis?'

She turns towards me. 'I'm going for a drink. Coffee won't do it for me today. I suggest you follow me. I want to know what this is about. What do you want so I can live my life without you in it?'

'That's not very sibling-like, is it?' I reply and then guffaw.

She orders a bottle of red wine. It's a good name, not the house crap and I tell her we'll share. We take a seat opposite each other next to the large windows of the bar. It gives me a sense of satisfaction that she chooses a public seat – shows me she's afraid of being in a dark corner with me. I have control. It makes my dick hard. Not for her.

She'll never do that for me, bitch. But the power. The control. I realise how things could have gone very wrong if I'd have slept with Sam. She didn't know we were related and I didn't know she was Melissa. The thought makes me boil with anger. The stupid bitch.

Melissa sits back in her seat.

'So what is this about?' She sighs. 'I know you met and fell for Jarrod.' She sees my reaction. 'Sorry, Inez. You met and fell for *Inez* at explorers. She told me. Then you moved to the estate to what, win her back?'

'Yes, and to take her from you.'

'So, part of this was not undying love and devotion for my ex but the need to get at me. Why? What did I ever do to you?'

I take a sip of my drink. 'Our mother wouldn't acknowledge me because of you.'

'I don't understand.'

I fill her in on all the times I visited our mother. Melissa's face pales but flushes with the wine she consumes to cope with what she's hearing.

'Ed. You were born out of wedlock at a time people didn't accept those things.' She tries to reason. 'It wasn't me that stopped you being accepted. It was the time of your birth.'

'No. She told me. She wanted me in her life, but it would upset you too much, so she chose you over me. She gave me away to my adoptive parents and then rejected me again for you. Twice I wasn't good enough. I watched you. You had everything. Loving parents, a great family home, a best friend who became a boyfriend and then husband. I had an adoptive father who was never there and a mother who killed herself. Then I got a stepmother with no morals. She knew me from my adoption as a baby and let me fuck her. Who in their right mind does that? You got the life that should have been *mine*,' I spit, droplets of red wine splash my chin.

Mel pulls at the top of her hair while she moves it away from her face. 'I am genuinely sorry that your life was not idyllic, but I can't apologise for being born, Ed. My mother made those choices – not me. She chose to have you adopted. She chose not to include you again.'

I realise then that it's Melissa who has the power. By seating us in a public place, I can't unleash my anger. Instead, I clutch the stem of my glass so hard, I fear it may break off in my hand.

'You're not the only one whose life was a lie, Edward. That's the joke in all of this. My *idyllic'—* she makes speech quotes with her fingers around the word –'life, was based on a mother who hid from me, and maybe even my father, that she had another child. And with them both deceased I have no way of asking either of them what the truth is. So you see, you've taken my so-called happy childhood and ruined it for me forever. Well done.' She slow hand-claps. 'As for my friend and boyfriend, well we all know how that turned out. Years of lies. You're not the only person who would like a do-over.'

She sits back and laughs. 'I was about to say that I wish I'd never met Jarrod, but I'd still have had you in my life, wouldn't I? Ready to destroy whatever path I'd have trodden. Did you ever love him? Or was it just to get back at me?'

'It started as getting back at you. I was going to steal your friend. That was all. But he showed me his true self, and I genuinely fell for him. I didn't try to make him something he's not.'

'Is that so? Because you named him Inez and you never let him make any decisions. That doesn't sound like someone who fell in love. You never let Jarrod be who he wanted to be.'

She puts her glass down on the table. 'That's why he's not seeing you, isn't it? You want Inez back, but he's not Inez anymore, is he?'

The bitch is clever. 'No. And that's down to you. You took him away from me.'

'Right back at you. Karma's a bitch.' She snorts.

'Are you happy with Dave, Melissa?'

She bristles at the mention of his name. 'Don't bring him into this.'

'But he's already involved, isn't he? He's part of the whole sordid evening. What happened that night, Melissa? What was it like when they took the foetus from your body. Was it already dead?'

I knock my wine over purposefully and the red spills over Melissa's top. She looks down at the blood red stains.

Tears spill down her face. I've never seen her weak, and it's glorious. I want to lick the tears from her face and rejoice in the salty taste on my tongue.

She takes a deep inhale and exhale. 'I won't answer those sick questions except to say that I could cope with your stealing Jarrod. I could have coped with finding out I had a brother. I would have welcomed you.' She mops at her stomach with a tissue. 'I always wanted a sibling. I used to nag my parents to death for one. I'd have loved you. But the evening of the accident, when I was hit by a taxi, you left me half-dead. Neither of you came up to help. I've never recovered from my loss and I never will. I'm happy with Dave. I truly am. My grandchildren are beautiful inside and out. But they'll never be mine. You took away the opportunity to do what I'd yearned for my whole life. To give life. I was so excited to meet my baby and then when I did–' She stops and cries again.

I wait until she composes herself.

'Are you the slightest bit regretful about what happened, Edward? Do you wish things could have been different?'

'No.' I tell her honestly. 'I wish I could bottle every tear on your face.'

'You sick fuck,' she spits.

I laugh. 'Oh, sister, there's so much more about me you need to know. Like, I'm not done. You're happy again, and I'm not. So, what's it to be? You help me get my wife back, or I make sure you don't have a husband – again.'

She throws the remainder of her glass of wine in my face. I wonder what anyone watching us is thinking?

I lick drops of wine off my lips. 'I wonder what Dave's blood would taste like?'

'You disgust me.'

I laugh and shrug my shoulders.

She sits back down. 'What do you want me to do?'

I leave the pub with a great sense of satisfaction. Looks like things are going my way again. I head to the rental property I've leased for myself and Inez when she returns. Work let me have an advance on my wages so I could get back on my feet. Inez will love the house. It's around the corner from our old home, and the layout of the property is the same. I've paid a deposit on a new puppy, the exact breed and look as Bounty. Everything will be back to normal soon. Once home, I get my gym kit out ready for the morning and place it on the chair at the end of the bed. I can restart my gym activities now I'm gaining strength and know I'm unlikely to be kidnapped again. Not if my dear sister Mel values that family of hers.

# CHAPTER TWENTY-EIGHT

Melissa

Dave's face reddens. His eyes protrude and a vein pulses in his forehead. 'He's never going to leave us alone then, is he? The man's psychologically disturbed. We've no chance against him. So let's just cut our losses and disappear.'

I shrug. 'And how do we explain that to the children? There's no way they are going to uproot everyone.'

He paces. 'What about the police?'

I look down at the floor. 'I think I'd have a lot of explaining to do.'

He runs his hands through his hair. 'God, this is such a mess.'

'Yes, well, having split them up, I now face having to get them back together again. What the fuck was any of the past few years for?' I throw a cushion at the wall, because I'm so damn frustrated, but I don't want to break anything. 'You're better off without me, Dave. I should have never come home.'

'No.' He rushes towards me, places his arms around my body.

'Then he's won. We'll think of a way, Mel. We will. We need him gone.'

I break away from him and sit in front of the computer and begin to type furiously.

'What are you doing?'

'I'm seeing if I can find any Bonham's in the area near to where I used to live when I was a teenager,' I tell him. 'It's a long shot but worth a try. Oh, my God, there's an I. Bonham. Do you think it could be a relation?'

'There's only one way to find out,' answers Dave with a weary sigh.

The next day I'm off to a nearby neighbourhood of my old haunts to see an Inez Bonham. I'm entirely fascinated by the fact that she has the same name Ed gave Jarrod. He said he shagged his stepmother, but wow, this is really fucked up. She wouldn't be drawn into any conversation on the phone, saying she wanted to meet me face to face.

I enter the block of four grey concrete coated flats. They look dilapidated, and as I open the door, the smell of stale piss fills the air. I ring the doorbell of the number Inez gave me and wait. A few minutes later the door opens. A grey-haired lady who looks to be in her mid-seventies opens the door. Her eyes fix on mine, her gaze sharp.

'Come in, Melissa.'

'How did you know—?'

'No one else visits, dear.' She strolls back down the hall.

I'm invited into a stark living room. It has a sofa that's seen better days and a wooden chair. There's a radio on the side, but I note there's no television. A newspaper on a coffee table at the side of the chair is open at a crossword, a pen lying on the paper. Inez's gait is strong for her age, and it would appear her mind is the same.

'I actually hoped I'd never hear Edward's name again. It's been years now. I thought I was free. Sorry, I'm being rude. Would you like a drink of tea?'

'No. I'm fine thank you.' I hover near the doorway.

'Actually, if we're talking about Edward, then sherry's probably more appropriate.' She passes me to go into the kitchen and returns with a bottle and two glasses. It looks like I'm having a drink whether I want one or not.

She sits on the sofa, then pours and passes me a small glass of sherry, nodding towards the chair. 'So, what brings you here?'

I take a seat. 'As I explained on the phone. My name is Melissa, and I've recently found out that Edward is my brother.'

'Let me guess. That's disturbed you. He's disturbed you?'

'It's a lot more complicated than that.' I tell her about Jarrod. I leave out that I kidnapped Ed. I let her know that he's obsessed and won't leave me alone.

'Oh dear.' Inez takes a sip of sherry. 'I know what that's like. It used to be me.'

I take a swallow before I speak. 'Edward said that you and he were lovers?'

Inez sighs. 'Oh, that old chestnut's back, is it?' She shakes her head.

'You mean you weren't?'

'No. We weren't. I was his stepmother, and I loved his father dearly. Edward had problems right from being around three years old. He exhibited very strange behaviour. Quite obsessional compulsive at times. Everything in his room had to be a certain way. He had to do things in a particular order. If not, he'd have a meltdown. His adoptive father worked away a lot, and he was left with his mother. No one realised the stress it put on her until it was too late. She took an overdose. Left a note saying the stress of caring for Edward was too much.'

'So she didn't do it because her husband cheated?'

'No. He didn't cheat.'

'He said you were the social worker who arranged his adoption.'

The corner of her mouth upturns. 'I was. Lucky me, eh? After Ed's mother died, Ed's father, William, came to see us. I was still working in the same department. He wanted to know if we could help with Edward. The department couldn't, but I became involved - too involved, and in the end, we married, and I became Ed's stepmother. His behaviour got worse. He was in and out of psychiatric units. He told them I'd slept with him. That led to quite intrusive investigations as you can imagine. He couldn't come home after that. He had to be fostered. Foster parents couldn't cope with him either. He ended up in care homes when he wasn't having psychiatric treatment. He's never changed his story though. He's convinced we had a relationship. It broke me and his father up in the end as the doubt was always in William's mind. There shouldn't be any doubt in a relationship, should there? There should only be trust.'

The sadness is etched on Inez Bonham's face. She clearly loved Ed's father, and yet it wasn't strong enough to survive Edward Bonham.

'When did you last see Ed?'

'Gosh, not since the late eighties. He came to see me to tell me he'd met someone. Couldn't stop going on about them. Said he knew it was meant to be. That was all he'd tell me. Not even a name. Anyway, after that, he left me alone. To be honest, I didn't care. His obsession with me was over, just like that.' She snaps her fingers.

'I'm afraid it wasn't,' I tell her. I tell her about Edward making Jarrod into Inez.

It makes me regretful of coming here when I see her tremble. 'Oh, dear God. I thought it was over.'

'The thing is,' I tell her. 'Inez is in a psychiatric ward being evaluated. It's all got too much. Now Ed wants me to get her back for him. I don't know where this will end. When is he going to leave us alone?'

Inez fixes me with those eyes of steel. 'When his obsession moves on, or when he's dead.'

We're quiet as I drink the rest of my sherry.

She asks me to excuse her for a moment and then returns from the room she had gone to. She hands me a piece of paper with an address and phone number on it.

'If you need me I'll be here,' she says pointing to the piece of paper. 'It's my niece's house. She always annoying me about going to stay. I don't feel safe here now. If that ex of yours doesn't go back to him, I don't know what Ed will be capable of. I'm not going to stay around to find out. I'm too old for his shit. I want to see my last days out in peace. Please don't let him get hold of this information.'

'I won't. He won't know I've been here. Thank you for seeing me. I'm sorry to bring up old memories.'

'When you have Edward in your life you're never completely free of looking over your shoulder.'

I nod, and after thanking her for the drink, I leave the house.

The next thing on mine and Dave's agenda is to get packed for the move to Handforth. We take the For Sale sign down on our house and take it off the market for a short time. That way, if Edward makes enquiries, he'll think we've changed our mind. Instead, we're escaping to my parents' old home until we can make plans to move. We only need to pack clothes and essentials as the house is furnished and has everything we need. A food shop and we'll be sorted. I take clean bedding. We fill up the car, and we're on our way.

Dave has never been to the house before, though he knew of it. We pull up outside. The weather today is dismal. It's been raining for days, and the uneven ground is full of puddles.

I pull my hood up and clutch my coat tighter around me. 'Come have a look around inside first, then we'll unpack.'

He nods.

I take him through the front door. The house is in dire need of decoration but is clean. From the small hallway, I show Dave through to the lounge. It's a long narrow room with an old wooden circular dining table at one end, complete with matching chairs with threadbare cushion pads.

'Gosh, it's like going back in time.' He laughs.

'It is. I never saw the point in spending money on it when it's virtually worthless.'

Dave looks out of the back window. 'So, the other houses are worthless?'

'Yes, and they're derelict after years of being left to rot. Roof tiles came off, windows cracked. The rain leaked in. I'm not sure if my house is entirely safe, but I've seen no signs of damp, so I've always assumed it's okay.'

'You little risk-taker you.' He laughs. 'We'd better take it steady in the bedroom. I don't want to bring the house down.' He winks.

He walks through to the kitchen giving it a cursory glance and then moves into the downstairs study where I hear him gasp. I follow him into the room, and my eyes follow his. I note him taking in the chain dangling from the wall. The tattoo equipment that remains in the room.

'What on earth happened here?'

'You don't need to know, but from what's here I'm sure you can guess.'

He moves to the window and sees the rectangular hole.

'Dug for psychological purposes only. I wasn't that hell bent on revenge.'

'The chain though.' He looks back at the wall. 'You kept him chained?'

'While I tried to destroy him, yes,' I bite out. 'Wasn't going to work very well trying to reason with him.'

'It's a shock, that's all. I'm not criticising. I'm trying to imagine this new side to my wife. I may have to get a tattoo.'

I smile. 'Would you really let me tattoo you?'

'I would trust you with my life.'

'And what would you have me etch on you?'

'A chameleon,' he says without hesitation. 'To remind me of you.'

I laugh. 'A chameleon? Is that what I am?'

'Yes.' He drags me to him. 'The outside of you changes but

inside.' He strokes my breast. 'Is the same woman I've always known, deep down. You adapt to your surroundings.' He begins to move out of the room. 'Tomorrow I'll fetch some filler and paint, and we'll give the study a little redecoration. Maybe you could fill that hole in the garden? It creeps me out.'

I shake my head. 'What a wuss. Come on, I'll show you the bedroom.'

The bedrooms are the only rooms I changed after my parents' deaths. New furniture and redecorated rooms that I did myself. I had taken the back bedroom for my own. I'd kept Ed in the front bedroom, and this would need to be cleaned out. I didn't want a trace of him left in that room. The bedrooms had to be changed as I didn't want to be reminded of my parents being sick and ill. They'd died within such a short space of time of each other, my father from leukaemia and my mother through a fall that led to pneumonia, though I'd say it was a broken heart that claimed her really. And she'd taken her secret to the grave. Never admitting to me at any point in her life that there was something I didn't know. Then a thought comes to me unbidden. The Solicitor stating that my mother had left some money to a charity, but she wanted it to be anonymous to everyone. It struck me as odd at the time as she'd never particularly donated anywhere. Had it really been to charity or had she left something to Ed? Had she lied to me even after death?

'Are you alright?' Dave's voice breaks through. I realise I've been sitting on the edge of the bed lost in my own thoughts for some minutes.

'I will be. I hope. It's knowing that every aspect of my childhood and life up to losing my baby was based on lies, Dave.'

He nods.

'None of it was how it appeared. It feels like a waste of all those years of my life.'

Dave places his arm around me. 'Mel. Were you happy? When you were living with your parents, and you had Jarrod. Right up until it went wrong. Were you happy?'

'Yes,' I tell him. 'My life felt perfect.'

'Then that's all that matters,' he assures me. 'You felt loved, and you were happy. No matter what came after. At the time of your childhood and young adulthood, you had health and happiness. Yes, people kept secrets. Most of us have secrets. Skeletons in cupboards.'

'Did you have a secret when you were younger?' I ask him.

'I did,' he says but adds nothing further.

I bump him with my hip. 'Tell me.'

'No.' He smirks.

I twirl my hands in his hair, 'I'll make it worth your while.'

He looks down at me. 'When I was in my late twenties, a young woman moved in across the street. Now, I was happily married with two young children, but hey, I wasn't blind. When she came to our house to get cooking lessons from my first wife, I used to try and sneak a peek down her top because her nipples used to show through her blouse. I used to imagine sticking her breasts in my mouth instead of the buns she used to offer me.'

'Is that right?' I ask him, removing my top to reveal my bra. Then I pull my bra down to reveal a breast.

'Were they like these?'

'Smaller, but I'm sure I can get just as excited at imagining these in my mouth,' he tells me.

And he does.

---

The following day is a Saturday, and Dave busies himself fixing the study and the wall of the front bedroom. We keep the windows open all day, despite the continuing rain, to let fresh air in and the smell of paint out. I clean and dust as if I can wipe out all traces of Edward having been in this house.

At one point, we break off for coffee and cake. I watch as Dave finishes eating but continues to chew his lip.

'What?'

'I don't quite know how to ask this, but it's bugging me.'

'So ask.'

'Bobby,' he says. 'You spent years with him. Was there ever anything between you?'

I stare at the lines of grief etched on my husband's face, so visible to me right now with the light cast from the window. He's spent all these years imagining the worst.

'You'll have to meet Bobby sometime. You'll like him. He's a character. But since we got together, there has never been anyone but you.' I move over to him and sit at his feet. 'There never will be, as far as I'm concerned, anyone but you.'

'There was Jarrod again. The video,' he says.

'I barely tolerated that. It made me sick to my stomach, but I had to do it. Do you understand that? I did what I had to do for the video, and I've regretted it ever since. I felt soiled.'

'But that's the point I'm trying to make, Mel. If it comes to it, for revenge, again, would you do it?'

'No.' I reach up and caress his lip. 'I only want you. Only you, Dave.' I undo the fly of his trousers and take him in my mouth, vowing to worship his body until the day he believes me again because right now he doesn't trust me and I don't trust myself.

I think back to the original Inez Bonham's words. *There shouldn't be any doubt in a relationship, should there? There should only be trust.*

I need to know that's what Dave and I have, and we can only have that if Edward is no longer in our lives.

# CHAPTER TWENTY-NINE

Inez

I've been having counselling, and I'm feeling so much better. Of course, I've not been able to talk about everything that's happened the past few years, but I've been able to discuss my feelings about not living the life I want. Ed is coming to visit today. I phoned him. Told him I wanted to chat. I've been told I can be discharged when I have a place to go and so I'm going to talk to Ed and see if I'm able to come home.

When he walks through the door at visiting time he looks weary. He approaches me, but where he would normally place his arms around me and gather me to him, he's hesitant. I don't blame him.

'Take a seat,' I say.

We're in the day room. A small room with large windows to one side that faces the industrialised city. There are a few nondescript chairs, a coffee table, and a television set.

Ed takes a seat at the side of me.

'How have you been?' he asks.

'I'm feeling a lot better.' I smile at him. 'They say I can come home. That's why I've asked you here. I need to tell you how I'm feeling now and see whether you want me back.'

'Inez-'

'No'. I put my palm up. 'My name is Lynne now.'

'The house was badly damaged in a fire.'

I place a hand to my mouth. 'What?'

'It needs thousands of pounds' worth of repairs. The fire brigade and insurers are insisting it was my fault, that I left a pan on, but I know I didn't. It would take all my savings to repair the house. All of them. She's fucked my life up properly.'

'No. We fucked her life up,' I answer.

His jaw tightens and his eyes narrow, but he stays silent. 'I've rented a place around the corner from our house. It's furnished. It's obviously not our house, but it's the same layout. I hope you'll come back to me, Inez.'

'My name is-'

'Stop it,' he yells, spittle flying from his mouth. 'You're Inez to me. That's all you have been. Please, if you need to change, can you give me some time?' He puts his head in his hands. I wait while he focuses, calming himself down. He peers back at me. 'I'm coming to terms with what that woman has done to us. Can we go to our new home and be us – the normal us – for a little while? Then we'll talk about who you want to be. I can't handle this right now. I can't.'

I nod. Then I bite my own lip. I'm the same subservient person I've always been. He orders me, and I obey. That's the reality of my life. I may as well accept it. I have no backbone. But no matter how controlling he is, I love him.

'Let's go home,' I tell him.

. . .

Ed is worrying me. I hear him muttering to himself as he walks around the house.

The place might have the same room formation, but with its dirty and broken furniture, it's not our comfortable home. I bought cleaning materials and did the best I could to clean the place up, but it's not the same.

I fix us an evening meal, and we sit at the small table. I have questions that feel like they want to burst out of me and I decide to ask them. Ed can only refuse to answer.

'How did Melissa capture you?'

His eyes narrow. 'She had a bloke helping her. The same one who tried to knock my work reputation. They knocked me out. Next thing I knew I was in a house in the middle of nowhere.'

'It sounds like her house at Handforth.'

'I don't know where I was. I wasn't conscious to see my entrance, and I was blindfolded for my exit. I had an occasional view out of the window.'

'Were there other cottages nearby, but in ruins?'

'I don't know. There were never any other signs of life, and the view from the window was the garden and then dirt.'

'It sounds like her parents' home. They left it to her when they died.'

For some reason this makes Ed clutch his plate so hard, the end of his fingers turn white. 'It's her parents house? She took me there? She tortured me in the family home? Oh, my God. She put me in the bed. Was it my mother's bed?'

'What are you talking about, Ed?'

'Melissa. I wanted to tell you but I couldn't until she'd suffered. I knew you'd try to protect her. She's my half-sister. Her mother had me out of wedlock, shoved me to one side, then had Mel and lived happily ever after.'

'You're lying.'

He backhands me across the face. I jolt back in my seat and put my hand on my cheek where it smarts.

'I do not lie.' Ed's face is mottled, his eyes wide, showing the whites of his eyes. I've never seen him like this.

'I- I'm sorry, I'm just, um, confused. Don't forget all that's happened lately. You've brought me home from a psychiatric ward, Ed. You'll have to forgive me if I'm questioning everything around me.'

He falls to his feet and grasps my hands. 'I'm so sorry. I never should have struck you. Please, forgive me, Inez. I love you.'

I nod and stroke the top of his hair. Why am I comforting him when I'm the one who got hurt?

When we go to bed, Ed wants to get close, intimate, but I tell him I'm not ready for that yet. He leaves the bedroom, and I hear a banging noise downstairs. I daren't see what's happening, so I lie in bed until the night turns dark and Ed comes back up and goes to sleep. Only then do I feel I can close my own eyes. The next day I find pieces of a dining room chair outside, and chunks of plaster out of the wall.

While Ed is at work today, I'm going shopping. I've agreed for him to call me Inez still, but I want to explore a different look again. I laugh as I realise I miss my friend Selma. She'd have advised me on what to buy. Then I shake my head. No. I tell myself. This is about you, and what you want. For God's sake decide for yourself.

I cook Ed's favourite meal for dinner, shepherd's pie, and wait for him to come home.

When he walks into the dining room that night, he stares at me as if I've grown an extra head. I'm wearing a new ash-blonde wig in a layered bob shape. It appears so much more natural than the long dark wig. I visited the makeup counter again, and they were very patient with showing me how to apply my makeup. I look a lot more how I'd always imagined myself. With a pair of grey wide-legged trousers and a white blouse, I still have a classy look in the style Ed always asked of me, but I've made it my own.

'What the hell's going on?' he growls.

My forehead creases. 'I'm not sure what you mean. Pull up a chair, I made your favourite, shepherds pie.'

He stalks towards me. 'Well, perhaps it's not my favourite anymore, *Lynne*.' Sarcasm drips from his lips when he says my new name. Perhaps I've decided on a change too?'

He grabs hold of the back of my neck with venom. His fingers pinch the top of my backbone. 'Has my money bought this shit?' he bellows. 'Last I knew, you weren't working. We're fucking skint, you silly bitch. You can take that back tomorrow. You look a complete cunt in it anyway. Where's the brown one?'

I wince under the pressure of his fingers. 'In the bedroom, in the chest of drawers.'

'Go and get it,' he snarls. 'Put it back on your head and remember that while we're together, you're Inez, and you have fucking brown hair, do you understand?'

He stands there while I remove my wig, then he rubs it through the shepherds pie, picking both up and throwing the lot on the floor. 'I'm going out,' he tells me. 'When I get back, this lot better not be here anymore. Make sure everything, including you'— he stabs his finger into my chest –'is back to normal.'

Then he grabs his car keys from the side and with a bang of the door is gone.

I slump onto a dining chair, clutching my head. Who the hell am I living with? There is none of the kind, loving husband I've lived with for all these years. The man who supported me through my change. Whatever Mel did to him, she's changed him. Are they really siblings or did she break his mind like she broke mine?

I need to see her. To ask her the truth. If she's back with Dave, then she's only around the corner. Tonight, I will tidy up, put my brown wig back on and play the game. Tomorrow I'll see Mel and seek the answers that will either mend my relationship with Ed or finish it forever.

Once I've tidied up I go into my bag and take out my phone. I study a couple of selfies of us and some other photos of Ed. I'm grateful Mel didn't delete the ones of me and my husband. After the fire, I have no other pictures of us. I stare at the man in the photos. The man I love. Or, the man I loved? Who is the stranger I've come to live with and is my husband ever coming back?

## CHAPTER THIRTY

Edward

Locks are so easy to break. If someone doesn't come to the door, well then, I'll just let myself in. I take note of the storage boxes and the suitcase.

'Going somewhere, stepmummy?' I ask her.

She sits back against the headboard, rubbing her eyes. Her skin as white as a sheet of plain paper. Ready to be doodled on. I laugh.

'It's been years, Edward,' she says. 'Why now? Why are you here now? Are you not back with your wife?'

How the fuck does she know about my wife? God, that bitch. Mel must have been here too. Interfering fucking cunt.

'That's the thing,' I say, withdrawing my belt from my trousers, 'I've lost my Inez. But then again, she never was you.'

She reaches over and switches on the light. It brings her lined face into focus. Her grey hair.

'Where's Inez?' I demand. 'You look like her. Are you her mother?' I begin to pace the room.

She gets out of bed and comes towards me.

'Edward. Look at me. You're ill again. It's me. I am your stepmother. I'm old now, Edward.'

'You lie,' I spit. What the hell is going on here? This is the address I've had in my mind for ages, recorded there. The address of Inez Bonham. 'Where's my stepmother?' I grab her throat.

'I am your stepmother,' she croaks out.

I drop my hold and look around. 'Inez has long dark hair, she's slim. We're lovers. She likes me to hurt her with this belt.'

'Edward,' the woman shouts. 'That never happened. How many more times do we have to go through this?'

I open wardrobe doors, searching for a clue as to the whereabouts of my stepmother. When I turn around, I see the phone in the old woman's hand.

'Oh no. I can't have you ringing anyone. Who are you phoning? Mel? Has she put you up to this? Are you her puppet?'

'No.' The old woman is crying now. 'I'm phoning my niece. I'm going to stay with her. That's why I'm packed. I'm letting her know she can fetch me now.'

I hold the belt up, wrapped around both of my fists.

'Oh no, sorry, you're going nowhere. Not until I find Inez,' I tell her. Then I take the phone from her hand.

## Inez

Ed doesn't speak to me when he gets home from work. In fact, he won't even look me in the eyes. He goes in the shower, changes into pyjamas, and then gets into bed. All night he mumbles my name, 'Inez'. I'm causing him pain, but I have to create more of a life for myself. I no longer want to be Inez Bonham. I know I'm changing. I'm so scared of the future. But I want to decide on my own appearance, not be told how to look. It's happened all my life. No more. Tomorrow morning, I will shop and replace the wig he destroyed. Lack of money or not. I will not lose this fight.

Ed is sombre at the breakfast table and unusually for him is not getting ready to go to the gym. I don't think he's entirely himself since his captivity. When he's a little calmer, I wonder if I might bring up the subject of counselling. He could have some psychological problems from being kidnapped.

'Could you pass me the milk please, Lynne?' he asks.

My eyes shoot up to meet his, but he's still not looking at me. Has he really come around to me choosing my name? That would be tremendous.

'You called me Lynne? Not Inez,' I say quietly.

'There's no more Inez,' he states, and picks up the newspaper from the table and opens it, separating our faces.

# CHAPTER THIRTY-ONE

Melissa

It makes the local news the next day. I'm on the internet when the post is shared on my feed.

**Witnesses sought in suspicious death of widow.**
It goes on to say how Inez Bonham had been found strangled at her house. I run to the bathroom where I lose all my breakfast. Dave is at work. It's got to have been Ed. Got to have been. I pace the bathroom trying to calm myself down. It will be a botched robbery. Nothing to do with Ed at all. I think of Jarrod. My God. Is he safe? I wanted revenge. I don't want him dead.

I reach for my phone.

. . .

'That's so strange, I was going to call around to see you today. Only Ed is saying the strangest things. He's saying he's your brother.'

There's no way I'm admitting to being the sister of a potential murderer unless I'm forced to.

'Inez.'

'I go by Lynne now.'

I pause. 'Good for you. Listen, Lynne. I don't know how else to say this, and with everything that's happened I don't expect you to trust me, but I have to try.'

I take a deep breath.

'Go on.'

'I don't think you're safe with Ed. They've just found his stepmother dead in her apartment, strangled.'

There's a loud laugh. 'I know he's controlling, but that hardly makes him a murderer.'

'His stepmother's name is, was, Inez Bonham. In her youth, she was slim and tall with long dark hair.'

'You're lying.'

'I don't expect you to believe me, but I met her. Edward was convinced they'd had a love affair. He was obsessed with her.'

'He loves me.'

'I agree, and I think he does, in his own strange way. I think you were a surprise he didn't expect in his life. But he's sick in the head. He's been in hospitals, and now his stepmother is dead. It's too much of a coincidence. How has he seemed to you?'

Inez sighs. 'Quiet. Mumbling'. There's a pause. 'A short temper. Oh, my God.'

'What? Lynne, what?'

'This morning. He said there's no more Inez. You don't think...?'

'All I know is that I don't think you're safe right now. Pack some belongings and get a taxi up to the house at Handforth. I've a spare room. We'll work out what to do.'

'I-' She hesitates.

'Forget everything from the past right now. I want a life. I can't have one while he's in it. Get here and then we need to phone the police. If he's innocent they'll let him go, won't they? No harm done. If he's not, you're safe here.'

'I'll be there as soon as I can.'

## Edward

I get home, and there's no food on the table.

No wife.

No Inez. My glorious Inez who I've adored all my life isn't here. My mind tries to fix on an image of her face, but it morphs into different ones.

I walk into the bathroom and realise her toothbrush has gone. I take the room apart. Some of her belongings are missing.

'Where the fuck is she?' I shout.

I sit on the floor and rock. I can't get my mind to hold a thought. I look at my hands, imagine them looping a belt around her neck. But that was an old woman, not Inez, wasn't it?

I couldn't concentrate at work today. Jack said they might have to let me go. So before I left, I hung him by his tie in the men's bathroom. That shut him up.

I pick up my mobile. Silly me. How could I have forgotten? I put a tracker on my wife's phone so that I always knew where she was.

I wait until it shows me her location.

Well, well. A little house in Handforth. What are the chances of that?

Looks like we're going to be having a family reunion.

# CHAPTER THIRTY-TWO

Melissa

We call the police, and a detective constable is sent to us. It's a long time since another car came down the long winding lane to my house.

'Gosh. I didn't know anyone still lived down here,' the DC says, his eyes taking in his surroundings.

'That's because they don't,' I tell him in clipped tones. 'We're only here because it's safe from Edward.'

The DC records the details we give him. That Edward is unstable. That he had a fixation with his stepmother, who has been found dead. That we have no proof he's involved, but it's worth investigating. I tell him that he gave our granddaughter glass shards through the window.

To my surprise, Lynne is open about being my ex-husband and having gender reassignment. She re-iterates that Ed was obsessed with his stepmother and groomed her to look similar, although she was unaware that this was his intention.

'Okay. Well, I'll head back to the station with this. We need to pick up Edward and bring him in for questioning.' The DC gets up.

'As I said, he'll either be at the gym or at home, as that's where he goes from work,' says Lynne.

'Thank you. We'll be in touch.'

'What happens now?' Lynne asks. Her name is giving me a headache. I want to call her Jarrod or Inez. Though who am I to talk?

An hour or so later I move to the kitchen to make a drink. Sitting around is not doing me any good. I feel edgy and jumpy. The atmosphere in the house is tense with Lynne there with Dave. The last time they met Dave beat her up. The sooner they pick up Edward, the better. I'm not religious as a rule, but I pray to God that he's arrested for murder or at the very least taken for psychological assessment. I move to the sink to fill the kettle, but movement at the periphery of my vision has me startle. The hairs on the back of my neck stand up as I stare at Ed on the other side of the window with a knife in his hand.

I scream and run for the lounge.

'Call the police. He's here.'

Dave quickly grabs the phone.

Lynne jumps up. 'How the hell did he know where we were?'

'I don't know,' I snap. 'He never saw the route when I brought him here.'

Lynne bites her lip. 'I told him you had property at Handforth. I'm sorry.'

I look at her in dismay. 'Sorry's a bit late when your psychopath husband is outside the kitchen window.' The last of my words are drowned out by the sound of glass shattering.

'He's trying to get in,' I shout.

Lynne runs through the lounge door and into the kitchen.

'What are you doing?' I yell.

'Barricade yourselves upstairs. I'm going out to him,' she says.

I look at Dave, his brow furrowed. 'Let's get upstairs to the toolkit.

Grab what you can. Screwdrivers, hammer. Anything we can use to keep him at bay,' he says.

We scurry upstairs and dash into the spare room where there are tools from the recent redecoration.

I hear voices from outside and walk over to the bedroom window. Lynne's outside now, talking to Edward. He's waving a knife around. She holds her hands up. I can only hear mumbling but can see she's trying to get through to him.

'What on earth was she thinking?' says Dave.

'She doesn't think. Just acts. That's always been my ex's problem. Now we wait to see who gets to us first. The police or Edward.'

Once again, my ex's actions could destroy my life.

## Lynne

I couldn't sit there and wait for the police. Edward has loved me for all these years. He wouldn't hurt me. I feel it deep down inside. Whatever has happened, there must be an explanation.

'Edward, darling. Put the knife down, and we can talk.' I put my own hands up. 'Look. I don't have anything. It's just me. Inez.'

He waves the knife. 'But you're not, are you? You're tricking me. I don't know what's happening. I picked up the signal of my wife's phone, and it brought me here. You look like her, but you don't.' He rubs his knife-free hand through his hair, agitated. Then he hits himself in the forehead. 'I can't remember what she looks like. I see long dark hair, but then I see an old woman. Then I see your face, but you're different.'

'You made me wear a wig. I have a different one on now. But this is me. Look.' I slowly remove the wig to reveal my own hair underneath.

'My Inez had proper long dark hair. It wasn't a wig. You're

tricking me. Why? You want me to go back there, don't you? To that kid's unit. They held me down. I won't be held down. Where is my wife?' He lunges, and the knife slashes the skin on my arm. It hurts like a bitch. He's startled to see the blood, and while he's still, I turn and run back into the house holding the door closed. When he comes to, he kicks and thumps the back door.

'Let me in. I want my wife. What have you done with my wife?'

I find it harder and harder to keep the door closed and then there's nothing. A reprieve? Is he trying to fool me that he's gone? Then I see his shadow at the window and hear him picking pieces of broken glass from the frame. Oh shit.

Then the strangest experience occurs. The house shakes. At first, it's a small tremble. Then it stops, and for a brief moment, I think I imagined it. Then it starts again. Items fall off the tops of the kitchen cupboards. I hold onto the door, but it's like the kitchen floor is suddenly made of liquid. It seems to ripple. What the hell?

Mel and Dave rush downstairs. 'Lynne. We need to get out. It's not safe. Something's happening to the ground.' I hear the front door open, and I know I should move, but it's like I'm frozen to the spot. I watch as Ed tries to climb through the window and then suddenly he's not there anymore. As the ground stops trembling again, my senses are alert. Adrenaline pumps and I run out of the front of the house as fast as I can.

# CHAPTER THIRTY-THREE

Melissa

We ran as fast as we could to the houses at the top of the street, Lynne closely behind. A paramedic checks us over and places some paper stitches on a cut on Lynne's arm. The police come to meet us. They tell me my garden is no longer there, and neither is the back part of my home. The noise has brought out the ambulance chasers and other nosy residents of the local area. I overhear their mumbles.

'No ones lived there for years. They should have knocked them down long ago.'

'My kids play down there. Could have been there when it happened. Wonder if I could sue?'

We're advised to get in the police car, and leave them all to it.

Later a detective fills us in. 'It would appear that heavy rain caused an old mine shaft to collapse. The safety of the area is being determined. Mrs Bonham, you say that your husband is somewhere in that shaft, but at approximately ninety metres deep, that will take some time to determine. We also have staff working at the crime scene of the deceased Mrs Inez Bonham to see if we can find any evidence to connect Edward Bonham with her death.'

We're free to go. I can't explain how I feel, other than shell-shocked. It's like dreaming wide-awake. Did any of this just happen?

We stand outside the police station. Myself and Dave are going back to our home. Our real home.

Lynne turns to me. 'What do we do now?'

I begin to laugh. So hard that rivers of tears run down my face.

'What do we do now?' I stand with my hand on my hip. 'Are you for fucking real? What you do now is fuck right off. Go and live the life you want, Lynne, because you're totally free.'

'I'll never be free. A person like me is never free.'

'Oh, stop playing the victim, it's getting old,' I snap. 'You're transgender. Get in groups, deal with it. There are plenty of people with problems to face. I'm the mother of a dead baby. We all have masks to put on, faces to portray to the outside world. You've made yourself Lynne. Is she a pathetic victim who blames everyone else for things that result from her own actions? Because that's how it seems. Exactly the same as Jarrod, and Inez before her. Anyway, I couldn't give a fuck what you are. I didn't want you dead, but I know I don't want to see you ever again. So don't stay in that rented house. Move away from me, or I'll make sure you don't get any quality of life here.'

She looks shocked. 'I thought when you asked me to come to your house-,'

'What? That we were becoming friends? You're as fucking mental as Edward. The only reason I asked you to come to my house is so your death wouldn't be on my conscience if he decided you were next.'

'So you do care, or you'd have left me to it.'

I sigh. 'Somewhere in there, is my best friend Jarrod, who I loved dearly. Maybe I tried to save him. That caring soul who'd do anything for me. Keep that part alive, Lynne.'

I take Dave's arm and walk away.

Leaving her alone for the first time in years.

We stay in our house. It was our family home, and now there's no reason for us to go anywhere else. Edward's body was recovered from the shaft. The earth did him a favour. The police found Jack dead at Bailey's, the same day as the mine accident. It had looked like a suicide. However, Jack had been found in an identical position to Jacobs, raising my suspicions, which I passed on to the detectives. It would appear Jacobs never took his own life after all. Police forensics confirmed that Ed had been responsible for the deaths of both his colleagues.

We've holidayed in Suffolk and Dave and Bobby finally met. They got on well. Bobby showed off his manwhore self, and Dave saw that we were more like brother and sister. That is, how you would imagine a proper brother and sister to be – nothing like my real sibling.

We received a postcard from Lynne. She said she'd moved to a supportive community. That she wouldn't send any more messages but she hoped I'd want to know she was okay and caring for others in a new job as a care worker, and that it was more fulfilling than working at a makeup counter. I threw the card in the recycling bin.

I'm baking biscuits with Millie when there's a knock at the front door. I turn off the hob, and swinging Millie up and into my arms, go to answer it – my paranoia has me looking through the window first.

'Hey there.' A young couple stand on my doorstep. The woman has a bottle of wine in her hand. 'We just moved in down the street, and we're bringing all the neighbours a bottle. Only,' she smiles, 'neighbours don't tend to socialise anymore, and we think that's a shame. We want to bring a sense of community back.'

I look at them. It could have been myself and Jarrod all those years ago.

'I'm sorry, that's kind of you, but I'm really busy.'

'It's only a bottle of wine,' says the woman. She looks at my apron. 'Hey, do you bake? Only I've always wanted to learn to cook.'

'I can't stand wine,' I say, and I shut the door in their faces.

'Grandma, are we going to finish our biscuits off now?' says Millie, her eyes burning with hope.

'We are, darling, and then would you like to make something else because for you I have all the time in the world.'

'When my little sister comes will we still bake?'

Joanne is expecting her second child, another daughter, any day now.

'Yes. We'll still bake. You are my best assistant.'

'Will you let Sarah bake?'

Sarah. That's what Joanne is calling her daughter after taking me to one side to speak with me. A tribute to the daughter who didn't get to live.

'I will, but I'm sure she'll never be as good at it as you are. Now, come on, before the biscuits burn.'

I put her down, and she runs into the kitchen, coming to an abrupt stop in front of the oven. 'I love you, Grandma,' she tells me.

'Love you more, Millie.'

'I don't want to share you, Grandma,' Millie says. 'You're mine.'

## THE END

Ready for another story that could take place on 'a street where you live'? Read on for BULLIED.

# BULLIED

# PROLOGUE

### Carla

They wondered why towns and cities were becoming lawless.

Well, just attempt to do things the right way. The way of the law. Like I did.

Go on. Try it. Call the police, report the crime, give the evidence. Give them leads to follow.

All I heard was:

*Can't do that.*

*Can't do that.*

*Can't do that.*

Victims live in fear and the perpetrators laugh.

Like the ones who invaded my life. Dressed like scrotes and chavs, they broke the rules, and laughed and clapped for their own damn selves, smug within their tiny little tribes, thinking they were the kings of the world.

But while the police did nothing, or rather the law *prevented* them from doing anything of any use, they taught me, indirectly. They were unaware of my processing every single thing they said.

But I did. Every crumb.

And now I would use it.

The victim shall be the victor.

The kings and queens shall lose their crowns.

Well, kind of. I fully intended to place a crown on Marcus Bull's head.

One made of barbed wire. A modern-day crucifixion.

Wire my heart is wrapped in because I've lost any semblance of emotion after burying my only daughter.

Marcus Bull killed her.

Marcus Bull will pay.

They say hell hath no fury like a woman scorned.

Ha. Make that woman a mother and hell shall look like a pilot light against a mother's inferno.

And a mother who no longer has her child? A woman with nothing to lose?

Satan would bow to her.

# PART 1

# 1

## CARLA

Sometime between 3:30pm and 4pm, I'd hear it. Loud voices and even louder giggles. It would start in the distance, and I'd wonder if they belonged to my flesh and blood. The decibel level would rise as they came closer to the front door. A pause in conversation, a key in the lock. Then the door would slam open, hitting the shoe cupboard. I'd hear shoes being kicked off, their thud echoing on the laminate floor, and the chatter would start up again, although now it wouldn't hold the secrets of teenage girls, not now they were within my proximity. The shoes would be abandoned in the middle of the floor, nowhere near the shoe cupboard. In fact, nine times out of ten at least one shoe would hit the wall or the skirting board, leaving a dirty smudge on the paintwork I'd later clean off with an anti-bacterial wipe. I'd put the shoes away and tidy up, telling myself that's what mums were for. That really, you had to pick your battles; especially with teenagers whose moods would sour like milk past its sell-by date for no obvious reason.

I bet you're wondering why the huge detail? After all, it's just a kid coming home from school, right? But you'll soon realise, at some point in my tale, that I now mull over every single detail about my daughter. Think of every hair on her head, every cell of her body, every wondrous part of her, even down to the whining and whingeing of a teenager being told no.

Yes, being the mother of a teenage daughter was a daily learning curve. I felt like a method actor. Today, I'd try to be cool; maybe tomorrow witty; the day after I'd lose my temper—not helped by my hormonal mood swings—and tell her she was an ungrateful little shit. Oh yes, I swore at her sometimes. I wouldn't have believed it, not even two years ago, if you'd told me that my golden girl, my little angel, would turn her mouth up in a sneer at me. Her eyes would fill with pity as if speaking to someone not all there mentally, and she'd have no gratitude whatsoever for the fact that her life was effortless and filled with everything her heart desired.

From her point of view life went from fabulous to fucked if the word, 'No', came out of my mouth.

Now where was I? Oh yes, Lena had just come home from school...

The living room door burst open and I looked up from my seat on the sofa. I worked from home as an accountant, loving the fact I didn't have to speak to barely a soul all day. I found dealing with other people wearing. The older I got, the more I liked my own company most of the time. Apart from Lena's now rarely given attention, I spent the majority of the evening the same way, either working or watching some mindless crap on the television. Even when I had lived with Lena's father, Ant, he'd spent most of his evenings working overtime, always some plumbing emergency happening. I didn't know most of the emergencies revolved around Natalie's plumbing until he packed his bags, and I didn't mean her central heating. My marriage had been fine until it wasn't. I'd thought we were okay.

"I'm going out, Mum."

I stared at Lena. At the eyebrows she'd filled in, so they sat like two slugs on her face. At her pouty lips filled in with the Charlotte

Tilbury Pillow Talk lipstick that she'd charmed me for. She was brilliant at that, was Lena. To ask to go shopping, for us to have a girly lunch. She knew that at this age I'd take any time with her I could. Then she'd fleece me for everything she wanted as she tried things on and they looked so good I couldn't refuse her. Once she'd got what she wanted and I thought about getting myself a little something, she'd say she was tired and could we go home and I'd realise I'd been played. Not with any malevolence. It was just a teenager's way.

I remembered doing similar things myself with her gran. A gran who passed two years ago now, leaving another gaping hole in my life. Fuck, I really needed to do something, maybe start dating again. Something to patch the leaks in my life before they flooded me and I just became a sole island.

But how did you start a new relationship when the last one left you questioning the entire thing? How did you trust someone new?

I realised I'd been daydreaming when I heard the door bang shut. I didn't get time to ask her what she was doing for dinner. It was another thing that drove me crazy. She'd flirt with a boy until he bought her a McDonalds, and the dinner I'd made her—the nutritious one a growing woman needed—would end up in the bin. Sighing, I abandoned my computer and padded into the kitchen where I opened a tin of soup.

The thing with being alone was I could lose myself in work. Self-employed hours were long, even longer in my case, and I filled my empty days with more and more work. I needed relatively little and so my earnings mounted up. I had enough *Coach* handbags to last a lifetime and so I spoiled my daughter. I knew I did, but hey, she had a shithead of a dad and if my worst crime was buying Lena too many designer sweaters, well then lock me up.

The smell of tomato soup sang to my now growling stomach. It was boiling away in the pan and I could hear my ex-husband's voice in my mind, 'You're spoiling it and ruining the pan'. Right barrel of laughs he was at times. He had a huge cock but proved he was an even bigger one in personality. Still, I missed that cock sometimes; it did great things. I put the pan straight onto my wooden lap tray and reached into the bread bin, where I released the peg off the wrapper and took out three slices of slightly stale white bread. To be honest, I preferred granary, but Lena would only eat white when she'd eat bread at all. I tore the bread up and put it in the soup just like my mum had done for me when I was little to make it more filling, and then grabbing a spoon I sat myself in front of the television and watched *The Haunting of Hill House* on Netflix, laughing when it made me jump.

I'd not heard any voices or footsteps, so when the front door banged and Lena yelled out, "Stupid bitch," I startled, spilling my last mouthful of tomato soup. Placing the tray on the coffee table, I rushed to the door, wiping my mouth and smearing orange sauce down my hands.

Lena stood in the doorway with a split lip. Blood poured down her chin.

For a moment, time stood still while my brain caught up to my vision. My heart thudded in my chest. It felt like it would give out any second. I sensed the blood draining from my face and my hands felt clammy. "What the fuck? Are you okay? Have you been mugged?" My voice was shrill and fast as I ran towards her. She shook my concern away with her hand and headed past me through the hallway, through the living room, the dining room, all the way into the kitchen where she grabbed a piece of kitchen towel, wetting it under the tap and dabbing at her lip.

"Can you please tell me what's going on?" My mind whirled with concern and my neck and shoulders were tightening. Did I need to phone the police? Was it just her lip? There was a weird smell around her, like burning rubber. I was on sensory overload while my brain tried to put the clues together because she wasn't answering my questions anywhere near quickly enough.

"Chill, Mum," she finally said, leaning back against the worktop, her face tightening. "I've just had enough of Chloe Butcher, that's all. She was in Costa acting all that, swinging her fake extensions around and telling everyone who would listen that I might have a Michael Kors bag and a Reiss coat, but my father was a plumber who liked to show his customers his pipe." She breathed through her nose audibly.

I'd heard similar before. Chloe Butcher was jealous of Lena. Lena who had naturally long hair, highlighted by the sun. Helped by straighteners, it hung like a halo around her face. Yeah, I was biased, but she was beautiful. There was no doubt in my mind at all. She looked like her grandmother, my mother, who had been a beauty queen back in the day. If it wasn't for the fact Lena was only five foot four, she'd have been modelling for sure.

I sighed. "But I told you to just ignore her. She's all talk."

"Yeah, well, usually I would, but this time she 'accidentally' walked past me with a lighter in her hand when I was walking past Costa on my way out with Sophie. She burned the end of my hair, the fucking stupid bitch. So I punched her in the face."

My eyes widened. My daughter had never even so much as pushed a child in playgroup, never mind punched someone in the face.

"Anyway, she hit me back and then we had a cat fight until Sophie and Tamsin separated us."

I recognised then what the disgusting smell was hanging in the air. It was my daughter's burned hair. I turned her so I was looking at the back, where the ends were now uneven.

"Is she for real? What a stupid, silly bitch." I let go and Lena turned back around to face me. I folded my arms across my chest. "Thank goodness it's Saturday tomorrow. I'll ring up first thing in the morning and get you booked in at Tracy's for a quick trim."

"She came off worse than me. I think I blacked her eye."

I sighed. "Is the rest of you okay?"

"I'm fine, Mum. Stop worrying. This has been coming for a long time. She just kept pushing and pushing and I know you always said speak with your words, but, Mum, she wasn't listening. I had to speak to her in a language she'd understand."

I nodded my head because I did understand. "Do you have her mum's number? This has gone beyond a joke now."

Lena crossed her own arms over her chest mirroring me. "No," she answered emphatically. "I don't need you getting involved. I've hit her and hopefully that'll be the end of it now."

God, I bloody hoped so. That girl was a grade A bitch and now Lena had shown her she wasn't a chickenshit after all, this might just be the end of years of snide comments.

"Was this fight witnessed?"

At that Lena gave me her first smile since she'd walked in. Although she winced as it hurt her lip. "God, yeah, we had a crowd around us, cheering us on. Probably gave half the lads of Berkley Edge a hard on watching us roll around on the floor."

I shook my head and smirked back at her.

All the time we'd been speaking, her phone had been beeping nonstop. Now our conversation was paused, she stared down at the screen.

"Right, I'm gonna talk to Soph. She stayed behind to make sure Chloe knew to leave me the fuck alone from now on."

With that she left the kitchen, going back through the house and I heard her feet stomp up the stairs, still in her shoes of course.

Once I heard her bedroom door bang shut, I tiptoed up the stairs until I reached her door and then I hovered there listening to one side of a conversation, trying to work out what was happening. She was definitely on the phone to Sophie. Most of the conversation was just teenage grunts and, 'Yeah, now she knows I'm not the wimp she accused me of being', type comments.

There were more beeps as notifications pinged.

And then I heard her say.

"They've been outside. She's taken a photo of the front of my fucking house telling me I need to watch myself or the house gets it."

I burst through her door, making her jump. My feet had moved before my brain had taken a chance to catch up.

"End the call," I told her sternly, my voice rising. She did, and then she looked up at me with indifference in her gaze. "It's just her acting hard, Mum, in front of the others. She'll not do anything."

"Show me the picture," I demanded.

Huffing, Lena tapped on her phone screen before passing it to me. There was a picture of my house. My front door, my drive. This was beyond threatening my daughter; this was threatening us both... and our home. I wasn't tolerating any of it.

"Can you save that?"

"Yeah, I can screenshot."

"Good. Do it and send it to me and let her know now that if she comes anywhere near you, threatens you, or us again, I'm going to the police."

"Okay, Mum." She took the phone back off me and I heard my own phone ping downstairs. "Done, okay?"

"Okay. Any more trouble and you let me know." I raised my eyebrows waiting for her confirmation.

"I will." Her phone continued to ping. "God, it's like I'm a local celebrity. Everyone wants to know the inside gossip on what's happened."

"As long as it all blows over," I told her.

But it didn't.

# 2
## CARLA

On Saturday morning, I got up earlier than I usually would and called the hairdressers to make an appointment, explaining why it was needed urgently today. Then I looked at Lena's phone plugged into the charger downstairs and saw there were a number of missed calls and some messages.

**I'm going to kill you, bitch.**

**You'd better not have said that about me or you're dead.**

I couldn't click into the phone as Lena had a password on it, so I snatched it off the worktop and took it upstairs with me, knocking on Lena's door and entering her room.

Lena hated my 'phone downstairs after midnight' rule, but I didn't trust her not to spend the night on it chattering to Sophie and it was exam year.

Her room was dark, and she hadn't stirred, so I pulled the curtains open just slightly to let a chink of the morning light in and then I pushed her arm to rouse her. After a few minutes of groaning, she opened her eyes and looked at me.

"What time is it?"

"Quarter past nine. You're booked in at Tracy's at half-ten. Wake up because you've a lot of messages and missed calls and some of them look a bit worrying." Sitting up, she rubbed at her eyes and took the phone from me. Her fingers glided across the screen.

"For fuck's sake," she snapped.

"What?" I was on high alert.

"Apparently I've been chatting shit about Tamsin and Alesha at school, so now they want to know if it's true and they're gonna end me." She rolled her eyes.

"I need to speak to their mothers. Do you know where they live?"

My conversation was interrupted by Lena's phone ringing. Her brow creased as she looked at the screen and as I mouthed, "Who is it?" she shrugged.

"Hello?"

Someone spoke on the other end of the line for a minute.

"Oh fuck off, Marcus. What's it got to do with you?" She hung up, her face a mask of annoyance.

"Who was that?" I felt like a nipping puppy, but I needed to know what was happening.

She let her head bang back against the headboard. Even tired she was beautiful. My perfect achievement.

"Marcus Bull. Complete fucking waste of space in the year below me at school. He's been hanging around with Chloe and her lot. He just told me he's going to punch me if he sees me."

My teeth ground. "I've had enough of this now. She's been harassing you for months and you finally put her in her place. That should be an end to it."

Her phone rang again. "Give it to me," I demanded and she handed it over.

"Hello?"

"You think you're so fucking clever now, but you'll not think that when I see you," a male voice shouted down the line.

"Hello, is that Marcus? This is Lena's mother. Just to tell you I'm recording this conversation," I lied. The line went dead. I passed it back to her.

"Hopefully that will be an end to it, but I'll walk up to the hairdressers with you and then for the rest of today, maybe just stay in the house and ask Sophie round if you like. There are pizzas in the freezer."

"Okay, Mum. Thanks."

Her thanking me in itself was a sign that she was wary. I touched her arm. "It'll all blow over soon enough. Just phone the other girls and tell them you've done nothing. If they don't believe you, then I will need to speak to their mothers."

"I'm beginning to wish I'd never hit her. It just seems to have made things worse." My daughter's lip trembled. I softly put my hand on her chin and tilted her face, so she was looking at me.

"She'd have carried on, love. You couldn't win. Like I said, anything further and I'm calling the police. You let me know if that weird boy calls again or tries to contact you."

She nodded. But the frown lines on her forehead didn't disappear and neither did the downturn of her mouth.

---

I thought it best to walk up to the hairdressers with her. She sat in the chair as Fiona neatened the edges and I sat near the reception talking to the salon owner, Tracy, who I used to go to school with too many years ago to mention.

"Kids these days. I wonder where the parents are? They just seem to do what the hell they like some of them, don't they? No bloody discipline, that's the problem."

I nodded.

"Anyway, there's no charge for Lena's trim. It's not like she wanted her hair cutting is it?"

My protests fell on deaf ears. Tracy's next customer came in and so she moved up to her chair. I sat back on the waiting area bench.

Picking up a worn magazine, I lost myself in weeks' old gossip until a commotion came from outside. Loud giggling and whooping got louder. A gang of kids without doubt and then I heard, "Ugly bitch." My daughter's widened eyes that flicked from the doorway to me told me all I needed to know. I launched for the door, meeting the gaze of several teenagers, some of whom I recognised. Others I'd never seen before, or they'd grown to be unrecognisable. Puberty did that. Most faces turned away from mine and the noise level went down. There were a couple of boys there, hoods pulled firmly up. I came face-to-face with Chloe.

"I don't care what happened last night. You had a fight or whatever, but it's done now, you hear? I've a good mind to give your mum the bill for this haircut. What were you thinking?" Chloe turned crimson while the others began to walk on, distancing themselves from the irate mother on the street. "Anything else and I'll be talking to your mother, and if I need to, I'll phone the police. We clear?" I finished my warning.

She just nodded. Satisfied, I turned back to the hairdressers and went inside.

"Sorry about that," I apologised, retaking my seat, but the staff all told me they understood. That they'd have done the same.

When we exited the salon, my daughter didn't have the same understanding. "Mum, what on earth? You've made a right show of me, being all ranty and embarrassing in the middle of the street. What if one of them had recorded you on their phone? I'd be a laughingstock."

I exhaled heavily. Kids and their pride. "It's much more important that she knows I'm not prepared to put up with it. It will have sent the same message back through the others as well." Lena was silent for the rest of the walk home. I could live with that. Teenage sulking. It might have lost her some cool points, but you couldn't put a price on safety.

The next few weeks passed without incident. I even saw Chloe's mum and we discussed the fight and I admitted I'd told Chloe off in the street. She agreed to speak to her daughter about it all. We swapped numbers and later she rang me saying that as far as Chloe was concerned it was done with now and they should just agree to ignore each other. I passed the news onto Lena, who said she was fine with that. With every day that passed with no more harassment, I breathed a little more calmly. Lena focused on revising for her exams and life carried on as before.

---

It was a crisp October morning when I left the house to go to an early dental appointment. My daily check of my car windscreen for ice had me rearing back in shock as I found shit smeared across it. I would have stayed staring in shock and wondering if I was seeing things were it not for the stench permeating my nostrils. I started to heave, stepping away from the car until I could take in gasps of fresh air. With time running out before my appointment, I was forced to leave the car on the driveway and head towards the bus stop so I wasn't late. I wasn't missing my appointment; I had a jagged edge to a tooth that kept causing me to cut my tongue. My whole journey there, I was consumed by what I'd just seen. What the actual fuck? Why would someone do that? I'd heard of people paying for manure to be dumped on people's paths, but actually smearing it was a bit much. It was no doubt dog poo. As my house was on a corner, I could only think it was someone who'd maybe thrown a dog poo bag over my wall and it had splattered. Despite poo bins having been placed around the grassed area near the end of my street, there was always some lazy bastard who couldn't be bothered to carry one or dispose of it properly. That was it. They'd have thrown it at my tree to hang it off a branch and it'd have been dislodged by a bird or something. There was a way for me to find out what had happened anyway. I had a security camera, and when I got home, I'd take a look and see exactly what had transpired. The thought of the trouble of a couple of weeks ago flitted through my mind. No, that was all sorted out. This wouldn't be connected. Anyway, Lena had stopped at Sophie's house last night, so wasn't even home.

Being a member of a local Facebook neighbourhood group, I often checked on what was happening in the area, so while on this bus I typed into there to see if anyone else had suffered the same fate, just as another possibility. There were a lot of kids around here with time on their hands and trouble on their minds. Nothing had been reported other than a couple of van break-ins. No reports of kids messing around.

After my dental check-up, where the dentist thankfully filed down the annoying tooth, I returned home and held my nose as I walked past my car. I hoped the large bushes from my front garden had stopped most of the early morning commuters from seeing it as they'd passed to go to the bus stop.

Somehow, I'd got to clean that off. Before I heaved again, I decided to grab a hot drink first, and get the manual out that showed me how to check the camera.

By the time I got to watch the video footage in the garage where I kept the monitor, a couple of hours had passed while I'd grown increasingly frustrated due to forgotten passwords and a general lack of technical knowledge. But finally, I found it. At 11:28pm someone walked onto our driveway. Physically and from their clothing, I'd guess they were a male youth, but it was someone wearing a large hood that covered their face. They also wore gloves, jogging bottoms, and trainers. They went out of vision while they ducked down in front of the car, and then a turd was placed on the window and the person used some kind of implement to smear it over the windscreen. Oh my fucking god. It was actual human shit. They'd squatted down, done a shit, and then coated my windscreen with it. Who the fuck would do something like that?

I left the camera paused, walked through into the living room and fell onto the sofa, my hand clutched over my chest. Who would do such a thing? Surely, no one would hold such a grudge against us so hateful they'd smear their own shit on my windscreen? I mean, Lena's fight was with Chloe and that was all sorted. I clenched my fists, annoyed because I didn't want to bother my daughter, but I knew I had to show her the video later to see if she recognised who it was who'd done this vile act.

Grabbing my laptop, I Googled getting rid of human excrement because I didn't want a disease while I cleaned my car. Of course, I couldn't find anything other than cleaning bird poo as it wasn't exactly a common activity was it? In the end I used my ice scraper to scrape as much as I could into a plastic bag while wearing my dishwashing gloves, and then I used a hosepipe. All the while I was cleaning it, I wanted to be sick. I sprayed a heavy dose of perfume into my scarf and wrapped it across my nose. Whoever had done this was seriously disturbed.

After that, I drove the car to a local car wash and had them wash it down properly.

By the time Lena came home from school, I was pacing the room, wanting to know if she knew who it was who'd done this.

As soon as she walked in and took a look at my face and the fact I was hanging around waiting for her, she knew something was wrong.

"Has something happened?" she said in a strained voice, her body stiffening.

I nodded. "Have you had any more trouble from anyone lately? You know, after the whole Chloe business?"

She shook her head. "No. Why?"

I exhaled deeply. "Because when I got up this morning there was shit all over the car windscreen."

Lena pulled a face. "Ew, what? Horse shit?"

I shook my head. "No. I looked at the security video. Someone took a dump and smeared it on the car. I need to see if you know who it was."

Her eyes widened. "I'm not watching someone take a shit."

I rolled my eyes. "You don't have to. You just have to watch them walk onto the driveway and tell me if you recognise them at all. They have a hood up, so you might not be able to tell, but it's worth a shot, right?"

Lena slung her bag down. "Okay, let me get changed and put my things away. You be lining it up."

Ten minutes later, Lena joined me in the garage, and I played her some of the footage.

"Well?" I asked.

I noticed Lena's arms were crossed over her body and she was rubbing at her shoulders. She knew who this was and it was winding her up.

"Well?" I repeated.

She sighed. "The trainers are Nike Air Max 270's. I also recognise the coat because he wears it all the time. I think that's Marcus Bull, Mum. Like, I'm 99.9% positive it's him."

Dear God. The boy I'd warned on the phone had exacted his revenge by shitting on my driveway and coating my car windscreen in it. The sick little fuck.

"Well, he made a huge mistake because it's all on camera," I told her, my arms folding across my own chest. "I'm going to call the police."

Lena nodded. "He's not right in the head, Mum, is he? To do that."

"God knows, but it's time to get the police involved and then hopefully that will be an end to it."

Lena nodded again, but her eyes left mine and as she looked away, I knew she didn't believe me that this would be over.

"Listen, don't mention it to anyone for now. Well, maybe Soph, but make sure she doesn't tell anyone else."

"Okay, Mum." She bit her lip. "I'm sorry. This all started because of what I did to Chloe."

"You weren't to know this idiot would try to join in, were you?" I said in a gentle tone. "The police will sort him out. You can't go round defecating on people's private property." I decided to change the subject. "Anyway, did you have a nice night at Sophie's?"

"Yeah it was fun. What's for tea?" she asked.

"It's only half past four! Grab some crisps or something," I told her. Then I giggled. "Or a Ripple because I think I've gone off anything a dark-brown colour now. Marcus might have actually helped me in my quest to lose a few pounds."

Lena pulled a face. "Ew, Mum, gross." But then she laughed, and I was pleased that with the literal shittiest of times, I could bring a smile to my daughter's lips.

## 3

## CARLA

You had to ring the number 101 to report a non-emergency crime. I found out later that you couldn't even phone 999 if you'd been threatened with a knife, if you'd managed to get away from it before ringing them. But at that moment in time, I was innocent to all of those things. I knew the police were short staffed, but to what extent I was unaware. As citizens we really did live a clueless life as to the reality of our police numbers.

I was 'on hold' for two hours. Two hours to get to speak to someone about the fact that someone had shit on my doorstep, so to speak. How many of us gave up, let crimes pass because we couldn't be bothered to hang around on the end of a line? It crossed my mind to hang up many times, but I didn't trust Marcus Bull. When I thought about his phone call and his latest actions, I had this gut feeling that he had to be dealt with. That he needed to be seen by the police. Eventually I was put through to someone who began to record the details.

"Okay, so we'll pass that onto your local police and you should hear something back within the next four days."

"Four days?" I replied, horrified. "But he could have done something else by then."

"If you see him on your property committing a crime, then call 999 immediately, but in terms of this other incident someone will be in touch."

I put the phone down, incredulous. Four days before someone would come to see us. All I had was a crime number written on the back of an old receipt and a general feeling of frustration.

---

For the next few days, every time there was a noise outside, I was at the curtain. My nerves were on edge, wondering if the strange boy I didn't know was out there. Lena started to get annoyed by my constantly asking her if he'd been in touch, if anything else was happening. I looked him up on Facebook. He wasn't on there anymore because all the teens had moved onto this bloody Snapchat. I had no idea what Snapchat even was. Instead, I looked at pictures of him on Facebook when he was younger, trying to work out what he might look like now, so that should I pass him in the street I'd recognise him. I found myself staring at every teenage boy I saw. I was entirely paranoid, especially of teens wearing hoodies; which, let's face it, was most of them. I wondered if he'd been there that day outside the hairdressers. One of the gang who'd jeered.

Finally, on the Friday, a policewoman called me and arranged to come and visit us. It was Monday before the PC and another female colleague were sitting in my living room with myself and Lena. They asked Lena to recount everything that happened and I helped fill in any blanks she left, or bits she'd forgotten.

"Okay, so if I could now look at the video," PC Tayburn asked.

After looking at security online, I'd found out how to put an app on my phone so that I could keep an eye on the house more easily. I located the incident via the app, showed her, and then she recorded it onto her own phone.

PC Tayburn took a deep breath before looking from Lena to me. "I'm going to be honest. You can't see his face. I appreciate how horrendous this is, but this video wouldn't stand up in court."

My forehead creased. "But his clothes. He wears the same clothes day in, day out apparently."

She shrugged. "Again, a judge would say these clothes are widely available and it doesn't prove it's him. Unless he wears something bespoke—a hand-knitted jumper by an auntie or something—it's not enough evidence. As crazy as it sounds, maybe if you'd have kept some of the faecal matter we could have proved it was him."

I began to get agitated, wringing my hands on my lap. "So I should have kept his crap on my windscreen and not cleaned it off? Maybe if you'd have been here earlier, the binmen wouldn't have emptied the bin with all the evidence in it."

I didn't miss the look that passed between the two policewomen. "I'm sorry. We've been dealing with emergencies."

I took a deep breath. "I understand that. Really, I do. I know you have more important things to deal with, but this isn't right. The lad is obviously disturbed."

"Look, I'll go to see him, okay?" PC Tayburn offered.

It was a peace offering, a gesture, and I leaped on it.

"Would you, please? I'd be so very grateful. It might just be enough to get him to stop."

She nodded. "I'll visit and talk to him and his parents. See what he has to say, and I'll warn him about harassing people by telephone. Obviously if he denies it all, there's not much I can do, but I'll give it a try. Do you know where he lives?"

"I don't, but I know what school he goes to."

She wrote the details down. "That's fine. I can get his address through the school. I'll be in touch, Mrs Haybrook. And if you see him on your property, call 999, okay?"

"Okay. Thank you. Thank you for your time."

They rose and I knew that was it. Yes, they'd go see him, but that was as far as this went.

After thanking them again, I watched them walk down the drive. A neighbour passed, her eyes widening at the police on my doorstep. Closing the door on her inquisitive gaze, I walked back to Lena. "Hopefully this will get him to stop."

She looked at me, her gaze dead. "He'll just deny it, Mum. We're no better off, let's face it. It's a waste of fucking time."

"Let's see, shall we? You never know."

But the truth was that deep inside me I felt the same way. Yet I had to have hope that the police would be able to help.

---

Later the next day my phone rang and PC Tayburn's voice came down the line.

"I went to see Marcus. As expected, he denied it all. He actually seemed like a nice lad, polite. Not what I'm used to, I have to say. Anyway, I gave him a warning to stay away from Lena and from your home and to not get involved with the argument any further. I explained that everything between your daughter and Chloe had now been settled. His mum said he wasn't the sort to do anything like that and got quite annoyed, but anyway it's done now. Hopefully, that will be an end to it."

"Thank you for going anyway. I really do appreciate it." My voice sounded over simpering even to my own ears while inside I was simmering with rage. 'Seemed like a nice lad'? Oh well, he couldn't possibly have done anything wrong if he was polite, could he? For fuck's sake.

The PC continued with her monologue. "No problem, and like I say, if you do see him on your property again. Call 999."

"I will. Thank you."

And I would, although I was wondering what the bloody point would be.

Against my expectations, it all stopped. Lena sat some mock exams and aced them all. She decided she was going to go to business college as she wanted to concentrate on business studies and hoped to move into retail. She aimed to manage some large fashion empire and then one day maybe even open her own shop. I encouraged every dream she had, told her to reach for the stars. She began to date a boy in her year at school. Lee was tall, quiet, and studious like her. They'd sit together at the dining table studying and then I'd give them money for a McDonalds or a KFC, or tell them there were pizzas in the freezer and I'd go shopping for a couple of hours to give them some peace.

"Carla." I heard my name being shouted while I stood in a clothes shop with a blouse in my hand. Turning around to the familiar voice, I found Sophie approaching me, her brown locks falling across her face messily.

"Hey, Soph. You spending all your pocket money?" I gave her a hug.

"We're just looking and dreaming about all the things we wish we could afford."

"We?"

"Yeah, I'm with some mates. They've just gone outside to buy cookies, so I'll need to catch them up." She looked at my hand. "That blouse is nice."

I held it up and looked at it again. "You think so? Usually I drag Lena with me so I can get some advice, but she's studying with Lee."

"Yeah, I know. I should be studying myself really, but the girls dragged me out. Though if you want, I can come round with you and help you choose some stuff?"

"Nah, don't be daft. You hang around with your mates. But thanks for taking pity on this old woman."

She smiled. "Don't be daft. I'd always make time for you. You're like a mum to me."

I squeezed her arm and smiled back. "What do you think to Lee?" I asked her while I had her there on her own. "He seems nice to me, nice and quiet, but I don't really know him. He's in your year, isn't he?"

She nodded. "I have some of my classes with him. He's nice, Carla. You don't have any need to worry. He's not one of the idiots. In fact, he's a lot like Lena. Quiet and studious. She'll be glad she can actually get some studying done, cos when she's with me I get bored easily and start chatting."

I laughed. "I can't believe the both of you are about to take your exams and move on."

"I know, bit different from when you were helping us learn our times tables. Now we need to know algebra, ugh." She pretended to shiver, and I laughed. Then she looked back at the doorway of the store. "Anyway, I'd better go. You need to get that blouse."

"Thanks. I will." I smiled. "She's not pushing you out, is she? I mean, you spent a lot of time together and now she's spending a heap of time with Lee."

"Nah. We're fine."

"Good, because I can't imagine not seeing little Soph at ours."

She giggled. "I don't think I'm so little now." She was right. She'd grown to five feet nine and was two inches taller than me. "We're growing up."

"You sure are." I wondered if Lena and Lee were sleeping together and if she wanted to get the pill. I'd given her condoms for her sixteenth birthday much to her embarrassment. It was a conversation for another day. My poor heart was struggling already with the thought of her growing up so fast. In two years' time she could be moving to a university miles away. The thought made my heart feel like it would break in two. It would be like losing a limb.

Sophie went off to meet her friends, and I tried on and then bought the blouse. Perhaps it was time for me to seriously look at dating again? I could wear this new blouse? Possibly.

After talking about the girls being little, I got home and as soon as Lee had left and Lena went to her bedroom, I went to my own room, grabbed my box full of photographs and I spent hours down memory lane looking at photos of Lena, and some of Sophie, shaking my head at how quickly those years had passed. Now they wouldn't pose for photos. The only ones they'd allow were the pics through filters. The ones they thought made them look like models when really their natural beauty was everything.

I hung my new blouse in the wardrobe, shoved thoughts of dating out of my mind, and carried on as usual.

---

It was three months later that a brick smashed our front window. Three months where there'd been nothing. No trouble whatsoever. Three months where Lena had settled into her final year at school. Three months where I'd started to breathe again, thankful that the incidents were over and that we could just get on with our lives.

This time the video showed two youths with hoods up. Lena once again recognised Marcus in the background, though the youth who'd thrown the brick was not him. Lena didn't recognise who the other person was.

"Are you sure you don't know?" I asked her again, frustrated.

"It could be any of his mates. It's too dark to see, Mum."

I arranged for the window to be temporarily boarded up and I left all the glass everywhere. The evidence. This time I wouldn't clear any of it up. I reported the crime.

It was another week before someone came. A week of glass all over my driveway and all over my living room. Lena told me I was an idiot not to clear it up, but I reminded her of what they'd told me last time. Maybe some of it was evidence.

I told her I wanted to see what Marcus looked like and so she found a photo of him on Instagram to show me. I didn't know what I'd expected. Actually, yes, I did. I expected someone who looked like a psycho, or mentally ill, but he didn't. Marcus had short blonde hair and was slim and tall. He was entirely average. He looked so different to the photos of him on Facebook where he was younger. The teen years changed kids so much. I thought about how much Lena had changed.

She'd become a lot more serious these days as her exams came ever nearer. Her relationship with Lee had fizzled out after six weeks, but she'd said she wasn't that bothered, that her exams were more important. Her head was down in her books most evenings. I was so very proud of her. She saw Sophie still a couple of nights per week, but on the whole, she spent more and more time in her room. I couldn't believe I actually found myself telling her to revise less!

When the police visited about the second incident, it was even worse than the first time. They told me they could do nothing at all. The footage in no way identified anyone. I was told it could just be nuisance kids in the area. The policeman wouldn't visit Marcus' house. He saw no point. All I had for my trouble was another incident number and a bill for the excess for getting the glass replaced.

And my anxiety back.

Yet again, I was at the window watching and waiting for something else to happen. I got colour cameras installed. I was constantly looking at the front of my own house. An average looking teenage boy was holding me hostage without even being there.

I hated him with a vengeance.

## 4

## CARLA

Two weeks later Sophie came through the door with Lena at home time and I heard her talking about stalkers. My ears pricked up at the word. I'd gone from listening and enjoying the sound of giggles to hanging around the front door at home time and making sure Lena was okay and eavesdropping on all of her conversations.

"He's just an idiot, leave it," Lena said. "And shh, because my mum will start kicking off again."

"You need to tell her what's going on."

That was enough for me. What did Sophie mean? I swung the living room door open and stepped into the hallway. I saw Lena roll her eyes in the direction of the ceiling. "Great."

"What *is* going on?" I looked from Lena to Sophie.

Sophie fidgeted, wringing her hands, but then spoke. "Marcus keeps running up to Lena before we get on the school bus. He says one day when she's not expecting it, he's going to push her in front of a car."

"He said what?" My voice had risen several octaves.

"Mum, he's been near me loads of times when I've been near roads. If he was going to do it, he'd have done it by now."

"That lad is dangerous. This is ridiculous, absolutely ridiculous." I turned to Sophie. "I want you to do me a favour, Sophie. The next time he does it, please can you try to record it somehow?"

She nodded. "I'll try. There's an app where you can record people speaking. I thought it was illegal to record people though?"

I shrugged my shoulders. "I don't know and I don't care. The lad's insane and if we get actual recorded proof of him threatening Lena, then it's some actual evidence for the police that they might be able to do something with."

I was shaking with rage because I needed to call the police again, but was there any point? I currently had no proof of what Marcus was doing, so what good would it do? It'd be another crime number, another week, and serve no purpose. I felt like we were just sitting targets and more than that, I was scared shitless for my daughter's safety. It wasn't like I could sit in the classroom with her. Though I could take her to school and back.

"From tomorrow I'm driving you to school and collecting you."

Lena looked at me in horror. "No, you're not. That'll just make things worse. It'll look like I can't stand up for myself."

I felt my temper rise. "Lena, until we manage to get him to stop, you'll do as you're told."

"He can still run up to me in school, Mum. Are you going to come to class?"

"When you have kids, you'll realise that you'll do whatever it takes to protect them. I'm taking you and bringing you home. Do you want me to pick you up as well, Soph?" Sophie didn't live all that far away from us and we passed her place on the way.

"Yes please."

"Okay, I'll come get you in the morning. Ten past eight. Right, you staying for tea?" I asked Soph.

"Yup, for a change." She laughed.

I was used to having Sophie around at mealtimes. She was the daughter of a single mum who worked a lot. She could either eat home-made food at mine, or a microwave meal or fast food at hers; so she came here, did her homework with Lena, had tea and then went home. She was here less at the moment because of them both studying, but still enough that I was happy she was eating okay. Sometimes I'd take her and Lena to the cinema, drop them off there and then pick them back up later. Occasionally on a Friday or Saturday night she'd stay over, though Lena mostly stayed over at her house at weekends, when Lou, Sophie's mum, tried to pay me back for having Sophie all week.

One weekend in four, Lena would relent and go stay over at her dad's, though she hated Natalie. Other than that, she mainly spoke to Ant on the phone.

"Can we get through the door, Mum, or are you going to stand there all night?" Lena gave me that teenage look of derision.

"This is not over, Lena. I'm not standing for it any longer. I'm going to go to his house myself. If the police won't do anything, I will. I'll talk to his parents."

"It's a waste of time, but it's your call." Lena kicked her shoes off.

"It's worth a try." Sophie said to her.

"Thank goodness someone around here agrees with me," I said, smiling at Sophie, "and put your shoes in the cupboard, Lena, for goodness' sake. How many more times do I have to say it?"

Lena cooked the pair of them a pizza each and they took it back up to her bedroom. I felt like I had ants in my pants. I just couldn't sit here a moment longer. Grabbing my car keys, I didn't bother shouting up to the girls, I just locked the door behind me and got behind the wheel. Usually I was so conscious to not break speed limits, but I could see myself pushing 33 in the 30 zones, my need to get to the address Lena had told me about on a previous interrogation overriding my usual sensibilities.

I didn't have an exact address from her. Just a description that the house had a navy-blue door and planters either side with spiky plants in them and there was a cut down tree in the small piece of grass at the side. It was a nice area, yet another thing that surprised me as I pulled up nearby. Seemed my mind was full of stereotypes and Marcus Bull wasn't one.

So there I was ready to show his parents the footage I had, because surely his mother would recognise her own son's clothes? And then we could end this ridiculous situation because I was getting to the end of my sanity. I needed a good night's sleep, and sorting this out tonight would give me that. I would be calm and reasonable.

Well, I thought I would be until the boy himself opened the door.

He stared at me. "Yeah?" he said, a sneer on his face.

"Is your mum or dad in? I'm Lena Haybrook's mother."

He blinked twice, like he couldn't believe I stood there.

"They're not here, they've gone shopping. But I didn't do anything, so—"

Just like that, I lost it. This teenage twat stood before me, lying to my face.

My body shook with rage and my voice wobbled with agitation. "Listen here, Marcus. I know for a fact it was you," I spat out. "We recognised you. Hiding behind a hood shows you for the pathetic fucker you are. But listen to me, lad. This ends here today. Believe me, you do *not* want me as an enemy and the day you fouled my car and broke my window you took this from being about just my daughter and involved me in it all. Stay the fuck away from us, otherwise you'll regret it. Do you understand?"

I didn't wait for a response. Instead, I turned my back on him and walked away. My body was shaking with adrenaline to the point it felt like my legs would give way and my heart would explode clean out of my chest. Part of me was annoyed that I'd lost my temper. The other part of me was joyous because I'd told him I wouldn't stand for his behaviour, had made myself entirely clear.

The police warning didn't do anything, maybe my own would.

God, I was still oh so naïve.

# 5

## CARLA

I was closing the curtains the following week when Marcus walked past the house with another four lads. They stared inside my windows as they walked past; all except Marcus who looked straight ahead. Why were they walking past my house? He was doing it on purpose, I decided. Goading me.

Not trusting him an inch, I went and sat on the sofa with the security app open on my phone. Just aimlessly sitting there and waiting.

They walked back again, and once more Marcus didn't look in. The others looked at my house and laughed. Every passing second a deeper hatred grew inside me, along with frustration, because I couldn't do anything about someone walking past my house even though it was winding me up.

Not five minutes later, they walked past again. I'd had enough. I grabbed my phone, switched on the camera, and walked down to the end of the street where they'd seen me and were standing around in a group.

"Could you tell my camera why you won't leave us alone?" I asked Marcus. He looked at me, a smirk on his face, and walked closer.

"You can't record me. You need to delete that."

"No." I looked at him over my phone. "I won't. I want you to tell me what you think you're doing."

"If you don't stop recording me, I'll make sure you have something else to occupy your time," he sneered.

I turned off recording. "Thanks, you little fucker. Threatening me and giving me the evidence. That's great. I'll just go phone the police now and you can look forward to a visit."

Triumphant, I stalked back to my house. Lena was walking down the stairs as I walked inside.

"Mum. What's happening? I heard the door and saw you tearing off after Marcus. Did he do something else?"

"He was walking back and forth past the house, driving me mad on purpose."

"You went out after him because he walked past the house? Mum, you need to stop this. Unless he does something that we can properly go to the police with, you might as well just get on with your life."

"He threatened me." I waved my phone at Lena. "I'm going to call the police again now. It'll no doubt be a week, but then he can have a visit from them again. The more he has the police visit, the more his parents will get fed up and the police will get fed up and then he'll go annoy someone else who doesn't ring the police every five seconds."

"Whatever, Mum," she said and went back to her room, banging her door shut.

I went on the computer, logged into the 101 page and posted my previous crime numbers, and my latest report.

It was nine days before a policeman was assigned to the incident. Another crime number, now our third, and yet another copper.

"Sounds like you're having quite a time of it," he said sympathetically. He told me he had children and understood my frustration. *Thank God*, I thought inwardly. *This one can empathise, he might help.*

I still had hope back then.

PC Lattimer listened to my recording. He sighed and grimaced.

"I'm afraid I can't do anything about that because it's not a direct threat."

"Pardon?"

He looked uneasy. "Yeah, he says he'll do something if you do, so he's not actually made a threat against you. Not directly. So there's nothing I can do. I appreciate it's frustrating, but..." He held up his hands.

"You can't even go see him and tell him to stop threatening me? He clearly says he will do something."

"Not directly. I'm sorry."

I stood up. "I'm sorry... to have wasted your time and mine."

PC Lattimer made his way to the front door.

"Could you tell me... Am I able to record them? He said I couldn't."

"If you're in fear for your safety, then do it. Hold the camera and point it at them. If it means they leave you alone, then let them know you're recording them."

"Thank you. That helps."

He nodded. "I'm sorry I can't do more. But if he threatens you directly ring 101 or send a report through online and in an emergency..."

"Dial 999." I sighed.

He nodded. Then he left, and I slumped on the sofa wondering just what you had to do to actually be dealt with by the police.

Flour came next. You can't phone the police for flour coating your car and windows, not really. It's harassment, it's a nuisance, but when the culprits are wearing hoodies, then there's nothing to call the police for.

And then came the scratches down the side of my car. Another crime number. Another visit. Now the culprits were in colour, wearing the same old clothes again, but still.

*We can't prove it's them without doubt.*

*We can't see their faces.*

When I went to bed at night, I struggled to sleep, because in my imagination, I was standing with Marcus, and I was picturing hurting him. This was the person I'd been reduced to being.

A nervous wreck with hate where my heart should be.

I'd picture a brick smashing into his face, busting his nose and mouth.

I imagine making him eat his own faeces.

Thoughts I didn't know I was capable of having flood my mind. Every day I was wondering what was next. It could be months, it could be days, hours, minutes. It'd already been over five months that this has been going on.

I just knew he wasn't finished.

He was still having too much fun.

# 6

## CARLA

April brought the Easter Holidays.

I'd said nothing to Lena, but I'd decided we'd move once she'd done her exams. I'd put the house up for sale and look for a rental property. We could live anywhere. I worked remotely and only needed a laptop, and I could choose a place with a highly recommended college for Lena. There'd not been any major trouble for a couple of months, but I wanted us to have a fresh start. Anyway, we'd gone periods of time with no trouble before and then BAM, something happened. Maybe Marcus liked us to think it was all over before he started again.

I needed a holiday too and had taken the week off my accountancy work. So I'd have time to look for a new place for us to live.

A fresh start.

It would be perfect.

---

Rightmove had become my morning break while I enjoyed a coffee. I opened it to see if there were any new rentals in a couple of areas I'd decided to focus on. Lena and Sophie had gone to the taco place that had just opened on our nearby small retail park. I'd dropped them off on my way to the supermarket. I didn't like Lena being out around the local area, but I could hardly stop her from going out and she was with Sophie and in broad daylight, so I felt reasonably assured.

That was until they came home and Sophie came to find me. That was one thing about Lena's friend. She'd risk Lena's wrath by confessing stuff if she felt I needed to know it. I guessed we were both looking out for Lena.

Lena trudged behind Sophie, and I was unnerved because instead of looking annoyed, Lena did actually look upset. Upset and tired. Worn down in a way that a sixteen-year-old shouldn't be. Exam stress was one thing, but this was a look I'd seen too many times on my own face and did not want to see on my daughter's. Despair.

"What's happened now?"

"Marcus came up to Sophie in the car park outside Taco Master. He said he wanted me to follow him to the staff car park so he could stab me," Lena confessed.

Sophie moved back to Lena and put her arm around her. "You're doing the right thing, telling your mum. You can't hide things like this."

Lena nodded.

"He came into Taco Master a few minutes later, and Carla, he actually had a knife in his bag."

"He what?"

"I'd got up to get some chilli sauce, and he was just in front of me in the queue. He had one of those man bag things. When he went in it for his money, I saw it," Sophie added.

"Are you sure you're not mistaken? It's more likely you saw his keys."

"It was a vegetable knife. I saw the handle. My mum has one the same."

"Okay. I'm going to call 999 because this is crazy." I felt frantic.

I picked up the phone and went through to the emergency number. A female operator answered.

"Hi, my daughter has just been threatened by a boy who said he wanted to stab her."

"Okay. Is she near him now?" the operator asked.

"No, she's at home now, but he's probably still near Taco Master because he'll be no doubt meeting his buddies."

"Okay, I'm going to have to ask you to call 101 because this is the emergency number."

"It is an emergency. There's a boy out in Berkley Edge with a knife in his bag threatening to stab people," I yelled.

There was a hesitation before the woman spoke again. Her voice was conciliatory, telling me in its tone that I was one of a long list of irate people she'd had on the line and she was giving me her, 'I understand but you need to calm down' timbre.

"Look. I need to clear this line because this is an emergency line. I'll call you straight back."

"Thank you," I said.

"What's happening?" Lena asked.

"Apparently we have to ring when he's actually holding a knife up to your throat or it's not an emergency. I can't fucking believe this," I said. The phone rang.

"I'm sorry, it's PC Stafford. I know it's frustrating, but it has to be an absolute emergency and your daughter is safe at home right now. I'm seeing if there is an officer who can go and investigate so can you tell me exactly what happened?"

I'm sure you know what came next.

An incident number. I was collecting them like tear-off strips on share packets of chocolate, but I didn't get to send them in for anything like a movie voucher. They were entirely useless. A series of useless letters and numbers that decoded would read: WE CAN'T FUCKING DO ANYTHING.

A policeman called me later on; yet another one I'd never spoken to before. Why wasn't everything pieced together like one case when it was about one youth? Instead, everyone held a piece of the Marcus Bull puzzle and no one had the full picture. The man told me an officer had just been to Taco Master but had found no one there.

"It's six hours after the incident happened. What was the point of going? He was unlikely to be there."

"I've requesting access of the video surveillance from outside the building."

"Oh." My heart rate soared and a small glimmer of hope kindled within me.

"Could take a few days, but I'll be in touch," he said.

Guess what? He called on the Wednesday.

"We looked at the footage. It just shows the boy talking to your daughter's friend. There's no sound and it's from a fair distance away. There's no sign of a knife, no immediate threat."

We.

Can't.

Do.

Anything.

---

Marcus Bull was getting away with everything.

I passed him on my way to the supermarket on the Thursday morning. He was alone. He looked at me and then looked away. Carried on walking.

That day I gripped my fists together so hard as not to punch him in the face that my nails bit into my palms.

---

"Do you want us to move?" I asked my daughter while we ate our evening meal.

"What?"

"To get away from Marcus. I could rent us somewhere."

"Mum. Marcus is an idiot. But if he was going to do something, I think he would have done it by now. And I'm leaving school soon, so he's bound to move on."

"Well, I thought we might move after your exams. Find somewhere new and a different college."

"But would it be far away? I'd not see Soph."

"I could rent a bigger place. Soph could have her own room. Stop when she likes. I'd make it not too far away, but it needs to be far enough to be away from Marcus Bull."

I could see Lena's mind working overtime.

"I'll think about it. Right now, I'm concentrating on my exams, not that dickhead."

"Okay, love."

It sounded like it wouldn't take much persuasion to get Lena to move. Maybe the promise of the master bedroom. Anything to get her away from Berkley Edge.

Just a few more weeks and we would be away from Marcus forever.

"Mum." Lena had that expression, the one where her eyes showed a frustration with her mouth. Where she clearly wanted to ask something but felt she really shouldn't.

"Yeah?"

"Why did you let Dad go so easily? Did you not want to fight for him?"

I sat back in my seat and put down my knife and fork. I could eat my dinner cold. My daughter had questions, and it was only fair I answered them.

"Do you think I should have tried to get him to stay?"

"Not if it was done with. I'm not someone who thinks you should stay for the kids," Lena said, sounding way beyond her sixteen years. I guessed that was what divorce did to children; grew them up faster as they faced a life where not everything was white picket fences and unicorns, though I'd tried to throw fairy dust where I could. It wasn't Lena's fault her dad couldn't keep it in his trousers.

"I didn't fight for him because he'd already gone." I'd always believed in telling my kid the truth, apart from the usual Father Christmas and Tooth Fairy shit and even then Lena had always been sceptical, even when so young she shouldn't have been looking at Santa and saying 'Mummy, he's just a man dressed up'. "When he confessed to the affair, it had been going on several months. That was too much for me. If it had been a mistake, then maybe we could have tried to work out what had gone wrong, but while I'd been living here thinking everything was fine, for your father I wasn't enough."

I could see what Lena was thinking. That she wasn't enough either.

"Your dad has always worshipped the ground you've walked on. It will hurt him that he doesn't get to see you every day. It's something he didn't consider when he slept with Natalie and started on a path to her door and out of ours. Led by lust. That's his mistake to live with, and your choice to make. He made his, you make yours. If you want to see your dad more, I will never stand in your way."

"You won't, but she will."

"Natalie?"

"She's so smug, Mum, when I go round. She's always touching him on the arm or kissing his cheek. It's like she's in competition to get his attention when I'm there. It's pathetic."

"She sounds insecure. But that's what she has to live with. She chose to sleep with a man who cheated on his wife. Every day she should be looking over her shoulder because leopards and all that."

"Don't you want to meet someone else? I mean, you seem lonely sometimes." Her voice sounded sad. I didn't want her thinking she had to worry about me.

"Sure, one day. I'd like to hope there's a guy out there for me. One who'll treat me right. But I can do all that after you've left home, can't I?"

"You can do it now, Mum." She eye-rolled me.

"I think about dating sometimes," I confessed. "But it's hard. I'm forty-one." Lost in my imagination for a moment, I smirked. "Oh God.

I can just imagine myself now, sat at a table in a restaurant across from a man I quite like the look of, and me going, 'so, if we get together will you cheat on me? Also, right off the bat, I think it's only fair for you to know, I've a sixteen-year-old daughter, and I don't like giving blow jobs."

"*Mum.*"

I cracked out laughing. "Your face. Do you want some dessert?"

"No, you've put me off food for life." She did a mock retch.

"I was only joking, I actually like—"

"Lalalalalalala," Lena put her hands over her ears.

Then we both burst out laughing. Afterwards she went up to her room. I noticed she went in the cupboard for a grab pack of Maltesers first. She'd not been put off food *that* much.

I cleaned up the dinner stuff and then retired to my usual spot on the sofa. Buoyed about the possibility of moving house, I opened my computer, clicked onto Rightmove and looked at more lettings, choosing different areas. And suddenly, there was my perfect home. Down a lane in a small village about thirty minutes from here. Detached. Three double bedrooms. A back garden with decking perfect for summer and a separate outbuilding where I could work. It was double my mortgage, but I could afford it. Obviously, I needed to go look at it, but things were looking up.

A new place and a fresh start for myself and Lena.

I closed the computer happy, curled up on the sofa and fell asleep.

---

When I woke, my neck hurt. It always happened when I fell asleep there. I never learned. Usually it was the lull of the television, along with a glass or two of wine that had me crashing out, but tonight it had been feeling a sense of peace for the first time in a long, long time.

Lena's exams would soon be over. Then it was prom, something her and Soph rarely shut up planning. It was costing me a small fortune with the dress, make-up and hair appointments, and the limo to take them; but it was a one-off, a rite of passage.

I remembered the house I'd found.

It was 9:47pm when I heard male voices shout outside, "Show us your tits, Lena." Then they burst out laughing. I flew to the door, and to the end of my driveway.

"God, she's here. The wicked witch," Marcus said to the others as he walked down the street like he owned it. This time he had seven other boys with him. All just laughed, whooped, and hollered as they walked past the house.

"One day, you'll get yours," I shouted after him.

He turned back and I could see his smug twat face from hundreds of yards away. "What are you going to do, old lady? Shout me to death?" Another cheer and another round of whooping. Like he was in the centre of a boxing ring and they were holding up his fist, declaring him the winner of the fight.

And he was right. As I walked back into my house and closed the door, resting my back against it and looking towards the top of the stairs, I realised that I could do nothing about him at all.

Nothing except move us away and hope that we left the problem of Marcus Bull behind.

As Lena hadn't rushed to the top of the stairs to tell me off for going outside and showing myself and her up, I figured she'd fallen asleep revising, so I made my way upstairs. My heart still thudded with the adrenaline of chasing after Marcus and I felt a little short of breath. You fucking idiot, I berated myself. Getting all worked up because of a kid.

I walked into Lena's room. She was sat up in bed typing furiously into her phone as usual.

"Oh, I thought you'd be revising?"

"Nah, needed a break, so I'm chatting to Soph. But I'm feeling beat, so I'm just trying to get her to accept I need some beauty sleep and then I'm going to settle down."

"Okay, sweetheart. Hey, no pressure, but I think I found a nice place for us to rent."

Her eyes widened. "Really?"

"Yeah, it's so cute. I'll show you in the morning."

"I'll look forward to it."

I was on my way out of the door when Lena called me back. "Mum?"

"Yeah?"

She got out of bed, walked over and put her arms around me.

"What's this all about?"

"You're moving on at last; from Dad I mean. New house, and you said you might date. You need this, a new focus. I'm glad. I love you, Mum. I want to see you happy."

"Love you too." She smelled of her Miss Dior perfume and coconut scented shampoo. I tried to take what I could from her hug without making her self-conscious. Finally, she stepped away from me and back toward her bed. I felt the loss of her body heat as the cool air of the room encircled me once more.

I didn't tell her about Marcus.

That could wait until tomorrow.

I'd let her have a good night's sleep.

Following her example, I got ready for bed earlier than usual. I still felt tired from earlier and the house, the chat, and now the hug wiped away Marcus' words. I'd checked on the app on my phone a couple of times while I was getting ready, but I didn't see him come past and in the end I made myself turn my phone off, so that I could turn my mind off too.

Snuggling down under my duvet, still feeling like I could smell my daughter's familiar scents in my nostrils, my last thoughts were that in the morning I'd make enquiries about our potential new home and then I'd make pancakes. Lena loved my pancakes and we'd not had them all holiday.

I'd not set an alarm with it being the school holidays and I woke up to find it had gone past ten am. It was the weekend, but that was enough of a lie-in for me, and I wasn't a parent who let their kid sleep in too late either. Putting my robe on, I pushed open the door of Lena's room.

"Lena."

Nothing. *Teenagers slept like the dead*, I thought, smiling to myself as I wandered over to the blackout curtains to pull them open. Lena couldn't sleep unless it was pitch black.

I tripped over something on the floor. That was another thing they did. Never fucking picked anything up.

I pulled back the curtain and turned to watch my daughter shriek from the light, ready to giggle at her screwed-up face and protests for me to close them again. Instead what I saw would never *ever* leave me.

My daughter's lifeless body.

# 7

## CARLA

I stood in a crematorium, just like I did two years ago for my mother, but this time the service was for my daughter. This was a joke, right? Any moment now Lena would spring out from behind a chair and tell me it was a prank for TikTok. I closed my eyes and prayed that when I opened them none of this was real.

That it was just one huge nightmare.

That Marcus Bull caused me a psychotic break.

That I was in an institution and this was a vivid hallucination caused by the medicines they'd put me on to bring my mind back.

But of course, the sounds of reality were still there when my eyes were shut. The background audio hum of talking and sobbing.

I opened my eyes to the truth of what was happening right now.

The room was full of family I'd not seen in forever; pupils from her school I couldn't be bothered with, including Chloe fucking Butcher and her parents; and my ex-husband and Natalie, who I'd had to act okay with. My ex-husband kept looking over at me. I kept meeting his eyes. Eyes that overflowed with his grief. I saw in Natalie's gaze as she watched him watching me that despite the fact our unspoken communications were mired in joint grief, the tightness in her eyes showed she was jealous and unsettled despite that. But then it took a selfish cow to steal a man from his wife and child, even though it took a weak man to let her.

Ant's sorrow would be overflowing with regrets about the time he never got to spend with Lena. My conscience was clear. That was the one thing about this. There was no guilt within me, as there was no room. All I was filled with was hate.

Hate for my husband who left us.

Hate for his girlfriend who tempted him away.

Hate for the teenagers there pretending to give a damn when they were here to make themselves feel better.

And hate for a teenage boy who didn't know what was coming.

---

Sophie and her mum were sitting at either side of me, both holding my hands. I was thankful to Lisa—even though after all these years I only really knew her on a surface level—for everything she'd done to help me since I'd found Lena a week ago.

But as soon as I'd done burying my daughter, I was done with all of these people.

Lena's body laid in a dark mahogany coffin at the front right-hand side of the room, and soon the curtain would close and she would become nothing but ashes.

Like my heart.

There was nothing of me left. It was all with her in that box.

My life was over.

I was dead.

The living dead.

I would join her, but before I departed this earth there was something I needed to do.

Marcus Bull shared the video where my daughter had stripped off to lose her virginity to her boyfriend. I knew it was him though he did it behind a fake Snapchat account as he knew he could.

I had no idea how he got the footage, but I would find out and whoever was involved would pay too.

My daughter's last words to me were not that she loved me and of her hope for my future, although now they seemed more poignant.

They were just two words written on a torn page.

**I'm sorry**

Lena's phone revealed to me about more taunts and bullying and Sophie's mum would tell me over those next hours after finding Lena's body about how Sophie had spent part of the night consoling my daughter about the video circulating around social media. About how my daughter said she was so tired of it all, and that she'd think about what to do about it in the morning. She'd told Sophie not to worry, that I was moving us away from there. Sophie had believed her. Why wouldn't she?

Sophie said Lee must have circulated the video, but I knew who would be behind it. He was behind everything.

Marcus Bull.

And now?

Marcus Bull would pay.

## 8

## CARLA

I took a minute at a time. Listened to the manure that came out of people's mouths as they passed on their condolences. That's how I saw it, shit spilling out of their mouths as they spoke. They dared to touch me. A kindly little squeeze of my arm. I was wound tight but outwardly cool, like a boxer before entering the ring.

My daughter moved on to the next life, whatever that was. I hoped she found peace. My mind was in purgatory, demons waited and languished in my brain.

This was the time Sophie took me outside and away from people. If anyone had any clue how I was feeling it was Sophie.

We walked around the grounds for a while. I was numb. Sophie wanted to help me or bond. I could see everyone's thoughts in their expressions these days. Poor Sophie. Our bond was gone. We were tethered by Lena and Lena was no more.

"My mum says she's cutting back her hours at work. She wants to spend more time with me."

"That's nice." *Shame it took for my daughter to die to show Lisa she could do better.*

"I'm sixteen years old. Up until now I've grown up with you and Lena mainly. She's too late. Where was she while I was studying for these exams? It's okay working and saying someone needs to pay the bills, but we could have lived in a smaller home. She could have bought less clothes and handbags. And when she was at home, she wanted 'me-time'. Now she wants to be around, but I'm used to her absence."

I didn't look at Sophie. I didn't need to. I'd known this girl for years. She'd be chewing the side of her cheek right now. That was what she did when she was mulling over a problem. A maths question, whether she wanted chips or a jacket potato with her tea, whether she wanted her mother in her life.

"Everything changed a week ago, Soph. Life is no longer what went before. Now I don't have a daughter, but you now have a mother. It's the yin and yang of life. My loss is your gain."

"Our loss," she said, her voice slightly raised.

"Yes, sorry, our loss."

We walked a few more minutes in silence.

"I'm moving to the rental I found. My house will go up for sale eventually, but right now I don't want to change anything in her room. Yet I can't bear to be near it either. I'm spending stupid amounts of my savings having two places, but I don't care. I need somewhere to be close to her and somewhere I can escape. Does that make sense?"

"Yes. Completely."

"We'd better go back. People are expecting us at the wake. Your mum will be calling you any minute."

"My phone is off."

Another minute of silence. All I could hear was our footsteps on the concrete.

"I wonder what he's doing while I bury my child?" I said quietly. So quietly it was a gamble whether or not Sophie would have heard me say it. Like I wasn't sure I wanted to say it out loud, but also I put it into the ether.

She unzipped her handbag, pulled out her phone and turned it on.

"What are you doing?"

"I have Marcus on my social media from a long time ago. You know, the times when you just accepted friend requests from anyone and everyone? I'd message him from time to time through Snapchat or Insta and tell him to leave Lena alone."

"You never said."

"I thought you'd tell me to sever the link and I didn't want to. I felt like I could keep an eye on him that way."

"Is there anything else I don't know?"

"He keeps his gang of friends because he buys them all weed. Maybe they do like hanging with him, maybe they just use him. I don't know. But that's what the gossip at school is. I didn't tell you that because Lena asked me not to. She thought you'd try to snitch about it to the police and she was scared you'd annoy a drug dealer or something."

I half laughed. "That sounds like Lena."

Her face as she looked at her phone contorted with fury.

"What is it?"

She shook her head. "You're better off not knowing. I know he did so many bad things and I know you hate him, but Lena would want you to have your fresh start, Carla. Forget Marcus Bull."

I snatched the phone from her hand. "You know I can't do that."

I stared at the photos on his Instagram grid. Standing with his homies, his little tribe. All staring at the camera like they were from the hood. Hoodies, masks, do-rags. It was pathetic. Acting like they were in a gang because, what, they'd played *Grand Theft Auto*? My hate for him knew no bounds.

"It's probably better you forget him now, especially if he's involved with drug dealers."

Huh. While my daughter's body rotted, his already rotten body lived on.

There was no justice in this world.

He'd got away with every damn thing.

I handed the phone back to Sophie.

"Yes, you're right. It's time I moved on," I lied. "Focusing on Marcus Bull just brings me more grief. I have to accept; *we* have to accept, that some things in life are evil, but we can live our lives away from them."

I turned to Sophie as we stepped off the concrete path and walked up the gravel driveway back to the crematorium car park and Lisa. "Let your mum back in. You've years to spend together yet if you're lucky. Take your second chances, Sophie, because I'd do anything to have a second chance with Lena. I'd have moved us away earlier and then she might still be alive."

It was the one time I let myself fall. I'd cried at the service, and my eyes felt like they were bruised, but this was the time where I visibly bled out my emotions while the gravel ripped into my black tights and through to graze my knees. I wrapped my arms around my head and I sobbed, my tears soaking through the gravel, as Sophie and Lisa's arms embraced me. Just for that one moment, I wished my own body would decompose right there and leach through the earth.

---

Anthony and Natalie had arranged the wake at a local pub. He'd insisted on arranging something when I'd told him I had no interest. They'd sat in my house while we spoke with the funeral director about what coffin to cremate her in. I'd chosen to have her buried in the prom dress she should have been wearing in July.

Jesus. That would still go ahead. While I continued to mourn, they would dance and celebrate the end of school life. Get pissed behind the teachers backs and some would no doubt fuck in a classroom.

I knocked back the sherry Ant had placed in my hand. Sherry. Was I his fucking grandmother? I wanted to go to the bar and ask for a bottle of vodka, but too many people kept interrupting me. More fake condolences to assuage whatever guilt they were carrying around. If only thoughts were visible whispers. I imagined them while they spoke to me.

*Shit, I hadn't seen them for six years.*

*I feel awful for saying I had a migraine the day they were due to visit.*

*Fuck, I don't want to be here talking to Carla. What do you say to someone who lost their daughter?*

*I wonder if there was more to it? I mean her father had cheated on her mother. Must take a lot for a child to kill themselves.*

They were all *sorry*.
   Sorry.
   Sorry.
   Sorry.
   *If you need anything, Carla, anything at all.*
   Yes. I need you all to take your hypocrisy and fake endearments and fuck right off. That's what I need.
   Fuck it. I decided to go to the bar. But before I could order a drink, some useless cousin of mine was beside me. "I'll get your drink, Car. What do you want, love?"
   Car?
   Love?
   He had no right to speak to me like this. The last time I saw him was at my mother's service. Today was just a dull repeat, but with more guilt in their eyes because 'at least Joanie had had a good innings'.
   Yes, that made me feel better about my mother's death, you fucking waste of sperm and eggs and the miracle of life.
   I spoke to the barman, not my cousin. "Double vodka please."

My cousin would be wearing a look of shock or understanding. I wasn't interested in either. I just grabbed my drink, muttered, "Thanks," in his direction and then I walked away, back to Lisa and Sophie, the only people I could stand to be near.

Of course, things came to a natural end. People didn't want to stay around real grief for long. Once they'd 'shown their face', their excuses were played out like I was stupid and they left.

*We need to get back, because you know, traffic... the dog... blah blah blah.*

Because you can't wait to get out of here. Me fucking too.

Wouldn't it be fantastic if I could just tell my truths?

I didn't because I wanted to respect my daughter in the last place I could.

But oh, how I wanted to tell every one of these people that they could go fuck themselves hard up the arse with a broom handle for all I cared. Stick their words up there while they were at it. Faecal words back where they belonged.

*You talk shit.*

*Get away from me.*

---

I told Lisa and Sophie to go. That I would be fine. Sophie wore a frown that would put a wrinkle between her eyebrows if she wasn't careful in the years to come.

For a moment I stood and imagined Sophie aging. She was very like her mum in looks and that's how she'd go. I'd never see Lena older. I'd never see my daughter again. Except for in my mind: in memories that would cruelly fade, in photographs that would destroy me to look at as much as they would delight me, and in my dreams and nightmares.

And again, my mind returned to him.

Marcus Bull.

Marcus who would sleep well every night because he didn't give a crap.

No, Marcus would not.

Marcus would sleep with one eye open soon.

Because if I had to stay alive to make sure he paid, then I was making my time worth it.

The law and police had failed my daughter and failed me.

So I'd spend my waking hours now letting him know how it felt to be the bullied one.

And if it drove him to take handfuls of tablets and leave the plastic bottles on the floor for his mother to stumble over in a morning before she opened the curtains to shine a light on his dead body then so be it.

# 9

## CARLA

Finally, there was just Anthony, Natalie, and myself. Time for me to thank them because it was the polite thing to do and somewhere my mother had installed this gene within me and then I could go.

Natalie had been helping the staff tidy up the remaining buffet food. At times her and Ant had been deep in conversation and whatever was being said, she wasn't happy.

I walked over to Ant and watched as Natalie made her way over too. As if she couldn't bear for me to have his company alone for even a second.

"I'm going to drive you home, Carla. I only had a pint."

My eyes flicked straight up to Natalie's. Her lips were pursed and her eyes narrowed, but it soon changed to a sympathetic smile as if I was a child in a shopping mall who'd lost her parents.

"He's not going to crowd you. Just make sure you're home safe, then he'll leave you to your own thoughts."

In other words. *He's not yours anymore, he's mine.*

And where I had fully intended to turn down any such arrangement, her expression had me do an about face, because guess what,

Natalie? You did what you did to me and my daughter and what you got for your conniving ways was my husband.

I got to suffer.

My daughter got to suffer.

And you had orgasms.

I'd not known how to spend the rest of my day other than plotting out how to derail a teenage boy, but now all I could see was a challenge.

*He was mine first, Natalie. You remember that, don't you? Especially now that it's clear we had something together you didn't.*

My God, I bet Natalie had even had a teeny, tiny bit, deep, deep inside that recognised and was even a guiltily bit pleased that there was no longer anything tying us together.

Our daughter was dead and Natalie Reardon would have had that thought whip through her mind. Not pleasure of her death. Pleasure of my exit.

*We're free of her now.*

I'd put money on that having been a whisper thread.

Now I looked at my ex-husband. At the caring gaze I remembered from the past.

"I'd really appreciate a lift. Thank you."

I grabbed my coat and thanked the staff at the pub and then we left. The car journey to drop Natalie off was stiff and awkward with her making polite conversation about it all going as well as it could.

All I could see in my head was a funeral bingo card and I wanted to yell 'House' after every line she rolled out, like 'I'm sure she was watching'. If there was a heaven, Lena would be up there looking at what cute guys there were, not at a bunch of miseries down on earth. I wanted to yell at Natalie that she knew nothing about my daughter and should keep her fucking nose out, but I didn't.

She needed to feel insignificant to me, like she made me feel all those years ago.

Ant pulled up outside my house.

"Ant, I know Natalie said you'd drop me off and that's okay, but if you want to come in, you can. It'd be nice for us to just talk about Lena for a bit without anyone else there."

He exhaled deeply. "I'd really like that, Carla." As he got out of the car, I saw he was trying to keep himself together. His body was shaking, and he started to make choking noises while placing a fist against his nose and mouth. Hurriedly, I unlocked the front door and he stepped quickly with me into the hallway, and then he burst into ragged sobs.

"It smells like her. I just want to see her one more time. Her run down these stairs. I want a do-over. I never, ever should have left."

I shrugged my shoulders. "There's no point in this, Ant. Come on, I'll get the vodka out. You can have a taxi home or stay here."

"Natalie—"

"Is not here and is not part of today," I yelled. "We just buried our daughter. *Our* daughter. So I couldn't give two fucking shits about Natalie, okay? We will talk about our daughter and we will celebrate her life with vodka and then you can go back home and Natalie can have you for evermore, but today, either you forget her, or you leave now, because today our daughter comes first. First, you hear me?"

I was so very annoyed with him that my fists beat at his chest. He grabbed them with his and held them away.

"You're right. I'm sorry, and it's why I wanted to come back here. I want us to remember Lena. I'll find the vodka. Please go get the photos from when she was little. When we were all together and happy. I need it, please."

Nodding my head, I walked upstairs and gathered the albums he wanted to look at.

We drank the vodka while pouring over pictures and reminiscing of better times.

"Why did I throw this all away?" Ant lamented, his eyes glassy from sorrow and vodka.

"Because you were ruled by your dick and another woman's attention."

Ant turned to me on the sofa. "I am so very sorry, Carla. I never said it before, but I am. You didn't deserve it."

"Something was wrong clearly. We just didn't know it until you broke us. If we'd have been as happy as I thought we were, then you wouldn't have strayed."

"There was nothing wrong with us. I just wanted to have my cake and eat it. And the cake was always decorated in tempting toppings and being flaunted in front of me."

*Like I said... weak.*

"When I look back, I remember things you used to do, habits, complaints, and I realise we were happy and yet at the same time you drove me mad," I confessed.

"That's marriage, Carla."

I smiled. "I guess so."

"That smile looks good on you. I hope in the future you have reason to smile more often."

I stared down at my flooring. "How do we manage to wake up each day now without her?"

It was my one honest question for him, where the part of my soul that loved him searched for the part of him that loved me.

"I don't know," he answered honestly and softly. "She's there every time I close my eyes. All these last years where I let her stay at yours because I knew she was angry at me, and that Natalie drove her mad. I could have taken her into town or told Nat to give it a rest. That I needed time with my daughter. There's so much about her in these last years that I don't know. I don't know how my beautiful daughter could have been so desperate that she felt her only option was to take a bunch of pills, and I know she'd been bullied and you'd been through all that shit, but I didn't take a single action myself. I only half listened when you phoned, thinking oh, Carla's on one again. If I'd followed him down a dark street and threatened him maybe she'd still be here now." He was crying again. I wiped away his tears with my hand. He clutched my hand again.

"I'm sorry," he said desperately. "I'm so, so sorry."

He leaned forward and kissed my forehead, and he moved to place his arms around me and tucked me under his chin in the way he used to do if something had upset me. His arms were warm and familiar, and I'd already made up my mind in the pub that if he made any move on me I would accept it, because I had a score to settle.

I would not initiate anything, but I wouldn't refuse it either.

Ant looked down at me, tilted my chin up, and kissed me. Soft, warm, and familiar, I knew I wouldn't regret a night in the arms of my ex-husband, treading familiar terrain. I could take comfort from his hands trailing and worshipping my body and when he lost himself inside me, I wouldn't care, because I was numb to anything but grief and my goals of retribution.

And that's what happened.

He stood and held out his hand. I reached out and took it and he led me upstairs. Up to our old room, as if he still lived there. Neither of us turned and acknowledged the closed door on the left.

He stripped me of my clothes before shedding his own. Then went into the wallet in his pocket and took out a condom. Who had a condom in their pocket at a funeral, was all I could think. Our clothes were discarded to the floor and then he climbed into my bed.

"Come warm me up," he said.

He'd always said that.

I climbed in and the coolness of the sheets hit me. And then I wrapped myself into the warm body next to me.

If I expected different moves from the person who'd had a different lover for so long, I was disappointed, but at the same time I was relieved as the same old routine was played out under the duvet, until such time as Ant decided I was sufficiently warmed up and he thrust inside me. As he bucked and writhed above me, all I could think of was what Natalie would think when I told her what had happened.

He came, and I faked my own pleasure. Then he gathered me into his arms.

"We were always so good together," he said, and then he fell asleep.

Once his breathing settled, I extracted myself from his arms and went to shower every bit of Anthony Haybrook from my body. Afterwards, I crept downstairs and took my mobile phone from my pocket. Back upstairs I snapped a photo of a naked Ant in my bed, the covers off his body showing his wilted penis. He stirred slightly so I quickly put my phone down and climbed back inside.

His phone began ringing an hour later, and I knew who it would be. I smirked in satisfaction. Now Natalie was the one wondering why her other half was so late home. But on just the one occasion. I'd been like it for months, only to be told a job had kept him back.

Ant and Natalie. At least they had each other. Or did they? I didn't care. It was time to send him home and send them both my goodbye.

His phone rang again, and I shook him.

"Ant. Ant. Your phone is ringing. Natalie will be wondering where you are."

Ant opened his eyes and looked at me, his eyes trailing over me lazily and hungrily. "Natalie can wait."

"No, she can't." I got out of bed. "Go home."

"But... I don't understand. We..."

"Fucked. We had a fuck, Ant. A drunken one at that. We were two people lost in grief who found solace in each other's bodies. It was no more than that. For me anyway."

His face downturned. "Fine." He began to shuffle out of bed and walked out and towards the bathroom.

I moved downstairs, busying myself in the kitchen with nonsense jobs like wiping down an already clean countertop until he stood waiting to go.

Walking up to him, I placed my arms around him. Surprised by my seeming change of heart he hugged me back.

"Thank you, Ant, for giving me Lena. For the sixteen beautiful years I had of our daughter, and thank you for helping with the funeral and for the time we shared when we got back, looking at photos and reminiscing, and for providing some, shall we say, comfort."

"You're welcome, Carla. I will always love you. You know that, right?"

I laughed, stepping out of his embrace. "I don't know what you truly feel, Ant, but I know what I feel. Like I died when our daughter died." His phone rang again. "There she'll be again. Natalie. Can't even let me mourn my daughter without her attention seeking. You did that, so go shut her up."

Ant looked at me, his eyes widening.

"I hate what you did to our family. I hate that you were weak. I've tried to hate you, but I don't. I can't because you gave me Lena and you were always a good father. You were just spineless."

"So what happens now?"

I couldn't believe he was asking me this.

"What happens now is you go back to the girlfriend you just cheated on with your ex-wife, and you answer all the questions she's going to ask you because she knows how you operate seeing as the last time she was on a different kind of receiving end." I smirked. "And you deserve every bit of nagging you get."

I opened my front door making it clear it was time for him to go and then as he left, I closed the door firmly behind him.

Going upstairs, I laid in my bed and picked up my mobile phone. I forwarded the photo of Ant to Natalie.

**Carla: Sending back the leopard to you. I'm done with him, and with you. My only question? Why is he carrying condoms in his pocket when you're sterilised?**

Natalie never wanted children. She'd made sure she couldn't have them by insisting on being sterilised at thirty-six. There was no room in Natalie's life for anyone but herself. I'd been secretly glad because it meant Lena didn't have to endure half-siblings.

My phone soon buzzed back.

**Natalie: What a hateful bitch you still are.**

I blocked her and Ant and huddled down under my bedcovers. I was indeed a hateful bitch and I felt like my revenge fuel tank was filling up nicely.

Ant had been the practice lap and now it was time for me to take the pole position.

The race to destroy Marcus Bull would start soon. I would avenge my daughter's death and then I could plan my own, just as soon as I could be confident total grief wouldn't trip me up.

## 10

## CARLA

The days moved along. Some had purpose. Days when I got in my car and drove from my house to the rental property and slowly moved from one to the other. Other days I laid in my bed in either house, whichever I was in when life beat me down into oblivion. I forced myself to eat when I was more with it.

I shopped for the few things I needed to exist and I dreamed of peace.

After some internal arguing with myself, I decided to sell the house after all. It was going on the market in the next day or two. Despite thinking I'd want to be around her things to feel close to her, I couldn't bear to be near or in Lena's room, and I'd not opened the door since the funeral. It was just too hard. Today I needed to go in and take apart the room that no longer held my daughter. Sophie had offered to help, but I'd said no. Instead, I'd invited her over last night and told her to go in and take whatever she wanted from Lena's jewellery box and the bits of ornaments on her side, things like bejewelled photo frames, some of which housed pictures of the two of them. She'd gone upstairs and returned not two minutes later saying she had all she needed: in her mind, in her photos, and in the friendship bracelet long ago worn off but kept in Lena's jewellery box. She'd held up the frayed threads and told me she kept hers in her own box and now she'd wrap them together so they could be friends forever.

I'd hugged her close and then made an excuse that I had to go to the other house, so I could drop her home. Sophie had worn an expression of sadness that went beyond Lena. It was a heavy resignation, an acceptance of losing her second home. But as much as I had loved Sophie, had known her since she was little, I couldn't find it within me right now, couldn't be there for her in her grief because my own was all consuming. I could only hope her mother's words weren't hot air and she did recognise the second chance she could get with her daughter.

So now I slowly pushed open the door of my daughter's bedroom. Her smell hit me the minute I walked in. Sinking onto her bed I breathed in Lena on the covers and I didn't move for hours. I sobbed and grieved for my daughter because this was my final goodbye.

Eventually, I sat up, got up, and went into the bathroom where I looked in the mirror above the sink at my red, puffy eyes that looked almost swollen shut. I splashed them with large amounts of cool water, and then held my mouth under the tap taking a few mouthfuls to quench my thirst.

Now was the time. With black plastic sacks, and packing boxes, I slowly worked my way through what was for the bin and what I was keeping. I was giving nothing to charity because I couldn't stand the thought of someone else being 'Lena'. I already had A4 boxes on the top of my wardrobe that housed collections of her artwork and cards to me, things that she'd done when young. A handprint picture. A Mother's Day card. One day I would look through them. Perhaps the night where I gave up on life myself. There was nothing like that now, just the occasional doodle of a flower in the corner of a schoolbook, but it seemed there was no room for diaries or journals. Life was recorded on social media, on places like Snapchat where you were seen and then deleted.

Lena was now deleted. Seen and gone.

When I'd finished, I put some cheap bedding and curtains I'd bought from the supermarket up. I was cheaply staging the house in order to hopefully get a quick sale. Not everyone would know the house had been where my daughter took her own life. Someone would see it as their dream home, not my nightmare.

---

A few weeks passed. It was June and most of Lena's classmates were in the middle of exams. I was now in my rental and I'd accepted an offer on the house. The estate agents and solicitors were handling everything. I was done with it. My appetite had improved and I found I was now comfort eating. My weight was increasing and I couldn't have cared less. I'd fought with my weight for years trying to keep myself from looking portly. Now my weight gain made me look different and I welcomed it. The first part of becoming insignificant.

I'd had my hairstyle changed in a salon I'd not been in before. The hairdresser hadn't understood why I wanted to chop my 'lovely long hair' short.

"But it must have taken so long to grow."

"I have cancer," I'd lied. "I want you to cut my hair short and turn it back to its natural colour as I expect it will fall out soon anyway."

She'd shut up then. "Oh my goodness. I am so sorry. Let me go mix the colour."

I hadn't liked having to lie, but people needed to think before their unwanted opinions flew out of their mouths. I'd rather not have had my gorgeous blonde streaked hair cut off, but it was a necessity as I didn't want Marcus recognising me. Plump, with short brown hair and a pair of clear specs, he'd have no clue. Not that I intended to be anywhere near him. Not at first anyway.

Needing access to Marcus' social media, I'd made fake Snapchat and Instagram accounts from a new phone. He wasn't stupid enough to accept my friend requests, but two of his friends were, and when they tagged him, I could see those photos, and they tagged him a lot. One boy in particular, Damon, liked to take photos of everything they did. Damon was a weakness to be exploited.

As 'Elise Wilson' I'd spent the last week or so sometimes commenting on the odd pic. Just hung around in the background of their social media, barely visible, adding comments like **Looks like fun** or **wish I lived in Berkley Edge**. I used photos of one of Ant's nieces. Took them off her own accounts and repurposed them. Lots of pouting at the camera. I'd made up some crap about having my account shut down and having to start a new one and I made sure I posted several times a day. I looked at what other teens posted: memes, jokes, selfies. It wasn't difficult. Damon would put emoticons of heart eyes.

Marcus was still hanging with his gang. They continued to post photos of themselves acting like they were some kind of street gods. Then he went home and played his Xbox until late into the night.

I knew because I watched his windows. I'd walked around the area where he lived as if I was just passing through carrying my shopping and going home. I needed to make sure the people in the area were used to me; so used to me I'd fade into the background. I'd smile at people and they'd say hello.

And then it happened. One tea-time I was there and Marcus was coming out of his driveway as I walked past. He looked at me, then looked away. I was insignificant. It felt amazing.

I could have easily bought a sharp knife and plunged it through Marcus Bull's throat. Watched as the blood sprayed out in satisfying spurts and the life drained out of him in minutes. But I didn't want his life to leave him fast like that. I wanted him to suffer. My game had to be slow and build, until the time came when Marcus no longer saw any point to his own insignificant life.

When I did begin, I started small. His father had a flash, black BMW. Brand new, it was clearly his pride and joy. I saw him on a couple of occasions washing it or polishing it as I did my walks.

To become invisible, I'd been taught that all you needed were joggers and a hoodie and so that's what I wore. In the early hours of an unremarkable July day, once the night was dark, I got out of my parked car some streets away and making sure none of me was able to be seen as anything more than 'not clear enough as evidence', I carved **MARCUS IS SCUM** into the side of his father's car.

My hands shook as I did it, but I didn't have a single regret. Even if they came outside while catching me in the act and pulled my hood back, what could they actually do to me? I was dead inside anyway. I didn't care. All I did was to avenge my daughter's death and I would start by making Marcus' home life hard.

Back home, I enjoyed a scalding hot bath and lit a scented candle of the same make Lena used to light in her room. I felt closer to her now if I could smell this scent. Then I fell asleep, content for once.

With my alarm set, the next morning I hurried to be back on Marcus' estate at 8:30am. I'd parked a few streets away again. This was around the time that his father left for work in a morning. I didn't have an exact time when Mr Bull set off, but I figured he'd not be rushing to get there on this particular morning given the circumstances. Dressed as if I was going to work, I came from the back of their estate and walked past in the direction of the bus stop on the opposite side of the street.

Marcus, his mother, and his father were standing on the driveway staring at the car. His father was puce in the face and shouting.

"You must know something about it. Who've you upset this time? Someone carved my fucking car up. Do you have any idea how much that's going to cost to repair?"

"I've already told you that I've done nothing," Marcus yelled back.

"People don't damage cars for no reason," his dad snapped.

"Peter, let's talk about this inside now," I heard his wife say. I'd walked as slowly as I could and now I couldn't be privy to any further conversation. I'd been lucky to arrive and hear what I had. Damn it. I realised now why murderers turned up to the funerals of their victims. You wanted to see the outcome of your efforts. To celebrate your achievements. On my way home I kept picturing the anger on his father's face. Such a small thing but it felt good.

Do you know what else felt good?

Later that day he accepted my friend requests on Instagram and Snapchat. On Insta I saw his post, a photo with his mates, where he declared, 'Pussies shouldn't hide'.

Was this a coincidence? That the day he accepted my request, he posted a message that was unknowingly directed at me?

I doubted he'd made the connection, but I'd make sure to stay alert.

---

A week later and Mr Bull's car was back on the driveway free of all blemishes. A small camera in his car windscreen flashed on and off. So he'd thought about security? I smiled. I knew all about these cameras. I knew that motion could make them start recording. But what was it going to record really? Some grainy picture that couldn't be used in court, that's what.

In any case, the camera couldn't record shit, when shit was thrown at the windscreen covering its view, and that's what I did next. Eight days after the first incident, I drove up nearby and walked down the street with my large plastic bag full of manure and a scraper. With dark glasses over my eyes and no part of me visible, I slapped the first piece of shit over where the camera was fixed and then I tipped the rest of the bag out and smeared it well. My final part was a rolled-up piece of paper that I stuck in the middle so it stood up. It was like a shit chocolate cake with one sad candle.

Whoever opened it would find the words.

### Marcus Went Too Far.
### Marcus Will Pay.

This time I went nowhere near the house after the event. It was time to calm my actions there, as they'd be especially cautious over the next week or two. With any luck, Marcus' parents would be looking out of their windows at any sudden noise or movement and then would berate him for the fact they were living that way. Now they'd feel the effects of their son's actions. They had to go in their pockets and pay for damage they didn't cause, and that would square with the fact that their entirely substandard parenting of their son meant I'd had to do the same. You reap what you sow, Mr Bull, and you sowed the seed of this pathetic child into his pathetic mother.

Social media had the odd mention of 'shit on your own doorstep' and similar, with laughing emojis from Marcus' mates. The best by far was one stating, 'brings a whole new meaning to BullShit'. I made a note of these people, I sent them friend requests, and I requested friends of friends of friends. I posted about new shoes I'd bought and how I was fed up of being single.

Damon commented on that. **You don't have to be.**

And so did Marcus. **Like you've a chance there, dickhead**, followed by laughing emojis.

I sent Damon a Snapchat.

**Elise: Ignore Marcus. I'm probably coming up to Sheffield at some point in the summer holidays if you wanna meet up?**

Damon responded back quickly. **Yes! Let me know when.**

From then he commented more on my posts and we started messaging. I spent evenings chatting shit to him, just hoping that by dropping him a crumb, he'd bite my hand off to feed. Every time I saw Marcus give him crap online, I'd just make sure to mention that I found him not very nice and thought he was supposed to be a mate.

Damon was apathetic and it irritated me. **Oh it's just banter,** he'd reply.

I started to feel strange. Like my skin itched, and I lost my appetite for a while. I felt nauseous at the fact Marcus wasn't suffering, not really. Something else needed to happen. The pressure needed turning up.

## 11

# CARLA

I left it two more weeks before I went back to the house. I knew that Marcus was still at school. They'd yet to break for the long summer term, and his parents both went out to work. My plan was to walk around to the back of the house and see if I could find an open window. If anyone stopped me, I was just going to say that I'd been asked to pop and make sure everything was okay given the recent events. But one thing about hiding in plain sight is that scarily no one bothers with you at all. Lifting up a plant pot at the front of the house, I was shocked to find a key under it. Given the alarm box on the wall was a fake arse shit one that I recognised from Ant getting the same thing, I was confident that once I was in this house I'd be undisturbed. Sure enough, the door opened, and I pulled my hood up and walked inside.

The house was immaculate, and I was guessing Mrs Bull kept it this way, almost to the point of a cleaning obsession. There wasn't a speck of dust to be seen. But I wasn't here to create housework, my intent was to quickly grab what I could from Marcus' room. I'd come here hoping to pinch a sweater off a washing line, but now I was actually inside.

His room smelled of fustiness; a window needed opening badly, but I wouldn't. No, I just needed to get something small and I needed it fast. I spotted a signet ring on his side with a snake emblem on it. Not real gold, just part of the image of the kid from the wrong side of the tracks Marcus wanted to display. This boy didn't want the silver spoon he was born with, he wanted gold grilles. I pocketed the ring. Opening his drawers and moving things carefully, at first, I found nothing useful, but then lifting his mattress, right in the middle was a rolled-up pile of money. Bingo. I counted it—five hundred quid—and I stuffed it in my pocket. I was in and gone within ten minutes and no one was any the wiser.

When I got back home, I immediately donated the five hundred pounds to Young Minds, a charity that helped kids being bullied. Fuck you, Marcus Bull. I only wished I could have left cameras in his room to see his face when he found his money gone.

These acts filled me with a sense of satisfaction, with warmth. I continued my accountancy work around thinking of what I could do next.

I re-watched the video from when the brick came through the window and I realised that Damon was the one who had thrown it. I'd not known before because I'd not known Damon, but now as I looked at his social media, I saw he tended to wear the same clothes in rotation. An Adidas tracksuit one week, a Nike one the next and repeat. And it was one of those he was clearly wearing in the video. Ooh, should I call the police and tell them I'd identified him, and then wait a week to be informed that even though we all clearly knew who it was, it wouldn't stand up in court?

Let's not waste our time, hey? Let's just take care of Damon ourselves.

Damon had been getting ever more involved in conversations with 'Elise', planning what we'd do in the holidays when we met up. It was boring, time consuming, but entirely necessary.

He got exasperated because Elise sent her Snapchats to pictures of her feet, or her bedroom, while he sent his chat across pics of his face. He wanted Elise to show her face, but Elise was 'spotty and didn't feel confident'.

**Damon: I think you're beautiful.**

I might have felt sorry for him were he not a part of the story that led to my daughter's suicide.

**Damon: You should be more confident.** He added on another.

**Elise: Do you ever get your house to yourself…?** I asked. **You know, for when I come over…**

The ellipses left blanks that Damon could fill in however he wished.

Of course the minds of teenage boys tended to go one way.

**Damon: There's just me and my mum and she works during the day, so we can hang out here when you visit. If you want to…**

**Elise: I want to.**

The good thing about Snapchat was that messages disappeared once opened and there was no chance at all of the police getting hold of any of what had been said. I knew this because they'd told me. If messages were screenshot, it informed the other person in chat. What these idiots seemed to forget though was that you could get a camera or another phone and snap a photo of what they'd written or posted that way.

So when the conversation eventually led to Damon sending Elise a dick pic, well of course after I wanted to be sick, because he was sixteen for fuck's sake and I was in my forties and no paedophile. I didn't screenshot, but I did take a photo of it with my own phone.

And then I stopped messaging Damon.

His panic was immediate. A pic of his face appeared in chat.

**Damon: Elise, I'm sorry. I thought that's what you wanted. Forget it. I'm just happy to chat with you. Please. Let me know, we're okay.**

**Damon: Elise, come on. I made a mistake. Forgive me, okay? We're going to have an amazing time when you come over. I've saved up to buy us lunch and everything.**

Message after message; each one got more desperate until he finally gave up for the evening.

**Damon: Okay, I'm sorry. I'll message you tomorrow.**

And he did. A few more desperate messages. Later that evening, there was a photo posted on social media of him, Marcus, and others in the local burger joint. Perfect. It was good that he told me where he was. I now knew that I could go visit his mother.

I put on my make-up, dressed in some decent clothes, and took my 'daughter's' phone and I went to visit Damon's house.

The door opened and a tired looking woman answered. Her blonde hair was highlighted and straightened. Her make-up was on her face but faded. She was dressed in jeans and a t-shirt. It was the tell-tale clues of someone who'd come in from work and got changed into something more comfortable.

"Yes?"

"Hello. I'm sorry to turn up unannounced, but are you Damon Caruthers mum?"

Those eyes narrowed on me. "Yeah, why?"

Instantly defensive. It made me feel smugger.

"He's sent my daughter a photo of his penis. I'd like you to get him to stop and I insist he not contact her anymore. She's extremely upset." I looked for shock, but Mrs Caruthers' face contorted in the defensive look of a mother who'd had plenty of practice of defending her 'innocent' son.

"Damon wouldn't do that." Her hands were on her hips and she looked like she wanted to punch me in the face. Yes, clearly one of those who knew her son was a waste of space but would protect him regardless.

"I can show you the photos and you can get him to stop, or I can go to the police," I snapped at her. No more Mrs Fucking Polite from me now. If she wanted to play it this way, then play it we would.

"Fine. Show me."

No, 'come inside'. Just a demand on the doorstep.

I passed her an A4 sheet of paper where I'd printed the messages and photo off my phone. As she looked at them, her shoulders sagged and the fight went out of her body. Oh she still wore the expression of a fighter on her face but her body betrayed the truth.

"I'll speak with him tonight. She'll not hear from him again."

"Thank you. Oh, and while you're at it, if you don't mind, can you ask him to tell Marcus to stop messaging her as well, only I don't know where he lives or anything."

"Why the fuck should I do that?"

"Suit yourself. Your son's 'friend' keeps talking shit about him and trying to get my daughter to choose him instead. They're both a nuisance. She doesn't want either of them."

"You sure about that? Sure your daughter's not being a prick tease?"

"Seriously, that's your angle? That my daughter might be at fault? Perhaps you can ask Damon if she sent him a photo of any part of her anatomy, can't you?" I began to walk away from the door.

"Come here again and I'll ring the police," she warned me. I walked back closer.

"If I come here again it will be because Damon has once again done something to my daughter, so you'd be more than welcome to call them. But don't worry, next time I won't give you the chance to speak and deal with him outside of the law, I'll phone them and he can be done for indecency. Another year of school to come, exam year. Waste of time sitting those if he's got a record for showing girls his cock don't you think?"

She slammed the door in my face. Good, I'd got to her. I went home. She'd already be on the phone to her son, demanding he come back, so I needed to be out of there.

Damon didn't send any further messages, but Marcus did.

**Marcus: What's your mother going on about? I never sent you any messages about us two. I don't know you.**

I messaged back.

**Elise: I don't know what you're talking about.**

**Marcus: Damon's mum told him you'd said I needed to stop messaging you. You're clearly some crazy bitch. Consider yourself blocked.**

**Elise: Whatever. Damon sent me a dick pic. He's obviously now trying to make out like I'm the crazy chick. Lost any money lately, Marcus?**

BOOM. Hahahahahaha. I sat back and waited for his response.

**Marcus: What do you know about missing money?**

**Elise: I know we were going on a date and he wanted to impress me and he said you owed him and he knew where you kept some cash.**

**Marcus: He wouldn't do that. He's my mate.**

**Elise: Then how come I know you have five hundred pounds missing from under your mattress? Goodbye Marcus, consider yourself blocked.**

I turned off the phone, walked out into the back garden and smashed it up with a hammer. And just as stray pieces of plastic moved on the path with the breeze, the pieces of destruction I'd just sent via telephone would drift through the friendship of Damon and Marcus.

A few nights later, I threw a brick at Mrs Caruthers' car's front window before I legged it down the street, got into my car and drove home. I made sure I dropped Marcus' signet ring by the front tyre.

I waited for the police to come. Waited for someone to have

caught my car on camera, security to have followed me via CCTV, but of course they didn't.

Because other than the person it'd happened to, no one cared.

Indifference.

"I don't want anything coming back on me." That's what I'd heard from one neighbour when I'd asked if he could check his CCTV after one of the incidents at our house.

So far I had got away with every damn thing.

Just like he had.

---

Sophie rang me. She rang every week to check how I was, bless her. I hoped as time went on that it would become less. Her mother was around more and making the effort still. That pleased me and I told her so.

"I hope you're being okay with your mum, Soph. You have a chance I'd love to have again with Lena."

"I am, don't worry. I can't be best friends forever with her though, just because she suddenly got the guilts after what happened with Lena."

"Yeah, I get that."

"I miss you, Carla, and I worry about you. Are you okay in that house on your own?"

"I'm fine, honestly. Just working a lot and doing a bit of decorating."

"Is my room ready yet?" There was a hopeful lilt in her tone.

"Pardon?" What was she talking about?

"My room. I know it's difficult with Lena and everything, but you were like a second mum to me, like an auntie or something. I miss you. Can't I come for tea one night?"

*No.* I thought, but that's not what I said.

"Yes, of course. Let me get a bit straighter, and just have a little more time to myself and then course you can come and have tea or something."

"Great. I can tell you all the latest gossip. Marcus and his mate Damon got into it last week. Massive fight. He knocked one of Damon's bottom teeth out."

"How'd you know that?"

"Chloe told me. Marcus got suspended. Him and Damon aren't friends anymore, and so he's not looking like the king of school so much now. Damon's more popular, weed or not."

"Good. I don't want Marcus living a happy life. Does that make me a bad person, Soph?"

"No, it makes you a mum. Well, I'll let you go. Hurry up and get that place straight, so I can visit, okay?"

"Okay, Soph." I hung up. Bless her. I did miss Sophie. Maybe I would ask her for tea. It's just we would talk about Lena, and then Sophie would tell me about her life, and try as I might to not think about it, I would wonder why Sophie was still here and Lena not.

And that wasn't fair. Sophie didn't deserve those thoughts. All she'd ever been was a good friend to my daughter. But her place was with her own mother. Maybe I had to be cruel to be kind with Sophie because someday soon I wouldn't be here myself and then she'd have another loss in her life.

I'd have to think about things. Because at the same time she was a route to information about Marcus.

And that was just too tempting.

## 12

## CARLA

I invited Sophie for tea. It was unfair of me really because I didn't do it to see her. I did it in case she could give me any information on Marcus.

My guilt was overridden by my desire for vengeance.

Lisa dropped Sophie off at the door three nights later. They both looked shocked at how different I looked, but neither of them passed comment.

"I'll pick her up about what, nine?"

I nodded. "Yeah, thank you. See you later." I waved Lisa off and turned back into the house.

Sophie grinned at me and I couldn't deny that it was good to see her. She'd been in a happy part of my life and the general enthusiasm she carried with her was kind of infectious.

"Come through. I've done your fave: pizza, chips, and beans. Bet you can't guess what's for dessert?"

Her eyes lit up. "Is it sticky toffee pudding and custard?"

"Might be."

She walked inside and looked around at my new place. "I know you're only renting, but I like what I've seen so far. It has a good atmosphere."

She threw her bag and coat across the back of the dining room chair. Her shoes were still on her feet. I'd told her to keep them on. I couldn't bear to see discarded footwear in the hallway. Not when I'd be begging for another pair to appear at the side of hers. I knew that this meal was going to be difficult, for her and for me. Because Lena wasn't here, and we would have to talk about it.

"I'll show you the rest later, but for now, wash your hands because I'm plating up." Everything was the same and it hurt because it was also different; my daughter wasn't there. I was just glad that I was in a different kitchen. I felt a little less guilty thinking that this wasn't the usual routine, not exactly, because all that had happened in our home, and this wasn't our home. Different kitchen, different appliances, different table and chairs; all belonging to the property owner who'd furnished the place, meaning I didn't have to sit amongst things that made me imagine Lena in them. I'd let a charity take all my furniture and dumped anything else because I wouldn't need it.

Sophie sat at the table.

"So how did your last exams go?" I asked her.

She shrugged. "I don't know. I did what I could. I'll hopefully get what I need for college." Sophie wanted to do hair and beauty.

"Well, that's all you need."

"Revising helped to occupy my mind. Funny really, that for all I didn't want to do it, in the end it was one of the only ways I could get through the day."

"It's hard," I admitted. "Every day is hard."

Sophie burst out crying. I rushed over to comfort her, and I began crying too. Damn this girl and her emotions making me realise deep down I still had a heart. We cried for minutes as I stroked her back, patting her. She was the one person who had some idea how I felt. After the sudden outpouring of grief, I moved away.

"I'm so sorry—"

"Don't feel sorry about grieving, Soph. It comes in waves and doesn't let you know when a huge one's about to crash. I hope you can find your appetite though."

She did and after we both rinsed our faces in the sink, we sat and ate and she caught me up on school life, and prom. It hurt again, reminding me my baby was wearing her prom dress in whatever came after we departed the earth, but I tried to make all the right noises, because I knew Sophie was trying to cheer me up, feeling guilty for crying.

"So have you heard anything else about Marcus?" I finally asked as I placed her pudding in front of her.

"He's become a complete loner. Doesn't have friends anymore. Not since it all kicked off between him and Damon."

"Good." I feigned disinterest. "It doesn't matter to me what happens to him now. I'm just glad he's not living his best life."

"He definitely isn't," she told me and she tucked into her dessert.

Lisa came and fetched Sophie back just after nine. I chatted to her on the doorstep as Sophie eye-rolled us both, left us to 'gossip about me', and went to get in the car.

"How's she doing?" I asked, before Lisa could ask me how I was doing.

"Cries a lot. It's all about time isn't it?" Lisa looked at me with sympathy. I didn't want it.

I nodded my head. "It is. It was strange her being here without Lena."

"I bet. But you've always been like an auntie towards Sophie. If you ever want to spend time with her, go get your nails done or whatever, just call. I'll never forget your kindness when I was struggling."

Smiling, I told Lisa that I'd better let them go, because the truth was if she said anything else to the tune of that I could basically borrow her daughter if I wanted to do the daughter things I couldn't do with my own now, I might just launch myself at her with my fists flailing.

The minute I got back inside the house it was like my crazy unleashed. I took a kitchen knife and stabbed it through a cushion, pulling and dragging and ripping with my bare hands and screaming and crying. Thank fuck I had no neighbours nearby because I was in the hold of madness. Nausea overwhelmed me and I just made it to the bathroom before I lost everything I'd managed to eat with Sophie, as if my body was saying to me, you can't eat with Sophie without Lena being there, you just can't. Exhausted, once I was sure I was done being sick, I dragged myself to bed and fell asleep.

When I woke, I felt an overwhelming urge to want to go to Lena's bedroom. Even though I'd emptied it, I needed to be there. Until it belonged to someone else.

I managed to force a piece of toast and a drink of coffee down myself to line my stomach and wake me up and then I drove to my former home.

As I got out of my car, my old neighbour was pruning her bushes in her front garden. She waved a hand at me. We'd said the odd hello over the years, but that was all. Out of politeness. An older lady and her husband, they'd once returned a ball Lena had accidentally kicked over their fence in the back garden sliced through with a knife. An empty, airless husk. Just thrown it back over the fence as a huge 'you'll not do that again' punishment. They'd never had kids and couldn't tolerate the noise. Always commenting about peace and quiet in earshot of me when she was out playing with Sophie.

"Hello, hello. How are you?" She beckoned me over. She didn't even know my name. Her sympathy card had come addressed to 'Number 15'.

I walked to her gate and she smiled. I did not. "In all the time we lived nearby you never once asked me how I was."

The smile slipped from her face.

"You'll not have to suffer the noise Lena made anymore at least now, will you? Now that she's dead. Empty of air like the football you threw back over that time because you hated her ever enjoying herself. Now my angel is dead, and yet, you... you spiteful old crone, still live." I turned on my heel and walked away.

While I was at it, I decided I'd call on the other neighbour. The one with the CCTV. Then I'd never come here again, because Lena was not here and seeing her room would just remind me of that. I needed to decide what was left to do to Marcus and then get the hell off this poisoned earth.

I banged on the door and the middle-aged guy who'd not given a damn answered. He looked shocked before a hesitant smile swept it off his features.

"Yes?"

"I just wanted to say you needn't worry about being involved in anything else to do with my daughter, now she's dead."

"I—"

I held up my hand. "Save it. I just wanted to say to you that I hope you fall down on your own driveway having a painful cardiac arrest and that everyone walks past and leaves you there, because they 'don't want to get involved'." I did pathetic air quotes. "I mean should someone do first aid and crack your ribs, you could sue. So yes, I hope it happens and I hope you die a very painful and frustrating death while passers-by just stare at you and let you get on with it."

His mouth was opening and closing like a dying fish.

"Yep, looking exactly like that." I pointed at his face. "And if you think I'm being evil, basically you just stood by while my own heart broke and did fuck all, so all I'm doing is wishing you the same. You're a despicable specimen of a human being."

I stalked off back to my house.

It felt good. I felt good. Adrenaline zinged through me, awakening my body and filling it with purpose.

I picked up the mail off the mat and flicked through it. There was nothing of interest to me and I threw it onto the side to dispose of and made my way upstairs. I sat on the floor of Lena's bedroom and just closed my eyes and somehow tried to feel nearer to her. As the adrenaline abated, exhaustion took over me and I must have nodded off, as I came to at some point later when the letterbox rattled.

I waited until I'd come round a bit and got my bearings because it would only be a charity collection bag. They were always posting them through. Standing up, I rubbed at my sore backside, and walked stiff legged onto the landing.

Oh for God's sake. A plain white envelope sat on the doormat. Another fucking sympathy card. If it was from the bitch next door or the other twat apologising, I would go shove it somewhere where a papercut would sting like a bitch.

Walking down the stairs, I knew I was never coming back to this place. Every day I felt wearier, like my body couldn't even be bothered anymore. Had given up.

I picked up the card and opened it. I couldn't help it. I had to open them all because often they said things they remembered about Lena, and they were extra glimpses of how she'd lit up other people's lives. So if I ignored it, I could miss a piece of Lena.

I gasped as I looked at the writing.

**I am sorry about Lena.**
**So very sorry.**
**MB.**

My hands shook as I dropped the card as if it was laced with Anthrax.

Sorry.

He was sorry.

The boy who killed her was sorry.

You'll be sorry all right Marcus Bull, I thought. Because the end was nigh.

## 13

## CARLA

How is one human body supposed to cope with an overload of sensations and feelings?

Hatred.
Frustration.
Anguish.
Desperation.
Fear.
Agitation.
Hurt.
Annoyance.
Rage.
Resentment.
Shock.
Short answer, it can't.

I couldn't stand still and I couldn't move. I couldn't think and at the same time thoughts were trying to spin around like a guy working the Waltzer just span my chair. I ran back upstairs and I was sick again. Marcus had literally made me sick.

My body was not coping with all this. Not with the grief, not with living. It was like it didn't want sustenance. Was giving up.

*I hear you,* I told myself.

*Let's finish this.*

I'd kept Marcus' Snapchat details and this time I sent him a request from my own name and my own phone.

He accepted it straightaway.

Now what?

I typed a message. No photo. I wasn't a teenager.

**Carla: I got the card.**

I felt like I was dragging a blade through unanaesthetised skin as I added.

**Thank you.**

Snapchat indicated he was writing back.

**Marcus: I never thought Lena would do that. I know you don't give two shits about me, but I'm sorry. Whoever sent that video went too far.**

*Whoever sent that video?*

So he couldn't even be bothered to tell me the truth now. But then again, he and his mates probably now knew about taking photos without Snapchat alerting them after the whole Elise business.

**Carla: Would you meet me, to talk about Lena?** I wrote, desperate. **Just anything you like really. I'm in Berkley Edge now and then I'm leaving for good. Somewhere private like near the old den? I promise, I won't keep you long.**

The little head poked up on Snapchat once again to tell me he was replying.

**Marcus: I don't know what I can tell you really.**

I didn't want to lose this chance. I was desperate.

**Carla: You could say sorry to my face, rather than through cowardly words on a piece of card. That would**

mean a lot. Give me some closure and then you won't have to see me again.

Another message being typed.

**Marcus: Okay. I'll be there in around fifteen minutes.**

As I closed the message, I felt like adrenaline might actually kill me this time. I felt faint, lightheaded, and my heart thudded insanely in my chest. What did I need? Nothing, except something to hurt Marcus with. I looked around me. Fuck, most things were packed. Aahh, but I'd left tools in the shed. Ones that belonged to Ant. Old rusted shit not really fit for any use. I sniggered. That'd be funny, if I wore gloves and Ant got arrested for whatever it was I was about to do.

I wouldn't think about what the next few hours held.

I would not speculate.

I would just act in the moment and go with what my mind and soul intended.

In the shed I found secateurs, a screwdriver, and an old pair of gardening gloves. It was a shame there was no knife, but I was sure I could do enough damage with a screwdriver. Anyway, the old den had plenty of shit dumped in it. There was probably a knife already waiting there in the bottom, thrown in after a mugging.

I put the items in my pocket and began my walk. We were due to arrive at roughly the same time. I would leave it all to fate.

There was purpose in my stride as I made my way down the overgrown path at the back of the nearby field. The field had been built at the side of a new housing estate. Below it were further farmers' fields and in between was a no-man's land, with an overgrown wood. They had built a path between it all where people could walk their dogs. A nice walk I'd done on my own when I'd needed time to think in the past. On that path, just a little off to one side was the old den. It'd been there for years. At the back of the path the soil sloped downwards into overgrown shrubbery and trees and set a little bit further back was just one wall of a previous building. What it used to be, I had no idea, but kids had hung around here on occasion and been warned about the dangerous wall. Lena had told me it was rarely used since the fast food places opened up nearby as instead of sitting in the cold, kids could sit with iPads in Maccys. Right now, most children were still in school and so it appeared Marcus was still suspended. The sun had moved behind the clouds and a wind had whipped up that was cool enough to make you need a jumper. Was there ever a full summer's day in the U.K.?

As I approached the turn off towards the den, I could see him. He had beaten me there. I looked at him from between the leaves of a shrub. He was kicking his feet and looking around while chewing the inside of his mouth. Nervous.

Good.

I walked around the corner and approached him. Jesus, here I was with the person responsible for my daughter's death, with no one in sight and tools in my pocket.

Taking my time, I came closer to him. He looked at me and looked away. Of course, I'd changed my appearance since I'd screeched at him on his doorstep.

Behind him was the den. The den where I'd thought I'd listen while he told me his reasons behind bullying my daughter, but now I was here in front of him, watching as he realised it was me and he opened his mouth and said, "Hello."

My answer for him was in my actions.

I pushed him.

I pushed him with all my force and he stumbled over the tiny two inches of wood marking the edge of the path. He toppled backwards and thudded down the slope landing on a piece of old fence. Old fence covered in rusty barbed wire.

He screamed. A waste of breath as no one could hear it except me, and I wasn't here to help him.

I made my way over the slope and down to him, ready to finish what I'd started.

Marcus was flailing, eyes wide. He was trying to get up but was wrapped in undergrowth. A quick look at the side of him revealed a broken piece of barbed wire.

Placing my hands in my gloves, I picked it up and I swung it with all my might at his thigh.

His scream was ear-piercing but pointless. I'd make sure to stuff a glove in his mouth though in a moment.

"Stop. P- please s- stop. T- tell y- you s- something," he whimpered.

I smirked down at him. "What is it like to be helpless, Marcus? To the point where you're on the point of extinction?"

"W- what?"

I spoke slowly, in no rush at that moment while adrenaline sparked my insides. "I'm going to kill you, Marcus. Or maybe I'll just cut you and let you bleed out slowly. I haven't decided yet. Actually, that sounds good because I don't know how long it took for Lena to die after she took the pills. Whether it was pain free, or whether it hurt. I know her life wasn't pain free. I know she had to go through mental torture to get to a point where enough was enough."

"Oh my god, oh my g- god."

"You may as well have fed her the pills yourself, Marcus, because that video was the last straw. I don't know why you bullied her and us so much. I'm not sure what you gained from it, but I'm sure you're regretting it now."

He tried to sit up again so I hit him with the wire once more. This time he retched.

"P- please. L- l – listen," he wailed.

"Fine." I stood back from him. "What are your final words, Marcus? I can assure you that they'll die with me, but I really am interested in what you have to say. A sorry might help before you go off to hell."

"B- blackmailed," he huffed out while sweat poured from his forehead. "Th- that's why. V- video of me, couldn't let o- out. It was g- graphic and would have m- made my own life not worth l- living."

Marcus was panting now beneath me, his face white as milk.

"G- grab... my... phone." He pointed to the ground at the side of him where it had fallen out of his hands on his way down and then his head lolled back. Tears rolled down his cheeks as he sobbed in pain. I turned to look at the phone. The screen was clearly broken, and I wasn't sure it would work. Anyway, this was all just a distraction so he could try to escape, try to beg and plead for his pathetic existence.

He raised his head a little and I could see he was close to passing out. "N- not lying. H- help me."

I took the screwdriver out of my pocket. "One false move and this goes through your neck," I informed him. "And if you are lying, I'll stab you twice."

I quickly swept up the phone. "So who's been blackmailing you then? Who will I be going after in your place?"

More sweat beaded on his brow, and he uttered the words, "Sophie Ellender."

# PART 2

## 14

## MARCUS

Maybe I wasn't ever meant to be happy. Some people were born lucky and on the surface I know it appeared like I'd lucked out.

When my parents had first moved into Berkley Edge, the estate we lived on had been brand new. New build houses with a new build price tag and my father had decided that was the place where we needed to be. From a man who'd owned a second-hand car lot, he'd grown his business until he had a sales showroom on the corner of a local thriving industrial estate. He'd positioned himself to sell expensive cars to the richer people of the surrounding areas, and in Berkley Edge he'd positioned himself in one of the largest houses on the new build estate, setting his stall as one of the most important and to be revered men there.

And as it was at work, it was at home. Mum was meek and did as she was told, and if I played up, I got smacked. Dad was a man's man. A macho, 'don't mess with me or I'll punch your lights out' kind of guy. It was how he succeeded so well in business, letting no one give him the run around, and it was how he failed miserably as a husband and father by being a despicable cunt.

The thing he'd seemed to pass onto me was his lack of height, and my mother had passed on her slight build. My early school days passed without problem. My mother gave me so much attention, because not only did she love me but she also over-compensated for my father, and I went to school showing my intelligence, top of the class and being given lots of praise because of it.

And then senior school started and suddenly all that positive attention from being brainy, turned into negative attention from my peers who were hitting puberty and now each other. Suddenly I was the runt of the litter; called a nerd, gay, and a little bitch, as well as a whole host of cuss words.

The estate we lived on was superseded by more new builds and my father's business did okay. The business got by but was no longer anything special. No matter what new tactics he tried, he couldn't raise the bar, so instead he raised his hand.

If my grades slipped. Whack.

If he thought I'd chatted back. Thumped.

And he put the fear of God into my mother. If she ever thought of leaving, he said he'd hunt us down and kill us both.

So we stayed.

And I took the grief from school, stayed small and hidden where I could, and suffered when I couldn't, because it was better to receive a taunt from school than a punch from home.

Until my own puberty kicked in.

My mum was small, but her brother and father were not. She'd inherited her own mother's genetics. Suddenly I bypassed my father's traits. Mum showed me some photos saying I looked like my uncle and grandad on her side. We were no longer in touch with family. Dad had cut that off long ago.

And so at fourteen years old, I found myself standing at six foot tall. Suddenly there was no more hiding. Because as my body changed and face altered, girls noticed. I'd always had long lashes and blue eyes but now they added to my features. I'm not being vain to say I was good looking. I wasn't the best looking boy out there, but I was enough to start to be noticed.

And of course my intelligence matured too and I worked out a way to be intelligent and survive. I used my mouth. Dad had taught me how to make people fear you and I found I could do the same. Being tall gave me the confidence to act tougher than I was.

So I still submitted my school work, but when Archie Hadley called me an arse licker, I flipped him the bird and told him it wasn't my fault I was gifted in all areas and then I winked. I flirted with girls I had no interest in, stuck my tongue down their throats even though it made me want to throw up, and found myself no longer a loser. I might be somewhere at the back of the gang of kids who hung around, but I was still there.

When Archie offered me a spliff, I didn't refuse it. When he told me how I could sell it to make some money, I eagerly signed up. I had one aim. Get enough money together so that on my eighteenth birthday I was out of my house and away from my father. Hopefully my mum would come with me, but if not, I was saving myself. And if I ever had kids, I would never treat them the way I'd been treated.

I wasn't proud of my behaviour with Lena Haybrook.

But sometimes we faced choices and we didn't know where they would lead us.

I had one mission. To survive. I didn't know that by doing what I did, someone else wouldn't.

---

A couple of times our group met up and hung around with Chloe Butcher and her mates. She was always bitching on about Lena. Clearly jealous, she'd moan on to Archie, who'd agree with whatever she said because it'd lead to a blow job for him in the park later on.

Even though I was a year younger, Chloe's friend Tamsin was trying to impress me, wearing increasing amounts of make-up and pushing up her tits in her low cut tops. It did nothing for me. When I thought no one was looking I was checking out guy's arses. Yes, I was gay. I'd known for a long, long time, and it was another daily torment because my father was not only a cunt, he was a homophobic cunt.

I thought no one noticed. That I was discreet, but it appeared that two people did.

---

It was a Friday teatime and as usual the Berkley Edge teenage population were hanging around fast food joints. I was with Archie and the others in the KFC that was next to the Costa when suddenly one of the lads, Damon, shouted. "Oooh, fight."

We all left our drinks on the tables and charged to the front entrance, piling out onto the concrete front where we watched as Chloe and Lena tried to tear strips out of each other before they were hauled back by their friends. Sophie Ellender had Lena, and Tamsin Doherty had Chloe. Lena had a split lip and Chloe had a rapidly swelling eye.

"You stupid fucking bitch, you'll pay for that," Chloe yelled.

"Wow. Two women fighting is fucking hot," Damon shouted to us.

I nodded my head in agreement, my mind not agreeing at all. In actual fact, I was bored. The guys I hung around with could be fun, but they could also be juvenile and stupid, and though I was a year younger than most, I felt that my life experiences had matured me quicker.

The fight stopped. Lena stomped off towards home, shouting something about Chloe being a crazy bitch and the excitement was all over. Chloe came waltzing over to us.

"Ha. I burned the ends of her stupid hair off. She'll learn who's fucking queen around here."

While Chloe showed off to Archie, my gaze rested on Sophie who was hanging around still, rather than having accompanied her best friend. It struck me as odd, but I soon moved my gaze away when she caught me looking at her and narrowed her eyes in my direction.

Chloe carried on showing off for a bit and then her and her mates went off to 'walk past Lena's house and show her I'm not scared'.

I returned to my boring Friday night. Well, I'd thought it was boring at that moment. Now I wish it had stayed that way.

---

We'd moved on to hanging around the local recreation ground, drinking various bottles of vodka and cans of flavoured cider. I'd had enough to seem chill and be buzzed. I'd offered everyone some weed for free which made me the cool kid. I almost felt like I belonged somewhere. Alcohol and bud mellowing the layer of torment I lived with.

The park was surrounded by houses on two sides but where we sat was halfway down and near a large rock next to the basketball court. A slightly raised hill, we sat undisturbed as barely anyone, except the odd bloke walking his dog, came down at this time of night when it was dark. The neighbours would say we were intimidating. We were just bored kids.

I needed a piss and walked down to where all the trees were. As I approached, I heard hushed female voices and I stopped as I recognised it was Chloe and she was talking to Sophie.

"I still can't believe you burned her hair, you stupid bitch. Her mother could have called the police on you."

"I couldn't help it. I got fucked off."

"You can't go around doing shit like that."

"Feeling guilty are you? Because you're the one who told me she'd been saying I was a thick ho. She thinks she's so fucking perfect, well now she's not. Now, even if only for tonight, her hair's wonky and stinks."

"You need to dial it back because her mum's livid. Especially because you sent that photo of the house. She's taking that personally."

"Look. I'll say a fake sorry, but I did it and right now I'm enjoying my moment. My eye might sting like a bitch, but I finally got to deck her. Now are we done here because I want to get back to the others?"

"Yeah, we're done."

I moved further into the trees and waited until they'd gone before I had my piss. When I returned, Chloe was with the group and Sophie was nowhere to be seen.

I sat back on the grass, laughed with my group at some of them acting like dicks because they were pissed up or bombed until my phone showed me it was time to go home.

Sighing, I got to my feet. "I'm off, I'll see you all tomorrow."

Archie got up. "I'll walk with you up to the trees. I need a piss."

We sauntered away from the group and Archie was chatting on about the fight and then Chloe and Tamsin.

"I'm surprised you didn't go for Tamsin," he said. "Older woman and all that." He laughed.

"She's not my type," I said truthfully. I was ready for home, bored with the whole night.

"Stand nearby while I have a slash, will you?" Archie said.

I turned and fixed him with an 'are you kidding me' look. "You scared of the fucking dark?" I laughed but shaking my head I wandered into the trees with him.

Archie moved closer to me.

"You fancy men, Marc?" he slurred.

My face drained of all colour. "Don't be fucking stupid. I just didn't want to go near that slag." I took a step back, but he grabbed hold of me.

"Suck my cock," he demanded. "I want to see if you do it better than Chloe."

"What? Let go of me. Chill out. I'm not gay and you're not funny," I said, trying to back away, but his grip tightened.

"I'm serious. I don't want a piss. I've got a fucking hard-on after that prick tease Chloe left me hanging and I keep seeing you looking at me weird. You're not the only one who's confused," he said.

"What?"

He lowered his voice. "Do it. I want to know what it's like. If we're not into it after, we don't say anything else about it, okay?"

I forgot about having to be home. Instead, as he opened his jeans and freed his cock, I dropped to my knees.

Unaware I wasn't the only one who could snoop about things.

---

Elation and fear danced together through my body as I made my way home. The truth that I'd had my first real sexual experience with someone I actually fancied had a triumphant grin cracking across my face. Archie hadn't returned the favour, but he'd said he might text me. I didn't care if he said it would never happen again. It had cemented what I'd thought about myself. That for me it was guys.

And then a voice sounded out behind me and any elation was gone forevermore. "Well, well, well. Thanks for teaching me about how to snoop among the trees, cocksucker."

I froze at hearing Sophie's voice behind me and at the content of her words. *Oh no. Oh hell no.*

Slowly, I turned around to face her. She stood with a hand on one hip, and the triumphant grin I'd been sporting appeared to have slid off my own face and crawled across the ground and up her body because now she was wearing it.

She waved her phone at me. She'd pressed play. There was a video showing me on my knees...

"Please, Sophie. My dad would beat the shit out of me. He doesn't get it."

"Marcus, don't worry," she said in a fake arse tone. "I don't intend to share it. I just need you to do a few things for me."

I exhaled deeply. "Like what?"

"Like keep your mouth shut about seeing me and Chloe talking and maybe I might need you to make Lena's life harder. Give me your number so I can contact you if I need to."

My forehead wrinkled in confusion. "But I thought Lena was your best mate?"

Sophie seemed to pause for a moment, and then she said, "She is. I don't have to explain myself to you though, do I?"

"No," I said in the tone of someone who had no choice but to agree with everything.

"Right." She nodded her head towards my phone. "I'm going to give you Lena's number. You might need that too."

And that was it.

Now I was at Sophie's beck and call.

Because if that video clip went anywhere, I might as well kill myself before my father did it for me, never mind what the teenagers of Berkley Edge's verdicts would be.

---

By the time I walked into the house, I was almost forty-five minutes late home. My father started the minute I walked in, arms-crossed in the hallway, the whites of his eyes standing out with his rage.

"Where the fuck have you been?"

"One of them was asking me about the business," I lied. "I figured I'd stay back and tell them what we sold, might be a sale in it. I should have phoned. I'm sorry."

"Yeah, you should have. Which one was it?"

"Samuel Bewley." The name slipped straight out of my mouth. He'd vaguely asked once. I'd have to mention the car business again tomorrow to cover my tracks.

"God, you stink of cannabis again. Go and get straight in the shower."

My dad and his principles. The first time I'd come home stinking of weed, he'd grabbed me by the throat until I'd said I needed to hang around with these kids no matter what they did because they were earning money through it and were the car buyers of tomorrow. Encouraged him that what I was doing was basically keeping my future customers as warm leads. Because my dad thought I'd be coming to work with him, carrying on his legacy, and even potentially taking it to a higher level. And so he tolerated the smell I walked in with clinging to my body, not having a clue that I was dealing it myself and hiding my earnings under my mattress. But for that night at least, I avoided a beating.

The next morning, Sophie told me that Chloe had set up a hate campaign about Lena, but I knew the truth. That it wasn't Chloe at all. But I had to ring Lena and make things even tougher for her. I was glad she had a supportive mum. I didn't like my actions, but I didn't have a choice. So I called her and told her that when I saw her I was going to punch her.

Lena called me a waste of space. She didn't realise it, but I happened to agree with her. Right now, I was nothing but the puppet of what other people wanted me to be. At some point in my life I hoped I would be able to be the real Marcus Bull, but that time was not now. Now, I was a puppet for Sophie and an actor in a play for my dad.

I called Lena again. "You think you're so fucking clever now, but you'll not think that when I see you."

But Lena wasn't on the other end of the phone. Instead, another voice came down the line. "Hello, is that Marcus? This is Lena's mother. Just to tell you I'm recording this conversation."

I hung up quickly, shock hitting my system, making me feel sick. For a while, I sat with my head in my hands and then I made a move to grab some breakfast because Archie had texted and the gang were meeting up again this morning. He didn't mention the previous evening and neither would I.

---

We were strolling down the Main Road and I was listening to Damon making up shit about how he'd escaped a mugging last night on his way home. I don't know why people let him get away with his crap, but we all did. His life was so boring it seemed he had to make up scenarios that made it sound more exciting. He'd always been the same. There'd been more threats to his life than to the entire cast of the soaps that my mum watched every night. But at least it masked the silence from me and most notably from Archie, who wouldn't even look at me. Fine. I'd got some experience and confirmation of my sexuality. I didn't need him. He could add himself to the long list of people who'd disappointed me.

I fell into line with Tamsin instead and winked at her. She winked back. Girls were weird. By the time fifteen minutes had passed she'd arranged to call for me later and had taken a selfie of the two of us, despite the fact I'd spent the previous evening treating her like shit.

We walked past the shops at the top of the main road and suddenly I caught sight of who was inside the shop. Lena. Made sense seeing as Chloe had burned some of her hair off.

I was done being the sheep at the back of this flock, it was time to steal the crown from Archie. If he was going to pretend I didn't exist, then I'd make it that no one saw him anymore.

"Lena's in there, Chloe. Wonder if they do plastic surgery as well?" I winked, getting her on side. She laughed. The group all whooped and hollered as we went past. I'd put my hood up, all us guys had. I yelled, "Ugly bitch," in the direction of the doorway and everyone laughed. Our group got louder.

Then she was there. Lena's mother stood in the doorway, her face full of hatred and rage. She made her way over to Chloe. The rest of us walked on ahead, but I heard her.

"I don't care what happened last night. You had a fight or whatever, but it's done now, you hear? I've a good mind to give your mum the bill for this haircut. What were you thinking? Anything else and I'll be talking to your mother, and if I need to, I'll phone the police. We clear?"

I didn't hear Chloe's response as by then we were too far in front, but I could take a large guess that she'd just nodded her agreement. A few minutes later, she caught up with the group.

"Fucking hell, she's a psycho bitch." Chloe huffed. "But I'd better calm things down for a bit, because she's threatened to call my mother and the police."

"We've got better things to do than focus on Lena Haybrook anyway, babe," Tamsin said to her. She'd now threaded her arm through mine.

"I can see what you wanna do." Chloe laughed.

That night I lost my virginity to a sixteen-year-old girl in the same trees where I'd sucked off Archie. I hated every minute of it, but it was a necessary evil.

# 15

## MARCUS

The weeks ticked on. Lena was ignored, after her and Chloe made a tentative truce to just ignore each other. I carried on 'dating' Tamsin, and Archie moved away from our group and made a new set of mates. I took his place. The group now had Chloe and Tamsin and a few other girls in it, and I led the whole thing. I saw Lena and Sophie around, chatting away and giggling like the best friends I'd always thought they were. Sophie didn't contact me and I'd thought it was all behind me. That she'd only wanted the phone calls to cement whatever she'd been up to the night of the fight. I could carry on like this, pretending to date Tamsin and run my crew until I could get away. I didn't like my life, but I didn't loathe it either. I could tolerate it.

But then October rolled around and another phone call from Sophie had me hating myself all over again.

It was a Saturday evening and I'd been lying in bed, listening to Spotify after catching up on homework when my phone rang.

I felt a lump form in my throat as I saw the name on my screen. I'd kept the number under SE, her initials. Dread filled my gut.

I pressed to answer and sighed, trying to brave it out.

"What?" I said in a bored tone.

"I want you to damage Lena's mum's car," she replied.

"What? Don't be ridiculous. Why would you want me to do that?" I sat upright against my headboard.

"You don't need to ask questions. You just need to do it, otherwise I'm showing people my recording."

I scrubbed at my forehead. "When do you want me to do it?"

I listened while she carried on giving me instructions and then she ended the call. Somehow I needed to get to the bottom of why Sophie was doing this and to either reason with her, or get something equally damaging on her, because I had enough crap in my life without her adding to it.

Turned out I'd soon have even more crap in my life...

---

Tamsin came for Sunday lunch. My mum and dad liked her. Mum fussed over her and Dad elbowed me when we were out of sight with winks—clearly I was a fully-fledged member of his 'all men together' club.

"Don't let her try to boss you about, son. They all do that. Make sure she knows who wears the trousers."

"I will." I agreed though I had no idea what he meant by this. Whether I was supposed to slap her one if she dared to challenge me about anything like he would do.

That night we went around to her house and I texted my dad to see if I could stay a bit longer than usual. His reply was embarrassing. He had no idea what a dick he really was.

**Dad: Course you can, son *wink emoticon*, just don't forget to wrap the beast!**

I left Tamsin's just after eleven that night, armed with my backpack, and I made my way to Lena's house, my heart beating faster with every step nearer.

Lena's house was on a corner, where large bushes in the garden obscured the view of passers-by, so I was able to pause there for a moment, checking around to see if anyone had noticed me. There was no one around. It was a cold winter's evening and people were tucked up warm. I wished I was. My stomach hurt. Fucking nerves; I needed a shit. While I delayed doing what Sophie had demanded it got worse and worse. For fuck's sake. What was I supposed to do? Run back home? I needed the toilet, but I had to damage the car. I didn't want to do it, but I had to. And then I had an idea. The most horrendous thing imaginable, but this way Sophie would surely be okay with my actions and Lena's mum wouldn't actually have to suffer a damaged car. And it took away the fact I needed the bog.

Pulling my hood up so that no one could make out it was me, I slipped into the driveway and crouched down in front of the car. My shit slid out easily because of nerves. It was putrid. I couldn't believe I'd just crapped on someone's driveway, but I needed to get this done and get home before someone saw me. I went in my backpack. I'd packed a pointy-ended trowel which was the only thing I'd managed to buy from the Asda that morning—when I'd fetched my dad a Sunday paper—that was sharp enough to do some damage to a car's paintwork. Instead, I used it to smear my shit across the windscreen.

It wasn't my finest moment, but it wasn't the worst moment of my life either. I packed everything up and walked back via the back lanes where overgrown hedges and fields yielded the perfect place for me to discard the trowel. I sprayed myself with Lynx in the hope that when I went in the house I didn't stink of shit given I couldn't exactly wipe my arse.

I messaged Sophie.

**Marcus: I've done something. I think it's better than car damage.**

Her reply came swiftly back. **SE: What did you do? You SHOULD do exactly what I asked. If you fucked up, the vid goes out.**

**Marcus: I didn't fuck up.**

I messaged what I'd done.

**SE: Oh man. You're a sick fuck, Marcus. But you can crack on with your sad life now hopefully.**

I breathed a hopeful sigh. Did this mean she was going to leave me alone now? Had I done enough?

---

I barely slept that night for fear someone would have seen me and recognised me. At school the following day, there was no talk of what had happened at all. I breathed a sigh of relief. It looked like I'd gotten away with it.

On Tuesday though I was walking down a corridor when I felt someone behind me. Too close to my personal space.

"What the fuck have I ever done to you, Marcus?"

I swung around to find myself facing Lena. Oh fuck.

"What are you talking about?" I put a sneer on my face.

"I recognised your clothes. I know it was you. Are you sick in the head?"

People were starting to make their way towards us. I didn't want anyone seeing me being yelled at. It wouldn't do my rep much good.

I was saved by her best friend coming to her rescue. Sophie appeared by her side. "What's going on?" She stared at me, eyes narrowed, obviously wondering if I'd grassed her up.

"I'm just telling this little shit, I know it's him. Little shit being the right word. I've never done anything to you, leave me alone."

"He's not worth it, Len." Sophie hooked her arm through her friend's, then she spun around to me. "You're disgusting. You'd better leave her the fuck alone from now on."

I stood there, silent. Just letting Sophie do her acting performance. They walked away, and I went back to my classes.

---

The next week passed without anything else happening, though I was permanently on watch. I took my annoyance out on Tamsin, telling her to fuck off being a clinger, and got shouted at by Chloe.

I was waiting for my mum to call me down for tea the following Tuesday night. It had been nine days since I'd visited Lena's house.

"Marcus." My mum's voice hollered up the stairs.

"I'll be down in a minute," I yelled. "Just finishing this game."

I heard her footsteps come up the stairs. Fuck's sake, why couldn't she just let me come to the table in a few minutes? It was my meal that would go a bit colder. A knock came to the door.

"What?" I shouted, snappily.

The door opened a fraction. "Can you come down, Marcus? The police are here," she said, looking at me with concern.

Oh fuck.

"W- what about?" I asked.

"Some incident with a car. I need to let them in. Come straight down and thank God your father is not home from work yet." Her gaze met mine with a shrewdness, like she was trying to get a read on me. "Is there anything I need to know about?"

"No," I protested. "I haven't done anything." I would protest my innocence until proven otherwise. She left the room and I composed myself, made sure I was looking presentable and I walked downstairs.

The two Feds looked up at me from their seats with assessing gazes. That's what my group called them, Feds. My mother was on the sofa and the Feds had taken a chair each. The clock showed it was just gone five. My dad would be home after six. If I'd bothered checking the time before, I'd have known my mum wasn't shouting me for tea.

But I'd been brought up with manners and so I stood straight, walked to the first Fed and said, "Hello, I'm Marcus," and I held out a hand for her to shake.

She took it and I saw the look that passed between her and the other Fed. The one that said, *this is not a boy who defecates on cars. This is a nice boy who was brought up well.* They were so stupid.

"I'm sorry to have to disturb you, Marcus. Sounds like you were at a crucial part of a game. Xbox?" The first Fed said introducing herself as PC Tayburn.

"Yeah." I smiled. "Don't worry about it. I just thought my tea was ready."

She laughed along with me and told me how she had a kid my age.

"So what can I help you with? Is everything okay? Is it about the fight I witnessed a week last Friday?" I asked innocently.

"We're not sure, that's what I'm hoping you might be able to help us with," the Fed answered. "Basically, there was an incident on Sunday evening at Lena Haybrook's house. That's the young lady who was in an argument with another girl called Chloe, right?"

I nodded.

"CCTV shows a youth defecating in front of Lena's mother's car and then they proceed to wipe the faeces across her windscreen."

Inside I froze. CCTV? Fuck, she had CCTV? But outwardly, I stayed calm because until PC Tayburn said they knew a hundred percent it was me, I could lie to myself and say it wasn't. That I never did that. Because the real me wouldn't have ever done that.

My mum gave me the few seconds I needed to pull myself together inwardly as she launched a screech at the Fed. "And how do you think my son is connected to that? He'd never do any such thing. He's been brought up right. He's the top in his class with his whole future ahead of him. He wouldn't be so stupid."

"Marcus?" The Fed turned to me.

"I'm sorry. I don't know anything about it. No one at school has mentioned anything about that happening either." Another lie given that Lena had accused me outright.

"Mrs Haybrook said she recognised you."

Sitting up straighter, I looked directly from one Fed to the other before returning my attention to PC Tayburn and speaking softly. "I don't even know her. I've only seen her once outside the hairdressers the Saturday after the fight when she came out shouting and bawling at me and my friends."

"She did what?" my mum said and I made what happened sounded like the antics of a madwoman.

The Fed was clearly done here, and her colleague had looked bored the moment she'd arrived. "I'm sorry to have disturbed you. I can see you're a nice young man, but I'm sure you understand I have to ask these questions. I'll leave you to get back to your game now."

"It's no problem and if I do hear any rumours about who might have done it, I'll let you know. You wouldn't say where you got the info from, would you?"

"No, of course not," she replied.

My mum dismissed me and I heard her read the riot act with the policewomen for even suggesting such a thing. She would not want them back anywhere near here for what consequences could be unleashed from my father and in her eyes I was a well-behaved son.

When they'd gone she came back up to my room. "Don't mention any of this to your dad."

"I won't."

She nodded. "And stay away from that Lena girl because her mother is clearly unhinged."

"She is. You should have seen her outside the hairdressers. Fancy telling the police it was me. As if I'd do anything like that."

My mum's jaw set taut. "If she does anything else, I'll make a complaint against her. She can't start accusing you of things without any evidence. That CCTV showed a kid in dark clothes. Could have been anyone."

"Thanks, Mum, for believing me."

She nodded. "Right, I'd better get on with the tea now, or your dad will be on one."

She closed the door, and I went back to my Xbox game, although my heart was no longer in it.

# 16

# MARCUS

Every time I thought Sophie had stopped, she'd be back with something else for me to do. After three months it was to put a brick through the window of Lena's home. I dared Damon to do that one. I promised him a bag of bud if he dared, so of course he did.

Then she wanted me to threaten Lena on a daily basis, so I kept having to go up to her and whisper threats. I had to be careful because I didn't want anyone else knowing what I was doing, so I did it on nights where Tamsin stayed behind for extra study classes. Lena never went to them.

One minute I was threatening Lena Haybrook, the next I was the good little student, the perfect boyfriend, and the goody goody son. None of it was real. None of it.

My parents had gone shopping one night when the doorbell rang. Mum'd told me the window cleaner might call round, so I picked up the envelope she'd left on the side and opened the door.

Mrs Haybrook stood in front of me.

It was the first time I'd seen her up close. I bet she'd been pretty when she was younger, but it was hard to see now through the bitterness nipping at her eyes and mouth. Wrinkles were beginning to eat at her face and grey peeked at her hairline. I threw the envelope onto the window ledge. I needed rid of her before my parents came back or Dad might find out about all the trouble and then me and Mum would be for it.

"Yeah?" I asked.

"Is your mum or dad in? I'm Lena Haybrook's mother."

"They're not here, they've gone shopping. But I didn't do anything, so—"

She started screaming and yelling at me. Spittle flying from her lips. "Listen here, Marcus. I know for a fact it was you. We recognised you. Hiding behind a hood shows you for the pathetic fucker you are."

Her rant went on at a hundred miles an hour and I only half listened as my eyes were fascinated by how crazy this woman looked now, when she'd first appeared at the door angry but composed.

"Listen to me, lad. This ends here today. Believe me, you do *not* want me as an enemy and the day you fouled my car and broke my window you took this from being about just my daughter and involved me in it all. Stay the fuck away from us, otherwise you'll regret it. Do you understand?"

She didn't give me a chance to answer. She turned, stomped off, got back in her car and drove away. I'd be lying if I said it didn't make my stomach twist, but the fact remained that Lena's mother's wrath would not be anywhere near that of my father's, so I wouldn't be stopping anytime soon. Not until Sophie finished this vendetta or at least kept me out of it.

But that didn't seem like it was going to happen in the foreseeable. Next, Sophie wanted me to make Lena and her mother anxious in their own home again, and so the following week I started walking past their house with my friends. Nothing else, just back and forth. There was a field near the end of their road that was part of a walking route and so no one would question a group of teens going in that direction, walking down the path and coming back. Sophie said Mrs Haybrook was constantly watching the monitors and it would wind her up. I still didn't know what Sophie was achieving with any of this. All I knew was that I had to tread carefully while doing her bidding as that footage of me with Archie's cock in my mouth could not get out. Soon, Sophie and Lena would be sitting their exams and leaving, and I just had to hope that when that happened Sophie moved on from me.

Once again, I came face-to-face with Mrs Haybrook as she ran down the street after me and my boys had just walked past. This time she was holding her phone up towards my face. The rest of the boys sniggered, and Damon yelled, "Crazy bitch."

"Could you tell my camera why you won't leave us alone?" she asked me.

I put a smirk on my face. I couldn't have my mates laughing at me. Then I moved closer to her.

"You can't record me. You need to delete that."

"No, I won't. I want you to tell me what you think you're doing," she said. I needed her away from me.

"If you don't stop recording me, I'll make sure you have something else to occupy your time," I sneered. I was confident that if she showed the police this video, she'd be facing a doctor and a series of questions about her mental health given she was chasing teenagers down a street. She wasn't aware but Damon was recording her yelling at us.

She held her phone down. "Thanks, you little fucker. Threatening me and giving me the evidence of it. That's great. I'll just go phone the police now and you can look forward to a visit."

She rushed back towards her house and I played along with being cool about it all while inside my stomach churned because I felt that something would snap soon. I couldn't keep on with this stuff and continue to get away with it. It wasn't how life worked, not my life anyway. It was all a ticking timebomb.

One that went off in a way I'd never expected.

The Easter holidays rolled around and the last time I'd been involved with the Haybrooks was a few days after my confrontation with Lena's mum when Damon had the idea to throw a bag of plain flour over her car in retaliation for her 'showing us up in the street'. He'd since told me he'd also scratched her car and I'd told him to leave it now. That we should quit while ahead.

I'd had no visits from the police and so it seemed that for once luck had actually been on my side.

I was going to get myself a taco when I spied Sophie and Lena making their way into the building before me.

Shit. I tried to turn around to go in the other direction, but Sophie came running up to me. I looked behind her. Lena headed into Taco Master and I saw her grab a seat, watching us.

"You okay, Marcus?" Sophie said.

"I was," I answered honestly. "Now, I'm not so sure."

"Meaning?"

I got angry then. My frustration with all of her blackmail and game playing was filling me up like a volcano on the point of rupture. "Sophie, are we nearly done? I've been following your instructions like a good little puppet now for long enough, and if I end up with the police at my door then I may as well just tell my dad everything because he'll beat the fucking shit out of me anyway."

"Yeah," she said arrogantly. "I'm done with you now. You're free. Go in and enjoy your taco. Thanks for being my bitch, but I don't need you anymore."

"And the video of me?"

"Well, obviously, I'll keep it safe, but I promise you've earned your freedom." She looked at me with what appeared like genuine remorse on her face. "I'm sorry it had to be this way and I hope that if you do like guys, you get to live a happy life with some dude somewhere down the line."

"You're crazy," I yelled.

She shrugged her shoulders. "I'm just doing what I need to do to make sure my own life turns out okay." She turned and went back into the shop. After a few minutes I went and got my own taco. Sophie stood behind me in the queue. I was aware of her the whole time she was there. I looked at her with a pissed off look on my face because it still felt like she was playing me somehow and I walked out of the shop the minute I'd been served.

I thought I'd worked out why she didn't need me anymore on Thursday when a video of Lena losing her virginity to a lad called Lee Swinton went viral around the teenagers of Berkley Edge and the surrounding areas. I didn't know how she'd managed to get hold of that, but it had been sent by a random account and I had no doubt she was behind it.

Damon wanted to walk past Lena's house. I tried to make out we had better things to do, but the rest of the boys were up for it, for winding Lena up, so as 'leader', I had to put my sneer on my face and act the part.

We reached the house. I could see Lena's top bedroom window was open. Damon shouted, "Show us your tits, Lena," at the top of his voice and everyone else laughed, including me. I had to, or they'd think I was being weird.

Of course, Lena's mother was out of the door by the time we got to the end of the road. "The madwoman's here," Damon laughed. I saw the others looking at him sniggering. My turn to act like the leader of this lot.

"God, she's here. The wicked witch," I shouted. The others laughed, whooped, and hollered.

"One day, you'll get yours," she shouted up the street.

I put my best sneer on my face. "What are you going to do, old lady? Shout me to death?"

She looked at us for a moment and then surprisingly, she turned and walked back to the house. Like she'd given up. I carried on walking around the estate, listening to the idiots I hung around with who were so entertained because they'd seen Lena naked. I hated them more every day. Hated this life more every day. But every day that passed was a step closer to freedom. I had to remember that.

Poor Lena. School on Monday would be hell for her. I wondered once more what Sophie's reasons were for all of this, and at what point she was going to stop.

But as it transpired, Lena wouldn't face anyone the next week at school.

Because on Friday morning the news broke out across our social media. Lena Haybrook was dead.

The message was posted in our group chat by Chloe. I'd picked my phone up because it wouldn't quit beeping and then I sat up fast. I read it over and over; maybe I thought if I stared at it long enough the words would change to say something else? Was this what Sophie had wanted? To drive Lena to suicide?

I found myself over the toilet retching. Picking up my phone, I messaged Sophie.

**Marcus: What the actual fuck? Did you want her to die?**

She didn't respond. No doubt the phone she'd used to message me was a cheap shit burner and it was now somewhere no one would ever find it. And that benefited me as much as it did her.

Guilt roiled through my stomach as I recalled everything I'd ever done to Lena or her mother. She'd killed herself. That's what Chloe had posted in our chat. Her mother knew the Haybrooks' neighbour. She'd heard the ambulance driver, or some shit like that. Speculation that would no doubt grow into made up stories.

All I knew was I felt sick. Was sick. Guilty and sick. But there would no doubt be many feeling the same way: Chloe, Tamsin, Damon. They'd all targeted Lena at some point. And most definitely Sophie Ellender.

My mind started flashing with thoughts of Lena's mum. She'd found Lena dead. All she'd done I knew was try to protect her daughter.

The daughter she no longer had.

Would she come to my door on one of her rants yelling that I'd done it?

I might not have killed Lena directly, but my guilt swirled within me. Would be in the ink of a suicide note, the fibres of a rope, a tablet or two of a bottle of pills. However she'd done it, I was partly responsible.

My mother found me over the toilet. "What's the matter, love? Do you have a temperature?"

I told her about Lena and her face went white. "Oh my goodness, that poor girl, and her mum. I know she got bullied a bit, but to go to those lengths. It doesn't bear thinking about." She passed me a tumbler of water to rinse my mouth. "There'll be people like Chloe feeling very guilty today, but they mustn't. You need to tell her that. People's minds can't be right anyway for them to get to that stage."

"Someone circulated a video of her losing her virginity," I told her, because she'd get to know soon anyway.

She gasped at that. "What on earth was someone doing videoing such a thing?" She shook her head. "I hope her mum has a lot of family and friends around her. She's going to need them."

When she checked I didn't need anything else, she patted my head like I was a poorly youngster again and when she left I closed my eyes and wished I could take the time back to when I was and that I could do my life all over again and make different choices.

Because the ones I'd made now had led to a girl's death.

A girl who, as far as I knew, had never actually done anything wrong except to trust the wrong people.

---

Two weeks later they held her funeral. Some kids from school attended including Chloe Butcher. There was no sign of Lee unsurprisingly. The rumours were that he was ill, but I doubted he'd be welcome anyway. Chloe was apparently insisting that at Prom they gave a toast to Lena and let off balloons. I was pleased I was in the year below and wouldn't have to witness any of it.

Chloe tried to extend a hand of friendship to Sophie. She told us all. But Sophie was broken, she said. No one saw Sophie for a few weeks and when Tamsin actually did, she'd been in the supermarket with her mum, morose, and saying she didn't know how to cope without her friend.

The weeks passed and exams started for those in the last year of school. Sophie returned to take her exams. I only saw her a couple of times from a distance. She kept her head down as if trying to look invisible. I recognised the stance as I'd done it myself lots of times in the past.

Tamsin finished with me as she started sitting her exams. We'd been toxic anyway. Always arguing. And I'd cared for her as a friend, but I'd never felt anything else for her. In return it seemed she'd used me too. Helped fit into the gang until the end of school came around. She also rolled out the excuse about Lena's death having made her look at her own life. She'd decided she wanted more, which translated as, *than hanging around street corners with a fourteen-year-old who sells weed and whose dad owns a car showroom.*

My own exam year would be next, but now the school holidays were almost upon us, and all I could think was I didn't want all that much space ahead of me with nothing to fill it except the mindless drivel that came out of Damon's mouth.

But life hadn't finished fucking with me yet.

# 17

## MARCUS

Life continued as normal. It seemed like you should live your life differently after someone you knew died, but only those directly affected live that way really. The only difference was that I no longer had a girlfriend and Damon couldn't stop talking about a girl he'd met through Snapchat.

We were sitting in my bedroom and he was boring me about her once more. I took his phone off him and stared at the picture of Elise. She looked like any other girl we knew on her photo, ie tons of make-up and posing. "You've got no chance." I wound him up. "She's not gonna let you smash her."

"Jealous, cos you're on your own now?" he jeered. It made me realise that something was changing. Damon was getting cockier by the day. When he'd thrown the brick and the flour he'd acted like he'd shot someone at point blank range. He seemed to be dealing with what happened to Lena by trying to act like he was some kind of gangsta. Part of me wanted to let him take over and for me to fade into the background again.

"Nah. I can get pussy any time I like, mate." I handed him his phone back. Elise had friend requested me, but I'd hesitated to accept. I liked my circle small. Didn't want to do anything that could change things.

Forgetting change was inevitable.

---

I was eating my cereal at the dining table one morning while staring at my phone. Dad said goodbye and went out of the front door. A moment later he was back, crashing through to where I sat, a vein bulging on his temple.

*What the...?*

Mum noticed the signs and came dashing over. "What's up, Peter?"

"What's up?" he said, his breath coming in sharp pants. "Let's all go outside and see, shall we?"

He yanked me out of my seat by my arm. It jarred and sent a pain shooting up to my armpit as he dragged me to the door, only letting go when he spotted someone walking down the street, looking towards us.

And then he pointed to the side of his car where someone had carved the words: **MARCUS IS SCUM**.

I reeled back. Who the hell would do this? I didn't have any enemies as far as I knew. Was it Sophie? Had she cracked up? Was it Lena's mother? She hated me. Fuck, she might do this. My mind was running ten to the dozen. Word on the street was Carla Haybrook had moved away. It wouldn't be her. But, fuck, if it was then how did I stop her?

Terror threatened at the corners of my mind. Once more, Marcus Bull did not get to breathe and be a teenager. He had to suffer. I only had to look at my dad's face to know a punishment was coming.

"So, who've you fucked off?" my dad said in a low, menacing tone that the neighbours couldn't hear.

"No one. I haven't done anything."

"You must know something about it. Who've you upset this time?" His voice rose as he finally lost it with me. "Someone carved my fucking car up. Do you have any idea how much that's going to cost to repair?"

"I've already told you that I've done nothing," I yelled back. I shouldn't have yelled. I knew the moment I did it, that I'd pay for my insolence.

"People don't damage cars for no reason," Dad snarled.

"Peter, let's talk about this inside now." My mother had noticed that Dad's temper had risen and that the neighbours were at their windows.

We all walked inside and my dad stepped towards me. My mum begged, "Just go to work, Pete, and let's talk about this when we've all calmed down, yeah? Maybe we'll know who did it by then."

He grabbed her by the throat. "You don't tell me what to do. I rule this house." He pushed her away and then he grabbed me, threw me to the floor and kicked me in the stomach hard. I curled up, almost blacking out through the pain. My dad left, slamming the door behind him and my mum rushed over, tears tracking down her cheeks.

"Oh, Marcus. Are you okay?"

She stayed with me until I could sit up again. "You need to sort whatever this is," she said. "We have to keep him calm."

"I honestly don't know who can have done it, Mum," I lied.

"Marc, you need to pass those exams, get a good job, and get as far away as possible," she told me.

"I'll get us both away," I said. "I promise."

"I should be able to protect you, but he… he." I found myself comforting my mum now. We sat on the floor for a few minutes speaking without words, and then I got up and got ready for school.

Once more Damon went on and on about Elise and how she was going to do this, that, and the other. So that night I accepted her friend request. Part of me wanted to steal her away from him, just to show him that life kicks you in the stomach, just when you think you're getting a break. Then I posted to anyone who might be watching my account: 'Pussies shouldn't hide'.

---

Dad got his car repaired and as one of the youngest in my year I had my fifteenth birthday. And because of the car repair, he said I got nothing. No celebration with my mates, no money for my birthday. If it made him feel like a man, then whatever. I had my own money. Bought my boys a Maccy's and shrugged off the idea of anything else saying it was cringe. Dad told me that some of my birthday money had gone towards a camera for the car. That if anyone did anything else he'd have them on camera.

Sad fuck. I knew how that worked. If people didn't want to be seen, they wouldn't. The days passed and with every one I waited for something else to happen and then one morning it did. Horse shit all over the car windscreen and a note stuck in the middle saying:

**Marcus Went Too Far.**
**Marcus Will Pay.**

But I was one step ahead this time. I'd gotten up early. Every morning now, I got up early to check. I cleaned the car down and destroyed the note. Told my dad I couldn't sleep so I'd washed his car. He looked at me funny.

As he got in the car to set off, I saw him check the camera. I held my breath, waiting to see if the motion sensor had been set off. If so, I was screwed.

"Fucking piece of shit thing. It's not working. I'll have to get Cliff to look at it. Amazon said this was the top one. Obviously paid for reviews."

He drove off and I closed my eyes while my breathing steadied itself. I needed to talk to Sophie because this had to stop.

I knew where she lived so I made excuses to my boys about going to the dentists and set off instead to her house. Chloe had been a daily source of knowledge about the aftermath of Lena's death, and I knew that Sophie's mum worked but was still very worried about her and trying to get her to enrol on the college course she'd wanted to do.

Peering through the window, I could see Sophie on the sofa in her living room, scrolling on her phone. I tapped gently. She jumped, turned to the window and her eyes widened. Then she ran to the door, opening it and looking around.

"What the fuck are you doing here?"

"You wouldn't answer my messages, so I had to come here. We might have a problem."

"Come in," she said and stepping back, she let me past.

I told her about what had been happening and she scrubbed a hand through her hair. "Fucking hell. Look, I'll contact Carla and if it is her, I'll get her to stop, okay? Don't worry about it. Just make sure you stick to not saying a word. Otherwise I'll add to your stress by circulating the video."

"Stop threatening me." I went on the attack. "I've told you I won't rat you out. Just check if it's Mrs Haybrook because I don't know who else would do this, but my dad is using me as football practice."

She hung her head. "I'll sort it. Listen, I'll get a new phone and message you, okay? I've got your number written down."

"You destroyed the other one?"

Dead eyes looked back at me. "What do you think?"

A few moments passed where there was silence between us and we just stood there. "Why did you do it, Sophie?"

As she looked at me her eyes filled with tears. "She wasn't meant to die," she said. "I was just supposed to live."

As I opened my mouth to ask her what she meant, her eyes turned cold. "Now get out, Marcus. You can't be here."

I told the group chat about the shit on the windscreen and asked them to keep it quiet, but if they heard anything about who could have done it to let me know. They ribbed me, calling BullShit, funny fuckers, but no one knew anything. I became more paranoid, but nothing else happened. Maybe it had been Carla Haybrook and maybe those two things were her revenge on my own actions. I'd understand if it was.

---

"Elise is coming over in the holidays and she's asked if my house will be free, so you know what that means." Damon elbowed me. He'd been to our house for tea and now we were in my room.

"That she clearly has a disability with her vision?" I quipped.

"Fuck off, you're just jealous. No one can ever have a better life than Marcus Bull," Damon said bitterly. "Right, I'd better get home now." He left my house and I watched him walk down the street from my bedroom window.

He was fucking me off big time. Getting louder with every day that passed. He'd started giving me shit about things I'd put about him on social media. I blamed this Elise. Fucking meddling girls. It was banter. It'd never bothered him before.

I wished she'd fuck off and incredibly I got my wish because idiot Damon sent her a dick pic and she sent her mother to his house. He was instantly sent for by his mother and grounded, but when he called me he said that his mother had told him to pass on that Elise's mum had said I'd been hitting on her and I should stop.

"That's not cool, bruh. I'd never do that to you. Thought you had my back?"

"Ask her for fucking proof. I've not done anything. Bitch is crazy," I replied.

When I ended the call, I messaged Elise.

**Marcus: What's your mother going on about? I never sent you any messages about us two. I don't know you.**

She replied. **Elise: I don't know what you're talking about.**

So she was playing it like that, was she?

**Marcus: Damon's mum told him you'd said I needed to stop messaging you. You're clearly some crazy bitch. Consider yourself blocked.**

I wasn't prepared for what came next.

**Elise: Whatever. Damon sent me a dick pic. He's obviously now trying to make out like I'm the crazy chick. Lost any money lately, Marcus?**

**Marcus: I don't know what you're talking about.** I answered, but while I waited for her to type a reply, I lifted up my mattress. My money was gone. All of it. I grabbed the phone and looked at her reply.

**Elise: I know we were going on a date and he wanted to impress me and he said you owed him and he knew where you kept some cash.**

**Marcus: He wouldn't do that. He's my mate.** I typed back furiously.

**Elise: Then how come I know you have five hundred pounds missing from under your bed? Goodbye Marcus, consider yourself blocked.**

She'd thrown my words back in my face and now my anger pulsed through my body. My fists clenched at the same time as I felt on the edge of just giving up. My money was gone. I was never going to escape this life of pain, not unless I did a Lena Haybrook and I didn't have the guts to do that. Not only that, but I was still convinced that one day I could walk away from all this. It just wasn't anytime soon.

I barely slept a wink as the realisation that Damon could be behind *everything* came to me. He could have scratched the car. He certainly could have thrown the manure. But then again, I'd not told him about what I'd done to Lena and her mother.

I felt like I could trust no one but myself.

One thing was clear though. The only person who had been in my room since the money was there and then not was Damon.

I spent the whole night before I finally managed to sleep feeling like I was being eaten up inside with torment and rage. How could he do this to me?

---

As soon as I saw him just inside the school gates, I pulled him to one side.

"Mate, where's my money? Elise ain't coming now, so if you haven't spent it, I want it fucking back."

Damon sneered at me. "What drugs you taken this morning? Cos they're bad."

"She told me. Said you took the money."

"Well she's a lying bitch." Damon had now rolled up his sleeves.

My breath was tensing, being held inside my body like a volcano on the point of eruption.

"How the fuck do you explain how someone I've never met knew where my fucking money was kept then, shithead? I want it back. Every fucking penny."

"I've no idea, but I know one thing. You've become a fucking loser, mate." He tapped at his temple. "And a nutjob."

That was it. White-hot rage flashed within me and I pulled back my arm and punched him straight in the face. He hit the ground hard just as teachers came running.

"Marcus Bull. Come with me," the assistant head demanded, pulling my arm. It reminded me too much of my father and so I pushed him off me, glaring, but I followed him back into school.

I got suspended and as I sat there waiting for my mum or dad to come collect me from the office, I realised I'd officially just turned into my father, beating someone to give me an answer. Damon had sworn it wasn't him. Maybe my dad had found my money and put it towards his 'Marcus' fuck-ups fund'. I felt like I was coming apart at the seams. If I had my father's traits deep down inside me then I didn't want them. It was, I thought, my worst nightmare.

Huh. I'd yet to meet my worst nightmare.

When my dad collected me from school, he first was called into the head's office without me. I knew I'd be in for a beating for embarrassing him. I thought about running away, but I had nowhere to go and no money now to help me.

The silence as we walked back to his car made me feel sick to my stomach and then once he'd started driving, all of a sudden Dad pulled off into a side street. *Oh fuck.*

Then my sick fuck father actually high-fived me for being suspended for fighting and said I was following a family tradition. That he'd been suspended when he was at school for the same thing. I just sat grateful that for once my body wouldn't sting from where he'd hit or kicked me.

---

My relief was short-lived as a brick was thrown through Damon's mum's windscreen and my ring was found at the side of it. I was being set up, but by who?

When she called Mum, we went around to her house, in order to try to prevent Dad learning about it. I sat in Damon's living room and told Mrs Caruthers how Damon had stolen my 'pocket money', seeing as I couldn't say it was five hundred fucking quid. I told her he had taken my ring and was setting me up. She argued back protecting her son and I reminded her that her son liked to send dick pics on social media and wasn't to be trusted.

Seeing the conversation was going around in circles, our mums agreed we should just avoid each other. That wouldn't prove difficult. My friendship with Damon was over, that was for sure.

"What is happening to you lately, Marcus?" my mum asked me before she said goodnight. "You need to keep out of trouble so that—"

"So that what, Mum? So that Dad doesn't try to beat the crap out of either of us? He liked it when I punched Damon. He's sick in the head."

"Sssh." Fear lit up my mum's features and I realised just how at risk she was if I shouted too loudly.

"I'm sorry, Mum. I'll sort myself out."

She breathed a sigh of relief, her shoulders falling down to normal levels, instead of being around her ears.

"Thank you. It's just until you can go."

I nodded, and she left and closed the door.

---

The following week while still suspended from school, I found myself walking past Lena's house. I spotted Carla's car outside. I wondered how she was doing. She'd been a bit batshit, but she'd never deserved to lose her daughter. I was sorry and although I didn't think she'd care, I just wanted her to know. Don't ask me what possessed me, but I walked back across the street to the supermarket, bought a plain card with a flower on and a pen and I wrote it out, leaning on the lottery station in the store.

**I am sorry about Lena.**
**So very sorry.**
**MB.**

Before I stuck it through the letterbox, I asked myself what I hoped to achieve. Why I felt I should do this.

And it came to me.

I'd wronged her and I wanted her to shout and scream at me for what I'd put her through and put Lena through.

Before I could change my mind, I posted it through the letterbox, and I waited.

Not long after I posted it, I received a Snapchat message. Immediately, I wondered how she knew my username.

Probably through Sophie. But then I just felt I didn't know anything anymore.

**Carla: I got the card. Thank you.**

Thank you? I wasn't expecting that response from her. Then again, I didn't know what I'd set in motion by my actions really. I typed back.

**Marcus: I never thought Lena would do that. I know you don't give two shits about me, but I'm sorry. Whoever sent that video went too far.**

I waited as she typed a response.

**Carla: Would you meet me, to talk about Lena? Just anything you like really. I'm in Berkley Edge now and then I'm leaving for good. Somewhere private like near the old den? I promise I won't keep you long.**

Was this what I wanted? To speak to Carla face-to-face? I hesitated and typed.

**Marcus: I don't know what I can tell you really.**

More typing from the other end.

**Carla: You could say sorry to my face, rather than through cowardly words on a piece of card. That would mean a lot. Give me some closure and then you won't have to see me again.**

Was this why I'd sent the card? To try and get some closure for myself? To make sense of what had happened over the past few months and try to get my own quietish life back where all that happened was people spat and shoved at me and called me names?

**Marcus: Okay. I'll be there in around fifteen minutes.**

I started to walk back towards where Carla's house was, but I took the longer way around, walking down a backstreet. My heart thudded and my mouth went dry, because I had absolutely no idea what would happen. I just hoped she'd listen and that we could indeed tell the truth. Well, I couldn't tell her about Sophie, but I could tell her I was an idiot. I just had to make sure she didn't record me.

I'd not been standing at the meeting place for long when a woman walked down the path towards me, but I didn't realise it was her until she got closer. Her hair was different and she'd put on weight. I took a deep inhale and said, "Hello."

Her answer for me was in her actions.

She rushed at me and pushed me backwards. It was completely unexpected and I sailed back, down the short embankment. My legs and back scraped as I fell past the shrubs and the breath wheezed from me as I landed on something hard.

It hurt and I was scared, so I screamed. I could see Carla sliding down the slope towards me and I just knew she didn't want my apology. She wanted to hurt me, the way my dad hurt me. I could take it. I took it from him. But I didn't like being stuck in this undergrowth, so I tried to sit up.

Oh my god, she was wearing gloves. Why was she wearing gloves? I saw too late when she grabbed at the piece of barbed wire and as it hit my thigh the pain was so excruciating that for a moment my hearing disappeared and white light blinded my vision. I needed words. I gasped for air.

"Stop. P- please s- stop. T- tell y- you s- something."

She smirked down at me. "What is it like to be helpless, Marcus? To the point where you're on the point of extinction?"

"W- what?" The pain. I needed to stay present. Please God, please. I felt so nauseous.

She leaned closer to me and whisper-shouted. "I'm going to kill you, Marcus. Or maybe I'll just cut you and let you bleed out slowly. I haven't decided yet. Actually, that sounds good because I don't know how long it took for Lena to die after she took the pills. Whether it was pain free or whether it hurt. I know her life wasn't pain free. I know she had to go through mental torture to get to a point where enough was enough."

"Oh my god, oh my god."

"You may as well have fed her the pills yourself, Marcus, because that video was the last straw. I don't know why you bullied her and us so much. I'm not sure what you gained from it, but I'm sure you're regretting it now."

I tried one last time to sit up, but she hit me with the barbed wire once more. This time I did retch.

"P- please. L- l - listen." I wailed.

"Fine." She stood up and from the edge of my consciousness I could see her face was composed. This was her swansong to me, her finale. "What are your final words, Marcus? I can assure you that they'll die with me."

"B- blackmailed." I screamed out, because my sexuality being revealed was preferable to death. "Th- that's why. V- video of me, couldn't let o- out. It was g- graphic and would have m- made my own life not worth l- living." I was running out of breath to plead, so instead my eyes looked around me wildly, searching for an escape, an answer. The pain wouldn't let me speak much longer. I spotted my phone in the undergrowth. The screen was cracked and I could only hope it worked. It didn't prove it was Sophie, but it showed the blackmail. That I was telling the truth. "G- grab my phone."

Her eyes narrowed on me.

"N- not lying. H- help me."

Carla took a screwdriver out of her pocket. Oh my fucking god.

"One false move and this goes through your neck," she told me. "And if you're lying, I'll stab you twice."

But she did reach for the phone and when she did, I closed my eyes because I was just about out of options other than to pray.

"So who's been blackmailing you then? Who will I be going after in your place?" she asked.

Sweat beaded on my brow, but I just managed to utter the words, "Sophie Ellender," and then it all went black.

# 18

## CARLA

For the last few months, I'd experienced a constant swirl of emotions, and now once more my body and mind had a hard time processing what they were experiencing. I'd think the boy was a liar were it not for how he'd begged and blurted out her name when faced with his last desperate pleas.

I knew because I'd been there.

When I was pregnant with Lena, I'd carried it all at the front. No one could tell from behind me. I'd not spread out around my backside or anything. I didn't waddle. At eight months pregnant one of my accounting clients had insisted on me meeting them at the local pub for a meal to celebrate my going on maternity leave. I was self-employed and only having the smallest time possible off. Really, they'd bought me some stuff for the baby and wanted me to get excited about it and I did. Every time I looked at tiny babygros and mittens and little hats, my heart soared with excitement. There was a genal at the side of the pub. One I'd gone down many, many times before to walk back home. But on this night as I walked down, my thoughts were full of the fact my baby was coming soon and not my own safety. So I'd never heard him approach.

Grabbed from behind, the man dragged me into the bushes before I had a chance to scream, but as he finally looked and stared at me his eyes widened in shock at my swollen and heavy stomach. I could only see his eyes. He had a hood up.

I prayed to everything there was. "Please don't hurt me. My baby. Anything but my baby," I pleaded. He ran out of the bushes, leaving me there.

In the moment of desperation, there was my truth. I'd have done anything he wanted as long as he didn't harm my unborn child.

Lena saved me that night from attack and it hurts so fucking bad that I couldn't do the same for her.

Coming back to myself, I stared at the boy lying against the fence. In his moment of reckoning he screamed that this was Sophie's doing. I looked at his phone and tapped into his messages. He had messages saved under SE.

I scrolled to the beginning.

**SE: I'm sending you this video so that you have your own reminder of what I'll send everywhere if you don't do exactly as I ask.**

I pressed play on the video until I saw the contents and then I switched it off. And then I turned to the boy lying there in pain and I realised that he might just have been fighting for his own survival in this cruel world. Guilt and horror swept over me at what I'd become. A vessel of hatred. While I had no idea if Sophie was truly behind this, I knew that I was done here. That I wouldn't touch another hair on Marcus Bull's head.

He groaned and opened his eyes.

"Marcus."

"Y- yeah?"

"Can I take you to my house? The one I'm selling. Will you let me get some stuff to get you patched up, or do you want to call the police? I don't mind either way, but if you come to the house, I promise we can properly talk after I get you some painkillers and stuff. You can tell me about Sophie and everything else and then if you want you can still call the police. Or I can drop you off at the hospital..."

"No hospitals. Take me to your house. I need painkillers please."

"Okay."

It took time to get back onto the path. Marcus was sore from the fall although he hadn't broken anything, and his leg was causing him a lot of pain from where I'd hit him with the wire.

I sighed as the truth hit me. "You will need the doctors, Marcus, because the wire was rusty. I'll take you to A&E. We'll go straight there."

Sweat beaded on his brow once more and he nodded. It took us a while to make our way back to my house. I managed to get him into the car so I could drive him to the hospital. We passed at least six people on the way from the den to the car and not one person asked a question or offered assistance. They saw a woman and a teenager and no doubt assumed that the teen had got into a fight or fallen and mum had come to help.

If only they knew the truth.

Marcus booked himself in at A&E and told them I was his mother. He said to the receptionist and then to the triage nurse that he'd been in a fight.

Then we took a seat each in the waiting room. Sat in a corner away from other people and began the long wait to be seen. And during that long wait, Marcus told me everything about his life and I in turn told him a lot about mine.

Finally, patched up and given painkillers that had him looking dazed, I told him I'd take him home and we could just tell his parents he'd fallen and I'd found him.

"I don't want to go home," he said through the drug fugue. "It might have been better if you'd just hit me over the head with a rock or something. Finished me off once and for all."

"You need to get away and start again and I can help you," I told him. At this point I still didn't know if it was Sophie who'd blackmailed him or someone else, but the truth was in his messages. He'd been a pawn in someone's game. And while he'd added to the pain my daughter went through, he'd just been trying to survive. I no longer hated Marcus Bull. I found myself wanting to parent him. I laughed out loud at that. I think the hospital must have given me some drugs too.

"Nothing can help me except time. Once I'm eighteen, I'm gone from there."

But that was another three years away and not good enough. Mr Bull was a bully and we all knew what I did to those.

Knocking on the door of his family home, his mother opened it, saw Marcus with his bandaged leg and then pulled him straight into her arms. He cried for her to 'get off him' in the way teenagers do when their mums aren't being cool, and then we told his mother the lies we'd made up about what had happened. That he'd been messing about and had fallen, and I'd been walking past having a stroll for a final time before I moved away from the area.

"Oh, you're..." his mum's voice trailed off.

"Carla Haybrook. Yes." I looked around. "Where's Mr Bull?"

"He's gone out for a drink with some business leads," she said. "Do you want a tea or coffee? It's the least I can do when you helped my son. I can't thank you enough."

I nodded my head. "I'd love a cuppa please. It's been a long day."

Marcus went up to bed, walking slowly with each step. He'd be asleep as soon as his head touched the pillow. I followed the woman who introduced herself as Kate through to the kitchen and then remembering, I went in my bag and took out the painkillers the hospital had given us.

She fixed me the tea and then passed it to me. "We can sit at the dining table." She nodded through to another room.

And then when we were seated, she said, "What I don't understand is why you sat in the waiting room with my son for hours and you never called me to come. What's going on, Carla?"

I blew over the top of my mug. "Your son did a lot of things to us, to me and to Lena, because he was being blackmailed. I've not got to the bottom of it all, but I will. Ultimately it led to the death of my daughter. I didn't call you because we were talking and I deserved to know the truth. You have a lifetime to spend time with your son. I no longer have the luxury of that time with Lena."

"Blackmailed for what?"

"Your son is gay. Do you know that?"

She scoffed at my words. "No, he's not. He just got out of a long-term relationship with a girl called Tamsin."

I threw her scoff back at her. "What would your husband do to a son he found out liked other boys, bearing in mind he kicks the shit out of him for much less?"

Her sharp intake of breath didn't stop me from talking. "He says your husband threatens you both all the time. That you live in fear. That he's waiting until he's eighteen and can escape." I fixed a glare at her. "What if Peter's gone too far by then? Hit him, or kicked him and ruptured an organ, made him fall and bang his head? He threatens to kill you both but he's slowly killing Marcus anyway."

The fire finally came out of Kate Bull as she blazed at me. "Who the fuck do you think you are? Coming here and telling me how to parent?"

I laughed. "I'm the woman with nothing to lose. Nothing at all. I'll tell you exactly what I think you need to hear because I can do what I like and no one can stop me, no one at all. I'm not afraid of your husband. I'd happily run a blade straight across his throat."

"You're unhinged."

I sat back and took a sip of my drink. "Yup, all because of a hate campaign against my daughter that led to her suicide." Once more I stared at her. "You're a whisper away from being me if you carry on with this life."

That hit home. Her hand trembled against her own mug. "I have nothing of my own. He's not stupid. I know there are hostels, but I wanted better for Marcus. He deserves the world."

I sucked at my top teeth. "My house is about to sell and I won't need the proceeds. I'm going to give you twenty grand if you agree to take Marcus away and move somewhere with an active gay community where he can live his true life."

Her mouth fell open. I held up a hand. "You don't have to answer now. Marcus knows how to get in touch with me." I got to my feet. "Right, I'll be off. I need to do some last bits at the house and then I'm out of Berkley Edge, for good."

She stood up to see me out. There was nothing left for us to say at this moment. Kate Bull had a lot to think about this evening. Just as we reached the dining room door, the outside door opened and in walked Peter Bull.

Calculating eyes looked at me and then at his wife. The king didn't like anyone he didn't know in his castle.

"Didn't know you were having a friend round?" he said guardedly.

"This is Carla Haybrook. She found Marc earlier. He'd fallen. She took him to the hospital. He's okay though."

"Painkillered up to the eyeballs and no doubt asleep." I smiled. "Anyway, I'd better be going. It was good to meet you both. Give my best to Marcus since I won't be able to myself."

"Oh?" Peter said, his head tilting to one side.

"My last day in Berkley Edge. Sold my house." I didn't miss the relaxation in his brow at the thought that this was a one-off, that I wouldn't be snooping around the place.

I said goodbye, walked down to my car, and got ready to lock up my old house for the final time.

As I clicked my key to open the car, I took a deep inhale. Tomorrow was set to be a busy day. First thing, I had to call the police and see if there had been any sexual assault cases in the area dating back from around sixteen years ago to the present time and then I had to give them Peter Bull's name and address. Because those cold, calculating eyes had been on me years ago. He might not remember me, but I certainly remembered him.

And then I had to see Sophie. Beautiful Sophie who I'd known for years and years, to see if she really had been an enemy, not a friend all along.

I'd thought I'd be able to say my own goodbyes soon, but I wasn't leaving this earth until I got answers for why my daughter had to die.

As I walked through into my new home, exhaustion hit hard. The adrenaline I'd been assaulted with all day was finally leaving my body, even though my mind remained full of unanswered questions. And though I'd thought sleep would evade me given everything that filled my brain, in actual fact I ended up crawling into my bed after just shrugging off my clothes and I knew nothing else until my alarm clock went off at its regular eight am.

# 19

## CARLA

If anyone asked me how I was—if anyone actually gave a rat's arse—I wouldn't have been able to describe where I was mentally or physically, other than maybe 'broken beyond repair'. My hair seemed to be a permanent straggle of grease, and spots had broken out around my chin. I ate scrappily and whatever took my fancy at the time, or not. Much of the time I skipped meals or ate a packet of crisps. What did it matter? The end was nigh.

When the alarm went off there were a blissful, few seconds where I wanted to live. In that brief space where all this had not happened, the reprieve between awakening and reality. It should be a place you could pause for a while. Let your mind be free of ruminating over everything and anything.

Like the fact it had been almost three months since my daughter left the earth and I still couldn't join her yet.

Sitting up in bed, waiting for my body to wake up enough that I could get out of bed, I closed my eyes and pictured her beautiful face. It was minutes before I realised that my face was soaking wet, tears dripping off my chin into the top of the duvet. Wiping my face on the duvet, I swung my legs out of bed. Fuck, I hadn't even got undressed last night; I was still in yesterday's clothes. I'd forgotten that. I took a shower, as if the water could drain away the shadows and darkness that coated me, before dressing and going downstairs.

I rang an anonymous police line about Peter Bull. I didn't know if that evening he had intended to mug me or rape me and that's what I said. They could do what they wanted with my report because somewhere along the line he'd lose Kate and Marcus anyway. And if Kate bottled out, she'd lose Marcus. I'd give him the money to escape all by himself. There would be places you could forge new identities for the right price. Or he could ring social services. I sighed and put my head in my hands. I didn't have space in my head for Marcus, but I couldn't leave him either. I blamed the mother gene, it triumphed above everything, even trauma.

Dialling Sophie's number, I waited for her to answer.

"Everything okay, Carla?" she said and I realised she was at work. She'd started at Primark that last week.

"Oh shit, Sophie. I totally forgot what day it was, and that you'd be out. I just wondered if I could meet you later?"

"Is everything okay?" she repeated.

"Yes, yes. I've just thought of something I wanted to talk to you about."

"Are you sure you're okay?" How many more times was she going to ask me? I wanted to tell her, 'No, I'm not okay. I want to know if you hurt my daughter'.

"Yes, but this can't wait. I just need to ask something about Lena and I'd rather do it face-to-face."

"I could get my mum to drop me off, if you want me to come to yours?" she answered, cheer in her voice.

"Oh no. I'm not in the mood to cook. I thought we could just go for a walk or something."

"You want to come back to Berkley Edge? You're worrying me."

"It's easier for me to come to you that's all."

"Okay. What about meeting at Costa at six?"

"Yeah, that works out great. And I'll get you a toastie or something if you'd like?"

"Sounds like a plan. See you later, Carla."

"See you later, Sophie."

---

I Snapchatted Marcus to see how he was.

**Marcus: Sore, but the drugs are good.**

**Carla: Am I guessing you added bud to the mix?**

**Marcus: *laughing emoticon***

**Carla: How was your dad?**

**Marcus: Not seen him yet. I pretended to still be asleep. Mum left me a bottle of water and a bar of chocolate at the side of my bed with a note saying to ring her at work if I needed anything.**

**Carla: Do you need anything?**

**Marcus: No.**

There was a pause and then he wrote again.

**Marcus: Do you believe me?**

**Carla: I believe you were blackmailed. I find it hard to believe it was Sophie. But now I know not to assume things and to find out the truth.**

**Marcus: She will share my video.**

**Carla: If she's done this, she will not be sharing your video. Trust me.**

I didn't know what my sentence meant because I couldn't imagine hurting a hair on Sophie's head, but then again, a few months ago I wouldn't have thought I was capable of pushing a teenager into a bush and hitting him with barbed wire, so I just let the sentence hang there.

I sent him my address.

**Carla: I don't know how long I'll be living here, but**

**if you need to escape your house, you get a taxi and come here. I'll leave enough money to pay for it under a plant pot next to the door.**

**Marcus: why are you doing this, after what I did to you?**

**Carla: Fuck knows. I'm just going with the flow. Offer stands. Maybe because your dad is a cunt?**

**Marcus: *laughing emojis* Sure is. Thanks.**

---

The rest of the afternoon stretched out ahead of me. I was still tired, but at least I was clean. I looked at the house and had an overwhelming urge to scrub it from top to bottom. So that's what I did, while my mind tried to work through things where there were no answers and it was on a futile quest.

Pulling into the Costa car park at a minute after six, I exited and walked into the coffee shop. Sophie waved at me from a seat in the window and I smiled and walked across. She jumped up and hugged me. I froze. I couldn't help it. It reminded me of impromptu hugs from my daughter. Also, Sophie smelled like Lena. She was wearing the same scent Lena had always worn.

"Your perfume..."

"Oh, yes. Fuck," Sophie said. "I've been wearing it since... you know. It makes me feel closer to her. I didn't think though."

"It's fine." I waved her off. "What do you want to eat and drink, Sophie?"

"I'll come with you," she said.

There was an awkwardness that had never been present before. It stayed while we ate, or rather while I picked over some salt and vinegar crisps and Sophie ate.

We were left with just our drinks.

"So why did you want to see me? Just missing me?" Sophie smiled.

"I came to talk to you about Marcus Bull," I answered.

"Oh God, what's he done now? Is he still not leaving you alone? I'll have a word."

I swallowed. "That's the thing, Sophie. He's told me you've already had a word. Several words. That you blackmailed him."

"That's ridiculous," she spat back. "You can't possibly believe him."

I sighed. "I don't know what I believe anymore, Sophie. All I know for sure is that my daughter is dead."

"Why are you calling me Sophie all the time?" Tears were blossoming at her lashes, threatening to course down, like a skier about to traverse the slope. "You call me Soph. You've *always* called me Soph."

I rubbed a hand down my forehead and over my right eye where a gentle throb came. "Because it's too hard. You were Lena and Soph and I can't have one without the other."

"All I wanted was to belong somewhere," she said as more tears ski'd down her face and off the slope of her top lip.

"What are you saying to me, Sophie?" I lowered my voice.

Her own voice broke. "She was never meant to die."

My chair scraped back. "What the fuck did you do? What the fuck, Sophie, did you do?"

She went in her bag and threw a book across the table.

I recognised my daughter's handwriting although I'd never seen the book before.

"When you asked if I wanted anything from her room." She looked down at the book and then went back into her bag and added two more. "I took her journals because I wanted to know what was in them."

Just when I thought nothing else could shock me. *My daughter wrote in journals?* Journals that had been stolen by Sophie. Taken from me when I could have had chance to listen to my daughter a final time.

"Why did you take them?"

"Protection."

I looked at her down my nose. Who was this girl? Another person who'd never shown me their true self?

"I never thought I'd see the day you looked at me like that, Carla. I always thought of you as my mum. Wanted you as my mum." She tapped the book. "You need to read them and then we can meet again. Tomorrow? Same time, same place?"

"Why? Why can't you just tell me what you did?"

"Oh I will. I'll tell you everything, but first you need to climb down from that pedestal you put yourself on."

"Pardon?"

"Oh I'm not the only one who drove Lena to suicide. You did too," she snapped.

"What?" I said, incredulous.

"Read the journals. See why Lena killed herself. It's all in there. See what *you* did."

I looked up at her in horror.

What *I* did?

# PART 3

## 20

## SOPHIE

Lena and I had been best friends since we were small. Now I had to learn to live without the person who'd been by my side for most of my life. As we'd grown up, we'd had fallouts, times when we weren't as close, but we always came back together.

Now though, there would never be Lena and Sophie. Not anymore.

And I had to live with my part in that and with a loss that left a gaping hole in my life. But you see Lena had one thing I'd always wanted and never had. Well, never *thought* I had. A loving mother.

With hindsight though... fuck... I'd read Lena's journals and seen that no matter what view we hold on other people's perfect lives, sometimes that's just far from the truth.

I thought I'd driven Lena to suicide, had taken her journals thinking they may somehow reveal something about the part I'd played. Wondered if Lena had discovered what I'd been doing behind her back, but her words revealed so much more. I needed to talk to someone about everything and I'd thought that person would be Carla, but now I wasn't so sure. Now I had to wait until Carla had also read her daughter's words and then see what she did.

So for now I would sit here in the coffee shop and ruminate over everything all over again. This was my life now. Memories on repeat.

---

As a child of a single mum, I'd spent a lot of time around childminders. Then at ten years old, all of a sudden Mum decided I was old enough to look after myself while she worked and that was that.

Microwave dinners packed in the fridge and freezer. I'd have one when I was hungry, Mum would have one when she got home from work. She'd ask if I'd done my homework and then she'd sit in front of the television before saying it was time for bed. Groundhog day Monday to Friday.

Weekends were better. She'd let us have a lie in, sometimes make me a bacon sandwich, but then she started going out on a Saturday night, 'now I was old enough to look after myself'. She'd come home at stupid hours of the morning while I'd been sitting in my room, curled up in my bed with the lights off, scared someone would find me home alone. Listening for my mum to come home so I could breathe again.

My mum would get up in the late hours of Sunday afternoon, make a Sunday lunch if she could face it and then it was back in front of the television.

---

One day life changed, because my best friend Lena invited me around to her house for tea. We were eleven and she'd mentioned to her mum how I had to stay on my own. Suddenly I was in another world, where I sat at a table with a mum and a dad and Lena. I'd pretend this was my family, that Lena was my sister. I became so attached to this family that sometimes I dreamed my mum let them adopt me.

Because the older I got, the less she bothered with me. I no longer slept scrunched up beneath the blankets being afraid of intruders. Now I snuck back downstairs, watched TV and had midnight feasts with whatever we had left around the place. It wouldn't be much as we were on a budget being 'not made of money'.

Mum relaxed even more once she knew I was having my tea at Lena's. Stopped asking if I'd done my homework because she knew Carla made us do it the minute we got home. She stopped asking me much of anything. "Everything okay?" she'd say.

"Yes, fine."

"Nothing to report?"

"Nope."

"Good."

That was the grand sum of things, except some weekends she'd let Lena stay over and when she did, she'd not go out that night. She'd pretend she was a proper mum, when really, she was nothing of the sort.

Carla was a proper mum.

When Ant left her for Natalie my young heart broke. It broke for her, for my best friend, and for me because I felt like I'd lost my 'dad' and I'd lost my dreams of them being my forever family.

But even though Carla was in turmoil, she never stopped protecting Lena. Lena came first and I loved her even more for that.

But I couldn't help but be jealous of my best friend.

Even though her parents had split up, she had two loving parents still, and Carla especially worshipped the ground her daughter walked on. She wanted for nothing.

If we were out and Lena saw an eyeshadow palette she wanted, Carla would grab it and then ask me if I wanted something. I'd always pick something cheap, but I'd have something, because my mum always said there was no money for anything like that, even though she could buy alcohol and pay for taxis home.

So that was how it was. Carla and Lena were my family. The one

I'd always wanted. Carla, in particular, the mum I adored. I didn't want my mum and my life. At night, I'd go to sleep praying that when I woke up Carla was my mother.

Of course, it never happened.

---

We grew up, Lena and I, and started talking about college and life away from home and I realised that there was a strong possibility I might lose both Lena's friendship and Carla as life moved on. That I may just be left behind. The invisible girl. So I decided to cause some trouble, so that Lena would realise she needed me in her life, her confidante, always, and that way I'd always be in Carla's life too.

It did piss me off sometimes though when Carla acted like Lena was a saint. Lena could be a right bitch like we all could and her and Chloe Butcher from our class had never really seen eye to eye. Stuff had rumbled away in the background between them for ages, but it had never gone beyond sassing each other.

But as we began approaching our final exam year even that was changing. They were largely just ignoring one another. Everything was heading towards the end of what I knew and I couldn't bear it.

I saw Chloe on her own one day which was rare. Usually Tamsin was glued to her side. Taking advantage, I wandered over.

"What do you want?" she huffed at me.

"Look, I know I'm Lena's best friend but this time she's gone a bit far."

Thick eyebrows rose. "What do you mean?"

I sighed. "She's telling people that you're a thick whore. I've told her it's not on and to stop but she's not listening. Don't say you heard it from me, but I thought I'd give you a heads up, so that maybe you can call her on it."

Chloe's eyes narrowed. "Is this a set up? Why would you help me?"

"Because I think Lena's wrong this time. But if you tell her I told you I'll deny it."

I walked away, expecting that what would happen would be another row between them, more shouting at each other and then I could offer a shoulder for Lena to unburden herself to. Lend my support. Remind her how important I was in her life.

But everything went out of hand on a Friday night in September.

---

"Oh God, Chloe, Tamsin, and Alesha are coming in." Lena rolled her eyes as she looked at me, having been staring out of the window.

My stomach churned a little as there'd been a few dirty looks from Chloe towards Lena at school, but this was the first time we'd bumped into them away from school property.

They got their drinks and sat themselves behind where Lena sat. She took a deep breath. "Look, I don't want them to think they're bothering me, so I'm not turning around. You just let me know if they start anything okay?"

"Yup, you can count on me. I'm your bestie."

Lena smiled at me, but she didn't say anything back.

She'd not been the same really since her parents split up. Lena didn't like to talk about it, but I knew she missed her dad and didn't like Natalie, her father's girlfriend. I guessed it was hard to have to be around your dad and someone who wasn't your mum. Plus, Ant hadn't done this quietly. Everyone in the area knew that he'd moved out of one house and straight to another still in Berkley Edge.

"Oh my paper cup's leaking. Does anyone know a plumber?" Chloe said a little too loudly. I saw my friend's shoulders tense up. She stared at me and closed her eyes for a moment.

"Ignore her," I said.

Lena nodded. "Yeah, I'm not giving her the satisfaction."

"She might have a Michael Kors bag and a Reiss coat, but it

doesn't disguise the fact her father was a plumber who liked to show his customers his pipe," Chloe added. Her two friends cackled.

Lena stood up.

"What are you doing?"

She picked up her bag. "Leaving here before I do something I'll regret."

I followed her out of Costa. Lena strode on ahead. "Hold on. I've not even got my coat on yet," I yelled.

As I caught her up the door had opened and the three girls were outside. Taking the piss, Chloe stomped past Lena. "Not so perfect now are you, you thick ho?"

I gasped as I saw what she'd done. She'd flicked on a lighter and singed Lena's hair. Lena grabbed her hair.

"What have you done?" Though she wasn't sure, she knew Chloe had done something and Chloe now stood in front of her, her hands on her hips laughing.

"Hair still looking hot, girl. Just in a different way."

That was it, before I even knew what was happening, Lena had drawn her fist back and punched Chloe in the eye. Chloe leapt forward shouting, "You stupid fucking bitch, you'll pay for that," and raining fists in the way girls do, anywhere and everywhere hoping one hits. I grabbed Lena and Tamsin grabbed Chloe and we pulled them apart, but I saw that Chloe had landed a hit on Lena's lip, blood running from it.

A crowd had gathered around, the boys of Berkley Edge watching and yelling, 'girl fight'. "Quick, get out of here," I said to Lena. "The Costa staff are coming out. I'll stay and make sure you don't get blamed. I'll come to yours as soon as I can."

"Thanks, Soph."

She rushed on towards home and I hung around making sure that Chloe did not drop my name into conversation. I tried to catch her attention, to warn her not to mention me, but it was impossible. She was gloating about having punched Lena. I'd have to try to get to talk to her later somehow. What on earth was she playing at?

That was actual assault. The last thing I needed was the police involved and Lena finding out I'd had any involvement, although I'd deny it.

One of the lads who was with Chloe's gang watched me. I caught his eyes and narrowed my own. *Fuck*, was he onto me? I figured I'd better get myself out of there and try to catch up with Chloe later.

I texted Lena to say I was on my way. I wasn't expecting her response.

**Lena: No, don't come. My mother's having a meltdown.**

**Me: But I can help. I can tell her it was all Chloe's fault.**

**Lena: It'll just wind her up. I'm in my room and I'm keeping my head down. She keeps coming to check I'm okay. If you come, she'll start asking you five thousand questions.**

**Me: I don't mind.**

**Lena: Well, I do. You've been amazing, Soph. Thanks for being my best friend and having my back.**

**Me: Anytime. You know that. I'll get home and then text you, yeah?**

**Lena: Yep, you can listen to me whine on about my mum lol.**

**Me: Huh, your mum's a saint. I'll trade you for mine.**

---

I walked home, feeling antsy that Lena didn't want me there, but glad she felt I'd had her back. Underneath though, I still felt like I was losing Lena, that she was growing away from me. A feeling I hated.

Once I got home, I texted Lena again and she told me that Chloe had been past her house, sending a photo and threatening them.

Fuck. I really needed to see Chloe. This was not what I'd meant to happen.

I called her.

"Yeah?"

"Where are you?"

"The rec, why? That bitch want a second round?"

"No. I need to talk to you. In private. Go to the trees. I'll come meet you."

The trees at the edge of the recreation ground were visible from my bedroom window. I watched as Chloe made her way there and I slipped out of the house.

"What's so important?" Chloe stared at me like she was bored shitless and sighed. Her head tilted towards me. "And hurry up because Archie's waiting for me."

"What's so *important*? What the fuck were you doing at Costa? Lena called you a thick ho. I thought you'd call her some names back."

"Yeah, well maybe I'd just had enough of Miss Fucking Perfect."

"I still can't believe you burned her hair, you stupid bitch. Her mother could have called the police on you."

Chloe kicked at some stones. "I couldn't help it. I got fucked off."

"You can't go around doing shit like that."

"Feeling guilty are you? Because you're the one who told me she'd been saying I was a thick ho. She thinks she's so fucking perfect, well now she's not. Now, even if only for tonight, her hair's wonky and stinks."

"You need to dial it back because her mum's livid. Especially because you sent that photo of the house. She's taking that personally."

"Look. I'll say a fake sorry, but I did it and right now I'm enjoying my moment. My eye might sting like a bitch, but I finally got to deck her. Now are we done here because I want to get back to the others?"

"Yeah, we're done."

I heard a twig snap from in another direction. Someone was there.

Chloe stalked off, and I pretended to, but instead I sat back near one of the trees at the back nearest my house. After a few minutes Marcus Bull walked out back to the others. He looked back towards where I lived, and I just knew he'd heard everything.

*Fuck.*

Now what?

I turned my phone to silent and sat propped next to a tree trunk and chatted to Lena, while I thought things through. If Marcus backed Chloe up, then that might give Lena doubts. I sat with my head in my hands. I was frustrated because this hadn't accomplished what I'd wanted. For Lena to use me as a shoulder to cry on. If anything, I seemed to have potentially risked our friendship for good.

Male voices approached. I made sure I was out of view but could hear and I listened in.

"You fancy men, Marc?" I heard a voice I recognised as belonging to Archie Hadley state. My ears pricked up because Chloe reckoned to be in with Archie, so I'd see if he said anything about her. And Marc? The boy who may have overheard me and Chloe talking? It wouldn't hurt for me to have one over on him, so what was Archie on about?

"Don't be fucking stupid. I just didn't want to go near that slag."

"Suck my cock," Archie demanded. "I want to see if you do it better than Chloe."

What? Archie was being a right twat to this lad. I had no problems with anyone being gay and Archie wasn't right to give him shit for it. But no matter how much people celebrated Pride month, the fact remained that gay remained a derogatory term around the male teens of Berkley Edge.

"What? Let go of me. Chill out. I'm not gay and you're not funny." I could hear twigs crack under feet as they argued. I switched my phone on to record the conversation.

"I'm serious. I don't want a piss. I've got a fucking hard-on after that prick tease Chloe left me hanging and I keep seeing you looking at me weird. You're not the only one who's confused," Archie said.

"What?" Marc replied.

Indeed. What was I hearing? Was Archie gay too? Whoa, that would certainly be one in the eye for Chloe Butcher!

Straining to hear Archie's voice now I moved closer, praying not to make too much noise, although the two seemed too deep in conversation to be aware of me. I made sure my camera was on them recording and I watched gobsmacked as to what was happening. I'd seen many people head for the trees from my bedroom window, but I'd never been in such close proximity before and for it to be two lads from my school.

"Do it. I want to know what it's like. If we're not into it after, we don't say anything else about it, okay?"

Archie opened his jeans and freed his cock and I watched as Marcus dropped to his knees.

Either of these two were now my willing slaves, but I would focus on Marcus first. Just in case he'd had any ideas on selling me out to Lena.

He left shortly after he'd made his friend come down his throat. I hung back awhile and then I quickened my pace until I'd almost caught up with him.

"Well, well, well. Thanks for teaching me about how to snoop among the trees, cocksucker."

He froze before slowly turning around to face me. I needed him to think I was cocky and sure of myself, so I stood with a hand on one hip, and wore a triumphant grin.

I held my phone up and pressed play. The video started.

Marcus went pale.

"Please, Sophie. My dad would beat the shit out of me. He doesn't get it."

"Marcus, don't worry," I said. "I don't intend to share it. I just need you to do a few things for me."

"Like what?"

"Like keep your mouth shut about seeing me and Chloe talking and maybe I might need you to make Lena's life harder. Give me your number so I can contact you if I need to."

His brow creased. "But I thought Lena was your best mate?"

*She is. She's my best mate, and that's why I've done this. Because I don't want to lose her. I want her to need me.* I realised I'd been staring into space. "She is. I don't have to explain myself to you. Right, I'm going to give you Lena's number. You might need that too."

I left him there and I went home, feeling a lot more secure now I had Marcus at my mercy.

## 21

## SOPHIE

I texted with Lena for the rest of the night until she had to put her phone on charge. Then I missed her in the silence of the early hours of the morning. My mum wasn't here telling me to put my phone on charge, something I knew Lena argued with her own about endlessly. My mum wasn't here at all. She'd started staying out now at weekends unless it was one where she let me have Lena stay over. She did that sometimes when I begged. Begged for her to let Lena stay, because when she did, she acted like a normal mother, like the one I'd always wanted.

Mum had never admitted to having any boyfriends even though I knew she must have. She also refused to tell me anything about my father. There were no photos, nothing. I was pleased I looked like my mum, because otherwise I'd have stared at any male who had my colouring wondering if I belonged to them and if they'd have made a better parent. I missed Ant Haybrook. He might have been a cheater but at least he existed. Was someone Lena had in her life.

I dozed off and when I woke it was just past half seven. Pushing myself up so I was resting against my headboard, I grabbed my phone and scrolled to see the latest posts. Tamsin and Alesha had posted stuff on their walls about Lena, calling her out for saying they were whores. So that was how Chloe had obviously decided to play it. To get her sidekicks to deal out more pressure to Lena without it coming back on her. As long as she kept her mouth shut about me. I chewed the side of my cheek while I considered contacting Marcus. Just to see if he really would do what I asked.

I needed a phone to contact him. One that wasn't mine. Some cheap shit. With a burning desire to find out if he'd resist me or do all I asked, I showered, dressed, and went to the local supermarket and bought a phone. Mum left me a tenner for food when she stayed out overnight and I saved it, so I was able to pay cash. I treated myself to a Maccy's bacon sarnie on the way home and after setting the phone up, I phoned Marcus.

"Yeah?" he said quietly, no doubt not wanting anyone to hear him.

"I want you to ring Lena and threaten her," I told him. "Tamsin and Alesha have started a bit of a hate campaign against her. I want you to add to it."

"Fine," he said. That was it. 'Fine'. No protesting against having to do it, just a one-word answer that he'd do what I asked.

I felt triumphant and then guilty that I was stooping so low as to blackmail someone. But I told myself this was just one time. That I wouldn't do it again. I was sure that once I proved I was the most supportive friend ever that I wouldn't need him to do anything else.

That was what I told myself anyway, to try to justify it to my own brain.

---

Lena texted me about all the vitriol she'd woken up to, that her mother was driving her batshit, but that she was going to the hairdressers to get her hair trimmed and after that Carla had said I could come over and hang out. I could stop for tea, there were pizzas.

**Lena: So please come over and help keep me sane because this is all just so ridiculous.**

**Me: You can count on me, I'll always have your back**.
I messaged in return.
**Lena: You're the best xoxo**

---

I arrived at her house for lunch. Carla made us a full cooked breakfast and even though I'd had bacon that morning, I eagerly ate it all. My own mother had yet to come home and here was Lena's mum cooking the works. She was fussing about all the trouble from last night and this morning. I listened and watched the interaction between the two of them. Their everyday conversations, how they looked at each other. A look of love, concern, and protection from Carla, and a rolling-eyes 'here she goes' gaze from Lena, not realising how much I'd love for my own mum to be so bothered about me that it caused me to actually want her to back off a bit.

We went up to Lena's room after lunch and she put some music on.

"So how are you really feeling about everything?" I asked her.

She shrugged. "I'm just hoping it all dies down. I thought my mum having a go on the main road in front of everyone might make things worse, but social media seems to have quietened down, thank fuck. It's just Marcus ringing that was a bit weird. I get that Alesha and Tamsin will do Chloe's dirty work, but what does any of our bitch fest have to do with him?"

"He hangs around with them though. He was there watching it all last night. No doubt he's wanting to get in one of their pants and so is showing off. They're all so pathetic."

"Yup. Thank God we only have this year with them and then we can go to college away from them hopefully. I tell you, the minute I'm eighteen, I'm out of Berkley Edge."

"Me too. We could share a flat somewhere maybe?"

"Yeah." Lena's eyes lit up. "Get completely away."

We chatted on making plans for a life away from Berkley Edge. A life that still had me in it and I was happy. Things were good. Change was coming, but I was part of it and that was okay.

When I got back home after tea, Mum was back. I beamed at her because I was in a good mood and she was my mum, I loved her. When I saw her I was happy. Happy she was back safe and always hopeful that this would be the time she'd say something to me like Carla would say to Lena.

"Hey, Mum. Did you have a nice night out?"

Mum scowled. "Bloody hell, Sophie, can you dial it down a notch? I've still got a hangover." She made no mention of tea, although I'd eaten at Lena's, and I realised that she just took that for granted now. She didn't feel the need to check, and anyway, she'd just say well there's stuff in the freezer.

"I'm going to catch up with Coronation Street. Have you seen it this week?" she asked me. I hated that programme, but I sat there sometimes while she watched just so I could be in her orbit.

"No."

"Come on then. Why not get your pyjamas on and grab some crisps and snacks?"

Another beam from me. Mum was suggesting a pj party.

We were sat watching the TV when I decided to tell Mum about Lena getting in a fight.

"Soph."

"Yeah?"

"I'm trying to watch TV. It's good Lena stuck up for herself, but tell me after."

I nodded and sat quiet. The programmes finished and Mum got up and told me she was going to bed.

With tears in my eyes, I went to my room, the truth apparent. My mum wasn't interested in me or my life.

I was a nobody.

And that's why I couldn't lose Lena and Carla.

I texted Lena when I went to bed.

**Me: Things still calm?**

**Lena: Yeah, nothing else thank God.**

**Me: Good. Listen, I know this is random but next time you go to your dad's for tea, can I come?**

**Lena: What? You want to go to the skank's house?**

**Me: Just haven't seen your dad in ages. It's weird.**

**Lena: If you saw him, it's still weird. He's like a different person. Just does whatever Natalie wants like a lapdog. I hardly go there myself because it's pointless. The minute he gives me any attention she starts crawling on his lap. Makes me want to barf. I was supposed to go this weekend, but I said no.**

**Me: Least you have one to turn down. I wonder who mine is. Any single person who walks past could be my dad. Hey, even your dad could be my dad!! We could be sisters and not know it.**

**Lena: Lol.**

Lol.

Funny was it, to think we could be sisters. Or was that just an awkward response to the subject of my not knowing who my dad was?

At least Ant wouldn't have babies with Natalie because Lena told me she'd been sterilised cos she didn't want any. She'd still always be her dad's golden child even if Natalie's pussy had temporarily taken his attention.

My dad might have other children. I might have brothers and sisters who'd want to spend time with me. I asked my mum again at breakfast the next day.

"Sophie. How many more times? You want to know about your dad? He wasn't anyone you would want to know. He was a complete waste of fucking air. Just drop this subject once and for all." She slammed the door and left for work twenty minutes earlier than usual.

---

Things calmed down between Chloe and Lena. They ended up making a kind of truce. An agreement that they wouldn't be friends, but they wouldn't bitch about each other either. Anyway, the focus of mirth at the moment was the fact Tamsin was dating Marcus. She was fifteen and he was fourteen. She braved it out, I'd give her that, saying he was a hottie and she was teaching him things. Yeah? I wanted to say like how to act heterosexual, but of course I didn't. I'd noticed Marcus and Archie no longer hung around together and indeed Marcus now seemed to be heading up his little gang.

I was excited about the future. Lena intended to do something in retail when she left school and so was going to do a business course or similar and I was going to the same college to do hair and beauty. Lena'd talk about having her own clothes store one day and I'd talk about my salon.

"Hey, just think, we could have our shops nearby and I could do their style makeover and then send them to you for a new wardrobe."

"Great idea," Lena said.

And so I dreamed of future businesses and future flat sharing until I discovered that while it was real to me, while I'd banked on it all happening, Lena was talking what my mum would describe as 'hot air'.

I was round for tea on a Saturday and chatting about how I'd like my salon to look.

"You need to get some savings behind you for that, Soph," Carla said.

"Oh I know. I'll have to get my qualifications, work my way up and then look into the business side of things, but I'll get there eventually."

"Would you stay here in Berkley Edge?"

I looked at Lena. "Hey, we never said where we'd live and work."

Lena shrugged her shoulders. "I'm not planning my life for the next God knows how many years. I'm just focusing on today."

"But we're going to flat share and have our shops near each other."

Lena talked through chewing her food. "Soph. Put your shop wherever you want. Don't build your dreams around me."

I was about to start arguing, but Carla interrupted. "God, there's plenty of time for you to plan your futures. Right now, you girls just need to focus on your exams. Otherwise you might not get into the college you want."

"Yeah, I need five GCSE's grade B or above to get into Brierly," Lena said.

"Brierly?" My cutlery clattered down onto my plate as I dropped them. "We're going to Tankersley."

"Oh, did I not tell you?" Lena looked confused. "I applied for Brierly Business College. Mrs Temberly thought I could get the grades and they have links to a few retailers like Sainsbury's. I might get work in their clothes department, projects etc."

"Th- that's amazing," I said, while thinking it wasn't amazing at all.

Brierly was out of my league. I would not get the grades to go there, even if I suddenly decided to switch to a business course.

So there was only one thing for it.

I had to make sure that Lena was so distracted, she failed to get the grades to go there either.

---

I called Marcus and told him that he had to damage Carla's car and I sent the video to him so he'd be reminded of what I'd send viral if he didn't do what I said. We arranged that it would happen on Sunday evening because Lena was coming to stay overnight at my house so I knew Carla would usually go to bed early.

All the time Lena was at my house I was fidgety, to the point where she asked me if I was okay.

"No, not really," I said and I confessed that my mum was staying out more and more and that what she put on around us was an act. That I could do with Lena moving in, so I had a nice mum all of the time.

"You are so dramatic." Lena laughed.

Yes, my life was hilarious to Lena who didn't believe me when I told her my mother ignored me.

I'd just get comments like, 'I wish mine would ignore me'.

She just had no idea because she was the perfect child in an almost perfect life. Perfect grades. Perfect face. Perfect body. Perfect hair. Mum and Dad who adored her even if they had split up.

And she didn't seem to even realise.

I felt my phone buzz in my pocket, so I excused myself to go to the loo and then I looked at my messages.

**Marcus: I've done something. I think it's better than car damage.**

My heart thudded in my chest. What the fuck had he done? He should have done what I told him. I typed quickly, my fingers flying across my keys.

**Me: What did you do? You SHOULD do exactly what I asked. If you fucked up, the vid goes out.**

**Marcus: I didn't fuck up. I needed a shit and so I smeared it across her windscreen. Meant I didn't make any sound that would alert her or anyone else of what I was doing.**

I almost gagged at the thought, but he'd actually done something I considered worse than damage, so I was okay with it.

**Oh man. You're a sick fuck, Marcus. But you can crack on with your sad life now hopefully.**

Hopefully, this would be enough to cause unrest in the Haybrook household and I could ramp up the tension myself.

It wasn't long after Lena got home from school the following day before she called me.

"You are not going to believe what's happened."

"Natalie kicked your dad out?"

"No, Marcus Bull smeared his own shit on my mum's windscreen. Sick fuck."

What? She knew who'd done it?

"He did what? How do you know?"

"Mum had the CCTV sorted after Chloe threatened the house. You can tell it's him cos of the clothes he wears although you can't make him out. She's ringing the police, but I doubt they'll do anything because the picture is grainy."

"What a sick fuck. Why would he do that?"

"It's obviously revenge for Tamsin. Chloe reckoned she'd called off her little bitches but looks like they still have a score to settle. Stupid prick, I'll kill him."

Fuck.

"You're better off ignoring him. If he's capable of doing that, what else is he capable of? Just let your mum handle it with the police."

She huffed. "Yeah, I suppose you're right. Just fucks me off. I've never done anything to him and neither has my mum. She had to clean his faeces off."

I made a heaving noise. "That's awful."

"Yeah and now my mother's paranoid again. I don't know how she expects me to concentrate on revising when she's in my room blathering on every five seconds."

"She's just concerned. At least—"

"Yeah, I know. At least I have a mother who's bothered. It's just—"

"What?"

"Nothing. I'm just wound up. I'll see you tomorrow, okay?"

"Call me later if you want?"

"I doubt I'll get the chance with my mother on one."

Despite Lena saying she'd let her mum and the police handle it, the next day at school I found her tearing into Marcus.

Fuck.

I legged it over as fast as I could.

"What's going on?" I panted, narrowing my eyes at Marcus.

"I'm just telling this little shit I know it's him. Little shit being the right word. I've never done anything to you, leave me alone."

"He's not worth it, Len." I hooked my arm through Lena's to lead her away and then spun around to Marcus. "You're disgusting. You'd better leave her the fuck alone from now on."

He said nothing. Later I texted him.

**Me: Make sure you keep your mouth shut. Don't think your dad would be too impressed with you shitting on cars. Could be his new slogan at the showroom: Shit cars a specialty.**

**Marcus: I won't say anything. Stop threatening me. I'm doing what you asked.**

---

It took an age for the police to visit Carla. When they did all Lena told me was they couldn't do anything.

I breathed a sigh of relief that I'd got away with it again.

Then the following night she told me the police had been around to see him. I thought I'd die on the spot. I thought she was phoning to tell me she knew everything. That he'd said it was me.

I could have passed out when she didn't.

"You didn't say the police were going round."

"I'll be honest, Soph. I'm sick of talking about it. My mother never shuts up. Anyway, hopefully now the cops went round that'll be an end to it. Right, rescue me, bestie, talk to me about hair and make-up or something. Tell me about our shops again."

I did so happily.

## 22

## SOPHIE

Time went on. Lena started dating a lad in our year called Lee. That didn't bother me. I was happy for her. Part of my own dream was to meet the love of my life, and live happily ever after with my own family. One I would love dearly. They would never know the feeling of being ignored. It also meant Lena was distracted from her studies cos she was in lurve. While she went out with Lee, I started hanging around with some other girls my age. Occasionally it'd be Tamsin, Alesha, and Chloe. They were all okay now, them and us. Still, when I bumped into Carla while out at the local shopping centre, I didn't want her to see them, so I told them I'd meet them outside the store and made my way over to Carla.

"Carla," I shouted. It was strange seeing her shopping on her own. She usually shopped with Lena or the two of us.

"Hey, Soph. You spending all your pocket money?" She hugged me and I lost myself for a moment in her warm hug.

"We're just looking and dreaming about all the things we wish we could afford."

"We?"

*Shit.* "Yeah, I'm with some mates. They've just gone outside to buy cookies, so I'll need to catch them up." She started to look around, so I quickly changed the subject. "That blouse is nice."

Carla held it up looking undecided. "You think so? Usually I drag Lena with me as you know so I can get some advice but she's studying with Lee."

*Huh, probably studying her bedroom walls while you're out.*

"Yeah, I know. I should be studying myself really, but the girls dragged me out." I had a thought. Maybe I could take Lena's place and help Carla decide on some outfits? "Though if you want, I can come round with you and help you choose some stuff?" I said.

"Nah, don't be daft. You hang around with your mates. But thanks for taking pity on this old woman," she said, smiling at me.

I smiled back. "Don't be daft. I'd always make time for you. You're like a mum to me."

She squeezed my arm and gave me a loving look and once more I wished that either my mum gave me that look, or Carla would adopt me.

"What do you think to Lee?" she asked me. "He seems nice to me, nice and quiet, but I don't really know him. He's in your year, isn't he?" She picked at imaginary fluff on the blouse. Carla worried too much sometimes but it showed she cared.

"I have some of my classes with him. He's really nice, Carla. You don't have any need to worry. He's not one of the idiots. In fact, he's a lot like Lena. Quiet and studious. She'll be glad she can actually get some studying done, cos when she's with me I get bored easily and start chatting."

Carla laughed. "I can't believe the both of you are about to take your exams and move on."

"I know, bit different from when you were helping us learn our times tables. Now we need to know algebra, ugh." I looked back towards where the girls had gone. "Anyway, I'd better go. You need to get that blouse."

"Thanks. I will." She put it over her arm. "She's not pushing you out, is she? I mean, you spent a lot of time together and now she's spending a heap of time with Lee."

"Nah. We're fine." I reassured her, because we were. Our friendship was solid. Lots of talk about what we'd do when we left school.

"Good, because I can't imagine not seeing little Soph at ours."

I giggled. "I don't think I'm so little now."

I said goodbye. Life was good. I was studying for my exams and while I wasn't a natural student I felt I'd get what I needed for my college course, and I was an important part of Carla and Lena's life, even if my own mother still continued to pretend she didn't have a child beyond my sitting watching the soaps with her in silence. She'd been making an effort to ask me if I was studying every day and was aware when my exams started which made a change, but I still would have been existing on microwave dinners were it not for the proper meals I got at Carla's a couple of times a week.

---

We did some mock exams. Despite the fact I'd tried to chatter through our revision sessions and she'd been seeing Lee, Lena sailed through them. It looked like if I couldn't persuade her to come to Tankersley with me then I might have to resort to getting Marcus on board again.

I knew what I'd done was wrong, but I couldn't help myself. Sometimes you could tell yourself your actions were excusable if you felt it was for the greater good. Lena needed me. I'd been with her throughout her life and through her parents splitting up, her first love break up when she'd been ten, her getting her period before me. She was my family.

After six weeks, Lee ended things with Lena. Once more I made sure I was a shoulder to cry on, but she didn't actually seem too upset. She did tell me she wanted to study though and she started to put me off coming round, saying she wanted to concentrate.

She was pushing me away again and I couldn't let that happen.

Over the next months I got Marcus to throw a brick through Carla's living room window. I got him to run up to her at school and threaten her. I found out flour was thrown at Carla's car and it was scratched and I hadn't even asked him to do that.

It brought her back to me a little, but Lena was still determined to study and ended our calls early to do so.

I told myself that it was just because she was studying and once the exams were over she'd be my close friend once more. But I wasn't sure I believed it. It was what led to my final moments of madness. I say final as in the last things I did to Lena, because after that...

She killed herself.

---

"Are you okay, love?" I looked up to see one of the Costa staff staring at me with concern.

I nodded, grabbing a napkin to wipe my eyes and nose. "Boyfriend trouble," I lied.

"Wait there." She said. I pulled myself together as the woman returned with a chocolate chip muffin.

"It's on me. It's not Ben & Jerry's but it's still tasty."

"Thank you." I smiled, though inside my heart was breaking. I made my way home.

"Hey, love. How've you been?" my mum asked the minute I stepped through the door. The mum I'd always wanted was in front of me. Asking how I was, making me proper dinners on the days she was off work. But now I felt like Lena must have done, like my every move was being watched.

Now I'd do anything to be able to turn back time and stop everything I'd done. Although she might have killed herself anyway, at least I wouldn't feel like I'd helped fill the tablet bottle.

I went up to my room, having told my mum I had a bit of a headache. I'd not told her I'd met Carla. Instead, I said I'd met Chloe, when really I'd seen no one since I'd left school. I laid down on my bed and thought about my last days with my best friend.

---

"Let's go get a taco, I'd kill for one." Lena begged. "You get my mum to agree, because she'll never say yes to me. She thinks I'm going to get attacked by Marcus every time I step outdoors."

So I did. I told Carla that she had to let us get tacos because it was law in the school holidays that you ate at Taco Master and that I'd be there to look out for Lena.

I could tell Carla wasn't happy, but she let us go.

We were just heading inside when I spotted Marcus behind us. Of all the people to bump into. But it made sense. Berkley Edge kids loved their fast food.

"Fucking hell, Marcus is here. I'll go and deal with him. You go get us a seat."

Lena had been happy up until that point and all the spark went out of her. "Jesus. I can't even enjoy my taco."

"I'll get rid of him. Go, get us a seat."

"You okay, Marcus?" I said once I'd reached him.

"I was," he replied. "Now, I'm not so sure."

"Meaning?"

I was shocked when Marcus' nostrils flared. "Sophie, are we nearly done? I've been following your instructions like a good little puppet now for long enough, and if I end up with the police at my door then I may as well just tell my dad everything because he'll beat the fucking shit out of me anyway."

"Yeah." I smiled. "I'm done with you now. You're free. Go in and enjoy your taco. Thanks for being my bitch, but I don't need you anymore.

"And the video of me?"

"Well, obviously, I'll keep it safe, but I promise you've earned your freedom." I looked at Marcus then and his face showed such utter relief that I was stopping using him, that for a moment I wanted to fall to my knees and apologise for what I'd made him do. "I'm sorry it had to be this way and I hope that if you do like guys, you get to live a happy life with some dude somewhere down the line," I said.

"You're crazy," he yelled at me.

I shrugged my shoulders. "I'm just doing what I need to do to make sure my own life turns out okay." I turned and went back into the shop.

"Everything okay?" Lena asked me. She'd ordered and received our tacos within the time I'd been outside.

"He was showing off as usual. Saying he was gonna stab you. Yeah, right?"

Lena's eyes widened.

"I'm just going to get some chilli sauce. You want anything else?"

"Just to eat this and get out of here. I'm losing my appetite."

"I won't let anything happen to you, Len."

I stood behind Marcus in the queue. He kept turning around to me looking pissed off. I definitely couldn't ask him to do anything else. I was lucky I'd got away with it this far. Anyway, there was always Archie. I'm sure he wouldn't want anyone seeing the video either, so I wasn't yet out of options.

Marcus left after he got his order.

I went back to our table.

"We need to go tell your mum, Lena. I saw in Marcus' bag. He did actually have a knife," I lied.

She didn't want to say anything, but I made her. Wanted to show Carla just how much I looked out for my best friend. Carla went apeshit and called 999. I knew they wouldn't do anything because of course I'd seen no such thing in Marcus' bag, so even if they found him there'd be nothing there.

I was the dutiful best friend until on Thursday, everything blew up.

It was half past nine in the evening and suddenly my phone was pinging with notifications. As I looked at what was happening, I immediately phoned Lena.

"Fuck, Lena. Where did they get the vid?" I asked.

"Well, it has to have come from Lee, doesn't it? He's the one who took it."

"Did you know he was filming you?"

"Of course not," she snapped.

"Sorry. Do you want me to come over?"

"And do what? You can't make it go away, can you?"

"No, but I can help you form a plan to deal with it."

"I'm tired, Soph. I can't be bothered to think about it tonight. I'm going to have an early night, turn my phone off and deal with it tomorrow. Mum said that she might have found us a new place to live, so that's something. She even mentioned a room for you."

"Really?" *Oh my god. A room for me? To stay sometimes or permanently?* I couldn't ask because I needed to be there for my friend, but maybe something good would come out of this. "Well, it's clear you're innocent in all this. Your mum will sort it. She'll need to call the police again."

"Tomorrow, Soph. Let's talk about it tomorrow."

"Okay, okay." I'd get off the phone and think about our potential new place.

"Night, Soph. Thank you for being my best friend. I love you."

"Love ya too, babes. Speak tomorrow."

She ended the call.

And then during the night, she ended her life.

---

The next morning when I called, her phone just kept ringing out and then it started going straight to voicemail. If I could have seen into Carla's house I would have known that she was dealing with having found Lena's body. That she turned off Lena's phone after seeing all the hate messages and mocking about the video. Couldn't cope with it. She'd phoned Ant.

Ant got my mum's number from Carla.

When my mum came through the door just after lunch, she looked at me in such a way that I just knew.

Lena hadn't answered my calls.

She never didn't answer me.

And my mum never came home in an afternoon and most certainly didn't wear a look of concern on her face.

"Sophie. You need to sit down."

"No, I don't. What's happened? Just tell me."

She moved closer.

"Lena died, sweetheart. She took some tablets. I'm so very sorry."

Time stood still.

I told my mum about my last conversation with Lena, about the video, and how she said she'd deal with it today. Then darkness descended because my mind could not process that my friend was no longer there.

Mum called a doctor and they gave me some sedatives to calm me down because I kept asking to see Carla.

"Carla and Ant will be busy, Soph. Look how upset you are. They need time to themselves."

"She's like a mum to me."

"Ouch," my own mum said.

I looked at her and grief made me spit out my every thought about my mother. I could see each one hit like an acupuncture needle, burning as it twisted.

But she still held me as I cried.

The woman who'd been a poor attempt at a mother, suddenly made changes. Cut down on her working hours. She apologised for being a shit mum and begged for another chance.

My feelings were mixed. Was this just guilt and would wear off? Then would everything return to usual?

What about Carla? She might need me.

I sent Carla texts but apart from the odd short reply there was no other communication. Even though I knew she was grieving, I couldn't help but feel abandoned. She'd not even spoken a word to me since this had happened. Just these few-worded text replies.

Guilt swarmed my system because I wondered how much of the suicide was attributable to what I'd set in motion.

I was in a living nightmare. So I let the sedatives help me through and let my mother act like a parent.

---

The next week was the worst week of my life to date. I couldn't cope with the thoughts in my own head. My mother was concerned, and despite her now being the mum I'd always wanted, at this time I didn't want her. She was suffocating me and I wondered if she thought I might try to do the same thing Lena had. I'd be lying if I said it hadn't crossed my mind. But no, someone had to make sure Carla was okay. Lena would want me to do that.

Eventually, the day of the funeral arrived and we sat either side of Carla in the funeral car while Ant and Natalie sat with us. It was a surreal experience as we slowly followed the hearse containing the coffin my best friend's body laid in.

None of it seemed real.

Carla seemed so alone. Anthony kept looking at her, but he was with Natalie now. My mum held Carla's hand the whole way through. They'd never actually been friends. My mum was just that to Carla, my mum; and yet now Carla hung onto my mum's hand like it was the only thing stopping her from floating away.

After the service, I could tell that Carla needed away from the people there.

"Do you want to have a walk in the fresh air?"

She nodded. Mum stepped forward to come with us, but I shook my head at her, so instead she held back.

As we began to walk down the path, I spoke.

"My mum says she's cutting back her hours at work. She wants to spend more time with me."

"That's nice," Carla replied.

No it wasn't 'nice', it was guilt. "I'm sixteen years old. Up until now I've grown up with you and Lena mainly. She's too late. Where was she while I was studying for these exams? It's okay working and saying someone needs to pay the bills, but we could have lived in a smaller home. She could have bought less clothes and handbags. And when she was at home, she wanted 'me-time'. Now she wants to be around, but I'm used to her absence."

She carried on walking. Didn't look at me. "Everything changed a week ago, Soph. Life is no longer what went before. Now I don't have a daughter, but you now have a mother. It's the yin and yang of life. My loss is your gain."

"Our loss," I said, not being able to help my tone. She wasn't the only one who'd lost Lena.

"Yes, sorry, our loss."

I felt guilty then, that I'd made it about me. We walked for a few more minutes in silence.

"I'm moving to the rental I found. My house will go up for sale eventually, but right now I don't want to change anything in her room. Yet I can't bear to be near it either. I'm spending stupid amounts of my savings having two places, but I don't care. I need somewhere to be close to her and somewhere I can escape. Does that make sense?"

"Yes. Completely."

"We'd better go back. People are expecting us at the wake. Your mum will be calling you any minute."

"My phone is off."

There was another pause in conversation while we walked.

"I wonder what he's doing while I bury my child," she said quietly, and my stomach turned over. She meant Marcus, of course. She blamed him for it all, and in doing so, she didn't know, but she blamed me.

I unzipped my handbag, pulled out my phone and turned it on.

"What are you doing?" she asked me.

"I have Marcus on my social media from a long time ago. You know, the times when you just accepted friend requests from anyone and everyone? I'd message him from time to time through Snapchat or Insta and tell him to leave Lena alone," I lied.

"You never said."

"I thought you'd tell me to sever the link and I didn't want to. I felt like I could keep an eye on him that way."

"Is there anything else I don't know?"

"He keeps his gang of friends because he buys them all weed. Maybe they do like hanging with him, maybe they just use him. I don't know. But that's what the gossip at school is. I didn't tell you that because Lena asked me not to. She thought you'd try to snitch about it to the police and she was scared you'd annoy a drug dealer or something."

Carla half laughed. "That sounds like Lena."

I selected a photo and made my face look annoyed.

"What is it?"

"You're better off not knowing. I know he did so many bad things and I know you hate him, but Lena would want you to have your fresh start, Carla. Forget Marcus Bull."

*Because I need you to let this go, so you don't find out what I did. Because then I'd lose you too and I couldn't stand it.*

She snatched the phone from my hand. "You know I can't do that."

The photo I showed her was of Marcus with his friends. They were all posing like they lived in the ghetto, not Berkley Edge.

"It's probably better you forget him now, especially if he's involved with drug dealers."

She handed my phone back to me.

"Yes, you're right. It's time I moved on."

Inside, relief flooded my body at her words. "Focusing on Marcus Bull just brings me more grief. I have to accept; *we* have to accept, that some things in life are evil, but we can live our lives away from them."

Then she turned to me. "Let your mum back in. You've years to spend together yet if you're lucky. Take your second chances, Sophie, because I'd do anything to have a second chance with Lena. I'd have moved us away earlier and then she might still be alive."

Her words hit home. It was all I'd ever wanted. For my mum to be a mum. Could she really change? Could that happen now? But it wasn't that simple. Carla had always been my mother figure. Lena was gone, but I was still here.

---

A week or so passed and Carla phoned to tell me she was at the house. She wanted me to come over and take anything I wanted from Lena's room.

I knew what I wanted.

Lena's journal.

She'd mentioned it once or twice. Said she wrote poems and thoughts in it. That it wasn't a diary, she didn't record her whole day, but it let her work through shit. She'd told me it was kept under her wardrobe, stuffed right at the back, in a place her mother never cleaned. She'd joked and said if anything ever happened to her, I had to destroy it.

Now I'd try to get it and see if she'd noted the things that had happened to her, that I was responsible for. See if I caused my best friend's suicide.

Standing at the door of Lena's house, I took a deep inhale and knocked lightly. It was the first time I'd been here since Lena died.

Carla answered and gestured me inside and told me to go up. She didn't hug me or anything. She looked distracted and tired and well... lost. So I nodded and made my way upstairs.

Pushing open the door, I was assaulted by the smell of Lena, of the scent she always wore that hung just slightly in the air. Or maybe

I imagined it because it had always been there? But I couldn't quit imagining seeing her dead body lying on the bed. I quickly got to the floor and reached for the journal. There were three, which surprised me. I stuffed them into my handbag and opened up her jewellery box. In it were the remnants of the friendship bracelet I'd made for her when we were eleven. I still had mine in my jewellery box too. I lifted it out and decided I'd weave them together, friends forever.

"I'm sorry, Lena," I said softly into the air. There had been so many, many good times happen between us. I couldn't face it if I found out that in trying to not lose her, I'd actually caused her to leave.

Making my excuses to Carla, who seemed glad for me to leave anyway, I went home and started to read the journals.

And I found out that the responsibility for my best friend's death hadn't been helped by my actions, but ultimately wasn't my fault at all.

## 23

## SOPHIE

I called Carla once a week. I'd made the decision to keep what I'd found in the journals to myself. There was nothing to be gained by anyone reading them. It would just cause more pain and heartache. I threw myself into my studies and my exams started. It was a way of existing, of managing to get through the days. I bought some Miss Dior and started wearing it so that I felt my friend was nearby. I was determined to do the best I could in my exams because my best friend had believed in me. She believed I could totally run my own beauty and hair salon and I would. I would make her proud.

But sometimes when I was alone in the house, when my mum was at work, the sorrow invaded and I could barely breathe.

The last thing I expected was Marcus Bull at my door.

But one day there he was.

"What the fuck are you doing here?"

"You wouldn't answer my messages, so I had to come here. We might have a problem."

I invited him inside, dread slithering through me. I'd thought all my ties to this boy were gone and done. It was dangerous for us to potentially be seen together because we weren't people who hung out. It would be gossip fodder.

I listened while he told me about his dad's car having been scratched and about shit on the windscreen and how he thought it could be Carla behind it.

The stress had me scrubbing a hand through my hair. I didn't see how it could be anyone else doing it, and if it was, she needed to stop before things escalated. "Fucking hell. Look, I'll contact her and if it is her, I'll get her to stop, okay? Don't worry about it. Just make sure you stick to not saying a word, otherwise I'll add to your stress by circulating the video."

"Stop threatening me," he spat out. "I've told you I won't rat you out. Just check if it's Mrs Haybrook because I don't know who else would do this, but my dad is using me as football practice."

Fuck. He was getting beat up by his arsehole dad for the trouble. Not only did I not want that on my conscience, but if pushed too far he might just tell all. "I'll sort it. Listen, I'll get a new phone and message you, okay? I've got your number written down."

"You destroyed the other one?"

Was he serious? "What do you think?"

There was silence then and I wondered what words hung unspoken in the air between us. "Why did you do it, Sophie?" he finally asked.

I felt the emotion burn at my eyeballs. "She wasn't meant to die," I said. "I was just supposed to live."

Seeing him open his mouth to ask me more, I couldn't cope. Because I would break down in front of this boy who was no one to me. So instead I yelled, "Now get out, Marcus. You can't be here."

His face wore the expression of someone not only kicked like a football physically, but also in life. Like he'd tried to connect with me in that moment, our lives entangled by what we'd overheard about each other, and I wondered if he really enjoyed being part of the gang he led, or if like me, he'd just been trying to survive.

In my calls to Carla, I'd ask if she'd been to Berkley Edge, but she denied it. Said she couldn't face being at the house at the moment.

Then as we turned into July, I heard Marcus and Damon had been in a fight and Marcus had been suspended. Chloe filled me in on all the gossip. How Damon had supposedly nicked Marcus' money and Marcus had in turn thrown a brick through his mum's car windscreen, accidentally leaving his signet ring behind as evidence.

Horrified, I wondered if Marcus' father had beaten him again. It looked like it was Damon who'd been behind everything then, not Carla after all.

Chloe also said that Marcus was starting to pull away from the group. I didn't blame him. I'd have done the same. I truly did hope that one day fate gave Marcus a helping hand, and got him away from his father, and away from people who couldn't accept his sexuality.

I'd last seen Carla physically in May. Though I understood she was still grieving, I wanted to see her and make sure she was okay. I also wondered how she was getting on with the house she'd been decorating and when I'd be able to stay over. I could talk about Lena and be a bit of company.

Every phone call started with the same topic of conversation from Carla though. My relationship with my own mother.

"I hope you're being okay with your mum, Soph. You have a chance I'd love to have again with Lena."

Here we went again. I told her once more that I couldn't suddenly be all besties with my mum after years and years of her not taking much notice of my existence.

"Yeah, I get that," she said.

Did she? Did she really? Or did she just want me and my mum to be perfect because her and Lena were no more? Did she want rid of me? I couldn't let that happen. I still needed Carla; she was the one person I had always been able to rely on.

"I miss you, Carla, and I worry about you. Are you okay in that house on your own?" I pressed, trying to give her a hint at inviting me round.

"I'm fine, honestly. Just working a lot and doing a bit of decorating."

"Is my room ready yet?" Shit. I couldn't help myself. It had just slipped out and now I sounded like I was pushing her.

"Pardon?"

"My room. I know it's difficult with Lena and everything, but you were like a second mum to me, like an auntie or something. I miss you."

She was quiet and I thought, fuck, I've pushed too far.

"Can't I come for tea one night?" I practically begged.

"Yes, of course. Let me get a bit straighter, and just have a little more time to myself and then course you can come and have tea or something."

My breath rushed out in an exhale of relief.

"Great. I can tell you all the latest gossip. Marcus and his mate Damon got into it last week. Massive fight. He knocked one of Damon's bottom teeth out."

"How'd you know that?"

"Chloe told me. Marcus got suspended. Him and Damon aren't friends anymore, and so he's not looking like the king of school so much now. Damon's more popular, weed or not."

"Good. I don't want Marcus living a happy life. Does that make me a bad person, Soph?" she confided.

"No, it makes you a mum. Well, I'll let you go. Hurry up and get that place straight, so I can visit, okay?"

"Okay, Soph."

I hung up. It looked like it hadn't been Carla after all. Of course, Damon had known everything. He'd clearly psyched Marcus out to take his place as gang leader. And soon—not now but soon—I could go and see Carla.

It turned out to be sooner than I'd thought.

Three days later I was being dropped off at Carla's new place by my mum. The first thing I noticed was her new haircut. She'd put weight on too. She looked different. It was like she'd tried to match her outside to her insides. Wearing grief in the greyness of her pallor and the drab brown of her hair. My mother's words, 'death warmed up' sprung to mind. How she used to describe herself after hangovers. But I didn't mention the change. It wasn't as if she'd had a glam makeover, was it?

My mum got out of the car and chatted to Carla on the doorstep about what time to fetch me home and then there were just the two of us.

I was pleased to be there because it meant that now Carla and I could help each other to heal.

It was so strange being in a different place. I took a seat at the table, but it was uncomfortable. I didn't know what I'd thought. That things would magically become okay? But of course they didn't.

"So how did your last exams go?"

I shrugged. "I don't know. I did what I could. I'll hopefully get what I need for college."

"Well, that's all you need."

"Revising helped to occupy my mind," I confessed. "Funny really, that for all I didn't want to do it, in the end it was one of the only ways I could get through the day."

"It's hard," she admitted. "Every day is hard."

That was it. The moment I realised that nothing would ever be the same again. That there would be no room for me here, no regular invite for tea. Carla Haybrook as I'd known her no longer existed.

I burst out crying. She flew over to me and I sank into the comfort of her arms as inside I said goodbye. We could only unite in grief I realised as Carla cried too. Eventually, Carla moved away from me.

"I'm so sorry—" I told her.

"Don't feel sorry about grieving, Soph. It comes in waves and doesn't let you know when a huge one's about to crash. I hope you can find your appetite though."

I made myself eat the food she'd cooked for me as she'd done all my favourites and I politely answered the questions about school and prom. I tried to make the sadness in her face lift a little, but it didn't.

"So have you heard anything else about Marcus?" she asked.

"He's become a complete loner. Doesn't have friends anymore. Not since it all kicked off between him and Damon."

"Good. It doesn't matter to me what happens to him now. I'm just glad he's not living his best life."

"He definitely isn't," I assured her, and guilt flooded through me once more as I thought of the boy I'd bullied.

---

When Carla's number appeared on my phone two days later, I was surprised, because she didn't phone me. The effort was always on my part. I was at work and not supposed to answer my phone, but I snuck into the toilets and pressed to answer.

"Everything okay, Carla?"

"Oh shit, Sophie. I totally forgot what day it was, and that you'd be out. I just wondered if I could meet you later?"

"Is everything okay?"

"Yes, yes, I've just thought of something I wanted to talk to you about."

She sounded desperate. I didn't like it.

"Are you sure you're okay?"

"Yes, but this can't wait. I just need to ask something about Lena and I'd rather do it face-to-face."

"I could get my mum to drop me off, if you want me to come to yours?"

"Oh no. I'm not in the mood to cook. I thought we could just go for a walk or something."

"You want to come back to Berkley Edge? You're worrying me."

"It's easier for me to come to you that's all."

"Okay. What about meeting at Costa at six?"

"Yeah, that works out great. And I'll get you a toastie or something if you'd like?"

"Sounds like a plan. See you later, Carla."

"See you later, Sophie."

I made up a story about having a migraine to get out of work early because something was clearly wrong with Carla and I had absolutely no idea what it was.

When I got home, I placed Lena's journals in my bag, just in case, and then when the time moved around to half past five, I walked to Costa and sat there waiting.

I watched as Carla's car pulled into the car park. She smiled as she approached and that settled me somewhat. Until I jumped up to hug her and she froze. Carla had never, ever frozen in my embrace, not even at her daughter's funeral.

Oh my god.

"Your perfume..."

"Oh, yes. Fuck," I said. God, I'd never thought. No wonder she'd frozen. I should have had a shower. She must have thought I was pretending to be Lena. "I've been wearing it since... you know. It makes me feel closer to her. I didn't think though."

"It's fine." She dismissed it. "What do you want to eat and drink, Sophie?"

"I'll come with you," I said.

All the time we were sat there, I waited for Carla to tell me why she was here, why she'd asked me to meet her. The suspense felt like I was on a slowly moving torture rack, and I was heading for the pain to start at any moment.

"So why did you want to see me? Just missing me?" I smiled, hoping that's all this was after all and that seeing me the other day had just brought back some memories of Lena she wanted to chat about with me.

"I came to talk to you about Marcus Bull," she said.

And there it was.

His name hung between us, dropped like a hangman's noose. I had to act stupid.

"Oh God, what's he done now? Is he still not leaving you alone? I'll have a word."

"That's the thing, Sophie. He's told me you've already had a word. Several words. That you blackmailed him."

"That's ridiculous," I said getting agitated now as I looked at her expression. One of disappointment and disgust. "You can't possibly believe him."

She sighed. "I don't know what I believe anymore, Sophie. All I know for sure is that my daughter is dead."

"Why are you calling me Sophie all the time?" Tears were beginning to run down my face as I realised the end of my relationship with the woman I'd thought a mother to me was here. "You call me Soph. You've *always* called me Soph."

"Because it's too hard. You were Lena and Soph and I can't have one without the other."

I wanted to throw up as my world tilted.

"All I wanted was to belong somewhere," I said, desperation in my tone.

Carla's voice dropped down. "What are you saying to me, Sophie?"

My confession fell from my lips. "She was never meant to die."

Carla recoiled. She pushed back on her chair, like I had a deadly disease. "What the fuck did you do? What the fuck, Sophie, did you do?"

There was no choice anymore. She had to read the journals for herself and see what she did too. I couldn't watch her blame me when that wasn't the whole truth.

"When you asked if I wanted anything from her room." I nodded towards the book and then added the others from my bag. "I took her journals because I wanted to know what was in them."

Her mouth gaped open as she saw the books in front of her. Words from her daughter she'd never seen. Words that right now she would hate I'd denied her, but not as much as she'd hate herself when she'd read them.

"Why did you take them?"

"Protection."

Pure loathing scorched her features.

"I never thought I'd see the day you looked at me like that, Carla. I always thought of you as my mum. Wanted you as my mum." I tapped the book. "You need to read them and then we can meet again. Tomorrow? Same time, same place?"

"Why? Why can't you just tell me what you did?"

"Oh I will. I'll tell you everything, but first you need to climb down from that pedestal you put yourself on," I snapped. I'd bear the scars of what I'd done, but I wouldn't carry Carla's punishment.

"Pardon?"

"Oh I'm not the only one who drove Lena to suicide. You did too."

"What?"

"Read the journals. See why Lena killed herself. It's all in there. See what *you* did."

She looked up at me in horror.

It was done now. We would all have to live with the truths of what we'd done. While Lena had suffered from it all.

Carla almost ran out of the coffee shop, and I wondered if she'd sit and read them in her car, but she didn't. She revved the engine and screeched out of there and I went home.

To tell my mother everything I'd done and why I'd done it.

---

After, my mother wanted to call Carla.

"No, Mum. We need to let Carla be. She will call if she needs us."

"I'm so very sorry." My mum apologised yet again. "I caused part of this. How I treated you, drove you to do what you did."

"It's not that simple is it, Mum? I've told you what the diaries said."

"Jesus Christ, Sophie. What a mess. When all this is done, maybe we should see someone. Help us process everything."

"I think we'd cause a psychologist to have a breakdown," I said.

My mum did a cross between a huff and a laugh. "Yes, I think we would," she replied.

## 24

## CARLA

I didn't know how, but I managed to get myself home before I read Lena's journals. I didn't remember the journey home, my mind racing with Sophie's words, her bombshell.

*What you did.*

What could she mean? All I had ever done was my best for my daughter. I decided Sophie's words were filthy lies.

Finally, on the sofa I began to read.

And I read and read.

It took a long time. As I battled through tears, as I paused to throw up, as I saw everything my daughter had written on lined pages. Poems, snatches of her thoughts. Things I'd not seen even though they'd stared me in the face.

My mind wanted to block out everything I'd learned, but I knew I needed to read it through again. Make sure of the facts before me, before I took action. I needed to speak to Lisa. Because while Sophie had asked for me to meet her again, I did not want our conversation to take place in a coffee shop. This was a conversation that required parents present. Whatever mixed feelings Sophie had about Lisa, the fact remained that she was her mum and the adult responsible for her.

And that was how I found myself the next morning sat in Lisa's living room while Sophie confessed to everything she'd done and I told her how I'd taken out all my hatred on Marcus before he'd told me his own story sat in A&E.

"I blame myself for what Sophie did," Lisa cried. "If I hadn't been such a shit parent she wouldn't have gone to these lengths, but it's just... I had my reasons." Lisa began to cry.

"Well, given what I just read, I think you have a rival for shit parent of the year," I replied.

"S- Sophie asks me from time to time, about her father, and I've always refused to tell her, but n- no more secrets. I will tell you and you tell me if there's anything else you've kept quiet and then we find a way forward. Okay?" She looked at Sophie and her daughter nodded, but her eyes met mine and she chewed on her cheek.

"I'd better go. This is private," I said, but Lisa shook her head.

"No, please. Don't go." She took a deep inhale and turned to Sophie. "The truth is. I don't know who your father is. I was attacked one night. I- I w- was too scared to tell anyone. It was months before I realised I was pregnant, and then your grandmother threw me out. She didn't believe me. I went to the doctors, but I was too far g- gone."

Sophie's face was ghost white. "My father was a rapist? You wanted to abort me?"

"I was fifteen, Sophie. Younger than you. I didn't know what I wanted. I'd been kicked out of my home. But no matter who your father is, you are the best thing I ever did."

"That's why you ignored me so much isn't it? You couldn't bear to look at me."

"No. N- no, that's not true."

Sophie left the room, slamming the door behind her and thundering upstairs. Lisa turned around to me and I asked her the question that had been hanging on my tongue for minutes now.

"Where were you attacked?"

And then I had to sit Lisa down and explain how she needed to call the police and how our tangled web had just potentially gathered more strands.

Because if Peter Bull was the father of Sophie.

Marcus was her brother.

# PART 4

## 25

## EXTRACTS FROM LENA HAYBROOK'S JOURNALS

13 August 2018

I'm not sure how to start! Do I say why I'm writing here? Do I write like I'm talking to a friend, or just randomly? I guess there are no rules, right? My God, can I actually do what I want here within these pages?

That's why I've decided to start a journal. I never had any interest in writing one as a kid, but I find myself writing one now at fifteen, because I need somewhere to just purge everything going on. Outside my life and inside me, because no one listens and no one sees me.

Not really.

Most people see Lena Haybrook, the perfect princess. With my perfect face and perfect hair and perfect grades. I'm punished for how I was born. But inside I am not perfect.

Far from it.

Inside I am broken, and bloody, and bruised.

I've spent the past year fighting a dark unknown enemy that can strike me down without warning. That lives within me. And as I write here, I'm trying to unburden myself of everything in the hope I can find a way through it.

I wrote a poem about it. I'm going to copy it here.

### A poem about depression by Lena Haybrook

> I'll put a smile upon my lips
> It doesn't reach my eyes
> I'll pretend it doesn't hurt me
> No evidence of my lies
>
> Tell myself I'm lucky
> I get to live and breathe
> But doubts and failure fill my mind
> Mostly without reprieve
>
> If at first you don't succeed
> I'll try and try again
> But when do you accept defeat?
> When do you refrain?
>
> Today the sun is shining
> I am well and I will fight
> Until the day is over
> And darkness takes the light

5 September 2018

My dad keeps asking when I'm going to his again for tea. When is he going to get it through his thick skull that while ever he lives with the evil bitch I'll try to not go at all? He left my mother and I understood, I really did. My mother is not the easiest person to live with.

But he's with a woman who chose to not have children. To have an operation to make sure of it. And she doesn't want me either. She's made that crystal clear.

I've tried to explain how she doesn't want me there and the things she says to me when he's out of earshot, but he doesn't want to hear it. I'm 'misunderstanding her' and need to 'give her a chance'.

So instead, I don't go at all, meaning she wins as I lose my father more and more, and as I was always a daddy's girl, this hurts.

And my mother? I can't say their names to her without a monologue on Natalie the whore and how my dad did *her* wrong. Her. It's always brought back to how it affected her. Never how it's affected me, the product of a broken marriage and a bitter divorce.

The worst thing was that my mum and dad always seemed so happy. Yes, he worked a lot, and yes, my mum was 'intense', but there were no huge arguments about things. They had silly squabbles about stuff like my dad eating my mum's last yoghurt from the fridge, but when the affair came to light it was a huge shock, to Mum and to me. But I was left to work it all out for myself while Mum got herself in one of her states. In fact, I ended up trying to console and reassure my mum.

My mum gets fixated on things to a degree that is exhausting. If it's possible to be loved too much, then my mother does that to me. And since my dad left, she's got worse. She's forever in my room asking me how I am and do I need anything. Asking if I want to go shopping with her. I don't but sometimes I go along just to let her buy me something and make her happy. Since the divorce she wants to be reassured that I'm still going to pass my exams because I need prospects.

She suffocates me with kindness and with what else it is that makes her so, well, I've already said intense and I can't think of another word for it. I know I sound like an ungrateful brat, but it's too much. It's hard to describe exactly how it is when someone is always on the periphery. Every move I make is watched or questioned. I can't breathe. I can't make the mistakes teenagers make: get drunk, hang out on street corners making out with boys. She tolerates my going to fast food places with Sophie because she knows there are adults there, but other than that I feel I almost can't move an inch without her permission and anxiety about what might befall me if I should ever actually go anywhere.

Mum's not only like it with me. If I ever got to speak to my father and I asked him why he went off with Natalie I'm sure he'd say it was to escape Mum. Because the minute he got in from work she'd expect a round up of his day. What jobs he'd done, who he'd seen, any more leads to further jobs? If he complained, she'd tell him she was just interested in his work and day and that she was sorry she bothered and then she'd be narky and Dad would have to apologise, so in the end he'd take the assault of questions until she went off to cook tea and then a look would pass between us, an eye-roll, before he switched the TV on and relaxed on the sofa until dinner was served and mum started up about something else.

I put it down to boredom. My mum didn't have friends and we'd done a little about mental health at school and I actually think she had a bit of social anxiety. She worked from home and I think her own life became so small that she widened it using us. Trouble was that once my dad had gone, her attentions focused more on me.

Thanks for that, Dad!

## 22 September 2018

Oh my god. Yesterday I was in Costa with Sophie, and Chloe fucking Butcher started up, taking the piss out of my dad having an affair. Like that's remotely funny. She burned my hair with a lighter! We ended up fighting and I punched her in the eye. I can't lie, it felt good. It had been a long time coming. I don't know why she's always having a go at me. I've never done anything to her. Well, actually I've talked behind her back a few times, but only in response to what she's done to me. Then she took a photo of our house threatening us. Sent it to me on social media.

But now it's made me wonder if hitting Chloe was worth it because Mum is mega wound up.

She took me to the hairdressers and went out and shouted at Chloe in the street. How fucking embarrassing. It was just supposed to be between me and Chloe, this beef, but now Tamsin and Alesha have started up, and a lad called Marcus has threatened me. My mum's just made things worse now, I'm sure. I was mortified. I hope Chloe shit her pants though when my mum shouted at her.

My mother has been listening at my door. She thinks she's quiet, but I know the sounds of this house. She also wants to know what's on my phone. This morning she woke me up to demand to see my messages and she's looking out of the windows all the time because the house was threatened.

I don't know which is worse. Chloe being a grade A bitch or my mother giving me no space. At least I only get Chloe in short bursts.

Soph came over. She's the one I can count on to help keep me sane. She got us into a conversation about sharing a flat. Sometimes it's good to play at being grownups lol. It'll be a long time before I've passed all my exams and started to earn enough money that I can get my own place, which sucks. I did try to talk to Soph last night about my mum, about how she is, but it was the same as usual. Soph always just says she'd rather have my mum than her own. Personally, I think if we could mix our mothers together somehow and combine their DNA, we might split them up and have two normal mothers!!! Sophie's ignores her and mine won't leave me alone. I'd love a week of her mother! Can we swap? Hahahaha.

4 October 2018

. . .

Things have been a bit better at school. Mum saw Chloe's mum and now me and Chloe have called a truce. I still can't stand her, but I'll not bitch about her. She told her mother I'd spread rumours about her being a thick ho which is a lie. Though the title fits her perfectly *snort*.

## 8 October 2018

Well, I didn't write much because up until now I haven't had anything I felt worthwhile to say. My mood has been bleak and getting out of bed has been hard, but Soph is always getting me out and about. It helps. Anyway, just a quick catch up before I get to the big stuff.

I finally got worn down by Dad and went for tea. Natalie was her usual self. She will wrap herself around my dad and put her tongue down his throat in front of me. It's disgusting and pathetic. He told her to 'calm it down' a bit. Her face! She made me a cup of tea and when I tasted it, she'd put salt in it, just enough that it tasted disgusting. I spat it out and she said she'd made a mistake. She has a fucking sugar pot with the name written on it. I can't believe that my dad was taken in by her 'being tired' lie. Later, when Dad went to the loo, she told me I should think myself lucky it was just salt.

It's the last time I eat or drink there. She's won that round.

Anyway, last night I went to Sophie's and I had a great time. Stayed overnight. Then I popped to Maccys on my way home from school. I felt happy. Silly me. I even wrote a poem while sat at the table.

**Cloud. A poem by Lena Haybrook**

> Sometimes they crowd
> Make it so dark
> But today they parted
> Left me outside
> A merry day
> Coat abandoned
> Along with the rules
> Sat at my table
> Watching the other humans
> Seeing who the clouds are gathering for next.

When I got home, I found out that being happy is a fleeting moment in time. We all strive for happiness and yet for most of us it's not a day-to-day reality. We're all wading through grey days and when that brightness of sunshine peeks its way through we feel ecstasy. We'd be better off accepting that mostly everything is grey.

But then, that's how I feel. Maybe others don't think that way? Maybe other people live in sunshine most of the time with only small patches of grey cloud? If they do, I envy them.

Mum greeted me at the door but not with her usual barrage of 'how has your day been?'. No making me recount every second of my existence since the moment she waved me off at the front door. No, this time she regaled me with the story of how she'd woken up that morning to find her car windscreen covered in shit and she'd watched the playback on the CCTV and it was someone who had actually done a real shit. She asked me to look at it. Thank God she meant the video. Anyway, I swear it's that Marcus. Same clothes and shoes. You can't tell one hundred percent cos the image is piss poor, but mum's calling the police.

I don't know Marcus that well, but he was known as a posh boy when we were younger. He's changed and looks like he's trying to look like a big man now. I don't get why he's smeared his shit on my mum's car. I can only think it's payback from Chloe. She said our house would get it after all. I thought we'd called a truce, but it seems she's as full of shit as Marcus!

12 October 2018

God help me.

My mother is constantly at the window, looking to see if anyone is out there. I've lost my temper with her today because she keeps asking me if Marcus has been in touch with me. I know she keeps listening outside my door again, as if I'm going to spill some great big secret to Sophie.

I haven't told my mum that I confronted Marcus at school. Soph dragged me away anyway.

Soph just helps me by talking about the future, about us having shops together side by side. I know it's only our imaginations, but it helps me feel like I'm escaping what's really happening now. Which is Marcus is a sick fuck and my mother is going ever more batshit.

15 October 2018

The police finally came and basically said they couldn't do anything. Mum was not happy. She went on and on until one of the policewomen said she'd visit Marcus to have a word. I could tell she didn't want to, but there was no way she was getting to leave our house without offering my mother something.

I need this to stop. My brain can't take it. I'm at the stage where sleep is the only place I find peace. I'm tired and what with exams,

Mum, and Natalie, on top of my fucked-up brain, it's just hard right now. I'm going to bed early to escape the fuss, welcoming the darkness of sleep and when I wake up, I pray for a better day.

Please let the trouble stop.

So Mum can go back to a normal level of fuss.

## 26

## LENA

14 November 2018

A boy called Lee in my year asked me out. I'd never really noticed him before. I don't have any classes with him. He's nice though. Quiet and studious. Thank God, when my mother met him she acted quite normal, although after he left she asked me sixty thousand questions I had no answers to. I even showed her his Facebook profile because I thought research him if you fucking want.

Dad called me tonight, upset that I haven't been round. I asked if he would meet me on my own and he told me to not be stupid, that I was being childish. Once more I explained about what Natalie does. When I said she'd done the salt on purpose, he said I was clearly going cuckoo like my mum. That Natalie was lovely and thought the world of me. Apparently, she's upset about my accusations and has told dad it's because she thinks I'm trying to get him and my mum back together.

I'm going to have to go round, but I'll just not have anything to eat and drink. And I'm going to call Natalie's bluff. I shall take flowers and chocolates and fake apologise and be so damn nice it messes with her head.

Just like she messes with mine.

## 30 November 2018

I've done some more mock exams. I did something else too, but I'm writing in a kind of code just in case. Something I was, I am no longer. It was okay actually. Better the second time. It still makes me chuckle that for my sixteenth birthday, part of my present from my mum was some condoms. I know she's a pain in the arse at times, but I love her dearly. She always has my best interests at heart. I'm leaving that package untouched though, because it would unleash a new round of lectures. Actually, I'm surprised she's not already brought it up. Does she seriously think we're studying *all* the time?

It's almost Christmas. All I want is for a peaceful Christmas and a brand new 2019 with no drama.

## 16 December 2018

Lee ditched me. Did I say I thought he was nice? Just before Christmas too. We'd had a great time the past six weeks, but he sent me a text saying I wasn't that great in bed and he could study on his own. I've texted him a bunch of times saying I just needed some more practice, but he's not even responded.

I'm gutted. I really liked him. I passed my mocks. Mum was more bothered about that, than my break-up. I think her words were that it was a shame but hardly the end of a marriage like she'd gone through. These days I just agree with what she says and then I come upstairs and scream into my pillow. I went through that break-up too. They both fucking hurt. They hurt a lot.

28 December 2018

Christmas was dreadful. First, spending the day with just Mum and television repeats. Sophie was home with her own. We texted each other about how bored we were.

Then I had to go to Dad's and this time I couldn't get out of eating there.

I bought Natalie a perfume. When she opened it, she asked me why I did that and fake cried. My dad asked her what was wrong and she said I'd had a conversation about what to get her for Christmas and she'd said anything but that she was allergic to jasmine and yet I'd bought her a perfume with it in. She asked why I hated her so much.

My dad's face when he looked at me was unbelievable. This was the father who'd worshipped my existence and he looked at me like he didn't know me at all. Likewise, Pops.

Natalie smirked the whole way through the dinner as I picked at my food. I pretended I wasn't feeling so good. I hate her with a passion. She won't accept that she has my dad most of the time. I only want a little bit of him, but she's taking him away. In fact, I feel I've lost him to be honest. He didn't even ask how my mocks went.

8 January 2019

So much for a happy new year. A brick was thrown through our front window. My mum's worse than ever. She won't clear up the glass that is all over the living room floor because it's 'evidence'. I've watched the video and I'm not sure who it is.

"Are you sure you don't know?" She must have asked me this twenty times.

Now she's insisted I show her Marcus on social media. I can only show her him on Facebook and that's years old.

I just went to get a snack and she's on her phone muttering about Marcus Bull even though she doesn't know it was him.

Time to stay in my room for the foreseeable.

### Who am I? A poem by Lena Haybrook

My father waited for my first word, 'Dada',
now he doesn't believe any of them.
My mother shouted, "You walked, you clever girl'.
Now she's nervous of every move I make.
A girl at school says she's okay with me now.
But bricks come through my window.
My boyfriend said he wanted my firsts.
Then he treated me like a second.
My best friend tells me she's there for me.
But when I speak to her, she's not listening.
Darkness tells me there's peace to be found.
But is that true, given nothing is ever as it seems?

4 February 2019

My mum now has colour security cameras. She can access the cameras by an app on her phone. Can sit there all day and all night if she wishes watching the outside of the house. The police told her they could do nothing.

Marcus has started coming up to me at school saying he's going to push me under a bus. It's just nonsense. I don't know why he's doing it, just to show off I think because he's not a crazy psycho even if he's being irresponsible. I confronted Chloe and she swore she had nothing to do with any of the window business. She told me Sophie was the one who said I'd called her a thick ho. Lying cow. She just wants to cause trouble between us. She's always been jealous of our friendship. Soph would never do that to me.

Then again, I didn't expect my own father to choose a thick ho over me, did I?

I know my bestie only has my best interests at heart, but she told mum about Marcus and now my mum is insisting on driving us to school and picking us up. That won't cause me to be the butt of any hilarity will it? Mum also asked Sophie to record Marcus threatening me. I can't deal with Sophie becoming like Mum, but she's on Mum's side. Why won't she listen to me? He's better off ignored.

Oh my god. Mum's been to his house.
    I can't take much more.
    Sophie keeps rattling on about our future life.
    I've got to survive the present first.

5 February 2019

My dad phoned to say he was thinking of proposing to Natalie on Valentine's Day. I told him Valentines was naff and asked if he'd thought of doing it on a nice holiday somewhere in the summer.

He thought my idea was fantastic.

I'm just hoping by then he's stopped thinking with his cock.

The last thing I need is to know Natalie is going to be a permanent fixture.

But I guess it's unavoidable.

18 February 2019

I heard the door bang earlier and looked out of my bedroom window and saw my mum run down the street. She had her phone held up and ran up to Marcus and some other lads. She looked like a proper nutjob.

When she got in, I begged her to stop, but she's not listening. I banged my door shut in frustration. Usually, she'd shout at me for that, but she's too obsessed with Marcus to know what's happening in front of her eyes.

She's not seeing me once again.

I'm begging and pleading and breaking and desperate in front of her eyes and she can't see for the blinkers with the name Marcus Bull embroidered on the front.

**Strangulated without hands. An acrostic poem by Lena Haybrook.**

**S**ay you'll remember me
**T**hough how will you, if you don't see me while I'm here?
**R**escue me
**A**llow me to be visible
**N**ot invisible
**G**rant me the audience I seek and let me speak
**U**p
**L**isten

**A**llow me to be believed
**T**ruth. It's what I speak.
**E**very word.
**D**enied again. I'm not sure what the answer is anymore, except maybe I'm being given it. That I should disappear, become the dark shadows.

## 29 March 2019

The first day of the school holidays and the time I need to make my mind up about whether or not I stay alive. Do I sound dramatic? I'm sure I won't off myself, but I need to get out there and remember the good things in life.

## 1 April 2019

Today is my best friend and tacos! I can't wait!

---

Huh, I hadn't even got in the doorway when Marcus appeared.
    Is he really stalking me now?
    How did he know I was there?
    Sophie says he threatened to stab me.
    Maybe he is crazy.
    Maybe I'm crazy.
    I don't know anymore.
    What I do know. Mum phoned 999. The police are coming again.

My taco was disgusting. It arrived cold, but with all the drama I didn't get chance to take it back.

Maybe it's a sign.

10 April 2019

**A glimmer of hope in a time of darkness. A poem by Lena Haybrook.**

A fresh start
A new place
A new dad?
Start it all again.
The past in the past.
The morons of Berkley Edge a distant memory.
A chink of sunlight in a dark day.

I had such a good chat with mum tonight. She actually said she was looking for a new place for us to live. A rental away from Berkley Edge. It inspired my poem above. I chatted to her about Dad and although she brought up again that he cheated on her, rather than us, she did say she was considering dating again and we even had a little giggle about things.

I think if we started afresh and she began dating again, things would be a lot better.

---

Okay universe, you win.

I can't do this anymore.

It's one step forward and what feels like six back. I feel I'm so far back now I can no longer go forward.

Lee recorded us having sex. I had no idea until tonight when his video had been circulated. I don't know if he did it, or Marcus got hold of it. It's from yet another 'unknown source' that I know will never be discovered. They'll get away with it like everything else.

But I won't get away with it.

This, a 'sex tape', will follow me for life, won't it? Escaping to a new house won't escape this. In any case I'm too exhausted for it all.

Sophie has phoned me with her plans to deal with it including phoning the police.

It's just a repeating pattern of crap.

I told Sophie I loved her.

My phone is pinging and I hear jeering outside my windows and my mother on a mission again, but I'm ignoring it all. No point in telling any of them to stop. They'll just ignore me.

Funny really. I wanted to be seen. Now my naked body is everywhere.

Be careful what you wish for.

I wondered about phoning my dad to tell him that I love him, but if Natalie was there then maybe he'd not take any notice. I'll text him instead. I'd have rather spoken to him, but I am far too exhausted to deal with Natalie's games.

I was telling Sophie that I'd sleep on everything and we'd sort it all tomorrow when Mum came in.

There was such worry on her features and I knew it came from a place of love, but I couldn't carry her troubles and my own. I got out of bed and told her I was glad she was moving on and that I loved her.

She just left my room.

I've just torn out a corner from my journal.

In a moment I will walk over to my wardrobe and kneel down. I'll reach to the back, underneath and put my journal back there into my place of secrets and I will get out the two plastic bottles I've filled with tablets.

If anyone ever does find and read this, then I am sorry. I know it might be you, Sophie, because I asked you to get them and destroy them if anything ever happened to me.

Please know there was nothing else for me to do.

I just needed peace.

And it's not meant for me in this life. No matter the events of late, the darkness has been on me for a while. The eclipse has come and I wait to hopefully find a new beautiful sunshine in the next life or peace if that's all that there is after.

I'm writing I'm sorry on the scrap of paper I tore off because I've nothing left except those two words. I know it won't be enough for my mum, but I've nothing left in me for anything more. I told her I loved her.

It's time now.

Time to put away the journals.

Time to take the tablets and climb into my bed.

Praying for peace.

## 27

## CARLA

Lisa is stunned by the bombshell I've just dropped on her. I tell her that he attacked me and he let me go when he saw I was pregnant.

She staggered to the sofa, her head in her hands.

"How will she ever come to terms with who her father was? What did I think I was doing, telling her? It was a mistake."

"I don't have any answers, Lisa. I wish I did," I said truthfully. "One thing though. In Lena's journals she said she wished Sophie and her could mix us both up."

Lisa's brow creased.

"She said you weren't enough, and I was too much and if we could be mixed and split then her and Sophie would both have a perfect mum."

Her jaw dropped as she took in my words.

"I have no idea if that is indeed the right mix of parenting, but it's worth a shot, right? So go see your daughter and tell her what she needs to hear. That you love her and you're there for her and then neither stay away from her or suffocate her. Somehow find the middle ground."

She nodded. "She really is the best thing I ever did in my life, no matter where she came from. I sometimes think fate made me not realise I was pregnant until it was too late. That she was meant to be."

"That's what she needs to hear." I sighed. "Right, I need to be going. I'm sorry, I know a lot has happened in the last few hours, but I read other things in Lena's diary that I need to deal with."

"Do you need me?" she asked.

I was shocked at that point. A woman in a state of emotional turmoil asked if I needed her.

"You have no idea how much I appreciate you asking, but no. Go see Sophie and tell her I said no more guilt. We all played a part in Lena's death, hers no more than most. I don't want Lena to have died in vain. She wanted Sophie to succeed."

Lisa nodded.

"You know where I am if you need me, Carla, but I'll not bug you. My offer is genuine though, not empty words. Anytime. Okay?"

"Thank you."

I turned down the path. I had research to do and places to visit, but now I also needed to call into a chemist or supermarket.

Because my conversation with Lisa made me realise that I didn't know the last time I'd had a period, though I did know the last time I had sex.

After my daughter's funeral. Almost three months ago. And even though we'd used a condom, I had to check.

# PART 5

## 28

## CARLA

Since Lena had died it had been a daily struggle to exist, to put one foot in front of the other. The only thing that had fuelled me to do so had been my need for vengeance. And then I found that nothing is what I'd assumed, and that some of the blame for my daughter's death lies with myself.

So many things transpired to take my daughter to a place where she felt ending her life was the only option, but she'd seemed hopeful with the thought of a fresh start. Until the video. Now it was time for me to find out who'd sent it.

I was in my living room and there were three different pregnancy test kits on the side. To be honest I'd not had the courage or strength to do them yet, but I knew I must. I told myself it was the menopause, but I was forty-one. It would be unusual to be in the menopause now. Not impossible, but unusual.

Then again, I'd experienced enough shocks of late to send my body haywire. Taking a deep breath, I walked upstairs to find out answers to a question I didn't want to ask. Not really.

Every test gave me the same answer.

I was pregnant.

And now I was in a worse state than ever because I'd thought it was almost time for me to say goodbye and join my daughter.

But my decisions were no longer that simple.

I decided to work with what I could handle. To try to find out more about the video and to forget what was physically growing inside me.

When Lena died, I'd never thought that Lee could be responsible for the video's release. Not for a moment. I'd just blamed Marcus for everything, and now? Now the boy I'd welcomed into my home could have been the person whose actions pushed my daughter to the edge of what she could handle.

I just needed to know the truth. It didn't really matter now about any further punishments. I'd already gone too far. What if Lee also had his reasons for what he'd done?

I knew I could call his mum, but I felt like I needed to search social media first. I didn't know what I expected to find, but maybe I could bring Elise back and trick the information out of him?

*No, Carla. No more games. Just get your coat on and go and ask.*

I was so weary. Putting everything down, I fell asleep on the sofa. What was one more day?

---

Nausea was my morning alarm call and once more I was sick, although now I knew why. Once again refusing to acknowledge it beyond these physical symptoms, I rinsed out my mouth and got ready to call Lee.

I wondered what sort of a boy Lee actually was? He'd presented to me as kind, caring, and understanding, but I knew now that many didn't show their true faces. I decided to switch on my computer and put on Facebook and I looked up Angela Swinton. If anyone was going to talk about their children's personalities it was a mother, even with their bias.

I found her straightaway and went down her feed, but she didn't post much and it tended to be posts about Animal Crossing. Her cover photo was of her son and daughter when they were younger but there was little else. I clicked onto her friends list to see if her husband had a Facebook account and then a photo on her friend's list made my heart skip a beat.

Natalie.

Natalie was 'friends' with Lee's mother.

It was a coincidence. It had to be.

I did a search on Angela's profile for Natalie and found a photo from six years ago. A family get-together for a fortieth birthday. Natalie was Angela's sister. Natalie was Lee's auntie.

*Do not jump to conclusions.*

*Do not jump to conclusions.*

*Do NOT jump to conclusions.*

I was dressed and out of the door before my brain had caught up to my feet.

---

I parked on the street outside and walked up a short driveway before knocking on the Swintons' door. After a minute Lee answered. He looked shocked to see me. "Mrs Haybrook. Are you okay? We weren't expecting you, were we? My parents are at work."

"I just have a question to ask you, Lee. Can I come in?"

He nodded his head and I stepped through the doorway.

I followed him through to the living room, having slipped off my shoes in the hall.

"You're lucky I'm in," he told me. "I'm usually at college but my tutor for the day is off sick."

"I'd have come back later. It's kind of that important," I told him.

He nodded his head. His eyes were widened. In fear.

"Oh, Lee," I said. "What did you do?"

"Wh- what do you mean?"

He was standing there looking guilty as fuck, but he clearly wanted me to spell it out for him.

"I'm guessing Natalie is behind all of this, Lee. The question is how guilty are you?"

The boy broke down and I realised I had yet another victim in front of me. "She made me date Lena. She made me make the video and she made me send it to her."

"And if you didn't?" I asked.

"She said she had evidence my dad has been cheating on my mum and she'd send it." He looked at the floor. "My dad cheated before, a long time ago, and mum said if he ever did it again that was it. I couldn't risk it. I didn't know Lena would kill herself. I just thought it would embarrass her and she'd want to move away from Berkley Edge. Then Natalie would be rid of you, and my family would stay as it was."

I didn't care whether his dad had cheated on his mum and I didn't care about Lee.

"Do not warn your auntie I know anything, or I'll tell your mum about your dad myself," I warned him and then I left him in his house.

---

I made an urgent appointment with my general practitioner. Due to the fact so many weeks had passed, they managed to get me a dating ultrasound booked there and then with the local maternity unit. I had a long wait at the hospital with a bladder full of pee, but I left with photos of a now very real unborn baby.

And in the early evening, I drove myself to Ant and Natalie's.

Ant answered the door and he gave me a guarded smile. "Hello, Carla, love. You okay?"

I shook my head.

"No, Anthony, and you aren't going to be okay either. Can I come in?"

He nodded, and taking my coat to hang up, he let me through. I walked into the living room.

"Who was it?" Natalie said without even looking up.

"Your worst nightmare," I replied.

She shot around to look at me, launching to her feet. "You'd better have a good reason for setting foot in my home."

"I have many. Now shut your fucking mouth while I talk to my ex-husband."

"You can't talk to me like that in my—"

I took the screwdriver out of my bag and brandished it in her face. "Unless you want this through your eyeball, I suggest you sit back down and shut the fuck up."

She asked Ant if he was going to let me talk to her like this, but she did sit down. Ant carefully walked over and stood between the chair Natalie sat in and the sofa I was on.

"Okay, Carla, we're listening and despite what's happened in the past, I'm here for you." He turned to a scoffing Natalie. "The woman just lost her daughter. Have some compassion."

Then he spoke to me again, in a soothing, 'let's calm the nutter down' way.

"I'm going to give something to you, Ant, but I need them back. They're Lena's journals. I didn't know she was keeping them, but Sophie gave them to me. It shows that there were many reasons why she killed herself." I looked over at Natalie who sat still.

"She was being bullied as you know, but the journals show it wasn't as simple as we thought. The lad who bullied her, Marcus, was being blackmailed by Sophie."

"Her best friend Sophie?" Ant asked, incredulous.

I nodded. "And Sophie was doing it out of some misguided notion that she could come live with us. It's complicated. You need to read it. She talks about us, Ant. Lena. About how I suffocated her and you with my intensity about things. About how she tried to talk to you about Natalie, but you ignored her.

"Oh yeah? What lies did she have to say about me?" Natalie spat out.

"Where do I start with what she said about you? Threatening her. Putting salt in her drinks instead of sugar."

"That was a misunderstanding," Ant said, still defending her now.

"What about her asking her nephew Lee to date our daughter, sleep with her, and then hand over a video for Natalie to circulate? Was that a misunderstanding too?" I said. "You know, the video that was the final straw before our daughter took her own life."

"She's a lying whore, just like her daughter was," Natalie ranted again.

That was it. She could call me what she liked, but she would not sully my daughter's name. But before my fist could reach her face, Ant's hand had slapped her across the cheek.

"'That's my dead daughter you're talking about." Ant was stunned. "You... you've always spoken about her so well. Now you're calling her a whore? What the hell's got into you?"

"You're mine, not theirs. You left them, for me. I didn't want Lena around. She talked about how wonderful her mother was on purpose. Trying to get you to leave. And I don't like kids. I hardly ever see my own fucking niece and nephew, why would I have wanted your kid around?"

Ant's jaw had dropped. "So are you telling me you did put salt in her drink?"

"While ever she was around, you were linked to Carla. I didn't think the silly cow would top herself. I just thought she'd leave eventually if I kept on at her. Anyway, you just said yourself." She turned back to me. "There were a few reasons why she chose to end her life. Probably one of which is because you're fucking cuckoo. Now get out of my house," she yelled.

"I'm not actually finished with what I came to say. But I'm sure you'll be the first to congratulate us." I turned to my ex-husband. "Ant, we're pregnant."

I didn't get a chance to see his response because Natalie launched from her seat in a fury and I had a body on me raining down blows on my stomach. "You fucking bitch. You did that on purpose. No. No. No. No."

She forgot I had a screwdriver to hand. I brought it up and shoved it straight into her neck.

I'm no medic. I didn't know I'd hit her carotid directly, but I wasn't sad when I did. My adrenaline pumped like the blood that spurted everywhere around us. Ant had leaped in to pull me away from Nat and we were soaked through as she bled out. Within thirty seconds, Natalie was unconscious.

"What do we do now?" Ant finally found his voice. I stared at him. We looked like we were in the movie *Carrie*.

"What you do now, is to look after our child better than we did our first," I told him. "Because I'll be in prison."

Ant grabbed hold of his mobile and I knocked it out of his hands. "I hit her carotid. She'll be dead within minutes, and anyway, I don't want her to survive. If she survives, what will she do to our new child?"

Ant seemed speechless and I didn't blame him. He'd just been told he was going to be a father, that the answers for our daughter's death laid in journals now on the chair, and his partner was dying on the sofa, killed at the hands of his ex-wife.

"I- I got a text from Lena, saying she loved me," he managed to say. It came the evening she died. I never responded to it. I told Nat about it and she distracted me with a blow job. What the fuck did I do to our family, Carla?"

He grabbed hold of the screwdriver and then pulled Natalie's still bleeding body onto himself.

"Get out of here, Carla. Look after that baby, and right all the wrongs we did."

I shook my head. "Don't be stupid. I killed her."

He felt at Nat's pulse. "No, she's not dead yet." And then he pulled his arm back and stabbed the screwdriver back through her neck.

The light faded from her eyes.

"I killed her," he said. "And my behaviour with Lena means I don't deserve a second chance at fatherhood. Go. But send me photos, won't you? Of our beautiful new baby?"

"I don't get it, Ant. We used a condom, but yet I'm pregnant."

He smiled. "Carla, that condom had been in my wallet from right back when I'd first cheated with Nat. It was ancient."

"Oh." There was nothing else to say and so I left the room, though I didn't know whether Ant would stick to what he said or whether the police would arrive at my door and arrest me for murder.

Carefully, covering my bloody clothing with my coat, I got into my car. We made sure I touched nothing on my way out of the house. Natalie and Ant lived on a quiet cul de sac in a detached house with a large private driveway. I could only hope no one had noticed me arrive and leave, but I'd leave it all for fate to decide.

Once home, I showered the blood from me and then I put my bloodied clothing in a black sack. If the police didn't come, tomorrow I would destroy it. I'd find somewhere to visit in the dead of night and burn it.

I realised I'd left Lena's journals at Ant's. Would I ever get them back?

The hours dragged on and I just sat there reliving everything over and over. All of it. Not just Lena's death but every single thing that had happened since Ant left me. If my 'intensity' had made him leave, then ultimately had I killed our daughter?

Or would depression have taken her anyway?

Did Marcus' actions contribute?

What Sophie did?

What Lee did? Natalie? Ant?

I'd never have a definitive answer.

If I weren't pregnant, I would have drunk to Natalie's death.

The police arrested Anthony for Natalie's murder. The local press went wild and I was glad I didn't live in Berkley Edge anymore.

My house sold and I moved. Far, far, away.

Where I could start all over again.

## 29

## SOPHIE

I might have been trying to get my head around my own parentage and my mum reporting a years old crime, but I heard the gossip about Anthony Haybrook and it shocked me to the core.

He'd killed Natalie.

Why? What had led him to do that?

I tried to call Carla, but her number was unobtainable. I guessed she was getting lots of calls about it.

A couple of days later I asked Mum to drive me to Carla's house.

But she wasn't there. There was no evidence of her living there. The house was furnished, but nothing of Carla's remained.

The day after that, a letter came.

*Sophie.*

*You will have heard the news by now about Ant and Natalie. I need to make a completely fresh start. I'm sorry to cut off our ties, but you need to focus on your own future. You have a loving mum who will do her best for you, I know. Please make the most of all opportuni-*

ties in life where Lena can't. I'm sure she's watching over you waiting for you to open your shop!

But even if you choose to follow a different path, as long as you're happy, that's what counts.

I know it will be hard to come to terms with who your father is, and if you need counselling for that, take it. But remember fathers come in many guises, not just biological, and you never know, your mum might yet bring a good one home for you one day!

And you have a brother. Be kind to each other. You've both been through so much. Maybe now you can be each other's support?

One day I just might come find you again, but right now, I had to get completely away.

I hope you understand.

I know it doesn't make up in any way for the fact I've left, but I wanted to help you put a deposit on that first business, or on a first home. I've given your mum a contribution. It's yours when you're eighteen.

Carla xoxo


I did understand, but it still crushed my soul.

Then my mum told me Carla had given me twenty thousand pounds.

## 30

## MARCUS

"You've got some mail," Mum said, passing me an envelope. She hovered nearby.

"I'll show it you once I've read it," I told her. She nodded and moved away, but not far. It made me smile.

Dad had been arrested on suspicion of carrying out several sexual assaults and was remanded in custody. He was trying to plead not guilty, but more women kept coming forward. Although, Dad's case had been knocked off the gossip charts by Ant stabbing Natalie.

I opened my letter.

*Marcus.*
*You will have heard about Ant and Natalie I'm sure.*
*I needed a fresh start and so I've moved away. I hope you can understand. I made a promise to you and your mum and I'm keeping that promise. You need to look in the place you've always kept your savings. Also, you need better security. Never leave a key under a plant pot.*

*I gave your money to a bullying charity, but now I'll cover that donation and I'm returning your money to you. Spend it wisely.*

*Get away from your father and live your true life.*

*Please keep in touch with Sophie if you can. I know you both have a lot to get your head around.*

*Live your best life. Carla.*

I flung the letter at my mum and ran upstairs. Under my mattress I found my five hundred pounds in cash in an envelope and then another envelope addressed to Mum.

By now, Mum had followed me upstairs and so I handed her the envelope with her name on it.

With a creased brow she opened it and slid out a cheque.

"Oh my god."

"What is it, Mum?"

"It's a cheque for twenty thousand pounds, Marcus."

Mum burst into tears.

We could leave.

## 31

## CARLA

My new home was near the beach. A rental because you never knew when you needed to move. I'd already had neighbours asking probing questions, especially once my pregnant belly had begun to swell.

I knew they were gossiping behind their closed doors.

They should be careful jumping to conclusions. It could set tragedy in motion.

I stroked my belly and my son kicked hard. Tomorrow, I was booked in for a c-section and I'd get to meet him.

---

He was perfect. Ten tiny fingers. Ten tiny toes. He had a smattering of dark hair, and rosebud lips. He smelled like heaven. Lena was never far from my thoughts, and I wondered if she was up in heaven laughing at me, saying, 'Look what I did. I got you and Dad back together even if only for a moment in time and now I have a brother that can stay where I could not'. It helped me to cope with her loss if I thought of it in those terms.

I had no idea what came next, but then none of us did. I was no different from any other parent in that respect.

I thought of Sophie and Marcus often and hoped they'd manage to try to move on. As far as Ant went, I had no idea of how much contact I'd have with him. For now, I'd send him the photos I'd promised but from post-boxes nowhere near where we lived. I didn't know what the future would bring.

Just as I had no idea what would happen if anyone ever tried to touch a hair on my newborn son's head...

## THE END

Want more psychological suspense? Read my Liar's Island suspense
BETRAYAL BEND

Sign up to my newsletter overleaf to keep updated with my new releases.
Thank you for reading. Please consider leaving a review.

## SIGN UP TO MY NEWSLETTER FOR UPDATES

Sign up to my newsletter and get another **A Street Where You** Live full-length novel **SAVE HER** for free.
I send news on work-in-progress, new releases, and offers.
Sign up here: https://geni.us/andreamlongsuspense

# BETRAYAL BEND

**Sometimes a good life is not enough…**

Shay Adler and her husband, Cam, run the Brew Love Coffee Company on Liar's Island. A gorgeous couple with sunshine smiles and a perfect marriage.

But behind Shay's smile lies unrest. She loves the husband she met in high school, but sometimes she feels trapped. Trapped by the island, trapped by her marriage and providing stability to her younger sister, and trapped by the whole 'good' ethos that underpins their company.

The tourists provide a distraction. They come, stay a short while, and leave again, and that leaves Shay with opportunities. Ones where she can not be such a good girl.

But on Liar's Island you can trust no one… so Shay's betrayal might not stay secret for long.

https://books2read.com/u/3R6wMj

# ABOUT THE AUTHOR

Andrea M. Long writes dark suspense. She's always thinking up new ways to torture someone.

She loves her job.

Andrea lives in Sheffield with her long-suffering partner and son; and Bella, her beautiful Whippet furbaby.